INVISIBLE POWER 2

for Dorothy —

Idealists of the world, unite!

Philip

INVISIBLE POWER 2

A Metaphysical Adventure Story

Philip Allott

Xlibris

To order additional copies of this book, contact:
Xlibris Corporation
1-888-795-4274
www.Xlibris.com
Orders@Xlibris.com
50271

CONTENTS

Instructions for the use of this book 9
Speaking parts 11
Speaking parts (by chapter) 13

Chapters
1. *Venice I.* 15
2. *Èze.* 20
3. *Venice II.* 26
4. *Beyond the Human.* 32
5. *Connecticut.* 36
6. *Beyond the Good.* 44
7. *Another World, Another Person.* 51
8. *End of a Beginning.* 55
9. *After Government.* 62
10. *Kreuzberg.* 69
11. *Parmenides Moment.* 72
12. *San Lazzaro degli Armeni.* 77
13. *Beginning to Mean Something.* 82
14. *Meeting of the Ways.* 89
15. *North Norfolk.* 95
16. *Into the Rose-Garden.* 100
17. *Gnostalgia for the Future.* 106
18. *Ideal Affinities.* 114
19. *World Mind Revolution.* 117
20. *Tying the Knot.* 131

ALLUSIONS EXPLAINED 135

Epigraphs. 136

Chapters

1. *Venice I.* 138
2. *Èze.* 145
3. *Venice II.* 154
4. *Beyond the Human.* 171
5. *Connecticut.* 182
6. *Beyond the Good.* 194
7. *Another World, Another Person.* 209
8. *End of a Beginning.* 224
9. *After Government.* 237
10. *Kreuzberg.* 244
11. *Parmenides Moment.* 250
12. *San Lazzaro degli Armeni.* 280
13. *Beginning to Mean Something.* 289
14. *Meeting of the Ways.* 300
15. *North Norfolk.* 309
16. *Into the Rose-Garden.* 331
17. *Gnostalgia for the Future.* 347
18. *Ideal Affinities.* 365
19. *World Mind Revolution.* 366
20. *Tying the Knot.* 389

Epigraphs. 391

Chapter 2 Appendices— 393

1. William of Occam and Francis Bacon. 393
2. Wyclif and Cranmer. 397
3. Hobbes and Locke and Jefferson. 398
4. Locke and Berkeley and Hume. 404
5. Adam Smith and Ricardo. 424
6. Burke and Owen and Bentham. 431
7. Newton and Lyell and Darwin. 443
8. Continental European mind. 447

Index 459

Plato has furnished for all posterity the pattern of a new art form, the novel,
viewed as the Aesopian fable raised to its highest power.
Friedrich Nietzsche.

The historian relates the events which have happened,
the poet those which might happen.
Aristotle.

This novel is certainly not a novel.
Jean-Jacques Rousseau.

. . . neque te ut miretur turba labores,
contentus paucis lectoribus.
Horace.

INSTRUCTIONS FOR THE USE OF
THIS BOOK

It is expected that the reader will have read
Invisible Power. A Philosophical Adventure Story
by the same author.

———

The present volume consists of two parts,
a story and an appendix explaining allusions
contained and concealed in the text of the story.

It may be read in one of three ways.
(1) Read the story, ignoring the appendix, treating the story
as a self-contained and self-referring thing-in-itself.
(2) (*Recommended*) Read the story first, then read the appendix.
(3) Refer to the appendix while reading the story.

An explanation of the prequel to the present story
may be found at the end of Chapter 2.

The reader is advised to read every word of the story,
and, if possible, every word of the Allusions Explained,
every word being a significant part of a total picture.

———

By the same author—

Eunomia. New Order for a New World
(Oxford, Oxford University Press; 1990/2001).

The Health of Nations. Society and Law beyond the State
(Cambridge, Cambridge University Press; 2002).

Towards the International Rule of Law
Essays in Integrated Constitutional Theory
(London, Cameron May; 2005).

SPEAKING PARTS

Mike Abi (MA)

Bunty Birmingham (BB)

Alsion Brand (AB)

Rupert Brand (RB)

Countess Frieda von Dorn und Graz (FDG)

Gabriele (Gabi) Dorn (GD)

Ingo Dorn (ID)

'Eunomia' (Thomas) ((E)

George Frampton (GF)

May Gaunt (MG)

Mr Gray (G)

Abraham (Abe) Green (AG)

David Greene (DG)

Hilda Greene (HG)

Jack Jackson (JJ)

Edmund Jenning (EJ)

Fred McDonald (FM)

Jane Meehan (JaM)

James (Jim) Meehan ('Boxcar') (JiM)

Luis Ortiz (LO)

Jake Plowman, V-P Planning (VPP)

Miss Spurgeon (MS)

Gregory (Greg) Seare (GS)

'Symbolism' (Isabella) (Sym)

Cardinal (Alvise) Trevisan (CT)

'Wednesday' (W)

SPEAKING PARTS BY CHAPTER

1. *Venice I.* AB, GD, CT.

2. *Èze.* G, FDG, GS, EJ, Sym, E.

3. *Venice II.* EJ, GS, GD, G, FDG, CT.

4. *Beyond the Human.* (GS).

5. *Connecticut.* AG, EJ, JiM, JaM.

6. *Beyond the Good.* VPP, GS, GF, BB, FM, MG, LO.

7. *Another World, Another Person.* ID, EJ.

8. *End of a Beginning.* G, ID, EJ, FDG, GS.

9. *After Government.* AB, MA.

10. *Kreuzberg.* (FDG).

11. *Parmenides Moment.* EJ, W.

12. *San Lazzaro degli Armeni.* GD, CT.

13. *Beginning to Mean Something.* EJ, G, FDG.

14. *Meeting of the Ways.* AB, JiM, JJ, AG.

15. *North Norfolk.* (GS).

16. *Into the Rose Garden.* EJ, RB, GD.

17. *Gnostalgia for the Future.* GS, CT, AB, DG, HG, MS.

18. *Ideal Affinities.* (EJ).

19. *World Mind Revolution.* HG, DG, AB, RB, GD, JiM, JaM, AG, GS, MG, JJ, MA, CT, FDG, G, EJ.

20. *Tying the Knot.* (GD), (EJ).

1

Venice I

'Have you ever met a cardinal before?'

'In my dreams. Literally.'

'You dream about cardinals?'

'More than once. I dreamt I was kneeling in front of a cardinal, in his scarlet robe and scarlet hat. I tried to kiss his ring, but he wouldn't let me.'

'Heavens!'

Alison Brand's original question had been meant as an offer of ecclesiastical advice, not an enquiry about the secrets of Gabriele Dorn's unconscious mind.

'I should probably have worked out a Freudian interpretation, but I thought it would be better not to try,' Gabi continued.

Alison tried to suppress even the thought, let alone the image, of Gabi—cheerful, charming, intelligent and very evidently a vigorous and healthy young woman—kneeling in front of any man, let alone a cardinal.

'I really don't think you need to do any of that for Cardinal Trevisan,' she said, steering the conversation back in the ecclesiastical direction. 'They make a point of informality nowadays. But Alvise Trevisan is definitely not a blue jeans sort of person.'

'God! I should hope not,' Gabi said. 'What's the point of being a prince of the Church if you're not willing to be princely?'

Terra firma in Venice never seems very firm. You step from the precarious watery medium onto fourteen centuries of impossible defiance. You hope that the blessed miracle—the marriage of denatured sea and unnatural land—will last a little longer.

The two women were helped from the taxi by a man who was apparently some sort of butler, wearing a green baize apron.

'*Grazie*,' Alison said.

'*Grazie*,' she said again, as the man helped her onto a steep stone step, abrupt frontier between intense light and intense darkness. Sensing that the man was treating her as if she were old, and in need of physical help, she felt a stab of anxiety. Would the Cardinal think that she was only there as some sort of chaperone, because she had thought that Gabi would need a chaperone when visiting a priest?

15

Fortunately, Cardinal Trevisan was not wearing jeans. But nor was he wearing red slippers. He was all in black, looking improbably, and probably unintentionally, fashionable. He was evidently in that stage of ultimate agedness when a man, or a woman, seems ageless, the processes of growth and decay having agreed to call it a day.

'My dear ladies,' he said. 'You make a very old man feel very much younger.'

The Cardinal spoke English with the best of English accents. But his manner was uniquely Italian, managing to suggest, as no Englishman would be able to suggest, that the very act of shaking the hands of these two strange women was itself one of life's particular pleasures.

'I bring warm greetings from Hilda Greene,' Alison said.

'I have the fondest memories of Sir David and Lady Hilda—and their delightful hospitality,' the Cardinal said.

'It's so good of you to let us intrude in this way.'

'You are here because you see me as the latest in a long line of saints and sinners whose words and deeds are as fascinating as my own are insignificant.'

'To tell the truth,' Gabi said, trying not to sound either too girlish or too forward, 'as I said in my letter, I am hoping you'll be able to help me solve a sixteenth-century mystery.'

The Cardinal led them into a room dominated by enormous windows looking out over the Grand Canal but in which there nevertheless seemed to be very little light. The small panes of yellowed glass in the windows were evidently designed to keep out the sunlight without interrupting the view.

'As you already know, Fräulein Dorn, the sixteenth century was not an altogether happy time for Venice or for my family . . .'

'Or for the Church . . .'

'Ah! The Church . . .'

The Cardinal filled the pause with an almost imperceptible gesture that managed to communicate quite clearly the sighing of an unsighed sigh and the shrugging of unshrugged shoulders.

'The Church . . . .'

Another pause.

'When was there ever a happy time for the Church?' the Cardinal said at last.

The servant in the green baize apron had brought lemonade in two-handled, almost translucent china mugs, with little piles of amoretto biscuits on matching plates. The gleaming oak floorboards squeaked pitilessly under the painstaking tread of his feet. The room smelled reassuringly of beeswax, like the parlour of a convent. The fruit of much labour seen, no doubt, as a form of prayer.

'Robinson's Barley Water,' the Cardinal said. 'The essence of old England, don't you think?'

Gabi decided that the time had come to state her case.

'As I think you know, my idea is that Venice had an opportunity in the sixteenth century to restore the unity of Christendom. That means, you had not only religious reasons but also diplomatic and pragmatic reasons for wanting to end the divisions.'

'If we did, then it was a strange—and I must say uncharacteristic—fantasy.'

'If I'm not mistaken,' Gabi persisted, 'a member of your family visited the Emperor in Leipzig in 1550. A lost opportunity—a last opportunity, perhaps.'

'What a marvellous might-have-been!' Alison said. 'No Wars of Religion, no Thirty Years War, no World Wars, no European Union.'

'An impossible might-have-been, I'm afraid,' the Cardinal said. 'War is a savage insanity of which human beings seem unable to cure themselves. There will always be those who find reasons for war. And they are as guilty as those who do the killing.'

The Cardinal led his two guests through a nest of rooms of different shapes and sizes. In one room, there were windows looking onto a *campo* filled with sunlight. A middle-aged woman was sitting on an upright chair, knitting what appeared to be a large sock in pink wool.

'May I introduce my niece Serafina?'

'How do you do? How do you do?'

'How do you do? *Piacere.*'

(Gabi seized the opportunity to demonstrate her command of Italian.)

There were two small boys lying face down in front of a television set.

'Come on, boys. Marco, Ludo. Come and meet my guests from England and Austria.'

The Cardinal said 'Orstria', in the old-fashioned way.

'The not-so-heavenly twins,' he said. 'They are the future. I am the past.'

The boys, aged about ten, were wearing long-sleeved white shirts, brown corduroys and sandals.

'Marc'Antonio. Ludovico,' they said, identifying themselves.

More 'how do you do's?' and *piaceres.*

'They should be at school.'

'It's June 2nd, Alvise,' Serafina said. '*Ricordi?*'

'*Il Giorno della Repubblica.* The Day of the Republic. How could I forget?'

At last they reached a room with a heavy metal door.

'We had to do this, after the *acqua altissima* of 1966. Fortunately our archives, such as they are, were already up here, but not well protected.'

The room was lined with metal shelves. Files and boxes were piled on the shelves and on the floor in a disorderly fashion.

'Whatever there is in here is yours to discover, Fräulein Dorn. I hope you will not be disappointed, but I fear that you may be.'

They returned to the reception room. The Cardinal led them out onto the balcony. Venice perennially observed. Venice perennially indifferent to those who observe it. Venice about which nothing can be said that has not been said before.

'Your Eminence, there is one other thing I should tell you,' Gabi said suddenly.

'My dear child . . .'

'I believe that a member of my own family was also at that meeting in Leipzig—a distant relative . . .'

'Then we must share the responsibility, your family and mine, for so many crimes and follies—the crimes and follies of European history.'

The Cardinal's voice now had a steely edge, reminding the women that he had spent the whole of his active life at the centre of power of the system of global power that is the Church of Rome.

'And, my dear child, since you have told me something that I did not expect to hear, I will tell you something remarkable that you did not expect to hear when you ladies so charmingly offered to grace me with your presence here today.'

Alison and Gabi had certainly not come to see the Cardinal expecting to be told anything portentous.

'In my old age, I am more or less a free man—free of all my former responsibilities, even of all my former loyalties—other than the life-long duties of the priesthood and the loyalty that is the loyalty of every child of God. And so I am free to think, to think for myself, to think about the future, as old men sometimes do. But I think about the future, not wistfully or bitterly, or hopelessly. I look for, and long for, another Martin Luther, another Reformation. But, this time, we must use religion to see beyond religions.'

'You are able to see light in the awful darkness of these times?' Alison said, with surprise and uncertainty in her voice.

'*Ecco! Lux in tenebris.*'

'And if the darkness will still not comprehend . . . ?'

'That is our God-given task, dear Mrs Brand, as it ever was. The divine spark in the human soul cannot be extinguished.'

Gabriele Dorn registered an irony. She, a young scholar, was an avid spectator of the tragicomedy of the human past. The ancient Cardinal had his weary eyes fixed upon a better human future.

Alison Brand registered a different puzzle. She wondered if she had heard the language of Inherent Potentiality and Ideal Possibility. Surely not? The Cardinal seemed to be someone who was a holder of great spiritual power but who had come to see that spiritual power in its old forms had come to the end of its useful life. Surely the Firm could not have not found its way into the hermetic caverns of the Vatican—an invisible power over the very visible power of those who act in the name of the most invisible of all powers?

As the Cardinal bade farewell to his two visitors as graciously as he had received them, Alison looked carefully. The Cardinal was not wearing a ring—a bishop's ring or a ring of any other kind—on the fingers of either hand.

They remained silent on the journey back to their hotel. Not that they were not thinking, each in her own way. Gabi was seeing in Venice the thrilling presence of the elusive past. When you are young, the future is, by comparison, a mere abstraction. Alison was seeing in Venice the illusion of the past, the ambiguity of the present, and the obscurity of a frightening human future.

'Now is come a darker day,' she said quietly, wanting Gabi to hear, but half-hoping that she would not.

The choppy water of the Canal lapped against the sides of the Cardinal's gondola, the familiar scenes gliding slowly past, the conscious mind at the mercy of the swaying of the jet-black boat, cradle and coffin, unconscious archetype of our first helplessness and our last.

*   *   *

2

Èze

Meanwhile, several degrees south in latitude and several degrees west in longitude, Mr Gray's yacht *Bellerophon* was tied up relatively inconspicuously in the Port Vauban at Antibes. It was wedged between two even larger vessels, one of which was provided with what seemed to passers-by to be a landing platform for a helicopter, if it was not an off-road parking-place for a couple of SUVs.

Mr Gray's guests had made their own way to the South of France. His yacht was their assembly-point. There was time to raise a glass of champagne to celebrate a particular piece of work satisfactorily accomplished. Then two cars, which had been waiting on the quayside, carried them high above the coast towards a village perched improbably on top of a mountain. A winding back road, no wider than the cars, brought them at last to their destination, a rambling house concealed behind ochre walls flowing with white—and red-flowered bougainvillea vines.

The Villa Montgenêt felt isolated, and yet it was barely a kilometre from the village of Èze. It seemed to be surrounded by masses of rock and vegetation and yet, from the terrace where dinner was served, there was a view stretching far into the distance over a green and grey and sun-burned landscape.

Mr Gray and the Countess offered no explanation of their connection with the house. Did they own it or rent it? Was it a property of the Firm? Their introductions of the guests had also been characteristically minimal. Edmund and Greg Seare were introduced to a man and a woman whom Edmund, at least, immediately recognised. Both had taken part in Mr Gray's laboriously staged exposition of the Invisible College in its Cabinet of Curiosities.

There was the woman who had sounded Italian, who resembled Isabella d'Este and who had spoken in the name of Symbolism (and whom we will refer to here as Isabella). And there was the lively man who had spoken, in English with a mildly French accent, in the name of Eunomianism, that is, the study of the ideal potentiality of human society (and whom we will refer to here as Thomas). (They were well-known public intellectuals under their own names.) To Edmund, who liked to be precise about such matters, they both seemed to be in the twilight zone of fortyishness.

'So now . . . ,' Mr Gray said.

In his role as an impresario of ideas, Mr Gray had, by his manner, tacitly decreed that the conversation at dinner would not include much in the way of small talk.

Observing yet again their unwavering seriousness and professionalism, Edmund reminded himself that Mr Gray and the Countess acted in the name of an institution—the Firm—which was a multinational corporation dealing in the commodity of Ideas or, more strictly speaking, dealing in the rather rarer commodity of the Best Ideas. It was an unusual sort of market, in which—as in the markets for Old Master paintings or top-rank footballers—demand and supply were always very limited.

The Countess Frieda implemented Mr Gray's unspoken decree.

'Thomas, would you like to begin?' she said.

'You, Dr Seare . . . ,' Thomas began.

'Oh, Greg—please.'

'You, Greg, and you, Mr Jenning . . .'

'Edmund—please.'

'You, Greg, and you, Edmund, are English.'

'We are,' Edmund said, speaking for both of them.

'You English have been the philosophers of Europe.'

'That's not what Nietzsche thought,' Greg said. 'Nietzsche thought the English had single-handedly destroyed the mind of Europe.'

'But, on other days of the week, he also thought that the mind of Europe needed to be destroyed,' the Countess said.

'The true history of the world is not the history of battles and buildings and machines and the making of things,' Thomas said. 'The true history of the world is the history of ideas.'

'And the history of the symbolic social structures made from ideas.' Isabella said.

Thomas and Isabella had gone into antiphonal mode.

'William of Occam and Francis Bacon made possible a new kind of philosophy.'

'And Wyclif and Cranmer made possible a new kind of religion.'

'And Hobbes and Locke and Jefferson made possible a new kind of democracy.'

'And Locke and Berkeley and Hume made a new kind of philosophy.'

'And Adam Smith and Ricardo made possible a new kind of economics.'

'And Burke and Owen and Bentham made the dialectic of modern politics.'

'And Newton and Lyell and Darwin gave humanity a new idea of itself.'

Isabella and Thomas were clearly acting out parts already written, for an audience now of four people, but which should some day be an audience of millions.

'Those people were bold adventurers of the mind,' Thomas said, 'pioneers and explorers and settlers in a New World—a new human world.'

'So there you have it,' Mr Gray said, almost triumphantly. 'The four great empires of the mind of the modern world—religion, science, capitalism, and democracy.'

'The English ideas may not have been the best possible ideas,' Thomas said, 'but they are the winning ideas. They are the survivors in the struggle for survival that is the human mind thinking about itself.'

'The English have a lot to answer for,' the Countess said, in a tone only slightly on the approving side of neutral.

'I suppose we can't really hold them responsible,' Thomas said, 'for all that the Continental European mind has chosen to do with their interesting ideas.'

'And now we're suggesting the exploration of yet another new world,' Isabella said, 'a new mind-world—the Eunomian world, a new word for a new kind of world.'

'Language is to the English what music is to the Germans,' Thomas said, 'the mirror of the national soul. Or what the aesthetic is for us in France—the aesthetic as rationality plus good taste. For the English, language is the means of freedom, the freedom to construct possible mind-worlds, possible places of human habitation.'

'The French and the Germans don't have a separate word for "mind",' Edmund said. "Did you know that?'

'And what cannot be named does not exist,' Greg said.

'So the French and the Germans are, strictly speaking, mindless,' Edmund said, 'despite much misleading evidence to the contrary.'

'But the French more than make up for it in *esprit*,' Greg said.

'And the French don't have words for "to like" or "to dislike",' Edmund said. 'It must be awful not being able to love or hate things *vaguely*—or people, for that matter.'

'Shakespeare is the English essence,' Isabella said. 'We greatly admire what you have written about Shakespeare, Greg. Shakespeare as the master of the fantasy of reality. Shakespeare as the master of the reality of fantasy. That is what you said.'

Thomas took up the theme.

'The play, the poem, the novel, the essay, the newspaper, the rhetoric of politics, the game of diplomacy, the consoling words of religion—the English have used them all, pragmatically, relentlessly, to construct their own mind, to enjoy their own mind, to make their own world of fact and fantasy.'

'I'm not sure that I recognise myself or us in all this,' Edmund said. 'If asked a direct question about such matters, I think most English people would say that everything is a game—except games—which are serious.'

'A game is symbolism embodied and enacted,' Isabella said.

'Metaphysics made physical,' Thomas added, sounding as if he, at least, understood what they were saying. 'And physics made unpredictable.'

'The English have learned the game of symbolism from the monarchy,' Isabella said. 'The monarchy is a metaphysical mirror in which the English people see whatever they want to imagine about themselves at any particular time—the good and the bad and the ridiculous.'

'They are believers who believe that they don't believe what they believe, and laugh at their believing and their non-believing,' Thomas said. 'That makes them particularly good at commerce.'

'I'm afraid I'm a complete failure as a lackey of capitalism,' Greg said. 'I seem incapable of desiring to possess anything. I can walk through the most glamorous of stores, full of things desperately pleading with me to buy them, and want to buy nothing.'

'You're a class traitor,' Edmund said. 'Those who have money to spare have a legal duty to spend it, as recklessly as possible. Capitalism is the economics of two laundries. If one laundry doesn't wash the dirty linen of the other, they'll both go out of business—and society will go with them. There's no opting out.'

'I can't desire to possess,' Greg continued. 'But I am very able to believe.'

'You're able to believe anything?' Isabella said.

'I suppose I have rather a special definition of belief,' Greg said, disappointing those of his hearers who had hoped that his intelligence might be an interesting mutation of what they would normally recognise as intelligence. 'By belief I mean affirming the truth of something by leading my life in accordance with it.'

'That is surely a special definition,' the Countess said. 'That would be why people are able to believe absolutely anything, and do great evil in the name of their belief.'

'It's strange,' Edmund said. 'I, on the other hand, seem to be just the opposite. I desire almost everything and everyone, but I find it difficult to believe anything. My head is in my heart.'

'Dr Seare is evidently a pragmatist,' the Countess said.

'I certainly am not,' Greg said. 'It's just that, for me, to think and to will are two sides of the same thing.'

'But most people don't actually will anything,' Edmund said. 'They just do things, as the slaves of desire. They live in a sort of entropic void. Things just happen. It takes a special effort of the mind not to do something. That's all our famous moral freedom actually is—the freedom not to do something, if we summon up the effort not to do it.'

'Mr Jenning is evidently a cynic,' the Countess said.

'I certainly am not. I think I may be an epicurean. And I think Greg is possibly a stoic—if we are anything labelable, which we may not be.'

'And you, Isabella,' Greg said, 'which are you, if I may ask—stoic or epicurean, pragmatist or true believer?'

'None of the above,' Isabella said. 'I observe, therefore I am.'

Her words served as the closing line of the well-prepared performance.

The light of the day had ebbed away. The terrace was half-lit by the light from lamps concealed in the surrounding foliage.

Edmund's tiny bedroom seemed like the cell of a cheerful sort of hermit. Bright yellow bedstead. Bright yellow wardrobe. Straw-seated wooden chair. Coconut mat on the pale brown floor-tiles. And, on the bedside table, a Moroccan lamp, metal with thick lenses of coloured glass, projecting a patchwork of shapes and colours onto the white walls and ceiling, stimulants for a vivid imagination.

Perhaps the room contained a message for him. He would withdraw from the world and spend the rest of a solitary life in a little cabin of clay and wattle, an ark on dry land, *chaste et pure*—chanting faint hymns to the fruitless moon—close to the heroically resistible temptations of the Côte d'Azur and Monte Carlo.

He stood at the open window-doors. Pine trees against the dark blue sky—*dichte Tannendunkelheit*—odoriferous tree-wings caressed by the warm night air—*soave zeffiretto*.

Scent of orange blossom. He closed the window-doors. *Scent of jasmine*. He closed a small square window high on another wall.

Jasmine and orange blossom and pine. Siren voices of a restless longing for the South—for Sicily or Andalusia or Greece or North Africa, where a north European native—pale eyes, pale skin and a pale soul—must try to find a new identity and a new morality, the morality of a purified sensuality. *Dahin* or not *dahin*? Always the question. Monastic seclusion?—not now—later, perhaps.

Sage, Welt, zu guter Nacht! Je demeure!

And the particular piece of work satisfactorily accomplished, celebrated with a glass of champagne on board the *Bellerophon*?

Gregory Seare has published pseudonymously a slim volume, a *lepidus libellus* with the intriguing title *Invisible Power*. It is selling well and attracting much intelligent attention. It is shamelessly cross-genre—novel, novelette, *nouvelle nouvelle*, essay, play, epic poem, neo-neo-Platonist film-script.

As novel, it is in the genre known as Ideal Realism or Magic Idealism, designed to imagine a new philosophy of personality—a post-Freudian idealist physiology of the mind—the ideal unreality of its hero being that he is a person unspoiled by parents or teachers.

It is a *novel of the mind*. It demonstrates how the human mind constructs its own world—in the private mind of each human being and in the public minds of human societies. Inevitably, it is a book that fails miserably to avoid those pests and parasites of artistic work—namely, ideas. It has a plot of raw facts and events, a sub-plot of interacting ideas, and a sub-sub-plot, a subconscious plot, of ideas in free association.

It is an anti-*Candide*, a tract against philosophies of pacifism and quietism, indifferentism and defeatism—the temptation to cultivate the garden as if the gardener were not also an integral part of the garden. It suggests that the great problems of the human world cannot be solved by politics or diplomacy or violence, but only by a change in the psychology of those people who have exceptional power over what happens in the human world—a change in their self-identifying, their emotional states, the symbolic reality that they inhabit.

It is a Eunomian book, the beginning of the imagining of a *new kind of human being* and a *new kind of human society*. And it is the partial lifting of the veil that conceals a benign conspiracy to use humanity's inexhaustible power of self-creating to bring into being a *new kind of human reality*. It is a *fiction* launched into the *fiction* that is the human world, telling a new story. New lyre, new story.

Such is the delicate task that has—so far!—been satisfactorily accomplished. Whether Greg Seare is the true author—given his notorious limitations—or whether he is merely the scribe, the writer of these lines leaves to the judgment of the reader.

A conspiracy that does not allow itself to be imagined as a conspiracy is not making full use of its *inherent potentiality*. A conspiracy that reveals too much of its hidden self is jeopardising some part of its *ideal possibility*. Imagination is the art of the possible.

A novel is a shared dream. A dream is a possible reality in which we live for a while.

*   *   *

3

Venice II

A table for six at the Cipriani. Mr Gray and the Countess had stayed for another week at the Villa Montgenêt and then travelled overland to Venice. Greg and Edmund had joined the *Bellerophon* on its circumnavigation of Italy. The dinner appointment had been made by telephone as the yacht was driving through a storm somewhere near the place where the Mediterranean and the Adriatic Seas cartographically converge.

Accompanied by two of the crew-members, the temporary, and not wholly convincing, sailors from England had taken time to visit, not for the first time, Paestum and Segesta and Selinunte and Syracuse. At Segesta, Edmund had sat down on the springy turf of the hillside opposite the noble wreck of the skeleton temple and, like a daughter of Jerusalem, he had wept—not a mere moistening of the eyes, but shoulder-shaking tears.

'*Eheu fugaces, Postume, Postume,*' was Edmund's simple response to the question—why the tears? '*O tempora, O mores! Fuit Ilium. Und so weiter.*'

He and Greg were sitting on wooden deck chairs, protected from the sun by a canvas stretched across the yacht's main deck. The yacht was gliding almost silently past an Italian coast that seemed near and far, a featureless strip between sea and sky.

'They weren't really tears in the ordinary meaning of the word,' Edmund said. 'More a liquefying of the brain. I had an Edward Gibbon moment. I saw the decline and fall of Western Civilisation. A three-thousand-year mind-empire in a wreck of ruinous perfection. *Lacrimae rerum. Lacrimae inanes.*'

'*Wo ist Athen? Entflohene Götter!*' Greg said. 'Or else you could say that the gods have disappeared from the temple, but the temple remains. We're still Athenians. We keep rebuilding their temple.'

'Temples in our own honour. God made Man. Man made God. The argument from despair.'

'The Athenians knew despair,' Greg said. 'The higher they flew towards the sun, the deeper they knew the fall of man had been.'

'Plato lived to be old and sad and bitter.'

'But, on the other hand,' Greg said, 'since I seem to be cast in the "on the other hand" role for the time being—on the other hand, Plato, you might say, never died. We're better Platonists than Plato. In our minds Plato is still thinking.'

'The ascent of man is the descent of man,' Edmund said, determined not to be reassured. 'The stairway to Paradise goes in both directions. Going up, we meet ourselves coming down. Lucifer tried to climb back into heaven but ended up on earth.'

Greg knew Edmund well enough to know that his intellectual moods were substantial but passing things. And he knew, and he knew that Edmund knew, that psychic healthiness requires a balanced diet of yea-saying and nay-saying, the pendulum between the smile and the tear.

Two days out from Venice the yacht anchored close to Marina di Ravenna. Greg and Edmund walked in the Pineta di Classe, carpeted with fallen pine-needles and empty pine-cones, the air full of the scent of sun-warmed pine-trees. They revisited the glories of Ravenna, where the Hellenic and the Hebraic meet in the Roman. They laid white roses at Dante's tomb. They were moved, beyond words and beyond tears, by the presence of a European past that had almost ceased to be a European present, a presence that would be absent from the European future.

The prospect of dinner in Venice was enough to fill both of them with a mood of intense yea-saying. It seemed like a Russian doll of pleasures—approaching Venice from the sea; a bath and a martini, or two, at their *pensione*; a gathering of people whom they were glad to know, to be with, in some sense to love; a meal that was to be a special occasion, a celebration—a celebration of Gabi's birthday.

Gabi herself, preparing for the evening in her *pensione*—which was on the Zattere next door to the *pensione* where the two men were staying—took particular pleasure in the thought that she was to attend a dinner in her honour with a group of people than whom there could not be a group of people less likely to sing 'Happy Birthday' in public.

On the other hand, it was a group of people by whom a newly minted twenty-three-year-old might reasonably feel somewhat intimidated. Her aunt and Mr Gray, Dr Seare and Edmund—each, in their own way, seemed unusually formidable.

And, as for the Cardinal, she could not decide whether to think of him as what he represented—the two thousand years of the *schwarzweiß* history of *unserer heiligen Mutter, die Kirche*—, or as what he seemed to her to be as a person—old and at peace, not merely alive but lively. If only Alison—good, reliable Alison—had not had to go back to London for her son Rupert's Easter half-term break.

'Life is a conversation—or so it seems to be,' Mr Gray said, meaning to break the ice rather than to propose a topic of conversation.

'Life is work, for most people,' the Countess said, meaning to sound severe.

'And family, for most people,' Greg added, meaning to sound conventional.

They had chosen a table in the main restaurant of the hotel, rather than on a terrace outside with fine, but distracting, *vedute* of Venice. Gabi had told Mr Gray and the Countess about the Cardinal's puzzling remarks about a new Luther and a religion beyond religions. They had agreed that they would use the opportunity of the birthday dinner to try to get the Cardinal to reveal more of his thinking.

'I have a confession to make,' Gabi said, refocusing the conversation.

'Ah, the Catholics,' Edmund said. 'Confessing in order to pay off their monthly credit-card account of sin.'

'*Debita nostra*,' Greg said.

'While I've been in Venice,' Gabi said, ignoring the interruption, 'I've being going each day to a church very close to my hotel.'

'The *Gesuati*,' the Cardinal said.

'Yes. It's an ordinary Baroque church in form, but amazingly perfect in every detail—down to the banks of white lilies which seem always to be fresh. Well, I asked Cardinal Trevisan to explain to me—a simple-minded sort of Catholic—why anyone would go to so much trouble and expense to honour a God who can be worshipped perfectly adequately in a monk's cell in the desert—or under a banyan or a bodhi. And I made the Cardinal promise to tell you his answer here this evening over dinner.'

'I'm not sure that my explanation will convince you,' the Cardinal said. 'All I can say—and this is what I said to Gabriele when we hatched this little plot—is that, if you regard God—among other things—as the perfection of all perfection, it's not surprising that you should want to present yourself to God in the context of some form of perfection—whether it is in the sublime simplicity of the desert or a beautiful place made by human minds and human hands.'

Edmund, who had himself recently experienced and resisted the eremitic temptation, was evidently not satisfied with the Cardinal's answer—or Gabi's question.

'Alvise . . . ,' he began.

When Gabi had introduced the Cardinal to the others, he had asked them to call him Alvise. Gabi herself felt unable to respect his request, for historical and ecclesiological and chronological reasons. She would try to remember to address him as Monsignore.

'. . . if I may,' Edmund continued after a hesitation, as if even he had some doubt about the appropriate form of address. 'I am not a Catholic, simple-minded or otherwise, but there is a very different question that many people ask, non-Catholics and perhaps even Catholics. Is it better to worship a God that is dead than no god at all?'

'Ha!' the Cardinal said, evidently delighted by Edmund's economical formulation of a classic provocation. 'The great question of the nineteenth century! It drove them all mad. When godliness is flouted, men go mad—and the gods notice!'

'Not least poor Nietzsche,' Greg said.

'Not least Nietzsche,' the Cardinal said. 'But countless others also. God cannot die—*ex hypothesi*. What can fail is the god-like in human beings—the god-like that is able to have an idea of god. That is what we owe to the recent past—we Europeans at least. The idea of God was eclipsed. A shadow passed over the face of God.'

'A hypothetical God, Alvise?' the Countess said, evidently intending to prompt the Cardinal into some sort of reassuring clarification.

'God's characteristics are hypothetical in the sense that we can only know them in the form that the human mind and human language are able to make available to us. We apply human characteristics to God and then negate them. We die, so we say God is immortal. We have a mind of limited capacity, so we suppose that God has a mind of unlimited capacity. We know that we are imperfect, so we say that God is perfect. We know that we are not all-loving, so we say that God is all-loving. But we also know that God's true unknowable nature is certainly not human nature, not even human nature negated.'

'You say that the face of God is in eclipse,' Greg said, 'but the world seems to be seething with religion, no less than it ever has been.'

'There is not *religion*,' the Cardinal said. 'There are *religions*. Spirituality is not co-ordinate with religion. There is good religion and bad religion. And bad religion—including bad Christianity—has done more evil than any other form of human institution—with the possible exception of nationalism, the evil form of patriotism.'

'From the gorilla to the death of God,' Greg said. 'From the death of God to the gorilla. The parabolic history of the human species. If God doesn't exist, Man is God.'

'Man the god and Man the beast,' Edmund said. 'People don't believe in the humanity of Man any longer, or the divinity of God. So Man-the-Beast has made God in his own image. The New Egolatry. If Hell doesn't exist, everything is permitted, isn't it?'

'Isn't it just the over-educated few,' Greg said, 'who are able to clear the idea of God from their minds?'

'But isn't it the over-educated few,' the Cardinal said, 'who have never been able to clear the idea of God from their minds, the over-serious few for whom religion is too much, and scepticism is not enough, for whom atheism is too much and agnosticism is not enough? Voltaire was a defiant sceptic and yet he couldn't believe his own unbelief. He was angry with God for not existing.'

'So was Nietzsche,' Greg said. 'He was a defiant nihilist and yet . . .'

'. . . and yet he was haunted by the Lutheranism of his early training—like Hegel. The defiant unbelievers give the non-existing-God other names—Spirit, Reason, Nature, History, Art, Science, Humanity, Progress, Eternal Return . . .'

'Denying divinely the divine,' Greg said.

'Incurable nostalgia for the All,' the Cardinal said.

The Countess leaned forward over the table, hesitated for a moment, holding the attention of the others who waited for her to speak.

'For me,' she began, 'the God in whom I can believe cannot be merely a god of the mind, an intellectual phenomenon, a necessary hypothesis. God must be an affective thing, to whom the whole of my being can attach itself. Not merely a projection of the human personality, and certainly not merely a collection of negations. God must be quite other, yet somehow within me. Isn't that the only possible meaning of a belief in God. God, the other, within us. Do I make any sense, Alvise? Forgive me.'

'My dear Countess,' the Cardinal said, gently and affectionately. 'I am moved by what you say, which is so close to what I myself try to believe. We human beings contain the universe. The universe is not an other. It is within us, and we are within it. But God *is* an other, beyond the universe, and yet within that part of the universe which is me. The human being, part of the universe, is able to know and to feel the presence of God.'

'So the universe also contains mind?' Mr Gray said. 'A strange form of matter.'

'It must be so,' Greg said. 'The universe contains a form of matter than can form an idea of the universe—so the universe must be a self-conscious universe.'

'It's strange, isn't it?' Mr Gray said. 'To us the universe seems to be something at the mercy of time, never the same from one moment to the next, but also something orderly—chaos and order, an orderly restlessness.'

'The whirligig of time,' Greg said.

'I think I may be the living embodiment of orderly restlessness,' Edmund said, 'the whirligig personified.'

'Are these also simply illusions caused by the limitations of the human mind and of human language?' Mr Gray persisted.

'On the contrary,' the Cardinal said. 'Edmund is right. We are each a microcosm of the cosmic. We have the dynamic power, the impulse of life, the creative power, and the power of self-ordering within us. That is the *god-like* within us. But also we act like anything else in the natural world, the cause of effects, good and bad—the *matter-like* within us.'

'As someone naturally inclined to belief,' Greg said, 'I would be glad to believe that we have a dual nature. As *things*, we do good and evil—like fire and water. As *humans*, we can *choose* to do good and avoid evil.'

'And we can love,' Edmund said. 'We can even be lovable.'

'We can love the true and the good and the beautiful,' Greg said, 'a very strange feature of physical matter, if ever there was one!'

'Yes,' the Cardinal said. 'I would call it *grace*. The supposed void that contains the universe is filled with grace, a gracious aether. And love is a form of grace, a reflection of the mind of God within us.'

'*Dia voluptas*,' Greg said. '*L'amor che muove il sole e l'altre stelle.* In San Vitale in Ravenna, we inwardly genuflected in the very place where Dante may have outwardly genuflected—in front of the image of Justinian, the image of Rome as an empire of law under the empire of the love of God.'

'As a man naturally inclined to desire,' Edmund said, 'I would love to believe that the sun and the planets are kept together by *love*—and that the nebulae are seething masses of love, with the occasional star bursting out, unable to contain its repressed love any longer, living and dying for a few million years of love.'

'Why not?' the Cardinal said. 'There are worse things to believe.'

'We should ask Gabi about her work here in Venice,' Mr Gray said.

'Yes, Gabi,' the Countess said. 'Have you made any great discovery? Are you about to re-write European history?'

'No. That is, it's really too soon to say,' Gabi said. 'I think I may *possibly* have found something that may *possibly* be important. But there's lots more work to do.'

'Can you yet say whether our respective families are indeed responsible for the decline and fall of Christian civilisation?'

'No, Monsignore. Not quite yet! I have found a reference in your family's papers to *la sedicente unione spiritale europea*—"the so-called European spiritual union". And I found another reference, quite separate, to *un modo di vivere* of the *città terrene* within the *città di Dio*—some sort of union between the City of God and the various Cities of Man.'

'That sounds like Dante's peculiar programme to re-make the medieval world into a benign world society,' Greg said. 'It fell on deaf fourteenth-century ears.'

'Well, I hope that Gabi finds that our respective families were on the right side, if there ever was such a debate in the *sixteenth* century.'

'And which would have been the right side, Alvise?' Greg asked.

'I will reserve my position on that, for the time being, if you don't mind,' the Cardinal said. 'The debate continues.'

They toasted Gabi and her work several times and in several languages and with the warmest affection.

After dinner, Greg and Edmund and Gabi took the Cardinal's gondola through the sleeping water of obscure side-canals, the mighty shadows of the buildings almost meeting above their heads, an occasional street light, the sound of voices in an empty square. They were wearing white carnival half-masks. Edmund and Gabi sat together, their legs stretched out in front of them, their arms resting along each other's shoulders, their light summer jackets neatly folded and placed like a sword between them. Facing them, Greg and the dark shape of the silent gondolier.

Greg began to sing softly, hardly above a whisper.

'Ti xe bela, ti xe zovene.
Ti xe fresca come un fior,
Vien per tutti le so lagreme:
Ridi adesso e fa l'amor!'

And then the Cardinal's gondolier broke his silence. Greg let him sing alone, the voice of a certain idea of Venice, *maestoso ma non troppo.*

'Coi pensieri malinconici
No te star atormentar . . .'

'We will not die,' Greg said. 'It cannot be!'

Venice, everlasting city of the troubled imagination, stealthy co-conspirator in ambiguous intimacies and anxious hopes.

*   *   *

4

Beyond the Human

Greg immediately recognised the invitation as the equivocal kind of invitation that suggests an unequivocal reply. It was an invitation he could not possibly refuse. It was an invitation he could not possibly accept.

The invitation was contained in a letter from the Vice-President (Planning) of Goldberg Pynch, the investment bank. The Vice-President (Planning) asked whether Greg would be willing to participate in the firm's Strategic Ethics Review Forum.

On the one hand, Greg saw that he could not possibly take part in such a thing, given his firm belief that ethics had nothing to do with business or, rather, that business had nothing to do with ethics. On the other hand, he could see that there would be a delicious irony in taking part in a charade in which profound bad faith was so shamelessly concealed behind a thin veil of good intentions. And there was the relevant fact that he would also be rewarded materially, with what the letter called 'appropriate compensation'—and an investment bank would probably have more exalted ideas of appropriate compensation than one would normally find in a British university.

Reading the letter again, he noticed something that resolved the dilemma unequivocally and definitively. The Vice-President's signature—'Sincerely, Jake Plowman'—was in severe black ink. But, in the first main paragraph of the letter, there were several underlinings in blue ink. The letter 'd' had been underlined each time that it appeared. The firm of Goldberg Pynch evidently and improbably harboured a member of the Firm.

In reply to Greg's acceptance of the part-time appointment, there came—by motor-bike courier from London—a bundle of papers 'to put you in the picture' and an invitation to a meeting in London during the following week. The urgency was explained by the fact that the bank was undertaking 'a review of long-term global developments in the light of the Executive Board's decision to present a Revised Global Orientation Framework to our investors by 30 September of this year.'

'It goes without saying,' the covering letter went on to explain, 'that the input of SERF to RGOF is seen as crucial.'

It was fortunate that Greg was on a term's sabbatical leave from the university. Perhaps somebody somewhere had known that fact. He would have to devote precious time and uncongenial effort to the peculiar background papers—**PERSONAL & CONFIDENTIAL : SERF MEMBERS EYES ONLY.** In the time available, he would have to form communicable 'ethical' judgments on the weighty matters to be discussed at the meeting in London.

The agenda was in two parts.

1. *COGNITIVE BIOLOGY.*
2. *COGNITIVE ENGINEERING.*

Under the general heading Cognitive Biology there were three sub-headings:

1.1 *Cognitive Genetics.*
1.2 *Cognitive Surgery.*
1.3 *Cognitive Pharmacology.*

Under the general heading Cognitive Engineering there were four sub-headings.

2.1 *Global Mind.*
2.2 *Global Culture.*
2.3 *Global Psychology.*
2.4 *Global Psychotherapy.*

An introductory paper ('The Ethical Scene') explained that the bank was faced with medium-term and long-term investment decisions in all the itemised fields.

'However,' the paper went on to explain, 'decisions in all such fields appear to be located at or beyond an Ethical Boundary that is essentially New in Quality.'

Greg had two immediate reactions to the list. (1) He had no ready-made ethical response to any of the items on the list. (2) Such matters—whatever precisely they turned out to mean—were probably not at the centre of the thinking even of professional philosophers, of whom Greg was not one, even in the United States of America.

Following from (1) and (2), it was also good to think (3) that it might be possible to approach such questions—whatever precisely they turned out to be—in an organised, not to say business-like, or even bureaucratic, manner. That would certainly make an interesting change from traditional—not to say academic—approaches.

And (4) it was even better to think that the new method might at last *solve* the insoluble problems that had been discussed by many people, in many countries and cultures, over the course of many centuries, not to say millennia.

Executive Summaries relating to each agenda item clarified matters obscurely, darkness made visible, at least.

COGNITIVE BIOLOGY refers to the ethical implications of handling mental processes as physical processes.

Cognitive Genetics refers to the genetic modification of human beings to produce appropriate mentalities.

Cognitive Surgery refers to the manipulation of particular human brains to produce appropriate mentalities.

Cognitive Pharmacology refers to the use of chemical compounds to produce appropriate mentalities.

COGNITIVE ENGINEERING refers to the ethical implications of the collective re-programming of mental processes at all levels from the personal to the global.

Global Mind refers to the replacing of the human brain, as store and processor of data, by socially organised electronic and post-electronic reservoirs and generators.

Global Culture refers to the replacing of existing socially generated mentalities by appropriate collective mentalities.

Global Psychology refers to the fashioning of appropriate paradigms of brain activity.

Global Psychotherapy refers to the adjusting of individual and collective mentalities in accordance with appropriate paradigms of brain activity.

Greg certainly had some immediate reactions to the Executive Summaries. (5) He wondered whether he was quite the right person to explore the ethical implications of any of the items on the list. (6) He wondered whether there would be much further use for the categories in which people like him had traditionally conducted their ethical discussions—freedom, duty, free will, justice, the good and the true, the ideal and the real, reason and rationality, knowledge and belief, cause and motive, altruism and the common interest, natural rights, sin, repentance and redemption, morality . . . .

Perhaps the whole history of philosophy and religion had been made obsolete, abandoned as a chronicle of wasted time.

It also occurred to him (7) that his idea of an 'investment bank' and, indeed, of commercial activity in general might need some revision, if the self-appointed leaders of the commercial world now saw it as a necessary part of their function to consider matters that had hitherto been seen as the special responsibility of philosophers, politicians, public intellectuals, and religious leaders. However, it seemed to follow, from (5) to (7) above, that (8) it would be interesting, and might even be a matter of duty in some obsolete meaning of that word, to experience this latest product of the insatiable and indefatigable creature known as *homo faber,* this new chapter in the story of the human will to know and the human will to power, the will that inspires and burns, the power that creates and destroys, the knowledge that excites and appeases.

When he had finished reading the Goldberg Pynch background papers, Greg found himself with two further reactions. It was obvious (9) that the whole exercise was suffused with Americanism or, at least, with a certain idea of America's ambiguity—an idea which Americans themselves promoted and which non-Americans, even intelligent non-Americans, were inclined to believe, with more or less reluctance.

There were copious signs of the optimism, the pragmatism and the recalcitrant innocence which together make up the *practical idealism* of the United States. There were copious signs also of the *practical realism* which is the other side of that idealism—arrogance, ruthlessness and recklessness—the certainty of rectitude, the end that justifies all necessary means, disdain for the different and the anomalous and the intractable and the obscure.

But it was also true (10) that Goldberg Pynch was not truly an American company. It had a registered office and a principal place of business in two American states, but its presence was truly supranational. Its staff, at all levels, were truly multinational. Globalised Americanism can surely no longer be classed as true Americanism?

And there was one more conclusion, a thought so unwelcome that Greg wished that he could immediately unthink it, a thought to which he would assign no programmatic number.

Why did this supranational mixture of practical idealism and practical realism seem so familiar? Where had he met it before? His own answer to his own question was not long in coming. The sinister union of practical idealism and practical realism has been the essence of the *practical fascism* of religions. Was the new globalism a new religion, a new road to a new kind of *monarchia*, a road and a destination that even the fertile globalising minds of Aristotle and Seneca and Cicero and Augustine and Aquinas and Dante and Suárez and Kant and Allott could not have imagined?

He prepared for a journey to an extra-human vantage-point from which to see the whole picture of human climate-change, a place where, no doubt, he would be seen as a harmless old Houyhnhnm among the aspiring Yahoos who were taking over, more or less unopposed, the under-capitalised and under-performing Academy of Projectors, the derelict meeting-place of those who had thought that they were the masters of those who know.

Command no more. Your rule is ended. Your day is gone.

*   *   *

5

Connecticut

'Ed, I'd like to adopt you as my son and heir,' Abe Green said.

'That's kind of you, Abe,' Edmund said. 'Very kind. But I think I may be rather too attached to my peerless and priceless independence to be much use as a son and heir.'

In fact, Edmund was not sure how to respond to Abe's strange statement. Was he meant to take it literally? Or was it a rather florid way of expressing approval or even affection? The tone of Edmund's reply was intended to hedge his bet on these rather different alternatives.

'I guess it would have more effect on me than on you—truth to tell,' Abe said.

So he did mean it literally. Edmund noticed that Abe showed no sign of shyness, reticence or embarrassment—in itself a strange fact, given the unexpected and unusual nature of the offer. But Abe Green did not do shyness, reticence or embarrassment. Instead, there seemed to be a deep, underlying, permanent sadness in him, something far more than the unquenched grieving of a father for the loss of an only child.

Edmund recognised in Abe Green that permanent accumulated subjectivity of suffering which, perhaps perversely, he detected in the Jewish people he had known, a subjectivity which seemed to him to make them into the most human and the most non-trivial of human beings.

'You're not like anyone I've ever known,' Abe said. 'Not remotely like anyone else.'

'I'm afraid I may not be all that I seem, or seem to be all that I am,' Edmund said, lapsing into Henry James mode.

'Who is?' Abe said. 'Not me, for sure.'

'But I think a sort of incurable isolation may be both of me, what I seem and what I am.'

'But don't misunderstand me. I wouldn't want to possess you, like a Ming vase or a Picasso, a deluxe object, to look at and display. It's just that . . .'

Abe hesitated, as if even he found the explanation difficult to utter, if not to formulate.

'It's just that I feel a need to protect you, to save you . . .'

'Heavens! From what?'

'I can't precisely say—but you know as well as I do—or, perhaps, not quite as well as I do—maybe you have not seen enough of what happens to people—they get ugly—not just ugly in their bodies, but ugly in their minds, their spirit, their soul.'

Edmund silently invoked the help of the spirit of Henry James, even of Henry's brother William. It had occurred to him that Abe Green might not be, socially and psychologically, quite like anyone Edmund had ever known.

Instead, it was the spirit of Greg Seare that came to the rescue.

'The corruption of the best is worst,' he said, quoting one of Greg's leitmotivs.

'Absolutely. Absolutely.'

'I think that may be my life's aim,' Edmund said, '—to find the secret of the beautiful soul.'

They were both silent for a while.

'Anyway,' Abe said at last. 'Think about it at least. It wasn't easy for me to say it. I'm sure it isn't easy for you to deal with such a proposition.'

In the interests of historical accuracy, it should be recorded that this brief but significant conversation took place at about nine o'clock on a sunny Sunday morning in late June, on the veranda of Abe Green's house, four miles from Westport, Connecticut, in the United States of America.

'I'd ask you, Ed,' Abe said, by way of a coda or envoi, 'not to say too much about what we've just been talking about here. You can imagine the headlines.'

'Of course, Abe.'

History should also record that Edmund would, indeed, make every effort to respect Abe's request. The writer of the present lines would ask the reader of the present lines to do no less.

The limits of Edmund's discretion were to be tested rather soon, since Abe Green's near neighbours, the Meehans—'two of my very favourite people—and really the reason why I've ended up in this place'—were due to join Abe and Edmund for brunch in about two hours time, on that very veranda, on that beautiful Connecticut morning.

Jim Meehan was the former editor of, and now a widely syndicated columnist on, the venerable Boston Courier. Jane Meehan was a published poet and an occasional art critic. She also had an art-gallery in her home, selling works by living artists. It was an elegantly understated enterprise, a sale seeming to be merely the coincidental exchange of a substantial cheque and a delightful object selected from Jane's personal collection.

The limits of Edmund's discretion were tested to breaking point as he watched Jim Meehan emerge from the passenger-seat of a dusty Range Rover. He recognised him at once as the newspaperman who had been known by the pseudonym of Boxcar at a certain meeting in a beautiful chalet in a beautiful place in Bavaria.

Boxcar did not give the slightest indication that he recognised Edmund. Such, Edmund told himself, was the loyalty and self-discipline that the Firm evidently inspired. On the other hand, it could simply be that he (Edmund) was a more forgettable person than he had reasonably supposed.

'How should I describe you, Ed?' Abe said, making the introductions. 'By the way, he's Ed as in Edmund, not as in Edward.'

'A *farniente*, perhaps?' Edmund suggested. 'Or at least *niente* of very much worldly significance.'

'I wanted you to meet him just for that reason,' Abe persisted, adopting what Edmund recognised as a familiar American practice of speaking approvingly in the third person singular about a person, in their presence. 'He's something rather special.'

'You make me sound like some sort of circus freak—subcutaneously freakish.'

'I'm sorry, Ed. But you know what I mean. One way of putting it might be this. Ed is everything that Jay Gatsby could have been, if only Jay Gatsby had also been a decent human being.'

'Well, I must say,' Jane Meehan said, 'that's as clear as mud. Now I feel I've always known you, Edmund.'

'I've always felt bitter,' Jim Meehan said, 'that no one ever gave me the chance to be Jay Gatsby, preferably as he was, but even as he might have been.'

'You'd have been no good at it, either way, Jim,' Jane said. 'You'd have talked all the *farnientes* into an even earlier grave. We're Irish-American, Edmund, born and more or less bred—you may have noticed.'

Edmund had, indeed, noticed that they had somehow managed to retain various attractive Irish characteristics—*her* pale blue eyes and very white skin, needing blood, as William Shakespeare might have said, of which *his* complexion evidently had some to spare. And they both retained the tribal trait of infectious conversational enthusiasm.

'What's an ethnic stereotype for, if not as a beacon of aspiration?' Jim said.

'Or a millstone about the feebler sort of neck,' Jane said. 'Are you Irish at all, Edmund?'

'I've really no idea.'

'Don't know—or don't want to know?'

'No, really. I know nothing of my parents.'

'Something to be said for that, all things considered,' Jim said.

'Jim, really!' Jane said.

'I may have floated into this world on the back of a swan. I could be spawn of a virgin and a devil—which would explain one or two things. But I feel entirely English—one ethnic stereotype is stereotype enough, for me at least.'

'You should try having three—Irish, American and liberal.'

'Since when is liberal an ethnic stereotype?' Abe asked.

'Well, a genetic type, then,' Jim said. 'The liberalish gene.'

'Every child that's born into the world alive . . . .' Jane began.

'Is either a little Liberal or a little Conservative,' Jim continued.

'You could stop being a liberal tomorrow, if you wanted to,' Abe said. 'There are many who have found the way to the right and to righteousness.'

'Yes, I could. And I could be a pitcher for the Boston Braves the day after, if I wanted to. It's Kismet. Like pattern baldness.'

'A good head of hair you can lose,' Jane said, 'and Jim has. Liberalishness grows grey and grizzly, but it's always there, lurking.'

Mrs Hägeström, one half of Abe Green's Swedish version of Edmund's indispensable Mrs Iolescu, had wheeled onto the veranda a trolley stacked with richly various forms of alcohol.

'You're lucky it's not a few weeks from now,' Abe said. 'Otherwise we might have been charmed by the sweet sound of a chain-saw.'

'Abe, really!' Jim said. 'Edmund, would you believe it? Abe is destroying a beautiful old New England apple orchard—and for why, for Christ's sake?'

'A very good and practical reason,' Abe said.

'To make a space for helicopters to land. I ask you. I keep telling him it's the Cherry Orchard all over again. Nothing good can come of it.'

'Abe's apple orchard is America,' Jane said, quoting Chekhov, more or less.

'We are the garden and the gardener,' Edmund said, quoting himself accurately and obscurely.

The very visibly aged Mr Hägeström, other half of Abe Green's housekeeping arrangements, came onto the veranda.

'Telephone, sir.'

'They used to work for *us* years ago,' Jim said. 'Old Haggie is quite Firs-like, actually. He wanders round mumbling about the general decline of everything.'

'Abe seems to be especially fond of you, Edmund,' Jane said.

'Yes. I sense that he's in the market for a substitute son-figure.'

'You're not in need of a father-figure?'

'Not really. I've got a pretty effective super-ego of my own already. Mother-figure, perhaps. We all need that.'

'Self-made man with a self-made super-ego,' Jim said. 'Saint Sigmund would have banished you to a footnote. Biologically impossible.'

'Actually, we've been quite worried about Abe,' Jane said. 'He seems a changed man since Carl died.'

'Carlton was a great guy—like his mother,' Jim said.

'He had his problems, Jim.'

'He sure had problems—but so do they all now—the over-privileged young.'

'He was a mess, and you know it, Jim. We don't have children. Do you hope to have children, Edmund?'

'Not just for the sake of it.'

'We've never decided what we think of it, not having children. Depends on the day of the week. Sometimes we have a bit of a weep. Other times we take off at a moment's notice, and go somewhere special—and think how lucky we are to be free.'

'I'd like children as a sort of immortality,' Edmund said. 'They sort of immortalise you.'

'The best and the worst of you,' Jane said. 'Very often the very worst.'

'And I'd like children to mould,' Edmund said. 'Like sculptor's clay.'

'Actually, to tell the truth,' Jim said. 'Jane and I have been thinking that maybe the new Abe could be a better Abe—deeper and broader, less focused.'

'He sure was focused,' Jane said. 'One-track—totally focused on making himself the Great American Dream Story—and keen for other people to share his dream.'

'Maybe Abe's orchard is Abe,' Edmund said.

'We're surely hoping he'll put down some roots here,' Jim said.

'They loved their house in free-spirited Vermont,' Jane said. 'But I always thought there was something spooky about it—surrounded by great sinister trees watching them the whole time.'

'Americans never seem to attach themselves to anywhere,' Edmund said. 'They're always moving somewhere else.'

'Land of the Free, Home of the U-Hauled,' Jane said. 'America is the Land of This Moment in Time. You can be born again in another State of the Union, up to forty-nine times—and as many times as you want in the District of Columbia.'

'Even a beautiful old New England house like this seems like a temporary intrusion into a more or less empty landscape, a surface phenomenon.'

'You have to remember, Edmund,' Jim said, 'in tiny Old England—or tiny Old Ireland for that matter—every blade of grass has been counted and colonised. America is vast and wild—the human presence is gigantic but marginal.'

'You probably think of Americans as permanent provincials,' Jane said. 'All English people do.'

'Or is it that Americans think that English people do,' Edmund said. 'But I think we *do* think of you as permanently deracinated, in the etymological sense of the word. Deeply rootless.'

'You may have noticed it, Edmund,' Jane said. 'There's another thing that puzzles Europeans. America is a land of extreme politeness—and extreme violence. "You may want to stand still while I blow your head off." That sort of thing.'

'And, therefore,' Jim said, 'a land of lawyers dreaming of fees.'

'There *is* an interesting difference between Europeans and Americans,' Jane said. 'We've worked it out, Jim and I—the fruit of long and bitter experience.'

'You Europeans have a layer of subconsciousness that is proud and tragic,' Jim said.

'We Americans have a layer of subconsciousness that is proud and confused,' Jane said.

'And the Canadians have both,' Jim said, 'and the Australians have neither. One breed of people, four kinds of mind. Very odd.'

Abe had returned.

'Hell! What did we do to deserve the Palestinians? Their own worst enemies.'

'Not while the Israelis are around,' Jim said.

They went inside and filled their plates from a generous buffet of cold dishes. They sat around a weathered refectory table in the kitchen. The Hägeströms hovered between the kitchen and the scullery, somehow managing to convey an impression of impatience and generalised disapproval.

'Who have more power,' Edmund asked, 'politicians or journalists?'

'Neither,' Jim said. 'We're all slaves of systems. Spinning the prayer-wheels of power. Treading the treadmills of dead ideas. Speaking our lines in a play we haven't written, and don't understand. Tell them, Jane. Jane has written a novel about all this.'

'Unpublished. The world is still waiting for it, though the world may not know that it's still waiting for it. We're all characters in many different stories. We write the story of our own life, but our life-story is only an incident in the life-stories of other people, as theirs are in ours.'

'And they're all just little stories in the big story of everything,' Jim said. 'The random and the necessary. We're the meeting point of the random and the necessary. The random is what we can't explain. The necessary is what we can't change.'

'It's certainly pretty random the four of us being here together now,' Edmund said. 'How many chances did it take to bring us here together now?'

'Random but necessary,' Jim said. 'We're here today—Jane and I—because a shortage of potatoes in the 1840's in Ireland left our families food-less, rent-less and house-less—thanks to you English. Random and necessary. Like birth. Everyone's conception is random, but conception and birth follow the laws of necessity.'

'Art is the only place,' Jane said, 'the only place where the random and the necessary are united, in a thing containing human consciousness that is thrown into the world of things—*geworfen*, as one might say—the random made necessary—a painting, a sculpture, a building, a piece of music—a novel even—assuming they're beautiful, that is.'

'And then there's Washington D.C.,' Abe said. 'Where the random meets the necessary and produces chaos. Nobody knows why we go to war or why someone wins an election. We just throw the cards in the air and, when they fall to the ground, Jim and his kind tell us what it all means.'

'We long to know the causes of things,' Jim said.

'*Rerum cognoscere causas.*'

'Couldn't have put it better myself. So we invent science, to tell us a story about the causes of things. And, when we can't find any cause of things, we say it's Free Will freely choosing, as if there could be any such thing.'

'Or the Will of God,' Edmund said. 'Or the General Will. Or the Forces of the Market.'

'Or the Great Architect,' Jane said. 'The Great Watchmaker, tinkering away for all eternity.'

'The Great Chess-Player in the Sky,' Abe said. 'The Great Illusionist.'

'The Ninety-Nine Names of God,' Edmund said.

'The Fourth Narrative,' Jim said.

'The narrative of all narratives,' Jane explained. 'Written by the Great Novelist in the Sky.'

Jim lifted his eyes heavenwards and raised the volume of his voice.

'Come on, Great Novelist in the Sky. What next? We're waiting.'

Silence.

'A dance to the music of power,' Jane said, as she stood up and made the round of the table refilling glasses.

'Democracy. A dance to the music of power and the magic of money,' Jim said. 'The glib and oily art of scurvy politicians. I'll tell you, Edmund, we journalists are court-appointed dancing-masters at the ramshackle Palace of Versailles known as democracy.'

'Journalists are parasites on the body impolitic,' Jane said, 'feeding on the waste-products of those who actually produce something.'

'Unlike art dealers,' Jim said. 'No. We tell people what to think—and they think they've thought it for themselves. We tell them what they want to hear—and they think that proves they're right. Democracy is a ritualised contest, like boxing or tennis, in which the voters place their bets on someone they hope will favour them and their kind.'

'Tell me,' Abe said, 'you people who think about these things—why have I always, throughout my life, lived with a sort of unspecific fear? Why can't I feel happy even when, just occasionally, I know that I could and should?'

'Existential anxiety,' Jane said. 'Angst, as we say in the Queen's English.'

'I don't know what it is,' Abe said. 'I can't remember a single moment of my life when I didn't fear the worst—that something dreadful could happen, at any moment.'

'Because something could,' Jim said. 'It's not a very unreasonable sort of feeling.'

'But it's kind of disabling,' Abe said. 'I can tell you that.'

'A more interesting question,' Jane said, 'is how other people manage to repress the nameless dread you're talking about, Abe—at least mostly, for most of the time.'

'How do we manage to find a satisfactory signal-to-noise ratio,' Jim said, 'psychologically speaking—at least for most of the time?'

'How is your signal-to-noise ratio, Edmund?' Jane asked. 'You seem a pretty calm sort of person.'

'Sometimes I think I may be pathological in that regard,' Edmund said. 'A pathological optimist.'

'Well, you're right,' Jim said. 'They lock people away for less than that.'

After lunch, Jane offered to drive Edmund to the beach, leaving Abe and Jim to talk—about politics, no doubt—about the goings-on of the Washington Paris-Garden—who's won, who's lost, who's out, who's in—the self-obsessed parochialisms of the world's principal parish-pump.

As Edmund said his goodbyes, Jim Meehan found a moment *à deux*.

'So how's the old firm?' he asked, winking excessively.

'Pretty good,' Edmund said, 'so far as I know. Good and getting better—I guess.'

The beach was immaculate and aggressively orderly, thanks to the totalitarian spirit of small-town American local government—each small town a centrally planned people's republic. Edmund swam for a while in the North Atlantic, and wished it were the Caribbean. He ran for a while along the water's edge, watching and wondering at some strange human species-behaviour. Hundreds of healthy young bodies, each one attached to an earpiece or a pair of headphones—supine and alienated in two senses of both of those words. Beautiful New England apple-blossom. Beautiful but barren.

He looked across at Jane Meehan—so intelligent, so lively, so interested—sitting calmly in her folding chair, reading a personally filleted version of the latest edition of the very big serial novel known as *The New York Times* (Sunday Edition). And he asked himself, not for the first time, why he was so very fond of so many Americans, and so much less fond of a certain American idea of America. Something wrong with the narrative of their narratives, presumably.

*   *   *

6

Beyond the Good

'Good—Afternoon—Mr—Miller—Welcome.'

'And good morning to you,' Greg said, pushing open a heavy glass door.

He had typed in his personal VAC (Visitor Access Code), as instructed. The disembodied voice was evidently either discreet or fallible.

'Fifteenth floor—meeting-rooms—A to C,' the lift announced, correctly.

The Vice-President (Planning) opened the meeting.

'We're glad to welcome Dr Gregory Seare, who comes to us from an ancient university, with its roots in another kind of world, but a place that seems to have been able to keep up with the times pretty well, over the centuries. I'd like to record our sorrow at the passing of Walter Werther who contributed so much to the work of this Board. We've greatly benefited from his wise and erudite input. In saying that, I'm sure I speak for all of us. Why he would want to put an end to his own life we cannot imagine and, I guess, we may never know.'

Intimations of agreement around the table, except from Greg, who wondered if he should, after all, have refused to accept the unrefusable and unacceptable—and possibly life-threatening—invitation.

'We've set aside a whole day to hear what you all have to tell us—although I'm sorry to say I'll be obliged to desert you all at about four o'clock. Plane to catch. It's a pretty full agenda, but we should be able to make some good progress on these complex matters. I don't need to remind you we're under a good deal of time pressure—so we'll need to get something rather solid from you today—so we can report to the GSB—the General Strategy Board—in about ten days time.'

They were sitting at a round table in a meeting-room on the top floor of an anonymous and unattractive office building in St Swithin's Lane in the City of London. The room was furnished in that style of interior decorating which manages to assimilate luxury offices and luxury hotels, each a home from home for their native populations.

In addition to the VP(P) and his two assistants, there were five ethics experts around the table—allowing for a majority vote, no doubt, on particularly divisive ethical issues. There were name-cards in front of each participant. Greg had read the potted biographies of his four colleagues in the pack of papers that had been sent to him. There were two men and two women. He knew all of them by name and, in two cases, by something they had written, but he knew none of them personally.

'So, without further ado—perhaps we should begin with a brief general discussion,' the VP(P) said, 'to re-orient ourselves a bit—and then we can take up the individual topics. I don't know whether Greg would like to share any general thoughts at this time.'

'Well, yes,' Greg said. 'I must say I read the papers for this meeting with a certain measure of amazement and also puzzlement. I come from a tradition of ethical thinking that is based on the autonomy of the individual human being. When I see that I am faced with a choice among different courses of action, I ask myself what could be judged to be a morally right thing to do, knowing that I will be responsible, personally and uniquely, for the choice that I make.

'I can't see how that sort of approach can be applied to the kind of thing you people are talking about—for which no individual human beings are responsible. They're all vast collective activities for which no one in particular is responsible. They are a frightening challenge, an impossible challenge really, for traditional conceptions of ethics.'

Intimations of consternation around the table.

'If I may say so,' said someone identified by his name card as George Frampton, 'it seems that you may be questioning a basic assumption of what we try to do in this group.'

'I think I may be,' Greg said.

'In the ethical tradition that I come from,' Frampton said, 'we find what you call "the right thing to do" by free and open discussion, analysing, weighing, balancing . . .'

'Balancing what exactly?' Greg asked.

'Considerations. All relevant considerations.'

'Are any of the considerations moral considerations?'

'Well, not as such, obviously. The morality is what we're trying to find. It's what we agree, at the end of the discussion, is the right thing to do.'

'Right in what sense, exactly?'

'Best in the light of all the considerations—and all the circumstances, of course.'

'Best in what sense, exactly?'

'What seems to us to be the best, assuming that we're responsible and rational and serious people.'

'And if we're none of those things?' Greg said. 'If you won't take seriously the problem of the nature of the good, how can you expect to deal with the problem of evil?'

'I wonder if I might throw my small oar into these rather troubled waters.'

One of the women was speaking, identified by her name card as Bunty Birmingham. Greg remembered reading a slim volume of hers with the title *What Good the Good? From Nietzsche to Wyczwycz*. He feared the worst.

'I think I may have some sympathy with Dr Seare's point of view.'

Greg winced noticeably.

'Don't we ourselves *en fin de compte* construct what we call by the name "moral"? But don't we also find some structures already out there, like pyramids in the desert or tracks in the forest—full of order and meaning, speaking to us—speaking to us with the voice of the peremptory, the *sotto voce* voice of the mother-father sign/signal?'

Greg wondered how the charmingly un*soignée* Bunty Birmingham managed both to sound like the White Queen in *Alice* and to look like the White Queen in *Alice*.

'I think we should perhaps return to our sheep, as the French say.'

The speaker was Fred McDonald, speaking with a soothing Edinburgh accent—a reassuring characteristic in a philosopher or a doctor. Greg knew him to be an ethical intuitionist—that is, a Calvinist soul in a Utilitarian body.

'We can't reinvent the wheel, here and now, can we?' he said. 'Shouldn't we focus on some of the specifics—see where we are and where we're going?'

The other member of the group—May Gaunt—remained silent, as she did for most of the morning. She sat with her head bowed, looking at nothing in particular. She seemed to be knitting mentally. This was surprising, as she was something of a celebrity, but not celebrated for remaining silent. Her career path had gone from plant genetics to professional philosophy, after a brief foray into Weberian sociology.

She had published very many books and articles of which, so far as he could remember, Greg had read only one—*Gods, Goods and the Bottom Line. Selling and Healing*. It was available in airport bookstalls—where Greg had bought his copy—and had sold in very large numbers. She regularly appeared on television, giving an ethical perspective on current issues and situations. She was a professor of Practical Theology, 'although not herself a believer', as the jacket of her books insisted. She was a shining example of those purveyors of sophism to the middle-class middle-brow, whose books the middle-brow middle classes give each other at Christmas.

'I'm sorry, but there's one other thing I really must say at this stage,' Greg said.

Intimations of impatience around the table.

'If you look at all the items on the agenda together, what do they add up to?'

'A privileged glimpse into an amazing future?' George Frampton said. 'A new humanity, scientifically re-created. A Eutopia—with an "eu" not a "u"—post-sex, post-disease, post-war.'

'A brave new human world that is really brave,' Fred McDonald said.

'The final dehumanising of humanity,' Greg said. 'A paradise of fools.'

'Oh, come on!' Frampton said.

'What you are discussing here,' Greg said, 'is the end of the world made by the Renaissance, the Reformation and the Enlightenment—the end of humanism—the end of the free self-creating activity of the human mind.'

'And would that necessarily be such a bad thing?' Fred McDonald said. 'The Enlightenment hasn't really enlightened us very much, has it? And the human sciences don't really seem to have improved us human beings very much, *qua* human beings. Natural science has no known limits—likewise, surely, natural *human* science.'

'Doing what, for heaven's sake?' Greg asked. 'For what purpose?'

'The greatest happiness of the greatest number doesn't yet seem to have produced very much happiness,' Frampton said, 'or not for very many people, if you ask me.'

'And isn't the wonderful power of science something that was produced by, and only by, what you refer to as humanism,' McDonald said, 'We got rid of the wretched superstitions of religion, and all other forms of self-imposed stupidity?'

'But, for most people,' Greg said, 'science is magic and mystery and miracles by other means, more mesmerising fairy-tales. Science is a sorcerer whose apprentice is technology.'

'Help me! Help me! Ye higher powers!' Bunty Birmingham said in a rather too theatrical manner. 'But whose, may we ask, but not only interrogatively, is the power over the higher powers?'

'Indeed,' Greg said speculatively.

'Who,' Dr Birmingham persisted, 'we *must* ask—we owe it not only to *ourselves* to ask—is to be the master, who are to be the masters, of our *ante mortem* unhappinesses?'

'Very true,' Greg said.

'You are forgetting one thing, Dr Seare.'

It was the voice of May Gaunt, at last. She spoke rather quietly, still looking downwards. This seemed to give her a spurious aura of the oracular, as if she were merely the humble conduit for some inspiration from a higher source. May 'Pythia' Gaunt. May Gaunt, *tricoteuse assoluta*.

'I am?' Greg asked.

'Business Decisions.'

'Business decisions?'

'Your analogy is not a good one,' May Gaunt said. 'The sorcerer is not science but Business Decisions. Without them there would be no Science and no Technology.'

She managed to convey capital letters in speaking the holy words. She said nothing more that morning. Perhaps Goldberg Pynch were not compensating her at the level to which she had become accustomed.

After these preliminary and pointless skirmishes, Greg also wanted to set his face like flint, and remain silent for the rest of the day. But he heard the *sotto voce* voice, not of the mother-father sign/signal, but of the Kantian Universal Legislator.

If everyone at such a meeting remained silent, there could be no such meetings at all. But did that imply a moral duty to speak or a moral duty to remain silent? No meetings at all might well be a Universal Good. And there was the matter of the 'appropriate compensation'. If everyone who was paid appropriate compensation did nothing to earn it, no one would ever do anything—or else no one would ever pay anyone to do anything—which, again, might not necessarily be a Universal Evil.

This was not the time or the place to have doubts about the Universal Legislator. There was always the Epicurean Third Way. Enjoy the unavoidable, so far as possible. Accept the inevitable, with mental reservations.

The meeting proceeded to plod through the agenda items. The course of the discussion will not be recorded here. It was discourse more suitable for summarising, if at all, in edited minutes of the meeting, rather than in the narrative of what aims to be, among other things, a novel.

Greg tried to treat the discussion of each topic with the seriousness that it merited.

He asked whether Cognitive Surgery might include *Cosmetic* Cognitive Surgery—for example, to make people more charming, or less boring. He wondered whether Cognitive Pharmacology would uncover the Ideal Form of the vodka martini, or merely regulate its public consumption.

He asked whether the new Global Mind would incorporate Irony-Filters. Would Appropriate Paradigms of Brain Activity include Invincible Stupidity or the Arrogance of Power, both of which could actually be very useful, Greg suggested, especially in the context of Collective Mentalities?

He explained that he would be obliged to withhold judgment on the project as a whole until he felt that he was in possession of reliable clarifications of such matters. The committee secretary said that Greg's statement of position would be reflected in the minutes of the meeting. Greg thanked him for that.

The lunch consisted of sandwiches, mineral water, yoghurts and fresh fruit, set out as a buffet in an adjoining room—a feeble offering, Greg thought, from an institution as ridiculously wealthy as Goldberg Pynch. Perhaps it was a statement of some kind—health-conscious capitalism, thrifty capitalism, ethical capitalism, or simply disdainful capitalism.

Greg found himself beside one of the VP(P)'s assistants whose name card had identified him as Luis Ortiz, a man of about thirty who looked as Spanish as his name—with jet black hair and eyes, and a sort of easy nobility in his features and his manner. Greg did not fail to see that Ortiz was wearing a gold signet ring on the middle finger of his left hand—something less unusual, perhaps, in Spain than in England.

Nothing ventured, Greg thought.

'Durchlaucht,' Greg said.

'Excuse me?' the other man said.

'Oops!' Greg thought, but did not say.

'No. Nothing,' he did say.

Significant pause.

'Durchlaucht!' the other man said at last, smiling broadly.

'Huh!' Greg said.

'What do you make of all this?' Luis asked.

'Utterly pointless, and somewhat worse than pointless. It feels to me like a classic case of malice in wonderland.'

'You five are, for us, a sort of focus group.'

'My first experience of such a thing, I have to say,' Greg said.

'You have probably guessed the real purpose of the meeting.'

'You might like to tell me.'

'Consultation with experts has three main purposes from our point of view. Number one—to show that there are at least as many opinions as there are experts, so that we can always say that whatever we decide to do has broad, if not unanimous, support. Number two—to discover the arguments of those who might object to what we decide to do. That's where you come in, judging by this morning. And number three—to fish for useful ideas to explain and justify what we eventually decide to do.'

'I think I'd guessed all that,' Greg said. 'It's what politics is all about. Democratic politics is the science of mental manipulation—mutual mental manipulation among the governing few, the rich few, the thinking few, and the long-suffering and tiresome, but unavoidable, many. Actually, so-called consultation with experts has a fourth purpose—to show that the expertise of experts is not worth very much.'

'They're not normally very galvanising, I must say.'

'These people have no idea what damage they do to the self-examining human mind with their feeble parody of philosophy. Intellectuals are—or should be—people who respect the past of the human mind, and who feel responsible for its better future. *These* people have no respect for the past of the human mind, and no moral commitment to its future. They are members of that breed of philosophers who have given philosophy a bad name. By the way—Jake Plowman—VP(P)—is he Canadian by any chance?'

'Yes, in fact he is.'

'He has that world-weary niceness that Canadians go in for. I think it may be a subtle form of anti-Americanism.'

'He's actually quite a big player in this place. People listen to him.'

'A cardinal of capitalism. I've always wanted to meet a cardinal of capitalism.'

'*À propos*,' Luis said quietly but correctly, 'you may like to know that there are microphones everywhere. Even in the lavatories. Experience suggests that people often speak more frankly in the lavatory. *In lotio veritas.*'

'Even when there is no *vino*?'

When the meeting reconvened after lunch, the VP(P) said that he felt he should, perhaps, clarify a couple of things—to avoid misunderstanding.

'I think you should know that the matters we've been discussing are not left-field, wild-eyed science fiction. In fact, they're not even possible projects. They're actual ongoing projects—even if some are still at an early research stage. Our role, in this house, is to assess what our financial and advisory contribution, our professional contribution, might be, should be.

'If we turn our back on such projects, they won't go away. Where it will all lead, none of us know. But it will lead somewhere, that's for sure. And I don't need to remind you that our job is to make money for our clients and, hopefully, for us also. We are not a charitable institution. We are not a public service.'

Greg felt that he might be in the cross-hairs of the VP(P)'s reproving sights—for what he had said during the morning's discussion—or for what he may have been overheard to say elsewhere.

'And, on the substance of what we're talking about here,' the VP(P) went on, 'I should just say this. This business of ours is in the business of ideas. Our main invisible asset is consciousness-capital—our own ideas, our ideas about the ideas of our competitors, our clients, governments, the public. Our terms of trade are determined by ideas. Our only possible USP is our better ideas. The wealth of a nation is the wealth of its ideas. And that's true for us too.

'We're living in a new world—a new world of new ideas—and we need to become makers of new ideas, including new ideas about how we make ideas—new ways of thinking—new ways of *being*, as you philosophers would say. Philosophy is a vital part of the story we practical people have to tell. Please be assured of that. You philosophers are people we *need.*'

The VP(P) managed to make his words sound spontaneous and heartfelt, but he was clearly speaking from a written text. Greg wondered if the paper might be a crafty emanation from the Firm. At least he himself was evidently not the VP(P)'s immediate target, after all. He might possibly be invited to another SERF meeting.

In the valedictory minuet at the end of the meeting, Greg made a point of offering his hand to the mysterious May Gaunt.

'I have so much admired your work, Professor Gaunt,' he said. 'I'm obviously going to have to do some new thinking, some new ideas . . .'

'Get lost,' she said—or words to that effect.

*   *   *

Another World, Another Person

E-mail.
From: Ingo Dorn
To: Edmund Jenning
Subject: Illumination/*Aufklärung*

My dear Edmund—

Greetings from India, from someone you knew as Ingo. Greetings from another world, another person.

If only you could be here with me. I would love to have shared all this with you—so you could see it all with your own eyes—your 'sparkling eyes'. What was the name of that poem Greg Seare made us read under the acacia tree?—'cheek by passion flushed' and 'sin no more'—that's all I can remember.

*Your garden in London—and me drunk—*inter alia*—with the scent of what you called your 'Old English' roses—seems so long ago and so far away—*und doch so nah.

Sometimes I feel that you are here with me—in more delirious and delicious moments—you and your young David aspectus—your pulcher, iucundus, jocosus aspectus—*minus the red hair.*

Dieux, quel bonheur d'être si beau! One must be beautiful to approach the beautiful. (Who said that? Plato?—who else?—could only be Plato.)

You won't know me when I return. If I return. I have a beard and my hair is long and I am very thin. But that is not what matters. The change is in me. Inside. Je. Qui ça? Je est un autre.

Everyone who comes to India discovers something. What it is, most of them don't quite know and can't quite say.

*I know—*und kann doch sagen! *I—Ingo Dorn—am many selfs. I am many selfs—plus several that I've never met before. Voilà! I've said it.*

> *There's the self among all other selfs. I-for-others.*
> *There's the self you see and love as a friend. I-for-you.*
> *There's the self who thinks of itself as me. I-for-me.*

There's the self within me I cannot know but can't escape. I-in-me.

There's the self that is part of everything else that exists. I-in-all.

And so there's a self that is the sum total of all the above. The self that thinks of itself as a Self. Ich.

But then there's a seventh self—part of all that is beyond all existing and seeming and thinking—a self that is not merely a self. ÜberIch.

And so there must be an eighth something (Etwas)—*the sum total of all the above.* Ich-ÜberIch. *Self-unself.*

And so there must be one thing (Etwas) *more—the sum total of my eight self-unselfs—the self that is neither a self nor an unself.* UrIch. NichtIch. *My true self that is a unique presence, but an inseparable presence, within the self of the All.*

I-am-who-am—and-who-am-not-I.

Metaphysical me has nine dimensions. Nine vibrating strings in timeless space and spaceless time.

And when I see beautiful things and sacred things my nine dimensions sing together.

Harmonia animi. Harmonia mundi. Und umgekehrt.

Ich will! Ich bin! Endlich!

I think I'm becoming a diamond.

I see you smiling, kindly. I hear you saying—what is he on? What oriental power or potion is talking? Ordentlich *Ingo a born-again hippy? Mother was not a 1960's person, I'm sure. My re-born multi-self isn't natural or nurtural. It is found! Waiting for me at the end of a dusty road.*

I have travelled a long way by train and bus and car and cart and rickshaw and on foot. I have slept in palaces and huts, and nowhere in particular, with only the sound of the sea. Someday I will re-imagine it all in words. My super-sensitive and super-intelligent Indische Reise *will be read and admired by all sensitive and intelligent people.* Indisch reisen *is exactly one thousand times more interesting than you-know-who's* Italienische Reise.

*In the meantime, I will reproduce some part of it here—and you will be my first super-super audience, trapped—*lang lebe das E-mail!*—like one of those people who come and sit beside you in a bar, and you can't escape. But please listen, Edmund. You may smile at what I say, but smile kindly—please, Edmund. Remember—I need you.*

It took me two hours after arriving in Delhi to change my view of the world for ever. That must be a record. Cutting a timid path through the crowded streets, I saw that every person seemed like a complete individual, self-contained, self-governed, self-confident. Nowhere in Europe had I ever had that feeling. The European-in-the-street seems the opposite—dehumanised atoms. India is the humanness of human beings.

Then—amid all the mind-churning chaos of the great Indian cities, moments of beauty—a face, a body, a sari, a shrine, a child, a tree, a flower, a gesture, a smile—that heart-wrenching Indian smile, as if the soul could smile. During the four weeks of my vagrant life here, these moments have been multiplied a thousand times. India is sparks of beauty strung together like pearls.

Then—when you breathe in here, you breathe religion—Hindu, Moslem, Sikh, Jain, Buddhist, Christian, usw. *In Europe, we breathed that atmosphere a thousand years ago—but our mental climate changed. I feel like a medieval European again—when our fourth self was a shared self. Now Europe's fourth self—the European soul—no longer knows much about gods.*

Did the millions of poor people in Europe—medieval or modern—know enjoyment of any kind—the peculiar pleasures of serfdom? Was the misère *of the masses always merely miserable? Some places suffer the cruel vertical integration of society better than others.*

More than once, I have watched as privileged little Indian girls and boys in the best of British school uniforms made their way cheerfully—skipping almost—through the rubble and the general mess of a village main street. I have exchanged the purest and warmest of glances with old men sitting crouched at the pavement's edge—men with no material possessions of any kind—living life in the total freedom of absolute poverty, the ultimate form of human indignity, the ultimate form of human dignity.

Edmund, even you could not imagine what it is like to be forced to think everything again, from the beginning. I can never go back to Tübingen—that's for absolutely sure. How could I pretend to want to know what I am supposed to discover there? I would be living a lie—a life of self-deceiving, deceiving no one, not even myself—to quote the wise words of Edmund der Weise. *Doctoral research. God help us! Doctor—first heal thyself!* J'ai lu tous les livres. Wahn! Wahn! Überall Wahn!

The truth, the human truth, of India is paradox. The present of India is so full of the past and, now, so full of the future. India—as old as the hills and as new as electronics—dashing into the future but looking back, facing the past—the past that is everywhere—ancient and more ancient India—with its procession of arrogant guests—Portuguese and Dutch and French—Moslem and British—Taj and Raj—making sure that India could never forget them.

And, now everywhere, the bulldozers and the cantilever cranes of modernising. Spotless laboratories—where I met people as excited and obsessed as anyone anywhere by the modern wonders of the world known as science and technology. Temples of capitalism full of people worshipping the new avatars of Vishnu—Production, Distribution and Exchange. The metaphysics of getting and spending.

Sensation without sentiment. Metaphysical India. Four-dimensional India. Sensation minus sentiment equals colour. Glowing, vibrating, gleaming, singing, blinding colours—colours that feeble European eyes have never seen before—sensation-seeking, sentimental European eyes.

India—microcosmos—overflowing with the insoluble contradictions, the cruel incompatibilities, the impossible possibilities, the restless stillness, the vigorous passivity, the warring peace of the human spirit.

All is struggle. Zucht und Haltung! Plaie et couteau.

Na gut!

Beyond the struggle is the All.
We form an idea of God because we cannot know the form of God.
I am in love with the formless God.
Licht! Licht! Überall Licht!

Edmund! I know now the science of all the sciences, even those that don't exist! And I have a hopeless hope and an unprayable prayer.

May India never take on the Grau in Grau *of the world made in Europe. May the Indias of the world—of a new world—help to heal a European civilisation with arthritis in its mental bones—dry brains in a dry season. May India, with its ageless memory, remember the future.*

The monsoon is coming and all our sins will be washed away. The sea has many voices, many gods, and many voices. I bathe in the poem of the sea. The rain also falls on the wicked. Blessed is the flower that smiles. The swan sings for joy. Sparge rosas. Alles endet, was enstehet. *Fare forward, voyagers!*

I know you will show this virtual letter to my mother. Tell her not to worry—as if she would be able not to worry. Remember what I have meant for her and what she means to me—at least, the 'I' and the 'me' that she has so much loved—too much loved. Try to comfort and support her, as if she were also, in some way, your own mother, the mother you never knew.

Remember me, Edmund ewiggeliebte—*remember me,* dein ewigliebende *Ingo, little friend of all the world.*

Licht! Licht! Überall Licht!

[Text lightly edited linguistically, and to repair e-mail syncopations and elisions.]

*   *   *

8

End of a Beginning

The Requiem Mass took place at the church of St Thomas d'Aquin. The early evening sun was shining on a Paris looking its majestic best. Not a funeral—no body to bury. No eulogy. Mr Gray read Ingo's virtual letter, his last words. Edmund read passages from the Katha Upanishad about the mind and the self. Gabi read a poem by Nietzsche (*Heiterkeit, güldene, komm!*). As the congregation left the church, the organ played Buxtehude's *Praeludium* in D, filling the peaceful street with the sound of the joy of life.

A person is never more wholly present in the minds of other people than in the ceremony that marks their final absence. Those who had known Ingo, and those who had loved him, filled only a part of the baroque splendour of the church in the heart of Saint-Germain which the Countess had chosen to treat as her parish church. Family members from Germany and Austria, friends of the family, fellow students from Berlin and Tübingen, colourful friends from the Kreuzberg district in Berlin where he had chosen to live. Senior members of the Firm, known only to the Countess and her brother, in a procession of imposing cars which had disappeared discreetly into the underground car-park beside the church.

Every person's death is a unique event with no single significance. Each mourner was filled with a particular idea of Ingo, each living a particular set of feelings, all of them trying to imagine the suffering of his mother, for whom Ingo was an only child, but in a relationship that seemed to be so much more than that of mother and child.

After the mass, the congregation walked the few steps to a reception in the Hôtel Montalembert.

To those who needed to know more, to understand more, about Ingo's death, Edmund showed the text of another e-mail.

E-mail
From: Annie Pleasance
To: Edmund Jenning
Subject: Ingo Dorn

Dear Edmund,

You don't know me. I found your name on a long mail that Ingo left on my laptop. I don't know how to say this—but it seems that Ingo is missing. We met in the ashram at Varkala. But, after a couple of days, Ingo left. He said it was commodity-spirituality—like Bayreuth or Lourdes—that's what he said. I didn't agree. I stayed.

So he left—and went up the coast for a few miles to a place he knew—where there was a derelict cottage by a deserted beach. He slept there in his sleeping bag. The people there told me—each evening he would watch the sunset, standing in the sea, walking into the sea up to his waist, wearing a white cotton loin-cloth, like a real old-style Indian. He said he liked to see the sun and the moon in the sky at the same time. He said he had fallen in love with a dancing star.

I went to look for him. The local people told me—one evening they saw him go into the sea as usual. They say they had told him about the terrible riptide—going along the coast. They say he was dragged under the water. They never saw him again. They say it's happened many times before. They say he'll never be found.

I'm so sorry, Edmund. I read that long letter—he really loved you—he really loved his mother. It must be awful for you. I loved him too. One of the nicest people I've ever met anywhere. So serious. So gentle. So loving. India was everything to him.

love and tears, Annie.

After the reception, the Countess and Mr Gray returned to the house on the Avenue Foch with Edmund and Greg.

'I am exhausted,' the Countess said. 'So many kind people to speak to, so little to be said. We had him when I was really too old, too old to be a proper mother. What a dreadful word that is—"had"! What a selfish thing it is to give birth to someone! People talk about a right to life. Mustn't there also be a right not to be born? The unborn. The fortunate ones. To give someone the burden of life for selfish reasons of your own . . .'

She hesitated.

'I had been ill. Ingo saved me—saved my life and saved my mind. His father died when the boy was fifteen. I was all that Ingo had. He was all that I had. We existed for each other. Was that a good thing? Maybe . . . Maybe not . . . Maybe to love too much is a sin—the most mortal sin—destroying two people by making half of two people into one.'

'He will always live within us, Frieda,' her brother said. 'We will always love him. He will always be with us.'

'I'm not sure he was ever happy,' the Countess said. 'Is any of us ever happy?'

'He was happy when he was with me,' Edmund said. 'I'm sure. He was like a brother—an ideal brother—someone you couldn't possibly be closer to.'

'We can dedicate our work to him,' the Countess said. 'The work of the Firm can be his life-after-death, the life of the world to come . . .'

'Having changed all our lives,' Mr Gray said, 'Ingo will change the world.'

'And now I must tell you two Englishmen something important,' the Countess said. 'You two ambassadors from the philosophical nation are here because you are especially dear to us, as you were especially dear to Ingo—but also—forgive me—you are here for a very practical reason. Tomorrow we will, indeed, talk about a new beginning, a new beginning in the making of a new world . . . But now it is time to rest. It has not been an easy day.'

The Countess and her brother left Edmund and Greg in the drawing room.

'What a remarkable woman the Countess is,' Greg said. 'Wisest, virtuousest, discreetest, best—with a sort of ancient gravity.'

'I seem to have loved her from the first day I met her,' Edmund said. 'And yet I feel that I hardly know her as she really is. Perhaps I love her for what she seems to be.'

Edmund then suffered a Proustian digression, somehow manifesting itself in Henry James mode. He wondered yet again at the fascinating aura of the Countess—a strange mixture of presence and absence, of reticence and power. She was as real and solid and knowable as Mrs Dalloway or Maggie Tulliver but as elusive and imaginary and unknowable as Virginia Woolf or George Eliot. This was, perhaps, the inherent potentiality of women. They are what they seem to be, but they are always something more than what they, for us others, seem. More even than figuratively, especially, they are a figure whose outline dissolves on our closer kind of inspection. And it is, therefore, an inherent potentiality of the man (a potentiality that is also an infirmity) that he is incapable of knowing whether he has fallen in love with what a woman is or with what she seems to be. For the woman, knowing this, the man is always less than what he seems to be, even if she sees, through the chisellings of time and the accumulatings of habit, that she may make him seem more than he had seemed, and more, that is, than he seems to himself—more, certainly, than he ever was. Even men, in this sense, have, one might say, a negative (but fructive) potentiality—to come to seem what they can never be or, at least, in the end, to be what they know they are not.

'We need Henry James,' Edmund said, 'to distil the essence of the Countess in diaphanous but well-chosen words.'

'God forbid,' Greg said, not knowing what he had missed.

'In church,' Edmund said, 'it occurred to me that what other people call prayer I call poetry, and what other people call poetry is really prayer. What do you, Greg, supreme arbiter of holy and unholy elegances, think of this, my newly minted prayer, in honour of the newly dead?'

> Unburied he sees the unseen world,
> Answers the answerless question.

'Seventeen syllables—but more India than Japan.'
'Well, this then?'

> The river returns to the sea:
> The dead mind rejoins the empty air.

'More physical, but too metaphysical.'
'Or this then?'

> The evening rose smiles
> When the sun and the moon meet
> And talk of love.'

'Ella Wheeler Wilcox, at her best.'
'So, Greg, what were *you* thinking about in church? It occurred to me that the strangeness and the discomfort of a Catholic church service must be a good inducement to higher thought.'
'I was using the time productively—re-arranging Shakespearean leaves of grass.'

> Farewell! Thou art too dear for my possessing,
> From hence your memory death cannot take.
> For summer and his pleasures wait on thee,
> And thee, away, the very birds are mute.
> To me, dear friend, you never can be old.
> Hearing you praised, I say, "'Tis so, 'tis true"
> And thou in this shalt find thy monument,
> When tyrants' crests and tombs of brass are spent.
> Now is this song both sung and past.
> Rejoice! Let me dream of your felicity.

'I can't understand people's attitude to death,' Edmund said. 'For the dead person in question, it must be rather nice—a great relief—not having to care about anything anymore—unless you believe awful things about judgment and damnation.'
'But it's the prospect of death that haunts every moment of life,' Greg said, 'as if we always know that our existence is only a temporary negation of our eternal non-existence—and non-existence seems the more natural of the two.'
'And non-existence,' Edmund said, 'lasts a good deal longer than existence. Probably.'
'To die is to resume another kind of life,' Greg said. 'From molecule to molecule.'
'When I first saw Ingo's e-mail,' Edmund said. 'I thought—I didn't tell you—I thought it was the lightning before death. When I heard of his death, I also thought of that time he mentioned in his e-mail—the three of us in my garden—a sort of ecstasy

of friendship—physical, mental, aesthetic—spiritual even—an intimation of ultimate co-existence.'

'That's what we really mourn,' Greg said, 'when we mourn the death of someone we love. We mourn our own loss—the loss of the possibilities of co-existence.'

'Ingo was seeking the impossible escape,' Edmund said, 'the escape from mere existence, escaping the unweeded garden.'

'*Plus tard on dira qu'il est.*'

'Or maybe not. I'm going to bed.'

Greg knew Edmund well enough to know that Ingo's death was much more than the death of someone he had loved. Among the *dramatis personae* playing their parts in the making of the new Edmund Jenning, Ingo had played an especially important role—as mirror and foil. His death had become a new part of Edmund's life, a new impulse of life within him. Every day we all die a little. Every day we can take a step, smaller or greater, on the way to becoming a new person.

In one respect at least, on the following day, the Countess was not a new person. At 09.30 precisely and in characteristically brisk fashion, she called the meeting to order. The meeting consisted of herself, Mr Gray and the two ambassadors from the philosophical nation, Greg and Edmund.

'Four weeks ago we had a meeting of our main sponsors,' the Countess said. 'Our *Erstes Gremium*, as we call it. We decided that there is now a new urgency. Beyond our projects of targeted influence and intellectual re-creating, we must urgently devote resources—material and psychic—to a third, perhaps the most difficult, of projects.'

'In schematic terms,' Mr Gray said, 'we say that beyond the first Philosophical Revolution—a new philosophy of the making of the mind of the *individual* human being—there will be a second philosophical revolution, the Metaphysical Revolution—a new philosophy of the mind's *collective* understanding of its own existence—a revolution in the way humanity understands its own situation—how it imagines its relationship to the natural world of this planet, to the universe of all-that-is—a new imagining of the meaning and purpose of human existence, a new self-creating of the human world, the world made by the human mind.'

'You may understand now,' the Countess said, 'why we began to talk about these things when you came to see us at Montgenêt . . .'

'. . . And why we were anxious to meet the remarkable churchman,' Mr Gray said, 'who is so kindly helping our niece with her academic work.'

Greg constructed from these two pieces of information the speculation that his sudden summons to take part in the SERF at Goldberg Pynch might be another effect of the same cause. And, at the very same moment, it occurred to Edmund to wonder if his pleasant visit to Abe Green's house near Westport, and his meeting with the very nice Meehans, might have been more necessary than random. It was Jack Jackson who had told Abe Green that Edmund would be in New York for a few days in June.

'The British have always seemed to observe the world from a distance,' the Countess said, 'thinking about the world with a strange sort of detachment, always plotting some new Reformation. Again and again, the British mind has produced the ideas that the world needs when the world needs them. The world needs new ideas now.'

'We need to imagine a new ontology,' Mr Gray said, 'making possible radical transformations of human consciousness and human behaviour. And to do that we need your help.'

'I'm afraid I'm not really able to think to order,' Greg said, 'like a bespoke tailor. That may be why I've not been very successful as a professional academic.'

'And I'm afraid *my* thinking tends to be rather feeling-led,' Edmund said. 'I don't think I was destined to be a philosopher, professional or otherwise. Cheerfulness keeps breaking in. I think I may be physically incapable of mental detachment.'

'Mental detachment is exactly what we do not want,' the Countess said.

'What we want—and what we believe you can give,' Mr Gray said, 'is originality and energy—originality of ideas and energy of the thinking process—those have been the characteristics of the somewhat disorderly and idiosyncratic activity of your country's public mind.'

'I suppose it depends who you see as the audience, the consumers, of the new ontology,' Greg said. 'Editors of learned journals and their guardian angels—the peer-reviewers—might be less attracted to philosophical originality and energy than you are.'

'Oh no!' Mr Gray said vigorously. 'We don't want to have anything at all to do with such people. Our Invisible College are studying, as a matter of urgency, how ideas—*pure* ideas—can be made *practically* operational in the new kinds of societies that we inhabit in the twenty-first century.'

'How do you change, at the deepest level, the general thinking of the public mind of today's society—and tomorrow's society?—that's the question,' the Countess said.

'O.K. Defensive gambit Number Two,' Greg said. 'Surely you could not have chosen a worse time to suppose that the human mind could induce in itself a self-enlightenment? Allott's Law of Enlightenments faces two rather serious objections. One—it supposes that there are patterns in human history that are real, and not merely retrospective illusions. Secondly, it supposes that there are always people capable of enlightening, and people capable of being enlightened.'

'Perhaps Professor Allott's Law of Enlightenments is rather the affirmation of an objective,' Mr Gray said, 'an energising ideal, a reminder of the possible rather than a prediction of the inevitable. The idea of a 21st-century Enlightenment is surely an energising idea.'

'Or else it is an idea that contains its own negation,' Greg said, 'a demonstration of what is no longer possible, not now or ever again. The twentieth century was the century of the fascism of government. Now we are living under a new fascism—a fascism of the mind—the three-headed totalitarianism of science, religion, and the economy. The history of the twenty-first century will be the history of the *inter se* struggle of the three totalitarianisms of the mind.'

'You might have added a third kind of challenge,' Mr Gray said. 'The new enlightenment will be universal—no longer merely European, or even American. Ingo's beloved India will play its part—and countless other cultures and traditions.'

'Your diagnosis, Greg, seems to overlook the amazing creative capacity of the arena of democracy,' the Countess said, 'where the social struggle is as unorganised in its conduct and as unpredictable in its outcomes as a revolution or a war.'

'Yes indeed, democracy,' Greg said. 'Democracy is, indeed, the arena—the arena where human beings are depersonalised, de-invidualised, and de-transcendentalised—precisely the dehumanising conditions required by the new totalitarianisms.'

'Speaking for myself,' Edmund said, 'I think I may have a character defect that would exclude me from being the prophet or the agent of a Metaphysical Revolution. I have the feeling that I am a heart-person rather than a mind-person. We card-carrying philanthropologists believe that the ontology of love—whatever that might be—is in the living of it, not in the saying of it. *Si vis amari, ama.*'

But Mr Gray and the Countess were purring with pleasure. And Greg and Edmund decoded that pleasure. The interesting challenge proposed by the Firm's mind-masters had taken possession of their English minds—and they had known that it would.

'So, Gregory Seare, English Stoic, and Edmund Jenning, English Epicurean,' the Countess said, 'we await your joint metaphysical prescription.'

'We await the redeeming word, or words,' Mr Gray said in a tone that was evidently intended to sound conclusive.

'If the Firm breathes collectively,' Greg said, 'tell it not to hold its collective breath.'

*   *   *

9

After Government

Over the years, Alison Brand's disguise had been remarkably successful. Even those who knew her well, such as Hilda Greene, had placed her in boxes marked Nice, Sensible, Intelligent, Brave, Efficient, Catholic, Widow, Working Mother, Mother, Devoted Mother. Hilda Greene herself was regularly placed in several of the same boxes by those who knew her well, but also in other boxes, including those marked Eccentric, Ancient, Intellectual, Convert, Wife, Devoted Wife, Her Own Woman. Such is the way we know each other. Such is the way we don't know each other.

In Alison's case, missing pieces of her composite portrait were known to those who knew of her other lives—not only her work for the Firm, but also her work for the British Government. Professionally, she was close to the top of her profession—number four or five in the administrative hierarchy of the British overseas security services. As such, she was a Woman of Power, although she herself resolutely refused to place herself in this box. To this extent, Alison did not know herself. She was more than she seemed to herself.

It is probably true that, unlike politicians in their more self-obsessed moments, senior civil servants never see themselves as Powerful. The fact that they determine, in the strongest sense of that word, the lives of other people—perhaps, the lives of millions of people, of hundreds of millions of people—seems less significant than the fact that there is an urgent memorandum to write, or a difficult meeting to attend tomorrow. Power chopped up into very small pieces seems more like Duty.

Admittedly, on this occasion, even as she took her place on a British Airways flight from London, Alison did recognise, in a diffusely anxious way, that she was on her way to a meeting of unusual difficulty and importance.

In the league table of smoke-and-mirror personalities, Michel Habai was at the very top of the Premier League, in a class of his own. He must have held the record for the number of cross-references referring to him in the file-indexes of both MI6 and the CIA and, no doubt, of many other overseas security services around the world. The British and the Americans even had him filed, among many other names and titles, under the name Pimpernel. His life was a web of deception carried to an almost sublime level. And there had always seemed to Alison to be something dangerous about him.

The relatively still point of the polytropic Mike Abi's many turning worlds was his employment in the International Relations Department at the Goldberg Pynch London office. At least that position gave people somewhere to contact him relatively straightforwardly. It also enabled him to meet many people and to travel a great deal.

On this occasion, his and Alison's separate trajectories—his, by way of Tunisair—were converging on a meeting-place in Tunis. It was to be a UN Roundtable on Security Issues in the New Middle East, but the title, and even the topic, were not of great interest to the potential participants. They attended so many such meetings—with titles as meaningless as a painting called Nocturne II or a sculpture called Free Form Fifteen—or a racehorse with the presumably non-descriptive name of Cheeky Chappie.

The participants had to keep reminding themselves what was this week's title and topic. Later, they would write a brief report—

'The meeting was well attended and we had a good discussion, albeit at a rather general level and, necessarily, not reaching any very definite conclusions. It was decided to meet for a follow-up session in Cancún, Mexico, in March next year.'

The report would be filed and the meeting would forgotten until next year. Every day of the year, all over the world, there are dozens of such meetings taking place, convened by the UN, its specialised agencies, and the other intergovernmental and non-governmental organisations whose ambition is the general improvement of the human condition.

The People and the Peoples of the World did not have—could not possibly have—any idea of the breadth and depth of the efforts being expended in their name and/or on their behalf. It was thankless work. For the time being at least, it had to be its own reward.

The rewards included travel to pleasant and/or interesting places, lodging in very agreeable hotels, much opportunity for cross-frontier and cross-gender (or even same-gender) socialising, and many opportunities for general cultural enrichment. But, always, there are a handful of people at such meetings who have an agenda, a personal agenda which is also an official agenda, an agenda which has little or no connection with the agenda circulated in advance of the meeting. They are people who are too busy to waste their time on foreign jaunts and jollities. They are people who are accustomed to using their time relentlessly and ruthlessly.

The meeting in Tunis was the first of many regional meetings convened by the newly established UNPAST (UN Palestine Advisory and Supervisory Team) to consider 'the functions and modalities of co-operation within purposes and projects relating to the New Situation in the Middle East'. The New Situation in the Middle East had recently caused the US Government and the European Union to announce an ambitious Marshall-type Plan for accelerated economic and social development in the Middle East.

And, coincidentally or consequentially, the Canadian Government had announced that it was convening a League of Sensible Countries (LOSC). LOSC, which would be 'pluripolar, that is, neither intergovernmental nor non-governmental', would organise

New Approaches on 'all situations which threaten World Public Order or constitute a Standing Affront to the Ideal of Social Justice'.

[In the International Arena (IA), the long and arduous march of social progress and the Acronymic Capitalising of Key Words (ACKWO) are seen as causally connected. ACKWO gives to such words a form of *Existenz* which is studied within the context of Semantic Existentialism (*Semantischexistenzphilososphie*) and the more practical discipline of Brand Nominalism (*Markenzeichenphenomenologie*).]

Alison's agenda on this occasion was certainly complex. She would be participating in the meeting in both her capacities—representing both MI6 and the Firm. In the former capacity, she carried with her the conclusion which she and her colleagues had recently reached—namely, that Mike Abi was the servant of two masters—or, at least, of two main masters. He and Goldberg Pynch were representatives of a new kind of public power over the past and the future of the human mind and the human world.

But Alison's two masters had formed the view that Abi's most important capacity might be as a leading member—perhaps even a founding member—of something called New Issues.

New Issues was not a listed corporation. It had no head-office. It was listed in no list of non-governmental organisations. It had, so far at least, remained beneath the radar horizon of the many busybody non-governmental organisations which saw it as their self-appointed and tiresome task to uncover the studiously covered-up.

NI was so informal that it produced no agendas, no reports, no paper trail or electronic trail of any kind. It imagined itself essentially as a club. It was not a think-tank. But it was, most certainly, a do-tank. Its purpose was to produce results, to cause effects, to exercise the ultimate form of power—the power over ultimate power.

So Alison's agenda for the meeting in Tunis was fourfold. (1) To discover whether Mike Abi—and hence NI and/or Goldberg Pynch—knew about the Firm. (2) To discover all that could be discovered about NI's membership. (3) To discover all that could be discovered about NI's plans and, in particular, whether it had some sort of Grand Plan (as some of Alison's colleagues in MI6 believed). (4) To form a view—a very tentative view—as to whether NI might be able to co-operate—in some way and to some extent—with MI6 and/or the Firm. Or must they be treated as the Opposition or even the Enemy? Might it even be possible to co-opt Mike Abi?

These were not the kinds of problem that could be resolved by direct questions. 'Oh, by the way, what are your plans for the future of the world?' Indeed, none of them could be referred to directly or explicitly. They were also not the kinds of question that espionage technology could possibly resolve. They called for the human touch—reading between the lines—inferentially, interstitially, indirectly, imaginatively, sympathetically—human intelligence in an older sense of the word 'intelligence'.

The great interest of governments—the thinking branch of the best informed governments—in the activities of NI was entirely pragmatic. The NI club-members were the rulers of industrial and commercial empires, empires that far exceeded in wealth and importance most of the world's state-systems. Their view of the world and their ambitions for the world had more effect on the future of the world than the views and ambitions of most, if not all, governments. They were the new self-appointed trustees of human happiness, foxes made into surveyors of the fold.

It seemed *a priori* that Alison's task would be complicated still further by the fact that Mike Abi was not staying with the other delegates at an international-style hotel in the centre of Tunis. He was staying in a charming hotel which was the former home of a pasha in the village of Sidi Bou Said, some twenty kilometres away, travelling to and from Tunis each day by train. However, as will be seen shortly, there proved to be a logistic advantage in this state of affairs.

If this were merely a novel, the 'dear reader' would now suppose that the diplomatic puzzle of international relations outlined above would be reflected in, and possibly even resolved in, a personal relationship of the most intimate kind between Alison and Mike—a labour of love satisfactorily consummated in the wider public interest.

However, the conventions, not to say the ethics, of a novel are not the same as those determining the behaviour of people like Alison and Mike, caught up in the unsentimental polygon of a very-large-scale international situation involving many governments and several kinds of supra-governmental system.

Diplomatic puzzles on such a scale are not resolved. They are, at best, developed in a positive direction. That was as much as Alison, or anyone else in her situation, could hope for. An account of actual events, even in fictionalised form, must respect this disappointing reality.

On the first evening of the conference, Alison and Mike both attended a dinner for the delegates in the conference hotel. On the second evening they excluded themselves from an expedition to another hotel where there was to be a 'Tunisian-style' buffet dinner followed by a 'folkloric manifestation'. Instead, they escaped to Sidi Bou Said by chauffeur-driven car.

They stopped briefly to inspect the remains of Carthage. Alison remembered a memory that was not her own, as she heard what the poet had called the clicking and the tapping of the mosaic-makers.

She was disappointed, but not surprised, to see that Carthage had, quite evidently, been as destroyed as history had related—one civilisation destroying another—a salutary reminder for the so-called civilisations of the twenty-first century. And she had duly remembered Dido, Queen of Carthage, and her fate—the fascinating Queen's colourful life terminally disrupted by a mysterious stranger from further to the East—a salutary lesson for any professional woman in a very responsible social position, especially a woman about to have dinner with a man born in Algeria who spoke Arabic and French as his mother-tongues, and English as if he had been born English or American, and who was evidently as crafty and as much travelled as Odysseus but a good deal less pious than Aeneas.

At the restaurant, Michel Habai was greeted by name. Winking nightlights on the light-blue wooden tables, *azulejos* everywhere, the warm evening air thick with the erotic scent of jasmine. Alison could see that she might, indeed, need to call upon reserves of

Carthaginian determination to keep control of an intrinsically uncontrollable situation, personal and professional.

She had only met Mike twice before. She first met him at a Christmas party given by the head of the International Relations Department at Goldberg Pynch. Mike had mentioned, very much in passing (or so it seemed at the time), that he was looking to appoint an assistant. Alison had immediately thought of Edmund—whose rather over-filled (and possibly imaginative) CV included various well-known corporate brand-names in the City of London—scenes from the story of the artist as a young man—but not the name of Goldberg Pynch.

'Your Edmund Jenning is an impressive person,' Mike said. 'I'm sorry we couldn't entice him into our little knot of vipers.'

They had ordered the meal. It was time for Act I—exploratory conversation.

'You really need more people like him in the Foreign Office,' Mike continued, 'his languages, his experience, his up-scale charm.'

Alison had always been, for Mike and other outsiders, an official of the Foreign and Commonwealth Office—and she was, as always, listed as such in the list of delegates attending this Roundtable in Tunis.

'We got to know rather a lot about him,' Mike Abi said. 'His interesting past, his likes, his loves. We tried quite hard to persuade him. But he resisted our blandishments.'

'He's not what you would call a team-player,' Alison said.

'Precisely. You need more such people.'

Alison had met Mike a second time at dinner in Edmund's house in Hampstead, when, in the face of Edmund's adamant rejection of what he called the sober-suited slavery of paid employment, Alison had mentioned the name of Luis Ortiz.

Luis was the son of very old friends of David and Hilda Greene. Hilda and Alison had spent a memorable week with Luis and his parents in a house in the foothills of the Sierra Nevada that had once belonged to the family of Federico García Lorca.

It was something of a coup for the Firm that Luis had now been transferred to the Planning Department, as assistant to Jake Plowman. Gregory Seare's replacing of the late, half-heartedly lamented, Walter Werther in the SERF was a useful consequence.

Alison's colleagues in the British delegation would report in traditional terms *mutatis mutandis* to their respective departments—

'. . . It was agreed that there would be a follow-up meeting in Marmaris, Turkey, in October.'

Alison herself would report to her own office—and also to the Firm—that she had taken the opportunity to speak to Mike Abi—*à deux*—over dinner—at some length.

I noticed that when Pimpernel uses the words 'we' or 'us' it is often not clear which of eight groups of people he has in mind.

(1) Me and him. (2) Him and Goldberg Pynch. (3) Him and people with a similar Arab-Middle Eastern-French colonial background. (4) Him and other

free-booters, soldiers of fortune, chancers, guns-for-hire. (5) Him and other privileged, resourceful and self-reliant people vis-à-vis the lumpen masses. (6) Him and the rest of the human race. (7) Him and those with whose world-mastering ambitions he feels himself associated (?NI). (8) An open-ended category of all those who are there for him to use in one way or another and all those who are on his side in whatever game he may be playing at any given time.

It follows from the above that it is more than usually difficult to determine what his plans may be at any given time—and whose plans he may be making his own at this particular given time.

However, mixing together into one inference (a) the agitated excitement with which he talked about Goldberg Pynch, (b) his excitement in talking about what he called 'the great struggle ahead', and (c) his insistence that I, and 'people like you in positions of power', should join 'us' in fighting 'the good fight, perhaps the last fight', I formed the modest, anally-retentive bureaucratic view that, at the least, he wanted to tell me that he had something important and urgent to tell me about Goldberg Pynch and NI, but he was not, then and there, in a position to tell me precisely what that thing might be.

Having arrived, rather laboriously, at this conclusion and having shared some more of the seductive Algerian red wine, Alison decided to try the Approach more or less Direct. To her own office, she reported the following conversation in general and abstract terms. To the Firm, she reported it *verbatim*.

'Edmund Jenning, for example,' I began. 'If you had to advise him—where do you think he should locate himself to make the most effective possible contribution in what you call the struggle ahead?'

'I see something of the younger me in him. We have a lot in common.'

'Well then,' I said, 'what would you have told yourself to do, at his age?'

'We each have to make our own choices. There is always a new choice to be made. Our choices now are like no choices that any human being has ever faced before—in the whole of human history. We can opt in, or we can opt out. Be careful who you call "us" and who you call "them". Choose your life-choices well. Join the slave-masters or learn to love your chains. Edmund Jenning surely knows all this already. Those who are not with us are against us, and may expect to be dealt with accordingly.'

The Approach more or less Direct seemed to be getting somewhere. I persisted.

'But how can Edmund know if he is with you or against you if he doesn't know who you are and what you are for?'

'It is we who name the forms of human evil. It is we who decide the nature of human nature. It is we who decide who is with us, and who is against us.'

'And the Goldberg Pynches of this world have the ultimate power—the power of money.'

'Money is not the ultimate power—making money or using money. The ultimate power is determining the meaning of money.'

'What people think about it?'

'It's people's imagination that makes the meaning of money. Control people's imagination and you control people.'

'And who controls the controllers?' I asked.

"They control each other.'

'Market forces?'

'Market forces are no longer enough. We are looking to something new. A capitalism beyond capitalism. Creative capitalism. World-making capitalism. The New Political Science.'

'And who, may I ask once again, are "we", in your scheme of things?'

'The makers. The creators. The master-builders. Without whom there would be nothing. The gods of fact, the masters of the gods of fantasy. The gods who really are—and will never fail.'

'And your Olympus, where you all meet, and survey your creation—where is that?'

'Nowhere and everywhere.'

And that was that. End of conversation. Cul-de-sac (in all three senses).

But not altogether wasted time. I had discovered—or seen clearly for the first time—an Interesting Possibility. I will call it the Brand Convergence Theory. Could it be that we and the Goldberg Pynches of this world are on parallel but converging tracks? IP meets NI somewhere this side of eternity?

Alison bought the *International Herald Tribune* and *Le Monde* at the airport.
US National Security Adviser resigns.
No mention of Abe Green's New England apple-orchard.

*   *   *

Kreuzberg

'The whole of human history can be explained by the fact that men are unable to imagine the mind of a woman when she is alone, in a room by herself. No man could ever know the distance of the woman's mind from the world that men's minds have made.'

Frieda von Dorn said these words to herself when she was alone, alone in what had been Ingo's apartment in Berlin.

'Men suppose that women merely think what they say and, when a woman is not saying anything, either she is not thinking, or else she is thinking what a man thinks he would think if he were in that woman's situation.'

The Countess certainly felt alone. When her husband died, she became half-alone. With the death of Ingo, she now had only the half-brotherly love of her loving half-brother.

'Freud hated women—he thought of them as a different species—peculiar domesticated animals with animal needs—a puzzle that men can't solve, but can't leave alone. Men fill their writings with the figures of women, all of them serving as magnifying glasses of the mind of men. *Madame Bovary, c'est nous.*'

'So women are left on their own to face the puzzle of men, and the evil that men do, and the price that women pay for the evil that men do.'

Frieda Dorn was suffering the loss of her only child. But she was not pitying herself. And she was not pitying another human being who had no more need of pity. She was pitying what life and death, both of them, mean for human beings—the pitiable meaning we have given to our life and our death.

'Even women writers—intelligent and articulate women writers—write about the woman in relation to the other people in her life, the woman as a self determined by others. What about the woman's self-determining self, alone, in a room by herself, with no others in sight or in mind, thinking—that is, living?'

Frieda tried to free herself from thinking about anyone else or anything else. She tried to erase from her mind every trace of the consciousness of suffering. She tried to stop herself thinking about other people's minds, about what the life and death of Ingo might mean for them. She tried even to stop thinking about Ingo, his life and his death. She wanted to think only about herself. And she could not do it.

Looking for her self inside herself, she found that there was no self there.

'I am all that isn't me,' she said to herself, aloud this time, in English.

As she said these words, she realised that, by the mere act of thinking, she had succeeded in increasing the burden of her own existence. Her self was the burden of the life she had lived, a burden that grew from day to day, a burden that she would carry with her to her own grave.

She could not escape from the burden of her self to find the self she could never know, the Ur-self of a person whose parents had decided that she would be known by other people as Frieda, but who was, in her own mind, nameless—a person who was, in her own mind, faceless, except as a face in a mirror, or a face glimpsed in the mirror of the faces of other people.

Ingo's tiny apartment was full of the presence of his absence. The Countess, surrounded by his personal possessions, could not bring herself to touch any of them. Someone else would have to dispose of them. She, who had respected his individuality while he was alive—how could she possibly violate his privacy merely because he would never return to the apartment, never again make use of anything in it, never want her to be there with him, never want her not to be there with him?

There were several photographs of a girl to whom the Countess had been introduced at the reception after the Requiem Mass in Paris. What was her name? What had she meant to Ingo? Frieda Dorn found herself staring at the photographs, trying to read into them a hypothesis, a possible story—not only the story of what might have been a life for Ingo, but what might have been a life for her, Frieda Dorn, the bearer of a separate and different burden of existence.

She would have been happy to share her love of Ingo with someone whom she could also love. At last she convinced herself that the face of the girl in the photographs was remarkably similar to her own face at a similar age, in her late twenties. And yet this girl could not possibly contain—or even imagine—what Frieda's younger eyes had seen, what the mind behind Frieda's younger face had experienced. To look at, they could have been the same person. To know, they could surely not have been more different.

We cannot know the burden of existence that another human being carries. Very often it is a burden that, if we knew it, would seem too heavy to bear.

For those of Frieda's generation whose life-texture was so dense and so complex, the shallow substance of the lives of the latest generation seemed like a permanent insult. How could the young pretend to be fully developed human beings when their experience of what human beings are capable of was so slight—the highest and the lowest of human potentiality—when their main experience of human life was in the form of electronic facts and fantasies manufactured by other minds?

The young now knew so little of the journey by which some human beings had struggled to reach even their present level of personal development. How could they possibly have any basis for judging an inheritance of which they were such unknowing, uncaring heirs?

How can you become a truly human being without suffering, without suffering greatly?

And then the Countess found herself staring at a different photograph—of Ingo and the girl together, side-by-side. Smiling. Self-confident. Eager.

At that moment, she remembered that she herself had once been smiling, self-confident and eager. She had once been another self. She was looking at the self she could have become, should have become. What had happened to her, to her generation, to her country, should not have happened. The young who had not known such suffering—Ingo, Edmund, Gabi, Rupert, this girl—they had been rescued from the past, born again in a sort of innocence. They would never see so much, feel so much—or be so much.

The Countess went to the window, looked out onto a very busy, very urban, very German, very un-German scene.

'Their future does not contain our past.'

At that moment, Frieda knew that her sanity was at risk, if sanity means the integrity of the imagined person with whom every real person shares a body.

But what if her imagined self was nothing but a ghostly presence of the past?

'No sane person can go on living with a ghost.'

She said this without any particular emotion, as if she were stating a simple and fatal fact.

She knew that her own future would be decided in the very next moment of her existence when she would, or would not, at last find the right answer to the obviously interesting question that any child might ask, and to which the priests had given answers that the child Frieda had never found satisfactory. Why did God make me?

'Why *did* God make me, troubled old woman, pathetic relic of a suffering world?'

An answer came to her as if from somewhere outside her, from outside her mind. And she was able to express it so clearly that she might have been shouting it out of the window.

'Eve is the name of the redeemer of her other self whose name is Adam. They loved each other in the presence of God.'

The self that she could not find outside herself was, as it always had been, in the presence of God. They—she and her son—were together, and always would be, in the loving presence of God. In Ingo's dying she had found the reason for living that she had always known, and he had surely found.

'We learn to love by loving a loving God. I am in love with the love of God.'

An observant passer-by might have seen an elderly lady, inappropriately well dressed, smiling to herself as she walked briskly towards the S-Bahn station.

You also would smile if you knew that you had corrected the sinister fantasies of the *Book of Genesis*—even if it was by way of a somewhat mysterious demystifying.

*   *   *

11

Parmenides Moment

'My existence is gratuitous. Caused but motiveless. Death is random and inevitable, but not always motiveless.'

Edmund Jenning was also making a metaphysical journey. Such is the effect on those who have loved them of the death of those they have loved.

A physical journey had taken him back to the north-west of Scotland, to a stretch of coastline so isolated that he could spend two days there without seeing another human being. The nearest places of human habitation were four miles away in either direction, at the end of rough paths. For two perfect high-summer days, he was as united as a human being can be—neither two nor one—with the natural world from which he had been formed—body and mind—and to which, some day, he would return.

For two days he had behaved as a natural being, more natural than human, an integral part of the first nature, the nature untainted by man's miseries. He felt pleasure in embracing the sea and the sand, feeling their pleasure in embracing him.

Then, for the first time in his life, he was holding in his hand a single grain of sand. His self-consciousness ceased. For a timeless moment, he shared the existence of another existence, inseparable parts of all existence.

The sea was cold, but he—his human mind—was able to give to this sea a special character and a special purpose. He knew something about the sea that the sea might not know about itself. He knew that the sea here was warmer than it would have been if its salty watery molecules had not begun to excite themselves somewhere in the Caribbean, off the coast of Antigua perhaps, and if those excited molecules had not chosen to socialise themselves into a great stream of warming energy with a view to warming the western coast of a sub-Arctic Britain which was in great need of their warmth. The warm sea met its death in the cold sea, having made the cold sea warmer.

'*Je m'offre au soleil*,' Edmund said, generously.

He wrapped his sea-washed body in the soft sand—another novice in the holy order of gymnosophists.

Eye-to-eye with the oystercatchers and the sandpipers, he watched them as they watched him, letting them know, what they may not have known, that they were oystercatchers and sandpipers, and he was a human being.

At night, he lay in his sleeping bag cradled in a hollow in the slope of the sand-dune, warmed by the warmth of his own body, observing a sky full of places older than the earth itself, in relation to which the earth itself was as nothing. But the universe of all universes had chosen to cause this particular and peculiar creature to exist, with the capacity to see other worlds, to guess their age and to respect their indifference, and with the capacity to imagine a universe of all universes—and something beyond all universes.

On the third morning—Wednesday—he saw footprints in the sea-swept sand. He was no longer alone.

The mind that gave names to oystercatchers and sandpipers gave the three names 'vagrant' and 'Old Man of the Sea' and 'Wednesday' to the man who must have been watching Edmund as he slept. He was sitting on a patch of soft grass at the edge of the beach. He had planted a wooden staff in front of him. He was dressed in odd bits of ragged clothing, hardly concealing the leathery skin of his sun-browned weather-worn body.

Edmund felt no fear. He knew he must speak to the man. He knew that each of them would explain himself to the other. He did not know that this vagrant would tell him something that he already knew but did not know that he already knew.

'My name is Edmund,' Edmund said.

'My name is Nameless,' the Old Man said. 'But who are you, named Edmund?'

'Being here alone,' Edmund said, 'I've almost forgotten who I am.'

'When you travel alone, like me,' the Old Man said, 'you travel in the best company. I know nothing about events. I'm the most interesting person I know, not really knowing anyone else. I'm enough to be getting on with. No part of the world I own, but wherever I am, I am at home.'

'Were you always alone?' Edmund asked.

'Everyone is always alone, but not everyone travels alone.'

'Am I a disturbance for you?' Edmund said. 'If so, I'm sorry.'

'We could kill each other,' Wednesday said, 'and no one would know—at least, no one would know the reason why—if there was any reason why.'

'My existence is as random as any existence could be,' Edmund said.

'And yet you always existed as a possibility. The universe always contained what you choose to call your existence, as a possibility. If you hadn't existed as a possibility, the universe would have been a different universe.'

'But I didn't choose to exist,' Edmund said.

'No. You were chosen to exist. You should feel honoured. You see those birds at the edge of the sea?'

'Oystercatchers.'

'You could have said—"birds" or "animals" or "God's creatures". We class them, but they are individuals. Thinking that we are individuals, we think that they are unique individuals, each with its own life-story, its own need to find its daily bread and to find a mate. The One and the Many.'

'The One and the Many?'

'From the Many our minds make the One,' Wednesday said. 'From the One our minds make the Many. We give one name to things that are many. We give many names to things that are one. You are one and many. Look at the sea.'

'I'm looking at the sea.'

'The sea divides. The sea unites. There is only one sea—the world ocean—and yet there are many seas. We divide and we unite.'

'I feel the world ocean inside me,' Edmund said, 'the One which is not Many.'

'Look at me,' Wednesday said.

'I'm looking at you.'

'No, you're not. I'm invisible. And so are you. What you're looking at is your idea of me. The Self and the Other.'

'The Self and the Other?'

'You think of yourself as a self because you think of me as a self. We create each other in creating our self. We create our self in creating each other. I am, therefore you are. You are, therefore I am.'

'And the oystercatchers,' Edmund said. 'They make you and me into us, human beings who are not-oystercatchers.'

'We don't know what the oystercatchers are thinking. Mind you, we don't know what anyone is thinking. No scientist, examining a human brain, will ever see the content of a single human thought.'

'What about all those pretty patterns on our brain-scans?'

'Thinking is the name we give to the brain's presentation of its activity to itself. Hence, *eo ipso* and *ipso facto*, not to mention *per definitionem*, a thought in one brain can never be present in another brain—only the thought of another person's thought.'

'How do you live without thinking about other people's thinking?'

'To talk is to write your own biography,' the Old Man said. 'We become what we say. Living is the name we give to the story we tell each other about ourselves, and the stories that other people tell about us, when they tell their own stories. As for myself, I don't talk to other people, so I don't really have what you might call a life.'

'I'm not sure I have a life,' Edmund said. 'I think I'm really just an imaginary character in a work of fiction. I keep turning the page of my life-story, to find out what happens next. I dream that I am, and sometimes I dream that I'm dreaming.'

'Your self is a crowd because it contains all other selfs. You are as many different people as the number of people who know you. For each of them you are a different person.'

'The problem is—I don't seem to be any single person, even for myself. I am Kim. Who is Kim? *Qui ça?* I am an enigma to myself. I change the whole time, depending on how I feel, who I'm with, what I'm doing. When I'm with someone else, I'm only half myself, at most, and the other person must feel the same way. I'm not sure I'd recognise myself if I met myself. Welcome to me, but really there's no me here.'

'When you say "I", you're really talking about two people—the *you* who does the thinking, and the *you* you think about. Each of you knows that the other is there—a sort of faithful travelling companion—always beside you—but somehow always just out of each other's sight.'

'I am a metaphysical illusion—self-deluding illusion of a person, deluding myself and other self-deluding illusionary people into imagining that we all exist.'

'No,' the Old Man said. 'You can't escape as easily as that. You're an illusion of a person, but you aren't *merely* an illusion of a person—convenient as that might be, from a practical point of view, not to say from a moral point of view.'

'So what am I really?'

'What you really are is a unique instance of the Impulse of Life.'

'Heavens! And I never knew it!'

'What is nothing cannot exist,' Wednesday said. 'What exists is something. You exist as much as anything else, everything else, in the universe.'

'A grain of sand . . . and the sea . . . and the sky . . .'

'Thou art that. And you are me, and I am you.'

'I had begun to suspect that you might be,' Edmund said.

'The Impulse of Life is the self-creating of the natural world—the making and the perpetual re-making of the sand and the sea and the sky . . . and the making and the perpetual re-making of the person known as Edmund.'

'The rather unstable chemical compound known as Edmund—relatively stable chemically, rather unstable subjectively.'

'Your outscape is an inscape, and your inscape is an outscape. So what are you?'

'I am a window,' Edmund said. 'Obviously.'

'Each part of the universe has its own perspective of the universe,' the Old Man said, 'its own point of view—its Inner Light—the subjectivity of the Impulse of Life.'

'Should I be able to see my Inner Light?' Edmund asked.

'Heavens, no! You don't *see* your Inner Light. You see *by* it. It leads you to imagine what you are—and to choose what you will become. It is your unifying principle.'

'My soul?'

'Your soul seen as a dynamic cause of effects—not merely as an inert essence.'

'How can I learn to become what I am, not merely what I seem to be?'

'You can't. What you *can* do is to learn to love the process of your own becoming,' the Old Man said. 'The journey of your soul.'

'I have a feeling that the journey of my soul may be somewhat beyond me,' Edmund said. 'To the weak the grasshopper is a burden.'

'A traveller is not a wanderer,' the Old Man said.

'I have been a wanderer,' Edmund said. 'I want to be a traveller.'

The Old Man of the Sea extended his arm, as if he would show Edmund the route to travel.

'There are three routes to travel,' he said. 'The way of power, the way of the ideal, and the way of resignation.'

'I have already chosen the way of the ideal,' Edmund said.

'Then you already know that the way of the ideal is the journey that has a definite destination, but a destination the traveller can never reach.'

'Your footprints in the sand,' Edmund said, 'the sea has washed them away.'

'What happens happens. Nothing is washed away. My footprints were leading nowhere and anywhere and everywhere. Every end is a beginning.'

'Thank you for making that clear.' Edmund said generously.

'The destructive illusion of time,' the Old Man said. 'I have no past. I have no future. I am not happy or unhappy. I simply am.'

'Without the past and the future,' Edmund said, 'there isn't a present, is there?'

'Anxiety is living in the future helplessly. Like a nightmare. A waking nightmare.'

'And happiness?'

'Happiness is living in a timeless present gladly.'

Edmund looked carefully and lovingly at the vagrant's weather-lined face, his cornflower-blue eyes, his wild white hair. *Durchlaucht* personified.

'*I am who am.*'

Edmund said this, slowly and quietly, as if he were talking to himself.

'Tell me what you are saying.' Wednesday said.

'You have reminded me of what a dear friend of mine said. He chose to *be*, and not to *become*. He found the All, and fell in love with it. He is near us now. He died in the arms of the world ocean.'

'Apollo is Dionysus, and Dionysus is Apollo. Love separates and love unites. You, dear Edmund, have within you a rare power—the power to love your *self* in loving those you love. The most beautiful human power in the beautiful superhuman universe.'

'At this moment,' Edmund said, 'I feel the harmonic of the soul of my ever-living dead friend Ingo. The ten strings of our souls are vibrating merrily. I accept the universe.'

'Good choice,' the Old Man said.

If you are going to be Zarathustraed, try to make sure that it is by someone who knows how to speak briefly and to the point. Edmund knew that he had been fortunate in this respect. But now he took hold of the Old Man's hand, as if he wanted to make him stay a little longer in that magical-metaphysical place, an imagined place that was real, a real place that was imagined.

Edmund heard himself praying—that is, his inward self was speaking self-transforming words—praying to the sea, perhaps, mother and lover of mankind.

I am who will. I will not die before I have lived. Genug des Werdens. Laß mich sein!

The Old Man had returned to the sea.

Like a bird he had come. Like a bird he had gone.

All that remained was his wooden staff, planted in the sand.

And a cup of strength containing the gladness of the world.

*   *   *

San Lazzaro degli Armeni

Cheerful uncomplicated Gabi Dorn was not liable to be tempted by metaphysical ruminations. However, she was very much interested in religion. And so, unsurprisingly, was Cardinal Trevisan.

Fifteen minutes by *vaporetto* from the centre of Venice, the monastery on the island of San Lazzaro had played an important part in the Cardinal's life. For George Gordon, Lord Byron, the monastery had been a refuge from his *terra firma* dissipations. For Cardinal Trevisan it was a physical refuge from the intensity, the complexity and the ambiguity of Rome and Venice and the Universal Church. It had been a spiritual refuge also, where Alvise could be himself, without titles or responsibilities, alone with the only person who could see him as he really was, the person in whom he believed and trusted as he believed and trusted in no-one or nothing else.

Gabi could not know what it meant to the Cardinal to take her to see the island and its monastery, to the place which he had always kept as some sort of a secret, even from those who were closest to him. His religion was of the old-fashioned kind, in which the sociable and the spiritual were separate worlds, separate ways of being.

Still more unlikely, he would share a picnic lunch with the young Austrian in the gardens of the monastery, sharing a stone bench, protected from the sun by the leafy branches of a cool green arbour. The bright eyes of this young woman were seeing the intensity, the complexity and the ambiguity of the world for the first time. For the old man, she represented something which was relevant to his own newness, to the latest, and least expected, chapter in the story of his own self-development.

He had been surprised to find that a human being, in very old age, can still want to be renewed. If the Church had permitted such a thing, he would like to have been re-baptised, in the way that married couples sometimes, late in life, re-affirm their marriage vows. For the Cardinal, Gabi was the image of the possibilities of every human life, the possibilities that had once been his.

'There is something that I object to in the Christian religion,' Gabi said.

Gabi's newness included an absence of reticence that was now the hallmark of the young.

'How is it,' she continued, 'that a religion centred on the idea of love should have its roots in so much evil?'

'You mean the story of Christ's suffering and death?' the Cardinal said.

'That, but not only that. From the Garden of Eden onwards, through the terrible story of ancient Israel, we are flooded with biblical images of evil. In *Genesis* they say that God saw that the world was good. And then, ten minutes later and forever more, God's world is all lust and lying and murder and mayhem. Imagine what the world would have been like if the *Book of Genesis* had never been written! The good-news of fallen humanity. Original gloom. A mythology of misery. An all-too-human God. At least the Greek gods seemed to enjoy using their peculiar powers and doing their dirty deeds.'

'But wasn't it all very prophetic, as things have turned out?' the Cardinal said. 'There has been a great deal of murder and mayhem and lust and lying, as you call it—an awful lot of sin, to use the traditional word.'

'But do you get people to stop sinning by getting them to wallow in the misery of other people's sins? It's a sort of sadomasochistic perversion—a pathological obsession. European art seems to be full of delicious scenes of the murder and mutilation of holy people?'

'Most people find the temptation to sin very real and very powerful.'

'I can't even listen to Bach's Passions,' Gabi said. 'For me, the whole New Testament Passion thing is a sort of sinister ecstasy of victimhood.'

'But remember, Gabi, the meaning of the death of Christ is in his victory over death, in an ecstasy of *life*. Bach also wrote an Easter Oratorio, you know.'

'I can understand God choosing to take on human nature for a while,' Gabi said, 'to remind us that we're not wholly bad—to remind us that we have some sort of god-like potentiality within us. But I can't see how the image of a murdered god could possibly transform the awful lives that people lead.'

'A murdered god who overcomes death,' the Cardinal said. 'A seed is re-born as a plant in order to bear fruit. Lazarus is us. We can also live a new life. Actually, I've been thinking recently about a different problem, but a problem that may be related to yours in some way. How can religion speak to people who have lived through the growth of individualism since the end of the Middle Ages—and then through the growth of the intense socialising of the modern world, since 1789?'

'But isn't individualism, the cult of the self, supposed to be the religion of the modern world? From theism through deism to meism—Europe's spiritual progress.'

'I'm afraid that's a grand illusion,' the Cardinal said. 'For a moment after the Renaissance the privileged classes imagined the idea of the sovereign individual human being—a sort of idealised version of themselves. And then, for a while after the Reformation, it was possible to believe in the lonely responsibility of the human being in the presence of a judging God. But then, with the rise of the modern state, individualism was transferred to the level of society, and the individual disappeared into the jaws of the self-obsessed leviathans of the modern state. The human being is withering away—the individual human being, not the state.'

'But doesn't that make a religion of redemption through love even more irrelevant?' Gabi said. 'Societies didn't originally sin, did they? They don't need redemption, do they? Christ proclaimed a new kind of kingdom . . .'

'And . . . ?'

'The dreadful old empires and kingdoms and republics remained, as bad as or worse than ever. And the Church itself became an empire.'

'I'm not sure I would express it quite like that,' the Cardinal said. 'But what you say goes to the heart of a very great problem. Religion in the hands of evil people is the perfection of evil. Righteous evil—the worst form of evil. How can we reconcile the idea of the redeeming power of love with the fact of the overwhelming power of societies?'

'Aren't societies just an illusion?' Gabi said. 'Aren't they just another name for people—good and bad people?'

'That is the great challenge of the twenty-first century. I'm sure of it. We've found that societies—illusion or not—behave like people. They can do good, but they can do great evil. Dare we say that holiness is not just an ideal for individual human beings but also for human societies?'

'Heavens!' Gabi said. 'A holy society sounds about as unlikely as a blue rose or fire in ice.'

They were both silent for a while, re-integrating some part of their respective worldviews in relation to the circumstances and the content of their conversation.

'Christianity has been such an awful disappointment,' Gabi said at last, 'hasn't it?—from a historical point of view. Christians aren't just very liberal Jews, are they? Wasn't it all meant to be something totally new? The Christian ideal must be the most beautiful idea the human mind could imagine.'

The Cardinal surprised her by taking up her line of thought.

'Yes. Human psychology re-imagined as a loving relationship of self-overcoming and self-perfecting, in a universe seen as intrinsically creative and benevolent. That is certainly a beautiful idea. But I'm afraid you're right, dear Gabi. That idea hasn't changed human nature. There has been no great mutation in the human species-mind.'

'It's as if the beautiful ideal was forgotten,' Gabi said. 'It's as if Christianity had never been tried as a real way of life.'

'We believe that God in the form of the Holy Spirit guides us,' the Cardinal said. 'But we may have misunderstood the message. We have built mountains of confusion on top of a simple and beautiful idea.'

'But isn't that true of all religions? All religions seem to get corrupted, make bad choices. Christianity seems to me to have made some pretty dubious choices along the way—buying into Bronze Age mythology, pagan sacrificial victimism, and Roman imperialism—*inter alia.*'

'Maybe you're right, Gabi. Maybe it is the Way of All Religions. They are human institutions, after all. And, sadly, the corruption of the best is worst, as the Romans used to say—in religions, as in everything else.'

'The most awful religions are very awful, aren't they?' Gabi said. 'About as awful as anything gets. They've got nothing much on the *credit* side of their accounts, and an awful lot on the *debit* side—xenophobia and genocide and murder and war—not to mention mass stupidifying.'

'The necessary conversion is the conversion of the Christians,' the Cardinal said. 'The conversion of Christians to Christianity.'

Gabi had assumed that the Cardinal would strongly oppose her pessimism. But she seemed to have uncovered something that sounded like a note of desolation in the Cardinal's voice, a desolation that might be the expression of a personal anguish.

It was much more than a pessimistic historical judgment. It was an anguish that the Cardinal could now, at last, face clearly and clinically, in the relative emancipation of his old age, inspired by the fearless lucidity of a fresh young mind.

'I'm sorry,' Gabi said. 'I didn't mean to sound so rude or so dismissive. I suppose it's just that I don't have much experience of talking about religion to a master of those who know, if I may call you that.'

'No, you may not,' the Cardinal said. 'Like you, my dear child, I am someone who would desperately like to know.'

The Cardinal's words sounded conclusive, as if he were saying that this part of their lunchtime conversation could go no further.

But the age-old conversation was far from finished.

'Maybe we *have* made a great mistake in what we have said as messengers of the most beautiful of all ideas. Could we imagine something new—a New Theism—leaving out what Gabi had called the Bronze Age mythology—but something still full of a very personal loving God—present in the universe and present in our souls?'

The Cardinal said this to himself. He could not—even now—say it to Gabi.

'Perhaps it was a mistake to use the threat and the promise of an after-life as the bait to catch the souls of the faithful—*do ut des*—a cruel deception, a relic of the covenant-based religion of a covenant-based society.

'What Gabi had called the most beautiful idea is an idea for here and now. We are still and forever in the Garden of Eden. We are already in eternity. We are redeemed by the love of God every time we do good and avoid evil.'

And then there was the final, and inescapable, anxiety of the faithful in any religion. When one is challenged and stimulated to think in a new way about one's own beliefs, there is always the possibility that one is hearing, not the voice of God, but the voice of a lively and intelligent alternative source of interesting ideas. And the Devil has one great advantage, as compared with God. You don't have to believe in the Devil to do the Devil's work.

As a very old Catholic, the Cardinal was familiar with the reasonable confusion and doubt of any true believer. Old people worry about sliding into what is known as senile dementia. Alvise Trevisan, prince of the Church, old man, was worried about sliding into a new and wholly unfamiliar state of mind, a terrifying state of mind in which doubt may end as despair, the dark night which contains no meeting with God and no necessary dawn.

Unlike Gabi's aunt Frieda, the Cardinal had certainly not solved the gruesome mysteries of the *Book of Genesis*. Unlike the Countess, the Cardinal was not smiling.

*   *   *

13

Beginning to Mean Something

Mr Gray and the Countess had thought hard about the problem of entertaining Rupert on his visit to Paris. He had come to attend a summer course to perfect his French, as the French generously describe it, at the Lycée Michelet at Vanves, near Paris. They already knew that he was an unusually serious and independent-minded youth, more *jeune homme* than *adolescent*, but essentially English in mind and manners. They decided that his visit was an opportunity to perfect also his *savoir-vivre*, as the French optimistically describe it.

Rupert was certainly not averse to being inducted into a certain idea of the French way of life. He knew that Mr Gray and the Countess were unlikely to lead him into any *nuits d'ivresse et d'extase* which, if French novelists and poets are to be believed, are an integral part of another idea of the French way of life, and a necessary part of a young man's initiation into the reality of real life, especially life as lived in Paris.

Apart from anything else, a bohemian life must surely be very uncomfortable and dispiriting for most of the time. It could surely only be the temporary fantasy of a bourgeoisie who know that they can eventually escape from it, re-living an alternative life intermittently through a collection of fading memories. Or so Rupert provisionally and conveniently assumed.

For Rupert, *the Countess and Mr Gray* were representatives of a generation whose experience of the worst of the twentieth century does not allow them simply to reconcile themselves to the cruel imperfections of the human world. On the contrary, such people seem to see their experience as obliging them to use every effort to make a better human future.

For the Countess and Mr Gray, *Rupert and Gabi and Ingo* were representatives of a generation that had not experienced the worst of the twentieth century, but who responded in different ways to the social conditions they had inherited.

Gabi was the kind of young person who is adjusting intelligently to her circumstances, through the merits of her own personality and her particular life-experience. *Ingo* was one of those young people for whom escape from the human world seems the only possible option. *Rupert*, on the other hand, was a rarity—that kind of young person who is in the process of being adjusted to the cruel imperfections of the human world, but who may yet be able to save himself, and others, by finding a viewpoint from which to understand, and then to judge, and then to change that world.

Such were the tortuous roots of the plan of the Countess and Mr Gray for marking Rupert's French coming-of-age. They would endeavour to give him something that few people have, and even fewer are able to have so early in life, with the possibility that it might determine one's understanding of the world for the rest of one's life.

They would let him see the world simultaneously from two different perspectives—a stereometaphysics. They would show him a second *manière de voir*, as the French say with deep meaning. They would relativise his understanding of social conventions.

'You can judge a nation,' Mr Gray said, 'by three things—the nature of its elite, its attitude towards religion, and its attitude towards history. That is the way to identify with precision the difference between England and France.'

'You must tell us about England, dear Rupert,' the Countess said. 'We will tell you about France.'

Rupert—aware that he had relatively little experience of life, let alone of real life, especially French real life—felt that this may already be quite a significant difference between England and France. In England people, so far as he knew, did not talk like this to people of his age—to people of any age, for that matter. Maybe, for French almost-eighteen-year-olds, such a thing was a normal occurrence.

'All France is divided into two parts,' the Countess said, 'Paris and *la province*, where most of Paris came from, and where most of Paris goes back to in August.'

'Paris is not a class society but a caste society,' Mr Gray said, 'horizontal castes of elites—old aristocracy and the highest bourgeoisie, the new aristocracy of business, those who play the game of politics openly or in the shadows, and the *énarques* and the self-admiring intellectuals who imagine that they wield the ultimate power, not merely the power of the mind, but the power of *the idea of mind*.'

'Two verbs define the mind of France,' the Countess said. 'To think, to doubt.'

'The Cartesian gospel,' Rupert suggested.

'Precisely—except that the French have never believed the rest of the Cartesian gospel. There is no end to thought and no end to doubt. There is no limit to scepticism and no limit to pessimism.'

'In France,' Mr Gray said, 'religion has always been the social aspect of scepticism. To believe in ideas is the same thing as disbelieving in ideas. Religion is a system of ideas that imply their own negation. The idea of the possibility of God's existence necessarily implies the idea of his non-existence. And the same is true of all human knowledge.'

'And the net result of these French ideas,' the Countess said, 'is that the only rational attitude to life itself is *enlightened pessimism*. Life is to be endured—rationalising its imperfections, minimising its inconveniences, avoiding its unpleasantnesses.'

'The French worldview is a gastronomic view of life,' Mr Gray said, 'making some kind of temporary pleasure out of a permanent necessity, a cosmetic of pleasure on the face of what Freud called *die Unlust—le déplaisir*.'

'So what do you think, Rupert—as an Englishman?' Mr Gray asked 'What is the English *manière de voir*, would you say?'

'I think we also know a good deal about *Unlust* in England,' Rupert said, 'although I guess English people don't usually call it that.'

'And what would you say is the English approach to *déplaisir*—generally speaking?'

'We are just not serious enough people, in England, to have any general views on *Unlust*—or *Un*-anything else, really. In England, we make a big effort to avoid the pale cast of thought. The Scots are more serious—and the Irish are more lively—and the Welsh are more articulate.'

'For the English, thinking is a form of action,' Mr Gray said. 'Your American cousins have made a whole anti-philosophy out of pragmatism.'

'That's probably what we think about religion as well,' Rupert continued. 'Religion without too much religion in it. That's the nice thing about the Church of England—beautiful, but not too much theological or moral complexity. Feel-good, if possible; do-good, when possible.'

'Religion as a subtle form of social control,' Mr Gray said. 'Your American cousins have made an anti-religion out of that—all in the name of Christianity—fundamentalist anti-religion.'

'And what about the English elite?' the Countess asked. 'What is their governing principle, would you say?'

'Gosh!' Rupert said, feeling that he might be getting close to the end of his personal store of general ideas about England and the English.

'I'm not sure I'd know the English elite if I ever met it,' he said. 'But I'd guess *you* might call the English ruling class a Mutual Unlust Society—a lot of shared unpleasure—beginning in school—punctuated by a lot of lust there and thereafter. The English ruling class seem always to have led miserable lives, but hectically and humorously.'

'Survival of the unfittest? Reverse Darwinism?' Mr Gray said.

'More a case of terminal insecurity, I'd say,' Rupert said. 'In England the rulers have never really felt like rulers—and the ruled never really felt like the ruled. And they each despise the idea of the other.'

'The ultimate noble lie?' the Countess suggested. 'If nobody rules, nobody is ruled. The exclusionary idea that excludes the idea of power—so that the powerful are left free to govern? No wonder the English taught the world democracy.'

Rupert felt unequipped to respond to the menacing tone of the Countess's challenge.

'One thing English people do think about,' he said instead, 'is the French. We're English because we're not French. Mostly we're rather weak on national identity. But I'm not sure that the differences aren't really imaginary, a sort of game, like charades—pretending.'

'The pretending that becomes real,' Mr Gray said. 'A thousand years of mutual misunderstanding? The narcissism of interesting differences?'

'Something the French still do much better than us,' Rupert said, 'is public spaces and public services. That's the advantage of being an *absolute monarchy*. In England we've always been a rather chaotic *republic*. We're starved of public demonstrations of grandeur and intelligence—and always have been.'

'We think it's important to emphasize the differences, Rupert,' the Countess said. 'We see the world as hungry for redeeming ideas—and new ideas grow from the opposition of ideas. What the French call *pensée unique*—everyone thinking the same—*le conformisme*—is the beginning of the end of thinking.'

'Some Germans,' Mr Gray said, '—and the Germans, I must say, have some experience of these matters—some Germans have called it the one-dimensional thinking of one-dimensional human beings in one-dimensional societies. That is truly the beginning of the end of the self-creating human mind. Totalitarianism of the mind is the death of the mind. *N'est-ce pas*, Rupert?'

'I decided some time ago,' Rupert said, 'that my vocation is to be a dreamer—that will be my career, my vocation. And I intend to be the dreamer whose dreams come true.'

'Yes,' the Countess said. 'We heard that from Edmund Jenning. And we liked what we heard.'

'And my anthropology is going to be of the optimistic kind—what Edmund calls philanthropology. And my ontology is going to be of the ideal kind. I don't know whether you'd call that English or French or German or something else.'

'For us,' Mr Gray said, 'the vital thing is multi-dimensional thinking, the richest possible kind of dreaming.'

'I think you left out a fourth way of judging a nation,' Rupert said. 'Its attitude to food. The narcissism of big differences?'

Rupert was glad to see that he had made the other two smile at least, at last.

'I detect a hint,' the Countess said. 'Don't worry. We're very nearly there.'

'I sometimes wonder if I might have French genes in me somewhere,' Rupert said. 'I do seem to be peculiarly interested in food.'

Unlikely as it may seem, the foregoing conversation took place partly in the house on the avenue Foch, but partly also in the car in which the three of them were being driven to a restaurant, with Rupert sitting on a *strapontin* facing his formidable interlocutors.

'Rupert, you will have to forgive us,' the Countess said. 'You may already have noticed. You will already know that my brother and I are especially interested—some people might say obsessed—by the problem of the education of the new generations.'

'I had noticed,' Rupert said. 'And Edmund told me that you are especially interested in the fact that he is self-educated.'

'We're exploring the possibilities of a new kind of education—but not just education for the young—permanent education, you might call it—for people at all ages—education in the widest possible sense of the word—education as self-empowering.'

'I'm supposed to be going up to Oxford in October,' Rupert said. 'But Edmund has promised to educate me in the holidays—that's what he said—education, in the widest possible sense of the word, whatever that means.'

Mr Gray and the Countess introduced Rupert to the people at Taillevent—*cher fils d'une chère amie à nous*. His hosts betrayed a certain pride in having Rupert as their guest. He looked unmistakably and wholesomely English—his fair hair orderly but cheerfully excessive, the healthy skin-colour of those who spend a reasonable amount time on outdoor activities, rather than the permanent urban pallor of young Frenchmen of the same age—light-grey summer suit—pale cream shirt—school tie—bright eyes, lively manner.

(His hosts might or might not have guessed that Edmund Jenning had already taken charge of Rupert's schooling in whatever is the English equivalent of *savoir-faire*—on the assumption that there is no English equivalent of *savoir-vivre*—including 'making the right appearance' on special occasions.)

They took all of ten minutes to choose the dishes for their respective meals, following detailed discussions with several members of the staff of the restaurant.

From the other side of the restaurant a woman walked across to greet Mr Gray and the Countess warmly—three kisses on the cheek for the Countess, two for Mr Gray, a gloved hand for Rupert. After Rupert had been introduced to Madame S., she began to speak in English.

'*Je suis là pour perfectionner mon français*,' Rupert said defiantly. '*D'ici deux semaines je le parle couramment*.'

'*Mais vous parlez déjà à la perfection, mon cher Rupert*,' the woman said, pronouncing his name in the English way.

Mildly, but noticeably, blushing, Rupert responded not only to the compliment addressed to him but also to what he recognised as the unique charm of this sort of Frenchwoman. She was wearing a two-piece suit in the palest faded-rose colour, with a dark paisley-patterned blouse gathered at the neck in a sort of ruff and, on one of the gently sloping lapels of the jacket, an amber broach.

Rupert, noticing these things as if he were used to noticing such things, decided that Mme S. was the living embodiment of *chic*, if *chic* means a perfect, and apparently effortless, union of the studied and the natural in the *tenue* of a woman of a certain age.

After Mme S. had returned to her table, the Countess leaned towards Rupert.

'The man she is with is a government minister and she is not his wife,' she said, her manner suggesting that she was merely conveying information, rather than making any sort of social or moral judgment.

'*Amour*,' Rupert said. 'To us English, the French attitude to love is a complete mystery. We're getting better at food, but *amour* is simply beyond us, beyond our comprehension.'

'Do you know,' Mr Gray said, 'in the French mind, there is a direct connection between love and intelligence? *On ne badine pas avec l'amour—avec l'intelligence non plus*.'

'And also between love and equality,' the Countess said. 'That sort of thing is a very special species of *amour* . . .'

She nodded towards the government minister and Mme S.

'Think of it rather as intimate friendship—*amour amitié* or else *amitié intime*—in which the aspect of intelligent friendship predominates over the physical aspect.'

'And friendship implies a sense of equality,' Mr Gray said. 'Such friendship dignifies both parties, man and woman, each treating the other as an equal.'

'At least for the purposes of their relationship,' the Countess said. 'That has been good for the status of women in France, especially mature women. But don't be deceived—there is more to the status of women in society than their status as intimate friends of vain men.'

'There's a spectrum from *amour-commerce*, at one extreme, to *amour folle*, at the other,' Mr Gray said. '*Amour-amitié* is somewhere in the middle.'

'Why is so much of literature and opera about *amour folle*?' Rupert said, 'I suppose intimate friendship is just not interesting enough. I seem to have read and heard an awful lot about the costs of love, and not very much about its benefits. Edmund has promised to teach me about the meaning of love—from the philosophical point of view, of course.'

'Love of that kind,' said the Countess, nodding once again in the general direction of the government minister and Mme S., 'love between mature people, has a big mental aspect, an intellectual aspect, if you like—I suppose you could say, a philosophical aspect.'

'The French have seen a great truth,' Mr Gray said. 'Life is a compromise between hope and fear—a compromise re-negotiated every day of our lives.'

'And so are love affairs,' the Countess said.

'It's a sort of shared pessimism,' Mr Gray said, 'a shared defiance in the face of what they see as the meaninglessness of the world, the meaninglessness of all human relationships, social and political and personal.'

'In that case,' Rupert said, 'I think we—we English—may never catch up with the French. Better restaurants, perhaps. But we're not clever enough to understand meaninglessness. "The meaning of meaning is a meaningless problem." I had to write an essay on that topic at school. I won a prize for it.'

'So you see, Rupert,' Mr Gray said, 'there is a worldview contained even in the smallest and most intimate aspects of life. Every moment of our lives contains a philosophy of life—a metaphysics—whether we know it or not.'

Rupert sensed that he was acting as a blackboard on which a particular chain of arguments—a theorem—was being inscribed.

'Every nation has its own metaphysics—its own theory of everything,' Mr Gray continued. 'Every person has their own metaphysics, even if they are unable to recognise it, let alone to express it in words.'

'For many people,' the Countess said, 'religion provides a convenient expression of a metaphysics, a useful theory of everything, causing them to become what they already think they are. Or, if it's not religion, then it's some sort of dominant ideology. No further thought is then required.'

'For most nations, their idea of their history is a sort of metaphysics,' Mr Gray said, 'a simplified worldview, allowing them to become what they imagine they already are.'

'So how do people live together—the French and the English, say—if they each have their own theory of everything—if every people in the world has their own theory of everything?'

'That, dear Rupert, is the great challenge,' Mr Gray said. 'Somebody has to find a metaphysics beyond existing systems of metaphysics, a religion beyond existing systems of religion, a morality beyond existing systems of morality—something new in the human mind that allows human beings to co-exist in a new way.'

'That is certainly a challenge.'

'But it's a challenge that has been faced again and again—one way or another, for better and for worse—since the beginning of human history. And we face it now, yet again, like everyone else who has gone before us—but it is a challenge which is now quite new in scale and urgency.'

Rupert sensed that the theorem had been completed. Q.E.D. *CQFD.* The meal had been as good as he had imagined and hoped. But it had also been hard work.

He believed that he was able to recognise a rite of passage when he saw one. He felt that he was not yet able to announce—like a distinguished predecessor: '*Je suis un adulte.*' But, as he prepared to enter man's estate, he felt that he could now volunteer the judgment: 'I now know the kind of adult I will be.'

By this he would mean to say that he had begun to be aware of other *manières de voir*, other *manières de vivre*. And that meant that he could tell himself—and would certainly tell Edmund—that he now knew, at last, how to become master of his own metaphysics, the maker of his own meaning-for-himself. He was no longer merely philosophy's apprentice. Rupert would now be the sorcerer of himself.

'*Savoir-vivre* plus *savoir-faire* equals *savoir-être,*' he reminded himself.

*   *   *

14

Meeting of the Ways

For Alison it was to be another challenging occasion. She was to meet Abe Green in New York—not on behalf of MI6 or the Foreign Office, but on behalf of the Firm. The Firm had learned—before it had become a matter of public rumour and speculation—that the Canadian Government had approached Abe Green with a view to offering him appointment as the first President-Director-General of the new League of Sensible Countries.

The Firm probably knew Abe Green better than the Canadian Government, but even they were unable to predict what his reaction to such an offer would be. They had been involved with the powerful American for some years, but surreptitiously and indirectly, without his knowledge. The time had come to take a risk.

There were good grounds for thinking that Abe, in his new state of mind, would sympathise with the general objectives of the Firm. He and Alison might both now be seen as representatives of a class of holders of governmental power who had come to see that governmental power in its old forms had come to the end of its useful life. The question was—would Abe be willing to associate himself with the practical work of the Firm?

It was a question that the Firm, with its new sense of the urgent necessity of a campaign of practical action on a broad front, must ask. And it was Alison's job to open exploratory talks. This evening she had convened a preparatory meeting at her apartment at 60th St and Third Avenue in New York.

'Your first problem is that it's not at all certain that the United States, in its present condition, would qualify as a sensible country. Now, a League of Strange Countries—it could be a Founding Member of that—no contest—no possibility of French *blackboulage* there.'

It was Jack Jackson, loyal and well-informed American diplomat, who raised this doubt.

'And there's another thing. Would Abe want to head such an organisation that didn't include the U.S. of A.? Or, to put it in another way, would Abe, in his present mood, want to belong to such an organisation that *did* include the U.S. of A.?

This further puzzle was proposed by Jim Meehan, the somewhat exotic newspaperman whom Alison had met answering to the name of Boxcar at the Firm's chalet in Bavaria. Edmund had given Alison a colourful account of his meeting with Jim and Jane Meehan at Abe Green's new home in Connecticut.

'I've talked to him since he left the NSC,' Meehan said, 'and he's got it in for everything and everyone.'

'I talked to him for a while last week,' Alison said, 'at that farewell lunch for your remarkable boss, the late lamented Secretary of State.'

'I won't ask you to parse that word "remarkable",' Jackson said. 'How did Abe seem?'

'We only talked generalities, but I agree with Jim. Abe seemed unusually grim, but also on some sort of high.'

'As you would, on emancipation from slavery, or release from gaol,' Meehan said.

'But that might be an attraction of the LOSC idea for Abe,' Jackson said. 'As I understand the deeply bizarre project, it won't be an intergovernmental thing at all.'

'Or a non-governmental thing either,' Meehan said.

'No. Not states or nations or governments or IGOs or NGOs. It's going to be a sort of international union of the ruling classes, in a wider sense of "ruling class"—people in leading positions across the board—the professions, academia, industry and business, the arts.'

'And the media already!' Meehan said. 'And sports! Nobody seems to have any idea how these paragons of civic virtue are going to be selected for their very obscure task.'

'The idea seems to be that there will be very little formal organisation,' Alison said, 'and very little in the way of formal powers, legal powers.'

'That's surely a major plus of the whole idea,' Meehan said. 'The world is reeling under the weight of IGOs and NGOs—thousands and thousands of them—a sort of self-appointed international mafia whose only shared purpose is to maximize the absolute power of governments, the absolute self-interest of lobby-groups, and the absolute arrogance of middle-class busybodies.'

'But a countervailing power to all such things wouldn't really be a power, would it,' Alison said, 'unless it had some real legal powers?'

'A plus for me is that people are saying that the working language of the whole thing is going to be the Universal Language . . .' Meehan said.

'. . . of which we here are fluent speakers of one of its dialects,' Jackson said.

'Two of its dialects,' Alison said, as Englishly as she could.

'The poor Canadians are facing a Unilateral Declaration of Independence by Quebec,' Jackson said, 'for having even hinted that LOSC might possibly have only one working language, and that would not be French.'

'Did you see their Governor-General has said that English is half-French in any case, so it's the Spanish or the Chinese who might have reason to object.'

'I think they've taken note of the sad case of the EU,' Alison said. 'The lack of a single language makes the EU intrinsically impossible—politically and philologically.'

'Great mistake giving up Latin,' Meehan said.

'Perhaps the French and the French Canadians would be happy if the Universal Language were called Frankish,' Jackson said.

'So, let's assume for a moment,' Alison said, 'that Abe agreed to become head of the thing, whatever it is. What should *we* do about that?'

'The Firm, you mean?' Jackson said. 'Do you know, I sometimes think he's already one of us. We were fixated on him for such a long time.'

'But to go from that virtual connection to a formal arrangement, that would be a huge step, Jack,' Meehan said. 'I don't envy your task, Alison. How on earth could you ask him without asking him.'

'Well, I hesitate to say such a thing,' Jackson said, 'but you have to know, Jim, that we spend a good deal of time doing something like that in the wonderful world of diplomacy—asking people to do things without actually asking them.'

'But you do it with gunboats and sanctions. Agree with us or else.'

'No, I'm thinking of our work at what you might call a more personal level.'

'Seducing innocent people into your nefarious plots and schemes.'

'The Firm has its tried and tested protocol for contacting people—we're all familiar with that,' Alison said, 'but not someone quite on the scale of Abe Green. He's in a position to do the Firm a great deal of harm, if he took things the wrong way.'

'I think it's simply a risk we have to take,' Jackson said, 'that *you* have to take, Alison. If Abe took on the LOSC project and if the Firm could net him, reel him in—two very big "ifs"—it could transform things—with all sorts of unforeseeable possibilities.'

'And the *Erstes Gremium*—the big guys—must have seen the same risk and the same possibilities,' Meehan said. 'Given that they're seeing the whole world situation in a sort of seismic shift condition—pending or actual—we must suppose they've simply decided that this is a time for exceptional risk-taking with a view to exceptional rewards.'

Alison had not mentioned an aspect of the situation that was still too delicate to talk about lightly, but which certainly was present to the minds of the *Erstes Gremium*. She and they knew that there was emerging a new global balance of power—symbolised, embodied even, in the embryonic LOSC and the shadowy New Issues—standard-bearers of a new kind of struggle, the struggle to take power over the future of the human mind.

The Firm's highest ambition was to involve itself in every aspect of that confrontation. Alison saw herself as a sort of personal centre of gravity between two exceptional people, holders of different kinds of power. And she felt privileged to know both of them, and to admire both of them in different ways—Abe Green and Mike Abi.

'Well, thank you, for your encouragement,' she said. 'I read you both as simply telling me to get on with it, and stop shilly-shallying.'

'That's about it, Alison,' Meehan said. 'It's your inning, as I believe one says in the language of cricket.'

After her two visitors left, Alison decided that, apart from a medicinal shot of cognac and a good night's sleep, she would make no further preparation for Abe Green's visit at ten o'clock on the following morning.

So be it, if it all went wrong. She had often thought longingly of early retirement, a wisteria-covered cottage, and a life of dignified leisure.

Time for the Approach Direct, again.

'Abe,' Alison began, and hesitated.

'Yes, Alison.'

'We were wondering what you think of the LOSC idea. Cranky, clever, or beneath your horizon of interest?'

'I'm flattered Her Majesty's Government should want to know the opinion of a has-been who never was as much as he seemed.'

'On the contrary, I can't think of anyone whose opinion would be more significant for us.'

'Well, in my new state of mental liberation, I have to tell you I don't any longer regard left-fieldism as necessarily cranky or necessarily clever—and this particular thing is certainly not insignificant.'

'Actually, I have to tell *you*,' Alison said, approaching still more directly, 'I'm not only asking you on behalf of HMG. There are some of us who meet occasionally, around the margins of things—try to take an objective view, an independent view of things—try to free ourselves a little bit from the mental constraints, the ideologies, we are paid to promote.'

'Free spirits inside the gulag?'

'Something like that. We're interested in the LOSC idea, but we don't see much chance that our governments will want to have anything to do with it . . .'

'. . . unless they see other governments having something to do with it. They're all like pathetic little children at playtime, aren't they? The mentality of governments is the mentality of the high school—my peers are my law—unless I'm much bigger than you.'

'But, as I say, we ourselves—among ourselves—don't want to allow the LOSC idea to disappear without trace, like practically every other interesting new initiative.'

'The League of Nations—General and Complete Disarmament—the partition of Palestine—the Havana Charter—Atoms for Peace—nuclear non-proliferation—the Oslo Accords—not to mention the dear departed United Nations Organization itself.'

'And the European Union,' Alison added, expressing a personal view, no doubt—*not necessarily reflecting the views of Her Majesty's Government*—as public officials say in anticipatory self-defence—the word 'necessarily' being pleasingly provocative.

'So, you people who think outside the little boxes, Alison—do you suppose you really have any power or influence?'

'That's one reason why we're especially interested in LOSC. We see it as a possible focus of real change—a very, very remote possibility.'

'And that is the official view of the Firm?' Abe said.

'The Firm?'

'The Firm.'

Recounting the conversation later, Alison would say that, at this interesting moment, she maintained her composure, 'didn't bat an eyelid'. However, the transcript of the conversation shows that Abe actually said:

'No need to look so surprised, dear Alison. We had known about you for some time. You confused us a bit at first. As you know, there are one or two other bodies hiding behind "Firm"-like names.'

'I think they all probably know that it's not-very-convincing camouflage—ineffective against those whose business it is to know about such things.'

'*Our* Firm—nestling in beautiful Langley, Virginia—is not terribly clever at dealing with such things. They have computer algorithms that assemble bits of apparently unrelated information and—Eureka!—from time to time, out pops a "provisional conclusion"—and we invade somebody, or the President makes a speech.'

'We had noticed.'

'And—Eureka!—one day out popped your gang as a provisional conclusion. We looked into you for a while and decided you-all were, on balance, benign or insignificant, or both. We have our hands rather full at the moment with people who, on balance, are unbenign and rather significant. So we decided to let you get on with whatever it is you're doing.'

'Well, that certainly simplifies matters somewhat. You can probably guess that *our* Firm is rather interested in LOSC and—if I may put it like this—rather interested in your possible position in relation to LOSC—your personal position, not the USG's.'

'You can probably guess that I'm giving it a good deal of thought myself. I wonder if this would be too much to ask. Would it be at all possible for me to have some sort of fairly structured discussion with you and your people? I'm very much on my own now—suddenly deprived of the shoals of people who were paid to help me think—and sometimes, occasionally, actually managed to think better.'

'That would be very possible, Abe,' Alison said. 'But I must tell you that such contacts would be unequally reciprocal. We would greatly appreciate your input. We're more into leftfieldism than you were in your official capacity. But our present view is that things are now at a sort of critical stage—a tipping-point between progress and chaos—if that metaphor works.'

'OK. Let's keep in touch, Alison.'

'I'll get back to you very soon—very soon.'

'I'm due to be in England in three weeks time.'

'I know,' Alison said. 'I think we will be seeing each other then, in any case.'

'Yes. They told me—my English cousins—of whom, I have to tell you, I have decided to become rather fond—in a strange sort of way—and rather late in life.'

The transcript of the conversation did not record that Abe embraced Alison as a farewell gesture, in a modified and rather reticent version of a continental European greeting—but with definite overtones of characteristic American warmth.

'Well done, Alison. Good work. It's an exciting moment.'

It was Mr Gray's voice. He and the Countess and one or two other people had listened to the conversation between Abe and Alison, in the Firm's headquarters in Potsdam, Germany, in real-time, as it happened.

Two days later, Alison received a telephone call from Abe.

'Alison, I've got tickets for the gala opening of the new *Magic Flute* at the Met. Would you like to come?'

Alison did not even look in her diary.

'I'd love to. That would be wonderful.'

*   *   *

15

North Norfolk

'Two last wars fatally self-wounded the European soul. America gave European civilisation the *coup de grâce*. And now the ghost of post-European civilisation is stalking the whole world. Soon all the world will be America.'

Greg Seare was talking to himself, sometimes even talking to himself out loud—a monologue as dialogue—the perennial essence of philosophy, that perpetual feast of nectar'd, but not always comforting, fruits.

He was staying with Cambridge friends at their weekend cottage in Wells-Next-the-Sea. While his hosts were at church Greg had taken the opportunity for a bracing walk on a sunny Sunday morning. He drove the few miles to one of his oldest and most favoured places of escape. The sandy beach, stretching out of sight in both directions, was almost deserted.

There was a family playing French cricket seriously, under the command of a domineering father. Another family, more easy-going, were trying to fly kites from the top of the sand dunes in a breeze that was mostly too feeble for kite-flying. It was a calm and safe sort of scene, with no apparent threat of metaphysical anxiety, and no obvious promise of metaphysical enlightenment.

The North Sea—with thousands of miles of the Eurasian landmass only a few miles away—is not in the same metaphysical league as the Atlantic Ocean, or even the Indian Ocean. It does not naturally inspire the oceanic feeling, even in those normally, that is to say abnormally, inclined to philosophise. Greg was so inclined.

'The World Spirit was an Unhappy Spirit long before there was Europe, let alone America. The March of God in the World has been the relentless rationalising of human misery. Thousands of years of mythologising and theologising and philosophising to explain and justify human misery. Call no man happy until he is dead. The angry ape that makes the angels weep.'

'Which came first—the unhappy human being or the unhappy human species—the unhappy private mind or the unhappy public mind—unhappy individual consciousness or unhappy collective consciousness?'

'Collective consciousness is human species-consciousness, the product of evolution by natural selection.'

'*We* think, therefore *we* are human beings.'

'*Individual* self-consciousness is a bizarre biological mutation, nature's evolutionary gamble, a daring experiment with a new principle of life.'

'*I* think, therefore I am not you thinking.'

'*Collective* self-consciousness is a product of the self-evolving of the new self-conscious species.'

'*We* think, because I am you thinking.'

'Philosophy is the mind's self-exploring. Bad philosophy is dangerous, but no philosophy is worse. In the twentieth century, megawatts of intellectual energy and forests of paper were wasted in the effort to disprove the claim of philosophy to find the truth. But philosophy never claimed—or never should have claimed—to find the truth. Philosophy is an orderly and laborious effort to think truly.'

'The rationality of philosophy is the morality of the self-ordering human mind thinking about itself. If people don't know that there is a problem about the nature of reality, they can't know that there is a problem about the nature of fantasy.'

'Philosophy is a fruitful union of the private mind, thinking alone, and the public mind, thinking together.'

'The post-European American mind—the mind of the unphilosophical nation—is the hegemony of the public mind over the private mind.'

'*We* think, therefore we are Americans, a chosen people.'

'America is a promised land of the collective imagination, ruled by imperious processes of the public mind—religion, law, capitalism, democracy, and pragmatism. Fundamentalist religion as a theology of social control. Law is rituals of social management. Capitalism is the totalitarian integration of labour and desire. Democracy is the disorderly absolutism of the general will. American Pragmatism is the ultimate socialisation of the thing formerly known as philosophy.'

'America is the place where communism succeeded. Communism of the mind.'

'The sudden emancipation of the masses in Western countries, after centuries of slavery, has left them in the same condition as the corrupt wing of the old ruling class—feckless, mindless, tasteless, and hopeless—led by a ruling class which has lost the will to lead, and a governing class who mistake social control for leadership.'

'Unhappy consciousness is to feel alone in a crowd—me and yet not me; not me and yet me. It is the burden of existing in-oneself but not for-oneself. Unhappy consciousness is the perverse self-denying of the self which may soon become the perverse self-denying of humanity.'

Greg, like the philosopher Immanuel Kant, was one of those people for whom there is nothing like walking to stimulate the stream of philosophical consciousness. Seeing him walk along the beach, you would not know that he was *thinking* in an orderly and articulate way, let alone that he was distilling a large part of his personal metaphysics.

And, with the words 'the self-denying of humanity', he had had reached a familiar omega point of his organised thinking.

At the same moment, he heard an unfamiliar sound. He heard the sound before he saw its source.

The sound was of a violin—distant but clearly audible. The sound of the violin and the image of the violinist were slowly approaching along the seashore. Greg remained perfectly still, as if any movement might dissolve the vision or disturb the sound. The violinist stopped some thirty feet away, watching Greg as Greg watched her.

Greg recognised the music—Heinrich Biber's fantastical *Representativa* Sonata in A major, with the sounds of frog and hen and nightingale darting from the violin into the soft morning air. The violinist—a new sea-borne Arion—was as pale and delicate as an orchid—dove-grey shirt, turquoise trousers, vermilion cummerbund, her feet bare.

The two families—cricketers and kite-flyers—stopped and stared, trying to make sense of the unlikely scene. There was some giggling among the younger children, as they heard the strange noises emanating from the violin.

Greg still did not move, the violinist still watching him, with a look that was both distant and embracing. They were interacting—each of them the producer and consumer of an unprecedented and unrepeatable experience for the other, both of them watching and watched.

They were alone together—alone together in the presence of a third thing—the music—together in a supersensory embrace, warm and enlivening, filled with something that seemed like the momentary possibility of a new kind of shared consciousness.

Then the young violinist turned away from Greg, turned to face the sea. The music changed.

A baroque sonata for solo violin, in a minor key. Music representing nothing and everything. Music full of a form of order not merely made in the minds of those who hear it, a form of order echoing in the inner order of those who hear it, an external-internal order for which the word *beauty* is the conventional word, but not the sufficient word.

Beauty, ladder from the particular to the universal, from the universal to the particular. Beauty, and its emotional counterpart for which the word *joy* is the conventional word, but not a sufficient word. Joy that sweeps aside all conflicting emotions and fills the mind, if only for a moment, with the possibility of another kind of existence for suffering humanity.

Freudenmeister for *Trauergeister*.

And now the cricket-playing children were dancing to the music—two boys and two girls, none more than ten years old—dancing, not in a silly childish way, but slowly, silently, as if in an amechanic trance, entranced by the music.

Then the image of the violinist and the sound of the violin were receding. Slowly the sound of the violin lost itself in the restless sound of the sea. And the image of the violinist dissolved into the placid picture of the seashore.

Strangely, the children were still dancing, as if they could still hear the music. They were dancing to the music of an unheard melody.

Then they stopped, returned to their game, as if nothing had happened, as if they did not know how to process in their minds a mysterious moment of metaphysical emancipation—momentarily unselfconscious children, their souls half-freed, for a while, from the prison of their half-formed bodies.

Greg felt his senses as sensations. He felt the soft air of the invisible breeze caress the skin of his face, the cold sand press against the skin of his bare feet. He heard the sound of the breaking waves, as if the sea were inside his head. He saw the sky stretched over him like a tent of pale blue silk.

Cheers of delight from the kite-flying family. The gentle breeze had become a light wind. Their bright red kite was flying high in the sky, gliding slowly and proudly, this way and that.

Holde Geige! Holde Kunst!

The inextinguishable trace of the music had insinuated itself into the depths of Greg's inner world, sparking metaphysical neural connections, new and old—sending a focused beam of light into the dark and secret place where the silence of the sub-unconscious mind can resonate with a universal harmony—revealing the outline of a possible personal paradise.

'The empiricists were wrong. There is plenty in the mind that was not first in the senses. Behind the painted veil there are other worlds.'

Greg had reached the age when we move from the haptic phase to the glyptic phase in the constructing of human personality—from the accumulating of personal character traits to the excising of characteristics extraneous to a more or less established personality.

For people who care, every thought is a form of action, engaging their moral responsibility. For Greg—a person who cared, if ever anyone cared—a metaphysical moment acts as a commanding voice speaking from, and to, the unchanging still centre of his self-creating self.

For people whose established personality is of the ascetic erotic type—and Greg had come to recognise himself as such a person—music at its most perfect can produce a paroxysm of sinless pleasure.

Time for the music-made metaphysical moment to speak, in the voice of this particular orderly and articulate human being!

'Our possible paradise has many dimensions. The order of the *individual human mind*—the self-ordering of a private world. *Social Order*—the collective self-ordering of a world made by many minds. The *Intelligible World*—the natural world re-ordered by the human mind. The order of the *Natural World*, of which human self-ordering is itself an infinitesimal part.'

'But there is a *fifth dimension*—the hidden order of all self-ordering—an order above and beyond and within and outside, a transcendental order.'

'To engage with the fifth dimension of our possible paradise is the wonderful purposeless purpose of human existence.'

Mr Gray and the Countess—defiant witnesses of human tragedy—had challenged Greg and Edmund, ambassadors from the philosophical nation—Greg, who was capable of extracting joy from the sadness of things—and Edmund, the incorrigible optimist who had wept at the destruction of a civilisation.

And they had embraced the aged Cardinal who had revealed to them his own defiant ambition, his final journey—to go in search of the religion beyond religions.

Greg, specialist in the study of the imaginative creations of the human mind—and especially the imagining of the tragedies of unhappy human consciousness—realised that he was in possession of a salutary philosophical message.

'The search for the meaning of *happiness* begins and ends with our consciousness of the dimensions of the mind. Happy consciousness is the harmonious co-existence of the concentric spheres of the self-ordering human mind, the solar system of which I am the sun.

'The all-too-human individuals of the Shakespearean world—Lear, Hamlet, Othello, Lady Macbeth, Richard III—like the all-too-human individuals of the Athenian tragic-imaginative world—Electra, Medea, Antigone, Orestes, Oedipus—are unique individuals sacrificed on the altar of the All in the name of the Many.

'The quixotic figure of Jesus Christ is a unique protagonist of a universal tragedy—the endlessly repeated failure of the endlessly repeated attempt of the Many to destroy the presence of the All in the One.

'Unhappy consciousness is the poisonous product of a disharmony in all the dimensions of our existence—from the first to the fifth. But there are fertile seeds even in a rotting fruit. Humanity *is* capable of happy consciousness. Self-wounding humanity *is* capable of self-healing.'

He spoke his defiance out loud, addressing the All that is One on behalf of the human animal that is One and Many.

'To be human is to be conscious of the impulse of life. To be conscious of the impulse of life is to have hope. To have hope is to be capable of the fullness of life.'

'Idealism is the science of hope, the most natural science, the science beyond all sciences, the science we must study, and then teach. The teacher's task is not merely to explain the earth. The teacher's task is to educate the earth. The teacher's task is to teach human beings how they might become immortal.'

'We will be the people of the Fifth Dimension!'

'To re-create the human race is a big task.'

A different genesis story.

He turned his back on a sea that is a small part of the World Ocean, to return to a Human World that is mostly still undiscovered, a Human World that is still only partly human.

*   *   *

16

Into the Rose-Garden

'Edmund has forty-three varieties of roses,' Rupert said.

'And two or three gardeners, presumably,' Gabi said.

'You're right,' Edmund said. 'Roses are difficult, very difficult. That's the only generalisation you can make about roses. Beyond that, every variety is a law to itself.'

'And people,' Rupert said. 'You could say the same about people.'

'Most roses smell nicer than many people,' Gabi said. 'That's another generalisation about roses.'

'But your assertion, if it were true, wouldn't invalidate Edmund's proposition,' Rupert said. 'Edmund's proposition and mine were, in Aristotelian terms, affirmative universals—all A is B. Your proposition is not an affirmative universal—either about roses or about people. In fact, Edmund proposed three affirmative universals—all A (roses) are B (difficult); and all C (other generalisations about roses) are D (untrue or impossible); and all E (varieties of roses) are F (incapable of being generalised about in other respects than their difficulty).'

'But my proposition had the distinct advantage,' Gabi said, 'that it can be fairly easily proved to be true—by olfactory inspection—of roses and people.'

'Gabi, really!' Rupert said. 'You can't compare olfactory inspection and Aristotelian logical necessity as grounds of truth.'

'A rose by any other name would smell as sweet,' Gabi said.

'But it wouldn't be a rose,' Rupert said. 'A rose is only a rose because it is called a rose. If a particular variety of rose were called a geranium, it might smell as sweet as a rose, but it would not be a rose.'

'Wouldn't you still be Rupert, even if you were called Griselda?'

'No, at best I'd be "Griselda, the person formerly, or also, known as Rupert". But if I'd always been called Griselda, even that wouldn't be true.'

'If someone asked—say, at a party—"who are you"?—would you say—"I am the person known as Rupert"?'

'Only, if they had asked "what is your name?" Then I might say "my name is Rupert".'

'Well, in that case, you agree that you are more than your name. You have a name. You are known by a name. Therefore you exist separately from your name.'

'But my existence—more strictly, my essence—is not to be the bearer of my name. I *was* before I had a name.'

'Roseness,' Gabi said, 'is the common feature or features of the plants that we happened to call "rose". I agree that a rose is more than its name, but not all that much more.'

'By common features do you mean the DNA that all roses share?'

'That's what plant classification is nowadays,' Gabi said. 'It used to be classification by morphology, structural bits they had in common. Now it's their DNA.'

'But since no two roses are the same,' Rupert said, 'what you call roseness can't be an essential part of being a rose—just as Rupertness can't be an essential part of two people called Rupert. Roseness must be something we imagine about roses. Universal affirmatives about roses can't be descriptions of characteristics of Edmund's prize roses over there. Roseness is like a photograph of a rose—it is not itself a rose.'

'But if you call it a rose, dear Rupert, you must be saying something about it—you're not merely talking about proper speech. If you say, "that is Edmund's prize rose" you're not merely wanting me to agree about the correct use of the word "rose". You're not just wanting me to agree that we would have made a mistake if we had called the same plant "Edmund's vaguely oriental summer-house".'

'Human beings are not human merely because we call them human,' Rupert said. 'But humanness is not something we infer from examination of all human beings.'

'What else can it be?' Gabi said. 'Either that, or else what you call universal propositions about human beings are inventions, fantasies, works of the imagination.'

'What makes some beings into human beings is their self-consciousness,' Rupert said. 'No one has ever looked at "all human beings", so you can't say anything universal about them. So you can't say "humanness" is a characteristic of all human beings, unless you mean that "humanness" is a word we choose to use to describe what we might want to be a characteristic of all human beings. But then you pay your money and you make your choice. I might say that what Edmund calls simianism—sex obsession—is a universal characteristic of human beings—or aggression or the herd instinct or addiction to gambling or ball-games.'

During this time, Edmund had been, with ostentatious concentration, working on a flower border. He had also been listening to every word that Gabi and Rupert were saying. He was judging them—according to a rather unusual scale of values. He judged people according to the usual criteria—appearance, class, intelligence, psychic and physical energy, moral purpose and moral integrity. All of us acquire the habit, and some of us develop great skill, in making such integrative judgments of other people—judgments which are sometimes more or less instantaneous, and which may determine not only our practical relations with them but also our affective relationship to them.

Can we co-exist with them? Could we co-habit with them? Can we work with them? Do we like them? Can we love them?

But there is another scale of values that Greg Seare and Edmund had come to call *metaphysiology*—the study of a person's personal metaphysics. To test a person's metaphysiology it is necessary to locate them on two scales—PQ and AQ—Plato Quotient and Aristotle Quotient.

Those scales together determine a person's mental hormonal balance. And the word 'hormonal' is not wholly metaphorical, since a person's metaphysiology is biologically determined to what is, no doubt, a substantial extent, even if that extent has not yet been convincingly determined, despite the best efforts of many leading philanthropologists.

Greg and Edmund had their own version of the Gilbertian law of mental pre-determinism. For them, every child that's born with feeling is either a little Platonist or a little Aristotelian. But one's natal platonic and aristotelian quotients are not wholly immutable. For example, there can be menopausal modifications in one's mental hormonal balance at an appropriate age, when one may suddenly become, for example, more conservative or more libertarian.

There can even be mid-life PQ/AQ crises, when one is tempted by some pretty trophy-metaphysics (say, environmentalism or evangelical religion). One may then risk making oneself into a laughing-stock, or a subject of uncharitable gossip.

Or else one may defiantly claim, and even believe, that one has suddenly been 'born again' and 'found' new mental co-ordinates. And one can, of course, be a metaphysical fashion victim—wearing this year's metaphysical in-label.

In testing a given person's metaphysiology, Greg and Edmund insisted that one should avoid what one might call *rorschachery*—the neo-behaviourist attempt to quantify wonderfully obscure and complex human characteristics through absurdly simple tests—and what might be called *traumocrancy*—the sub-Freudian attempt to assign simplistic and perverse meanings to the blissful obscurity of our nocturnal dream-life.

Instead, they suggested, in judging a person metaphysiologically we should simply have in mind a set of rough-and-ready Diarchic Indicators (DI) to which people are invited to respond indicating their personal preferences and inclinations in relation to the two terms of a given DI.

PQ ↔ AQ.

Ancients ↔ Moderns. Authoritarian ↔ libertarian. Being ↔ becoming. Belief ↔ knowledge. Bolshevik ↔ Menshevik. Burke ↔ Bentham. Calderón ↔ Lope de Vega. Calvinist ↔ Lutheran. Catholic ↔ Protestant. Classic ↔ romantic. Conservative ↔ Socialist (in the U.S., 'liberal'). Country ↔ town. Custom ↔ law. Expressionism ↔ Impressionism. Father ↔ mother. Gothic ↔ Romanesque. Greece ↔ Rome. Hegel ↔ Kant. Hinayana ↔ Mahayana. Hobbes ↔ Locke. Ideal ↔ purpose. Ideal ↔ real. Individuality ↔ sociability. Inner-directed ↔ other-directed. Introvert ↔ extrovert. Jesus Christ ↔ Paul of Tarsus. Kant ↔ Hegel. Leonardo ↔ Michelangelo. Love ↔ law. Marx ↔ Hegel. Mind ↔ matter. Nation ↔ State. Nature ↔ Nurture. Orthodox ↔ Reform. Patriotism ↔ nationalism. Philosophy ↔ Science. Plato ↔ Aristotle. Psychic health/wealth ↔ physical health / wealth. Pure reason ↔ practical reason. Renaissance ↔ Reformation. Revolution ↔ reform. Right ↔ Left. Rousseau ↔ Voltaire. Shakespeare ↔ Racine. Soul ↔ body. Sufi ↔ Sunnite. Thought ↔ action. Unreasonable optimism ↔ reasonable optimism.

Greg and Edmund had collected these, and many more such constitutive binaries, in the course of a beach-combing holiday in south-west Spain, combing beaches for the metaphysical flotsam and jetsam of successive waves of human intrusion over the course of thousands of years—from real but imagined Trojan exiles to pitiful boat-people from Africa.

A person's set of preferences and inclinations in relation to such constitutive binaries determines that person's overall PQ/AQ balance, that is to say, their individual metaphysical nature. The experienced and sensitive metaphysiologist may get to know us better than we know ourselves. Edmund was listening carefully to the young woman and the still younger man as they interacted metaphysically.

Animi exercendo levantur. Edmund had been teaching Rupert what Greg had taught Edmund. The mind and the body must be exercised every day, like the work of thoroughbred racehorses every morning on Newmarket Heath. They must be tended as carefully as favourite plants. For most people, dementia and deficia—decay of the mind and the body—set in from an early age, usually from about the age of twenty-six, in some cases even earlier. The mind must think, read, speak, write difficult things as much as possible, every day. The body must be used to do difficult things as much as possible, every day.

'So, Gabi,' Rupert said, engaging his and her mental laterals, as it were, 'do you have a purpose in life?'

'I can't say I've got any particular general purpose in life, no.'

'So your life is purposeless?'

'Not at all,' Gabi said. 'I suppose I must have purposes for the things I choose to do—such as they are.'

'But how do you choose among possible purposes for the things you choose to do, unless you have some purpose that determines your choice among purposes?'

'Well, I suppose I must have values, as one might call them, values that let me weigh up possible alternatives.'

'But then it's just the same problem—one step back,' Rupert said. 'How do you choose among possible values, unless you have some transcendental value—values for weighing up possible values?'

'So, Rupert—what is your purpose in life, your transcendental value? I suspect you were about to tell me, in any case.'

'To become what I am.'

'That's the kind of saying that has the shape of something true, but I've never known what it means. People keep saying it, but what can it possibly mean—practically speaking—or even poetically speaking?'

'An organic thing is not a thing but a process of becoming,' Rupert said. '*Ipse dixit* Aristotle. A human *being* is a human *becoming*. And it's a becoming in a given direction—and a direction is a purpose.'

'For most things—for every thing, perhaps—becoming is decay and death,' Gabi said. 'Look at Edmund's roses. Soon they will have finished flowering.'

'And in a few months they'll be full of life again.'

'And in a few years they'll be dead, as we will be,' Gabi said. 'So—on your argument—death must be the purpose of their lives—and ours.'

'Living is a way of dying,' Rupert said, 'but living is also a way of not dying—and there are better and worse ways of living—and dying.'

'I wonder if roses think that we are immortal,' Gabi said

Edmund intervened.

'That's why we gardeners garden,' he said. 'It's a conspiracy between Humanity and Nature. We try to actualise the ideal of Beauty to try to defeat Time, for a while.'

'But Nature always has the last word, doesn't it?' Gabi said. 'There's a lot of agony in the garden, isn't there?'

'Nature takes a look at our plans and purposes,' Edmund said, 'and passes judgment on our efforts. Nature to be commanded must be obeyed.'

'Imagine the world without roses!' Gabi said. '*Voilà les roses!*'

'*Conjuguant le verbe aimer*,' Edmund said.

'God was the first gardener,' Rupert said. '*Ipse dixit* Francis Bacon.'

'A garden is a garden of the soul where God walks,' Edmund said. 'A gardener is a metaphysical lover of the sensual.'

'Well, then you are a saint, of sorts, Edmund,' Gabi said. 'Creating transcendental beauty.'

It is true that Edmund's garden was becoming something very beautiful. With the help of Lady Greene he had designed what he calls a Metaphysical Garden—Hampstead Metaphysical Garden. It would not be opened to the public—except, perhaps, to the occasional select band of fellow *illuminati/ cognoscenti /dilettanti*.

There are two sweeping borders with parabolic curving edges. One (which Edmund calls *Lyceum*) is full of foliage of every shape and shade, with great grey rocks distributed here and there, randomly and with great care.

The other border (which Edmund calls *Academy*) is fifteen metres long, full of roses, their petal-shades and scents combining and competing, sight and smell in an intense embrace. And, amid a mass of dark pink *rosa centifolia*, a great block of polished porphyry, four feet high, washed by a silent stream of blood-red water flowing from its summit, as if the crystalline rock itself were melting.

Between the parabolic borders, at the far end of the garden, there is a stately acacia tree, with its deeply gnarled bark and delicate foliage. Under the acacia tree stands Edmund's vaguely oriental summer-house, which he rather ambitiously calls *Temple of Apollo*, with a curving pitched roof and intricate geometrical fretwork in strong colours, its back wall a mass of richly scented white-flowered jasmine. *Sehnsucht nach Süden*, in Hampstead.

On a frieze above the entrance to the summer-house is an inscription in classical Arabic which, being translated, says (approximately)—

GREEN AND FLOWERING HARMONY.

Edmund took his throne-like seat in the summer-house to pass judgment on the two young people lying on the grass in front of him—two young people than whom he felt so much older, two young people of whom he was very fond and about whom, for that reason, he worried—not least about Rupert, soon to be exposed to the cruel misanthropologising of a modern university.

Greg and Edmund had always known that the true focus of their shared life-work is the *anatomy of optimism*, the uncovering of a blessed potentiality in the human soul. And now they had found an instrument of diagnosis which is also an instrument of prognosis. Metaphysiology is astrology of the soul. One is born with Plato or Aristotle in the ascendant.

Gabi's AQ seemed to be at somewhere around 70%. Rupert's PQ was in the general region of 60%.

Edmund and Greg had decided that Greg's PQ was somewhere around 80%.

And, in the mind-clearing atmosphere of Andalusia—definitely not *fría y pura*, more *cálida y dura*—they had made an amazing discovery about Edmund himself.

A meticulous biopsy of Edmund's mind had revealed that both of his PQ/AQ quotients were firmly fixed at 80%—which was not mathematically or metaphysiologically possible. There was no escaping the fact. His constitutive binaries were not binaries. Edmund was more of an Aristotelian than Aristotle, more of a Platonist than Plato.

This seemed to lend weight to the conjecture that there had indeed been something miraculous about Edmund's birth—a double Virgin Birth—no human father, no human mother. Perhaps the all-perfecting power and order and love of the God of the All had intended that all human beings should be like Edmund, but the tiresome vagaries of Animal Evolution by Natural Selection—the true Serpent in the Paradise Garden—had intervened and decreed otherwise.

And then, in this particularly English paradise, this materialising of the garden of his soul, Edmund was looking beyond the flower-borders, beyond his young friends, beyond beauty and beyond time.

He was looking at a small tree, standing alone, its silver-green leaves shimmering in a pool of sunlight.

The wooden staff left in the sand by the Old Man of the Sea, whom Edmund had called Wednesday, had chosen to be what we, who call ourselves human, have chosen to call an olive tree.

And an olive tree is a strange thing—defying time, defying human transience, possessed by a self-absorbed pride in its beauty and its usefulness, a pride that owes nothing to the human being who beholds it, or the human beings who use it.

Ideal potentiality of a sacred grove, in Hampstead.

*   *   *

Gnostalgia for the Future

They had been to the July Races at Newmarket. Now they had retreated to the warm stillness of a summer evening at Borthwill Park. It was a sequence of experiences which had no doubt been re-enacted by each of the eight or nine generations of those whose home Borthwill had been, and for whom Newmarket, through the centuries, had been the heartland of a parallel world, accessible and ambiguously attractive, elegant and louche at the same time.

'I love horse-racing,' Greg said. 'not just for what someone called its crackling, sensuous excitement. I see it as an image of the union of the natural and the human—a sort of loving union between the human being and a noble and handsome animal—producing something orderly and dynamic and beautiful.'

'And a perfect example of the union of necessity and chance,' Cardinal Trevisan said. 'Physical causes producing effects which must be wholly predictable in principle but are wholly unpredictable in practice.'

'The Quantum Mechanics of Horseracing,' Greg said.

'My putting money into the pockets of undeserving bookmakers is highly predictable,' Alison said.

'You got a winner,' Greg said, 'which is more than I did—I who am a loyal reader of the Racing Post.'

'Chance, pure chance. I wouldn't have known I'd won, if you hadn't remembered the name of my horse.'

'Hilda says: where do you want to eat?—inside or out?'

David Greene had come out of the house still wearing his race-going brown tweed suit and brown felt hat, the Premier Enclosure tag still hanging from the lapel of his jacket. He had changed from aged brown brogues into fluffy pink bedroom slippers.

'Depends what we're eating,' Alison said. 'I'll go and consult with Hilda.'

'Oh, there's Abe,' she said over her shoulder, as she went into the house. 'Found his way back.'

They had thought that Abe Green had used the excuse of a solitary evening walk to escape from what they themselves saw as their rather relentless, but non-threateningly free-ranging, conversational company.

'I need to collect my thoughts for a while,' he had said, setting off in no particular direction, but a direction that led to an area of not very well managed marshland.

'He looks a bit more cheerful,' Greg said. 'Coming back quicker than he left. Always a good sign.'

'Marsh Harrier,' Abe said. 'Pretty sure that's what it was. Bit smaller than our Northern Harrier. A close relative, obviously.'

'You were lucky,' his cousin in the pink bedroom slippers said. 'Not many people have seen *Circus aeruginosus*, even in East Anglia.'

'Isn't that just something! I can't wait to brag to my Audubon friends.'

'Who can frame the sources of civilisation's contents and discontents?' Greg thought, but did not say.

'Were you talking about me in my absence?' Abe asked.

'We were thinking about you,' Greg said, 'but not exclusively.'

'I was thinking about us all,' Abe said, 'and about all the other little human microcosms—millions of them gathered around in millions of places—places not all as favoured as this—little groups of people, talking to each other—person to person—free—natural—sharing—human beings being human.'

Abe's solitary foray into the Suffolk marshland had clearly been more fruitful philosophically than the post-racing relaxation of the others.

'Nostalgia for the life of the cave,' the Cardinal said. 'The human family, the only natural human society.'

'Nostalgia for the camp-fire,' Abe said. 'And the circle of wagons.'

'The yesterdays of our lost innocence,' Greg said.

'Families—proper, functioning families,' Abe said, 'seem to be becoming rarities, the exception rather than the rule, at least in so-called advanced societies. I speak as one who had a family, and now does not have a family.'

'As someone whose way of life has precluded the making of a family of my own,' the Cardinal said, 'I may not seem to be best placed to extol the virtues of family-life. And yet the idea still seems to me to be a beautiful idea—a form of human society held together by a natural and spontaneous form of love.'

'Speaking as one who bitterly regrets having failed to create a *genetic* family of my own,' Greg said, 'I preach—and try to practise—a new kind of social institution—the *generic* family, a philial family ("philial" with a "ph", not an "f")—held together by shared concerns and interests, held together by the many possible kinds of affection.'

'Isn't there a danger,' the Cardinal said, 'that your *generic* family would really be a sharing of selfishness? A *genetic* family is essentially a generous family, a sharing of generosity, giving life to children in an atmosphere of security and affection.'

'I have known a lot of families,' David Greene said, 'and I can tell you, Alvise, security and affection are not the words I would choose to describe most of them. Precarious peace and permanent rebellion, more like.'

'The thing I like about old-fashioned families,' Greg said, 'is that they are the last refuge of individualism. They seem to be nothing but socialising machines, but, in fact, they are places where children struggle to find their individuality.'

'But then,' Abe said, 'almost at once, they have the individuality knocked out of them—not least by other children.'

'What exactly do you mean by individuality, Gregory?' David Greene asked. 'Nowadays I find it hard to remember who is who, let alone names and faces—and that's not just because old men forget. People are less memorable nowadays.'

'An individual is a person who sees the universe from a unique point of view,' Greg said, 'and whose whole life is determined by that point of view.'

'A formidable woman,' the Cardinal said, 'suggested that the soul should learn to imagine that there is nothing in the universe but it and God.'

'*El Castillo Interior*,' Greg said.

'Yes, Gregory! Precisely,' the Cardinal said. 'I think your idea of the true individual is rather like that—a solid fortress in which, and from which, we become more fully ourselves.'

'Are you saying that one can learn to be an individual?' Abe Green asked, '—that you can learn it as a sort of life-skill?'

'Why not?' David Greene said. 'If people are made to learn to be sociable, why shouldn't they be made to learn to be individual?'

'But isn't such a thing deeply unfashionable in Christianity nowadays?' Abe Green said. 'The whole thing seems to be just a vast machine for imposing and enforcing social conformism. Certainly is in the United States. Us and our God. Not God and me.'

'McCalvinism,' Greg said. 'Silly sheep.'

Alison Brand had returned to her place on the terrace silently, not wanting to interrupt the conversation. She listened as the conversation approached asymptotically one of the Firm's leading projects. She assumed that this had been Greg Seare's intention, and she was grateful to him for it. To associate Abe Green intellectually and practically with the work of the Firm was now very nearly a mission accomplished.

Alison was also pleased that the Cardinal was there, contributing enthusiastically to their collective thinking process. The Firm was eager that he should share with them the fruits of his own personal project, his search for what he had called 'the religion beyond religions'.

'We're going to compromise,' she said. 'We'll have dinner in the Orangery, so-called—halfway between inside and outside.'

The Orangery did not contain any orange trees. It was a glass structure leaning against one side of the house, a product of the Victorian-British-imperial vogue for compelling tropical flora to survive in the impossible British climate. There were several tall, vaguely palm-like trees and a motley collection of tubs and pots containing evidently exotic, but not easily identifiable, plants. This evening it still held the warmth of the day's sunshine.

'Between the castle of the individual and the kingdom of God there is an awful lot in-between,' Abe said, as they walked to the Orangery. 'An awful lot seems to have got itself into the space between the One and the All, between me and God.'

'The problem is that the One of the human individual is very many,' Greg said, as they took their places at a solid oak table whose aged wood had been bleached by the intensified rays of the sun. 'And the All of God is many gods.'

'And for each wretched religion,' David Greene said, 'their wretched God is supposed to be the One and Only.'

'I prefer to see religion as an uneasy truce between hope and experience,' Greg said. 'We know more than we want to know about the past life of religion. But we can't get rid of the idea that there must be something more than the world of appearances, something more than the universe as the eye of the human mind happens to see it.'

'And the eye of the human mind sees something even more mysterious than the universe, Greg,' Alison said. 'It sees what human beings have made of their little bit of the universe, the human universe. The eye of the human mind sees itself . . .'

'. . . and doesn't very much like what it sees,' Greg said. 'It judges itself.'

'It wouldn't be difficult to construct a completely rational religion, would it?' Abe said. 'You could even invent a religion that took account of science, couldn't you?—science integrated with religion.'

'But what would be the point, Abe?' Greg said. 'Don't religions take pride in being irrational—or, at least, preaching a different sort of rationality?'

'And wasn't it the whole point of science to be something other than religion?' Alison said.

'The Americans have got it right,' David Greene said. 'Make religion into a commodity, with lots of different brands—then get people to choose a brand and stick to their favourite brand—like a washing-powder or a football team.'

'Free-market religion,' Greg said. 'Survival of the market-leader.'

'Junk religions make a lot of money,' David Greene said. 'Fast religion, fast buck. People will believe anything. The more preposterous the dogmas, the more prosperous the religion.'

'Like scent,' Hilda Greene said.

She came to the table carrying a large yellow salad-bowl. She was followed in processional formation by Miss Spurgeon, the long-serving and long-suffering Borthwill housekeeper, carrying plates of cold meats on a vast tray. Miss Spurgeon, who had long since become detached form her Christian name, had a strangely theatrical walk—a relic of the time when she did, indeed, tread the boards—more gracefully, presumably—in the corps de ballet of the Royal Ballet. Lady Greene had rescued her, in obscure circumstances that neither would be able to—or would want to—recall with precision.

'Put some smelly water in a bottle,' Miss Spurgeon said, 'give it some silly name, and idiotic people will pay anything for it.'

'At least holy water doesn't smell, Spurgeon,' Hilda said.

'What about the odour of sanctity?' David Greene said. 'Smell it a mile off.'

Alison glanced at Cardinal Trevisan, to gauge his reaction—not that a defender of a particular faith is obliged to defend all faiths—especially if his particular faith happens to be the One True Faith, as it were, definitive and infallible.

'I can't see why people keep fulminating against religion as such,' Greg said. 'Every conceivable argument has been made countless times—against religions in general, and particular religions in particular . . .'

'. . . with much greater power and elegance than the modern iconoclasts can manage,' the Cardinal said.

'It's strange, isn't it?' Abe said, 'that people spend so much time worrying about law and war and government and so on, when the really worrying thing is what people think, and what makes people think what they think.'

'I know some rather sinister people who think that it is going to be for *them* to decide what people will think,' Greg said. 'They think they will decide what people will be like. They will manufacture people, and the people they manufacture will think what they are programmed to think.'

'But isn't that what *religions* have always done, Greg?' Hilda said. 'Or tried to do. Make people conform to a certain type.'

'Yes, Lady Greene. But *these* people are proposing to do more or less what Abe was talking about before—integrating religion with science. There will be nothing beyond their control—not even people's ideas about the One and the All.'

'Maybe they'll just chuck the whole ghastly religion thing overboard,' David Greene said. 'Imagine that!—a world without religion—bliss at last—heaven on earth!'

'These people you are referring to, Greg,' the Cardinal said, 'Do you know what exactly they are planning to do about religion—and philosophy as well, for that matter?'

'They are definitely not philosopher-kings,' Greg said. 'They intend to be kings of philosophy—and, presumably, kings of religion also.'

'Oh no!' David Greene said. 'You mean they might decide that religion is a good thing after all?'

'Yes, they might, especially if they thought that some form of religion would be sociobiologically advantageous, as they would say—a human vector with positive potentiality, as it were.'

'Potentially positive human vector, my foot! God help us!'

'Mental totalitarianism isn't exactly a new thing,' Hilda said.

'It isn't,' Alison said. 'But I think Greg is talking about something which *is* new—a non-governmental form of absolute power—a power even over governments themselves—let alone over the toiling masses.'

'So?' Hilda said. 'The Popes used to give orders to kings, if I'm not mistaken.'

'And Puritans in the American colonies,' Abe said. 'They ruled people's minds—or tried to, for a while.'

'No—that's different,' Alison said. 'The people Greg is talking about see religion and philosophy as a side-show, peculiar survivals from a darker age—to be dealt with pragmatically, like everything else that they find lying around the place.'

'So they've got an ideology?' Abe said. 'An ideology that explains everything, has an answer for everything, like Marxism-Leninism?'

'No,' Greg said. 'They don't have a pre-determined ideology. They're inventing ideology as they go along—*passim* and *à la carte*—custom tailored—to suit some practical purpose. They see themselves as beyond politics. They're not left-wing or right-wing. They see themselves as making and managing a post-political world.'

'And the process has already begun,' Alison said 'The emptying of people's minds. The first step is to get rid of the idea of *memory*, including historical memory—who needs to remember anything when everything is remembered electronically?'

'And the next step after that is the elimination of *knowledge*,' Greg said, 'knowledge as collectively accumulated thought. And then, after that, you get rid of *thinking* itself, as a private and public process of understanding and judging. Who needs to think when machines can do it better?'

'And so, on the way,' Alison said, 'you can get rid of *education*, the handing-on of knowledge, and of the capacity for thinking and new thinking.'

'And where shall we build the Ark,' the Cardinal said, 'to hold the survivors from this destruction of what we have called civilisation?'

'Will there *be* any survivors?' Hilda said.

Momentary silence. The only sound the sound of collective chewing. What could one do but to try to digest inwardly and collectively the prospect of yet another End of History? Previous inhabitants of that particular and privileged place in Suffolk had had to digest collectively, since Neolithic times, the prospect of one terminal existential threat after another—as the ugly faces of yet another set of barbarians had appeared over the horizon.

'What I'll miss is right and wrong,' Miss Spurgeon said at last. 'Particularly right.'

'Without wrong there can be no right, Spurgeon,' Hilda said. 'It takes a lot of wrong to make a little right.'

Momentary silence. Now they were floundering in their collective thinking. Not merely—who will survive? but also—what will survive?

'Compasses,' David Greene said. 'People must have got around before there were compasses.'

'The sun and the stars,' Miss Spurgeon said. 'They had the sun and the stars.'

'Without magnetism there'd be no compasses,' Hilda said.

'There's got to be purpose behind purposes,' Alison said.

'And desire behind desires,' Greg said. 'And truth behind truths.'

'To hope for something,' Abe said, 'you have to believe in hope.'

'To be lovable you must love,' Miss Spurgeon said, on a slightly diverging philosophical track, probably led off-course by the compass of her own unfathomable psychology.

Her grey eyes were staring bleakly, through grey-metal-rimmed spectacles, into a middle distance that only she could see.

The Cardinal had not joined in the escalation of desolate whistling in the darkness. But his silence seemed to the others to be both eloquent and pregnant. They waited for him to bring forth encouraging words. After all, *c'est son métier*, they reminded themselves.

'Miss Spurgeon is right,' the Cardinal said. 'Love is not a matter of rational calculation. But nor is it isolated from the other capacities of the mind.'

He spoke as if he were speaking to himself. The others, individually and collectively, decided to remain silent, overhearing his conversation with himself.

'If the whole universe suddenly became conscious, what would it say? Would it speak about God?

'It would be conscious of itself not merely as a being but also as a process of becoming. And it would try to imagine the principles governing that process of becoming. Why am I, the universe, as I am, and not something else? The religion of a conscious universe would be a metaphysics—a philosophy of physics.

'If a human animal suddenly became fully conscious, but without any knowledge of the religions that already exist, what would it think? Would it think religiously?

'It would be conscious of itself as a process of becoming, a living thing. And it would ask: why am I as I am, and not something else? It might try to imagine the principles governing its process of becoming.

'As a small part of the universe of all-that-is, the human animal recognises that it is subject to the same principles of becoming as every other part of the universe.

'But the consciousness of the human animal has a strange characteristic. The human animal supposes that it is in a position to determine, or at least to modify, its own process of becoming. Its religion must also be an ethics—a philosophy of what to do next. What shall I choose to become?

'Physics and metaphysics and ethics are responses of the reasoning capacity of the human mind challenged by two interesting questions—what am I?—what shall I choose to become? Together they can form a single science of human existence.

'We have the capacity to desire to become what the order of the universe confers upon us as a possibility. I now see that that is the meaning of what we have called the Love of God.

'Is and ought are inseparable.

'Faith and reason are inseparable.

'The religion beyond religions is the religion before religions.'

(Reproduced from the transcript of the Firm's recording of the conversation.)

More silence, pregnant but not eloquent. The others now looked to Gregory Seare for an appropriate reaction to the Cardinal's utterances. After all, that sort of thing was also his *métier*.

'*Synousia*,' Greg said, 'and *synoikia* and *sympatheia* and *symmetria* and *symphonia*.'

'And *harmonia*,' the Cardinal said.

'And *eunomia*,' Greg said.

The Cardinal then resumed his self-communicating manner.

'The order that the human mind finds in the universe is reflected in the self-ordering of the human mind through reasoning thought. The power that the human mind finds in the self-creating power of the universe is reflected in the power of human self-creating through purposive action. The binding force of the universe is reflected in what the human mind recognises as its natural capacity for loving affection.'

Greg was surprised and moved by the Cardinal's words, signposts on a road parallel to a metaphysical road that he and Edmund had only recently discovered.

'Cardinal Alvise, you may remember that you have met a young friend of ours,' Greg said, 'an unusual person who has tried to take power over his own process of becoming.'

'The charming Edmund,' the Cardinal said. 'Of course. I remember him with affection.'

'I want you to know that he and I feel that we are on the way to a destination not unlike that which you have just described. We think we may be the first of the *neo-gnostics*, potential thorns in the side of the out-dated *agnostics*.'

'I am not surprised to hear that,' the Cardinal said. 'In extreme old age I seem to have become as young in my mind as I am old in my body. The withering of the body may conceal a new flourishing of the mind. How is such a thing possible? One's true age is the age of one's soul—and the soul is ageless.'

'Oh no,' Miss Spurgeon said. 'No. No.'

Miss Spurgeon had taken off her grey-metal-rimmed spectacles. She was wiping their lenses with a corner of her table-napkin, as if she were wiping away hidden tears.

*   *   *

18

Ideal Affinities

Somewhere else—no particular place—at some other time—no particular time—Edmund Jenning also found himself in the presence of his more or less ageless soul.

He had, of course, always known that the person known as Edmund Jenning was not the same thing as that person's much desired body and much admired personality. He knew now that the life-story of Edmund Jenning, of which he was a co-author, the life story of the outward man, was not the same thing as the life of his soul, the life of the inward man.

Like everything else in the universe, he was less than he seemed to be, and more than he seemed to be—something of which one could only have an *idea*, but also something which no *idea* could encompass.

At this moment, as if he were touching something tender and delicate, he allowed himself to remember, as diffusely as possible, how he had discovered the infinite smallness of the stuff from which human beings are made, and the infinite greatness of the stuff from which the infinite smallness of human beings is made.

And, at the same moment, he reassured himself with some metaphysical relativism. The small seems small only because the great seems great, and the great seems great only because the small seems small, the idea of each forming the idea of the other. He, able to imagine both the great and the small, must choose to imagine himself—the inward and the outward man—as something somewhere between the two.

And then he saw, for the first time clearly, that, even if the category of physical *quantity* may be relative, the category of metaphysical *quality* is not.

Edmund had always felt the *beauty* of beautiful things with a physical intensity that was almost painful. He knew now that the beauty of beautiful things was something that all beautiful things share. He knew now that beauty was an idea of something present in beautiful things, something that his mind was able to *recognise* as such. His mind made the beautiful beautiful, but the beautiful did not need his mind to make beauty beautiful.

Edmund had always felt the *goodness* of good people, with an intensity that was a sort of delight. He knew now that the goodness of good people was something that all good people share. He knew now that goodness was an idea of something present in good people, something that his mind was able to *recognise* as such. His mind made goodness good, but goodness did not need his mind to make goodness good.

Edmund had always felt the *truth* of speaking truly, with an intensity that was a sort of craving. He knew now that the truth of true speaking was something that all true speaking shares. He knew now that the truth of speaking truly was an idea of something present in the effort to speak truly, something that his mind was able to *recognise* as such. His mind made the truth of speaking truly, but truth did not need his mind to make truth true.

And there was a further step that he was able to take—now, at last. He could see now that, in recognising the beautiful, the good and the true, his mind was recognising something that they *share*. Given his over-sensitive and over-affectionate personality, it was not difficult for Edmund to form in his mind the idea of what is shared by the beautiful, the good, and the true.

Surely, he now tells himself, and will soon tell everyone else who needs to know, they are all forms of *love*, the binding force of the metaphysical universe.

They are desirable in themselves, not because of the purposes that they serve, or the effects that they cause. They teach us to desire what is desirable *in itself*, not merely what is desirable *for us*. They are not merely *ideas*. They are *ideals*. They cause us to choose to be not merely what we *will* be, but what we *should* be—not merely what we *are*, but what we should *become*.

But there was one more thing that Edmund's more or less ageless soul had to tell him. And this happened as an event at a given time and a given place, a time and a place that he was not, however, later able to identify with complete precision, when he recounted the experience to others, some of whom were accordingly sceptical.

A sudden flood of warmth and light in his immaterial soul came close to causing a syncope in his very material body. (Perhaps body and soul are not, after all, different substances!)

He now knew, as if he had always known without knowing it, that the perennial and universal and relentless human search for *happiness* is the search for a state of the totality of our inward and outward being. The search for happiness, he now tells himself, and will soon tell everyone else who needs to know, is a journey to a *metaphysical* destination, far beyond all ideas and all feelings.

The ideal of human happiness is the permanent possibility of inward perfection.

And, in Edmund's now pleasantly agitated mind, one new idea led to another.

The inward eye that recognises the attraction of the ideal is a single eye shared by all human minds. The soul of each human being recognises itself in the souls of all other human beings.

To be a human being is to see the universe from a particular point of view, but a point of view that is capable of being a universal point of view.

The time has come for the single eye of the human species to see the universal idea of human happiness.

He tells himself these things, and he tells himself that these are things that he and Greg, ambassadors from the philosophical nation, must include in the unlikely report that they will make to the Countess and Mr Gray.

*   *   *

19

World Mind Revolution

David and Hilda Greene felt as if they were under siege in their own house in London. The house seemed to be full of people they knew, half-knew, or did not know at all. Alison Brand had simply taken command. She had even engaged 'caterers' to do whatever 'caterers' are supposed to do.

'And who's paying for it all, might I ask?' Hilda asked. 'Caterers, or whatever they are, don't come cheap—from what I remember.'

'Search me,' her husband said.

In fact, the whole thing was being paid for by the Firm. It had been good of the Greenes to allow Alison to use their house in this way. But their London home had the great advantage of offering a dining-room with a dining-table large enough to seat up to sixteen people comfortably. And there was a large sunny drawing-room, opening onto a balcony stretching across the whole width of the house and overlooking a charming formal garden, with a view of leafy Holland Park beyond.

'LOSC and MOTH,' Alison said firmly, as if she were calling a meeting to order. 'We're here for what we all hope will come to be seen as an historic occasion. A sort of *Jeu de paume*, if you will.'

'Or a nailing of theses to the door,' Rupert Brand suggested.

'Not,' said Gabi Dorn.

'Or a Boston lunch-party,' Jim Meehan said.

'Not,' Jane Meehan said.

'We are here to inaugurate something very rare in the history of the world,' Alison continued. 'A purposive mental revolution, I suppose you could say.'

'You-all don't look like revolutionaries,' Rupert Brand said. 'You must be the most middle-class-looking revolutionaries since the French Revulsion.'

In preparing the seating-plan for lunch, Alison had taken particular pleasure in seating Durchlauchts and non-Durchlauchts alternately, as thoughtful hosts try to alternate men and women at the dinner table, or try to protect interesting people from bores. The assembled company included eight Durchlauchts and six non-Durchlauchts. Only the former were in a position to appreciate this aspect of Alison's skill as a hostess.

Alison Brand

Greg Seare (D)		Abe Green (D)
May Gaunt		The Cardinal
Jim Meehan (D)		Mr Gray (D)
Mike Abi		Jane Meehan
Jack Jackson (D)		Edmund Jenning (D)
Gabi Dorn		Rupert Brand

Countess Frieda

David and Hilda Greene were certainly not revolutionaries. They were the kind of people who have learned to adjust to the notorious imperfections of the human world, and can see absolutely no reason to believe that things will ever be very much different, or very much better, than they have always been. *Tout passe*, or not, as the case may be.

'History teaches only one lesson,' they were both inclined to say. 'Those who think that they can change things for the better always end up making things worse.'

And so they had taken refuge in Hilda's dressing room upstairs, fortified by their own private supply of the delicate but expensive food that Alison's caterers had managed to produce from the Greenes' kitchen, which was well-equipped, but was not very often called upon to produce large quantities of very *haute cuisine*, however delicate.

'You don't all know each other,' Alison said. 'You're here because either Greg Seare or I, or both of us, know you and appreciate you—and we know that you'll all be interested, at the least, in what we're trying to do. As it turns out, you're a rather representative group—in point of age and experience—public life, the life of the spirit and the arts, the business world, the media, the university.

'I've asked Abe Green kindly to say a few words about LOSC, by way of introduction. And then Greg will say something about MOTH—and then we hope to have a more general discussion in the drawing room. So, Abe, if you would like to start us off.'

'Well, I'm surely glad to be associated with all this—even if my own personal background has probably not conditioned me to be a very convincing revolutionary. You all know more or less what the League of Sensible Countries is all about.'

'Enough is enough already,' Rupert said.

'Yes, that's the idea, in slogan form,' Abe continued. 'We're trying to get together socially responsible people who have simply lost patience with the way the world is. We're trying to encourage responsible people to take social responsibility for redeeming the failure of those who are supposed to be in charge, but who seem to have lost their way in the human jungle, lost control of the whole mess of the human world.

'The responsible people we have in mind are people who exercise significant social responsibility but are not directly involved in politics or government. They are people who see, from their own experience, that we human beings are at the end of the road. We are at a dead-end. The party's over. Humanist civilisation is moribund. The possibilities of existing social structures—national and international—are exhausted.

'The existing ruling classes are incapable of rescuing the human species from its crazy self-wounding and self-destroying. People who hold public power cannot solve the problem. They are the problem. They cannot cure humanity of its death wish. They carry the mental virus within them in its most virulent form.

'The representatives of the Sensible Countries are people who see the situation and refuse to look away, refuse to surrender to despair.

'We're at the very beginning of thinking how the Sensible Countries will work together in LOSC. One thing we're pretty sure about is that we'll have no written constitution, no committee structures, no office-holders. We'll gradually evolve some new kind of unwritten constitution for ourselves—and for the world. We'll be a kind of constitutional Convention, in permanent session.

'So far I've spoken to people from New Zealand, Norway and Switzerland—and, of course, from Canada—not that they're the only sensible countries in the world. But we've got to start somewhere. There are no precedents for what we're going to do, no experience to draw on, no road map.

'We want and need to hear all your thoughts and suggestions—today and hereafter. We're going to need a lot of help, a lot of hope and, probably, a lot of prayer.'

'Thanks, Abe,' Alison said. 'We're delighted that you've been willing to take a leading role in this exciting venture—this highly peculiar and highly speculative venture.

'LOSC is an experimental vessel carrying pilgrims and pioneers from a very tired Old World to a New World that is still only a world of the imagination—a New and highly hypothetical Atlantis.

'And now, Greg, would you like to say something about MOTH?'

'Abe has spoken about responsible people taking social responsibility for the future organisation of the human world,' Greg began, 'and that is the purpose of the League of Sensible Countries. But there's a wider and a deeper problem—the other great task and challenge that we face.

'What kind of human future do we want? That is the task and the challenge for the Movement of Thinking Humans.

'The MOTH is definitely not a mass movement. The minds of the masses are not their own. They are mind-slaves held in the iron cages made by mind-masters who corrupt and dehumanise them with a diet of junk education, junk politics, junk religion, junk information, junk entertainment, junk ideas.

'MOTH is a movement of the middle class. The middle class is, and always has been, the creative class, the energetic class, the class with the biggest practical stake in the successful self-creating of society, the revolutionary class, the class that makes governments, and should be able to break them, if the governments are no good.

'As an exclusionary tactic and as a sort of pledge, we will require the middle classes of the world to pay a substantial sum of money per person per annum to register their names with us. In return they will find that they have acquired nothing much more than the right to take part in the making of a reformed and reinvigorated human consciousness.

'And that new right will carry with it a strange obligation. The Thinking Humans will be obliged to think, relentlessly and creatively and purposively, to think dialectically, about all those things that human beings at their best have always thought about, all the things that human beings have lost the courage to think about.

'So—the members of the Movement of Thinking Humans will pay good money to enter into a vocation, as philanthropologists, that is, as philanthropic philosophers acting as self-appointed mind-leaders with a life-time commitment to thinking about the making, the re-making, and the self-perfecting of humanity.'

Differing degrees of scepticism—from determined disbelief to amused condescension—could be read in the faces and the body-speech of some members of Greg's audience. Others—the Already More or Less Enlightened Ones, as it were—showed distinct signs of enthusiasm, in differing degrees.

Under rather intense, and sometimes acerbic, questioning, Greg defended a manifesto which seemed to him to be a good deal less strident, and obviously much more realistic and practical, than the ill-fated Communist Manifesto.

MAY GAUNT: 'Dr Seare, how can you imagine for a single instant that the middle class, of all people, are capable of thinking any thought that is not about the protecting and promoting of their own self-interest?'

Greg hesitated. May Gaunt was, for him, the embodiment of the greatest intellectual obstacle to the self-transcending of humanity—namely, the anti-philosophy of fundamentalist pragmatism—and a living symbol of the sickness of the human spirit.

'Self-interest is not a simple phenomenon,' he said. 'There are different horizons of self-interest, horizons of time and scope. The middle class have a material interest in the successful functioning of society—and that means they have a direct material interest in the short-term and the long-term aspects of its functioning, and everything in-between. It means that they have a direct material interest in aspects of society that affect them directly and immediately.

'But they also have an interest in aspects of society that affect them more distantly and indirectly, when those aspects are liable to affect the general efficiency and prosperity of society. And that includes even phenomena beyond the frontiers of their own country. It even means that they must have a personal interest in the most general questions of human life. Man is born and dies and is unhappy. Why? Man is born and dies and wants to be happy. How? The perennial challenges for religion and philosophy.'

MAY GAUNT: 'Where have you been for the last two hundred and fifty years, Dr Seare—for heaven's sake? Some of us have made some progress. Anthropology tells us what we are. Sociology tells us how to live together. Psychology tells us what we want. The old religions that still haunt the world are crazy relics of dead civilisations. We go on paying the price for their terrible fantasies—and not only in the misery of the so-called

Holy Land. [*Dry scornful laugh.*] You may like to know that some of us have liberated ourselves from mad religions and nonsensical philosophies. Philosophy is a useful part of the story that practical people have to tell. That's all there is to it.

'Don't you think you should stick to Shakespeare, Dr Seare? People are interested in him.'

Greg did not need to hesitate.

'Anthropology, sociology and psychology have taught us nothing about anything human,' he said, 'except about the human mind's capacity for self-impoverishment. They are moral-responsibility-by-pass strategies. If termites decided to study themselves, they we would not choose to study themselves as if they were worms. The human sciences are nihilism thinly disguised. Religions have given religion a bad name. Philosophers have given philosophy a bad name. But—whatever people of your kind may think—good religion and good philosophy are still possible. And never more urgently needed. And Shakespeare, of all people, were he living now, would see that, I can assure you.'

JIM MEEHAN: 'You disapprove of psychology, Greg. But isn't psychology precisely a study of how we might cure ourselves of our unhappiness, a possible therapeutic protocol, if not an exact science of happiness? Wouldn't termites tend to think of themselves as primarily, perhaps even exclusively, social animals? Shouldn't you concentrate your efforts on reforming or re-forming social consciousness? We are social animals, surely, not merely socialised animals.'

Greg hesitated. Jim Meehan, homme moyen sensuel *quite evidently, but an important person, a private mind that had direct and immediate access into the public mind of America—a master of tribal story-telling. Greg knew that Jim's mind was the better sort of American Mind, but he also knew, from experience, that you have to go carefully in trying to work with even the better sort of American Mind.*

'I'm sorry, but there can be no such thing as psychology, still less any such thing as social psychology, if they purport to be *sciences* of the mind. There can only be more or less valuable philosophies of mind. Freud himself knew that he was not a scientist. He was a philosopher of mind and/or a human biologist and /or a faith-healer—stirring up a witches' brew containing large helpings of Gloom of Schopenhauer and Scream of Nietzsche, and much other toil and trouble besides.

'Our first and greatest task is to rescue the individuality of the human individual by inventing a new kind of human being. The unlimited potentiality of human society reflects the unlimited potentiality of the human individual. The sickness of human society is a product of the sickness of human minds. The good health of human society is a product of the good health of human minds. The private mind and the public mind produce each other, in sickness and in health. A new kind of human being and a new kind of society will create each other.

'Civilisation is the collective sublimation of the impulse of life—the drive to reproduce, to create and to change. Civilisation uses the animal power of the impulse of life to cure the human animal of the worse kinds of animal behaviour. It can also use the animal power of the human animal to destroy and to corrupt.'

JACK JACKSON: 'If I may, I want to go a little bit further with Jim Meehan's comment. Whether we like it or not, individual consciousness has now become residual in relation to social consciousness. We are ruled by great social systems whose force-fields now cover the whole of planet Earth. Those of us who work in government should feel a rush of imperialising power in such a situation, but somehow, for some reason, we don't. We surely don't. I very much agree with what Abe Green said earlier. Public officials see themselves as the victims of events, not as masters of any universe. We feel as if we spend our energy and waste our souls trying to sweep back a sea that seems always to be at flood tide—leading to good fortune randomly, if ever.'

Greg hesitated. Jackson was another important person—an exceptionally effective player in the Great Game of government. Greg tended to see him as a sort of laboratory animal, testing two alternative hypotheses. Are those involved in the business of government at the highest level still capable of re-imagining their situation and reforming their practice? Or are they, through no personal fault of their own, but as the price of their professional competence, prisoners of the particular form of consciousness that makes a particular form of government possible?

'As I see it, Jack, the situation is even worse than you suggest. It's not merely individual consciousness that's now residual. It's social consciousness too. We're moving into a state of human society in which our lives will be ruled by autonomic social systems—systems that no human beings control, but which control all human beings. Capitalism, democracy, science and technology, religion, the Internet—they're all systems in the strict sense. They process human inputs mechanically—inhumanly—to produce outputs that determine human behaviour. They are nightmare versions of Rousseau's General Will and Adam Smith's Invisible Hand—nightmare versions of the Will of God and the Laws of Nature. We may have one last opportunity—if it's not already too late—to master our new masters.'

RUPERT BRAND: 'But, Greg, I also have a problem—less cosmic, but no less urgent. What should I study? Should I study at all? I already have one foot, and part of my mind, inside the hallowed walls of a certain place of higher learning. Education seems to be merely a way of learning more sophisticated ways to be unhappy. And, in any case, I'm already working hard on my own *manière de voir* and my own *manière de vivre*—the unfolding *curriculum vitae meae*—more or less self-determined and self-taught, with a little help from my friends. I'm not sure if I'm ready to abandon my mind and become other-determined, especially if the other is not very much to my liking.'

Greg hesitated. He saw Rupert as a sort of spiritual grandson. He, who did not have children of his own, had learned, in his association with Edmund, the weight of responsibility that rests on anyone who is in a position to influence the development of the mind and the personality of a young person. But how can one—how far should one—risk sowing the seeds of either illusion or disillusion in young minds? That is the conscientious dilemma for anyone involved in such a situation.

'You are about to enter one of the Universities of Misanthropology—Umis. Latin motto: *nil desperandum nisi spes*—which, being translated, means: 'nothing is hopeless except hope itself'. You'll find that the facilities are excellent, admirably suited for their purpose.

'There's the Bertrand Russell Auditorium—where the class of all classes meets. No one knows if it can be a member of itself, so there's never anyone there. Then there's the John Rawls Liberal Swimming Pool—perfectly circular, perfectly fair; no start, no finish; no winners, no losers. And Jacques Derrida House—always under construction, no foundations, no roof. And, not least, the Ludwig Wittgenstein Centre for the Study of Silence. The students like to go there because students nowadays are good at staring vacantly into electronic space. And the Great Books Library has ten million books, with the better books shelved randomly, so that no one ever reads them.'

'But Greg, you haven't answered my question,' Rupert said.

'But I have,' Greg said. 'Can you imagine a more challenging and stimulating environment for one who already has an idea of the *iter vitae suae*? Remember—philosophy is dialectical, mind struggling with itself. Go and do some struggling in an overgrown botanical garden of the mind, one of the holy places of the New Ignorance. It is on the rubble of a fallen civilisation that we can climb higher, as one might say.'

MIKE ABI: 'It seems to me that there runs through everything you say a profound unreality—as if the main lesson of human history were not the absolute inevitability of evil. In the end, evil always wins. Pseudo-religious thinking is just as hopeless as pseudo-scientific thinking when it comes to challenging the absolute power of evil. In democracy and capitalism we have surely found a highly efficient way to turn private vice into public benefit, to integrate self interest and public interest.'

Greg hesitated. He knew Mike Abi only by reputation, as a Prince of Darkness, the embodiment of the brutal efficiency of naked capitalism, that dismal but enthralling alchemy of money breeding money. The prophets of naked capitalism had every reason to be proud of its world-transforming achievements. Their indomitable self-assurance was the age-old state of mind of conquerors and tyrants, agents of raw power whose success justifies itself, seeing no need to play games of aesthetic or political or moral disputation.

'Post-religious and post-political capitalism is the work of the devil. Capitalism is a system of state-sponsored usury on top of a system of state-sponsored slavery. Capitalism without the voice of conscience, and capitalism without the dialectic of solidarity, is an instrument for de-humanising humanity. Democracy is capitalism's loyal assistant. Democracy is the subjection of the masses through a fiction of freedom. The governed are told that they are the government, so that the government is left free to govern as it sees fit.

'Alongside the history of the grandiose achievements of communalised greed there is the history of the splendid achievements of communalised love—the love that tames the chaos. Beyond the pursuit of material wealth there is the search for a form of wealth that is psychic or spiritual, a form of healthiness that people sometimes call happiness. The true wealth of nations is the health of nations, measured by their gross national product of human happiness. The humanising of *homo economicus* is a very urgent and very interesting challenge for Thinking Humans.'

CARDINAL TREVISAN 'We would be foolish not to recognise that people have seemed—still seem—to feel a great need to believe the irrational, the incredible, the absurd even. But I now know that there *is* a religion that could accompany the re-forming of the human world that you have in mind, Greg.

'It is a religion that believes in the *God before God*, before the human mind tries to put God into words and images; the *God of the universe*, reflected in the mind-conceived order of the natural universe; the *God in us*, reflected in the ideal of the self-ordering of human societies; and the *God in me*, the God of my soul, reflected in the ideal of my own self-ordering as a human being, and my loving self-identifying with other human beings.

'It is for us to decide what shall be the presence of God in our own daily life, and the nature of our affective relationship with God—a relationship that we may, if we wish, share with others, in a community of shared belief and commitment.

'The function of religion is not to fill the minds of the people with nonsense, or to increase the power of the powerful, but to make the best possible use of the self-consciousness of human beings, as integral parts of the universe that transcends them.

'That is what I now know.'

Greg hesitated. For him the Cardinal was the living presence of a Christianity which had been a compendium of all religions, an archetype of all religious traditions, ranging from the crudest superstition and revolting cruelties, at one end of the scale, through devoted lives of simple goodness and mystical intensity, to the most sublime limits of human thought, at the other end of the scale. Greg knew that the Cardinal himself, in his old age, had the desire to rediscover, within the lived reality of religions, their most noble potentiality.

'I think you would agree, Cardinal Alvise, that history and our personal experience show that the human mind *is* capable of transcending itself, that the human race *is* capable of seeking to perfect itself in accordance with its highest ideas, the ideas we have traditionally called ideals. Why would a species that has discovered within itself the capacity to think beyond itself, and to choose its own self-perfecting, seek to deny and destroy that capacity? It is like a gifted athlete seeking to maim himself. It is like a gifted painter seeking to blind herself.'

COUNTESS FRIEDA: 'We might say—people do say—that we are living in exceptionally tragic times. Some people—irrationalists, admittedly—even speak of "the end times". Greg, I know that we—we at least—believe that it is possible for human beings to find within themselves, yet again, the courage to look beyond the actual, to see the possible, to want the ideal.'

MR GRAY: 'But there is a prior problem that is really a practical problem. How can we possibly convince other people—good-hearted and thoughtful people—that we are not merely pathetic victims of our own wishful thinking?'

Greg hesitated. He saw the Countess and Mr Gray as representatives of a generation that had been born into suffering, with an exceptionally tragic sense of human life. It seemed that in every century of human history there has been a generation born into suffering. But, remarkably, it has typically been such people who have been the prophets and the leaders of revolutionary change. Greg knew something that some other people in the room did not know. The Countess and Mr Gray—in the hidden work of the Firm, and now in their support for the public action of LOSC and MOTH—were the most discreet of all prophets, and the most subtle of all leaders of revolutionary change.

'People speak of a Clash of Civilisations. We would do better to speak of a Clash of Irrationalities. There are the gross irrationalities flowing from the most irrational forms of religion. But there are also the gross irrationalities of a collective fantasy world, ruthlessly and relentlessly corrupting the human mind, shamelessly and relentlessly filling the human world, the mind of every human being, with images of vice and violence.

'Democracy is the sedation of the masses by an illusion of freedom. Popular culture is metaphysics for the masses, putting into their minds an idea of reality confected by someone else.

'It is not wishful thinking to believe—soon it may no longer be possible to believe—that we can still find the highest human values within ourselves and that the highest human values could be the seeds of humanity's self-redeeming.

'The future already exists as a possibility. Prometheus must redeem Prometheus.

'The great struggles of the 20th century were struggles between good and evil. The great struggles of the 21st century will be struggles between different conceptions of the good.'

ALISON BRAND: 'I don't see how you can have any effect unless you organise the Thinking Humans into a powerful political force. Powerful people only respect

power—power in all its forms, from the crudest to the craftiest. The three greatest
murderous monsters of the twentieth century used ideas to help them to gain power and
to maintain their power. But the only thing that such people trust is violence, killing
bodies and killing minds—one-by-one and by the tens, the hundreds, of millions. At
some point, won't you have to man the barricades—you and the few thousand other
thinking humans—a few thousand, if you're lucky?'

*Greg hesitated. Alison represented for him an exciting possibility—the possibility that
the distinctive identity, experience and mentality of women might, at long last, have a
transforming effect on the making of the human future. Perhaps Alison was an exceptional
woman—powerful and unspoiled by power—but surely far from unique. The future of
the human world—if the human world has a future—may depend on the metaphysical
emancipation of such women.*

'If, as I do,' he said, 'you think of Evil as a failure of the Good, then it follows,
almost by definition, that Evil will never be finally defeated by the Good. We accept
that, Alison. Indeed, we think it's possible that Evil may finally defeat the Good—if
most people finally lose the capacity to distinguish between good and evil.

'Ideas are changed when the reality of the streets demands new ideas, and when there
are ideas—good ideas and evil ideas—ready and waiting to form a new reality.

'As to numbers, we're aiming at the Pareto twenty per-cent of thoughtful people.
The Thinking Humans have no action-programme, no enforceable orthodoxy. We have
only a foundational belief—in the power of the mind to make and re-make reality. And
we have a foundational value—the value of value. Our revolutionary programme is the
revaluation of values through the revaluing of the idea of value. The only power over
power is the power of ideas. The only power over bad ideas is better ideas. Our revolution
is a revolution in the mind, not in the streets.'

JANE MEEHAN: 'I'm with Oscar Wilde in thinking that art is the telling of beautiful
untrue things, expressing nothing but itself. Art is the art of the possible. I'm with André
Malraux in thinking that the artist overcomes misery by creating the world that he/she
would have made if she/he had been God. I'm with Camus in thinking that, when we
create, we live a second time. I'm with Beckett is thinking that a novel or a play is not
about something. It is something. And, of course, I'm with Plato—a society is as good as
the state of its imagination. Am I right, Greg, in seeing the MOTH project as really an
artistic enterprise—imagining a more beautiful world, telling the people a more beautiful
story. It's not really meant to be a sensible practical enterprise at all, is it?'

*Greg hesitated. He could see that Jane Meehan was, like her husband, a representative of a
fascinating part of the American Mind in which an American re-imagining of European
civilisation is experienced as a sort of permanent bitter-sweet anguish—a clinical condition
known as Mid-Atlantic Ridge Syndrome (MARS) or Jamesianism. Greg had always been*

uncertain how to respond to such people. Patronising but not disdainful. Sympathetic but not collusive. A perennial social and intellectual dilemma for sensitive Europeans.

'A work of art is the consciousness of one human being made into an object that is beautiful, an object whose beauty enters the consciousness of another human being, penetrating the subunconscious mind that they share. A work of art is an act of love. Soul embracing soul. On certain days of the week, I'm with William Blake in thinking that Art is the Tree of Life, and Science is the Tree of Death—with Blakean capital letters *ad libitum*. People accuse Plato of *imagining* an ideal society, as if a society could be a *work of art*. But all societies are works of the imagination, fragile card-houses made of ideas. Why shouldn't we try to imagine a society that is beautiful?.

'The ultimate aims of LOSC and MOTH are the same—laying the foundations of the City of Good. The first step in the MOTH project is to remind people that human history has been the author of some very terrible social fictions. The second step is to remind people that the human mind can always imagine something better, tell a better story. The third part of the project is to remind people that we have the power to turn our new and better ideas of human reality into a new and better human reality. If thinking human beings are artists, then it follows that, like any other artist, we are capable of creating something beautiful.'

GABI DORN: 'That's the amazing thing I've discovered in my life-long—well, four years so far—my very extensive study, let's say, of pre-modern European history. *Everything could have been different.* Isn't that an amazing thought? If this person or that had done this or that slightly differently, then everything would have been different. There's the Cleopatra's Nose theory of history—history as the fall-out from random human interactions. Then there's the Martin Luther's Constipation theory of history—the Reformation needn't have happened if Brother Martin had eaten his Bran Flakes. Or, when it happened, the *Reform* needn't have collapsed into such a dreadful mess. The Enlightenment needn't have happened. Or, when it happened, it needn't have done so much collateral damage.

'Why is it, Greg, that people, who know perfectly well what is the right and good thing to do, then go off and do all sorts of wrong things and bad things? And why is that the ruling class seems always to be the ruining class—leaders as misleaders—hijacking and perverting the few really good ideas that people have invented—building the City of Evil, brick by wretched brick?'

Greg hesitated. Gabi's challenge was the most challenging of all—the age-old unsolved puzzle of humanity's fractured, fallen existence. He knew also that it is normal, inevitable perhaps, that intelligent and thoughtful young people will, at some moment, see beyond the masks and mirrors of the human world, but will then, normally and apparently inevitably, put that painful vision to one side—both because they see all other intelligent and thoughtful people doing the same thing, and because they sense that it is simply not possible to live with such a vision as a sane well-adjusted member of society.

'The crimes and follies of mankind, the sad pageants of men's miseries, the passions of people-devouring kings and foolish peoples, are diseases of the public mind originating in the pathologies of the private mind. Our personal values determine whether we choose to do good or to do evil. To judge our values is the work of the higher values that lie beyond the values that determine our choices. To judge our higher values we must re-discover the value of all values—and that is what we call the revaluing of value.

'I'm sorry, Gabi. I'm only saying what many people before me have said, in many places over many millennia. But our aim now is to involve all Thinking Humans—not merely mystics and philosophers—in the great task of re-imagining the value of our values. Evil breeds evil. But good also breeds good—notwithstanding a great deal of evidence to the contrary.'

EDMUND JENNING: '*I am becoming what I am. I am not yet what I should be.* That is what *I* now know—and *those* should surely be the slogans of MOTH. They may be a bit too recherché for mass distribution through the *grandes surfaces* of popular culture, a bit too interesting for the wizened minds of the *grandes écoles*. But *noblesse*, such as it is, surely *obliges*—especially *noblesse* of the mind.

'Greg, you've spoken today as if we revolutionaries of the mind were rational, cerebral, sensible people—architects and engineers of the city of the future, the City of Good, a better world. We're not.

'We're slaves of passion, with an uncontrollable desire to change the world—fierce, unquenchable, overwhelming desire—fired by anger, and, yes, by resentment that the wicked and the worthless should flourish in the manure of rotting minds and rotten societies.

'We're filled with a terrible sense of the human tragedy, an unbearable pity for all the self-inflicted torture, the miserable waste, of the human world and human lives, human lives terrorised by false dogmas, false moralities, and false politics. How can anyone speak calmly, elegantly, intelligently about the horror of it all, the pity of it all?

'Ours is a sort of physical desire for humanity's other possibility, the beautiful potentiality of humanity—a desire to save the human mind from itself, to make the human mind into its own saviour, using its own inexhaustible power of self-creating, self-recreating, self-overcoming, self-perfecting. We want human beings to imagine what human happiness could be—and we want them to want it and work for it and find it.

'Surely that's what we have to say to people. We have to tell people that it's good to love what is lovable, to want the best for those we love, to want as much as possible of what we love. We've got to tell people about the seven types of love—from love of my own soul to the love of God.

'We have to beg them to believe that the only wealth that really matters is the wealth that can't be measured in money—the inexhaustible wealth of the good and the true and the beautiful. Humanity's own natural resources—imperishable and inextinguishable.

'We've got to say these things, Greg, haven't we?—shout these things from the rooftops.'

Greg hesitated, but only briefly. He could not say, even to himself, all that Edmund meant to him—Edmund, new human being, unfallen man, unspoiled by parents or teachers—Edmund Euphues, beautiful in body and mind and soul, incarnation of moral elegance. How could he explain to the others the idea *of self-transforming Edmund—living actuality of a human potentiality, ideal form of a possible transforming human energy?*

'I'm sorry, dear Edmund. An intellectual is what I have been—whatever else I might have desired to become. And I think we are *all* now becoming something more. We are becoming what human history now requires us to be. The life of a prophet is dedicated to the service of ideas. But there are true prophets and false prophets. The life of a true prophet is dedicated to the service of good ideas.

'I now see clearly what I had previously only seen dimly and tentatively. A pious hope has become a transforming belief. The crimes and follies, the savage passions and the endless miseries of human history, the dark side of humanity's species-life, have *not* destroyed the self-surpassing power of the human mind.

'We all-too-human human beings *can* undertake a new kind of *journey of the mind.*

'In *nature* you saw, for a moment, the order of your *soul*—the order of the universe reflected uniquely within each unique human being. You heard the voice of your soul.

'Through *music* I knew, for a moment, the idea of universal order that all human beings share in their subunconscious mind—the idea that allows us to form an idea of what it is to be *truly human.*

'And—perhaps—our dear friend Ingo discovered, for a moment, a string theory of his soul, pure and practical theory of universal consciousness, at the limits of a human mind whose limits the human mind cannot know.

'And there is something that you and I found, deep inside the order of all order, ruling the reality of all realities—*the binding force of love.*

'The love that binds together each human self—desiring to be what it can choose to become.

'The love that binds human beings together—desiring to be what human beings together can choose to become.

'The love that binds together the being and the becoming of the universe itself. Some people have called it *the love of God.*

'Edmund and I are pilgrims on the road to Eutopia. We are becoming *Enthusiasts.* People of the Fifth Dimension. Born-again Enthusiasts.

'Why shouldn't all thinking human beings become Enthusiasts? Why should the human world default itself into despair, left to the miserable mercies of the Pragmatists and the Nihilists?

'*Idealism is the new realism, the science of hope. Social idealism is the new humanism, the new conservatism, and the new socialism.*

'This is what we now know, and the human world needs to know.

'Long live the union of soul and body! Long live the union of mind and heart! Idealists of the world unite! Things need not only get worse! To change the world we need only change ourselves! Human being is human becoming!'

Greg was not alone in thinking that to speak in exclamation marks, even on such a self-consciously solemn occasion, and even in the capital city of the philosophical nation, was to come close to committing a major social solecism of several different kinds.

He had been half-standing, and half-sitting on the arm of an armchair, in the Greenes' drawing room. He stood up and took a bow. He was acknowledging a burst of improbable, and not uniformly enthusiastic, applause—applause for his performance, if not necessarily for his candour or the force of his arguments.

May Gaunt's applause was ostentatiously limp.

'The mind that thinks itself undeceived is the mind that is most deceived,' she said, as if she were quoting, probably from her own copious writings.

'A closed mind is a sleeping mind,' Edmund said, 'waiting to be wakened by a kiss.'

Did May Gaunt blush? There are those who say that she did.

*   *   *

20

Tying the Knot

Brompton Oratory looked unusually pretty, almost skittishly pretty, like a venerable dowager made to look young again. There were banks and mounds and drifts of late-summer flowers and foliage. The place was full of people and music and sunshine.

A marriage had been announced and, rather soon thereafter, Abe Green and Alison Brand found themselves, equally embarrassed, on an unlikely stage, the focus of an unfamiliar kind of attention.

It was a transatlantic dynastic wedding worthy of the fortunate old days of imperial Austria. The congregation included several Presidents and Prime Ministers and ambassadors, and more than one Cardinal, together with many other faces more or less recognisable from newspapers and newscasts. Many representatives of the Sensible Countries and the Thinking Humans. Many members of the Firm from all over the world. People who had always known each other, people who had not known each other, people whose lives were now intersecting in the converging lives of the happy couple.

At the reception in the Victoria and Albert Museum, there were abundant opportunities for the intersecting of those who were now involved, whether they knew it or not, in the new global class struggle—the struggle between the masters and slaves of the Old World and the prophets and pioneers of a New World.

In church, Edmund and Gabi had intersected on a rather smaller scale. At a particularly intense moment in the course of the marriage service, Edmund had taken hold of Gabi's left hand with his right hand—a non-gratuitous and non-providential event which was the effect of a determinable cause—namely, Edmund finding himself suddenly in his sentimental and sensualist mode. Gabi turned to look at Edmund without any trace of sentimentality or sensuality in her expression.

Edmund was uncertain how to read Gabi's look, definitely a look with the mind, and not merely with the eyes. It was not—'Edmund, we're in church!' It was probably not even—'I didn't know you cared!' Then Gabi smiled, not the mysterious smile of interior voluptuousnesses but, rather, a salvific Anglican smile. Edmund read that smile as meaning—'isn't this nice, and aren't we all nice?' And Edmund felt inclined to agree. The reader of these lines may be surprised to learn that there are—that there still are—such people in this world.

Later, as people at a wedding are inclined to do, Edmund and Gabi were both thinking about the future. Or, more strictly speaking, they were both thinking, with their different life-histories and their different mentalities, about their (respective) futures. And, as people thinking about the future, especially in an ecclesiastical setting, are inclined to do, Edmund was also thinking about the past—in narrow and broad terms.

'It's good that I didn't know my parents,' he told himself. 'It means I'm free to imagine that they were as remarkable as the remarkable DNA they left inside me. I suppose you could say the same thing about us human beings in general. Offspring of human parents with some of God's DNA still inside us. Grandchildren of God.'

Edmund Jenning. Son, presumably, of man and woman. Self-begotten descendant, perhaps, of a self-revealing unknown God.

Edmund found that he was, as it were, praying.

'The alchemy of the soul can turn gold into prayer,' he thought—in substance, if not, until recounting the event later, in those precise words.

The story of a life—his life—so far.

*   *   *

The gods take notice, when godliness is flouted
And men go mad.
Sophocles.

None said "Let darkness be!" But darkness was.
George Eliot.

A nobler spirit lived not among the sons of men. Thy intellectual powers were
truly sublime, and thy bosom burned with a godlike ambition. But of what use
are talents and sentiments in the corrupt wilderness of human society? It is a
rank and rotten soil, from which every finer shrub draws poison as it grows.
William Godwin.

We should consider what is natural not in things which
are depraved but in those which are rightly ordered
according to nature.
Aristotle.

Why may not we have our heaven here
(that is, a comfortable livelihood in the earth)
and heaven hereafter too?
Gerrard Winstanley.

If we see things as they are, we shall live as we ought,
and if we live as we ought, we shall see things as they are.
John Smith.

Vain is the discourse of a philosopher by which
no human suffering is healed.
We must philosophise
and laugh at the same time.
Epicurus.

'Tis the Lord of us all,
The Dreamer whose dreams come true!
Rudyard Kipling.

Ego multa tacui.
Cicero.

ALLUSIONS EXPLAINED

X-ray of a Possible Universe

'If people don't know that there is a problem about the nature of reality,
they can't know that there is a problem about the nature of fantasy.'
(Page 96. Gregory Seare speaking.)

This appendix explains allusions contained or concealed in the text of the story.

An 'allusion' is an indirect or obscure reference, or the product of an association of ideas. Beneath the surface of mind-made human reality there is a turbulent ocean of hidden mental complexities and connections, the network of a hidden mental reality.

The word 'allusion' is derived from the Latin verb *ludere*, to play—as is the word 'illusion'.

Ideally, the explanation of an allusion should cause a cascade or effervescence or implosion of further allusions, and associations of ideas, in the reader's mind.

Cross-references to allusions already contained in the Allusions Explained appendix to *Invisible Power. A Philosophical Adventure Story* are given in the form: 'I.1, I.2'—meaning that the explanation is to be found in the section of that appendix relating to Chapter 1, Chapter 2, and so on, of that volume.

ALLUSIONS EXPLAINED

Epigraphs

— **Friedrich Nietzsche** (I.19). *The Birth of Tragedy* (1870-71), §XIV (tr., F. Golffing). Nietzsche argues that the ancient Greeks experimented with different ways of representing and exploring human existence—in epic poetry (Homer), in tragic drama (Aeschylus, Sophocles, Euripides) and, finally, in philosophy.

But philosophical ideas were already present in the plays of the third of the tragedians, Euripides (480-406 BCE), and, says Nietzsche, Plato (427-348 or 347) translated the (unwritten) philosophical radicalism of Socrates (470-399) into a new art form (the 'dialogue'), presenting abstract ideas through the medium of the interacting consciousness of actual and fictionalised human beings. Aesop's *Fables* (6th century BCE) had presented problems of personal and social morality in a form in which human characteristics are attributed to animals.

Nietzsche's own idiosyncratic and disorganised writings, typically either aphoristic or poetic in style, are a sustained polemic demanding a new kind of philosophy, including a new metaphysics and a new ethics. Human experience in the twentieth century has made his voice seem both prophetic and tragic.

— **Aristotle** (see I.13). From the *Poetics*, 9.2. Aristotle goes on to say that poetry (imaginative writing) is more philosophical than history, since poetry deals with the universal, history with the unique. (The ancient Greek word *poieō*, from which the English word 'poetry' is derived, is a wonderfully general verb covering all kinds of creating, making, inventing—'calling something into existence that was not there before': Plato, *Symposium*, 205b.)

Aristotle, Plato's pupil, established a non-imaginative form of philosophical presentation—a *prosaic* form which, for better and for worse, has remained the standard form to the present day. (The word 'prose' may be etymologically related—via French and Latin—to an ancient Greek word meaning 'pedestrian'!)

— **Jean-Jacques Rousseau** (see I.1, I.19). '. . . *ce Roman n'est point un Roman.*' In a *Second Preface* (1763) to his epistolary novel *Julie, ou la nouvelle Héloïse* (1761), Rousseau imagines a conversation with a sceptical reader of the book who objects, among other things, that this cannot be a novel because a novel should be a

136

realistic portrayal of recognisable people in extraordinary circumstances, not about extraordinary people in very ordinary circumstances—including two people who are so pure and virtuous that they might be creatures from another world.

In fact, the novel takes the form of proto-Joycean or proto-(V)Woolfian multiple streams of consciousness, conveyed through letters between people who are often present in the same house (on one occasion in the same room), but with a polemical-philosophical sub-text exploring the obsessive Rousseauesque target-area of the agonistic interaction between the individual and society. Julie and Saint-Preux, her tutor, seventeen and nineteen years old at the start of the novel (Voltaire said that her parents must be idiots to employ a nineteen-year-old tutor), are entangled in a web of personal, family, and social relationships. *S'il y a quelque réforme à tenter dans les mœurs publiques, c'est par les mœurs domestiques qu'elle doit commencer . . .'* 'If we are to try to reform public standards of behaviour, we must begin with domestic standards of behaviour . . .' (present author's trans.).

Rousseau is expressing in novel form his most heartfelt belief, to the effect that it will require a fundamental transformation of humanity's traditional ways of living and thinking, including a re-imagining of the nature of education, to allow human beings and human societies to become what they are naturally capable of being.

The three epistolary novels (novels in the form of letters) of the English writer Samuel Richardson (1689-1761) had suggested the form of Rousseau's novel. *Pamela: or Virtue Rewarded* (1740) is regarded as the first English-language novel in what would become the canonical form, presenting the outer and inner lives of imaginary, but recognisable, human beings. Richardson said that his novels were designed to entertain and to instruct, causing the reader to form judgments about the behaviour and thoughts of the characters in the novel, especially judgments about problems of social and moral propriety.

Such novels are thus a form of philosophy in disguise, or philosophy by other means. That such novels may give rise to intense debate, vilification, and parody—for example, Henry Fielding's *Shamela* (1741)—demonstrates their intended or unintended secondary effect as more or less subliminal philosophical discourse—a novel, and not a novel.

Richardson was 'disgusted' by the social and moral improprieties of Rousseau's novel. Voltaire, who also used the novel form to convey philosophical ideas (*Zadig*, *Candide*), said that Rousseau's novel was 'stupid, impertinent, boring; but it has a fine piece on suicide which makes you want to die.' (letter to d'Argental).

In Rousseau's tantalising claim quoted here as an epigraph, there is also a pre-echo of an intentionally philosophical painting by the Belgian artist René Magritte (1898-1967) entitled *La trahison des images* ('The Treachery of Images') which consists of a realistic image of a pipe above a written text: *Ceci n'est pas une pipe* ('This is not a pipe')—a challenge to our understanding of what we mean when we say that anything 'is' or 'is not'.

— **Horace.** *Sermonum liber primus* (*Satires*), I.10, lines 73-4.

CHAPTER 1. *Venice I.*

— **Cardinal**. Holder of the second highest office in the Church of Rome, appointed by the Pope in his capacity as head of the Church. The Pope (*Il Papa*, in Italian) is elected by the cardinals meeting as a collective body known as the College of Cardinals. In Italian, *papa* means 'papa' or 'daddy'. Cf. the ancient Greek παππασ—*pappas* ('papa' or 'daddy'), μαμμα—*mamma* ('mama' or 'mummy').

— **Kissing his ring**. A cardinal is normally also a bishop. Bishops wear a gold ring symbolising their attachment to the Church. It is traditional for the faithful to kiss the ring as a mark of respect.

— **Freudian interpretation**. The first major psychoanalytical publication of Sigmund Freud (I.7, I.19) was *The Interpretation of Dreams* (*Die Traumdeutung*) (1900) in which, in his own words, he endeavoured 'to elucidate the processes which underlie the strangeness and obscurity of dreams, and to deduce from these processes the nature of the psychic forces whose conflict or cooperation is responsible for our dreams.'

Although Freud continued to develop his understanding of the dream, placing more emphasis on the symbolic nature of their manifest content, he maintained his view that a dream is a disguised fulfilment of suppressed or repressed wishes, usually of a sexual nature, and that the study of dreams offers 'the royal road to a knowledge of the unconscious activities of the mind,' a place not otherwise available to introspection or investigation. More than thirty years later, he said that the book contains 'the most valuable of all the discoveries it has been my good fortune to make. Insight such as this falls to one's lot but once in a lifetime.' (Preface to 3rd English ed.).

As an epigraph to the book, Freud places a quotation from Book VII of Virgil's *Aeneid* (I.13): *Flectere si nequeo superos, Acheronta movebo* 'If I cannot move the powers of Heaven, I shall stir up the depths of Hell.' (Juno, Jupiter's wife, speaking.) Many of the dreams of which he offered interpretations were his own dreams, but he admitted that discretion prevented him from revealing the full substance or significance of those dreams. He seems to have had an obsessive, almost pathological, interest in the related phenomena of sexuality and religion, perhaps stemming from his relationship with his own father. Indeed, essential characteristics of his philosophy/biology of mind might be seen as reflections of his own troubled mind. It may be that such a thing is inevitable. The unconscious mind must also have power over our ideas, however abstract or concrete or neutral or superficial they may seem to be.

Carl Jung (I.20) broke free from the psychic domination of Freud and his obsession with problems of sexuality as the ultimate explanation of mental pathologies. He said that Freud seemed to suppose that sexuality was 'a sort of *numinosum*' (an aspect of divinity). Jung quoted Freud as saying that his 'sexual theory' was a bulwark 'against the black tide of mud . . . of occultism'. Jung himself is reported as saying that he avoided 'unsavoury details' in talking to patients—because it was awkward if one later met them at dinner. This might remind us of a saying attributed to St. Teresa of Avila, to the effect that 'some of the things in [the seemingly erotic Biblical book known as] the Song of Songs might have been put differently'.

— **Cardinal Trevisan**. The Trevisans were one of the aristocratic families recognised in accordance with the rules of the so-called 'Closing' (*Serrata*) of the Great Council (1297) which constituted Venice as a republic ruled by an hereditary aristocracy, from among whom the Doge, the republic's temporary monarch, was elected. Marc'antonio Trevisan was Doge in 1553. He is the subject of a portrait (1554) by Titian (I.20), now in the Museum of Fine Arts, Budapest. Five members of the Trevisan family died in the fall of Constantinople in 1453 (I.14; and below, under 'the Church'), an event that has been seen as a catalyst of the Italian Renaissance.

— **Prince of the Church**. When the Church of Rome is perceived as a virtual monarchy, this phrase refers to its lesser royalty or leading courtiers.

— *Terra firma*. In Latin, 'solid ground, the mainland.' Here used to refer to the land area of Venice itself, as opposed to the sea that surrounds it and the canals that form its thoroughfares. However, the Venetians themselves use *terra ferma* (the equivalent in the Italian language) to refer to the *Italian mainland*.

— **Unnatural land**. The buildings of Venice were originally constructed on wooden piles driven into the mud and marshland of islands in a coastal archipelago. The Adriatic Sea is enclosed as a lagoon (in Italian, *laguna*). An extensive and urbanised island facing the open sea is known as the *Lido* ('seashore', in Italian).

— *Grazie*. In Italian, 'thank you'.

— **Red slippers**. Traditionally worn by the Pope and (until 13 April 1969) by Cardinals, following the example of the Roman Emperors—for example, the Emperor Constantine at the Council of Nicaea in 325CE (I.16), a fashion-note particularly noted by those who wrote accounts of the Council.

— **Grand Canal**. Venice's (water-filled) high street.

— **The Church**. In this context, the Church of Rome, that is to say, the institutional centre of Roman Catholic Christianity in Rome, the head of the Church (the Pope—see above) being also Bishop of Rome.

Constantine (reigned 306-337) founded the new imperial capital of Constantinople on the site of the ancient city of Byzantium. A distinct Eastern Church gradually established itself at Constantinople, reflecting the growing separation of the Roman Empire into eastern and western branches. (The last emperor of the Western Roman Empire was deposed by the invading 'barbarians' in 476. The Byzantine Empire continued until 1453 when Constantinople was taken by the invading Ottoman Turks who made it their capital under the name of Istanbul.)

The Eastern Church rapidly divided into a collection of distinct communities, each with its own subtle theology. What came to be called the Orthodox Church established a dominant presence in Byzantium and subsequently in Greece and

Russia. Roman Christianity struggled to retain its unity in the face of a series of dissenting movements, culminating in the 16th century Reformation (see below, under 'Christendom'). The Orthodox Church, originally 'in union with' the Roman Church, has been separated from it ('schismatic', from the point of view of Rome) for one thousand years.

— **Labour seen as prayer.** An echo of a principle of Benedictine monasticism—'to work is to pray' (*laborare est orare*, in Latin)—in which the daily routine of the monks should include a period of physical labour.

— **Robinson's Barley Water.** A proprietary British soft drink (diluted with water).

— **Christendom.** Christianity seen as a particular culture or civilisation, or as the place where that culture or civilisation predominated. As a consequence of what came to be called the Protestant Reformation (from about 1520), the unity of Christianity (in the Church of Rome) collapsed, and has not been recovered (see Appendix 2 below). The Reformation failed in its effort to reform the Church from within, focusing on what had long been seen (at least since the fourteenth century) as major failings of the Church of Rome. The Church responded to the Protestant Reformation by what came to be called the Counter-Reformation, especially through decisions taken at a Council of the Church held (intermittently) at Trento (in Latin, *Tridentum*) and Bologna in Italy (1545-1563). The outcome was that northern Europe became predominantly Protestant (outside the Roman Church) and southern Europe remained predominantly Roman Catholic, with Germany divided between the two.

— **The Emperor in Leipzig.** The Reformation was a major challenge for the Holy Roman Empire of the German People (I.12, under 'Ettersberg'), with its Europe-wide interests and connections. In 1521 Luther was condemned by an imperial Diet convened by the Emperor at Worms in Germany. Thereafter, the Emperor endeavoured to bring about reconciliation on various occasions.

Venice, with its trading interests across Europe and far beyond, was careful not to align itself firmly with either side, but generally supported the Roman Church, and made some effort to prevent the disintegration of Christendom. A member of the Trevisan family is recorded as having been sent on a special mission to the Emperor in Leipzig in the context of these efforts.

The Venetians were the first great European masters of what would come to be known (in the late-18th century) as 'diplomacy', that is, pseudo-personal relations among imagined polities (generically known as 'states') represented by their rulers (generically known as 'governments') in pursuit of their supposed self-interest (generically known as 'foreign policy').

— **Wars of Religion.** The struggle between 'Catholics' (supporting the Roman Church) and 'Protestants' (opposing the Church) took a violent form in various countries, especially in France (1562-98). See I.21, under 'Pont Neuf'. Such conflicts were characterised by remarkably high levels of brutality, reflecting a long tradition of bloody wars among (Christian) European countries.

'. . . did the heathen ever make war on each other as continuously or as savagely as Christians among themselves?' 'The things which are done in wars between Christians are too obscene and appalling to be mentioned here.' (Erasmus, see under 'savage insanity', below.)

— **Thirty Years War.** (1618-1648). One part of a fifty-year struggle for European dominance, primarily between France and the Imperial Hapsburg powers (Spain and Austria), but in which most other European powers became involved (other than England, which was preoccupied at the time with its own form of revolutionary constitutional transformation—the so-called 'English Civil War'). The war reduced still further the formal power, let alone the actual power, of the Holy Roman Empire over the numerous and disparate polities of Germany (Treaties of Westphalia and Münster, 1648).

— **World Wars.** The multi-state wars of 1914-19 and 1939-45.

— **The European Union.** The official name (since 1993) of a constitutional union formed after the end of the Second World War (originally consisting of three 'European Communities') and presently comprising twenty-seven member states.

— **Savage insanity (of war).** The Cardinal is evidently recalling the diatribe against war that Erasmus (I.5, I.6, I.11) included in the 1515 edition of his *Adages*. He is discussing the saying *Dulce bellum inexpertis* ('War is sweet to those who have not experienced it.') (The English translation quoted here is by Margaret Phillips; Cambridge University Press; 1964.)

'There is nothing more wicked, more disastrous, more widely destructive, more deeply tenacious, more loathsome, in a word more unworthy of man, not to say of a Christian.'

'Nor are there lacking lawyers and theologians who add fuel to the fire of these misdeeds and, as they say, sprinkle them with cold water [as water is used in forges]. And the result of all this is, that war is now such an accepted thing that people are astonished to find anyone who does not like it; and such a respectable thing that it is wicked (I nearly said heretical) to disapprove of the thing of all things which is most criminal and most lamentable. How much more reasonable it would be to turn one's astonishment to wondering what evil genius, what a plague, what madness, what Fury first put into the mind of man a thing which had been hitherto reserved for beasts—that a peaceful creature, whom nature made for peace and loving-kindness . . . should rush with such savage insanity, with such mad commotion, to mutual slaughter.'

'Whatever evils war brings, must be put to the account of those who find reasons for war.' 'What is war, indeed, but murder shared by many, and brigandage, all the more immoral for being wider spread? But this view is jeered at, and called scholastic ravings, by the thick-headed lords of our day.'

Erasmus goes on—in this most passionate and impressive indictment of the practice of war—to discuss a threatened war against 'the Turks', a war, he says, whose alleged purpose is to convert the Turks forcibly to Christianity and/or to defend Christian civilization against the threat of the use of force by the Turks and/or to get hold of their wealth. (Suchlike pretexts for war have been echoed on countless occasions, up to the present day.)

And we may recall Tolstoy: 'And drowning the despair in their hearts with singing, debauchery, and vodka, torn away from peaceful labour, from their wives, their mothers and their children, hundreds of thousands of simple, good-natured men, with weapons of murder in their hands, will trudge off where they are sent. They will march; will be frozen, will be hungry, will be sick, dying of disease; until at last they reach the place where they will be murdered by thousands, and will themselves, not knowing why, murder by thousands men whom they have never seen, who have done them no wrong, and can have done them no wrong.' L. Tolstoy, *Christianity and Patriotism* (1894).

'But war's a game, which, were their subjects wise, / Kings would not play at.' W. Cowper (1731-1800), *The Task*.

See also, 'Law and war—a sinister partnership', and 'War, law and the psychopathology of human societies', in Ph. Allott, *Towards the International Rule of Law. Essays in Integrated Constitutional Theory* (hereafter *Towards the International Rule of Law*).

— *Campo.* In Italian, literally 'field'. In Venice, the word is applied to city squares.

— *Piacere.* In Italian, 'pleasure (to meet you)'.

— **Not-so-heavenly twins.** In ancient Greek mythology, Castor and Pollux, sons of Zeus and Leda, were known as the *dioscuri* (in Greek, 'sons of God') or 'the heavenly twins'. The star-constellation known as 'Gemini' (in Latin, 'the twins') is named after them.

— *Ricordi?* In Italian, 'do you remember?' (familiar form, second person singular).

— **Day of the Republic.** It recalls the day in 1946 when the Italian people, in a referendum, approved the constitution of the new Italian Republic, replacing the monarchy which had been established following the unification of Italy (1866).

— *Acqua altissima.* In Italian, 'very high tide'. From time to time, the water in the Venetian lagoon rises above ground level (referred to as *acqua alta*, high tide) and causes flooding, especially in the Piazza San Marco (St Mark's Square; the central square of Venice). In 1966, exceptional rainfall in Italy caused serious flooding in several cities, including Florence and Venice, causing substantial damage to buildings and their contents, including works of art, books and archives.

— **Venice observed.** The echo is of the title of a play by Christopher Fry, *Venus Observed* (1950). The leading character is an amateur astronomer, giving a metaphysical overtone to the play's love-story.

It contains a fine working of a familiar and charming theme—applicable also to Venice, perhaps, where we are conscious of all those who have observed it before us: see below, under 'Now is come a darker day'.

'I'm looking at the same star / That shone alone in the wake of Noah's / Drifting ark as soon as the rain was over, / That shone on shining Charlemagne / Far away, and as clear / As the note of Roland's homing horn. / Alone so long, and now casually / Descending to us, on a Thursday midnight:/ Saturn, who once glinted in the glass /Of Ariadne's mirror at the moment / When she died and melted out of Naxos.' (II.2).

The same beautiful idea was expressed in his *Ode to a Nightingale* by the English Romantic poet John Keats (1795-1821).

'Thou wast not born for death, immortal Bird! / No hungry generations tread thee down; / The voice I hear this passing night was heard / In ancient days by emperor and clown: / Perhaps the self-same song that found a path, / Through the sad heart of Ruth, when, sick for home, / She stood in tears amid the alien corn . . .'

Unlike stars and planets and birdsong, the timeless sharing of the experience of great works of art may be ruined by their vulgar 'restoration'.

Venice Observed is the title of a book (1956) by the American writer, Mary McCarthy (1912-89), who was notably sensitive to the unfathomable Venetian spirit. She recalls the familiar saying—'there is nothing to say about Venice that has not already been said' (including that saying itself!).

— **Your Eminence**. Traditional form of address for Cardinals.
— **Crimes and follies**. See I.13.
— **Martin Luther**. I.15; and above, under 'Christendom'; and Appendix 2 below.
— **Reformation**. See above, under 'Christendom' and Appendix 2 below.
— *Ecco!* In Italian, 'there!' or 'so!'
— *Lux in tenebris.* In Latin, 'light in the darkness'. Alison and the Cardinal evidently have in mind a passage at the beginning of the [Christian] Gospel of John (1.5). *Et lux in tenebris lucet et tenebrae eam non comprehenderunt.* 'And the light [of God] shineth in darkness: and the darkness did not comprehend it.' John is explaining the need for God's new self-revealing in Christ. Light and darkness have been, at all times and in many cultures, key metaphors to express the self-surpassing and self-perfecting capacities of the human mind.
— **Divine spark**. In many philosophical traditions, including the western tradition originating in the Pythagoreans and Plato (see I.13, under 'Platonic gospel', and *passim* below), humanity is conceived as containing some aspect or potentiality akin to the nature of a god or gods. Plato refers to it as 'the divine principle within us' (*Timaeus*, 90d). 'God, being generous, desired that all things should become as like as might be to himself.' (*Timaeus*, 29c). Augustine (I.19) calls it 'the spark of reason' from humanity's being 'made in the image of God' (*scintilla rationis in qua factus est ad imaginem Dei*) (*City of God*, XXII, xxiv).

— **Caverns of the Vatican**. The echo is of *Les caves du Vatican*, the title of a novel by
André Gide. See ch. 11, under 'we could kill'.
— **Now is come a darker day**. From P.B. Shelley (1792-1822), *Lines written among
the Euganean Hills* (1818). The English Romantic poet, having been sent down
from University College, Oxford, for publishing an essay in defence of atheism, led
a brief and tragic life. With his second wife Mary (see ch. 3 below, under 'Dante's
tomb'), he visited Byron in Venice (see ch. 12 below).

> 'Sun-girt City, thou hast been / Ocean's child, and then his queen; / Now is
> come a darker day . . .'

Venice had declined in the 18th century—'magnificent in her dissipation, and
graceful in her follies,' according to the art historian and social critic John Ruskin
(1819-1900), *Stones of Venice*, I.1. It had been occupied by French forces under
Napoleon in 1797. It was under Austrian rule from 1815 until its incorporation
(with help from Bismarck's Prussia) into the new Italy in 1870.

Venice has always been much visited and, usually, much admired. The Florentine
poet-humanist Petrarch (born in Arezzo where his family were living in temporary
exile) visited Venice in 1332: 'a city rich in gold, but still richer in beauty'. Philippe
de Commynes, on a diplomatic mission for the French King in 1494/5, said that
the Grand Canal was 'the most beautiful street in the world'. Friedrich Nietzsche
said that Venice was 'the only place on earth that I love'.

John Ruskin, obsessive observer of its art and architecture of which he made
much idiosyncratic use in expounding his universalising theories of art and
architecture, even admired the pigeons.

Herbert Spencer (1820-1903), stern post-Darwinian social philosopher,
disapproved of the buildings on the Grand Canal—as have many others before
and since—on the ground that they were merely decorated facades—as are many
other much-praised buildings. Many visitors over the centuries took away as their
dominant memory the smell of the (then) unsanitary canals.

The *acqua altissima* of mass tourism is Venice's new darker day.
— **Gondola**. Flat-bottomed boat rowed by a gondolier (*gondoliere*) standing in the
stern.
— **Cradle and coffin**. An image taken from no. 8 of the *Venetian Epigrams*, a set of
poems by J.W. von Goethe (see I.12, under 'Ettersberg').

> *Diese Gondel vergleich ich der sanft einschaukelnden Wiege, / Und das Kästchen
> darauf scheint ein geräumiger Sarg./ Recht so! Zwischen der Wieg und dem Sarg
> wir schwanken und schweben / Auf dem grossen Kanal sorglos durchs Leben dahin.*
> ('I compare this gondola to the gently rocking cradle, / And the little box on
> top to a spacious coffin. / Rightly so! From cradle to coffin we sway and float
> through life carefree on the great canal.' (present author's trans.).

— **Archetypes**. Birth and death, the universal human experiences, are especially likely to produce universal archetypes in humanity's 'collective unconscious', if there is such a thing. See I.20, under 'valley of the shadow'.

CHAPTER 2. *Èze*.

— **Èze**. Pronounce to rhyme with 'days'. A medieval hill-village in the Alpes-Maritimes department of France. With its strategically important fort dominating a much-disputed part of the Mediterranean coast-line, it has had an interesting history within the drama of Provençal history, including occupation by the Saracens in the 9th century and by Barbarossa (Khayr al-Din) in the 16th century.
— **SUV**. Sport Utility Vehicle. A hypertrophic form of motor vehicle.
— **Old Master**. A general term for leading pre-19th century European painters.
— **Nietzsche and the English mind.**

> 'They are no philosophical race, these Englishmen: Bacon signifies an *attack* on the philosophical spirit; Hobbes, Hume, and Locke a debasement and lowering of the value of the concept of "philosophy" for more than a century. It was *against* Hume that Kant arose, and rose; it was Locke of whom Schelling said, *understandably, "je méprise Locke"* ['I despise Locke']; in their fight against the English-mechanistic doltification of the world, Hegel and Schopenhauer were of one mind (with Goethe) . . .'
>
> 'Finally, we should not forget that the English with their profound normality have once before caused an over-all depression of the European spirit: what people call "modern ideas" or "the ideas of the eighteenth century" or also "French ideas"—that, in other words, against which the *German* spirit has risen with a profound disgust—was of English origin; there is no doubt of that . . . European *noblesse*—of feeling, taste, of manners, taking the word, in short, in every highest sense—is the work and invention of France; European vulgarity, the plebeianism of modern ideas, that of England.'
>
> F. Nietzsche (see I.19), *Beyond Good and Evil* (1886), §§252, 253. (tr., W. Kaufmann).

— **Antiphonal mode**. A liturgical form in which short verses of a text are spoken or sung by two voices alternately. From the ancient Greek *antiphōneō* (to respond).
— **William of Occam and Francis Bacon**. See Appendix 1.
  Wyclif and Cranmer. See Appendix 2.
  Hobbes and Locke and Jefferson. See Appendix 3.
  Locke and Berkeley and Hume. See Appendix 4.
  Adam Smith and Ricardo. See Appendix 5.
  Burke and Owen and Bentham. See Appendix 6.
  Newton and Lyell and Darwin. See Appendix 7.

— **Continental European mind.** See Appendix 8.
— **Empires of the mind.** 'The empires of the future are the empires of the mind.' Sir Winston Churchill, speech at Harvard University, 6 September 1943.
— **Eunomian world.** A human world giving effect to the principles of Eunomian social idealism (I.19).
— **Monarchy a metaphysical mirror.** The idea of the fantastical and illusionary character of the British monarchy is at least as old as Shakespeare. The deep-structural constitutional significance of the idea was most lucidly examined by Walter Bagehot (1826-77; editor of the *Economist* newspaper) in his *The English [sic] Constitution* (1867/1872).

> 'We have no slaves to keep down by special terrors and independent legislation. But we have whole classes unable to comprehend the idea of a constitution—unable to feel the least attachment to impersonal laws. Most do indeed vaguely know that there are some other institutions besides the Queen, and some rules by which she governs. But a vast number like their minds to dwell more upon her than upon anything else . . . A *family* on the throne is an interesting idea also. It brings down the pride of sovereignty to the level of petty life. No feeling could seem more childish than the enthusiasm of the English at the marriage of the Prince of Wales. They treated as a great political event, what, looked at as a matter of pure business, was very small indeed . . . A Republic has insinuated itself beneath the folds of a Monarchy.'

— **Mind** (in French and German). Ancient Greek and Latin have words which we feel able to translate into English as 'mind' (*nous* and *mens*). Italian and Spanish have *mente*.

French has *esprit* (which also means 'spirit' and 'wit'), *conscience* (which means both 'consciousness' and 'conscience'), *mentalité* ('mentality') and *raison* ('reason').

German has *Geist* (which also means 'spirit' and 'ghost'), *Bewusstsein* ('consciousness'), *Gedanke* ('thought'), *Verstand* ('reason', 'sense').

None of these is precisely equivalent to 'mind' seen as the specific organ of thought, that is, the totality of what (at least for the time being) we suppose to be the non-material aspect of the functioning of the brain.

— *Esprit.* Greg is referring to the French word as the equivalent of the English 'wit'. In this sense, *esprit* is something more than mere 'humour' in the English sense. It contains undertones and overtones of cynicism and scepticism and moral autonomy and mental vigour.

It may also be worth noting that there is no adequate equivalent in English of the French word *ennui*—which is something much more than 'boredom' and contains flavours of *accidia* and *anhedonia* and *amechania* and *Angst* and the blues.

— **Like and dislike.** The French have to say *aimer bien* ('to love well') and *ne pas aimer bien* ('not to love well'). The position is much the same in German.

— **Lackey of capitalism.** 'The jargon peculiar to Marxist writing (hyena, hangman, cannibal, petty bourgeois, these gentry, lackey, flunkey, mad dog, White Guard, etc.) consists largely of words and phrases translated from Russian, German or French.' G. Orwell, 'Politics and the English language' (1946). 'Lackey' is a more or less pejorative name for a minor servant in a royal or noble house.

Greg is no doubt familiar with the saying attributed to Socrates by Diogenes Laertius (3rd-century summmariser of the various schools of philosophy). 'How many are the things of which I have no need.'

— **Two laundries.** A traditional image of a simple, and apparently pointless, form of co-operative economic system in which two people undertake to wash each other's dirty clothes. However, the most sophisticated of economic systems is a transformation of such a simple exchange into something which can mysteriously increase the wealth and/or well-being of both parties. See Appendix 5 below.

— **Pragmatist.** There is a popular use of the word 'pragmatism', referring to a way of thinking which is dominated by a calculation of the practical effects of possible choices of thought or action.

The word is also used to refer to a development in post-Kantian thought, especially in the USA. It is difficult to generalise about American pragmatism. It took many forms—one writer identified thirteen forms. And, in the work of each of its three leading exponents—William James (1842-1910), C.S.Peirce (1839-1914) and John Dewey (1859-1952)—it is not possible to find any settled and coherent set of ideas, let alone a set of ideas that they all share.

However, it is possible to hazard a generalised view of the relation of their ideas to the perennial Western philosophical tradition.

(1) They saw themselves as post-philosophers, traditional philosophy having run into the ground. But they recognised that the perennial and ultimate challenges of philosophy—the relation of mind to matter, the functioning of the mind, the meaning of 'truth', the meaning of 'the good'—were real and continuing challenges. (We are told that, in his youth, Peirce had studied Kant's *Pure Reason* for two hours a day for three years!)

(2) They thought that these puzzles could not be solved by remaining in the territory of the old philosophy, that is to say, seeking a solution by constructing an internal model of the mind, what we have above called a metaphysics of the mind, seen merely from the point of view of the mind.

(3) They proposed what we might call (they did not) an *exteriorisation* of the functioning of the mind, taking Kant's model of the co-operative effort of mind and matter two steps further. (a) We should focus on the mind in action in the world. (b) We should focus on the interaction of minds.

(4) It followed that they rejected supposed 'truth' based on logic, intellectual or religious authority, or abstract (a priori, metaphysical, transcendental) thinking. In Peirce's words: 'The opinion which is fated to be ultimately agreed upon by all who investigate is what we mean by truth, and the object represented by this opinion is real.' (*Collected Papers*, vol. V, at 407).

(5) They especially admired the success of the scientific method, which seemed to respect (3) and (4) above.

(6) But the great problem remained—how do you apply exteriorised collectivised thinking to things other than the observable phenomena of the material world without diluting the ideas of 'truth' and 'the good' into transient products of some more or less disorderly form of social consensus, or controversial interpretations of the highly equivocal record of human experience?

(7) This problem greatly troubled the American pragmatists, especially as they faced the dramatic developments (many of them extremely negative) in Western society in the late-19th and 20th centuries. Not to be able to speak confidently about 'truth' and 'the good' in the face of such events seemed like some sort of moral catastrophe.

(8) However, it must be said that a form of 'pragmatism' which reflects both the popular and the intellectual uses of the word is recognised, by Americans themselves, as being a deep-structural component of 'the American mind' and a distinctive feature of American society, from the founding of the Republic to the present day. This broad pragmatism somehow manages to co-exist with countless forms of highly socialised religion whose roots stretch back much further—to the founding of the first British settlements in America. See further in chs. 5 and 15 below.

— **Entropic void.** 'Thus it is no surprise that the two things that seem to be productive of movement are desire and practical thinking. [But] it is because of the movement started by the object of desire that the thinking produces its movement . . . Thus there is really one thing that produces movement, the faculty of desire.' Aristotle, *De anima*, III.10. (tr., H. Lawson-Tancred). (Pre-echoes of David Hume! See Appendix 4 below.)

The *Second Law of Human Thermodynamics* suggests that human beings with very low energy/desire/libido levels are liable to lead a quiet life, but are also liable to depersonalise and dematerialise, prematurely returning to the formless void.

Edmund certainly also knows the *Third Law of Human Thermodynamics*. Those who divert high levels of energy/desire/libido in creative and constructive directions may lead a less entropic life, but will have to learn to live with the ever-present threat of serial frustration and haunting despair!

— **Cynic. Epicurean, Stoic.** Plato and Aristotle, the ultimate reference-points for all subsequent Western philosophy, inspired this set of dialectical variations in their Greek successors, led respectively by Diogenes (c.410-c.23 BCE), Epicurus (341-270

BCE), and Zeno (c.335-c.254). Their ethical teachings share a common focus: the nature of the good life of the human individual (rather than the good life in society). They advocated moral autonomy. The individual human being is responsible for understanding the nature and demands of virtue. The Cynics emphasized the intrinsic freedom of the individual. The Epicureans emphasized the duty of the individual to find the best form of happiness by discriminating prudentially among sources of pleasure and pain. The Stoics emphasized the duty of the individual to seek happiness by conforming to the natural order of the universe in which human beings participate.

— **Patchwork of colours.** Knowing him as we do, we may expect that Edmund associates this phenomenon with a description of a childhood experience of the narrator in *Du côté de chez Swann* (1913), Book I of Marcel Proust's novel *À la recherche du temps perdu* (I.19).

> *On avait bien inventé, pour me distraire les soirs où on me trouvait l'air trop malheureux, de me donner une lanterne magique dont, en attendant l'heure du dîner, on coiffait ma lampe; et, à l'instar des premiers architectes et maîtres verriers de l'âge gothique, elle substituait à l'opacité des murs d'impalpables irisations, de surnaturelles apparitions multicolores, où des legendes étaient dépeintes comme dans un vitrail vacillant et momentané.* ('Someone had had the happy idea of giving me, to distract me on evenings when I seemed abnormally wretched, a magic lantern, which used to be set up on top of my lamp while we waited for dinner-time to come: in the manner of the master-builders and glass-painters of gothic days, it substituted for the opaqueness of my walls an impalpable iridescence, supernatural phenomena of many colours, in which legends were depicted, as on a shifting and transitory [stained-glass] window.' (tr., C.K. Scott Moncrieff).

For Proust's narrator, the lamp only made him more miserable, by alienating him from a room which he regarded as an integral part of his personality.

Edmund is of a more cheerful disposition.

— **Cabin of clay and wattle.** From *The Lake Isle of Innisfree*, a poem by the Irish poet W.B. Yeats (1865-1939): 'I will arise and go now, and go to Innisfree, / And a small cabin build there, of clay and wattle made.'

— **Ark on dry land.** 'Already he had begun dreaming of a refined Thebaid, a desert hermitage equipped with all modern conveniences, a snugly heated ark on dry land in which he might take refuge from the incessant deluge of human stupidity.' From a charmingly *fin de siècle* novel by the French writer J.-K. Huysmans (1848-1907), Against Nature (*A rebours*) (tr., R. Baldick), in which a young man detaches himself from the world and devotes himself to a life of aesthetic (in the narrower and wider senses of the word) pleasure.

— ***Chaste et pure*.** Echoes a fine aria in *Faust*, an opera by the French composer C. Gounod (1818-93): *Salut! Demeure chaste et pure* ('Hail dwelling! Chaste and pure'). Faust is addressing the place where Marguérite, his prospective lover, lives. In the opera, as in Goethe's Faust Part I (see I.20), the drama ends tragically but ambiguously. As Marguérite (Gretchen in Goethe's poem) dies, Méphistophélès (Mephisto) shouts 'Damned', but a heavenly choir sings 'Saved'!

— **Chanting faint hymns**. 'Therefore, fair Hermia, question your desires; / Know of your youth, examine well your blood, /Whether, if you yield not to your father's choice, / You can endure the livery of a nun, / For aye to be in shady cloister mew'd, / To live a barren sister all your life, / Chanting faint hymns to the cold fruitless moon.' W. Shakespeare, *A Midsummer-Night's Dream*, I I. i (Theseus speaking).

— *Dichte Tannendunkelheit.* 'The dense darkness of pine-trees.' From *Einsamkeit* ('Solitude'), a poem by J.B. Mayrhofer (1787-1836), German poet and friend of the composer Franz Schubert (I.7) who set it to music (D620; 1818). *Gib mir die Weihe der Einsamkeit / Durch dichte Tannendunkelheit / Dringt Sonnenblick nur halb und halb, / Und färbet Nadelschichten falb.* ('Give me the consecration of solitude. / Through the dense darkness of the pine-trees / the gaze of the sun hardly reaches / half-gilding the fallen pine-needles.' (present author's trans.).

— **Odoriferous tree-wings**. '. . . now gentle gales / Fanning their odoriferous wings dispense / Native perfumes, and whisper whence they stole /Those balmie spoils.' J. Milton, *Paradise Lost*, bk. 4.

— *Soave zeffiretto*. From a duet sung by the Countess and Susanna in the opera *Le Nozze di Figaro* (The Marriage of Figaro) (1786) by W. Mozart (I.2). *Che soave zeffiretto / Questa sera spirerà / Sotto i pini del boschetto.* ('What a gentle breeze will breathe this evening under the pine-trees of the little wood.') They are planning an unpleasant surprise for the Count.

    Zeffiretto, in Italian, is a diminutive form of *zeffiro* (breeze). In ancient Greek mythology, Zephyr is the West Wind. In the South of France, the west wind may sometimes come from Andalusia and North Africa! See below, under '*Dahin*'.

— **Siren voices**. 'Your next encounter will be with the Sirens, who bewitch everybody that approaches them. There is no home-coming for the man who draws near them unawares and hears the Sirens' voices . . . For with the music of their song the Sirens cast their spell upon him, as they sit there in a meadow piled high with the mouldering skeletons of men, whose withered skin still hangs upon their bones.' Homer, *The Odyssey*, bk. XII. (tr., E.V. Rieu). The goddess Circe is warning Odysseus of the dangers facing him and his crew, as they seek to return home to Ithaca after the Trojan War.

— *Dahin*. 'Thither', in German. The echo is of a charming poem *Mignon* by J.W. Goethe (I. 12), expressing the lure of the South.

> *Kennst du das Land, wo die Zitronen blühn, / . . . . / Kennst du ihn wohl? Dahin, dahin / Geht unser Weg./ O Vater, lass uns ziehn!* ('Do you know the land where the citrus trees bloom . . . Do you know it well? There, there goes our way. Oh father, let us be carried there!' (present author's trans.).

Ein Fichtenbaum steht einsam / Im Norden auf kahler Höh. / ... Er träumt von einer Palme ... ('A spruce-tree stands alone, in the North on a bare hill-top ... It is dreaming of a palm-tree.') H. Heine (see Appendix 8 below), *Lyrisches Intermezzo* XXXIII. (Is the waspish Heine here *parodying* German Romantic sentimentality?)

— **Later, perhaps**. Edmund would certainly have in mind an unlikely prayer that Augustine (I.19) attributed to himself. 'But I wretched, most wretched, in the very commencement of my early youth, had begged chastity of Thee [God], and said, "Give me chastity and continency, only not yet." For I feared lest Thou shouldest hear me soon, and soon cure me of the disease of concupiscence, which I wished to have satisfied, rather than extinguished.' (*Confessions*, bk. VIII; tr., E.B. Pusey). His wish was granted, and the cure delayed, for a few more years.

— *Sage, welt, zu guter Nacht!* ('Say, world, good night'). From *Komm, Jesu, komm* ('Come, Jesus, come'), a beautiful chorus and aria (BWV 229) by J.S. Bach.

— *Je demeure! Vienne la nuit sonne l'heure / Les jours s'en vont je demeure.* From *Le Pont de Mirabeau*, a poem by the French poet Guillaume Apollinaire (1880-1918). ('Let the night come, let the hour sound / The days go by, I remain.')

— *Lepidus libellus*. In Latin, 'charming little book'. The Roman poet Catullus (85-54 BCE) so described one of his own books of poetry.

— *Nouvelle nouvelle*. 'New short novel', in French. An ironical reference to the expression *nouveau roman*. In the 1950's some French novelists began to produce novels in a form which came to be called *le nouveau roman* ('the new novel'). Especially advocated and exemplified in the work of Alain Robbe-Grillet (1922-2008), such a novel aims to avoid what it sees as the traditional function of a novel as a vehicle of mere story-telling, replacing it with a narrative that seeks to convey a direct re-presentation of the natural and human worlds. As is always the fate of claims to novelty, this claim to novelty was challenged by those who pointed to previous examples of novels in atypical forms. (In French, a *nouvelle* is a work of fiction whose scale is somewhere between the short-story and the novel.)

— **Neo-neo-Platonist**. Plato's successors (including Aristotle and those mentioned under 'Cynic, Epicurean, Stoic' above) sought to improve Platonic thinking (as they supposed). Neo-Platonism then sought to re-platonise Plato, improving his thinking by suggesting what Plato would have said, had he been able to understand himself more deeply. Plotinus (c.205-270), in particular, influenced Christian theology as it began to philosophise itself to a high intellectual level.

After Albert (c.1193-1280) and Aquinas (1225-1274) had revived and improved Aristotle, Plato was, once again, restored to glory in the Italian Renaissance (Platonic Academy, Florence; Pico della Mirandola). Somewhat surprisingly, in 17th-century Cambridge, a group of philosopher-theologians made intriguing use of Platonic themes (Cambridge Platonists) (see ch. 11 below, under 'no scientist'). G.W.F.Hegel

(I.19, and Appendix 8 below) believed that he was, among many other things, a direct heir of Plato, at last completing the Platonic enterprise.

— **Ideal Realism**. An ironical reference to the expression Magic Realism which is used to refer to 20th-century art-forms, especially prose fiction, whose method is halfway between realism and surrealism. Everyday realities are re-imagined in forms which are not possible realities, from a conventional or literal point of view, but which, because they can be imagined by the human mind, have a claim to be possible realities in some other sense. The form came to public attention especially in relation to the novels of certain Latin American writers, such as Jorge Luis Borges and Gabriel García Márquez.

    Ideal Realism would thus probably be an artistic form which imagines a *better* reality with a view to its becoming *actual*.

— **Post-Freudian**. Like the deceased owner of a great, but ramshackle estate, Sigmund Freud (I.7, I.19) left a rich legacy of stimulating ideas, but also a wealth of confusion, dispute and revulsion. His followers in the apostolic succession have defended a Freudian orthodoxy hip and thigh, albeit with much revisionism, and even if it is difficult to find any steady-state orthodoxy in his quicksilver writings. However, the Freudian challenge to thinking about the functioning of the human mind, and about the roots of human personality, is inescapable. All those who indulge in such thinking are, in this sense, post-Freudian, even if they are also anti-Freudian.

— **Pest and parasites**. '"Les Palais Nomades" [The Nomad Palaces; a collection of poetry (1887) by the French symbolist poet G. Kahn (1859-1936)] is a really beautiful book, and it is free from all the faults that make an absolute and supreme enjoyment of great poetry an impossibility. For it is in the first place free from those pests and parasites of artistic work—ideas. Of all literary qualities the creation of ideas is the most fugitive.' G. Moore (1852-1933), Irish writer, *Confessions of a Young Man* (1888).

    'We hate poetry that has a palpable design upon us.' J. Keats (1795-1821), letter to J.H. Reynolds, 3 February 1818. We may recall also Keats's fine (but discussable) 'axiom' about poetry. 'That if Poetry comes not as naturally as the Leaves to a tree it had better not come at all.' (letter to J. Taylor, 27 February 1818).

    W. Hazlitt (see Appendix 6 below), who often influenced Keats' thinking, had recently said: 'It is, indeed, one characteristic mark of the highest class of excellence to appear to come naturally from the mind of the author, without consciousness or effort.' (W. Hazlitt, 'On posthumous fame—whether Shakespeare was influenced by a love of it?' (1814). Hazlitt argues that Shakespeare was not so influenced.)

    'Life is 'monstrous, infinite, illogical, abrupt, and poignant'. A work of art is 'neat, finite, self-contained, rational, flowing, and emasculate'. R.L. Stevenson (1850-94), quoted in Leon Edel's *Henry James*.

    'The chief defect of the novel of ideas is that you must write about people who have ideas to express—which excludes all but about .01 per cent of the human race.' A. Huxley (1894-1963), *Point Counter Point* (1928).

However, we may also recall a discussable saying of the French writer Albert Camus (1913-1960). *Un roman n'est jamais qu'une philosophie mise en images. Et dans un bon roman, toute la philosophie est passée dans les images.* ('A novel is always only a philosophy put into images. And in a good novel, all the philosophy is conveyed in the images.') Review of J.-P. Sartre's *La Nausée*, in *Alger républicain*, 1938.

— **Ideas in free association.** 'Association of ideas' is an idea used in the philosophy of mind (see Appendix 4 below). 'Free association' is a practice, used especially by Freud and Freudians, designed to reveal unconscious contents of the mind by asking the patient to respond spontaneously to a word or image.

— **Anti-*Candide*.** On the (ambiguous) defeatism or quietism of Voltaire's *Candide*, see I.22.

— **Pacifism. Quietism.** Attitudes of detachment and passivity in relation to the threats and challenges of human life, especially of human social life. In Latin, *pax*, 'peace'; *pacificus*, 'peace-making'.

— **Garden/gardener.** For Greg's and Edmund's response to the supposedly Voltairean thesis that we should resign ourselves to merely 'cultivating our garden', see I.21, and I *passim*.

— **Fiction of the human world.** 'Why could the world which we are concerned with not be a fiction? And if someone then asks "But doesn't an author belong to a fiction?" could he not be fully answered with Why? Does not this "belong to" perhaps belong to the fiction?' F. Nietzsche (I.19; and 'Epigraphs' above), *Beyond Good and Evil*, §34. (tr., I. Johnston).

— **True author of IP (?Greg Seare).** Echo, perhaps, of M. Cervantes (1547-1616), Don Quijote de la Mancha (1605-15).

> Llegando a escribir el traductor desta historia este quinto capítulo, dice que le tiene por apócrifo, porque en él habla Sancho Panza con otro estilo del que se podía prometer de su corto ingenio, y dice cosas tan sutiles, que no tiene por posible que él las supiese.
>
> ('As the translator of this story reaches the writing of this fifth chapter, he must say that he thinks it is apocryphal because in it Sancho Panza speaks in a style other than that which his limited intelligence would permit, and says things that are so subtle, that it is not possible that he could know them . . .'). (present author's trans.). (Sancho Panza is the simple, but relentlessly common-sensible, peasant who accompanies the Don.)

— **New lyre.** 'For behold, Zarathustra, new lyres are needed for your new songs.' F. Nietzsche, *Thus spoke Zarathustra*, III.2. (tr., W. Kaufmann).

— **Inherent potentiality / ideal possibility.** Iconic phrases used by the Firm to express their optimistic view of human nature and the human world. See I *passim*.

— **Art of the possible.** Otto von Bismarck (1815-98), German statesman, said that *die Politik ist die Lehre vom Möglichen* ('politics is the theory of the possible') in a conversation (1867) with F. Mayer von Waldeck. The saying was used as the title of a memoir by the British politician R.A.Butler (1902-82) who, after leaving politics, served as Master of Trinity College, Cambridge (1965-78).

— **Shared dream.** 'All poetry we ever read / Is but true dreams interpreted.' (Hans Sachs, in *Die Meistersinger von Nürnberg*, text and music by R. Wagner (see ch. 7 below, under '*Wahn!*').

For C.G. Jung (1875-1961), Swiss psychiatrist, the fact that the dreams of different people exhibit common forms and common substantive content suggests that the unconscious layer of the mind, in which dreams originate, contains forms and content shared by human beings in general.

Or else we might say that shared dreams suggest that human beings share the mental process known as imagination. Shared imagination makes art possible, including the art of fiction.

CHAPTER 3. *Venice II.*

— **Cipriani.** A hotel on La Giudecca, one of the Venetian islands.
— **Paestum. Segesta. Selinunte. Syracuse.** Paestum in southern Italy is the site of an ancient Greek city (Poseidonia) which was taken over by the Romans in 273BCE and re-named Paestum. It contains the remains of 6th—and 5th—century Doric temples of exceptional beauty. Segesta, in Sicily, has the remains of an unfinished 5th-century temple and a theatre—magnificent buildings standing in splendid poetic isolation among high green hills. They are all that remains of a city which had the misfortune to be destroyed successively by Carthaginians, Romans, Vandals, and Saracens. In Selinunte and Syracuse (Siracusa, in Italian), also in Sicily, are other wonderful remains of Greek public buildings. Archimedes was born in Syracuse, and Plato went there twice to inspect the reality of a state, ruled by his friend Dionysius II, which was very different from Plato's visionary republic.
— **Noble wreck.** In Act III of *Manfred*, a verse-drama by Byron (I.15), Manfred (having lived in isolation in expiation of an unidentified crime or sin, and now about to die) recalls a visit to the ruined remains of Imperial Rome, including the Colosseum (where gladiatorial combat took place): '. . . amidst / A grove which springs through levell'd battlements, / And twines its roots with the imperial hearths, / Ivy usurps the laurel's place of growth; / But the gladiators' bloody Circus stands, /A noble wreck in ruinous perfection! / While Caesar's chambers, and the Augustan halls, /Grovel on earth in indistinct decay.'
— **Daughter of Jerusalem.** An echo of passages in the (Jewish/Christian) biblical *Book of Psalms* and in the (Christian) New Testament. In the former, the Jews in exile in Babylon think about Jerusalem: 'By the rivers of Babylon, there we sat down, yea, we wept, when we remembered Zion.' (Psalm 137). The 'daughters of Jerusalem' are addressed in the Song of Solomon (ch. 8). In the New Testament (*Luke*, ch.23), Jesus Christ, on the way to his execution, spoke to women in the crowd: 'Daughters

of Jerusalem, weep not for me, but weep for yourselves, and for your children. For, behold, the days are coming, in the which they shall say, Blessed are the barren, and the wombs that never bare, and the paps which never gave suck.' (King James Bible, 1611). This is presumably, among other things, a prophecy of the destruction of Jerusalem by the Romans in the year 70, leading to many other forms of exile for the Jewish people.

— *Eheu fugaces*. From an ode (addressed to Postumus) by Horace (I.4). *Eheu fugaces, Postume, Postume, / labuntur anni nec pietas moram / rugis et instanti senectae / adferet indomitaeque morti* . . . 'Ah! Postumus, Postumus, fast fly the years, / And prayers to wrinkles and impending age / Bring not delay; nor shalt assuage / Death's stroke with pious tears.' (tr., J. Marshall). In Latin, *eheu* (like *ei*) is an interjection expressing pain or grief (*eheu me miserum*: 'woe is me!'), unlike *eia* which is an interjection expressing surprise or joy.

— *O tempora, O mores*. From Cicero's First Speech against Catiline (8 November 63 BCE). *O tempora, o mores! Senatus haec intellegit. consul videt; hic tamen vivit. Vivit? immo vero in senatum venit* . . . 'What an age we live in! The Senate knows it all, the consul sees it, and yet—this man is still alive. Alive did I say? Not only is he alive, but he attends the Senate . . .' (tr., C. Macdonald). Lucius Segius Catilina (usually referred to as Catiline in English) agitated, conspired, and eventually led an armed uprising against the Roman Republic. Cicero had been elected consul (the highest office in the Republic) in the election of 63. Catiline (c.108-62BCE) was from an old patrician family. Cicero was by comparison a *novus homo* (a 'new' man). (Catiline spoke next after Cicero in the Senate, referring in passing to Cicero's *novitas*.)

And, typically, it was the 'new man' who expressed a sentiment—What is the world coming to? Is this the end of civilisation as we have known it?—which has figured again and again in European public discourse from ancient Greece to the present day. The Greek poet Hesiod (8th century BCE) had already charted human decline from a Golden Age to the contemporary Iron Age.

Such rhetoric has been matched by equal and opposite predictions of a 'new age'. 'Now is come the last age of the song of Cumae; the great line of the centuries begins anew . . . ; now a new generation descends form heaven on high. Only do thou, pure Lucina, smile on the birth of the child, under whom the iron brood shall first cease, and a golden race spring up throughout the world!' Virgil, *Eclogues* IV. (tr., H. Fairclough). (The Cumaean Sybil had prophesied a new age following the Age of Iron.) The poem is celebrating the arrival of Augustus as master of the Roman republic/empire (see below, under '*fuit Ilium*').

Early Christians understood Virgil's reference to a child as prophesying the coming of Christ. There is another, less mystical explanation of the reference to Lucina's child.

— *Fuit Ilium*. In Latin, 'Troy was [is no more]'. From Virgil, *Aeneid* (I.13), Bk. II. *vix ea fatus eram gemitu cum talia reddit: / venit summa dies et ineluctabile tempus / Dardaniae. fuimus Troes, fuit Ilium et ingens / gloria Teucrorum; ferus omnia Iuppiter*

Argos / transtulit; incensa Danai dominantur in urbe. 'Scarcely had I said these words, when with a groan he answers thus: "It is come—the last day and inevitable hour of Troy. We Trojans are not, Ilium is not, and the great glory of the Teucrians [Trojans]; in wrath Jupiter has taken all away to Argos; our city is aflame, and in it the Greeks are lords.' (tr., H. Fairclough). Aeneas, in telling the story of the taking of Troy and the destruction of Trojan civilisation by the Greeks, here recounts the answer of Panthus to his question: 'How fares the state?'

According to the legend, Aeneas escapes to Italy and helps to found the kingdom (Latium) from which his descendant Romulus will found the city (and future republic and empire) of Rome. Virgil even suggests that Aeneas was the ancestor of the Julian family which would produce Julius Caesar and Augustus (63BCE-14CE), the first Roman Emperor and Virgil's contemporary and, to some extent, patron.

— **Und so weiter**. In German, 'and so forth'.
— **Liquefying of the brain**. *Qu'est-ce qui me fait pleurer ainsi? . . . Il n'y a rien ici qui puisse attrister. C'est peut-être de la cervelle liquefiée.* ('What is it that makes me weep like this? . . . There is nothing here that could make me sad. Perhaps it's liquefied brain.') S. Beckett, *L'Innomable* (The Unnamable) (1953). Edmund may also have in mind an image from *The Grey Monk*, a poem by W. Blake. 'For a Tear is an intellectual thing, / And a Sigh is the sword of an Angel King, / And the bitter groan of the Martyr's woe / Is an arrow from the Almighty's bow.'
— **Edward Gibbon moment**. 'It was at Rome, on the 15th of October 1764, as I sat musing amidst the ruins of the Capitol, while the bare-footed friars were singing vespers in the Temple of Jupiter, that the idea of writing the decline and fall of the city first started to my mind.' E. Gibbon (I.19), *Memoirs of My Life and Writings* (Gibbon's intended title for a book published posthumously (1796) as his *Autobiography*). (It is now generally supposed that his rather precise recollection of the event is more symbolically than factually true.)

In Chapter 38 of his *Decline and Fall of the Roman Empire*, Gibbon ponders anxiously the question of whether Western European civilisation might suffer the same fate as the Roman Empire. He reaches a tentatively optimistic conclusion, largely based on the fact that European civilisation has made so much progress in so many fields. 'We may therefore acquiesce in the pleasing conclusion that every age of the world has increased and still increases the real wealth, the happiness, the knowledge, and perhaps the virtue, of the human race.' More than two centuries later, we may feel even less certain of such optimism.

Gibbon himself also utters a warning. 'Yet this apparent security should not tempt us to forget that new enemies and unknown dangers may *possibly* arise from some obscure people, scarcely visible in the map of the world.'
— **Mind-empire.** See ch. 2 above, under 'empires of the mind'.
— **Ruinous perfection.** See above, under 'noble wreck'.
— **Lacrimae rerum.** In Latin, 'tears of things'. *Sunt hic etiam sua praemia laudi, /sunt [hic etiam] lacrimae rerum et mentem mortalia tangunt.* Virgil, *Aeneid*, bk. I, lines

461-2. 'Here, too, virtue has its due rewards; here, too, there are tears for misfortune and mortal sorrows touch the heart.' Aeneas, on his journey of exile from Troy, is contemplating the thriving city of Carthage, minutes before his fateful meeting with Queen Dido (I.13). *Restitit Aeneas claraque in luce refulsit,/os umerosque deo similis; namque ipsa decoram / caesariem nato genetrix lumenque iunventae/ purpureum et laetos oculis adflarat honores; / quale manus addunt ebori decus, aut ubi flavo/argentum Pariusve lapis circumdatur auro.* 'Aeneas stood forth, gleaming in the clear light, godlike in face and shoulders; for his mother herself had shed upon her son the beauty of flowing locks, with youth's ruddy bloom, and on his eyes a joyous lustre; even as the beauty which the hand gives to ivory, or when silver or Parian marble is set in yellow gold.' (lines 588-94) (tr., H. Fairclough). Rather unnecessarily, the goddess Juno uses Cupid to enflame Dido with love of Aeneas, but first the Queen asks Aeneas to tell the story of the fall of Troy, which he proceeds to do, at length, in Book II of Virgil's epic poem.

— ***Wo ist Athen?*** In German, 'where is Athens?' From a poem *Der Archipelagus* (The Archipelago) by F. Hölderlin (I.8). *Sage, wo ist Athen? ist über den Urnen der Meister / Deine Stadt, die geliebteste dir, an den heiligen Ufern, / Trauernder Gott! Dir ganz in Asche zusammengesunken, / Oder ist noch ein Zeichen von ihr, dass etwa der Schiffer, / Wenn er vorüberkommt, sie nenn' und inrer gedanke?* 'Tell me, where now is Athens? Over the urns of the masters / Here, on your shores, on the holy, sorrowing god, has your city / Dearest of all to you perished, utterly crumbled to ashes, / Or does a token, a trace remain, just so much that a sailor / Passing by will mention her name, will notice the site and recall her?' (tr., M. Hamburger).

— ***Entflohene Götter.*** In German, 'gods that have fled'. From another poem by Hölderlin, *Germanien* (Germania). *Entflohene Götter! Auch ihr, ihr gegenwärtigen, damals /Wahrhaftiger, ihr hattet eure Zeiten!* ('Gods who are fled! And you also, present still, / But once more real, you had your time, your ages!') (tr., M. Hamburger).

— **God made Man. Man made God.** An ironical reference to the central Trinitarian doctrine of Christianity—the incarnation of God in the person of Jesus Christ and, hence, Christ as one of the three 'persons' of God. Dissenting forms of Christianity have denied the divine nature of Christ (especially Arianism and Unitarianism). The doctrine does not mean that, by taking on the form of a human being, God became merely Man, still less that Man became God.

— **Argument from despair.** An ironical reference to one of the traditional arguments seeking to offer a rational *proof* of the existence of God. The 'argument from design' suggests that the orderly and ingenious design of the created universe shows the necessity and the nature of its creator.

— **The higher they flew.** A reference to a story in ancient Greek mythology. Daedalus made wings to enable him and his son Icarus to fly across the Aegean from Crete. Icarus flew too high and fell to his death, the sun having melted the wax holding his wings. Daedalus is seen as a mythical progenitor of technology (and, perhaps, of its ambiguities), having supposedly created the Cretan labyrinth and invented tools such as the saw and the axe.

— **Ascent of man.** In *The Ascent of Man* (*Lowell Lectures*) (1894), H. Drummond argues that Darwinism contains a 'great error' in its failure to recognise the question of how the human species became 'human', a problem that far exceeds in complexity and importance the 'history' of how the human animal evolved from other living species. In *The Descent of Man* (1871/1888), Darwin had said—'In what manner the mental powers were first developed in the lowest organisms, is as hopeless an inquiry as how life itself first originated.' On Drummond's views, see further in ch. 5 below, under 'mother-figure'.

The Ascent of Man is also the title of a television series and a book (1973) by J. Bronowski (1908-74), exploring human progress from the earliest times to the present, especially in the fields of mathematics, science and technology.

— **Stairway to Paradise.** In the (Jewish/Christian) biblical book of *Genesis* (ch. 28), Jacob (son of Isaac who was the son of Abraham) had a dream in which he saw a ladder leading up to heaven on which angels were ascending and descending. In *Paradise Lost* by John Milton (I.20), Satan, the angel who somewhat mysteriously rebelled against God, does a great deal of travelling between heaven and earth and hell.

— **Lucifer.** In Latin, 'bearer of light'. Popularly, if mistakenly, used as another name for Satan (the devil).

— **Substantial but passing.** An echo, perhaps of a poem, *Contention of Ajax and Ulysses*, by the English poet James Shirley (1596-1666): 'The glories of our blood and state / Are shadows, not substantial things; / There is no armour against fate, / Death lays his icy hand on kings.'

— **Yea-saying. Nay-saying.** *Ja sagen/nein sagen*, in German. These phrases occur throughout Nietzsche's work, but not in an entirely consistent way. The central idea—which was one of Nietzsche leading themes—is that the time has come to say 'no' to almost every aspect of the existing human world—religious, moral, social, political, personal. And the time has come to stop saying a feeble, unthinking, conniving 'yes' to the evil and nonsense that passes for normal and reasonable reality. See I.19 and 'Epigraphs' above; below, under 'poor Nietzsche'.

The tiresome 'yea' and 'nay' in some English translations of his works are attributable to the wish to make his texts (especially *Thus Spoke Zarasthustra*) sound ancient and prophetic. They are also due to the obscure fact that Nietzsche uses the ass as a symbol of the mindless yes-sayer and, in German, the noise made by an ass is represented by *J-ai*, which sounds somewhat like 'yea' in English.

— **Pendulum between the smile and the tear.** From Canto IV of *Childe Harold's Pilgrimage* by Byron (I.15), in which Byron is in Rome—

'Oh Rome! My country! City of the soul! / The orphans of the heart must turn to thee, / Lone mother of dead empires.' (LXXVIII).

'Admire, exult—despise—laugh, weep,—for here / There is such matter for all feeling:—Man! / Thou pendulum betwixt a smile and tear . . . !' (CIX).

An echo also, perhaps, of *Joy*, a poem by W. Blake (see above).

'Man was made for Joy & Woe; / And when this we rightly know / Thro' the World we safely go. / Joy & Woe are woven fine, / A Clothing for the Soul divine; / Under every grief & pine / Runs a joy with silken twine.'

However, the relentless pessimist A. Schopenhauer (see ch. 4 below, under 'will to power') insists again and again that we must face a simple fact:

[Das Leben] schwingt also, gleich einem Pendel, hin und her zwischen dem Schmerz und der Langeweile. ('And so [human life] swings, like a pendulum, to and fro between pain and boredom.') *The World as Will and Idea*, §57.

— **Marina di Ravenna**. A seaside resort, some twelve kilometres from Ravenna.
— **Pineta di Classe**. A forest of pine-trees set in sand dunes, admired by Dante and Byron.

'Sweet hour of twilight!—in the solitude / Of the pine forest, and the silent shore / Which bounds Ravenna's immemorial wood, / Rooted where once the Adrian wave flowed o'er, / To where the last Caesarean fortress stood, / Evergreen forest! Which Boccaccio's lore / And Dryden's lay made haunted ground to me, / How have I loved the twilight hour and thee!' Byron, *Don Juan*.

Dante refers to it in Canto XXVIII of *The Divine Comedy: Purgatory*. *Tal qual di ramo in ramo si raccoglie / per la pineta in su 'l lito di Chiassi*. '. . . as gathers from branch to branch in the pine wood on the Chiassi [Classe] shore.' (tr., J. Sinclair).

— **Ravenna**. City in north-west Italy with a chequered history characteristic of European history in general. Founded by the Greeks, taken by the Romans, made the capital of the Western Roman Empire when the Visigoths attacked Rome, scene of the end of the Western Empire when the Goths and then the Ostrogoths disposed of the last Emperor (476), taken (510) into the Eastern Roman Empire (Byzantium) under Emperor Justinian, taken by the Lombards (752), given to the Papacy by a French king, taken over by Venice, returned to the Papacy (1509), taken by Napoleon, restored to the Papal States, integrated into the new kingdom of Italy 1870, resisted Mussolini, much damaged in the Second World War. The Italian poet Dante (1265-1321) died in Ravenna (in exile from Florence). His tomb is an 18th-century reconstruction of a 15th-century work by the sculptor Pietro Lombardo. The town contains fine buildings and artworks, especially from the Byzantine period.

— **Hellenic and Hebraic.** In *Culture and Anarchy* (1869), Matthew Arnold (I.19) suggested that European culture had been produced by an interaction between two forces—the Hebraic (from ancient Israel) and the Hellenic (from ancient Greece). The resultant of the two forces has changed constantly.

'And these two forces we may regard as in some sense rivals,—rivals not by the necessity of their own nature, but as exhibited in man and his history—and rivals dividing the empire of the world between them ... The final aim of both Hellenism and Hebraism, as of all great spiritual disciplines, is no doubt the same: man's perfection or salvation.' (This and following extracts are from ch. IV.)

'At the bottom of both the Greek and the Hebrew notion is the desire, native in man, for reason and the will of God, the feeling after the universal order,—in a word, the love of God. But, while Hebraism seizes upon certain plain, capital intimations of the universal order, and rivets itself, one may say, with unequalled grandeur of earnestness and intensity on the study and observance of them, the bent of Hellenism is to follow, with flexible activity, the whole play of the universal order, to be apprehensive of missing any part of it, of sacrificing one part for another, to slip away form resting on this or that intimation of it, however capital. An unclouded clearness of mind, an unimpeded play of thought, is what this bent drives at. The governing idea of Hellenism is *spontaneity of consciousness*; that of Hebraism, *strictness of conscience*.'

'As Hellenism speaks of thinking clearly, seeing things in their essence and beauty, as a grand and precious feat for man to achieve, so Hebraism speaks of becoming conscious of sin, of awakening to a sense of sin, as a feat of this kind.'

'No one, however, can study the development of Protestantism and of Protestant churches without feeling that into the Reformation too,—Hebraising child of the Renascence and offspring of its fervour, rather than its intelligence, as it undoubtedly was,—the subtle Hellenic leaven of the Renascence found its way, and that the exact respective parts in the Reformation of Hebraism and of Hellenism, are not easy to separate.'

In *On the Genealogy of Morals* (1887), F. Nietzsche (above) took a similar schematic view, contrasting the Hellenic-Roman and the Jewish strains in European civilisation.

'For thousands of years, a fearful struggle has raged on earth ... The symbol for this struggle, written in a script which has remained legible throughout the whole of human history up until now, is called "Rome against Judaea, Judaea against Rome" ... Which is in the ascendant at the moment, Rome or Judaea? . . . there is no doubt that Rome has been defeated. Admittedly, during the Renaissance there was a simultaneously glittering and sinister re-awakening of the classical ideal, of the noble mode of evaluation, beneath the weight of the new Judaicized Rome, which assumed the appearance of an ecumenical synagogue and called itself "the Church", the old Rome itself moved like someone re-awakened from apparent death: but Judaea triumphed again immediately, thanks to a fundamentally plebeian (German and English) movement of *ressentiment* [in Nietzsche's vocabulary, bitter and envious resentment], known as the Reformation . . . In an even more decisive and profound sense than previously, Judaea triumphed once more over the classical ideal with the French Revolution.' (extracts from the *First Essay*; tr., D. Smith).

Discounting the provocative language (somewhat expurgated by the present author in the above extracts), Nietzsche, like Arnold, is raising fundamental questions about the nature of European civilisation, questions that are relevant to any consideration of its present and future states.

— **Dante's tomb**. 'I have seen Dante's tomb, and worshipped the sacred spot.' P.B. Shelley (1792-1822), English Romantic poet, letter (15 August 1821) from Ravenna to his wife Mary Wollstonecraft Shelley, who was the daughter of Mary Wollstonecraft and William Godwin (see Appendix 6 below) and who was the author of the novel *Frankenstein*.

— **Russian doll**. A collection of wooden dolls of decreasing size, set one inside another. A characteristic Russian craft-product. Because they are often decorated with the image of a stout female figure, they are called in Russian *matryoshka* (big mother) dolls.

— *Pensione*. In Italian, 'small hotel'.

— *Zattere*. Le Zattere ('the lighters', in Italian). A waterfront quay in Venice which takes its name from its original function as a place for unloading cargo-boats.

— *Schwarzweiss*. In German, 'black and white'.

— *Unsere heilige Mutter.* 'Our Holy Mother the Church'. A symbolic expression used to refer to the Church by members of the (Roman) Catholic Church.

— *Debita nostra.* In Latin, 'our debts'. The Lord's Prayer (*pater noster;* Our Father) is considered by Christians to have been instituted by Jesus Christ himself. One of its pleas is: 'Forgive us our trespasses, as we forgive those who trespass against us'—in Latin, *dimitte nobis debita nostra, sicut et nos dimittimus debitoribus nostris. Debita nostra* is generally understood as referring to sins, and is so translated in some English-language versions. The word *debita* is translated as 'trespasses' in the Anglican Book of Common Prayer of 1662 (see Appendix 2 below), and in the version of the prayer commonly said by English-speaking Roman Catholics. 'Confession' is a sacramental practice in the Catholic Church in which the faithful confess their sins to a priest. It is also a confession of faith in the possibility of forgiveness.

— **Gesuati.** Church designed by G. Massari (1736), located on the Zattere (see above), in a style which might be described as post-Palladian-baroque—that is, in the manner of A. Palladio (1508-80), but with greater elements of freedom and fantasy. The French historian and art critic, Hippolyte Taine (1828-1893), in *À Venise—Voyage en Italie III* (1866), was not impressed by the church . . . . *un luxe froid, un étalage de mignardises coûteuses. Le dix-huitième siècle italien est encore pire que le nôtre. Nos oeuvres gardent quelque finesse; pour eux, ils s'assoient triomphalement dans l'extravagance.* ('A cold luxury, a display of costly affectations. The Italian eighteenth century was even worse than ours. Our works retain a certain delicacy; theirs share in a triumphant extravagance.') (present author's translation).

As regards Venice as a whole, Taine was enthusiastic. *C'est la perle d'Italie; je n'ai rien vu d'égal; je ne sais qu'une ville qui en approche, de bien loin, et seulement pour les architectures: c'est Oxford.* ('It is the pearl of Italy; I have seen nothing that equals it; I know of only one city that approaches it, but far behind, and only for the architecture: that is Oxford.')

— **Baroque.** A style of European art, especially in the seventeenth century. It is a characteristic of the history of European art (and, it may be, of other artistic cultures with a long history) that there is a permanent dialectical tension between tradition and the challenging of tradition. In Europe it has meant that all the arts—including the visual arts and architecture, literature and music—are in a constant state of change and self re-imagining. The dialectic of art is an intensely fruitful phenomenon.

Baroque art challenged the classicism of the Renaissance, itself a re-imagining of medieval art under the inspiration of models form Greece and Rome. The baroque represents the side of the dialectic in which a sense of artistic freedom challenges the sense of order, the power of the imagination challenges the rule of reason, the restless dynamic of real life challenges the static presence of any work of art. As in so-called 'Romantic' art of the early 19th century, *feeling* contaminated the act of *narrating*. As in so-called 'modernist' art of the 20th century, *image* began to be as significant as *idea*.

The baroque seemed to grow out of the spirit of the Counter-Reformation of the late-16th century, when the Roman Church, among many other things, rediscovered its vigorous and sensual aspect, in opposition to the coldness of the extremer forms of Protestantism.

The highest art—archaic Greek sculpture (before the 5th century BCE), Homer, Dante, Shakespeare, Mozart, Turner, Dostoevsky—seems to contain and overcome the dialectical tensions of art. It reveals the highest ideal of art—to create something that is universal and utterly particular, perfect so far as the given medium allows—something whose essence contains the all-too-human existence of the artist, and which becomes part of the essence and the existence of the all-too-human spectator. The highest art makes human strangeness beautiful. On the nature of art, see further below, chs.15 and 19, and *passim*.

'There is no excellent beauty, that hath not some strangeness in the proportion.' F. Bacon (see Appendix 1 below), essay *On Beauty.*

— **Banyan.** A tree sacred to the Hindu religion.

— **Bodhi.** A tree on the bank of the Nairanjana river, under which, according to a Buddhist tradition, Siddharta Gautama (6th century BCE) sat in meditation, leading to his enlightenment as Buddha, following years of ascetic living. Also according to a tradition, he was born at Lumbini, close to the city of Kapilavastu where his father was the leading citizen. Lumbini and Kapilavastu in Nepal are places of pilgrimage for the Buddhist faithful.

— **Eremitic temptation.** Hermits who seek to lead a life of holiness and mystical intensity by living in total solitude, especially in the desert (in Greek, *eremia* means 'desert', 'wilderness', 'solitude').

— **Monsignore.** Italian title of respect, especially accorded to the holder of a senior office in the Roman Catholic Church ('monsignor', in English).

— **God that is dead.** Gabi no doubt has in mind: 'Better to worship God in this shape [as an ass] than in no shape at all.' F. Nietzsche, *Thus Spoke Zarathustra*, Pt. Four ('the pope [of the Ass Festival]' speaking).

In this and his many other references to the matter, Nietzsche (see under 'poor Nietzsche' below) was expressing in crude terms what was the focus of extreme existential anxiety for all sensitive thinking people in the 19th century. How could humanity exist and survive without the stimulus and the control of religion? The anxiety drove many such people to the edge of madness.

In England, the novelist George Eliot (Mary Ann Evans) (1819-80) set an example of a cooler approach to the problem. She translated from German into English two of the books that had contributed greatly to the crisis of growing unbelief—David Strauss, *Das Leben Jesu* (*The Life of Jesus*; 1835), which re-classifies the trickier parts of the New Testament as 'myth'; and Ludwig Feuerbach, *Das Wesen des Christentums* (*The Essence of Christianity*; 1841), which treats the life and teaching of Christ as symbolic representations of humanity's longing for transcendence and perfection; but a falsely transcendent idea of God alienates the human mind from the God-idea as human potentiality.

However, Eliot was also representative of her class and generation in retaining a nostalgia for the ideal and the absolute. There is an account, possibly somewhat improved in the telling, of a revealing incident.

'I remember how, at Cambridge [in about 1868?], I walked with her once in the Fellows' Garden of Trinity, on an evening of rainy May; and she, stirred somewhat beyond her wont, and taking as her text the three words which have been used so often as the inspiring trumpet-calls of men—the words God, Immortality, Duty—[she] pronounced, with terrible earnestness, how inconceivable was the first, how unbelievable the second, and yet how peremptory and absolute the third. Never perhaps, have sterner accents affirmed the sovereignty of impersonal and unrecompensing Law. I listened, and night fell; her grave, majestic countenance turned toward me like a sibyl's in the gloom; it was as though she withdrew from my grasp, one by one, the two scrolls of promise, and left me the third scroll only, awful with inevitable fates.' (Recalled by F.H. Myers, a Fellow of the College, writing in 1881.)

The German writer Jean Paul (pen-name of Jean Paul Friedrich Richter; 1763-1825) uses a particularly powerful image: of Christ himself searching the universe for God, and finding only an empty heaven. *Und alle riefen: "Jesus! Haben wir keinen Vater?" Und er antwortete mit stromenden Tränen: "Wir sind all Waisen, ich und ihr, wir sind ohne Vater".'* ('And everyone shouted: "Jesus! Have we no father?" And he answered with streaming tears: "We are all orphans, I and you, we have no father".') (present author's translation).

— **When godliness if flouted.** 'The gods take notice, in their own good time, / But without fail, when godliness is flouted / And men go mad.' Sophocles, *Oedipus at Colonus*. (Oedipus is speaking to Theseus, king of Athens, shortly before Oedipus is mysteriously taken away by the gods.) (tr., E.F. Watling).

— **Poor Nietzsche.** Whether they know it or not, the ghost of Friedrich Nietzsche (1844-1900) haunts the minds of the people whose earnest conversations are recorded in the present volume. His was the prophetic and tragic voice of the 19th century's spiritual anguish and the 20th century's spiritual exhaustion. His father and both of his grandfathers were Lutheran pastors. He himself was nicknamed 'the little pastor' at the age of twelve. He lost his religious faith, and the whole of his life thereafter—until his mental breakdown in 1889—was devoted to the project of re-imagining what a human might be—or, rather, might become—in a post-religious world. His life was characterised by extreme personal isolation, deep pessimism, and an extreme sense of failure—but also by an ineradicable belief in a better human potentiality. His barely readable writings are concerned with problems which seem, to those who have experienced the 20th century, more troubling than ever—a century in which all previous attempts at intellectual redemption—renaissance, reformation, enlightenment, positivism—withered away as realistic possibilities of a new form of redemption.

— *Ex hypothesi.* In Latin, 'in accordance with the hypothesis'.

— **Hypothetical God.** There have been many attempts to construct rational forms of religion in which God is a reasonable hypothesis. John Locke (see Appendix 4 below) suggested that reason could lead us to the idea of God, but such an idea is not sufficient without the further truths taught by 'revelation', including the special revelation coming from the life and teaching of Jesus Christ. (*Reasonableness of Christianity*, 1695).

Deists jettisoned the second part of Locke's view. Reason itself could supply an idea of God fully sufficient to serve as a guide for the living of a good life. Needless to say, there have been countless others (not least David Hume; see Appendix 4 below) who see religion as meeting obvious psychological and social needs, and capable of being 'rationalised' to serve those purposes, but with no possible claim to be itself a necessary product of reason. On deism, see further in ch. 12 below, under 'theism/deism'

— **From the gorilla to the death of God.** Greg is no doubt thinking of a (Nietzschean) passage in Part I, ch.3, of *The Possessed* (1873) (also translated into English as *The Devils*), a novel by the Russian writer F. Dostoevsky (1821-81). The following extracts are from C. Garnett's translation. The narrator is talking to Shatov.

'Man fears death because he loves life. That's how I understand it,' I observed, 'and that's determined by nature.'

'That's abject; and that's where the deception comes in.' His eyes flashed. 'Life is pain, life is terror, and man is unhappy. Now all is pain and terror. Now man loves life, because he loves pain and terror, and so they have done according. Life is given now for pain and terror, and that's the deception. Now man is not yet what he will be. There will be a new man, happy and proud. For whom it will be the same to live or not to live, he will be the new man. He who will conquer pain and terror will himself be a god. And this God will not be.'

'Then this God does exist according to you?'

'He does not exist, but He is. In the stone there is no pain, but in the fear of the stone is the pain. God is the pain of the fear of death. He who will conquer pain and terror will become himself a god. Then there will be a new life, a new man; everything will be new . . . then they will divide history into two parts: from the gorilla to the annihilation of God, and from the annihilation of God to . . .'

'To the gorilla?'

'. . . To the transformation of the earth, and of man physically. Man will be God, and will be transformed physically, and the world will be transformed and things will be transformed and thoughts and all feelings.'

Shatov is a characteristic young Russian of his time—torn between patriotism, revolution and religion—possibly a self-portrait of the author. In a conversation (Pt. II, ch. 1) with (the even more peculiar) Stavrogin, he says—

'To cook your hare you must first catch it, to believe in God you must first have a god . . . .'

'I only wanted to know, do you believe in God, yourself?'

'I believe in Russia . . . . I believe in her orthodoxy . . . . I believe in the body of Christ . . . . I believe that the new advent will take place in Russia . . . . I believe . . .' Shatov muttered frantically.

'And in God? In God?'

'I . . . I will believe in God.'

Nietzsche, in a letter (23 February 1887): 'I did not know the name of Dostoevsky just a few weeks ago—uneducated person that I am . . . The instinct of kinship (or how should I name it?) spoke up immediately; my joy was extraordinary.' (ed. and tr., W. Kaufmann).

— **Man the God. Man the beast.** (1) Although Aristotle says that 'man is by nature a political [social] animal', he also says: 'But he who is unable to live in society, or who has no need because he is sufficient for himself, must be either a beast or a god: he is no part of a state.' *Politics*, I.2. (tr., B. Jowett).

(2) 'And rest assured that it is only your body that is mortal; your true self is nothing of the kind. For the man you outwardly appear to be is not yourself at all. Your real self is not that corporeal, palpable shape, but the spirit inside. *Understand that you are god.* You have a god's capacity of aliveness and sensation and memory and foresight; a god's power to rule and govern and direct the body that is your servant, in the same way as God himself, who reigns over us, directs the entire universe. And this rule exercised by eternal God is mirrored in the dominance of your frail body by your immortal soul.' Cicero, *Scipio's Dream*—a meditation on the after-life; it is all that has survived of his book *On the State*. (ed. and tr., M. Grant).

(3) *Simia quam similes, turpissima bestia, nobis quam similes.* ('How like the monkey we are; filthiest of beasts, how like us.') Cicero, *De natura deorum* (On the Nature of the Gods), I.35.

(4) 'Man like an angry ape plays such fantastic tricks as make the angels weep.' W. Shakespeare, *Measure for Measure*, II. ii.

(5) 'For certainly man is sicker, less secure, less stable, less firmly anchored than any other animal; he is the sick animal.' F. Nietzsche, *The Genealogy of Morals*, Third Essay, XIII. 'Once you were apes, and even now man is more ape than any ape.' (*Zarathustra*, First Part, prologue).

(6) 'He who understands baboon would do more towards metaphysics than Locke.' C. Darwin, *Notebook M* (1838).

— **Egomania.** 'When the god is not acknowledged, egomania develops, and out of this mania comes sickness.' C.J. Jung (I.20), Commentary on *The Secret of the Golden Flower*. Jung's commentary is directed to R. Wilhelm's translation into German (1931) of this Chinese book on techniques of meditation.

— **If God does not exist.** 'If there is no God, then I am God . . . If God exists, all is His will and from His will I cannot escape. If not, it's all my will and I am bound to show self-will.' F. Dostoevsky, *The Possessed* (see above), Pt. III, ch 6 (Kirillov speaking, shortly before his suicide).

— **Nothing is true, all is permitted.** '"Nothing is true, everything is permitted": thus I told myself . . . Alas, where is that mendacious innocence that I once possessed, the innocence of the good and their noble lies!' F. Nietzsche, *Thus Spoke Zarathustra*, Part 4. (tr., R. Hollingdale). (Zarathustra's shadow speaking).

— **Voltaire and religion.** The attitude of Voltaire (I.15, I.21) to religion is an insoluble puzzle. Certainly he was bitterly opposed to superstitious and fanatical religion—*écraser l'infâme* ('crush the infamous thing') was his war cry (mainly referring to the Roman Catholic Church).

However, it is equally clear that he was neither a fully committed atheist nor a fully committed deist nor a believing theist (that is, one who believes in a personal god who takes an interest in human affairs). 'God cannot be proved, nor denied, by the mere force of our reason.'—he wrote, in English, in one of his early *Notebooks*.

Over the doorway of a chapel that he built in the garden of his house at Ferney he placed a witty inscription—*Deo erexit Voltaire* ('Voltaire erected this for God')—echoing, perhaps, Rousseau's complaint: 'How many men between God and me!'.

It also seems inappropriate to call him an agnostic, to the extent that that word suggests indifference, or even contempt, in relation to a religious response to ultimate questions of human existence. Beneath a surface of cynicism and wit, he was a rather passionate and sensitive person. He could see the role that religion played in human life—for better and, usually, for worse.

His case is reminiscent of that of Sigmund Freud for whom religion is an infantile illusion and delusion, but who seems also to see it as a special defensive neurosis by which people seek to save themselves from a more general form of neurosis. It is as if both Voltaire and Freud (and Rousseau) would have liked religion to be a believable thing for rational people, but they were unable to satisfy themselves that it ever could be.

— **Lutheranism.** A form of Christianity originating in a movement led by Martin Luther (from 1519) to rescue Christianity from the hegemony of the Church of Rome, and from what Luther (among many others, including many of the Roman Catholic faithful) saw as the social, moral and intellectual corruption of the Church. The demand for reform had been heard for centuries (see Appendix 2 below). What came to be called Protestantism thereafter took very many forms, of which Lutheranism was one, especially in northern Continental Europe.

— **Denying divinely the divine.** From *A Vision of Poets* (1843) by the English poet Elizabeth Barrett Browning (1806-61).

> 'Lucretius, nobler than his mood, / Who dropped his plummet down the broad / Deep universe and said "no God" / Finding no bottom, he denied / Divinely the divine . . .'

The poem, of more than six hundred lines, surveys the higher peaks of the history of poetry. Browning said that the purpose of the poem is to show 'the necessary relations of genius to suffering and self-sacrifice'. On Lucretius, see below under '*dia voluptas*'.

— **Projection.** An idea used in the Freudian philosophy of mind. It refers to a form of thinking which transfers (*projicere*, 'to throw', in Latin) troubling ideas and feelings onto some external object or person. The idea has seemed to be particularly relevant to ideas about God, which may easily be interpreted as the projection of ideas about

human beings and human relationships. Freud saw Judaism as a 'father' religion, and
Christianity as a 'son' religion. The idea is present in many previous philosophers of
mind, including Schopenhauer and Nietzsche. On anthropotheism, see I.20, under
'we invent gods'.

— **Collection of negations.** A perennial and apparently universal form of theological
discourse seeks to suggest the nature of spiritual reality, such as the nature of God,
negatively (the *via negativa*—'the negative way', in Latin)—that is, by identifying
the attributes that such reality does *not* possess.

— **Whirligig of time.** 'And thus the whirligig of time brings in his revenges.' W.
Shakespeare, *Twelfth Night*, Act V. i. (Clown speaking).

— **Grace.** *Gratia*, in Latin. The name used in Christianity for an idea which is present
in various religions. It refers to a continuing active divine presence in the human
world, assisting human beings to behave in conformity with the demands of a
divinely inspired holy life.

— ***Dia voluptas.*** In *De rerum naturae* (*On the Nature of the Universe*), Lucretius
(c.100 BCE-c. 55) presents an explanation of the phenomena of the natural
universe reflecting the philosophy of Epicurus (see ch. 2 above, under 'Cynic, Stoic,
Epicurean'). The central theme is that natural phenomena are all explicable without
resort to supernatural causes.

> 'In the face of these truths, some people who know nothing of matter
> believe that nature without guidance of the gods could not bring round the
> changing seasons in such perfect conformity to human needs, creating the
> crops and those other blessings mortal are led to enjoy by the guide of life,
> divine pleasure [*dux vitae dia voluptas*], which coaxes them through the arts
> of Venus to reproduce their kind, lest the human race should perish.' (bk.
> II; tr., R. Latham).

In the introductory proem to the poem, Lucretius invokes 'life-giving' Venus,
paradoxically it might seem: 'it is your doing that under the wheeling constellations
of the sky all nature teems with life . . . Through you all living creatures are conceived
and come forth to look upon the sunlight.'

These poetical images might rather be read as referring to the dynamic nature
of the universe in which a universal force of attraction causes change through the
coupling of different causes. (See further ch.4 below, under 'will to know', and ch.17
below, under 'binding force'.)

— ***L'amor che muove il sole.*** In Italian, 'the love that moves the sun'. Echo of the last
lines of the final Canto (XXXIII) of Dante's *Divina Commedia: Paradiso* (I.16 and
above, under 'Dante's tomb').

*All'alta fantasia qui mancò possa;/ma già volgeva il mio disio e 'l velle,/ sì come rota
ch'igualmente è mossa,/l'amor che move il sole e l'altre stelle.* ('Here power failed

the high phantasy [the mind's capacity of representing phenomena]; but now my desire and will, like a wheel that spins with even motion, were revolved by the Love that moves the sun and the other stars.') (tr., J. Sinclair).

T.S. Eliot (I.18) said that Canto XXXIII was 'the highest point that poetry has ever reached or ever can reach.'

Dante's mystical epic journey has taken him through Hell and Purgatory to Heaven—and to a vision of the light that comes directly from God—the *light* being intended as a physical representation of God's *love*. The whole poem is infused with the metaphysical theology of Catholic Christianity, revealing that theology's debt to Plato and Aristotle, as mediated, in particular, through the minds of Bernard of Clairvaux (1090-1153) and Thomas Aquinas (1225-1274).

But the great power of the work, especially for those for whom that theology is of more than academic interest, lies in the ever-present *person* of the poet in every scene of his journey. Even in the presence of this final 'beatific vision' emanating from God (an event which may possibly correspond to some actual mystical experience of Dante himself), the poet's response is modestly human—he admits that he cannot adequately understand or even describe what he is experiencing.

For those who read the poem merely as poetry, Dante's Hell is more interesting than his Paradise, rather as Milton's Satan is more interesting than his God, and his Paradise Lost is more interesting than his Paradise Regained.

— **San Vitale.** The Basilica of San Vitale in Ravenna (see above) dates from the sixth century. It contains fine mosaics from the early sixth century, including a depiction of the Emperor Justinian surrounded by soldiers and courtiers.

— **Justinian.** Roman (Byzantine) Emperor (c.482-565). A member of the *premier grand cru classé* of historical figures (with, say, Moses, Julius Caesar, Jesus Christ, Mohammed, Charlemagne, Napoleon, Bismarck, Lenin, Mao Tse-Tung). (The classification is a judgment in terms of their world-historical effect, and is not necessarily a seal of approval of their respective actual world-historical effects.) Justinian (Flavius Petrus Sabbatius Justinianus) rescued and enhanced Greco-Roman civilization by force of arms, by law and government, and by religious and artistic and intellectual patronage.

— *Città terrene.* In Italian, 'earthly cities'. The echo is of *The City of God* by Augustine (I.19). (*De civitate Dei contra paganos*—to give it its full title—Of the City of God, against the Pagans). The book is, like so many of the greatest products of the human mind, a response to critical real-world events—in this case, the sack of Rome in the year 410 by the Visgoths under Alaric.

Augustine was responding to the claims of non-Christian Romans ('pagans') that the fall of the Roman Empire was due to its Christianising. The acceptance of Christianity in the Roman Empire was normally ascribed to the Emperor Constantine (Edict of Milan on religious freedom, in the year 313). Or was the truth, rather, that the Roman Church sagaciously co-opted the Emperor as an ally in its great struggle with the heresy of Arianism (see above, under 'God made Man')?

Augustine uses the occasion to argue that, beyond all the 'cities of man', ruled by selfishness, lust for power, and material greed, there is a 'city of God' (*città di Dio*) inhabited by those whose faith in God requires from them a different kind of life, including a different kind of social life. On this view, the decadence of Rome prefigures the withering-away of all human institutions rooted in evil.

— **Mighty shadows.** Perhaps another echo of Byron's evocation of Venice in the Fourth Canto of *Childe Harold's Pilgrimage* (see above, under 'pendulum').

> 'But unto us she hath a spell beyond / Her name in story, and her long array / Of mighty shadows, whose dim forms despond / Above the dogeless city's vanish'd sway.'

The last Doge of Venice had abdicated in 1797, when the Great Council surrendered the government of the city to General Bonaparte. Byron was in the city for the first time in 1816.

— **Jackets like a sword.** The echo is of the 'sword of chastity' which figures in medieval romances—above all, in the story of Tristan and Iseult, in the version of Béroul, an Anglo-Norman troubadour of the 12th century.

Tristan is sent to Ireland by Mark, king of Cornwall, to bring Iseult to Cornwall to be the king's bride. Tristan falls in love with Iseult. When the king discovers their betrayal he sentences Tristan to death, and Iseult to live with a hundred lepers. They escape and live in a forest for three years. One day, Mark happens to come across the two sleeping in the forest, with Tristan's drawn sword between them. Mark, rather oddly, takes this to be evidence of their innocence. He replaces Tristan's sword with his own sword—another mysterious fact, full of Freudian and Jungian resonances, and highly characteristic of the dream-like quality of the most powerful works of the human imagination.

The German composer Richard Wagner (1813-83) made an opera out of his own version of part of the story (*Tristan und Isolde*, first performed in Munich in 1865), using it to convey a characteristically high-octane vision of the power of love.

— *Ti xe bella.* From a poem in Venetian dialect—*Sopra l'acqua indormenzada*—by P. Pagello (1807-98), set to music by Reynaldo Hahn. 'Thou art beautiful. Thou art young./ Thou art fresh as a new-born flower./ Though all must bear their shame of tears, / Laugh while you may: come now, make love!' (tr., J. Day).

— *Coi pensieri.* From the same poem—'Do not torment thyself / With melancholy thoughts.'

— *Maestoso ma non troppo.* 'Sadly, but not too much'—an instruction by the composer of music as to the appropriate emotional tone for its performance.

— **We will not die.** Echo of the closing lines of *A Toccata of Galuppi's* by the English poet Robert Browning (1812-89), addressed to the Venetian composer Baldassaro Galuppi (1706-85).

'Butterflies may dread extinction,—you'll not die, it cannot be! / As for Venice and her people, merely born to bloom and drop, / Here on earth they bore their fruitage, mirth and folly were the crop: / What of soul was left, I wonder, when the kissing had to stop?'

— **Venice, everlasting city**. *Eternal city* is a term traditionally used to refer to *Rome*. The place was probably first settled in the 8th century BCE. Legend gives a peculiarly precise date of its founding by Romulus and Remus—753BCE. Roman years were traditionally calculated *ab urbe condita*—'from the founding of the City'.

CHAPTER 4. *Beyond the Human.*

— **Bad faith**. Greg probably has in mind something more complex and elusive than the term in its general use. To act 'in bad faith' normally means that a person acts in a way which conceals from someone else a bad intention behind a seemingly good intention. But, especially under the influence of J-P Sartre (I.20), in the existentialist phase of his intellectual life, the term (*mauvaise foi*, in French) has come to be used also to refer to a form of dishonesty designed to deceive *oneself*, to conceal the truth about *oneself* from *oneself*.

For the existentialist philosopher, human consciousness implies freedom, and freedom includes the freedom to think oneself into existence, including one's existence in relation to the self-creating consciousness of others. It also includes the possibility to think of oneself as if one were an 'other' in relation to oneself. This is not merely a pretence or a game or a tactic—it is a self-deceiving that is liable to deceive even oneself. (See further in ch. 20 below, under 'Gabi's hand'.)

It may be that Greg is seeing the Goldberg Pynch project as being not merely a capitalist money-making enterprise of a highly sophisticated kind, concealed behind a pretentious façade. He may also see it as an instrument for the *de-humanising* of human beings claiming to be *improving* human beings—an ultimate form of bad faith.

— **Clarified obscurely**. Greg will have in mind the phrase as spoken by Don Rodrigue in *Le Cid* (IV. iii) by the French dramatist P. Corneille (1606-84). *Cette obscure clarté qui tombe des étoiles* ('that obscure light that falls from the stars'). The play displays a struggle between love and honour in the life of of the Spanish 11th-century knight and hero, known as *El Cid Campeador*.

— **Darkness made visible**. Echo of a description of the Hell in which the fallen angel, Satan, found himself in Book I of *Paradise Lost* (I.20) by J. Milton.

'A dungeon horrible, on all sides round, / As one great furnace flamed; yet from those flames / No light; but rather darkness visible/ Served only to discover sights of woe, / Regions of sorrow, doleful shades, where peace / And rest can never dwell, hope never comes . . .'

The phrase 'darkness visible' was one of those to which Richard Bentley objected. He emended it to 'transpicuous gloom', on the ground that 'visible darkness' is impossible. Bentley's edition of Milton's epic was designed to 'improve' it by correcting errors, and removing offences against good taste, good sense, and propriety.

Bentley (1662-1742) was a leading classical scholar (a scholar of Greek and Roman literature) who became Master of Trinity College, Cambridge in 1700.

He had been educated at Wakefield Grammar School and St John's College, Cambridge. Efforts to remove him from the mastership led to a thirty-year war between Bentley and the Fellows of the College, and the Bishop of Ely, who had disciplinary jurisdiction over the Mastership.

The matter found its way to the High Court in London on many occasions, and even to the House of Lords, which ruled (1733) that the Bishop was legally entitled to consider twenty of the sixty-four articles of accusation against Bentley, including the following—

'Why did you of your own Head pull down a good Stair-case in your Lodge, and give Orders and Directions for building a new one, and that too fine for common Use?' (From the Articles Against Dr Bentley, 1710).

Bentley's staircase remains in the Master's Lodge. The Fellows did not object to the landscaping (1717-18) of the fields behind the College (the Backs) in the best contemporary style, and at considerable expense to the College.

The Bishop deprived Bentley of the Mastership in 1734. Several writs of *mandamus* from the High Court ordered the enforcement of that decision. But Bentley remained with his family in the Master's Lodge until his death in 1742. He is buried close to the altar in the College chapel.

In his last years, he was cheerfully working on his own edition of the Homeric epics. He was particularly proud of being able to make use of his discovery of the *digamma* (double 'g') in ancient Greek. He had established that the sound of the letter was known in Homer's time, but the letter had mysteriously disappeared from the Greek alphabet. Its restoration would definitely improve the Homeric texts. 'I shall render multitudes of places intelligible which the stupid scholiasts [commentators on classical texts] could never account for . . .'

We may be reminded of another leading classical scholar, A. E Housman (1859-1936), who was Professor of Latin at University College, London and then at Cambridge, where he was a Fellow of Trinity College from 1911 until his death. 'I wish they would not compare me to Bentley . . . I will not tolerate comparison with Bentley. Bentley is alone and supreme.'

Housman, like Bentley, was a master of 'textual criticism', which he defined as 'the science of discovering error in texts and the art of removing it.' He devoted much of his scholarly life to an edition of the *Astronomy* of Manilius, an obscure 1st-century Latin poet—a very poor poet, according to Housman.

Housman was himself a much admired, even a best-selling, poet (*The Shropshire Lad*). But, late in life, he said that his proudest achievement was a particular emendation involving an iota subscript (another element of written Greek).

For a while in the 1930's, he was the downstairs neighbour (in Whewell's Court, Trinity College) of the equally *eigenartig* L. Wittgenstein (I.20).

— **Chronicle of wasted time**. From W. Shakespeare, Sonnet CVI. 'When in the chronical of wasted time . . .' The poem refers to medieval courtly love-poetry, 'in praise of ladies dead and lovely knights'. But it is a different challenge to sing in praise of the beauty of a real living person.' For we, which now behold these present days, / Have eyes to wonder, but lack tongues to praise.'

— ***Homo faber***. In Latin, 'the human being as maker' (from *fabricare*, 'to form, to make'). Greg no doubt has in mind the contrast between rational man (*homo rationalis*) and man the maker or doer, and also the contrast between the *vita contemplativa* (life of the mind) and the *vita activa* (life of action). The American writer Hannah Arendt, in *The Human Condition* (1958), analyses human history as a constant process of change in the meaning of these categories, and in their relative weight in the life of different societies at different times.

She also distinguishes *homo faber*, who creates through the application of purposive thought (the tool-maker), from the *animal laborans* who simply works, as a slave or as part of an integrated social process. Central to the historical development in European societies was a transformation caused by Christianity (as part of its inheritance from its Hebraic past). It put 'human life', the survival and immortality of the individual human being, before everything, including political life and the natural world. Man became the measure of all things.

Christianity declined, Arendt says, not as the result of 18th-century atheism or 19th-century materialism—'but rather [due to] the doubting concern with salvation of genuinely religious men, in whose eyes the traditional Christian content and promise had become "absurd".'

But the human-life-centred ethic persisted and, with it, the idea that 'labour' designed to develop and prolong human life was an ultimate and absolute value—together with the idea that natural science is the perfect tool for this human self-rule. To put the idea in a form which Arendt did not use explicitly—*homo sapiens* and *homo rationalis* and *homo faber* and the *zoon politkon* (or *homo socialis*) and the *vita contemplativa* and the *vita activa* have all now been fused together into a sort of all-embracing *vita laborans*—humanity enslaved by a ceaseless struggle to *make itself in its own image*. (See further in chs.15 and 19 below.)

Arendt ends her book on a wanly hopeful note. Perhaps *thought* might come to take its place once again as the highest form of *activity*.

'For if no other test but the experience of being active, no other measure but the extent of sheer activity were to be applied to the various activities within the *vita activa*, it might well be that thinking as such would surpass them all.'

— **Monarchia**. In ancient Greek, 'monarchy, absolute power' (from *monos*, only; single; *arche*, rule). The idea that the species-unity of humanity could be expressed in a global form, even a global social form, has been expressed repeatedly since the beginning of religious and philosophical thought, even as lesser social formations (especially the 'nation' and the 'state') came to dominate the human world.

The idea of the species-unity of humanity has been expressed in various different ways—*humanitas* (the Stoics); the *humana universitas* (Dante), the 'universal society' (Suárez), the 'great and natural community of mankind' (Locke), the *civitas maxima* (Wolff), the 'great city of the human race' (Vico), the 'general society of the human race' (Rousseau), a 'perfect civil union of mankind' (Kant), the 'international society of all human beings, the society of all societies' (Allott).

In his *Monarchia*, Dante (ch. 3 above) uses the idea of world government polemically in relation to contemporary (medieval) struggles, suggesting that the world be placed under the authority of the Holy Roman Emperor (I.12), to avoid its being subjected to the Pope of the Roman Catholic Church.

— **Will to know, will to power.** Greg is no doubt thinking of the work of F. Nietzsche, but especially of the work of the German philosopher Arthur Schopenhauer (1788-1860), the last philosopher in the great tradition of Western philosophy—before K. Marx and F. Nietzsche and S. Freud heralded the decline and fall of Western philosophy in the 20th century.

Schopenhauer sought to reconcile Berkeley and Hume and Kant with the originators of the tradition—the pre-Socratics, Socrates, Plato and Aristotle—as 'that notorious charlatan Hegel' (as he called him) had tried and failed to do.

Like Berkeley and Hume (see Appendix 4 below), of whom he approved, he published his influential works at a remarkably young age—his doctoral dissertation *On the Fourfold Root of the Principle of Sufficient Reason* in 1813 and his main work, *The World as Will and Idea* (*Die Welt als Wille und Vorstellung*), in 1818 (with a second and enlarged edition in 1844).

The latter work (like Hume's *Treatise*) was greeted with loud silence. Schopenhauer had few students at his lectures in the University of Berlin. He had wilfully timed them to coincide with Hegel's lectures. Hegel was an early example of those academics who acquire star status and a fan-club. (Like the Pharisees, they have had their reward.) Schopenhauer left academic life in disgust.

Schopenhauer follows Hume and Kant in seeing the work of the mind, even in the natural sciences, as the constructing of a metaphysical world whose relationship to the physical world—things-in-themselves—is unknowable, since we can only know the contents of our own mind.

'Consequently that Kantian principle implies in turn a further principle: that the objective world exists only as idea.' (*World as Will and Idea*, Bk. I: supplement; tr., J. Berman).

But Schopenhauer then takes a corrective view of *idealism* similar to that which is suggested in the Chapter 2 Appendices below—especially Appendix 1, under 'William of Occam', Appendix 4 under 'Berkeley', and Appendix 8.

'Idealism is, in spite of all that one may say, more persistently and repeatedly misunderstood than anything else, in that it is interpreted as meaning that one is denying the empirical reality of the external world . . . True idealism, on the contrary, is specifically not the empirical, but the transcendental. This leaves the empirical reality of the world untouched, but maintains that every object, in other words, the empirically real in general, is conditioned by the subject [the thinking human mind] twice over; in the first place materially or as object generally, because an objective existence is conceivable only in relation to a subject and as that subject's idea; and in the second place formally, in that the mode or manner of the object's existence—its being perceived per space, time and causality—follows form the subject, and is predisposed in the subject. So the simple or Berkeleian idealism which concerns the object in general, is closely succeeded by Kantian idealism which concerns the specially given mode and manner of objective existence.' (Bk. I, supplement).

However, Schopenhauer reduces Kantian reality-constituting categories of the mind to one single category—causality—that is, reality imagined as a series of events in time and space which the mind connects into 'cause' and 'effect'. But what he calls *aetiology*—explanation in terms of causality—is still not an account of the real nature of external reality.

'Consequently, the most complete aetiological explanation of the whole of nature can never be more than an inventory of forces which cannot be explained, and an authoritative statement of the rule according to which phenomena appear in time and space, follow and make way for one another . . . Thus we see already that *from without* we can never arrive at the real nature of things. However much we investigate, we can never reach anything but images and names.' (Bk. II.§28).

But then—as the second fundamental aspect of his work—Schopenhauer does a remarkable thing. He tells us how we *can* know external reality. *We know reality because we participate in reality.* Our mode of participation in reality is not simply the indirect activity of forming *ideas*. It is the direct activity of what he calls *will*.

'This will of which we are speaking he [the reader] will recognise as the inmost nature not only in those phenomena which are closely similar to his own, in men and animals, but further reflection will lead him also to recognise the force which stirs and vegetates in the plant, and indeed the force by which the crystal is formed, that by which the magnet turns to the North Pole, the force whose shock he experiences form the contact between different metals, the force which appears in the elective affinities of matter as repulsion and attraction, separation and combination, and, lastly, even gravitation, which pulls so powerfully through all matter, draws the stone to the earth and the earth to the sun—all these he will recognise as different only in their phenomenal existence [their appearances], but in their inner nature as identical, as what is directly known to him so intimately and so much better than anything else, and which, in its most direct manifestation, is called *will*. Only this use of reflection forbids us to stop at the phenomenon, and instead leads us beyond it to the *thing-in-itself*. Phenomenon means ideas, and nothing more. All idea, of whatever kind it may be, all *object*, is *phenomenon*, but the *will* alone is *thing-in-itself*. As such, it is emphatically not idea, but *toto genere* [in its whole nature] different form it; it is that of which all idea, all object, is the phenomenal appearance, the visibility, the objectification. It is the inmost kernel, of every individual thing, and also of the whole. It is manifest in every force of nature that operates blindly, and it is manifest, too, in the deliberate action of man; and the great difference between these two is a matter only of degree of the manifestation, not in the nature of what is made manifest.' (Bk. II, §22).

This fascinating theory of *will* might be said to be an *idealist materialism*, or else a *materialist idealism*.

'I hope that in the preceding book I have convincingly shown that what in the Kantian philosophy is called the *thing-in-itself*, and appears there as so important and yet so obscure and paradoxical a doctrine, and . . . was considered a stumbling block, and the weak aspect of his philosophy—I hope to have shown that this, if it is reached by the entirely different route by which we have arrived at it, is nothing but the *will*, when the sphere of that concept is extended and defined in the way I have shown. I hope, further, that after what has been said there will be no hesitation in recognising the definite grades of the objectification of the will, which is the inner reality of the world, to be what Plato called the *eternal Ideas* or unchangeable forms (εἴδη); a doctrine which is regarded as the principal, but at the same time the most obscure and paradoxical, dogma of his system, and has been the subject of reflection, of controversy, of ridicule and of reverence, to so many and such different minds down the centuries.' (Bk. III, §32).

(It must be said that, for an *idealist* philosopher in the best senses of that word, the preceding paragraph is a source of intense aesthetic delight—a perfect example of philosophy as the eternal recurrence of the human mind's self-contemplating, always the same and always new.)

Schopenhauer's use of the word 'will' (*Wille*, in German) had an unfortunate consequence, given that that word's primary meaning is in relation to the forming of an intention before we take action, and given that there is a vast accumulated mass of thought and writing on the problem of the will, especially the 'freedom of the will'. Nietzsche's use of the word, in his key concept of the 'will to power', owes much to Schopenhauer, but adds a further source of misunderstanding. Nietzsche also did not mean 'power' merely in the social or political sense.

The Schopenhauerian-Nietzschean word 'will' should be understood in a metaphysical sense. Like 'force' or 'gravity' it is a mental construct designed to express the dynamic character of the universe—the becoming of being—which is neither purposeful nor purposeless, but which seems to act as if it were moving itself in a particular direction. This 'will' manifests itself in an infinite variety of forms. Sentient animals experience it in a particular way. Human beings experience it in a form which they present to themselves in their mind.

It follows that human beings are an absolutely integral part of the universe and of the process of the universe, but have the interesting characteristic that they can 'know' themselves as such. From this knowledge stems the whole substance of the human comedy, its grandeurs and its miseries.

There are echoes in this of Spinoza and Leibniz, but also of the Hinduism of the Upanishads. See further in ch. 11 below, under 'that art thou'.

The third element in Schopenhauer's work is the most notorious. He takes a view of the way in which *will* manifests itself in the *human being*. It is not a pretty picture or a happy story.

'Each and every human life flows onwards between desire and its attainment. The wish is, of its nature, pain; attainment quickly produces satiety: the object of desire merely *seemed* to be that; possession takes away its fascination; the wish, the new, reintroduces itself in a new form; when it does not, then follow desolation, emptiness, boredom, against which the struggle is just as painful as against want . . . What we might otherwise call the most beautiful part of life, its purest joy (if only because it lifts us out of real existence and transforms us into disinterested spectators), is pure knowledge to which all willing is alien, pleasure in the beautiful, true delight in art—this is granted only to a very few, because it demands rare talents, and even to those it is granted only as a fleeting dream. And then their higher intellectual power makes even those few susceptible of far greater suffering than dull people can ever feel . . . But to the great majority of mankind, purely intellectual pleasures are not accessible.'(Bk. IV, §58).

'If, finally, we were to show everyone the terrible sufferings and miseries to which life is constantly exposed, he would be seized with horror; and if we were to conduct the most confirmed optimist through the hospitals, infirmaries, and surgical operating-theatres, through the prisons, torture-chambers, and slave-barracks, over battlefields and places of execution; if we were to open to him all the dark dwellings in which misery cringes from the glance of cold curiosity . . . then he, too, would finally see just what this "best of all possible worlds" is like. For where else did Dante get the material for his hell, if not from our real world?'

(For 'best possible world', see I. 22, under 'garden to cultivate'.)

His discussion of good/bad and good/evil, of Christianity, of asceticism and the 'denial of the will to life', of guilt and conscience, anticipates remarkably the work of Nietzsche (especially in the latter's *Genealogy of Morals*), as does the tone and vigour of his writing. Nietzsche called Schopenhauer 'my great teacher'.

Schopenhauer regards sexuality as the fundamental human motivating force, the ultimate explanation of every kind of behaviour, good and bad. He wonders why no philosopher before him has investigated the matter: 'So I have no predecessors either to make use of or to refute.'

'It [sexual love] is the ultimate goal of almost all human endeavour, exerts an adverse influence on the most important affairs, interrupts the most serious business at any hour, sometimes for a while confuses even the greatest minds, does not hesitate with its trumpery to disrupt negotiations of statesmen and the research of scholars, has the knack of slipping its love-letters and ringlets even into ministerial portfolios and philosophical manuscripts. Every day it contrives the worst and most intractable quarrels, destroys the most valuable relationships, ruptures the most durable bonds. It requires the sacrifice sometimes of life or health, sometimes of wealth, rank, and happiness . . . Generally, then, it plays the part of a malevolent demon who is trying to pervert, confuse, and overthrow everything.' (Bk. IV, supplement 'On the Metaphysics of Sexual Love').

Schopenhauer's anticipations of Freud are remarkable. (Thomas Mann said that Freud turned Schopenhauer's metaphysics into psychology.) Freud, in his *Autobiography*, understated his debt to Schopenhauer and Nietzsche (and to other people: see L. Whyte, *The Unconscious before Freud*). He said that he had not read Schopenhauer until his own ideas were long since formulated. 'Nietzsche, another philosopher [other than Schopenhauer] whose guesses and intuitions often agree in the most astonishing way with the laborious findings of psycho-analysis, was for a long time avoided by me on that very account.' (According to F. Sulloway (*Freud, Biologist of the Mind*), Freud had, in fact, belonged to a Viennese student reading society who treated Schopenhauer and Nietzsche as intellectual heroes.)

Schopenhauer's notorious pessimism is almost entirely unrelieved by either *sweetness* or *light*—the 'two noblest of things', according to J. Swift (ironically) in

The Battle of the Books and M. Arnold (earnestly) in *Culture and Anarchy* (ch.3 above, under 'hellenic'). Like Nietzsche's, his voice seems both prophetic and tragic in the light of the painful experience of the twentieth century.

However, it is not without interest that the generally benign William James said: 'The sallies of the two German authors [Schopenhauer and Nietzsche] remind one, half the time, of the sick shriekings of two dying rats.' (*Varieties of Religious Experience*, lec.2. See ch.5 below, under 'Henry's brother William'.)

If only Schopenhauer and Marx and Nietzsche and Freud had been happy people! The history of the twentieth century might have been different. The natural gloom-level of the human world is high, without any need for philosophers to seek to raise it artificially. It is not the job of those who think for a living to find new ways to make people unhappy.

Dr Johnson's friend Edwards said: 'You are a philosopher, Dr. Johnson. I have tried too in my time to be a philosopher; but, I don't know how, cheerfulness was always breaking in.' (J. Boswell, *Life of Johnson*, entry for 17 April 1778).

On Schopenhauer's remarkable and influential—and much less gloomy—views on art and music, see ch. 15 below, under '*holde Kunst*'.

— **Extra-human vantage-point.** H. Arendt (see above, under '*homo faber*') suggests that natural science has given humanity the power to find an Archimedean point outside the earth, from which to investigate the universe.

> 'Only now have we established ourselves as "universal" beings, as creatures who are terrestrial not by nature or essence but only by the condition of being alive, and who therefore by reasoning can overcome this condition not in mere speculation but in actual fact . . . What ushered in the modern age was not the age-old desire of astronomers for simplicity, harmony, and beauty . . . It was rather the discovery . . . that Copernicus' image of "the virile man standing in the sun . . . overlooking the planets" was much more than an image or a gesture, was in fact an indication of the astounding human capacity to think in terms of the universe while remaining on the earth, and the perhaps even more astounding human ability to use cosmic laws as guiding principles for terrestrial action.'

Arendt says that mathematics is 'the leading science of the modern age'.

> 'With the rise of modernity, mathematics does not simply enlarge its content or reach out into the infinite to become applicable to the immensity of an infinite and infinitely growing, expanding universe, but ceases to be concerned with appearances at all. It is no longer the beginning of philosophy [as Plato had taught], of the "science" of Being in its true appearance, but becomes instead the science of the structure of the human mind.' (*The Human Condition*, ch. 36).

— **Harmless Houyhnhnm.** One of Gulliver's travels was to a country dominated by
orderly and rational and acute and judicious horses who spoke their own language
and called themselves 'Houyhnhnms' (which may be pronounced as 'whinwhins').
They are served by human-like creatures whom they refer to as Yahoos. In heavy-
handed satire, Swift contrasts the elegant rationality of the horses and their society
with the animal-like debasement of human beings and human society. Gulliver's
horse-mentor cannot believe Gulliver's account of life in mid-18th century England,
seemingly dominated by irrationality, vice and misery. *Gulliver's Travels* (1726), by
the Irish writer J. Swift (1667-1745), Part Four.

— **Academy of Projectors.** In Part Three of *Gulliver's Travels*, he visits Laputa and is
told about academies for 'putting all Arts, Sciences, Languages, and Mechanicks
upon a new Foot'. Swift then satirises, with delightful ingenuity, the new post-
Galilean-Baconian fashion and passion in Europe for experimental science, and for
practical 'projects' designed to improve human life.

The Royal Society 'for improving natural knowledge by experiments' was
established by royal charter in 1662. Discussion about how to make use of the
'New Philosophy or Experimental Philosophy' had been taking place since 1645
in London and, during the Civil War, in John Wilkins' rooms in Wadham College,
Oxford. (Bacon had died in 1626; see Appendix 1 below.) The *Proceedings of the
Royal Society* began publication in 1665.

(There had been an *Academia Secretorum Naturae* (Academy of the Secrets of
Nature) in Naples from 1560 (suppressed by the Inquisition). In Rome there had
been an *Accademia dei Lincei* (Academy of the Lynxes—*i.e.*, lynx-like experimental
scientists) from 1603. Galileo Galilei (1564-1642) was a proud member. The
Academy ceased to exist in 1630 after the death of its then secretary. After various
attempts to re-found a scientific academy, the Academy of the Lynxes was re-
established in 1847 and is now known as the *Accademia Nazionale dei Lincei*. The
French *Académie des Sciences* was founded by Louis XIV's chief minister Jean-Baptiste
Colbert in 1666.)

'To this End they procured a Royal Patent for erecting an Academy of
PROJECTORS in Lagado: and the Humour prevailed so strongly among
the People, that there was not a Town of any Consequence in the Kingdom
without such an Academy. In these Colleges, the Professors contrive new Rules
and Methods of Agriculture and Building, and new Instruments and Tools
for all Trades and Manufactures, whereby, as they undertake, one Man shall
do the Work of Ten; a Palace may be built in a Week, of Materials so durable
as to last for ever without repairing. All the Fruits of the Earth shall come to
Maturity, at whatever Season we think fit to chuse, and increase an Hundred
Fold more than they do at present; with innumerable other happy Proposals.
The only Inconvenience is, that none of these Projects are yet brought to
Perfection; and in the mean time, the whole Country lies miserably waste, the

Houses in Ruins, and the People without Food or Cloaths.' Gulliver's Travels, Part Three, ch. 4. Gulliver goes to Lagado to see the principal Academy.

'In another Apartment I was highly pleased with a Projector, who had found a Device of plowing the Ground with Hogs, to save the Charges of Plows, Cattle, and Labour. The Method is this: In an Acre of Ground you bury at six Inches Distance and eight deep, a Quantity of Acorns, Dates, Chestnuts, and other Maste or Vegetables whereof these Animals are fondest; then you drive six Hundred or more of them into the Field, where in a few Days they will root up the whole Ground in search of their Food, and make it fit for sowing, at the same time manuring it with their Dung.' (Part Three, ch. 5).

'I had hitherto seen only one Side of the Academy, the other being appropriated to the Advancers of speculative Learning.'

Gulliver then meets a professor who has invented a machine 'for improving speculative Knowledge by practical and mechanical Operations'.

'Every one knew how laborious the usual method is of attaining to Arts and Sciences; whereas by his Contrivance, the most ignorant Person at a reasonable Charge, and with a little bodily Labour, may write Books in Philosophy, Poetry, Politicks, Law, Mathematicks and Theology, with the least assistance from Genius or Study.'

The machine consists of wires holding small pieces of wood on which every word in the language, in every mood, tense and declension, has been written. The assistants turn various handles, and words are brought together randomly to form parts of sentences.

'. . . the Professor shewed me several volumes in large Folio already collected, of broken Sentences, which he intended to piece together; and out of those rich Materials to give the World a complete Body of all Arts and Sciences.'

(Swift does not tell us the professor's name, which could, of course, have been anything from Gargle to Gurgle—but probably not Yahoo.)

We may also recall the characters known as Bouvard and Pécuchet in G. Flaubert's wonderfully post-modern (and mercifully unfinished) novel that bears their name (1881). They devoted their lives to accumulating all that had ever been written or said, including masses of clichés and conventional wisdom (*idées reçues*), about how life should be lived. They found that it was impossible to make sense of the meaningless morass of conflicting ideas. Their *leitmotiv* was: *Où est la règle alors?* ('So where is the rule?').

Flaubert took his inspiration from a saying of Nicolas Chamfort (1740-1794), the Oscar Wilde of his day: 'You can be sure that every public idea, every

conventional opinion, is stupid, since it has suited the largest number of people.'
Compare: Erasmus (I.5): 'If a thing displeases the vulgar, that is a presumption in
its favour.'

We may also recall the wise words of the Austrian-British philosopher K.
Popper (1902-94).

> 'I see in science one of the greatest creations of the human mind. It is a step
> comparable to the emergence of a descriptive and argumentative language, or
> to the invention of writing. It is a step at which our explanatory myths become
> open to conscious and consistent criticism and at which we are challenged
> to invent *new myths*.' *Objective Knowledge. An Evolutionary Approach* (1972)
> (emphasis added).

— **Masters of those who know.** Dante so describes Aristotle—*il maestro di color che
sanno*—in *Inferno* (Hell), the first book of the *Divine Comedy* (Canto IV).
— **Command no more.** As the end of the tragedy *King Oedipus* by Sophocles
(c.495BCE-406), the self-blinded Oedipus is led away into exile. He asks that he
should be accompanied by his children. The children were born to him and Jocasta,
whom he had married, not knowing that she was his own mother, after he had,
without knowing it, killed his own father, Jocasta's husband. Creon, his successor as
king of Thebes, refuses his request: 'Command no more. Obey. Your rule is ended.'
(tr., E Watling).

Dr Seare surely cannot suppose that philosophers and academics and intellectuals
were ever the real rulers of the world or, if they were, that they would surrender that
status without a fight or, at least, a symposium.

CHAPTER 5. *Connecticut.*

— **Connecticut.** As a resident of New England, Abe Green is living in one of the
World Intellectual Heritage Sites (as one might, but does not yet, say)—alongside
such places as Mesopotamia, Egypt, China, Athens, Rome, England, Florence, and
France.

Connecticut is a state in the North East of the United States of America,
bounded by the states of New York, Massachusetts and Rhode Island. One of the
thirteen original British colonies, founded by emigration from Massachusetts in
1636. The emigration was led by Thomas Hooker, a Puritan minister and theologian,
who had at one time been a Fellow of Emmanuel College, Cambridge. He was one
of the authors of the new colony's written constitution—the Fundamental Orders
of 1638—perhaps the earliest of all written constitutions. (Connecticut is known
as 'the Constitution State'). Another colony was founded at New Haven, with its
own written constitution (1639). New Haven colony was merged with Connecticut
under a royal charter of 1662.

The Fundamental Orders are a rare and remarkable example of an *explicit* social contract—a phenomenon which, in classical democratic theory, is supposed to be *implicit*.

'We the Inhabitants and Residents of Windsor, Hartford and Wethersfield are now cohabiting and dwelling in and upon the River of Conectecotte [a first attempt to anglicise the Algonquin name] and the Lands thereunto adjoining; And well knowing where a people are gathered together the word of God requires that to maintain the peace and union of such a people there should be an orderly and decent Government established according to God, to order and dispose of the affairs of the people at all seasons as occasion shall require; do therefore associate and conjoin our selves to be as one Public State or Commonwealth . . .'

The settlers who came to be known as the Pilgrim Fathers had adopted (1620) a virtual social contract when they were still on board the Mayflower, the vessel that had brought them from Plymouth, England. Bad weather had driven them north, away from the mouth of the Hudson River, their intended destination in 'Virginia' (the generalised name—honouring Queen Elizabeth I—of the main royally-authorised settlement in America). They eventually landed and settled in Cape Cod Bay, at a place to which they gave the name of Plymouth, and there established the Plymouth Colony. The Colony was merged with the Commonwealth of Massachusetts in 1661.

'We whose names are underwritten, the loyal subjects of our dread Sovereign Lord King James, by the Grace of God of Great Britain, France and Ireland, King, Defender of the Faith, etc. Having undertaken, for the Glory of God and advancement of the Christian Faith and Honour of our King and Country, a Voyage to plant the First Colony in the Northern Parts of Virginia, do by these presents solemnly and mutually in the presence of God and one of another, Covenant and Combine ourselves together into a Civil Body Politic, for our better ordering and preservation and furtherance of the ends aforesaid; and by virtue hereof to enact, constitute and frame such just and equal Laws, Ordinances, Acts, Constitutions and Offices, from time to time, as shall be thought most meet and convenient for the general good of the Colony.'

Massachusetts had been founded by a group of investors established under a royal charter of 1628 as 'The Company of the Massachusetts Bay in New England'. Under the leadership of John Winthrop (who had studied at Trinity College, Cambridge, and who would become Governor of the colony in 1630), the investors in the project drew up (in Cambridge, England) an Agreement (1629), under which it was agreed that the settlement would not be administered by the Company in England, but would be entirely self-governing in New England.

Newtowne in Massachusetts was re-named Cambridge in 1638. New College was founded in 1636 and was re-named Harvard College in 1639 in honour of its first substantial testamentary benefactor (£779 and 260 books), John Harvard (1607-38), a graduate of Emmanuel College, Cambridge. Harvard College became Harvard University in 1780. The name Harvard College now applies only to the undergraduate section of the University.

These highly purposive society-making events, which pre-date the social contract theories of both Thomas Hobbes and John Locke (see Appendix 3 below), reflect a period in human social history when theocratic and democratic ideas might still be seen as compatible, perhaps even inseparable.

The self-conscious secularising spirit of both the American and French Revolutions obscured, but did not finally exorcise—far from it!—the age-old problem of the place of religion in social and political order. Abe Green is certainly aware of this deep-structural complex in the inherited consciousness of New England, which remains a deep-structural complex in the inherited social consciousness of the United States of America. For further discussion, see ch. 15 below.

— **Henry James mode.** The American novelist Henry James (1843-1916), who spent most of his life in Britain and was naturalised as a British subject (and appointed to the Order of Merit) in 1915, had an inimitable (but parodiable) style of writing whose density and obscurity reflect his intensely serious artistic purpose. He attempted to represent and analyse the consciousness of people living socially privileged lives, on both sides of the Atlantic, and especially the intricate interacting of their minds at a level below that of their explicit social and personal relations. His published letters seem, by comparison, limpid. (See further in ch. 8 below, under 'Proustian digression'.)

— **Ming vase.** Made in China during the Ming imperial dynasty (1368-1644). From the time (about 1500) when the Portuguese began to bring Chinese and Japanese art into Europe, it was highly prized for its remarkable beauty. Europeans were already familiar with the high aesthetic value of Islamic art. As art works from other places (Korea, India, pre-Columbian America, Africa) were introduced into Europe, European aesthetic sensibility was greatly enhanced by this globalising of aesthetic experience.

— **Picasso.** Pablo Picasso (1881-1973), Spanish painter who was also a master of several other art forms.

— **Henry's brother William.** William James (1842-1910), American philosopher of mind/psychologist. The brothers were members of a family, and of an extended intellectual family, which was at the heart of the remarkable cultural flourishing of Boston and Cambridge (Massachusetts) in the mid-19th century. For a while, Boston seemed to be the 'hub of the universe', as they said—until it was displaced by New York City. They and their kind were the intellectual wing of the 'Boston Brahmins' (*brahmin*, highest caste in the Hindu caste-system), an aristocracy of birth (rather than of money) who set the tone of the late (and, on balance, late lamented) WASP (White Anglo-Saxon Protestant) ascendancy in the US.

The James family, like so many other 19th-century intellectuals, on both sides of the Atlantic, were plagued by illnesses of body and mind—and of body-mind (the term 'neurasthenia' appears frequently in the biographies of such people). The intellectual Bostonians were painfully high-minded, generating a form of philosophical religion—'transcendentalism' (prophet: R.W. Emerson—1803-82)—which seemed to grow naturally out of the Boston mental *terroir*—a sort of Anglicanish deism.

William James brought a cool intelligence to the study of religion, especially in his very remarkable *The Varieties of Religious Experience* (1902), and to expounding for a wider public the philosophy of what he called 'pragmatism' (see ch. 2 above, under 'pragmatist'). C.S.Peirce, a close, and even more troubled, friend of James, had preferred the name 'pragmaticism'. 'Perhaps it would be correct, and just to all parties, to say that the modern movement known as pragmatism is largely the result of James's misunderstanding of Peirce.' (R.B. Perry).

— **Corruption of the best**. A fine Latin saying: *corruptio optimi pessima* ('the corruption of the best is worst'). The saying is not found, in so many words, in any classical Latin author. But the idea was familiar to the Romans, perhaps originating in a saying of Aristotle's: 'That which is the perversion of the first and most divine is necessarily the worst.' (*Politics*, IV.2; tr., B. Jowett). And so, he says, tyranny is the worst form of government because it is a corruption of monarchy, which is (potentially) the best.

— **Leitmotiv**. In German, 'lead-motif'. A repeated musical phrase expressing and recalling some particular aspect of a person, place or event. A significant feature of the music of the operas of R. Wagner (see ch. 3 above, under 'jackets like a sword').

— **Westport**. Small and notoriously affluent coastal town within commuting distance of New York City.

— **Coda or envoi**. *Coda* : in Italian, 'tail, end, foot'. It is used in classical Western music for the last section of a musical composition. *Envoi* : in French, 'a or the sending'. It is used in Western literature for verses at the end of a poem, usually addressing the poem to some named or unnamed recipient.

— **Range Rover**. A brand of motor vehicles, which were designed for use in the countryside and on rough ground, but which, like foxes, have found a precarious foothold also in town.

— **Boxcar**. The Firm's *nom de guerre* for Jim Meehan.

— *Farniente*. In Italian, 'idleness' (from *fare*, 'to do', and *niente*, 'nothing'). Most often used in the phrase *dolce farniente* (pleasant idleness). Compare: *fainéant*—in French, 'idler' from *faire*, to do, and *néant*, nothing). Cicero (*Pro Publio Sestio*) spoke of *cum dignitate otium* (dignified leisure), an ideal of the more sensitive members of the Roman privileged classes.

Compare: 'I could never bear to be idle, it saps one's energy.' S. Beckett (ch. 11 below, under '*qui ça?*'), *Molloy* (1951). Or Charles Eliot Norton (who became President of Harvard University at the age of 34) in a letter to Henry James:

> 'Born and bred in New England as we were, where the air we breathe is full of the northern chill, and no other philosophy but that of utilitarianism is possible—it is not easy to learn to be content with the usefulness of doing nothing. Italy is a good place, however, for deadening the overactive conscience, and for killing rank ambition.'

— **Jay Gatsby.** The leading character in *The Great Gatsby* (1925) by the American writer Francis Scott Fitzgerald (1896-1940). He is a rich and dissolute and charming young man, an archetype of a *time*—the Twenties and Prohibition (the constitutionally decreed, and criminally circumvented, prohibition of the manufacture and sale of alcohol in the United States)—and of a *place*—New York and Long Island (the latter, adjacent to New York City, containing the houses of rich New Yorkers, the pretentious stage-setting for wasted time, and much *otium sine dignitate*). Gatsby ends badly—shot by a husband whose wife he had seduced, she having recently been killed by a woman driving Gatsby's car, a woman who was the wife of a friend of Gatsby's and whom he had also seduced. Fitzgerald's novel is admirably and mercifully short—120 pages—*vita brevis, ars brevis*.

— **White skin, needing blood.** Distant echo of a sonnet (LXXXII) by W. Shakespeare: 'I grant thou were not married to my Muse.' The poet says that his beloved's beauty needs no exaggerated poetical devices to describe it. Let such things be saved for those who are in need of embellishment.

> 'Thou truly fair, were truly sympathised / In true plain words, by thy true-telling friend; / And their gross painting might be better used / Where cheeks need blood; in thee it is abused.' (spelling here modernised).

— **Millstone.** An echo of words attributed to Jesus Christ. 'And Jesus called a little child unto him, and set him in the midst of them, And said, Verily I say unto you, Except ye be converted, and become as little children, ye shall not enter into the kingdom of heaven. Whosoever therefore shall humble himself as this little child, the same is greatest in the kingdom of heaven . . . But whoso shall offend one of these little ones which believe in me, it were better for him that a millstone were hanged about his neck, and that he were drowned in the depth of the sea.' (*Gospel of Matthew*, ch.18; King James version).

— **Floated on a swan.** 'The Grail therefore resolved to despatch as a rescuer, Lohengrin, the son of Parsifal. Just as he was about to place his foot in the stirrup a swan came floating down the water drawing a skiff behind him. As soon as Lohengrin set eyes upon the swan, he exclaimed: "Take the steed back to the manger; I shall follow this bird wherever he may lead me".' (Legend as recounted in O. Rank, *The Myth of the Birth of the Hero,* 1914). In Act I of R. Wagner's opera *Lohengrin*, this scene is represented.

Wagner's sometime patron King Ludwig II of Bavaria (I.12)—splendid and sad hero-prince of suffering sensualist aesthetes—was peculiarly fond of swans. He rebuilt a family castle at Hohenschwangau (High Swan Place), whose décor had been full of swan-images, creating a fantasy-castle which, after his death, would come to be called Neuschwanstein (New Swan Rock)

Although himself unmusical, he was for years manically infatuated with R. Wagner and the romantic mythology of Wagner's operas, especially Tannhäuser and Lohengrin. He re-enacted on the Alpsee Lohengrin's swan-journey (artificial swan) with his (at that time) very close friend Prince Paul von Thurn und Taxis standing in the boat dressed as Lohengrin. He built a grotto (modelled on the Blue Grotto on Capri) at his castle of Linderhof where, dressed as Lohengrin, he could travel on a boat in the shape of a cockle-shell (accompanied by swans, but rowed by a servant).

His artistically inclined grandfather (Ludwig I) had been forced to abdicate after (among other things) he had become romantically involved with Lola Montez, a Spanish dancer (a.k.a. Mrs Eliza Gilbert; a.k.a. Gräfin von Landsfeld). She later married (?bigamously) a British Old Etonian. (There were even those who referred to Wagner as the young Ludwig's Lolus or Lolette.) Ludwig II had an aunt who believed that she had swallowed a glass grand piano.

— **Spawn of a virgin and a devil.** The alleged parentage of Merlin, Arthurian wizard or wise man, depending on whom you believe (on both matters).

— **Every child.** 'I often think it's comical / How nature always does contrive / That every boy and every gal / That's born into this world alive / Is either a little Liberal, / Or else a little Conservative.' W.S. Gilbert (author of the lyrics), in W.S. Gilbert and A. Sullivan, *Iolanthe*, Act II.

— **Boston Braves**. A leading NFL (National Football League) team located in Washington DC in the USA.

— **Kismet**. Fate, destiny. A Turkish form of an Arabic word.

— **Mr and Mrs Hägeström.** They share their surname with the Swedish philosopher A. Hägeström (1868-1939) who was a leader of a school of Sandinavian legal philosophy, of a severely realist or positivist kind, which excludes transcendental values from the essential nature of law, and sees law as a product of the actual social processes of given societies. We may be inclined to suppose that Abe Green's Mr Hägeström would be sympathetic to such views.

— **Cherry Orchard**. *The Cherry Orchard* is a play (1904) by the Russian writer Anton Chekhov (1860-1904). Its setting is the breakdown of the old Russian social order in the period after the emancipation of the serfs in 1861. A landowning family faces financial ruin, including the loss of a prized cherry orchard at their country estate. There is desultory discussion about the new social situation, but the family and their friends seem unable to respond to it in any effective way. The property, including the cherry orchard, is bought at auction by a friend of the family, a member of the class of the new rich, who begins to destroy the orchard even before the family leave the house for the last time.

— **We are the garden and the gardener.** A slogan invented by Edmund Jenning in opposition to the apparent theme of Voltaire's *Candide* (see I.22). In working in the garden of human life, the gardener cannot avoid working on him/herself.

— **Firs.** The name of an aged servant, formerly a serf, in *The Cherry Orchard* (see above). He is a touching character, driven to the edge of insanity by the collapse of the old social order in Russia. At the end of the play, he is simply abandoned by the family, presumably left to die in the empty house that is no longer their home. The symbolic connection between the action of the play and the situation of 19th-century Russia is eloquent. Could there be a more-than-symbolic connection between the situation of 19th-century Russia and the contemporary situation of the United States or, indeed, of the Western world in general?

— **Son-figure.** In the Freudian and Jungian descriptions of the mind, the mind is liable to re-construct reality using abstracted ideas of human characteristics, ideas that are, however, liable to take effect as if they were real—for example, a father-figure (*Vaterfigur*) acting as a representation of authority (*Autoritätsfigur*). Oddly, Freud and Jung saw themselves (and at other times refused to see themselves) as *Vaterfigur* and *Sohnfigur* (son-figure) respectively.

— **Super-ego.** English version of S. Freud's *Über-Ich*. It is the mind's internal and internalised system of self-control. Like every other mental process, it may develop in a distorted and diseased way during the course of life-experience.

— **Mother-figure.** Edmund may like to recall: '*Amor matris*, subjective and objective genitive, may be the only true thing in life.' J. Joyce, *Ulysses*, Stephen Daedelus speaking.

He is referring to the fact that the Latin phrase can mean either 'love of the mother for the child' or 'love of the child for the mother'. Compare the two directions of the phrase 'the love of God', forming a *circuitus spiritualis*—spiritual circuit—between God and the human being. (See ch.11 below, under 'thou art that').

'The Evolution of a Mother . . . was the most stupendous task Evolution ever undertook.' 'Is it too much to say that the one motive of organic Nature was to make Mothers? It is at least certain that this was the chief thing she did.' 'Love is the final result of Evolution.' H. Drummond, *The Lowell Lectures on the Ascent of Man* (1901), ch. VIII.

Edmund may not want to recall: 'the mother is the first seductress of her boy.' S. Freud, *An Outline of Psychoanalysis* (1938).

— **Free-spirited Vermont**. A state in the North Eastern USA contiguous with Canada. Although it was not settled as a colony, the British established a fort there in 1724. With the French loss of Canada to the British (Treaty of Paris, 1763), *les Monts Verts* (in French, 'the Green Mountains') ceased to be a potential French territory and were settled by pioneers from the colonies to the south. (On the Seven Years War (1756-63), see ch. 19 below, under 'Boston lunch-party'.)

Under the name of Vermont ('the Green Mountain State'), it declared itself an independent republic in 1777. It joined the United States in 1791, as the first member state not among the original thirteen founding states.

There is a Vermont independence movement, proposing secession from the United States of America. Vermont has a slightly larger population than Malta, a member of the UN and the European Union.

— **Land of the Free**. 'And the star-spangled banner in triumph shall wave / O'er the land of the free and the home of the brave.' From *The Star-Spangled Banner* (1814), by F.S.Key. His poem was originally entitled *Defence of Fort M'Henry*—written to commemorate an event in the War of 1812-15 between the US and Britain—of which the White House and the Library of Congress were among the material casualties. The war was caused by American resistance to British interference with American shipping in support of its ongoing war with Napoleonic France (1793-1815). A modified version of Scott's poem was made the national anthem of the USA by Act of Congress in 1931.

— **U-hauled**. U-Haul, a company which rents self-drive removal vans in the USA.

— **District of Columbia**. Administrative area containing Washington, federal capital of the USA, with a special status, not being itself a state of the Union.

— **Lawyers dreaming of fees**. In W. Shakespeare's *Romeo and Juliet*, Mercutio describes the nature and work of Mab, queen of fairies. '. . . she gallops night by night / Through lovers' brains, and then they dream of love; / O'er courtiers' knees, that dream on curtsies straight; / O'er lawyers' fingers, who straight dream on fees . . .' (I. iv).

— **Prayer-wheels of power**. As a sacred ritual, Tibetan Buddhists turn cylinders or wheels on which prayers are inscribed.

— **Treading the treadmills**. A treadmill is a machine in which a wheel is rotated by a person treading on successive planks attached to the wheel. Used for practical purposes, such as the raising of water from a well, it was also formerly used as a form of punishment in prisons.

— **Story of our life**. In W. Shakespeare's *The Tempest*, Prospero, on his last night of exile on the island, says that he will tell Alonso (who improperly replaced him as King of Naples) 'the story of my life / And the particular accidents gone by / Since I came to this isle . . .' (V. i).

— **Shortage of potatoes**. In 1845, disease caused a failure of the potato crop in Ireland, at that time a part of the United Kingdom. There followed a shamefully long period of famine in Ireland (1845-49). There was terrible hardship, much loss of life, and substantial emigration, including to the USA.

— ***Geworfen***. Jane is no doubt thinking of the existential philosophy of the German philosopher M. Heidegger (1889-1976) who rejected the idea that human beings have an *essence*. All we have is *Dasein*—that is, *da* ('there') and *sein* ('to be'). We are simply 'thrown' (*geworfen*) into the world of being. Thereafter we have to make our own *existence*. We come into *being* out of *nothing*, and then makes ourselves into *not-nothing* by the way we choose to lead our *existence*.

For Heidegger, therefore, we cannot *know* our human thing-in-itself (reality-behind-the-appearances), even as an *idea*—rejecting Kant's *noumenon* behind the *phenomena* (see Appendix 8 below). Nor can we *experience* ourselves as thing-in-itself through our activity in relation to all other things-in-themselves (rejecting Schopenhauer's *will* (see ch. 4 above).

There is *simply no such thing* as the human thing-in-itself. There is no there there (as Gertrude Stein said, but not of the putative human thing-in-itself—see ch. 10 below, under 'no self there').

So we are left able only to know the appearances (*phenomena*) of being human, appearances behind which there is no other or deeper reality—just as we know only the appearance (phenomena) of the rest of what we think of as reality.

Philosophically, we are left with *phenomenology*—the study of human existence as a collection of phenomena.

Heidegger was consciously looking back to the earliest philosophers in the Western tradition, of whose philosophies we have only tiny fragments—especially Parmenides (see further in ch. 11 below), for whom the essential philosophical question was apparently the question of *being* (what is it to cease to be nothing?) and Heraclitus (c.550-c.480 BCE) for whom *being* was apparently to be understood not as a thing but as *a process of becoming within time*.

Heidegger's main work is entitled *Sein und Zeit* (Being and Time). The main work of his (sometime) disciple J-P Sartre is *L'être et le néant* (Being and Nothing).

In the long-suffering and intellectually orphaned 20th century, *phenomenology* thus joined forces with the other perverse self-denying post-philosophical forms of discourse—*Marxism* (all ideas, including philosophical ideas, are socially determined, ultimately through relations of social power); *Freudianism* (the mind, even at its most supposedly rational, is ultimately the victim of mental contents that it cannot control, or even express in rational linguistic forms); *logical positivism* (the only form of *truth* that the human mind can find within itself is the provisional hypotheses of the natural sciences); *linguistic philosophy* (philosophy cannot aspire to be anything more than the exploration of linguistic puzzles that the mind sets for itself); *pragmatism* (the mind cannot transcend its own activity, an activity which is essentially social); *behaviourism* (the mind can be led by appropriate procedures to believe or unbelieve anything).

— **Rerum cognsocere causas.** In Latin, 'to know the causes of things'. Jim and Jane are recalling lines from Virgil (I.13), II *Georgics*, 490-92.

> *Felix, qui potuit rerum cognoscere causas, / atque metus omnis et inexorabile fatum / subiecit pedibus strepitumque Acherontis avari.* ('Blessed is he who has been able to win knowledge of the causes of things, and has cast beneath his feet all fear and unyielding Fate, and the howls of hungry Acheron!') (tr., H. R Fairclough). Acheron—'river of distress' in Hell—from *achos* (Homeric Greek for *Angst*).

— **Free will**. One of the most immediate (and most difficult) problems that the self-contemplating human mind finds within itself is the question of whether human actions can be self-determined, produced simply by a movement within the human mind, or whether human actions are determined by something else—especially by natural processes (including human physiology) or by a supernatural determinant (such as Fate or the Will of God).

In other words, how can human actions possibly be excluded from the universal system of *cause and effect* of the natural world?—or how can they escape the power of an all-knowing and all-powerful ruler (or ruling principle) of the universe?

The problem of free will was made into a crucial controversy within Christian theology by the writings of Augustine (I.19), especially his *De libero arbitrio* (c. 393 CE), on the origin of evil and the freedom of the will.

He took the view that the Fall of Man (the sin of Adam and Eve) described in the biblical *Book of Genesis* (see further in chs.10 and 11 below) meant that humanity was naturally inclined to do evil, except to the extent that the manifestation of God on earth, in the life and death and resurrection of Christ, and the permament benevolent intervention of God—in the form of 'grace' (*gratia*)—save us from doing evil.

This problem would be at the centre of a disintegration of Christianity into rival versions of Christian orthodoxy (especially Roman Catholic and Protestant), leading to internecine wars and persecution (see ch.1 above, under 'savage insanity'). It is a problem that is still actual and anguishing. (See further below, *passim*.)

— **Will of God.** Various religions have ascribed to a god or gods, or to some form of personalised destiny, an anthropomorphised power of sovereignty over the universe and hence over human life, generating a corresponding duty or inclination to submit to, or to endeavour to conform to, its demands.

— **General will.** John Locke (see Appendix 3 below) spoke of 'the public will'. The head of the *Executive* is 'the Image, Phantom, or Representative of the Commonwealth, acted by the will of the Society, declared in its Laws ... But when he quits the Representation, this public Will, and acts by his own private Will, he degrades himself, and is but a single private Person without Power.' (*Second Treatise on Government* (Laslett edition), §151).

Hobbes had defined the 'Common Power' or 'Sovereign' as being the means by which the citizens ensure that 'all their Wills' are reduced to 'one Will'. (*Leviathan*, II.xvii).

But it was J.-J. Rousseau (I.1) who brilliantly identified an idea which would take its place at the centre of modern ideas of liberal democracy. The 'general will' is not merely an aggregation of individual wills or a polling of opinions. It is a mysterious and complex process by which a society generates collectively an idea of the common interest capable of being transformed into law.

> 'There is often a great deal of difference between the will of all and the general Will; the latter considers only the common interest, while the former . . . is no more than a sum of particular wills.' *Social Contract*, ch. III. (tr., G.D.H. Cole).
>
> 'The body politic, therefore, is also a corporate being possessed of a will; and this general will, which always tends to the preservation and welfare of the whole and of every part, and is the source of the laws, constitutes for all the members of the State . . . the rule of what is just or unjust.' *Discourse on Political Economy*. (same trans.).

Rousseau says that subordinate societies and individual citizens have their own ideas of the public interest, manifesting their particular wills, and such ideas can help to modify the general will.

Rousseau's conception of a General Will is accordingly remarkably analogous to Adam Smith's conception of an Invisible Hand (see Appendix 5 below).

— **The forces of the market**. See Appendix 5 below.

— **Great chess-player**. An echo, perhaps, of the *deist* idea of God as a watch-maker who designed the universe with remarkable skill and set it into motion, with no further sense of responsibility for, or interest in, its functioning.

There is also, perhaps, an echo of A. Einstein's saying that 'God does not play dice with the universe' (that is, there cannot be uncaused random events).

And there might be an echo of the suggestion of William James (see above, under 'Henry's brother William') to deal with the problem of 'free will'—imagine God playing chess with an eight-year old novice: they both know the rules of the game, but God knows more.

For deism, see ch. 12 below, under 'theism/deism'.

— **Ninety-Nine Names of God**. To be found as calligraphic inscriptions on the sides of the tomb of Mumtaz Mahal (1593-1631), wife of Shah Jahan, in the Taj Mahal, the mausoleum that he dedicated to her at Agra in India.

> *O Noble, O Magnificent, O Majestic, O Unique, O Eternal, O Glorious . . .*

— **Dance to the music of power**. *Dance to the Music of Time* is the English title of a painting (*Ballo della vita humana*—painted in Rome; now in the Wallace Collection,

London) by the French artist Nicolas Poussin (1594-1665). It shows four dancing figures who have been variously identified. The English art-historian Anthony Blunt (1907-83), a leading Poussin specialist, eventually came to accept the view of a 17th-century biographer of Poussin, to the effect that the figures represent Poverty, Labour, Wealth, and Pleasure—which might allow Jane Meehan, and us, to view the decorative Italianate work as some sort of social and moral commentary.

Dance to the Music of Time is the title of a vaguely Proustian series of twelve novels by the English writer Anthony Powell (1905-2000).

— **Glib and oily art**. 'I want [lack] that glib and oily art / To speak and purpose not [not intending to do what one says].' King Lear speaking, about politicians, in W. Shakespeare, *King Lear*, I. i.

— **Scurvy politicians**. 'Get thee glass eyes; / And, like a scurvy politician, seem / To see the things thou dost not.' King Lear speaking, in W. Shakespeare, *King Lear*, IV.vi.

— **Palace of Versailles**. Hypertrophic but splendid royal palace near Paris, built for King Louis XIV (1638-1715). It set an impossible precedent of architecture and garden design on the grandest scale. It set a bad example for other self-glorifying monarchs and presidents wishing to waste the sweat and the money of the people on feeble imitations.

— **Body impolitic**. Ironical reference to 'body politic', the metaphor for an organised society (*polis*) seen as an integrated system, like the human body—used by countless political theorists, including Aristotle (*Politics*, V.3).

J.-J. Rousseau takes the trope rather far in his *Discourse on Political Economy* (1755).

'The sovereign power represents the head; the laws and customs are the brain . . . : commerce, industry and agriculture are the mouth and stomach . . .'

Rousseau may or may not have been inspired by John of Salisbury (c.1115-80), who in his *Polycraticus* (a treatise on government) distributes the parts of the body politic in still greater detail. The prince is the head of the body, the peasants and workers are the feet, and the government's protection of the people is the footwear. John was an aristocratic, but learned, English churchman who became Bishop of Chartres in France. He was present at the assassination (instigated by King Henry II) of Thomas Becket, Archbishop of Canterbury, in Canterbury Cathedral in 1170.

— *Angst*. In German, 'anxiety'. Used in a special sense in the context of the philosophy known as Existentialism, where it refers to the psychic burden of being free to create ourselves through our own actions. See above, under '*geworfen*'.

— **Washington Paris-garden**. Paris-garden—a bear-garden. A metaphor for a disorderly place, originating in a place for bull-baiting and bear-baiting in Tudor London, on land which had belonged to Robert de Paris in the 14th century.

— **Who's won, who's lost.** Echo of another comment on public life by King Lear, in mental distress shortly before the death of his daughter Cordelia and his own death.

> 'We two will sing like birds in the cage / . . . /And pray, and sing, and tell old tales, and laugh / At gilded butterflies, and hear poor rogues / Talk of court news; and we'll talk with them too, / Who loses and who wins; who's in, who's out.' (V.iii).

— *À deux.* Between, or involving, two people.
— **Old firm.** Jim Meehan is referring to the benevolent conspiracy (which sometimes calls itself 'the Firm') which is described in *Invisible Power. A Philosophical Adventure Story*, and to which he and Edmund belong.
— **People's republic.** Centrally planned Communist states have sometimes been denominated in English as 'people's republic'—*e.g.*, the People's Republic of China—or else as 'democratic'—*e.g.*, the German Democratic Republic.
— **Supine and alienated.** Two senses of the words. *Supine* : lying on one's back (from the Latin *supinus*). But also, metaphorically in English : 'passive' or 'inert'. *Alienated*: having become the property of another person (from the Latin *alienus*). But also, metaphorically in English : mentally adrift, not at one with oneself or one's situation in life.

CHAPTER 6. *Beyond the Good.*

— **Tradition of ethical thinking.** Greg Seare is presumably referring to ethical philosophy in the Western tradition, originating in ancient Greece. However, it is hard to imagine that there has been a single society or culture in human history that has not been conscious of the problem of identifying the source and the substance of the self-regulating of human behaviour.

In the Western tradition, stemming form Plato and Aristotle and their predecessors, the problem has been seen as the challenge of integrating three axes of order—the self-ordering of the human mind, the self-ordering of human society, and the self-ordering of the universe. Every society and culture contains—perhaps, every society *is*—a permanent process for finding, and constantly re-finding, its own response to this challenge.

Greg is probably familiar with a work of which this is the central theme: Ph. Allott, *Eunomia. New Order for a New World* (1990/2001)—in which the discussion is taken to the level of *the society of all-humanity*.

On this occasion, Greg is evidently expressing a concern about two aspects of the intellectual legacy of the troubled public mind of the 20th century.

(1) The trend towards an absolute hegemony of the *social* dimension of human self-ordering, to the virtual exclusion of both the personal and the transcendental.

and (2) the trend towards treating ethical problems as *pragmatic* problems, or even as *biological* or *physiological* problems. Greg evidently sees both these trends as symptoms of a long-term *dehumanising* of human beings, treating human beings as not personally and ultimately responsible, and a *naturalising* of humanity, treating human beings as if they were things.

— **Problem of evil**. The ethical search can be seen as a never-ending effort to give meaning to the idea of 'the good'. But the idea of the good seems necessarily to imply an idea of evil. Each may be used reciprocally to identify the other.

Is the human being naturally inclined to do evil and/or naturally capable of doing good? Human evil seen as a *problem* has been seen as originating in a familiar tendency of human beings to choose to do evil in a given situation, even when they are aware of what it is to do good in that situation. *Free will* (see ch. 5 above) has been understood as a capacity to choose to do evil as readily as to choose to do good.

And, for those whose religious beliefs include a belief in the absolute goodness of a creator-God, there is the special problem of how God can have made a creature capable of doing evil.

> 'It is important to understand that evil is essential to the order of the world and to the birth of the good.' Voltaire, *Zadig* (the angel Jesred speaking).
>
> 'Knowledge of good bought dear by knowing ill.' J. Milton, *Paradise Lost* (I.20), IV (recounting the *Genesis* myth: see ch.10 below, and *passim*).
>
> 'We know and recognise what is right, but we do not act on it, for we are in the grip of passion.' (Euripides, *Hippolytus* (I.4) (Phaedra speaking). 'The mind commands itself and is resisted.' Augustine (I.19), *Confessions*, VIII.
>
> '. . . *je vois le bien, je l'aime, et je fais le mal*' ('I see the good, I love it, and I do evil.') J.-J. Rousseau, *Profession de foi du vicaire Savoyard*, in *Émile*. (See further in ch.11 below.)
>
> 'The whole of history is the refutation by experiment of the principle of the so-called "moral world order".' F. Nietzsche (I.19), *Ecce Homo*.

The permanent challenge of the problem of the nature of evil includes a more particular challenge—why should we seek to do good, when doing evil may profit or please us more? Many religions have supposed that the quality of the life we live on Earth may determine the quality of the life we live after death. (On 'Pascal's wager', see I.20. See also the discussion in ch.12 below.)

> *On a beaucoup ri d'un télégramme que Mauriac a reçu peu de jours après la mort de Gide et ainsi rédigé : "Il n'y a pas d'enfer. Tu peux te dissiper. Préviens Claudel. Signé André Gide."* (Julien Green, *Journal*, entry for 28 February 1951.)
>
> 'We laughed a lot about a telegram which Mauriac received a few days after the death of Gide, reading as follows: "There is no Hell. You can dissipate yourself. Warn Claudel. Signed, André Gide".'

A. Gide (!869-1951), French writer, was a seriously free spirit. F. Mauriac (1885-1970) and P. Claudel (1868-1955), French writers, were seriously (Roman) Catholic.

The tragic approach to evil is a reflection within Christianity of the Hebraic tradition (see ch. 3 above, under 'Hellenic and Hebraic'; and see further in chs. 10 and 12 below) as opposed to the Hellenic tradition of ethical philosophy, discussed above. A Buddhist tradition originating at much the same time as the Hellenic tradition takes the view that human beings are essentially good, and hence that the practice of holiness is like the refining of gold, gradually removing the impurities that are the cause of evil.

— **Wyczwycz** Withold Wyczwycz (1926-86) (pronounce approximately as: 'wit-old wodge'), post-philosopher of Polish-Hungarian origin who 'lived' for most of his life in Paris. (He himself always inserted inverted commas, written or spoken or signalled, around the word 'live'.) His early neo-dispositionist ethics (late in life he became rather more of a post-repositionist) was popular with the revolting young on the *Rive gauche* of Paris in the late-1960's.

In 1964, with his protégé Jacques Méridoux (I.16) as co-author, he published the literally seminal and literally groundbreaking *Vivre pour mourir* ('Living to die'), which was subsequently published in the United States under the not-wholly-accurate title *Living Death*. It led to a wave of 'die-ins' on American university campuses, and to a number of romantically staged, and sometimes fatal, student 'pseudocides'—from the Greek *pseudēs* ('false') and the Latin *caedere* ('to kill').

The early Wyczwycz believed (as the later Freud did not) in Freud's principle of a 'death instinct or drive' (*Todestrieb*), which seemed to Freud, for a while, to be explanatorily necessary, if biologically unlikely and psychically dispiriting, in order to balance dialectically his peculiarly unpleasant 'pleasure principle' (*Lustprinzip*). 'The aim of everything living is death.' *Das Ziel alles Lebenden ist der Tod.* S. Freud, *Jenseits des Lustprinzips* (Beyond the Pleasure Principle) (1919). See ch. 19 below, under 'death wish'.

In his earlier (pre-1919) formulation of a struggle within the mind between a 'pleasure principle' and a 'reality principle', Freud came close to an analysis of the dynamics of the mind suggested by Socrates/Plato.

> '. . . within each one of us there are two sorts of ruling or guiding principle that we follow. One is an innate desire for pleasure, the other an innate judgment that aims at what is best. Sometimes these internal guides are in accord, sometimes at variance; now one gains the mastery, now the other.'
> Plato, *Phaedrus*, 238d. (Socrates speaking) (tr., R. Hackforth).

See also ch. 11 below, under 'self is a crowd'.
— *en fin de compte.* In French, 'in the end'.

— *sotto voce.* In Italian, 'in a quiet voice'.
— **mother-father sign/signal.** Dr Birmingham is evidently meaning to invoke the *façon de parler* (speech-mode) of *semiology* (*sēma,* in ancient Greek: sign, signal; *logos*: rational study), which considers the way in which language (human communication of all kinds) conveys *meaning.*

Semiology draws particular attention to the fact that the *meaning* of a word or sign has a life of its own, and a history of its own. A particular word or sign may seem to represent some particular thing ('mother', 'father', 'truth', 'God', Stars and Stripes, a swastika), but its effect in consciousness (its meaning) is infinitely more complex and unstable than its surface form suggests. It is hard to think of words more saturated in meaning than the words 'father' and 'mother', not least in their role in the internalising of ethical ideas.

Plato makes Socrates discuss this problem in his dialogue *Cratylus.* What is the relationship between a name and the thing it names? By making Socrates go through a long and laborious and ludicrous effort to deconstruct a long succession of Greek words to find their 'real' relationship to the things they represent, Plato shows that the meaning of words has a completely different source which it is, ultimately, the task of *philosophy* to recosntruct.

Medieval *nominalist* philosophy had taken the view that words are merely names, so that it is not possible to infer from the fact that a thing is named that that thing exists. See Appendix 1 below.

C.S. Peirce (see ch. 2 above, under 'pragmatist') advocated a form of study that he called 'semiotics'. Indeed, one view of his *pragmatism* is that it is a science of meaning.

'Every thought, or cognitive representation, is of the nature of a sign. "Representation" and "sign" are synonyms. The whole purpose of a sign is that it shall be interpreted in another sign; and its whole purport lies in the special character which it imparts to that interpretation. When a sign determines an interpretation of itself in another sign, it produces an effect external to itself, a physical effect, though the sign producing the effect may itself not be an existent object but merely a type.'

From a draft book review in which Peirce summarises with relative clarity what he sees as the essence of pragmatism. Reproduced in H. Thayer, *Meaning and Action. A Critical History of Pragmatism* (1968).

In the 20th century semiology became an intellectual industry, alongside linguistics (the study of the underlying, and presumably universal, structures of language), especially under the influence of posthumously published lectures by the Swiss linguist F. Saussure (1857-1913).

'Advertisements for *Omo* also [like advertisements for *Persil*] indicate the effect of the product . . . , but they chiefly reveal its mode of action; in doing so,

they involve the consumer in a kind of direct experience of the substance,
make him the accomplice of a liberation rather than the mere beneficiary of
a result; matter here is endowed with value-bearing states. *Omo* uses two of
these, which are rather novel in the category of detergents: the deep and the
foamy. To say that *Omo* cleans in depth . . . is to assume that linen is deep,
which no one had previously thought . . . As for foam, it is well known that
it signifies luxury . . .' R. Barthes, 'Soaps and Detergents', in *Mythologies*
(1957). (tr., A. Lavers).

If one were to attempt a semiology of semiology, one would place it within
the field-force of *phenomenology* (see ch. 5 above, under '*geworfen*'), part of the vast
20th-century enterprise to replace the study of substance by the study of surfaces, a
flight from *meaning* to the *meaning of meaning*—the title of a book by C. Ogden and
I. Richards (1923/1926) which crudely demystified the phenomenon of language, to
the delight, in particular, of those who find the most serious uses of language to be
uncongenial. This general intellectual movement was related to *modernism* in the arts
and literature and music, where the medium itself becomes the centre of attention,
where the medium itself (the surface phenomenon) is the main message.

One of the most quoted and silliest sayings of the semiologist L. Wittgenstein
(I.20) is: *Wovon man nicht sprechen kann, darüber muss man schweigen.* 'Of what
we cannot speak about we must remain silent.' *Tractatus Logico-Philosophicus*
(1921), §7.

This saying particularly pleased those who feel mildly ashamed of their ignorance
of philosophy and those for whom natural science is the only reliable form of abstract
speech. They could forget about 'philosophy'. *Die Lösung des Problems des Lebens
merkt man am Verschwinden dieses Problems* 'The solution to the problem of life is
seen in the disappearance of the problem.' (§6.521).

The silliness of these sayings is in the prescriptive words 'cannot' and 'must'. Why
cannot we talk about things that the most thoughtful people have thought about for
thousands of years? Why *must* we stop talking about things that go to the root of
the anguished self-consciousness of human beings and their troubled consciousness
of the worlds (natural and human) that they inhabit? How can the problem of life
disappear when it clearly always remains to torment people's minds?

Even if we (good and intelligent people) perversely choose not to speak about
such things, we can be sure that others (bad and intelligent people—political
extremists and religious fanatics, among others) will certainly go on talking about
such things, often at immense human cost.

At least Wittgenstein had the good grace, or the tactical sense, to distance
himself from the ranks of 'professional philosophers'. '. . . from the bottom of my
heart it is all the same to me what the professional philosophers of today think of
me; for it is not for them that I am writing.' (letter to M. Schlick; 8 August 1932;
quoted in R. Monk, *Wittgenstein. The Duty of Genius*, ch. 14).

The *T L-P* (all 71 pages of it, in the English version) was the only book that Wittgenstein published in his lifetime. (He later said that he had been 'forced to recognise grave mistakes in what I wrote in that first book.') *Philosophical Investigations* (1953/58/74) and *Culture and Value* (1977/78/80) were edited and published by others after his death, making use of some of his intellectual *disiecta membra*.

In these books, he reveals himself finally as a semiologist. *En fin de compte*, we may say to him, as Milton said to the late lamented Shakespeare: '. . . each heart/ Hath from the leaves of thy unvalu'd Book, / Those Delphick lines with deep impression took.' (His tribute to Shakespeare was Milton's first (anonymously) published poem, written while he was a student at Christ's College, Cambridge, and placed as a frontispiece by the publisher, Robert Allott, in what is known as the Second Folio of Shakespeare's plays (1632). The poem was later revised. The word 'heart' in the above quotation is from the 1640 version.)

In *The Gutenberg Galaxy* (1962) and *The Medium is the Massage* (1967), the Canadian social philosopher M. McLuhan (1911-80) created enormous public interest in the idea that civilisations have turning-points connected to changes in their methods of social communication. He suggested that western civilisation in the 20th century had moved into a mode dominated by electronic communication and the ethos of journalism and advertising.

He quotes Socrates in Plato's *Phaedrus* (275a) telling the story of an Egyptian king refusing to accept the idea of the alphabet. 'If men learn this, it will implant forgetfulness in their souls; they will cease to exercise memory because they rely on that which is written, calling things to remembrance no longer from within themselves, but by means of external marks.' (tr., R. Hackforth).

He quotes the French poet and politician A. Lamartine (1790-1869), writing in 1831: 'Before this century shall run out journalism will be the whole press—the whole human thought . . . Thought will be spread abroad in the world with the rapidity of light; instantly conceived, instantly written, instantly understood at the extremities of the earth . . .'

He quotes himself: 'Today we're beginning to realize that the new media aren't just mechanical gimmicks for creating worlds of illusion, but new languages with new and unique powers of expression.'

(McLuhan deserves high praise not least for regularly using a plural verb with the word 'media'—the plural in Latin of the Latin word *medium*. In French, the regrettable form *les medias* is now being used.)

— **Unsoignée.** *Soigné*, in French 'elegantly well-dressed' (with an extra 'e' in the feminine form).

— **White Queen**. A particularly un*soignée* character in *Through the Looking Glass* (ch. V) by L.Carroll (I.19). She conducts an earnest conversation with Alice.

Alice asks her: 'Can *you* keep from crying by considering things?" 'That's the way it's done,' the Queen said with great decision, 'nobody can do two things at once, you know.'

Alice objects to one of the Queen's odder assertions. 'One *can't* believe impossible things,' Alice said. 'I daresay you haven't had much practice,' said the Queen. 'When I was your age, I always did it for half-an-hour a day. Why, sometimes I've believed as many as six impossible things before breakfast.'

The Queen objects to Alice's idea of memory. 'It's a poor sort of memory that works backwards.' The Queen says that memory means that pain should be felt *before* it is caused, and crimes should be punished *before* they are committed.

— **Return to our sheep.** The French phrase is *revenons à nos moutons* ('let us return to our sheep'—meaning: to get back to the point of a discussion after a digression).

Is it possible that Fred McDonald had also experienced an involuntary association of ideas, linking Bunty Birmingham and the White Queen in *Alice*? Later in her conversation with Alice, the Queen apparently turns into a sheep in a shop, with characteristics that seemed to Alice to pose idealist-metaphysical problems about the nature of reality.

> 'The shop seemed to be full of all manner of curious things—but the oddest part of it all was that, whenever she looked hard at any shelf, to make out exactly what it had on it, that particular shelf was always quite empty, though the others round it were crowded as full as they could hold.
>
> "Things flow about so here!" she said at last in a plaintive tone, after she had spent a minute or so in vainly pursuing a large bright thing, that looked sometimes like a doll and sometimes like a work-box, and was always in the shelf next above the one she was looking at. "And this one is the most provoking of all—but I'll tell you what" she added, as a sudden thought struck her, "I'll follow it up to the very top shelf of all. It'll puzzle it to go through the ceiling, I expect!"
>
> But even this plan failed: the "thing" went through the ceiling 'as quietly as possible, as if it were quite used to it.'

Was Alice looking for the Aristotelian *essence* or *substance*? Or was she, at the early age of seven-and-a-half exactly, experiencing for the first time the *phenomenological* temptation?

— **Ethical intuitionist.** Someone who believes that we have an innate capacity to distinguish between good and evil. Besides David Hume (see Appendix 4 below), 18th-century Scotland produced several influential philosophers who explored the ground covered previously by Locke and later by Kant (Appendix 8), in particular the question of how to understand our apparent capacity to make *moral judgments*, especially moral judgments about our own behaviour.

F. Hutcheson (1694-1746) suggested that we have a 'moral sense'. T. Reid (1710-96) suggested that we have a 'common sense', in addition to the five physical senses, which enables us to integrate experience and volition.

At least as seen from an English point of view, such as that (presumably) of Greg Seare, these Scottish philosophers, other than Hume (who seems essentially English in this respect), seem to be reluctant to dismiss the idea of morality (the inescapable spirit of Scottish Calvinism, perhaps), while being led by their cool rationality to favour a morality of intelligent utilitarian calculation (see further below, under 'happiness').

— **Weberian sociology.** We are not told whether May Gaunt approved of the dismal sociology of Max Weber (1864-1920). Like Nietzsche, Weber seems to have been psychically overwhelmed by the prospect of the 20th century. At the wrong time (1919—when Germany was reconstituting itself after the War), in the wrong place (Munich, where Hitler was waiting in the wings), he told students a very wrong story.

> 'In the last analysis the modern state can only be defined sociologically in terms of a specific means (*Mittel*) which is peculiar to the state, as it is to all other political associations, namely physical violence (*Gewaltsamkeit*). "Every state is founded on force (*Gewalt*)", as Trostsky once said at Brest-Litovsk. That is indeed correct . . . In our terms, then, "politics" would mean striving for a share of power or for influence on the distribution of power, whether it be between states or between the groups of people within a single state.' '. . . the state is a relationship of *rule* (*Herrschaft*) by human beings over human beings, and one that rests on the legitimate use of violence (that is, violence that is held to be legitimate).'

Weber goes on to state the three 'inner justifications' which can legitimate the power of the state—custom, charisma of the ruler (the prophet, the war-lord, the plebiscitarian ruler, the demagogue, the leader of a political party), and legality (respect for the law). *Politik als Beruf* ('The Profession and Vocation of Politics'), lecture to the Union of Free Students, Munich and Leipzig. (tr., R. Spiers).

On German constitutional psychology, see Ph. Allott, 'The Crisis of European Constitutionalism', in *The Health of Nations*, ch. 7.

— **Bottom line.** The last line of a balance-sheet where the totals of profit and loss, or assets and liabilities, are stated, and a balance is drawn between them. Now used metaphorically to identify the most solid explanation or justification or possible outcome of some human activity.

— **Sophism.** Soft-core philosophy, giving simple answers to complicated questions simply expressed, often with a view to the reassuring or consolation of those who are liable to be consoled or reassured by such things.

From the Greek, *sophistēs*, professional philosopher in Athens. Socrates and Plato used the example of the *sophist* to show, by way of contrast, the nature of the true *philosophos*, 'lover of wisdom'. See further below, under 'humanism'.

— **Middle-brow**. Somewhere between high-brow and low-brow, in relation to things of the mind, but not normally able to recognise itself as such. It has no necessary connection with social class.

— **Eutopia**. See I.22.

— **Brave new human world**. 'O, wonder! / How many goodly creatures are there here! / How beauteous mankind is! O brave new world, / That has such people in't!' W. Shakespeare, *The Tempest*, V. i. (Miranda speaking).

    Brave New World (1932) is the title of a presumably unEutopian—and notably prescient—novel by the English writer A. Huxley (1894-1963), describing a human future dominated and determined by science and tehnology.

— **Paradise of fools**. A common expression describing a situation supposed to be good, but only on the basis of illusion, delusion or error.

    It derives from an idea connected with the Christian idea of *Limbo*, as (1) a place reserved for the after-life of the pre-Christian prophets of Christianity, who would eventually be received into heaven; (2) a place for the after-life of children who die before they can be baptised into Christianity; and (3) a place for the after-life of idiots ('fools') who could not be held responsible for their bad deeds.

    The expression received notorious, capitalised recognition in a passage in J. Milton's *Paradise Lost* (bk. III), where it seems to be referring to (4) the Roman Catholic Church as the propagator of an illusory paradise.

> '. . . and now at foot / Of Heaven's ascent they [Satan and friends] lift their Feet, when lo /A violent cross wind from either Coast / Blows them transverse ten thousand Leagues awry / Into the devious Air; then might ye see / Cowles, Hoods and Habits with their wearers tossed / And fluttered into Rags, then Relics, Beads, / Indulgences, Dispenses, Pardons, Bulls, / The sport of Winds: all these upwhirled aloft / Fly over the backside of the World far off / Into a *Limbo* large and broad, since called / The Paradise of Fools.' (spelling modernised).
>
> 'Relics', 'indulgences', 'pardons', '[Papal] bulls [edicts]' were well-established polemical sign/symbols, for Protestant Christians, of the deep corruption and venality of the Roman Church.

    The whole passage (lines 443-97) was excised by R. Bentley—'a silly Interruption of the Story'—in his new improved *Paradise Lost* (see ch. 4 above, under 'darkness made visible').

— **Spirit of the spiritless**. 'Religious distress is at the same time the expression of real distress and the protest against real distress. Religion is the sigh of the oppressed creature, the heart of a heartless world, just as it is the spirit of a spiritless situation. It is the opium of the people. The abolition of religion as the illusory happiness of the people is required for their real happiness. The demand to give up the illusion

about its condition is the demand to give up a condition which needs illusions.'
K.Marx (I.19), *Critique of Hegel's Philosophy of Right* (1843).

— **Humanism**. Protagoras of Abdera (c.486-c.410 BCE) was, to 5th-century Athens, what David Hume was to 18th-century Europe, or Nietzsche to 19th-century Europe—a necessary intellectual irritant and stimulant.

'Man is the measure of all things'—a saying already famous in his own day—has been understood in various different ways—

(1) as a denial of any transcendental, especially religious, explanation of anything;
(2) as an affirmation of relativism or pragmatism: there can be no way of deciding finally among contradictory propositions and opinions—'. . . on Protagoras' view it is what appears to anyone that is the measure [of truth, beauty and goodness].' Aristotle, *Metaphysics*, 1062;
(3) as an affirmation of empiricism or phenomenology: there is no hidden reality behind the appearance of the world;
(4) as an appeal to humanism: if we leave gods and fate and metaphysics out of our thinking about things human, we can take full responsibility for making human things better.

Socrates/Plato and Aristotle took Protagoras the Sophist (see above) seriously. In Plato's dialogue *Protagoras,* he is the main interlocutor of Socrates. Protagoras reveals himself as the prototype of a certain kind of professional philosopher still familiar today—articulate, self-confident, with ready views on all matters, open-minded, unchallenging, rewarded by society with esteem and income.

The 'humanism' (as it later came to be called) of the Italian Renaissance of the 15th century contained two interlocking originating strands, which might be characterised respectively as Greek and Roman. One strand sought to incorporate into Christian theology substantial elements of Platonism (and, especially, of the neo-Platonism of the second and third centuries) under the leadership of Marsilio Ficino (1433-99), who translated into Latin the surviving works of Plato and founded the Platonic Academy in Florence. There had been a previous Hellenising movement (incorporating Aristotelian ideas) in the (later so-called) 12th-century Renaissance. (See ch. 2 above, under 'neo-neo-Platonist'.)

The other (Roman) strand was the effect of an intense revival of interest in Roman society and Roman law which had medieval origins and was epitomised in the work of Francesco Petrarca ('Petrarch') (1304-74). Since ancient Rome had been 'pagan' (non-Christian because pre-Christian), in the eyes of Christians, this strand of humanism was detached from the mainstream of Christianity and gave rise to a secular form of *humanist idealism*—spiritual, intellectual and artistic—aimed at *human self-perfecting*.

With the organisational disintegration of Christianity, following the 16th-century Reformation, this secular form of humanism took effect as a form of psychic liberation, manifesting itself in the scientific revolution of the 17th century, the Enlightenment of the 18th century, and the optimistic universal scientism of the 19th century.

It was possible for A. Comte (1798-1857), dogmatic philosopher of the new positivist 'social science', to seek, late in life, to give humanism a religious aura in what he called a 'religion of humanity'. (The Victorian public intellectual *par excellence* T.H. Huxley (1825-95) called Comte's unreligion an 'incongruous mixture of bad science with eviscerated papistry' and 'Catholicism *minus* Christianity'.)

It was also possible for a fierce apostle of secularism to claim to be an heir of a humanist tradition. *L'homme n'est rien d'autre que ce qu'il se fait. Tel est le premier principe de l'existentialisme.'* ('We are nothing other than what we make ourselves. That is the first principle of existentialism.') J.-P. Sartre, *L'existentialisme est un humanisme* (Existentialism is a Humanism) (1946/71).

Late in the 20th-century, among some Christians, especially 'fundamentalists' (see ch.19 below, under 'fundamentalist pragmatism'), the word 'humanism' came to have an opprobrious connotation: 'humanism' as a negation of religion.

— **Greatest happiness**. One's idea of 'happiness' is a direct correlative of one's governing philosophy of life. Every substantial philosophy has expressed or implied a governing idea of happiness. Many ancient traditions of philosophy and religion devoted much attention to the problem of human happiness. The word lived a particularly active life in the public mind of 18th-century Europe.

The *Characteristics of Men, Manners, Opinions, Times* (1711) of Anthony Cooper, 3rd Earl of Shaftesbury (1671-1713), pupil and patron of John Locke (see Appendix 4 below), proposed a platonic-stoic view of happiness as a human response to the good and the beautiful, which are, in turn, our response to the order of the natural world. (See further in ch.19 below, under 'soul embracing soul'.)

Shaftesbury's integrating of the moral and the aesthetic would have a dialectical influence—leading towards a *rationalising* of morality and aesthetics (most notably in the work of Immanuel Kant—see Appendix 8 below), but leading also, by way of negation, to a *subjectivising* (especially in the work of D. Hume—see Appendix 4 below) of both moral and aesthetic experience, culminating in the Europe-wide Romantic movement of the late-18th century).

The word 'happiness' even found its way into political philosophy, as a way of expressing the controlling purpose of society, government and law. Francis Hutcheson (see above) graduated from Glasgow University (founded 1451) in 1712. His writing shows the influence of Shaftesbury.

'In comparing the moral Qualities of Actions, in order to regulate our Election among various Actions proposed, or to find which of them has the greatest moral Excellency, we are led by our moral Sense of Virtue to judge thus; that in equal Degrees of Happiness, expected to proceed from the Action, the Virtue is in proportion to the Number of Persons to whom the Happiness shall extend; . . . so that, that Action is best, which procures *the greatest Happiness for the greatest numbers*; and that, worst, which, in like manner, occasions Misery.'

F. Hutcheson, *Inquiry into the Origins of our Ideas of Beauty and Virtue, in Two Treatises* (1725), 3.8. (Emphasis added; spelling modernised).

D. Diderot (1713-84), a leading activist of the French Enlightenment, published a translation of Hutcheson's *Inquiry* in 1745. C.A. Helvétius (1715-71) proposed that the search for happiness is the search for pleasure, which is the governing principle of private life, and should be seen as the governing principle of social life. Accordingly, the aim of society is the greatest happiness of the greatest number of the people. His *De l'Esprit* (On the Mind) (1758) was much read in the period before the American and French Revolutions.

Helvétius himself followed closely in the path of T. Hobbes (see Appendix 3 below), whose profoundly influential view of human nature (mollified somewhat by J. Locke) might be summarised as: *happiness* is maximised *pleasure*; pleasure is obtaining what we *desire*; what we desire we call *good*. So, for Hobbes also, society is a system of collectivised self-interest in which government and law provide the conditions for maximising the self-interest of all.

The American Declaration of Independence hallowed the word 'happiness' in the formula 'life, liberty and the pursuit of happiness'—an ominous variant of the admittedly equivocal (John) Lockeian trinity of 'life, liberty and property'. Th. Jefferson, main author of the Declaration, had read Hobbes and Locke and Helvétius. He objected to what he saw as the latter's crude morality of egoism and self-interest.

J. Bentham (see Appendix 6 below) acknowledged his debt to Helvétius, using the 'greatest happiness' principle to bring out a radical aspect of the latter's thinking, an idea which would also be central to R. Owen's *socialist* project. Society can, through rational law and government, improve *the quality of the lives* of the people. But also, especially through rationally organised education, society can even improve *the quality of the people themselves*.

As might be expected, S. Freud was not a great believer in happiness. 'One feels inclined to say that the intention that man should be "happy" is not included in the plan of "Creation".' *Civilization and its Discontents* (1930).

The German title is more accurate: *Das Unbehagen in der Kultur* ('The Discontent within Civilization'). Freud had previously considered two other titles—'Happiness (*Glück*) and Civilisation' and 'Unhappiness (*Unglück*) in Civilisation'. He might better have chosen 'The Unhappiness of Civilisation (*Die Unglück der Kultur*)'.

Less expected is the testimony of Goethe (I.12).

*Man hat mich immer als einen vom Glück besonders Begünstigten gepriesen; auch
will ich mich nicht beklagen und den Gang meines Lebens nicht schelten. Allein
im Grunde ist es nichts als Mühe und Arbeit gewesen, und ich kann wohl sagen,
daß ich in meinen fünfundsiebzig Jahren keine vier Wochen eigentliches Behagen
gehabt.* ('People have always thought of me as a person especially favoured
with happiness, and I won't pity myself or complain about the way my life
has gone. Only deep down has it been anything but trouble and work, and I
can truly say that, in my seventy-five years, I have hardly had four weeks of
contentment (*Behagen*).')

P.Eckerman, *Gespräche mit Goethe in den letzten Jahren seines Lebens*
(Conversations with Goethe in the Last Years of His Life), entry for 27 January
1824. (present author's trans.).

Did Goethe know a certain poem by Michelangelo (*Madrigal* LII)?

*Ohimè, Ohimè, pur reiterando / vo 'l mio passato tempo e non ritrovo / in tutto
un giorno che sia stato mio!'* ('Alas, Alas. I keep going over my past time and do
not find in the whole of it one day that has been mine!'). (tr., G. Kay).

— **Science is a sorcerer.** See next entry. See Appendix 7 below.
— **Help me, ye higher powers!** Dr Birmingham is quoting a line from J.W. von
Goethe's *Der Zauberlehrling* (Sorcerer's Apprentice) (1779).

Helft mir, ach! ihr hohen Mächte!

The poem is based on a story by a late Roman writer about a magician whose
curiosity leads him to create effects that he cannot control. Humanity's mental
history shows an interesting process of separation of astronomy from astrology,
chemistry from alchemy, physics from magic, natural philosophy (natural science)
from metaphysics.

A non-scientist is liable to detect a residue of the latter in the former, in each
case. Greg Seare apparently sees the natural sciences as a form of sorcery which is
now beyond the control of the form of society that has made it possible.

— **Pythia.** Priestess of Apollo at Delphi who emitted oracles, foretelling the future
with fatal obscurity.
— ***Tricoteuse assoluta.*** *Tricoteuse*—'woman who knits', in French. During the French
Revolution, the public were invited to attend the Convention that would order the
execution of King Louis XVI. Women were paid to attend and, to pass the time,
they knitted. They tended to support violence and, during the Terror, they would
sit, still knitting, beside the guillotine—or so it is said. The scene was made familiar
by its depiction in Th. Carlyle, *The French Revolution* (1837) (see ch. 9 below, under
'pimpernel').

Prima donna assoluta. In Italian, 'absolute first lady'. *Diva assoluta,* 'absolute goddess'. Titles of honour sometimes conferred on very leading opera singers.

Prima ballerina assoluta. In Italian, 'absolute first ballerina'. Title of honour sometimes conferred on very leading ballerinas.

— **Set his face like flint**. A (Judeo-Christian) biblical echo. 'For the Lord God will help me; therefore shall I not be confounded: therefore have I set my face like a flint, and I know that I shall not be ashamed.' *Isaiah*, 50.7. (King James English version, 1611). Flint is a particularly hard form of rock.

— **Kantian Universal Legislator**. The 'problem of evil', see above, includes the question of the possible *rationality* of morality. Is there a form of self-control that causes people to do good and avoid doing evil *on rational grounds*—and not merely for extrinsic reasons, such as the pursuit of pleasure or the avoidance of pain.

Challenged by the moral scepticism of D. Hume (Appendix 4 below), Kant, in his *Critique of Practical Reason* (1783), proposes an ingenious solution (Appendix 8 below).

In terms of Kantian *practical reason*, to act morally is to act *in order to do my duty*. It is acting in such a way that the principle that determines my action could be the principle determining the action of any other person seeking to do their duty in the same circumstance.

This 'principle' of my decision is not the same thing as a *motive* for action. My actual motive on the given occasion (my psychological state, as it were) does not determine the morality of my action. Morality is not merely a matter of intention. It is a matter of carrying out one's *duty*. Moral action is thus action for which a reason can be inferred which is *not a self-interested* reason. It is a universalisable reason. In this sense, when I act morally, I act as a sort of *universal legislator*—by giving effect to a form of self-regulating which could be a form of self-regulating for human beings in general.

This argument has not, for obvious reasons, convinced moral sceptics and moral reductionists. But, at the risk of trivialising Kant's idea, it may be said that there is even some sort of *psychological truth* in the idea.

The question—what if everyone did that?—*can* be a relevant part of a *conscious* effort to avoid a bad course of action. And *empathy*—trying to put ourselves in the position of someone else, or of others, who might be affected by our action—can be another part of the same kind of effort.

— **Epicurean Third Way**. On Epicurus, see ch. 2 above, under 'Cynic, Epicurean, Stoic' and ch. 3 above, under *'dia voluptas'*.

— **Ideal Form (vodka martini)**. Unfortunately, Plato fails to discuss explicitly the (Platonic) Ideal Form of the vodka martini. However, it may be that there is a clue to his view on the matter in the *Timaeus*. Timaeus, in the course of explaining the origin and nature of the universe, says that wine 'warms the soul as well as the body' (60a).

— **Vodka martini (social regulation of)**. The elderly Plato is more circumspect.

'. . . the souls of the drinkers grow softer as they are heated, like heated iron, and become more juvenile, and consequently more ductile in the hands of one who has the power and skill to train them and mold them, much as when they were still youthful, and the molding should now, as formerly, be the task of the good legislator . . . Then if wine and merriment were used in such fashion, would not the members of such a party be the better for it and part, not, as they do today, on terms of enmity, but with an increase of friendship, seeing their intercourse would have been regulated throughout by laws, and they would have followed the path marked out by the sober for the unsober?' Plato, *Laws*, 671b-e. (tr., A. Taylor).

— *Durchlaucht*. Term used by the Firm to identify participants in its conspiracy (see I, *passim*).
— **Malice in wonderland**. A familiar ironical echo of the title of L. Carroll's *Alice in Wonderland* (I.19).
— **Focus group**. An illusory and delusive form of public participation favoured by the governing classes in the most advanced forms of liberal democracy. On the related delusive concepts of 'governance' and 'civil society', see 'European governance and the re-branding of democracy', in Ph. Allott, *The Health of Nations*, ch. 6.
— *À propos*. In French, 'by the way, but relevantly'.
— *In lotio veritas*. The familiar Latin phrase is *in vino veritas* ('people are inclined to speak frankly under the influence of alcohol'). In Latin, *vinum*, 'wine'; *veritas*, 'truth'. In Latin, *lotium*, 'urine'.
— **Left-field**. A common expression, derived from baseball, indicating a wild or aberrant idea, situation or person.
— **Cross-hairs**. An image, usually a cross formed from two thin lines at right-angles, used in the focusing mechanism of an instrument, especially in the telescopic sight of a rifle.
— **Terms of trade**. A concept of international economics identifying the relationship between the price which a country obtains for an exported product or products and the price paid for an imported product or products. The relationship is relevant to the country's overall *balance of payments* and hence, ultimately, to the *wealth of the nation*.
— **Wealth of a nation**. The echo is of the title of Adam Smith's *Wealth of Nations*, itself presumably an echo of the title of Turgot's principal work (see Appendix 5 below). The VP(P) seems to be seeking to turn the supposedly dismal science of free-market economics into something richer and stranger—a free-market *philosophy à l'américaine*, perhaps.
— **USP**. Unique Selling Point. A competitive advantage of a particular product or service. Seen as a highly desirable phenomenon in the metaphysics of capitalist commerce.

CHAPTER 7. *Another World, Another Person.*

— **Another World.** Observing an alien form of culture with a view to enlightening oneself about one's own culture and one's own identity is a practice at least as old as the keen interest that the culture of ancient Greece took in the very different cultures of its neighbours—especially Egypt and Persia—for example, in the writing of Herodotus (I.17). Especially in the 1960's (see below), India seemed to offer, to privileged young westerners in particular, the ideal counter-example to Western culture, a tantalising dialectical negation, a possible basis for a new kind of personality.

Satirising a given form of human existence by describing another form, actual or imaginary, has been a common literary form. Aristophanes (c.445-c.386 BCE) and Lucian (c.125-c.192 CE) inspired modern writers—from Erasmus (I.5) and Thomas More (I.11) and Francis Bacon (I.11) and Voltaire (I.15, I.22), to W. Morris (1834-96) and S. Butler (1835-1902) and George Orwell (1903-50). It is not always easy to say whether a given author—except, perhaps, Plato in his idealising *Republic* (I.16)—is meaning to describe a *eutopia* (good place), a *utopia* (no place) or a *dystopia* (bad place—a word suggested by J.M. Patrick in 1952).

Another World and Yet the Same is the English title of a severely dystopic and mock-scientific book published pseudonymously in Latin (*Mundus Alter et Idem*) in 1605, apparently by Joseph Hall (1574-1656), Puritan churchman and prolific writer—graduate and sometime Fellow of Emmanuel College, Cambridge. The narrator travels to societies in the furthest South Atlantic where all human vices are treated as virtues. In his other writings, Hall made still clearer his view that European civilisation had reached the depths of depravity and would soon destroy itself.

In France, a movement opposing 'globalisation' (*mondialisation*; 'world-isation') is called *altermondialisme* ('another-world-ism'). In Latin, *alter*, 'other'.

— **Sparkling eyes.** 'Take a pair of sparkling eyes'—a song from *The Gondoliers* (1889)—lyrics by W.S. Gilbert, music by A. Sullivan. The charming poem also includes the following Edmundlike lines, which Ingo might well have recalled, had he been familiar with the G & S opera. 'Live to love and love to live—/ You will ripen at your ease, / Growing on the sunny side—/ Fate has nothing more to give.' But see next entry below.

— **Cheek by passion flushed** It is more likely that Greg recited, and Ingo has remembered, an excited passage in one of the more excited poems of George Byron (I.15), *English Bards and Scotch Reviewers*.

> '[Orpheus] Who in soft guise, surrounded by a choir / Of virgins melting, not to Vesta's fire / With sparkling eyes, and cheek by passion flush'd, / Strikes his wild lyre, whilst listening dames are hush'd?'

The poem is a lengthy and fierce attack, responding to a bad review in the Edinburgh Review in 1808 of his first published book of poetry. It is also a satirical polemic on good and bad poetry (rather different from E.B Browning's Olympian review of the history of poetry—see ch. 3 above, under 'denying divinely the divine'). He later said that it had been written when he was 'very young and very angry, and has been a thorn in my side ever since.'

In the poem he took aim at an obscure Cambridge poet, Hewson Clarke. In a Postscript to the second published edition of the poem, he spoke of Clarke as 'a very sad dog, [who] for no reason that I can discover, except a personal quarrel with a bear, kept by me at Cambridge to sit for a fellowship [of his College] and whom the jealousy of his Trinity contemporaries prevented from success, has been abusing me'. Byron is referring to the story, also recounted in one of his letters (to Elizabeth Pigot, 26 October 1807), of his having kept a tame bear in his rooms when he was an undergraduate at Trinity College, the College rules having prohibited the keeping of a dog in College.

— **Old English roses.** Rose varieties from before the 20th century which have become fashionable in recent years, not least because they seem less artificial, and more interesting, than modern roses produced by much genetic modification through selective breeding. On Edmund's garden, see further in ch. 16 below.

— **Inter alia.** In Latin, 'among other things'.

— **Long ago and far away.** The title of a memorable song (1944) by Jerome Kern, with lyrics by Ira Gershwin.

— *Und doch so nah.* In German, 'and yet so near'.

— *Aspectus pulcher* In Latin, 'beautiful appearance'. *Jocosus.* In Latin, 'cheerful', 'witty'. *Iucundus.* In Latin, 'pleasant'. The echo is of a passage in the Latin (Vulgate) version of the biblical *First Book of Samuel*, 16.12, in which God tells Samuel that he has chosen to favour his son David (future king of Israel—see ch. 12 below, under 'ancient Israel').

> . . . *misit ergo et adduxit eum erat autem rufus et pulcher aspectu decoraque facie et ait Dominus surge ungue eum ipse est enim.* 'And he sent, and brought him [David] in. Now he was ruddy, and withal of a beautiful countenance, and goodly to look to. And the Lord said, Arise, anoint him: for this is he."' (King James English version, 1611).

— **Dieux, quel bonheur.** Echo of a poem—*Cantate de Narcisse (Cantata of Narcissus)*—by the French poet, Paul Valéry (1871-1945).

> *O ma beauté . . . Ma chair . . . Ma peau . . . Dieux, quel malheur d'être si beau!* ('Oh my beauty . . . my flesh . . . my skin . . . Gods, what misfortune to be so beautiful!'). (Narcissus (I.21) speaking!). Ingo changes the words 'what misfortune' to 'what good fortune' (*quel bonheur*).

— **One must be beautiful to approach the beautiful.** Ingo might better have referred to the Alexandrian philosopher Plotinus (205-270 CE) (see ch. 2 above, under 'neo-neo-Platonist') who expressed even more explicitly than his master Plato the idea that our appreciation of beauty involves a concordance between the state of our soul and the form of that which is beautiful. So it follows that the more beautiful we make our soul, the more intensely we may know beauty.

> 'For he that beholds must be akin to that which he beholds, and must, before he comes to this vision, be transformed into its likeness. Never could the eye have looked upon the sun had it not become sun-like, and never can the soul see Beauty unless she has become beautiful. Let each man first become god-like and each man beautiful, if he would behold Beauty and God.'
> Plotinus, *Ennead* I, sec. 6. (tr., T. Taylor).

Plotinus takes up Plato's analysis (especially in the dialogue known as the *Symposium*) of the forms of beauty, rising from its physical form to its most spiritual form, each participating to a differing degree in the ultimate Form (or Idea) of Beauty, which is (like the Good and the True) itself a reflection of the nature of God or the One. For Plato, and for Plotinus, *education*, in the fullest sense, is an ascent of the human being, a self-perfecting, as we set aside those things which block and cloud our appreciation of such ultimate ideals.

We might hope that Ingo is looking beyond Edmund's physical appearance and seeing something beautiful in self-creating Edmund's soul. If so, he himself has reached a higher place on a Platonic spiritual ascent.

In one of his first works—*The Birth of Tragedy*—F. Nietzsche (I.19) made extensive use of an ancient distinction between the Apollonian and Dionysian aspects of our inheritance form ancient Greece. In a formula which Nietzsche himself did not use, we might say that there is a useful distinction in that inheritance between what might be called the Apollonian—centred on the soul and ideas and beauty—and what might be called the Dionysian—centred on nature, the body and the emotions. See further in ch. 11 below.

For a strangely distasteful attempt to combine the two aspects in a single work of fiction, see *Der Tod in Venedig* (Death in Venice) (1912) by Th. Mann (I.5). It is the story of a German writer who becomes obsessed with a handsome youth during a stay in Venice. The integration of the physical and the spiritual aspects of the relationship is unconvincing and unenlightening.

— *Je. Qui ça?* In French, 'I. Who is that?' From *L'Innomable* (The Unnameable), a novel by the Irish writer S. Beckett (1906-89). The puzzling form of the novel has been the subject of much learned debate about its philosophical and literary significance.

The novel seems to be nothing but the interior monologue of a person who sees their only existence as being in their speaking, as their being nothing but a voice, saying nothing in particular to no one in particular. The voice says: 'I have no voice and must speak' (there is no 'I' separate from the voice); and: 'it seems impossible to speak and yet say nothing' (our speaking seems to make us, rather than the other way around); and (the novel's closing words): 'I cannot go on speaking. I must go on' (to exist is to speak, if only to oneself).

The 'I' that speaks is apparently not the author or the narrator, or even a character in a novel. It seems to be neither dialogical nor single-voiced (in Bakhtinian terms) but no-voiced. It is as if the novel itself is the only existence of the source of the voice, the only thing that makes the source of the voice something rather than nothing. It suggests that 'I' am merely a story I tell myself and, if I choose to stop telling myself the story, I can cause myself to cease to exist.

It may be this is what Ingo has in mind, in his e-mail message which seems like a final interior monologue that he is sharing with others by means of the placeless and soundless electronic medium. As a student at Tübingen (see below), he will also have considered a perennial theme of Western philosophy (see Appendices 4 and 8 below)—the idea that personal identity is a logical inference from the fact that there is thinking, that fact suggesting that there is a source of the thinking, a source that may, in thinking, choose to recognise itself as 'I'.

But Ingo will also have been influenced more recently by perennial aspects of Eastern religion and philosophy which see the world and life, and even human identity, as illusory, with self-consciousness being our futile attempt to overcome the illusion.

See further under '*Ich*' below. On Edmund's and Greg's encounters with these matters, see chs. 11 and 15 below.

— **Je est un autre.** In French, 'I is an other'. Words used by the French poet Arthur Rimbaud (1854-91) in a letter (15 May 1871) to P. Demeny. Commenting on an array of previous French poets (and French critics)—a review more succinct but no less opinionated than that of Byron noted above (under 'cheek')—he reveals his own way of poetic creation, in which the poem seems to be something that happens to him, as if he were not wholly responsible for it.

> *Les romantiques, qui prouvent si bien que la chanson est si peu souvent l'œuvre, c'est à dire la pensée chantée et comprise du chanteur ? Car Je est un autre. Si le cuivre s'éveille clairon, il n'y a rien de sa faute. Cela m'est évident : j'assiste à l'éclosion de ma pensée : je la regarde, je l'écoute : je lance un coup d'archet : la symphonie fait son remuement dans les profondeurs, ou vient d'un bond sur la scène.* ('The Romantics who show so well that song is so rarely a work, that is, the singer's sung and communicated thought? For I is an other. If brass wakes up and finds that it is a bugle, it is not its fault. That is obvious to me: I witness the hatching of my thought: I look at it, I listen to it: I shoot an arrow: the symphony stirs the depths, or leaps onto the stage.') (present author's trans.).

Rimbaud capitalises the word *Je* ('I') in the crucial sentence, although the word is not at the beginning of the sentence, as if to suggest that he has in mind his identity as an idea or a phenomenon or a thing.

We may recall the similar view of J. Keats (see ch. 2 above, under 'pests and parasites') and also his conception of 'negative capability'—'that is, when man is capable of being in uncertainties, Mysteries, doubts without any irritable reaching after fact & reason' (letter of 21 December 1817 to G. and T. Keats).

We may recall also the opinion of W. A. Mozart that his best experience of composing was when the piece came to him, not as a succession of notes, but as a single thing (*Alles zusammen*)—'like a picture or a beautiful person'—which he could then write out without much trouble. (O. Jahn, *Life of Mozart*.)

— *Und kann doch sagen*. In German, 'and can indeed say'.

— *Voilà!* In French, 'There!'

— *Ich*. In German, 'I'. It seems likely that, before he came to India, Ingo has been studying the work of the German philosopher J.G. Fichte (1762-1814). A main focus of his philosophy is the perennial problem of the nature of the self, *das Ich*. As for other idealist philosophers, for Fichte external reality is known to us only as a product of the mind, and personal identity is the cause and effect of our thinking about reality. The idea of the self is produced by the mind acting as the subject (*Ich*) and object (*Nicht-Ich*, 'not-I') of its own thinking.

Fichte applied such a dialectical method to all rational thought, interpreting the philosophy of Kant in a way which prepared the ground for the philosophy of Hegel (see Appendix 8 below)—using the terms *thesis*, *antithesis* and *synthesis* to express that method—terms which his successor Hegel did not himself use in his own deeply dialectical philosophy.

— *ÜberIch*. In German, 'over-I'. S. Freud uses the term *Über-Ich* to express the internal self-regulating mechanism of the mind. He was displeased with the Latin words used in the English translation of his key terms ('Ego' for *das Ich*—'Id' for *das Es* ('It'); 'Super-ego' for *das Über-Ich*), especially given the hallowed status of the term *Ich* ('I') in German philosophy. He thought that the Latinisms sounded too scientific, too remote from introspection as their true source.

A similar problem relates to the unfortunate English translation—'superman'—of Nietzsche's *Übermensch* ('beyond-person'—a person who has gone beyond the present dehumanised form of the human being). See ch. 19 below, under 'revaluation of value'. Freud borrowed the term *das Es* from Nietzsche, and the ideas of *repression* and *sublimation* from Schopenhauer and Nietzsche.

— *Etwas*. *UrIch*. *NichtIch*. In German, 'some thing', 'original I', 'not-I'.

— **I am who I am**. 'And Moses said unto God, Behold, when I come unto the children of Israel, and shall say unto them, The God of your fathers hath sent me unto you; and they shall say to me, What is his name? what shall I say unto them? And God said unto Moses, I AM THAT I AM: and he said, Thus shalt thou say unto the children of Israel, I AM hath sent me unto you.' *Book of Exodus*, 3.13-14 (King James Version, 1611).

Ingo may also have in mind a passage in *Die Bestimmung des Menschen* (The Vocation of Man) (1800) by Fichte (see above, under 'Ich'). 'I am that which I am, because in this particular position of the great system of Nature, only such a person, and absolutely no other, was possible.' (tr., W. Smith).

Fichte took the view that human life was absolutely determined by its place in the order of Nature, but our moral consciousness puts us in the unique position that we can choose how we act—a solution, to the perennial problem of human self-determination within the pre-determined order of Nature, which is a bridge between Kant's 'practical reason' and Schopenhauer's 'will'. (See Appendix 8 below, and ch. 4 above, under 'will to know'.)

— **Nine vibrating strings**. See ch. 11 below, under 'ten strings of my soul'.
— *Harmonia animi. Harmonia mundi.* In Latin, 'harmony of the soul', 'harmony of the world'. The musical metaphor of harmony has been much more than a metaphor for those philosophers, beginning with Pythagoras (c.570-c.480 BCE), for whom the mysterious harmonies of music and the remarkable patterns of mathematics are an integral part of harmonies and patterns that extend up to the ordering of the whole universe.

> 'Since, then, the whole natural world seemed basically to be an analogue of numbers, and numbers seemed to be the primary fact of the natural world, they [the Pythagoreans] concluded that the elements of numbers are the elements of all things, and that the whole universe is harmony and number.' (Aristotle, *Metaphysics*, 985).
>
> 'There is another theory about the soul that has come down to us, which many people find the most plausible one around . . . They say that the soul is a kind of attunement (*harmonia*), on the grounds that attunement is a mixture of and compound of opposites, and the body is made up of oppositions.' (Aristotle, *On the Soul*, 407b. (tr., D. Ross).
>
> 'There seems to be in us a sort of affinity to harmonies and rhythms, which makes some philosophers say that the soul is a harmony, others, that she possesses harmony.' Aristotle, *Politics*, VIII.5. (tr., B. Jowett).

It is the central—and most beautiful—theme of Plato's *Republic* that the human soul and human society each have a 'spiritual constitution' (*Republic*, 444a) whose tendency is to find harmony within itself ('justice'), a harmony which reflects and re-enacts the harmonious order of the universe.

On the nature of music, see further in ch.15 below.

— *Und ungekehrt.* In German, 'and vice versa'.
— *Ich will. Ich bin. Endlich.* In German, 'I wish', 'I am', 'at last'. Ingo is surely recalling a saying of F. Nietzsche (I.19) (*Will to Power*, §940). *Du sollst. Ich wll. Ich bin.* In German, 'you must, I wish, I am'.

One might interpret this as expressing with ultimate concision what is perhaps Nietzsche's most characteristic idea—the idea of a possible moral progress of human beings. *You must*—moral dependence. *I wish*—selfish interest. *I am*—moral autonomy, personal authenticity.

— **I think I'm becoming.** According to the not-always-serious Roman historian Suetonius (*Lives of the Twelve Caesars*), the dying words of the Emperor Vespasian (reigned 69-79 CE) were: *vae puto deus fio* ('Oh dear, I think I'm becoming a god'). What did he mean? Was he regretting, or making fun of, the deifying of Emperors. (Suetonius thought he was joking.) One of the better Roman Emperors, he was (*nolens volens*; whether he liked it or not) deified by the Senate shortly after his death.

— **Becoming a diamond.** Perhaps Ingo has come into contact with a form of Buddhism—the Vajrayāna, or Diamond Vehicle (*vajra* : in Sanskrit, 'diamond' or 'thunderbolt')—originating in northern India, but influential across the different forms of Buddhism, and especially in Tibet. It seeks to cause a rather rapid (possibly within one lifetime) 'transmutation' in the body and mind of the initiate by intense yogic and ritualistic practices under the influence of a guru. Its aim is to produce a Siddha, a person 'who is so much in harmony with the cosmos that he is under no constraint whatsoever, and as a free agent is able to manipulate the cosmic forces inside and outside himself'. (E. Conze).

It is also possible that Ingo—Tübingen doctoral student—is familiar with the mystical experiences of the remarkable Spanish religious leader Teresa of Avila (1515-1582). 'I began to think of the soul as if it were a castle made of a single diamond or of very clear crystal, in which there are many rooms, just as in Heaven there are many mansions.' (*The Way of Perfection*).

— *Ordentlich.* In German, 'orderly'.

— **1960's person.** Within Western civilisation in the 1960's, a mental and social rebellion swept through society, especially among otherwise privileged members of society, challenging traditional rules and values in the name of 'freedom'. The movement withered away, either because the pleasures of such 'freedom' proved illusory and ultimately unsatisfying and/or because the power-structures behind society's rules and values (especially those of democracy-capitalism) are more than able to resist poorly organised collective violations.

— *Indische Reise. Indisch reisen.* In German, 'Indian journey', 'Indian journeying'.

— *Italienische Reise.* In German, 'Italian Journey'. The title of a book by J.W. von Goethe, published only in 1829, but containing the letters and notes that recorded his impressions during his first visit to Italy (beginning in September 1786 and lasting some two years).

Under the influence of his father and of his own nature, he had acquired an early longing to go to Italy (a *Sehnsucht nach Süden*; see ch. 2 above, under '*dahin*'). But it was especially Greek and Roman Italy that attracted him rather than medieval or Renaissance Italy. And the book is, like Ingo's e-mail, really a story of a significant stage in Goethe's mental development. He returned from Italy a different person. Italy would serve as a mental staging-post for many other sensitive people, especially German-speaking people—Heine, Nietzsche, Wagner, Freud, Thomas Mann . . . escaping from 'heavy northern thoughts' (H. von Treitschke).

— *Lang lebe das E-mail.* In German, 'long live e-mail.'

— *usw. Und so weiter.* In German, 'and so forth'.

— *Misère.* In French, 'misery' (especially social and economic deprivation).

— **Vertical integration.** In the structuring of capitalist enterprises, a group of corporations may be said to be vertically integrated when they operate at different stages of an industrial and/or commercial process (e.g., the extraction of oil, its refining, and its wholesale distribution and retail sale)—as opposed to horizontal integration, in which companies at the same stage of an industrial or commercial process are associated.

— *Tübingen.* The University of Tübingen (near Stuttgart in south-west Germany) was founded in 1477. In the 19th century, initially under the leadership of F.C. Bauer, it was the focus of a new era in theology—turning the long tradition of 'biblical criticism' in a new post-Enlightenment direction, a new way of reading and understanding the Christian bible (Old and New Testaments) in broader historical and cultural and intellectual contexts. This new way co-existed precariously with still more radical and destructive forms of religious criticism. (See ch. 3 above, under 'God that is dead').

— *Edmund der Weise.* In German, 'Edmund the Wise'. The echo is of *Nathan der Weise*, the title of a play (1779) by the German writer G. E. Lessing (1729-81). The play suggests that the three religions with a common origin—Judaism, Christianity and Islam—should respect each other as three ways to serve the same God.

— **Doctor—first heal thyself.** Apparently a saying already well-known in ancient Israel at the time when Jesus Christ referred to it as a 'proverb'. *Gospel of Luke*, 4.23. In the original Greek text: Ἰατρε θεραπευσον. In the Latin translation (Vulgate): *medice cura teipsum.* He was evidently using it to make the point that the old forms of religion had not succeeded in making their adherents holy. The phrase has become universally proverbial.

— *J'ai lu tous les livres.* In French, 'I have read all the books'. Ingo is recalling a fine poem, *Brise marine* (Sea Breeze) by the French poet Stéphane Mallarmé (1842-98).

> *La chair est triste, hélas! Et j'ai lu tous les livres / Fuir! là-bas fuir! Je sens que des oiseaux sont ivres / D'être parmi l'écume inconnue et les cieux! / Rien, ni les vieux jardins reflétés par les yeux / Ne retiendra ce cœur qui dans la mer se trempe* ('The flesh is sad, alas! And I have read all the books. To escape, to escape over there! I feel the birds intoxicated by being in the unknown sea-foam and the skies! Nothing—not even the old gardens reflected in the eyes—will hold back this heart which soaks itself in the sea.' (present author's trans.).

— *Wahn! Wahn! Überall Wahn!* In German, 'Madmess! Madness! Everywhere madness!' Ingo is quoting the opening words of the monologue of Hans Sachs in Act 3 of *Die Meistersinger von Nürnberg* (The Mastersingers of Nuremberg), text and music by R. Wagner (see ch. 3 above, under 'jackets like a sword').

> *Wahn! Wahn! / Überall Wahn! Wohin ich forschend blick / in Stadt—und Weltchronik, / den Grund mir aufzufinden, / warum gar bis aufs Blut die Leut sich quälen und schinden / in unnütz toller Wut? in Flucht geschlagen, / wähnt er zu jagen; / hört nicht sein eigen Schmerzgekreisch, / wenn er sich wühlt ins eig'ne Fleisch, / wähnt Lust sich zu erzeigen!*
>
> 'Madness! Madness! Everywhere madness! I search in the chronicles of the cities and of the world, to discover the reason why do people spill blood, tormenting and abusing each other in pointless and foolish fury? Forced to flee, he thinks he is hunting, and cannot hear his own screams of pain, as he digs into his own flesh, and thinks that he is feeling pleasure.' (present author's trans.)

— **Facing the past**. In Varkala (see ch. 8 below) Ingo may have heard of Sutra 211 of the (Hindu) Nandinatha Sutra—about the preparation for death of those who are about to die, including the practice of facing their past.

  In some traditional cultures, humanity is seen as facing the past (which exists and can be known) rather than the future (which is an unknowable void). Western culture has been manically forward-looking, at least since the 14th century, a characteristic which is an integral part of the fiercely impatient social process known as 'globalisation'.

  Ingo is apparently hoping that India will not fail to look to its past as it becomes so intensely concerned with its future.

— **Taj and Raj**. *Taj* (an Arabic word for a headdress or crown). *Raj* (a Hindi word for 'rule'). A crude way of referring to two aspects of India's more recent past—the Mughal empire (from the middle of the 16th century) and British India (formalised as such from 1858, although the British had been in India since the 17th century). India became fully independent in 1947, in the separate states of India and Pakistan (and, from 1971, Bangladesh). India (as a single entity) had been a founding member of both the League of Nations and the United Nations.

— **New avatars of Vishnu**. In Hindu theology, the god Vishnu has become present on earth in the form of various *avatars* (in Sanskrit, 'coming down').

— **Getting and spending**. An echo of a sonnet by the English Romantic poet W. Wordsworth (I.10).

> 'The world is too much with us; late and soon, / Getting and spending, we lay waste our powers: / Little we see in Nature that is ours; / We have given our hearts away, a sordid boon! / This Sea that bares her bosom to the

moon; / The winds that will be howling at all hours, / And are up-gathered now like sleeping flowers; / For this, for everything, we are out of tune, / It moves us not.'

The poet is referring to the new spirit of materialism, dominating British society as a by-product of what would come to be called the Industrial Revolution (from about 1770).

— **Sensation without sentiment**. Could Ingo be recalling distantly the great and continuing debate surrounding the writing of the Austrian music-critic E. Hanslick (1825-1904), especially his *Vom Musikalisch-Schönen* (On the Musically Beautiful) (1854)? Hanslick is the leading exponent of the very reasonable view that it is not the nature or function of (serious classical) music to convey emotion. (See further in ch. 15 below, under 'music').

— **Microcosmos**. Microcosm. Smaller version of something large. Formed from two Greek words—*mikros* ('small') and *kosmos* ('world' or 'universe').

— **All is struggle**. A perennial philosophical idea, traditionally traced back, in western culture, to two sayings attributed to the Greek philosopher Heraclitus (c.550—c.480 BCE). His strange sayings only survive as fragments, but he had a significant influence on the thinking of the philosophers of the 5th century BCE, and hence on those whom they influenced.

> 'It is necessary to realize that war is common, and strife is justice, and that everything happens in accordance with strife and necessity.' (Diels 80). 'War is father of all and king of all.' (Diels 53).

The idea of *dynamic creative duality* became a central, perhaps the central, structural principle of creative thinking in the most diverse intellectual arenas.

Metaphysics (being and nothing, essence and existence, being and becoming, mind and matter). *Epistemology* (dialectic of competing ideas, idealism and realism). *Logic* (true and false). *Ethics* (good and evil, right and wrong, freedom and necessity). *Religion* (the divine and the human, body and soul, mortal and immortal, orthodoxy and heresy). *Social philosophy* (justice and law, freedom and subjection, right and duty, self-interest and the common good, citizen and alien). *Politics* (elections, the party system). *Law* (law and justice, right and duty, plaintiff and defendant). *Criminal law* (guilty and innocent, adversarial criminal procedure). *Biology* (life and death, evolutionary struggle). *International society* (war). *Physics* (rest and motion, action and reaction).

For the application of *dynamic creative duality* to the social philosophy of *social idealism* (up to the level of the society of the whole human race), in the form of the *perennial dilemmas of society*, see Ph. Allott, *Eunomia*—and ch. 11 below, under 'the self and the other' and 'the one and the many'.

— **Zucht und Haltung**. In German, 'breeding', 'discipline'. Words used in respect of thoroughbred racehorses. But Ingo is probably thinking of them as the stifling ideals of solid bourgeois society, as reflected, perhaps, in the novels of Thomas Mann (I.5).

— **Na gut!** In German, 'sure!' (with ironical overtone).

— **Plaie et couteau**. In French, 'wound and knife'. Echo of a poem in *Les Fleurs du Mal* (1857), a collection of poems by the French poet C. Baudelaire (I.19).

> *Je suis la plaie et le couteau! / Je suis le soufflet et la joue! / Je suis les membres et la roue, / Et la victime et le bourreau!* ('I am the wound and the knife! I am the slap and the cheek! I am the limbs and the wheel! And the victim and the executioner!') From *L'Héautontimoroumenos* (self-tormentor—formed from three Greek words: *heauton timorou menos*).

— **Licht! Licht! Überall Licht!** In German, 'Light! Light! Everywhere light!' Compare above, under '*Wahn! Wahn!*'

— **All sciences, even those that don't exist**. Ingo has evidently read, or heard about, *Vathek*, an eccentric novel (1782, in French; 1786, in an English translation) by the eccentric William Beckford (1760-1844). He used his great wealth to create, among other things, Fonthill Abbey, a Gothic fantasy mansion in Wiltshire (England), the main part of which collapsed (for the third time) in 1825. The novel purports to be the story of the Caliph Vathek who (not unlike Beckford) devotes his life to sensual pleasure and various vices and ends badly—'in an eternity of unabating anguish. Such was, and should be, the punishment of unrestrained passions and atrocious deeds!'

> 'He had studied so much for his amusement in the life-time of his father, as to acquire a great deal of knowledge, though not a sufficiency to satisfy himself; for he wished to known every thing; even sciences that did not exist.'

— **Unprayable prayer**. Ingo evidently has in mind a passage from *The Dry Salvages*, the third of *The Four Quartets* by the American-British poet T.S. Eliot (I.18). (Eliot explains the title as follows—'The Dry Salvages—presumably *les trois sauvages* [in French, 'the three savages']—is a small group of rocks, with a beacon, off the N.E. coast of Cape Ann, Massachusetts. *Salvages* is pronounced to rhyme with *assuages*.')

> 'Where is there an end to it, the soundless wailing, / The silent withering of autumn flowers / Dropping their petals and remaining motionless; / Where is there an end to the drifting wreckage, / The prayer of the bone on the beach, the unprayable / Prayer at the calamitous annunciation?'

— **Grau in Grau.** In German, 'grey in grey'. Ingo is recalling a dispiriting and much-quoted phrase in the Preface to the *Philosophy of Right* (1821) by G.W.F. Hegel (I.19, Appendix 8 below) where he discusses the relationship between social reality and philosophical ideas.

> 'One word more about giving instruction as to what the world ought to be. Philosophy in any case always comes on the scene too late to give it. As the thought of the world, it appears only when actuality is already there cut and dried after its process of formation has been completed. The teaching of the concept, which is also history's inescapable lesson, is that it is only when actuality is mature that the ideal first appears over against the real and that the ideal apprehends this same real world in its substance and builds it up for itself into the shape of an intellectual realm. When philosophy paints its grey in grey [its picture of an aged world], then has a shape of life grown old. By philosophy's grey in grey it cannot be rejuvenated but only understood. The owl of Minerva spreads its wings only with the falling of the dusk. [*Die Eule der Minerva beginnt erst mit der einbrechenden Dämmerung ihren Flug*].' (tr., T.M. Knox). (Minerva was the Greek goddess of wisdom.)

However, it is worth recalling that, in a letter (to Niethammer, 28 October 1808), Hegel also said: 'Every day I become more convinced that theoretical work achieves more in the world than practical work. When the realm of representation (*Vorstellung*) is revolutionised actuality cannot hold out.'

— **Dry brains in a dry season.** Ingo has in mind a line from *Gerontion*, a poem by T.S.Eliot (I.18). 'Thoughts of a dry brain in a dry season.' The poem contains the somewhat terminal thoughts of an old man (in Greek, *geron*, 'old man').

The image of 'dry' seemed to have had a peculiar hold over Eliot's mind—symbolising spiritual and psychological aridity.

> 'In this decayed hole among the mountains, / In the faint moonlight, the grass is singing / Over the tumbled graves, about the chapel / There is the empty chapel, only the wind's home. / It has no windows, and the door swings, / Dry bones can harm no one.' (*The Waste Land*).
> 'We are the hollow men / We are the stuffed men / Leaning together / Headpiece filled with straw. Alas! / Our dried voices, when / We whisper together / Are quiet and meaningless / As wind in dry grass / Or rats' feet over broken glass / In our dry cellar.' (*The Hollow Men*).

A possible connection has been noted between Eliot's peculiar and powerful phrase 'dry brain' and words spoken by Jaques in Shakespeare's *As You Like It* (II.7). He had been speaking to 'a fool' who had said—

'. . . from hour to hour we ripe and ripe, / And then from hour to hour we rot and rot, / And thereby hangs a tale.' Jaques says that the fool has a brain 'Which is as dry as the remainder biscuit / After a voyage . . .'

There is also a mysterious and interesting saying attributed to Heraclitus (see above, under 'all is struggle'). 'A dry soul, a beam of light, is wisest and best.' (Diels 118).

— **All our sins will be washed away.** Ingo has in mind Psalm 51 (I.16) (in Eastern Christianity, Psalm 50), one of the seven psalms known to Christianity as the 'penitential psalms', expressing a sense of sinfulness and of sorrow for sin.

> 'Have mercy upon me, O God, according to thy loving-kindness: according unto the multitude of thy tender mercies blot out my transgressions. / Wash me thoroughly from mine iniquity, and cleanse me from my sin. / For I acknowledge my transgressions: and my sin is ever before me. / Against thee, thee only, have I sinned, and done this evil in thy sight: that thou mightest be justified when thou speakest, and be clear when thou judgest. Behold, I was shapen in iniquity; and in sin did my mother conceive me. / Behold, thou desirest truth in the inward parts: and in the hidden part thou shalt make me to know wisdom. Purge me with hyssop, and I shall be clean: wash me, and I shall be whiter than snow.' (King James version, 1611).

The powerful image of water as the agent of purification, in the second and last verses of the above, is beautifully expressed in the Latin (Vulgate) version as follows.

> *Amplius lava me ab iniquitate mea: et a peccato meo munda me./ Asperges me, Domine, hyssopo, et mundabor: lavabis me, et super nivem dealbabor.*

— **The sea has many voices, many gods and many voices.** Ingo is again quoting from Eliot's *The Dry Salvages* (see above, under 'unprayable prayer').
— **Bathe in the poem of the sea.** Ingo is recalling a poem *Le Bateau ivre* (The Drunken Boat) by A. Rimbaud (see above, under '*Je est un autre*'), a poet whose poetry, but especially whose turbulent brief life, appeals particularly to the young.

> *Et dès lors, je me suis baigné dans le Poème / De la Mer, infuse d'astres, et lactescent, / Dévorant les azurs verts; où, flottaison blame / Et ravie, un noyé pensif parfois descend . . .* ('And then, I bathed in the Poem of the Sea, infused with stars, and milky, devouring the blue-greens; into which, pale and ravished floating, a thoughtful drowning man sometimes descends.' (present author's trans.).

The voice of the poem is that of the waterlogged, sinking boat. Later, there is the line: *Ô que ma quille éclate! Ô que j'aille à la mer!* ('Oh that my keel would break! Oh that I might sink down into the sea!')

Did Ingo sense his own imminent fate?

— **Rain also falls on the wicked**. 'But I say unto you, Love your enemies, bless them that curse you, do good to them that hate you, and pray for them which despitefully use you, and persecute you; That ye may be the children of your Father which is in heaven: for he maketh his sun to rise on the evil and on the good, and sendeth rain on the just and on the unjust.' *The* (Christian) *Gospel of Matthew*, 5.44-45. (King James Version, 1611).

— **Flower that smiles**. Ingo is recalling a delightful poem by the English poet R.Herrick (1591-1674), *To the virgins, to make much of time.*

> 'Gather ye rosebuds while ye may, / Old time is still a-flying: / And this same flower that smiles to-day / To-morrow will be dying.'

— **Swan sings for joy**. Reference to the idea of the 'swan song'.

> 'Evidently you think that I have less insight into the future than a swan; because when these birds feel that the time has come for them to die, they sing more loudly and sweetly than they have sung in all their lives before, for joy that they are going away into the presence of the god whose servants they are.' Plato, *Phaedo*, 84e. (tr., H. Tredennick).

— ***Sparge rosas***. In Latin, 'spread roses'. From a notably sensuous poem (*Odes,* III.19) by the Latin poet Horace (I.4), in what would now be called the Symbolist style.

In poetry, following in the footsteps of the French poets P. Verlaine (1844-96) and A. Rimbaud (see above, under 'Je est un autre' and 'bathe in the poem'), the main exponents of symbolism include S. Mallarmé (see above, under '*J'ai lu*'). In different art-forms (poetry, drama, painting, music), the Symbolists rejected 19th-century naturalism and formalism. Poetry, in particular, should appeal to the mind through the senses, thorough its sounds and its images. The English-language poets Ezra Pound (1885-1972) and T.S. Eliot (I.18), among very many others, were strongly influenced by the Symbolist spirit.

Horace's poem is about pleasure. It has been suggested that the background to the poem is that, at a dinner-party, the guests have been bored by the tedious talk of one Lycus (?an academic). We are here to enjoy ourselves, the poet says. The relevant passage is—

> *Cur pendet tacita fistula cum lyra? / Parcentis ego dexteras / odi: sparge rosas; audiat invidus / dementem strepitum Lycus, / et vicina seni non habilis Lyco.*

('Why when we drink / Hangs the flute idle with the lyre laid by? / The stingy hand at feasts I hate! / Fling roses! Let sour Lycus hear the din! / And our fair neighbour, ill-matched mate / Of dotard Lycus, let her list [listen] within!') (tr., J. Marshall).

— *Alles endet, was enstehet.* In German, 'everything that comes into being comes to an end.' From a song by Hugo Wolf (1860-1903), setting to music a text adapted by W.H. Robert-Tornow from a poem by Michelangelo.

> *Alles endet, was entstehet. /Alles, alles rings vergehet, / Denn die Zeit flieht, und die Sonne / Sieht, daß alles rings vergehet, / Denken, Reden, Schmerz, und Wonne; / Und die wir zu Enkeln hatten / Schwanden wie bei Tag die Schatten, / Wie ein Dunst im Windeshauch.* ('Everything that comes into being comes to an end. / Everything, everything everywhere passes away. / For time flies, and the sun / Sees that everything everywhere passes away / Thinking, speaking, pain and joy; /And those who were our grandchildren / Have faded away like shadows in the light of day, / Like mist in a breath of wind.') (present author's trans.).

Michelangelo's poem begins with the words—*Chiunche nasce a morte arriva /nel fuggir del tempo; e 'l sole /niuna cosa lascia viva.* ('Everyting that is born ends in death / As time flies, and the sun / Leaves nothing alive.')

— **Fare forward, voyagers**. Also from *The Dry Salvages* by T.S. Eliot (see above, under 'unprayable prayer').

> 'O voyagers, O seamen, / You who came to port, and you whose bodies / Will suffer the trial and judgement of the sea, / Or whatever event, this is your real destination. / So Krishna, as when he admonished Arjuna On the field of battle. / Not fare well, / But fare forward, voyagers.'

(Might we be right to infer that Ingo has with him a copy of Eliot's *Four Quartets*? They are poems which are liable to have a significant effect within the intellectual and spiritual development of those who read them, and who are among those who are aware of their own intellectual and spiritual development.)

— *Ewiggeliebte. Ewigliebende.* In German, 'ever-loved', 'ever-loving'.
— **Little friend of all the world**. The name given by the Indians to Kim O'Hara, the hero of *Kim* (1901), a picaresque (I.4) novel by the British writer R. Kipling (1865-1936). The orphan Kim lives in a space of his own between India's different worlds—finding his own way in India's overwhelming confusion of overlapping spiritual, geographic, historical, ethnic, social, and political worlds.

— *Licht! Licht!* See above. Characteristically ambiguous dying words have been attributed to J.W von Goethe (I.12): *Licht. Mehr Licht* ('Light. More light.') Or, possibly (ecstatically and metaphysically): *Licht! Mehr Licht!*

There is a fine saying of Augustine (in Nietzschean mode and mood): 'There is, indeed, some light in men: but let them walk fast, lest the shadows come.' *Confessions*, X, xxiii.

CHAPTER 8. *End and Beginning.*

— **End and beginning**. 'In my beginning is my end' is a line repeated several times in *East Coker*, one of the *Four Quartets* by T S. Eliot (I.18).

There are two sayings to similar effect attributed to Heraclitus (see ch.7 above, under 'all is struggle').

> 'The beginning and the end are shared in the circumference of a circle' (Diels 103).
>
> 'The way up and down is one and the same' (Diels 60).
>
> 'Now this is not the end. It is not even the beginning of the end. But it is, perhaps, the end of the beginning.' From a speech given by Winston Churchill (I.16) in November 1942, shortly after a first victorious battle in World War II at El Alamein in North Africa.

— **No body to bury**. Eliot's *East Coker* also contains the lines—'They all go into the dark . . . / And we all go with them, into the silent funeral, / Nobody's funeral, for there is no one to bury.'
— **Requiem Mass**. Christian liturgical form marking a person's death. It takes its name from the opening prayer (*Introit*) of the Mass (in Latin): *Requiem aeternam da eis, Domine* ('Eternal rest give unto them, O Lord').
— **St Thomas d'Aquin**. The French version of the name of the Italian Dominican (I.14) philosopher-theologian Tommaso d'Aquino (1224/25-1274)—in English, Thomas Aquinas. His much-travelled life including periods of teaching in the University of Paris. He visited London for a meeting of the Dominican order in 1263. His reconciling of the philosophical inheritance of ancient Greece, especially the Aristotelian inheritance, with Christian theology had effects in European culture going far beyond its significance in the intellectual history of Christianity.

The Parisian church dedicated to his name is located in a street close to the Boulevard St Germain, not far from the site of the ancient heart of the University of Paris, and not far from the even more ancient abbey-church of St Germain. The church was consecrated in 1683. In the period of the suppression of religion during the French Revolution, the church was a Temple of Peace used for the celebration of Theophilanthropy (a newly invented near-religion based on reason and nature). Later it was a meeting-place of the Jacobin Club, a leading revolutionary faction which gained a reputation for violence from its participating in what came to be called the Terror.

— **Katha Upanishad**. Edmund probably read the following splendid passage—

> 'Beyond the senses are their objects, and beyond the objects is the mind. Beyond the mind is pure reason, and beyond reason is the Spirit in man. Beyond the Spirit in man is the Spirit of the universe, and beyond is Purusha, the Spirit Supreme. Nothing is beyond Purusha: He is the End of the path. The light of the Atman, the Spirit, is invisible, concealed in all beings. It is seen by the seers of the subtle, when their vision is keen and clear. The wise should surrender speech in mind, mind in the knowing self, the knowing self in the Spirit of the universe, and the Spirit of the universe in the spirit of peace. Awake, arise! Strive for the Highest, and be in the Light!' (tr., J. Mascaró).

The Upanishads are sacred texts of Hinduism, the oldest of them originating between the 8th and 4th centuries BCE. The Katha Upanishad is among the oldest. It recounts the teaching of a young man who is seeking enlightenment. He is instructed by Death, the god of the after-life.

There are remarkable shared resonances in the teaching of the Upanishads, idealist philosophy in the ancient Greek tradition, aspects of Buddhism and Taoism, and aspects of Christian thought. There are those who have been tempted to see these resonances as evidence of a common underlying condition of the human mind faced with the mystery of human life within a mysterious universe—a condition which happens to have been expressed in different, culturally determined, forms. (For Schopenhauer's view of Indian religion, see ch. 11 below, under 'grain of sand'.)

— ***Heiterkeit***. Gabi evidently read the last part of Nietzsche's poem whose first line is *Die Sonne sinkt* ('The sun sinks'), a poem written shortly before his mental breakdown in 1889. Tragic conscience of the 19th century, tragic prophet of the 20th century, Nietzsche died on 25 August 1900.

> *Heiterkeit, güldene, komm! / du des Todes / heimlichster süssester Vorgenuss! /—Lief ich zu rasch meines Wegs? / Jetzt erst, wo der Fuss müde ward, / holt dein Blick mich noch ein, / holt dein Glück mich noch ein. / Rings nur Welle und Spiel. / Was je schwer war, / sank in blaue Vergessenheit, / müssig steht nun mein Kahn. / Sturm und Fahrt—wie verlernt er das! / Wunsch und Hoffnung ertrank, / glatt liegt Seele und Meer.*

> 'Cheerfulness, golden, come! / you most secret, most sweet foretaste of death! / Did I run my way too fast? / Now, as my foot gets weary, / your gaze catches up with me, / your happiness catches up with me. / All around nothing but waves and playfulness. / What was always a burden, / has sunk into blue oblivion, / now my boat is at rest. / Storm and voyages—how they

are forgotten! / Desire and hope are drowned, the soul and the sea are calm.'
(present author's trans.).

Another part of the poem (*Tag meines Lebens*) was set to music by the German
composer P. Hindemith (1895-1963).
— **Buxtehude**. Dietrich Buxtehude (1637-1707), German composer. His splendid organ
and choral music prefigures that of J.S. Bach and G.F. Handel, who acknowledged
their debt to him. His Prelude in D major (BuxWV139) is a particularly joyful
work.
    Hermann Hesse's Sinclair (see below, under 'dancing star') was much moved
when he heard Pistorius play an organ Passacaglia of Buxtehude.
— **Saint-Germain**. A prosperous and elegant district in Paris (7th *arrondissement*), a
favoured place to live and/or work for the contemplative wing of the French ruling
class.
— **Kreuzberg**. A district in Berlin (see below, ch. 10).
— **The Firm**. The benevolent conspiracy described in *Invisible Power. A Philosophical
Adventure Story* sometimes calls itself 'the Firm'.
— **Hôtel Montalembert**. Elegant hotel beside the church of St Thomas. C.F.
Montalembert (1810-70) was a French politician and public intellectual.
— **Varkala**. A town in southern India (Kerala) on the shore of the Arabian Sea. A holy
place of Hinduism, it attracts people, especially 'westerners', seeking 'enlightenment'.
Sea currents at the many fine beaches in the area are notoriously dangerous.
— **Bayreuth**. Small town in Bavaria (Germany) where R. Wagner (1813-83) (see ch. 3
above, under 'jackets like a sword') established (1876) an opera-house (*Festspielhaus*)
devoted to the performance of his operas. After his somewhat peripatetic life, he
settled there (1872) with new his wife Cosima (daughter of the composer Franz
Liszt), living in a house to which they gave the name *Wahnfried* ('escape from
anxiety/trouble/madness/delusion') (see ch. 7 above, under '*Wahn! Wahn!*'). Bayreuth
is a holy place of Wagnerism—a place of pilgrimage for Wagnerites.
— **Lourdes**. Small town in South West France, close to the Pyrenees. In 1858 a local
peasant girl had visions of Mary, the mother of Jesus Christ. The scene of the visions
became, and remains, a major place of Christian pilgrimage.
— **Fallen in love with a dancing star**. Like countless other German and Austrian
adolescents form 1919 to the present day, Ingo will certainly have found a sort
of consolation and perhaps inspiration, in the novel *Demian* (1919) by H. Hesse
(1877-1963; Nobel Prize for Literature 1946). It is a *Bildungsroman* (I.4, under
'picaresque') full of Jungian archetypology (I.20).
    It tells the story of the struggle of an intelligent and sensitive young man
(Sinclair) who is trying to 'become himself' with the help of an ideal saviour figure
(Demian), an ideal mother-figure (Eva, Demian's mother), and a mysteriously wise
musician (Pistorius). Could Ingo possibly see reflected in those figures the (real and
not archetypal) Ingo and Edmund, the Countess and Gregory Seare?

It is also a *Bildungsroman* full of Freudian and Spenglerian gloom about the end of a western civilisation overwhelmed by materialism (despiritualisation) and the herd-instinct. O. Spengler (1880-1936) made a valiant contribution to the gathering gloom with his *Der Untergang des Abendlandes* (The Decline of the West) (1918-22).

But it is also, inevitably, a *Bildungsroman* haunted by the spirit of Nietzsche.

'Alas, the time is coming when man will no longer shoot the arrow of his longing beyond man, and the string of his bow will have forgotten how to whir! I say unto you: one must still have chaos in oneself to be able to give birth to a dancing star. I say unto you: you still have chaos in yourselves. Alas, the time is coming when man will no longer give birth to a star. Alas, the time of the most despicable man is coming, he that is no longer able to despise himself. Behold, I show you the *last man*.'

    F. Nietzsche, *Thus Spoke Zarathustra,* Prologue; Zarathustra speaking. (tr., W. Kaufmann).

    'And she [Eva] told me [Sinclair] about a young man who was in love with a star. He stood by the sea, held out his hands, and worshipped the star; . . . But he knew, or thought he knew, that a star couldn't be embraced by a human being . . . Once he was standing by the sea again at night, on the high cliff, looking up at the star and blazing with love for it. And in a moment of supreme longing he jumped into the void, in the direction of the star.' *Demian*, ch. 7. (tr., S. Appelbaum).

— **Riptide**. Or rip current. A powerful current in the sea, flowing away from or parallel to the coast.

— **Right not to be born**. Perhaps the Countess is recalling words spoken by the Chorus in Sophocles, *Oedipus at Colonus*: 'Say what you will, the greatest boon is not to be; / But, life begun, soonest to end is best, / And to that bourne from which our way began / Swiftly return.' (tr., E. Watling).

In *La Vida es Sueño* by P. Calderón de la Barca (I.16), Prince Segismundo says: *pues el delito mayor / del hombre es haber nacido* ('for man's greatest crime is to have been born'). This gloomy idea must have pleased the gloomy Schopenhauer (see Appendix 8 below, and above and below, *passim*). He refers to it on two separate occasions in *The World as Will and Idea*.

We may also recall W. Shakespeare, *King Lear*, IV.vi.

'When we are born, we cry that we are come / To this great stage of fools.' (Lear speaking).

— **Mortal sin**. In Christian moral theology, a sin so serious that it may exclude a person from the possibility of salvation after death.

— **Wisest, virtuousest.** A passage in Book VIII of *Paradise Lost*, by the English poet
John Milton (I.16, and above *passim*), in which Adam describes Eve (the first human
beings, according to the biblical *Book of Genesis*). It is a finely lyrical passage, unlike
so much of the harsh style of the rest of the poem, reminiscent of the Italian poet
Dante at his most expressive.

> 'Yet when I approach / Her loveliness, so absolute she seems / And in herself
> complete, so well to know / Her own, that what she wills to do or say, / Seems
> wisest, virtuousest, discreetest, best:/ All higher knowledge in her presence
> falls / Degraded; Wisdom in discourse with her / Loses discountenanced, and
> like Folly shows; / Authority and Reason on her wait, / As one intended first,
> not after made / Occasionally; and, to consummate all, Greatness of mind
> and Nobleness their seat / Build in her loveliest, and create an awe / About
> her, as a guard angelic placed.'

— **Ancient gravity.** Greg may have in mind a phrase—*prisca severitas* (in Latin, 'old-
fashioned dignity')—used by Cicero in one of his Senate speeches (*De haruspicum
responso*; 56BCE). Praising admirable figures in ancient Roman history, he mentions
Claudia Quinta: *cuius priscam illam severitatem sacrificii mirifice tua soror existimatur
imitate* ('whose ancient gravity in self-sacrifice your sister wonderfully admired by
imitation'). Claudia, the noblest of Roman matrons, had supervised the bringing to
Rome (203BCE) of a Greek image of the goddess Cybele, who was then venerated
in Rome as the Great Mother (*magna mater*).
— **Proustian digression**. See I.21.
— **Henry James mode.** The writing style of the American-British novelist Henry James
(see ch. 5 above, under 'Henry James mode') is unfortunately too easy to parody.

> 'He had run up, in the course of time, against a good number of "teasers;"
> and the function of teasing them back—of, as it were, giving them, every
> now and then, "what for"—was in him so much a habit that he would
> have been at a loss had there been, on the face of it, nothing to lose. Oh,
> he always had offered rewards, of course—had ever so liberally pasted the
> windows of his soul with staring appeals, minute descriptions, promises
> that knew no bounds. But the actual recovery of the article—the business
> of drawing and crossing the cheque, blotched though this were with tears of
> joy—had blankly appeared to him rather in the light of a sacrilege, casting,
> he sometimes felt, a palpable chill on the fervour of the next quest.' M.
> Beerbohm (1872-1956), 'The Mote in the Middle Distance', in *A Christmas
> Garland* (1912)

The 'he' in the above passage is trying to guess what is in the Christmas stocking
at the end of his bed on Christmas morning. Beerbohm was a friend of James. James

was amused by the parody but said that 'whatever he wrote now, he felt that he was parodying himself.' (S.Waterlow/L. Edel).

Another friend, the American novelist Edith Wharton (1862-1937), said that James suffered from a *furor syntacticus*, treating the English language as 'infinitely syntactically malleable . . . but without the system of case-endings that make a Latin sentence comprehensible in whatever order, more or less, the words are placed.'

Wharton recounts James's own story of what happened when he suffered a stroke—'in the very act of falling . . . he hears in the room a voice which was, distinctly, it seemed, not his own, saying: "So here it is at last, the distinguished thing".' We might compare this with one of the psychosomatic episodes (1912) in the life of S. Freud, another chronic neurotic. When Freud collapsed after an argument with C.J. Jung (the apostle who would betray him), Jung lifted him from the floor and carried him to a couch. Jung says that Freud's first words on recovering his speech were: *Es muß süß sein zu sterben* ('It must be pleasant to die.').

— **Mrs Dalloway**. The central figure of a novel *Mrs Dalloway* (1926) by the English writer Virginia Woolf (1882-1941), one of Woolf's imaginative reconstructions of self-consciousness, so effectively achieved that subsequent writers attempting to be novelists of self-consciousness may be inclined to give up in despair.

It recounts a day in the everyday mental life of Clarissa Dalloway, a woman typical of her kind and class—a day very different from (and mercifully shorter than) the day in the mental life of Leopold Bloom recounted in James Joyce's *Ulysses* (1918/22). In focus and texture and ethos, it might have been written by H. James, if he had not written English as if it were a foreign language. There is much of the mind of V. Woolf herself in the novel, but transmuted into the minds of her created persons.

— **Maggie Tulliver**. A central figure of a novel *The Mill on the Floss* (1860) by the English writer George Eliot, the pen-name of Mary Ann Evans (ch.3 above, under 'God that is dead'). Like Clarissa Dalloway, we get to know Maggie Tulliver very well, but in the manner of the 19th-century novel, that is to say, in the context of a great tapestry of events and relationships, involving relatively ordinary people, but full of high tension and tragedy. There is certainly a connection between her situation and her subjectivity and those of George Eliot, her creator, but that connection does not seem to have the novel-transcending effect that it has in the writings of V. Woolf, at least for those of Woolf's readers who are somewhere close to her in abnormal sensitivity.

— **Arbiter of elegances**. Edmund is referring to a passage (XVI.18) in the *Annals* of the Roman historian Tacitus (c.55-c.120CE) about Caius Petronius, an associate of the Roman emperor Nero (reigned 54-68CE) who appointed him as *elegantiae arbiter* (in Latin, 'arbiter of elegance', 'judge of taste'). Tacitus describes him as *non ganeo et profligator, ut plerique sua haurientium, sed erudito luxu* ('not a debauchee and spendthrift, like most of those who squander their substance, but a man of refined luxury'): *inter paucos familiarium Neroni adsumptus est, elegantiae arbiter,* *dum nihil amoenum et molle adfluentia putat, nisi quod ei Petronius adprobavisset* ('he became one of Nero's few intimate associates, a judge in matters of taste; and the emperor considered nothing luxurious to be pleasing or elegant if Petronius did not approve of it').

— **Seventeen syllables**. Edmund has offered three poems in *haiku* form (see I, final epigraphs).

— **Metaphysical**. Greg is no doubt referring to certain English poets of the 17th century who have come to be referred to as 'metaphysical poets'—including J. Donne, A. Marvell, and G. Herbert (these last two being alumni of Trinity College, Cambridge). The description was applied to some of them by Samuel Johnson (see Appendix 4 above, and *passim*), who was, among so much else, a pioneering literary critic.

Writing in 1921, the poet and literary critic T.S. Eliot (I.18, and above *passim*; Nobel Prize for Literature, 1948) suggested that the particularity of the metaphysical poets is that they incorporate ideas into poetry without surrendering the appeal of poetry to the imagination and the senses, thus expressing a unity of sensibility that has since been lost in English poetry:

'. . . it is the difference between the intellectual poet and the reflective poet. Tennyson and Browning are poets, and they think; but they do not feel their thought as immediately as the odour of a rose.'

Eliot's own poetry at its best expresses such a unity of sensibility.

— **Ella Wheeler Wilcox**. A popular American poet (1850-1919) who specialised in life-enhancing poetry.

'Laugh, and the world laughs with you; / Weep, and you weep alone; / For the sad old earth must borrow its mirth, / But has trouble enough of its own./ Sing, and the hills will answer; / Sigh, it is lost on the air; / The echoes bound to a joyful sound, / But shrink from voicing care.' ('Solitude', from *Poems of Passion*, 1883).

In fairness to her, it should be recalled that the English poet John Keats (see ch. 1 above, under 'Venice observed') took one of his first steps on the road to immortality with a poem whose first line is: 'A thing of beauty is a joy for ever.' (*Endymion*, 1818).

— **Shakespearean leaves of grass**. Echo of the title of a book of poems *Leaves of Grass* (1855, several later editions contain additional poems) by the American poet Walt Whitman (1819-92). Whitman is the American Baudelaire (I.19) or the American Catullus (see ch. 2 above, under '*lepidus libellus*') or an American Nietzsche, expressing sensuality in explicit terms, in a way calculated to shock a middle-class sense of propriety.

However, a major focus of the poems in *Leaves of Grass* is a sensual response to Nature. But it is nature-poetry of a kind which makes the English Romantic poet Wordsworth seem like an anaemic spinster. It has the over-masculine tone which will become a feature of American imaginative writing and the American visual arts—an over-asserted masculinity, often accompanied by alcoholism and promiscuity, as if it were necessary to compensate for a possible American public perception of artistic creation as an unmanly activity.

Greg's patchwork of verses contains lines from the following of Shakespeare's sonnets—86, 81, 97, 97, 104, 85, 107, 107, together with lines from two poems by Wyatt—an ode ('My Lute Awake') and a sonnet (first line: *You that in love find luck and abundance*). It was Th. Wyatt (1503-42) who introduced the sonnet-form into England from Italy, where it had been perfected, above all, by Petrarch (see ch. 1 above, under 'now is come'). Wyatt had been a student at St John's College, Cambridge.

— **Molecule to molecule.** Compare the biblical *Book of Genesis* (3.19): 'In the sweat of thy face shalt thou eat bread, till thou return unto the ground; for out of it wast thou taken: for dust thou art, and unto dust shalt thou return.' (King James version, 1611). This passage is echoed in the burial service of the (Anglican) *Book of Common Prayer* (see Appendix 2 below): 'earth to earth, ashes to ashes, dust to dust'.

— **Lightning before death.** From Romeo's last speech, thinking aloud before he drinks the poison, in W. Shakespeare, *Romeo and Juliet*, V. iii.

> 'How oft when men are at the point of death / have they been merry! Which their keepers call / A lightning before death: O! how may I / Call this a lightning?'

His dying words are: 'Thus with a kiss I die.'

— **Intimation of co-existence.** Edmund will no doubt have in mind the title of a poem (I.21) by W. Wordsworth, *Ode: Intimations of Immortality from Recollections of Early Childhood.*

— **Unweeded garden.**

> 'How weary, stale, flat, and unprofitable / Seem to me all the uses of this world. / Fie on't! O fie! 'tis an unweeded garden, / That grows to seed; things rank and gross in nature / Possess it merely.'
> W. Shakespeare, *Hamlet*, I. ii.

Hamlet is thinking aloud, after being in the presence of his mother and her new husband, the new king, the murderer of his brother, Hamlet's father. A particular *frisson* of the play comes from what seems to be Hamlet's retarded Oedipal closeness to his sinful mother.

— *Plus tard on dira qu'il est.* In French, 'some day, people will say that he is.' An echo of a saying attributed to the French novelist Hélène Bessette (1918-2000), whose work was ignored during her tragic lifetime: *plus tard on dira que je suis* ('some day, people will say that I am').

— *Dramatis personae.* In Latin and English, the cast of characters in a play. In Latin, *persona* (plural, *personae*) means the mask worn by an actor, the character played by an actor, and oneself as a person (the part one plays in the world). On the problem of personal identity, see ch. 11 below, and Appendix 4 below.

— *Erstes Gremium.* In German, 'first (supreme) committee'.

— **The British from a distance**. Could the Countess have in mind a phrase in the first Eclogue of Virgil (I.13): *et penitus toto divisos orbe Britannos* ('[we could visit] the Britons completely cut off from the rest of the world')?

— **Planning some new Reformation**. 'But 'tis the talent of our English nation, /Still to be plotting some new reformation.' From the prologue written by John Dryden (I.16) for the play *Sophonisba, or Hannibal's Overthrow* by his friend N. Lee (c.1653-92) who, like Dryden, had been a student at Trinity College, Cambridge.

— **Ontology**. Formed from a part of the Greek verb, *eini*, to be. *Onta*, things that are, reality. Ontology is the philosophy of being. Metaphysical philosophy. Contemplating the word 'is'. What *is* reality? See further in ch.11 below, and *passim*.

— **Cheerfulness keeps breaking in**. Remark of Dr Johnson's friend Edwards. See ch. 4 above, under 'will to know, will to power'.

— **Peer-reviewers**. To help them to decide whether to publish an article, editors of academic journals may seek the opinions of specialists in the given field—a jury of the author's peers, as it were. They surely have in mind Article 39 of *Magna Carta* (1215). 'No freeman shall be . . . in any way molested [*aliquo modo destruatur*] . . . unless by the lawful judgment of his peers [*nisi per legale judicium parium suorum*].'

— **Invisible College**. The intellectual wing of the Firm. See I.19.

— **Pure ideas practically operational**. We derive from Aristotle a distinction—which has been very influential in the history of philosophy—between 'practical' thinking, designed to be put into practice, and 'pure or speculative' thinking, which is thinking abstractly.

> 'For example the carpenter and the geometrician alike try to find the right angle, but they do it in different ways, the carpenter being content with such precision as satisfies the requirements of his job, the geometrician as a student of scientific truth seeking to discover the nature and attributes of the right angle.' *Ethics*, I.vii. (tr., J. Thomson).

For an application of such a distinction to the philosophy of *social idealism*, in the form of 'pure theory' and 'practical theory', see Ph. Allott, *Eunomia*, §§2.45ff. In *Eunomia*, a third form of theory is also identified—*transcendental* theory, that is, the theory of theory, ideas about the formation of ideas, including ideas about the possibility of values and ideals.

The self-constituting of a particular society is a continuous actualising of all three forms of theory simultaneously. This is true of every kind of society from a football club to the *international society* of the whole human race, the society of all societies.

For example—*democracy* can take the form of the principles of a particular constitution (practical theory), or else ideas about 'liberal democracy' (pure theory), or else ideas about how we form explanatory and regulatory ideas and models concerning social phenomena (transcendental theory).

— **Defensive gambit**. A metaphor taken from the game of chess—a tactical opening move designed to counter an opening move played by the opponent.

— **Allott's Law of Enlightenments**. See I.19. According to that Law, a New Enlightenment is due in the 21st century.

European cultural history contains a cycle of enlightenments at three-century intervals since the end of the Roman Empire in the West. Western monasticism (6th century), especially under the Rule of Benedict of Nursia. The Carolingian renaissance (9th century), centred on the court of the Emperor Charlemagne. The 12th-century renaissance, centred on the University of Paris. The 15th-century renaissance, centred on Italy, especially Florence. The 18th-century Enlightenment.

See Ph. Allott, *The Health of Nations*, §§3.18 and 5.61.

— **Energising ideal**. The powerful idea of the *ideal* is clearly a central feature of the present stage of the spiritual journeys of Greg and Edmund.

J.G. Fichte (see ch. 7 above, under '*Ich*'), in his *Third Address to the German Nation* (1807) describes (in Platonising language) an idealising education of a young person.

> 'He is also . . . a link in the eternal chain of spiritual life in a higher social order. A training which has undertaken to include the whole of his being should undoubtedly lead him to a knowledge of this higher order also. Just as it led him to sketch out for himself, by his own activity, an image of that moral world order *which never is, but always is to be,* so must it lead him to create in thought by the same self-activity an image of that supersensuous world order in which *nothing becomes, and which never has become, but which simply is forever;* all this in such a way that he intimately understands and perceives that it could not be otherwise.' (tr., R. Chisholm; emphasis added).

The italicised words express well the idea of *the ideal*, as a target which is always beyond our reach, a standard of 'what always will be, and never is' (*immer wird, nie ist*), which simply is forever, but which can determine and energise our action.

— ***Inter se***. In Latin, 'between or among (if more than two) themselves'.

— **Philanthropologists**. See I.5.

— **Si vis amari, ama**. In Latin, 'if you want to be loved, love.' From one of the *Moral Epistles* of the Roman writer and Stoic philosopher Seneca (c.2BCE-65CE). Epicurus (ch. 2 above), in one of his letters, had discussed the question of whether a wise person needs friends—or should the ideal person be self-sufficient, free of all emotions, including the need for friendship.

Seneca takes up the discussion. He says that the wise person can do without friends, in the sense that he can take the absence of friends with equanimity. But he should want friends (not, as Epicurus suggested, for practical reasons—for example, to have someone to be there for him when he is ill), but to help him to bring out his own best qualities.

And there is a simple prescription for making friends. *Hecaton ait, 'ego tibi monstrabo amatorium sine medicamento, sine herba, sine ullius veneficae carmine: si vis amari, ama.'* ('Hecaton says: "I will show you a love-potion without medicines, herbs, or witch's spells: if you want to be loved, love".') Hecaton was a Greek Stoic philosopher, often cited by Seneca.

— **Stoic, Epicurean**. See ch. 2 above, under 'cynic, stoic, epicurean'.

— **Redeeming word**. The 'word of God' or the 'word of the Lord' are frequent expressions in the Judaic Bible and the Christian Old Testament. For Christians, the words and deeds of Jesus Christ, recorded in the New Testament Gospels, are the direct 'word of God' and constitute a prescription for redemption, that is, a transformation of personal life in accordance with the ideal expressed in those words and deeds.

However, in the tradition of Christian theology, a more complex idea has developed, apparently under the influence of Greek and neo-Platonist philosophy (see ch. 2 above, under 'neo-neo-Platonist') and especially the work of Philo of Alexandria (c.15BCE-c.50CE), a Jewish philosopher who sought to reconcile Judaism and Greek philosophy. This is the idea of λογος (*logos*)—the word, the explanation, the underlying order of the universe.

Philosophical thinking naturally generates the problem of explaining *being* (how and why anything is) and *change* (how and why anything becomes something else while remaining itself). Different cultural traditions have proposed different kinds of answer—a plurality of gods, a single god ruling the universe, a universal material substance (either, fire, air, water), or a universal deep-structure (atoms and a void).

As in certain other cultural traditions, especially those of Asia, some of the ancient Greek philosophers postulated an underlying *metaphysical unity* of the universe.

In a few words attributed to him, Heraclitus (see ch.7 above, under 'all is struggle') expressed the conceptual foundation, not only of western metaphysical philosophy, but also of natural science—that is, the metaphysical re-construction in communicable forms of the presumed unity and uniformity of the universe.

In a saying reported in *De mundo* by Aristotle (or someone purporting to be Aristotle)—ἐκ πάντων ᾿εν καί ἐξ ᾿ενος πάντα (*ek panton hen kai ex henos panta*—'the one is made of all things, and all things come from the one'). In a saying reported by Hippolytus—εν πάντα ειναι (*hen panta einai*—'[we should agree that] everything is one').

In another saying (reported by Clement) Heraclitus spoke of a universal order (κοσμος—*kosmos*) which is the same for all, which no god or man has made, but ever was and is and will be. And in another saying (reported by Sextus Empiricus) he said that it is possible to give an account or explanation (λογος—*logos*) of the universal order, an account or explanation capable of being shared by all human minds.

The sayings of Heraclitus are uncertain—truly or falsely attributed—and always obscure—he was nicknamed 'the riddler'. Their correct translation into English is much disputed. But the significant fact is that, whatever their authenticity or meaning, they have had an effect on the minds of all those who have heard them over the course of twenty-five centuries.

Diogenes Laertius (ch. 2 above, under 'lackey of captialism') tells the story of Euripides giving Socrates a treatise of Heraclitus. Socrates (allegedly) said: 'What I understand is splendid; and I think that what I don't understand is so too—but it would take a Delian diver to get to the bottom of it.' (tr., J. Barnes).

The human mind is capable of finding within itself an idea of the order of the universe, because the human mind is itself part of the order of the universe.

So, for the most sophisticated of early Christian theologians living in a cultural ethos (1st century CE) full of Greek philosophy, the question was—is Christ, who is an incarnation of the one God, a manifestation of the *logos*?

In what came to be accepted as a fourth book of the Christian 'new testament', the *Gospel of John* opens with the words—

— (in the original Greek) εν αρχη ην ὁ λογος και ὁ λογος ην προς τον θεόν και θεος ην ὁ λογος (*en arche en ho logos kai ho logos en pros ton theon kai theos en ho logos*);
— translated into Latin (the Vulgate) as: *in principio erat Verbum et Verbum erat apud Deum et Deus erat Verbum* ;
— translated into English (King James Version, 1611) as: 'In the beginning was the Word, and the Word was with God, and the Word was God.'

For almost twenty centuries, rivers of ink have flowed in controversies about the interpretation of this sentence, especially (among several others) about the meaning of the words *arche—principio—beginning* and *pros—apud—with*. What can it mean to say that, originally, the order of the universe is (or ! was) related to God?

The better (!!) view might be as follows.

(1) *arche* (like *logos*, a notoriously multivalent word in ancient Greek) is here referring to the *origin* of the order of the universe, not merely in a temporal sense (as the King James version might seem to suggest), but in the sense that the *order* of the universe (*logos—verbum—the Word*) is inseparable from the *existence* of the universe—each originates the other.

(2) And hence, for theists (I.20; and ch. 12 below, under 'theists/deists'), God is related to the order of the universe in the same way as God is related to the universe itself.

(3) So, if the God of theists is the author and ruler of the universe, God is also the author and ruler of the order of the universe.

(4) And so the order of the universe must contain a (Platonic) reflection, as it were, of God—an impression, as it were, of its origin.

(5) But the order of the universe is an order which, as Heraclitus said, can be known through the rational capacity of *all* human minds (including the minds of those who do not believe in God) and hence the order of the universe can be spoken of independently of God (by those who believe in God and, especially, by those who do not).

(6) And so, for theists, the 'creation' of the universe can be spoken about in two ways—either (a) in speaking about *the order of the universe*, a context in which 'creation' may suggest an origin of the universe in the dimensions of time and space—the specific ordering categories of the human mind (see Appendix 8 below);

or (b) in speaking about *God*, a context in which the order of the universe suggests the origin of the universe in the nature of God, without reference to time and space—the presence of the universe in 'God's world', as it were.

(7) And so, for theists who are Christians, God's 'incarnation' (in the person of Jesus Christ) would then be the perceptible appearance of God, in time and space, *within the order of the universe*—'the Word' made able to speak 'the word of God', the words of redemption, in human language, in the human world—that is, the human world seen as part of the natural order of the universe, which is itself part of God's world. ('Incarnation' means 'being made flesh'—*Verbum caro factum*—in Latin, 'the Word (*logos*) made flesh'. In Latin *caro*, 'flesh'.)

And so, in one tradition of Christian practice, the concept of 'transubstantiation' (see Appendix 4 below) might be seen as referring to an event in God's world without a corresponding perceptible event in the (natural) order of the universe. The bread and wine retain their natural form as such.

(8) And so also, for some Christians, the idea of what is called the *Trinity*—of a God who is three-in-one—is the idea of a *God* whose *love* is manifested in Jesus Christ and whose *mind* is manifested in the Holy Spirit, all three being manifestations, in a form appropriate to the nature and capacity of the human mind, of a benevolent order of the universe.

(9) So, for Christians, human beings live in both worlds—in the natural order of the universe (seen as an order in time and space) and in God's world (seen as an order apart from time and space), with Christ acting as a bridge between the two—or, rather, a ladder—the humanising of God enabling human beings to find the godlike within themselves.

From all the above it follows that a more accurate (if less poetic) English version than the King James version of the controversial text might be—

In the origin of the universe is its order, and its order is from God, and its order is of God.

In looking for a 'redeeming word or words' from Edmund and Greg, the Countess is, perhaps, asking them to produce good new ideas about the *logos* of *the human world.*

CHAPTER 9. *Beyond Government.*

— **MI6. CIA.** See I.3.
— **Premier League** The name of the highest professional football (soccer) leagues in England and Scotland.
— **Pimpernel**.

> 'The Scarlet Pimpernel, Mademoiselle,' he said at last 'is the name of a humble English wayside flower; but it is also the name chosen to hide the identity of the best and bravest man in all the world, so that he may better succeed in accomplishing the noble task he has set himself to do.'
> 'Ah, yes,' here interposed the young Vicomte, 'I have heard speak of this Scarlet Pimpernel. A little flower—red?—yes! They say in Paris that every time a royalist escapes to England that devil, Foucquier-Tinville, the Public Prosecutor, receives a paper with that little flower dessinated in red upon it.'

From *The Scarlet Pimpernel* (ch. IV), a novel by Baroness Orczy (1865-1947). The man in question is an elusive English aristocrat who specialises in rescuing French aristocrats from the guillotine. The novel was inspired by *A Tale of Two Cities* by C. Dickens (1812-70), a novel (1859) set in the French Revolution, which was itself inspired by *The French Revolution. A History*, by Th. Carlyle (1795-1881), published in 1837.
— **Sublime level (of deception).** People who work in government and who know Mike Abi might remember the description *splendide mendax* (in Latin, 'splendidly deceitful') used in one of the *Odes* (III.xi) of Horace (I.4).

The poet uses the phrase to describe Hypermnestra, one of the Danaides, the fifty daughters of Danaus. In a strange episode of Greek mythology, which seems to have Freudian or Jungian overtones, Aegyptus required the fifty daughters of Danaus to marry his fifty sons. Danaus ordered his daughters to kill their husbands on their wedding night. Alone of the daughters, Hypermnestra failed to do so, having fallen in love with the son who had been assigned to her. Together they were the progenitors of a royal dynasty.

— **Something dangerous about him.** Echo, perhaps, of W. Shaklespeare, *Hamlet. Prince of Denmark*, V. i. 'Yet have I in me something dangerous.' (Hamlet speaking).

— **Still point of Mike Abi's many worlds.** 'At the still point of the turning world. Neither flesh nor fleshless; / Neither from nor towards; at the still point, there the dance is, / But neither arrest nor movement. And do not call it fixity, / Where past and future are gathered. Neither movement from nor towards, / Neither ascent nor decline. Except for the point, the still point, / There would be no dance, and there is only the dance.'

From *Burnt Norton*, one of the *Four Quartets* by T.S. Eliot (see ch. 8 above).

— **Goldberg Pynch.** See I.22.

— **Nocturne II.** From the Latin, *nocturnus* ('by night'), from *nox* ('night'). Used as the title of art-works in various forms, including musical compositions.

The American painter J.A.McN. Whistler (1834-1903) gave the title *Nocturne* to several of his paintings. One of them—*Nocturne in Black and Gold. The Falling Rocket* (1875), now in the Detroit Institute of Arts, an impressionistic night-scene (more black than gold)—was the subject of a fierce attack by the art historian and social critic J.Ruskin (I.16) in his *Fors Clavigera. Letters to the Working Men and Labourers of Great Britain* (!).

He said that the Grosvenor Gallery in London was charging two hundred guineas for what was close to a 'wilful imposture' by an artist who was 'flinging a pot of paint in the public's face'. Whistler sued Ruskin for libel and was awarded one farthing (one quarter of a penny) in damages.

The naming of thoroughbred racehorses is a minor art-form. Their names may contain not more than 18 letters or spaces, according to traditional rules. 'Nocturne II' would not be permitted as a name, for another reason: it contains a final numeral.

— **Cheekie Chappie.** A cognomen adopted by Max Miller (1894-1963), a British music-hall comedian who strongly influenced later generations of comedians.

— **The People and Peoples of the World.** Compare the opening words of the US Constitution. 'We *the People* of the United States.' Compare the opening words of the United Nations Charter. 'We *the Peoples* of the United Nations.' Compare Article 1 of the International (UN) Covenant on Civil and Political Rights (1966). 'All *peoples* have the right of self-determination' (italics added in all three cases). The benign-sounding idea of 'a people' (as distinct from 'people') is presumably intended to refer to a collection of people with some sort of collective identity which is not, however, that of 'a state' or even 'a nation'.

It is an idea which has insinuated itself into international parlance, trailing controversies about its meaning and its practical application. The UN Charter wisely and all-too-realistically goes on to say—'our respective *Governments* . . . have agreed to the present Charter'. And the International Covenant wisely and all-too-realistically (and fatally—since they are essentially rights to be claimed against the state) goes on to provide that 'the *States* Parties to the present Covenant . . . shall promote the realization of [*inter alia*] the right of self-determination, and shall respect that right.' (italics added in both cases).

— **Jaunts and jollities**. Echo of the title of a collection of stories—*Jorrocks's Jaunts and Jollities* (1838)—by the English writer R. Surtees (1803-64).

— **UNPAST.** See I, ch. 18.

— **Marshall-type Plan.** In a speech at Harvard University in 1947, US Secretary of State George Marshall initiated a programme under which the US Government assisted European economic recovery after World War II. The motives and the causes and the effects of the programme are the subject of continuing controversy, reflecting the obscurity of human motivation, even at the institutional level, and the complexity of dynamic economic phenomena.

— **Servant of two masters.** Echo of an admirably poetic passage in the King James Version of the (Christian) *Gospel of Matthew* (ch. 6)—a passage which, in style and substance, recalls Hindu or Buddhist sacred writing.

> 'Lay not up for yourselves treasures upon earth, where moth and rust doth corrupt, and where thieves break through and steal: But lay up for yourselves treasures in heaven where neither moth nor rust doth corrupt, and where thieves do not break through nor steal: For where your treasure is, there will be your heart also. The light of the body is the eye: if therefore thine eye be single, thy whole body shall be full of light. But if thine eye be evil, thy whole body shall be full of darkness. If therefore the light that is in thee be darkness, how great is that darkness! No man can serve two masters: for either he will hate the one, and love the other; or else he will hold to the one, and despise the other. Ye cannot serve God and mammon.' (In ancient Greek, *Mammonas*, Syrian god of riches, and hence 'wealth' in general.)

— **Trustees of human happiness.** In 'Professor Malone', one of the humorous fictions in *Some People* (1927) by Harold Nicolson (I.18), Nicolson describes a meeting of the Council of Four at the Paris Peace Conference (1919), at which sovereignty over the (fictional) island of Palur was to be decided. The British Prime Minister, David Lloyd George, improbably but all-too-probably, reminds his colleagues that they are 'the trustees of human happiness'.

— **The fox made surveyor of the fold**. From *Henry VI*, Part 2, a play which may or may not have been written, in whole or in part, by W. Shakespeare.

> *Duke of York*: 'Were it not all one an empty eagle were set / To guard the chicken from a hungry kite, / As place Duke Humphrey for the king's protector?' *Queen Margaret*: 'So the poor chicken should be sure of death.'
> *Duke of Suffolk*: 'Madam, 'tis true: and were it not madness, then, / To make the fox surveyor of the [sheep] fold?'

The scene is set in the Abbey at Bury St Edmunds (I.14), where an out-of-town session of Parliament was held. The play reflects a power-struggle in England at the end of the Hundred Years War (I.16), yet another miserable power-struggle, which came to be called the War of the Roses, from the emblematic white and red roses of the competing aristocratic clans, and which ended with the passing of the throne from Richard III (who was the subject of a play certainly written by Shakespeare) to Henry VII (reigned 1485-1509), who was the first of the Tudor royal dynasty, who was the subject of a biography by Francis Bacon, and who was succeeded by his son Henry VIII (sponsor of the importation of Renaissance and Reformation into England), father of Queen Elizabeth I (sponsor of the idea of England as a possible imperial power).

Such is the way of history. Profound social change may have its origin in despicable events.

— *A priori*. In Latin, 'from what has gone before'. Especially, an argument based on previously established abstract principles or assumptions, rather than (argument *a posteriori*) from observation or experience.

— **Sidi Bou Said**. A village twenty kilometres from Tunis which takes its name from a 12th century holy man who retired to the place to lead a life of contemplation. In this context, *sidi*—an Arabic title of respect—is equivalent to the English word 'saint'.

— **Carthage**. A place close to Tunis with a very remarkable history. Its rivalry with Rome could well have ended differently, with profound world-historical consequences. Europe might instead have had a Carthaginian Empire as a principal part of its genetic inheritance.

The city of Carthage was founded by the Phoenicians—according to legend, in the 9th century BCE, by Dido (I.13 and I.16) from Tyre, another Phoenician city. The Phoenicians built a maritime empire in the western Mediterranean, in constant conflict (see below) with the Greeks and the Romans, and developed a sophisticated society based on international trade. They were leaders in the modernisation of agriculture. Their alphabet is at the root of western languages. Among the other cities that they established is Gades (present-day Cádiz) in south-western Spain.

— **The clicking and the tapping**. Alison's involuntary memory is clearly of an onomatopoeic passage in *Cape Carthage*, a poem by Gregory Seare, published in

1980 in the (late lamented) *Cambridge Review* under the defensive pen-name of Ph*l*p A**o**. The opening lines are as follows.

> 'Emirs between prayers planned gardens of delight, / Particular paradises from Granada to Baghdad, / Where the dazzling future danced on jets of water / And never came, or rode with the fixed stars / And passed away. No jewelled hand / Planted this genetic bazaar at this crossroad, / Intercontinental slack water, brown sail / Made good with brown patches, shroud and grail. / Among the ruins, enough time regained for one day, / The clicking and the tapping of mosaic-makers stop. /Scipios descending from air-conditioned buses / Will not destroy their work, guarded by official ropes.'

— **Carthage destroyed**. There were two major periods of war between Carthage and Rome—the so-called Punic (Phoenician) Wars of 264-241 and 218-201BCE. In the second war, Hannibal, the Carthaginian leader, came close to success but was finally defeated by the Romans, under their leader Scipio Africanus, at the battle of Zama in North Africa.

Having shown signs of a revival, the city of Carthage was totally destroyed by the Romans in 149BCE, in fulfilment of a policy expressed in a saying which acquired legendary status—*Carthago delenda est* ('Carthage must be destroyed'). The Romans set an unfortunate precedent, of which there have been modern copies, of wiping a human settlement off the face of the earth and, in the traditional account, sowing the Carthaginian earth with salt to prevent a revival of agriculture.

The Romans later re-founded a city on the site, a city which was taken over by Byzantium, and then destroyed in an Arab invasion in the 9th century—leaving the Roman mosaic pavements and other vestigial remains which have been the object of excavation and limited restoration.

— **Dido—forget her fate**. See I.13 and I.16.
— **Odysseus**. See I.22.
— **Aeneas**. See I.13 and I.16.
— *Azulejos*. In Spanish, 'tiles'.
— **Artist as a young man**. Echo of the title of a novel, *Portrait of the Artist as a Young Man* (1916), by the Irish writer James Joyce (1882-1941). The novel describes the mental development of a young man living in Dublin, whose experiences seem likely to be close to those of the young Joyce.
— **Sierra Nevada**. In Spanish, 'snow-covered mountain ridge'. An area north of Granada, in the province of Andalucía, Spain.
— **Federico García Lorca**. Spanish writer (1898-1936). Born and died in Andalucía. Assassinated by Nationalists under General Franco, who led an insurrection against the Spanish Republic which had displaced the monarchy in 1931, leading to a Civil War (1936-39). Franco was Spanish head of state from 1939 until 1975, when the

monarchy was restored. Lorca's poetry and plays reflect the Spanish imagination and Spanish traditional culture in a powerful way.

— **Knot of vipers.** *Le Noeud des Vipères* (1932) is a novel by the French writer F. Mauriac (1885-1970) (ch. 6 above, under 'problem of evil'). The novel is the written confession of the father of a provincial bourgeois family whose life has been poisoned by an obsession with money and by many forms of self-hating and bitterness. It is also a story of his thinking himself in old age into a form of redemption, as he comes to realise the potentiality of the life that he could have led, including its possible spiritual dimension.

The metaphor of a knot of vipers—poisonous animals writhing together in inextricable intimacy—may or may not be suitable as a metaphor for a troubled 'heart', as the narrator says, or as a metaphor for a troubled family, including several generations, which he painfully describes. It certainly seems to be a possible metaphor for the world that Mike Abi and Alison inhabit—the co-habitation of political and governmental and economic actors in a mutually sustaining and mutually corrupting embrace. (It is a world depicted in a novel with the apt title *The Nest of Vipers* (1997) by L. Davies.)

It is difficult to avoid an echo also of the Roman sculpture known as the Laocoön, which shows Laocoön and his sons dying in the grip of sea-serpents. G. Lessing (see ch. 7 above, under 'Edmund the Weise') uses the sculpture as the crux of a discussion (*Laocoön*, 1766) about the central and perennial question of aesthetic philosophy—what does, or should, a work of art (a work of any of the arts) represent? See ch. 15 below, under 'music', and ch. 7 above, under 'sensation without sentiment', and ch, 19 below.

— *Mutatis mutandis.* In Latin, 'those things having been changed that should be changed'.

— *à deux.* In French, '[a situation, conversation] involving only two persons'.

— **Lumpen masses.** An echo of the German word *Lumpen*, 'rags'. *Lumpenproletariat* ('proletarian rabble') was a favourite expression of K. Marx and F. Engels, for whom the actual consciousness of such people was less easy to imagine than that of the 'proletariat' considered as an abstract social category capable of revolutionary consciousness.

— **Anally-retentive.** A characteristically unpleasant and pejorative heuristic category in the psychobiology of S. Freud (I.5, and above *passim*). It was used to refer to a stage in the development of the child which may be reproduced in the mentality of the adult, involving a high degree of self-controlling and self-restricting behaviour (surely not always considered to be a bad characteristic).

— *verbatim.* In Latin, 'word for word'.

— **Love your chains.** Echo of a text in the *Social Contract*, bk. I, of J.-J. Rousseau (I.1, and above *passim*). 'Aristotle was right; but he took the effect for the cause. Nothing can be more certain than that every man born in slavery is born for slavery. Slaves lose everything in their chains, even the desire of escaping from them: they love their servitude . . .'

Rousseau is referring to a passage in Aristotle's *Politics* (bk. 1) where he argues that there are 'slaves by nature', who have the mentality of slaves, as opposed to 'slaves by law'. Aristotle does, however, discuss at length the view that slavery is 'a violation of nature'.

— **Those who are not with us are against us**. A sentiment echoed by tyrants and revolutionaries and ideologues throughout the ages. Reflected also in an uncharacteristically harsh saying of Jesus Christ recorded in the (Christian) *Gospel of Matthew* (12.30). The milder, reverse form of the statement—'he that is not against us is with us'—is reported in the *Gospels of Luke* (9.50), and *Mark* (9.40).

— **Meaning of money**. The status of money as money is a product of human imagination, of social convention, of social practice, and/or of law. It is not possible to identify any precise 'essence' of money, and, hence, there is, notoriously, no generally agreed definition of the word. At the least, money is something that serves three functions—as a measure of value, as a medium of exchange, and as a store of wealth. (G. Crowther, *An Outline of Money*, 1941). The recent development of electronic financial transactions, with no other physical substance, suggests that money is becoming ever more imaginary.

However, Mike Abi is right to suggest that the determination of what is to take effect as money in a given society is the exercise of one of the most powerful of all social powers, incidentally determining the unequal distribution among society-members of countless other social powers.

— **Who controls the controllers?** An echo of a Latin saying—*quis custodiet ipsos custodes* ('who will guard the guards?')—now used as a rhetorical commonplace. Its source is in a passage in a *Satire* by the Roman poet Juvenal (c.60-c.130 CE). Satire VI is about the ways of women. a*udio quid veteres olim moneatis amici, / 'pone seram, cohibe.' sed quis custodiet ipsos / custodes? cauta est et ab illis incipit uxor. / iamque eadem summis pariter minimisque libido, nec melior silicem pedibus quae conterit atrum / quam quae longorum vehitur cervice Syrorum.* ('I hear all this time the advice of my old friends—"Put on a lock and keep your wife indoors." Yes, but who will ward the warders? The wife arranges accordingly and begins with them. High or low their passions are all the same. She who wears out the black cobble-stones with her bare feet is no better then she who rides upon the necks of eight stalwart Syrians [horses, presumably].') (tr., G. Ramsay).

The facile overuse of the saying can obscure the profound importance of an idea which lies at the heart of the greatest challenge of social organisation. How can society's higher values be imposed on those who exercise great social power? It took centuries of painful experience to begin to make into a reality an idea which had always been familiar to philosophers—an idea that has come to be called 'the rule of law' (*Rechtsstaat*, in German; *état de droit*, in French)—the idea that the propriety of the exercise of legally conferred social powers is to be determined in accordance with the law, interpreted and enforced by an independent judiciary.

Alison Brand and Mike Abi are referring to a formidable new aspect of the ancient problem—who is to control, in the name of the common interest of society, the exercise of the vast *economic power* now held by public and private corporations and individuals—power that determines the lives of all human beings everywhere as much as the public powers of governments?

— **Market forces**. The dynamic energy acting in a capitalist market imagined as an intelligent machine. See Appendix 5 below.

— **Master-builders**. The fully qualified members of medieval craft-guilds were called 'masters'. The guild controlled access to the given trade by controlling the training of 'apprentices'. A so-called master's degree awarded by a university is a survival of such a system, the medieval university having been a guild of teachers or a guild of teachers and scholars (the apprentices).

> 'When those particular incorporations which are now particularly called universities were first established, the term of [seven] years which it was necessary to study, in order to obtain the degree of master of arts, appears evidently to have been copied from the terms of apprenticeship in common trades, of which the incorporations were much more ancient.'
> (A. Smith, *Wealth of Nations*, Bk. 1, ch. 10).

With the Teutonising, and then industrialising, of the modern university, the medieval ghost walks again.

The term 'master builder' is now inevitably associated with *The Master Builder* (1892), the accepted English title of a play (*Bygmester Solness*) by the Norwegian dramatist H. Ibsen (1828-1906). The play recounts the decline and fall of a builder who has sacrificed his affective life to success in his trade. When the life he might have led returns to haunt him in the person of a young woman, he fails to respond to her challenge, and dies in an accident caused by her provocation.

— **Gods who will never fail**. Echo of the title of a book *The God that Failed* (1949), edited by R. Crossman, in which a number of former Communist intellectuals explained their conversion to, and apostasy from, communism.

— **Olympus**. In ancient Greek mythology, the mountain home of the gods.

— *Cul-de-sac*. **(three senses)**. In French (literally), 'bottom of the sack'. In French and English, 'dead-end street', 'dead-end [of any kind]'.

CHAPTER 10. *Kreuzberg.*

— **Kreuzberg**. (In German, 'Hill of the Cross', 'Crosshill'). (Pronounce as 'Croits-berg'.) A district in Berlin notable for its ethnically mixed population, but also subject, in recent years, to some gentrification (*Gentrifizierungseffekte*).

— **Woman in a room by herself.** In 1928 Virginia Woolf (see ch. 8 above, under 'Mrs Dalloway') delivered lectures at Newnham College and Girton College, Cambridge—two colleges for women founded in 1871 and 1869 respectively. (Women students at Cambridge did not have the same formal status as male students until 1947. Girton now has men and women students.)

In 1929 the lectures were expanded and published under the title *A Room of One's Own*. From the starting-point of the question of the role of women as fiction-writers, the discussion goes far wider—to survey the historically determined status and psychology of women, and to investigate the social and psychological function of fiction-writing. The style of the lectures is remarkably similar to the style of Woolf's own fiction-writing—an account of her own states of mind as she thought her way into, and through, both the narrower and the wider topics. She begins with a much-quoted conclusion.

'All I could do was to offer you an opinion upon one minor point—a woman must have money and a room of her own if she is to write fiction; and that, as you will see, leaves the great problem of the true nature of woman and the true nature of fiction unsolved.'

She reviews the way in which male writers—obsessively, it seems—present women and their psychology in works of fiction.

'Why are women, judging from this catalogue, so much more interesting to men than men are to women?'

'A very queer, composite being thus emerges. Imaginatively she is of the highest importance; practically she is completely insignificant. She pervades poetry from cover to cover; she is all but absent from history. She dominates the lives of kings and conquerors in fiction; in fact she was the slave of any boy whose parents forced a ring upon her finger. Some of the most inspired words, some of the most profound thoughts in literature fall from her lips; in real life she could hardly read, could scarcely spell, and was the property of her husband.'

On the nature and purpose of fiction-writing she says—

'If one shuts one's eyes and thinks of the novel as a whole, it would seem to be a creation owning a certain looking-glass likeness to life, though of course with simplifications and distortions innumerable. At any rate, it is a structure leaving a shape on the mind's eye, built now in squares, now pagoda shaped, now throwing out wings and arcades, now solidly compact and domed like the Cathedral of Saint Sofia at Constantinople. This shape, I thought, thinking back over certain famous novels, starts in one the kind of emotion that is appropriate to it. But that emotion at once blends itself with others, for the "shape" is not made by the relation of stone to stone, but by the relation of human being to human being. Thus a novel starts in us all sorts of antagonistic and opposed emotions. Life conflicts with something that is not life.'

— **Freud hated women.** The Countess may be expressing the matter rather too strongly or, at least, too clearly. But there is no doubt that Freud's miscellaneous writings about the psychology of women are suffused with a negative and distancing attitude. His view of human psychology in general is predominantly cold and gloomy (see ch. 1 above, under 'Freudian interpretation'), but 'the problem of woman' seems to have been particularly painful for him.

'Throughout the ages the problem of woman has puzzled people of every kind . . . You too will have pondered over this question in so far as you are men; from the women among you that is not to be expected, for you are the riddle yourselves.' S. Freud, 'The Psychology of Women', in *New Introductory Lectures on Psycho-Analysis* (1933). (tr., W. Sprott).

These lectures, written in the form of lectures but not delivered as such, were a continuation of his *Introductory Lectures* delivered in 1915-16. Freud had expressed views on the psychology of women on various previous occasions, but now, at the age of seventy-seven, he still found the psychology of women to be a puzzle.

Freud seems to have taken the view that women are very much the secondary sex in civilised life, closer to the earth and nature, psychologically determined by motherhood (the Freuds had six children), by a natural tendency to passivity, by an innate feeling of inferiority (*Minderwertigkeitsgefühl*) in relation to the sexually potent male, and by their useful function as a permanent stimulation to sublimation of sexuality on the part of males, a sublimation which generates the benefits of civilised life—a consoling thought for women, no doubt.

Freud sometimes suggests that such views are 'scientific', in the sense of being reasonable generalisations from observed behaviour of women in all places and at all times. But he also frankly admits that, if the status of women were as he had described it, it might be a product, in whole or in part, of cultural causes, and/or that his own views might themselves be a reflection, in whole or in part, of the cultural prejudices of his class and culture.

Freud also leaves us confused by saying that, of course, many women do not conform to the woman-type, and that we are all, in any case, more or less bisexual, men and women, with especially creative people being especially bisexual. Also, without evidence or further discussion (and alongside many derogatory remarks about women), he makes the remarkable assertion that the relation between a mother and her son is 'the most complete relationship between human beings' and that a mother teaches a son how to love. (Had Freud read *Ulysses* (1922) by J. Joyce (1882-1941)? 'Mother's love the only thing in life.')

We, who have the benefit of possessing the extended self-analysis that is Freud's written *oeuvre*, might tend to think that his views on women could have, in whole or in part, a rather specific and personal origin.

— **Madame Bovary, c'est nous.** In French, 'Madame Bovary is us (men).' The echo is of a saying—*Madame Bovary, c'est moi, d'après moi* ('Madame Bovary is me, drawn from me') attributed (but without a source in his writings) to G. Flaubert: (1821-80), the author of the novel *Madame Bovary. Moeurs de province* (Madame Bovary. Provincial Manners) (1857).

From its first publication, the novel, which minutely dissects the adultery of the wife of a provincial doctor, has given rise to intense controversy as to its psychological significance. Is it a depraved work, failing even to suggest the culpability of Emma Bovary and her lovers? (Flaubert was prosecuted for indecency, but not convicted.) Is it a work of pure realism—'a work of petrified feeling', in the words of the English critic M. Arnold—in which the emotional states of the characters are described with repulsive clinical objectivity?

Is it, as suggested by the novelist H. James, a work of a writer simply incapable of expressing psychological truth, especially the psychology of women—the distinguishing mark of the great novelists? Is it simply a work of beautiful imaginative power, whose moral significance (if any) is entirely a matter for the reader, as suggested by the French poet C. Baudelaire? Or is it a work of passionate distaste (almost Nietzschean or Marxian or Baudelairean or Satrean in spirit—among many other bourgeoisie-haters), by an author who saw provincial life as the symbol of the way in which social convention stifles, and ultimately destroys, those who have an idealistic or romantic view of human potentiality? The ruined potentiality would then be that of both Emma Bovary *and* Charles Bovary, of both Emma Bovary *and* Gustave Flaubert himself. On this view, Madame Bovary would be all of us. *Madame Bovary, c'est nous tous.*

Flaubert may have suggested his own answer to the puzzle in a saying that does have a definite source in his correspondence. *Si vous me connaissiez davantage vous sauriez que j'ai la vie ordinaire en exécration. Je m'en suis toujours personnellement écarté autant que j'ai pu.* ('If you knew me better, you would know that I loathe everyday life. I have always personally detached myself from it as much as I could.') Compare the main title of Flaubert's novel about a woman—*Madame Bovary* (1857)—with the title of Tolstoy's novel about a woman—*Anna Karenina* (1875-77)—or the title of Ibsen's play about a woman—*Hedda Gabler* (1890).

— **The evil that men do.** Echo of the words of Mark Antony speaking to the Roman crowd after the assassination (44 BCE) of Julius Caesar, in Shakespeare's play. 'Friends, Romans, countrymen, lend me your ears; / I come to bury Caesar, not to praise him. / The evil that men do lives after them; / The good is oft interred with their bones; / So let it be with Caesar.' (III. ii).

Antony was presumably using the word 'men' to refer to human beings of both genders. The Countess evidently is not. Caesar had paid, and Antony would pay, a price for their love of Queen Cleopatra VII of Egypt (reigned 51-30 BCE) See ch. 19 below, under 'Cleopatra's nose'.

Caesar was a larger-than-life figure, akin to a modern 'celebrity' in his private life. Suetonius (see ch. 7 above, under 'I think I'm becoming'), the great biographer of imperial Rome, who liked to share unsavoury biographical details with his readers, quotes Curio the Elder, in a diatribe (55BCE) against Caesar, calling him 'every woman's husband and every man's wife' (somewhat of an exaggeration in one respect, if not in the other). But he also quotes Marcus Cato as saying that 'Caesar was the only sober man who ever tried to wreck the constitution'.

— **Thinking, that is, living**. An echo, perhaps, of a saying of Cicero (106-43 BCE) (see above, *passim*): *vivere est cogitare* ('to live is to think') (*Tusculan Disputations*, v.38). A different formulation of such an idea—*cogito, ergo sum* ('I think, therefore I am')—would be the solitary indubitable idea found by R. Descartes within the self-doubting human mind, an idea that would enable him to reconstruct the rational activity of the mind (see Appendix 8 below).

— **No self there**. A distant echo of a saying of the American writer G. Stein (1874-1946) in her autobiography *Everybody's Autobiography* (1937). She had published a previous volume of autobiography under the title *Autobiography of Alice. B. Toklas* (1933), purporting to be the autobiography of her partner of that name, in which Stein referred to in the third person. The saying refers to Oakland, California, her place of birth, to which she returned on a book tour of the United States. (She had been normally resident in France for many years.)

> 'What was the use of my having come from Oakland . . . there was no there there.' In fact, her remark meant something slightly more complex than it appears to mean. She was saying that all the places in Oakland that had been significant for her in her childhood (her school, her synagogue . . .) had disappeared. The 'there' of her subjective destination was no longer there.

The saying may not be inappropriate to describe the strange emptiness that we may encounter when we try to revisit past states of our consciousness, looking for a unity of consciousness, the single self that must presumably have been the subject of all those past states of consciousness. See *passim*, M. Proust (I.19), *À la recherche du temps perdu*.

— **Ur-self**. *Ur*, in German, a prefix indicating ancient or original. In looking for her *Ur*-self, Frieda (Austrian Countess with German ancestors who may have known Goethe) could not fail to associate her search with a notorious *Ur*—the *Urpflanze* (original plant) of Goethe (I.12).

Throughout his life, Goethe interested himself, among his countless other interests, in aspects of natural science and, especially, physiology and botany. He shared a Romantic (Blakeian) and German idealist disgust for what was seen (mistakenly) as Newtonian materialism and mechanism—the idea that the whole universe is explicable on the basis of ascertainable physical laws.

But he sought obsessively to show that the universe (inorganic and organic) could be explained by understanding the inner processes of development that cause its different manifestations in rocks and animals and plants. He invented the word 'morphology' (*Morphologie*, in German) to refer to the theoretical study of the dynamic process of formation of the particular forms (*morphos*, in Greek, 'form, figure, shape') of the contents of the universe.

At least in an earlier period of his thinking, he thought that plants, for example, were all manifestations of a development from an original plant-form (*Urpflanze*). Later, he took the view that all plants followed the same forms of morphological change—in other words, he was proposing a sort of scientific idealism, that there is a hidden order of the universe that is not Platonic (ideal metaphysical forms) nor Kantian (unknowable real reality whose order is produced by our minds) (see Appendix 8 below). On the contrary, this inner ordering was ascertainable—a sort of mediation between the order of the mind and the hidden (and absolutely real) order of nature.

The evolution of *flowers* remains a complete mystery—perhaps they, if nothing else, were the result of *Intelligent Design* by an especially pleasure-loving designer.

If the Countess is well versed in Goetheianism, it may be that she is trying to find—as philosophers and psychologists try to find—the self-forming unity of her own self, as an instance of the self-forming unity of all selfs(!). See further in ch. 11 below.

— **Suffering greatly.** Echo of words spoken by the Chorus in the tragedy *Antigone*, by Sophocles (c.495-406 BCE): 'This law is immutable: / For mortals, to live is greatly to suffer.'

— **They would never see so much.** Echo of the closing words of *King Lear* by W. Shakespeare. 'The weight of this sad time we must obey; / Speak what we feel, nor what we ought to say. / The oldest hath borne most: we that are young, / Shall never see so much, nor live so long.' (The Duke of Albany speaking, immediately after the death of Lear, and in the presence of his body.)

— **Why did God make me?** A traditional answer given to that question in the instruction of Roman Catholic children in English-speaking countries (the so-called Penny Catechism for children) is—'God made me to know Him, love Him and serve Him in this world, and to be happy with Him forever in the next.' If Frieda had also been taught this as a child, it may be that she would rather have hoped to be happy with Him also in *this* world.

— **S-Bahn station.** An overground railway in Berlin is called the *Strassenbahn* ('street railway').

— ***The Book of Genesis.*** The first book of the Jewish Torah (and the Christian Old Testament) was given the Greek title *Genesis* ('source', 'origin', 'birth') in its original Greek translation (the Septuagint; translated from the Hebrew and Aramaic by Greek-speaking Jewish scholars in the last centuries BCE). It includes an account of the creation of the universe by God. It also includes a story of God's creation of the first human beings, Adam and Eve, and their defiance of the will of God. It is the source of a doctrine of Christian theology known as 'original sin' (I.19, and ch. 6 above, under 'problem of evil').

Controversial in the extreme, in general and in detail, the doctrine suggests that the defiance of Adam and Eve was 'the Fall of Man', the source of an innate human tendency to do evil, a tendency that may, on one view of the matter, be overcome with the assistance of God ('grace').

The Countess clearly has particularly in mind the commonly held view that the Genesis story also suggests that man was a primary creation and woman a secondary creation, and that the 'original sin' was initiated by the woman.

Compare the story of Pandora in ancient Greek mythology. Zeus made her the source of human evils and sufferings, as punishment for an act of god-defiance by a man, Prometheus (I.22)—a more equitable myth. (The account of this myth by the Greek poet Hesiod (8th century BCE) came many centuries after the writing of Genesis, if that book was written, as tradition holds, by Moses. Two centuries later, the Greek philosophers and the philosophers of Buddhism and Taoism would offer other explanations of the nature and causes of evil.)

It is impossible to overestimate the effect that the Genesis story has had on Christian minds and Christian societies for almost two thousand years. If the Countess were able to satisfy herself that she had 'corrected' that effect, she would not be the first person to suppose so (I.10). In postulating Adam and Eve as two aspects of the single human being who is capable of redeeming him/herself, she would, at least, be offering a more encouraging interpretation of the ancient story.

CHAPTER 11. *Parmenides Moment.*

— **Parmenides.** Greek philosopher (c.515—c.440 BCE). He has been regarded as a founder of metaphysics and epistemology in the Greek philosophical tradition. He asks the question—what is it to *say* that something *is*? Or, to put the question in another form—what is the nature of *reality*?

As with so many others of the so-called pre-Socratic philosophers (preceding Socrates and Plato), we have only fragments of the writings of Parmenides, but he had a strong influence on the minds of those of whose ideas we know more.

The Parmenidean challenge—which Edmund faces fully for the first time in his life, in the isolation of a remote Scottish seashore—leads in three directions which have determined the agenda of philosophy in the Western tradition.

(1) What causes anything to exist—to emerge out of 'nothing', as it were?
(2) What causes our minds to see what exists in the way that we see it?
(3) What is the nature of existence in-itself, not merely existence in the form that is available to us in our minds?

Among the very many possible answers to those questions, some became central themes of Greek philosophy, and remain as central topics of philosophy to this day.

(1) Either (a) the *religious* answer—a 'creator God', perhaps, or some other putative supernatural source; or (b) the *scientific* answer—ascertainable processes of material change.

(2) Either (a) the *mentalist* answer—because that is the way in which the human mind works and the way in which human minds communicate with each other; or (b) the *materialist* answer—because the human mind is merely an aspect of the functioning of the human brain in its relation to the natural world, of which the human brain is itself an integral part.

(3) Either (a) the *idealist* answer—there is a more real reality of which the reality that we see is only a shadow or a reflection; or (b) the *realist* answer—we cannot know any reality other the reality that we know through the functioning of the brain in its participation in the natural world.

The aspects of the philosophical tradition which are discussed in the Chapter 2 Appendices below reflect these questions and answers.

'In my opinion, the distinctive faculty of the active and intelligent being is to be able to give meaning to the word *is*.' J.-J.Rousseau, *Profession de foi du vicaire savoyard* (Profession of Faith of a Vicar from Savoy), in Book Four of *Émile, ou de l'éducation* (Emile, or On Education) (I.19).

Rousseau uses a seemingly unsophisticated country priest (a Wednesday-like figure) to express Rousseau's own views on ultimate philsophical questions. He tells the young Emile that metaphysics has done nothing but fill philosophy with absurdities. Instead, we must consult our 'inner light' (*la lumière intérieure*).

Voltaire (I.15) said that the *Profession* contains 'forty pages against Christianity, among the boldest ever written'. Rousseau called Voltaire 'that poor man, weighed down, so to speak, by fame and prosperity, bitterly complaining about the wretchedness of this life'. 'Though Voltaire has always appeared to believe in God, he has really only believed in the Devil, because his so-called God is nothing but a malicious being who, according to his belief, only takes pleasure in doing harm.' (*Confessions*, bk. 9) (tr., J. Cohen). For Voltaire's views on relgion, see ch. 3 above, under 'Voltaire and religion'.

In Ph. Allott, *The Health of Nations*, ch. 1, it is suggested that human beings inhabit a place called *Istopia,* formed from all the uses to which we put the word *is*. For 'Parmenides Moment', see §1.6 of that work.

— **Moment.** The word is here used in two senses. A moment in time. But also a moment in the sense that the word is used in Mechanics—the turning-effect of a force. Edmund is experiencing a moment of philosophical enlightenment which has the capacity to alter the direction of his personal existence. The moment when a thoughtful person becomes aware of the Parmenides problem of the nature of reality—the Parmenides Moment, as it were—is a significant event in that person's process of mental self-constituting.

With the help of the Old Man of the Sea, Edmund discovers for himself some of the great questions and answers surrounding the word *is*. He thereby begins a new stage in the making of his own personal metaphysics, a process that every human being undertakes, more or less consciously, more or less coherently. On *stereometaphysics*, see ch. 13 below. On *metaphysiology*, see ch. 16 below.

— **Gratuitous existence**. The idea that human existence is meaningless, purposeless, absurd, gratuitous, and valueless is a default position of human consciousness.

From Greek sceptical philosophers to modern anarchists and nihilists and existentialists, it is not difficult to lead people to the view that meaning and purpose cannot be intrinsically present in the universe as whole, or in any part of it, such as human existence in general, or the existence of any particular human being.

And so it is not difficult to lead people to see a corollary to the effect that, if meaning and purpose are ascribed to the universe or any part of it, then that is an act of interpretation produced by the human mind from within itself, a more or less arbitrary construction of reason and/or imagination.

In the 20th century, many forms of artistic and literary creation and intellectual discourse exploited these positions, in a period of human history when the real world seemed to be demonstrating in dire practice their irrefutable validity. Modernism, surrealism, existentialism in literature and drama, the theatre of the absurd, and postmodernism—all of these seemed to reflect, in different ways and to different extents, a contemporary human reality which seemed to be exceptionally meaningless, purposeless, absurd, gratuitous, and valueless.

Edmund is not alone in discovering that the more interesting aspect of nihilism is the *post-nihilist* challenge. If humanity must find its own meaning and purpose—inherent in existence, or fabricated by the human mind—what meaning and purpose *shall* we give to our existence?

> *Au bout de ces ténébres, une lumière pourtant est inévitable que nous devinons déjà et dont nous avons seulement à lutter pour qu'elle soit. Par delà le nihilisme, nous tous, parmi les ruines, préparons une renaissance. Mais peu le savent.* ('At the end of this darkness, however, a light is unavoidable, a light that we already detect, for which we need only fight for it to come to be. Beyond nihilism, we are all, among the ruins, preparing a renaissance. But few people know it.' From the last chapter of *L'Homme revolté* (The Human Being in Revolt) (1951) by the French writer A.Camus (1913-60). (present author's trans.).

The book is a searing analysis of the state of Western civilisation. This last hopeful note is unexpected, and is not further elaborated.

— **Untainted by men's miseries.** Echo of *Invocation*, a poem by P.B. Shelley (I.16).

> 'I love snow, and all the forms / Of the radiant frost; / I love waves, and winds, and storms / Everything almost / Which is Nature's, and may be / Untainted with men's misery.'

— **Grain of sand.** Edmund certainly knows the poem (*Auguries of Innocence*) by the English poet W. Blake (I.16), which contains much quoted lines.

> 'To see a world in a grain of sand / And a heaven in a wild flower, / Hold infinity in the palm of your hand / And eternity in an hour.'

He may also know a saying attributed to the elderly I. Newton (I.16).

> 'I seem to have been only like a boy playing on the seashore, and diverting myself in now and then finding a smoother pebble or a prettier shell than ordinary, whilst the great ocean of truth lay all undiscovered before me.'

He may possibly know another of Blake's poems.

> 'Mock on, mock on, Voltaire, Rousseau; / Mock on, mock on; 'tis all in vain! / You throw the sand against the wind, / And the wind blows it back again. / And every sand becomes a gem / Reflected in the beams divine; / Blown back they blind the mocking eye, / But still in Israel's paths they shine./ The Atoms of Democritus / And Newton's Particles of Light / Are sands upon the Red Sea shore, / Where Israel's tents do shine so bright.'

Edmund may possibly also have in mind a passage in *L'infini dans les cieux* ('The Infinite in the Skies'), a poem by the French poet A. de Lamartine (1790-1869) where the poet also thinks metaphysical thoughts on a seashore.

> *Oh! Que suis-je, Seigneur! Devant les cieux et toi? / De ton immensité le poids pèse sur moi,/ . . . Et je m'estime moins qu'un de ces grains de sable, / Car ce sable roulé par les flots inconstants, / S'il a moins étendue, hélas! a plus de temps; / Il remplira toujours son vide dans l'espace / Lorsque je n'aurai plus ni nom, ni temps, ni place . . .* ('Oh, what am I, Lord? Before the skies and Thee? The weight of your immensity rests heavily upon me . . . And I value myself less than one of these grains of sand, for this sand, moved by the changing waves, may have little space but, alas! it has more time. It will always fill its own gap in space, when I no longer have name or time or place.') (present author's trans.).

— **Stream of warming energy.** The Gulf Stream, a current of warmer water flowing from the Caribbean to the North-East Atlantic, is a small-scale side effect of very large-scale events in the geological history of the Earth's surface.

It is responsible for causing a temperate climate in the United Kingdom whose climate would otherwise be closer to that of northern Canada, which is at a similar latitude.

— *Je m'offre au soleil.* In French, 'I offer myself to the sun.' Edmund no doubt has in mind lines in *Air de Sémiramis* a poem by the French poet P. Valéry (see ch. 7 above, under '*Dieu! quel bonheur*').

> *Enfin, j'offre au soleil le secret de mes charmes! / Jamais il n'a doré de seuil si gracieux !* ('At last, I offer to the sun the secret of my charms! Never has he covered with gold a more gracious threshold!')

— **Gymnosophists.** From the ancient Greek—*gymnos* ('naked') and *sophistes* ('wise man'). The Greeks used the composite word to refer to the most ascetic of the Indian holy men known as *sadhus.*

— **Vagrant.** From the Latin, *vagare*, 'to wander'. Edmund's meeting with Wednesday distantly echoes Zarathustra's meeting with his own shadow in Part Three of *Thus Spoke Zarathustra* by F. Nietzsche (I.19). The shadow says:

> 'I am a wanderer, who has already walked far at your heels: always going but without a goal and without a home . . . "Nothing is true, everything is permitted": thus I told myself. I plunged into the coldest water, with head and heart. Alas, how often I stood naked, like a red crab, on that account!'

Zarathustra then has a sleep in which his soul seems to be speaking to him:

> 'Precisely the least thin, the gentlest, lightest, the rustling of a lizard, a breath, a moment, the twinkling of an eye—*little* makes up the quality of the *best* happiness.' (tr., R. Hollingdale).

— **Old Man of the Sea.** In Book IV of Homer's *Odyssey* (I.22) Menelaus recounts the story of the adventures of Odysseus, as told to him by Proteus in the form of the old man of the sea (*halios geron*).

In Canto I of *Purgatorio*, the second part of the *Divina Commedia* of Dante (see ch. 3 above, under 'Pineta di Classe'), Dante and his guide (Virgil), as they enter Purgatory, meet an old man who gives them advice.

> 'I saw an old man standing by my side / Alone, so worthy of reverence in his look, / That ne'er from son to father more was owed.'

He is Cato of Utica (95-46 BCE), known also as Cato the Younger, great-grandson of Cato the Censor (234-189 BCE), both of them renowned as icons of rectitude. Cato the Younger followed the principles of stoicism (see ch. 2 above, under 'cynic, epicurean, stoic'). He committed suicide after losing a battle against Julius Caesar. Utica was a city in North Africa older than Carthage which, after the fall of Carthage to the Romans (146BCE), became the capital of the Roman province of *Africa*.

In *The Rime of the Ancient Mariner* (1798), a poem by the English poet S.T. Coleridge (1772-1834), an old man, with 'long grey beard and glittering eye', causes a wedding-guest to stop on his way to a wedding-feast. He recounts a story of a sea-voyage full of tragic and supernatural events, a story with metaphysical and moral resonances. Having heard the story, the wedding-guest is said to be 'a sadder and a wiser man'. Edmund's meeting with another Old Man of the Sea will surely leave him a wiser man, but perhaps also a happier man.

The Old Man and the Sea is the title of a novel (1952) by the American writer E. Hemingway (1899-1961), in which a boy learns existential lessons through his association with the existential struggle of an old fisherman.

The 'wise old man' is one of the major archetypes of the Jungian collective unconscious (I.20). Edmund is certainly privileged if he has had the opportunity to meet a Jungian Unconscious Archetype, in person and in bodily form, and in a pedagogic, but unusually unprolix, mood.

— **Wednesday**. Edmund evidently has in mind the name 'Friday' which Robinson Crusoe gave to the man who intruded into his isolation on a Friday in *Robinson Crusoe* by the English writer D. Defoe (1660-1731), a novel whose utopian character takes the form of the solitary life of the survivor of a shipwreck on a remote island totally cut off from 'civilisation'. Crusoe gradually recreates the characteristics and benefits of 'civilised life', and teaches them to Friday, who has had no previous experience of 'civilisation', and who may come to have legitimate doubts about the benefits of such 'civilisation'.

Edmund's Wednesday/Old Man of the Sea is recreating for Edmund the characteristics and benefits of what one might call 'metaphysical life', the human mind's inheritance of ideas about its relationship to what it sees as 'reality'.

— **Something that he already knew but did not know that he already knew**. In *Meno*, an early dialogue, Socrates/Plato explores the idea that we are born knowing certain things, but we may need to be led to discover what we already know. A slave boy is led to discover some principles of geometry for himself—'the spontaneous recovery of knowledge' (*anamnesis*; 'unforgetting'). The focus of the discussion is *virtue*. Nobody can say what it is. But could we be led to discover its meaning for ourselves?

'And if the truth about reality is always in our soul, the soul must be immortal, and one must take courage and try to discover—that is, to recollect—what

one doesn't happen to know, or, more correctly, remember, at the moment.'
Meno, 86b. (tr., W. Guthrie).

The idea that there is a source of transcendental knowledge available to the
human mind becomes a central idea in Plato's works and in Platonism.

— **My name is Nameless.** In Book IX of Homer's *Odyssey* (see ch. 2 above, under
'siren voices'), Odysseus and his companions reach the land of the Cyclops, where
they are captured by the one-eyed giant Polyphemus. After he has eaten six of the
men, he asks Odysseus to say his name. Odysseus replies: 'No-man' or 'Nameless'.
Polyphemus says that, as a guest-gift, he will eat No-man last of all the men. Having
blinded the giant, Odysseus and his men escape, clinging to the underside of the
giant's sheep.

— **No part of the world I own.** Echo, surely, of *The Traveller*, a poem by the English
writer O. Goldsmith (1728-74).

> 'My fortune leads to traverse realms alone, / And find no spot of all the world
> my own.'

The poem also contains a memorable opinion that Wednesday might share.

> 'In every government, though terrors reign, / Though tyrant kings, or tyrant
> laws restrain, / How small, of all that human hearts endure, / That part which
> laws or kings can cause or cure!'

— **Wherever I am, I am at home.** Edmund may hear in Wednesday's words an echo
of lines in a song (D870) by F. Schubert (I.7) *Der Wanderer an den Mond* ('The
Wanderer Speaks to the Moon'), setting a poem by J.G. Seidl. The wanderer envies
the moon wandering freely around the whole world.

> *Und bist doch, wo du bist, zu Haus /* . . . *O glücklich, wer, wohin er geht, / Doch
> auf der Heimat Boden steht.* ('And wherever you are, you are at home. Oh
> happy he who, wherever he goes, yet stands on his native soil.')

— **When you travel alone.** A possible interpretation of *Waiting for Godot*, a play
(written originally in French, 1948/49), by the Irish writer S. Beckett (1906-89),
is that the two characters, who seem doomed always to be in each other's company,
and to travel without ever arriving, are two aspects of a single person.

Cicero quotes (*De officiis*, III) a saying attributed to Scipio Africanus to the
effect that he was 'never less alone than when he was alone.' (For Scipio, see ch.9
above, under 'Carthage destroyed'.)

'The lion is alone, and so am I.' G. Byron, *Manfred*, III.1 (see ch. 2 above, under 'noble wreck'). Manfred's isolation is an obsessive theme of the drama.

— **We could kill each other.** Edmund evidently has in mind the marginally philosophical problem of the so-called *gratuitous act*. Can there be such a thing as a wholly free, motiveless, causeless, meaningless act, an act beyond moral judgment or reasonable explanation?

In *Les caves du Vatican* (1914) by A. Gide, the rigorously uninteresting 'hero' pushes an unknown fellow-passenger out of the door of a train for no particular reason.

In *La Nausée* (1938) by J.-P. Sartre, the relentlessly miserable 'hero' experiences the meaninglessness of the human and natural worlds.

In *L'Étranger* (1942) by A. Camus, the remarkably low-energy 'hero' is unable to feel any feelings either about the death of his mother or about his killing of an unknown man on a beach.

Neither Nietzsche nor Dostoevsky would recognise in these examples the profundity of the questions that they had raised about human autonomy and human dependence.

— **Existence as a possibility.** 'I am that which I am, because in this particular position of the great system of Nature only such a person, and absolutely no other, was possible.' J.G. Fichte (see ch. 8 above, under *'Ich'*), *Die Bestimmung des Menschen* (The Vocation of Man) (1800), Book One (tr., R. Chisholm).

— **We class them.** Wednesday is recalling a perennial problem of philosophy—the seemingly organic tendency of the brain/mind to integrate its experience into abstracted classes. What is the relation between a particular thing and the universal class/classes to which it belongs? Does a particular thing contain a universal aspect? Or is this merely a side-effect of the nature of human language? In what sense is a particular oyster-catcher also a bird, an animal, an organism, an arrangement of matter, a particular part of the universe?

Aristotle's *analysis* of language, and of its possible capacity to convey 'truth'—a study that would come to be called 'logic'—begins with the idea that, in referring to something by a particular word, we are already placing it into a class of all the things to which that word could also apply.

He even suggests that language uses a very limited number (approx. 10) of classifying words ('categories') which are the basic programme, as it were, of descriptive or representative language—for example, *substance* (e.g., 'oyster-catcher'), *quantity* (e.g., 'far'), *quality* (e.g. 'warm'), *relation* (e.g., 'twice'), etc. Whatever the merits of his particular list of categories, it is part of what might be called the Aristotle Moment when one sees that language has this classifying and universalising effect. (For I. Kant's use of 'categories', see Appendix 8 below.)

Aristotle also identified three principles of rational thought without which we could not efficiently communicate with each other. They cannot be 'proved' (because their proof would itself require their being used), but they are simply necessary assumptions of what we regard as rational discourse.

$A = A$ ('A is what it is'—identity).

A cannot be both B and not-B (e.g., 'both true and not-true'—contradiction).

A must be either B or not-B (e.g., 'either true or not-true'—excluded middle).

One exciting aspect of this idea is that much of our most interesting talk knowingly or impliedly violates or plays with these principles—including metaphor (A is B: 'gluttonous death'—Donne), paradox (B and not-B are both true: 'the death of God'—Nietzsche), imagination or belief (A is both B and not-B—Don Quijote and the windmills); dialectic (B and not-B produce C—'God is everywhere; God is nowhere').

Aristotle also suggests that sentences that combine individual words to say something general about the world ('propositions')—typically of the form 'All A is B'—can also be analysed to discover their truth-conveying capacity. And, furthermore, when particular propositions ('premises') are combined (in a 'syllogism') to suggest the truth of another proposition ('conclusion'), it is possible also to analyse the potential truth-conveying capacity of such combinations.

The merits, if any, of this aspect of Aristotelian logic have been the subject of vigorous debate until the present day. However, it seems difficult to deny that some underlying self-ordering system of human language makes possible the most effective kinds of human communication. It is a striking and mysterious fact—analogous, perhaps, to the mysterious certainties of mathematics—that we can often—somehow, and without the benefit of any study of 'logic'—*recognise*, as it were, the truth or the untruth of a conclusion that seems to be drawn from seemingly true premises.

Philosophers are thoughtful people. Intelligent people are thoughtful. Therefore philosophers are intelligent people. False conclusion.

How do we *recognise* this falsity from the *mere relationship* of the sentences? It is not merely a matter of the definition of the words. It is not a judgment based on our observation of philosophers, thoughtful people, or intelligent people.

No great philosopher was ever married (Nietzsche, *Genealogy of Morals*, 3rd Essay). *X is an unmarried philosopher. Therefore X is a great philosopher.* False conclusion.

Lazy people shun work. Some unemployed people shun work. Therefore unemployed people are lazy. False conclusion.

False conclusions are especially characteristic of political debate.

Much would be gained if wider attention were paid to L. Carroll, *Alice in Wonnderland*, ch. VII, where the Hatter rightly tells Alice that 'I say what I mean' is not the same as 'I mean what I say'. The Dormouse helpfully adds: 'you might as well say that "I breathe when I sleep" is the same thing as "I sleep when I breathe".'

Within the unending debate which Aristotle's ideas have caused, especially that between the 'idealists' and 'realists' (see Appendices 1 and 4 below), there were those who asserted the absolute reality of *particulars*, that is, unique self-existing entities or substances which the human mind identifies as such immediately and directly, without resort to universalising concepts. This so-called *principium individuationis* ('principle of individuation') is particularly associated with the name of the Scottish philosopher Duns Scotus (c.1266-1308).

There have also been those who argue that the universe must ultimately consist of particular and unique substances which cannot be further divided—such as the *monads* of the German philosopher G.W. Leibniz (1646-1716) (see further below, under 'I am a window')—or else that the universe itself must be a single substance—such as the *Deus sive Natura* (God/Nature) of the Dutch philosopher B. Spinoza (1632-77).

The human mind is surely privileged in being able to journey so freely, in both directions, between the particular and the universal.

'Schopenhauer has described for us the tremendous awe which seizes man when he suddenly begins to doubt the cognitive modes of experience . . . If we add to this the glorious transport which arises in man, even from the very depths of nature, at the shattering of the *principium individuationis*, then we are in a position to apprehend the essence of Dionysiac rapture, whose closest analogy is furnished by physical intoxication.' F. Nietzsche, *The Birth of Tragedy*, I. (tr., F. Golffing).

— **The One and the Many.** Wednesday is recalling another perennial problem of philosophy—the relationship between what we see both as a unity and as a collection of constituent parts. An atom, a cell, a plant, an animal, a human being, a human society, the material world, the universe—they are all both One and Many.

In each case, it seems that the unity and the multiplicity are not merely ways of seeing, or speaking about, the situation. Each aspect (one/many) seems to be an intrinsic or essential or necessary aspect of the other—something that we find in the situation, and do not merely invent or imagine.

Is it possible that Wednesday, in a former existence, may have known, among countless other discussions of the problem, passages in Fichte's *Vocation of Man* (see above, under 'existence as a possibility')?

'In every moment of her duration Nature is one connected whole; in every moment each individual part must be what it is, because all others are what they are; and you could not remove a single grain of sand from its place without thereby (although perhaps imperceptibly to you) changing something throughout all parts of the immeasurable whole.' (Book One).

Wednesday, like Fichte, apparently sees the vocation of the human being as essentially spiritual and, in religious and metaphysical philosophies of East and West, the *spiritual* is regularly seen as an aspect of the *unity of everything*.

'Man is not a product of the world of sense, and the end of his existence cannot be attained in it. His vocation transcends time and space, and everything that pertains to sense . . . he must be able to raise his thoughts above the limitations of sense . . . and the truly human mode of thought, that which alone is worthy of him, that in which his whole spiritual strength is manifested, is that whereby he raises himself above those limitations, whereby all that pertains to sense vanishes into nothing—into a mere reflection in mortal eyes of the one, abiding Infinite.' (Vocation, Book Three).

Wednesday may also be familiar with the sacred Hindu text known as the Katha Upanishad (see ch. 8 above):

'Beyond the sense is the mind, and beyond mind is reason, its essence. Beyond reason is the Spirit in man, and beyond this is the Spirit of the universe, the evolver of all.' (tr., J. Mascaró).

The Hindu sacred writings, written in Sanskrit, 7th-5th centuries BCE, became available in the West in the early 19th century. Fichte cannot have known them in 1800, but Schopenhauer did—and respected them highly.

Wednesday may even be aware of Ph. Allott, *Eunomia. New Order for a New World*. The One and the Many is there identified (§§4.24*ff*) as one of the five Perennial Dilemmas of Society—one aspect of the multiple and interactive process by which a human society constitutes itself through a never-ending, ever-more-complex series of resolutions of constitutive oppositions. See ch. 8 above, under 'pure ideas practically operational'.

The *Eunomian* dilemma of the One and the Many is a permanent struggle between a society's striving towards unity and the assertion of the individuality of its members. On this view, constitutional systems, such as 'democracy', are evolved systems for organising this dialectical struggle. On this view also, a society's self-constituting reflects the dialectical self-constituting of the personality of the individual human being.

In one of Plato's dialogues, Socrates describes the excitement of a young man when he first learns about the problem of 'the one and the many'—'for really it is a remarkable thing to say that many are one, and one is many . . .'

> 'We get this identity of the one and the many cropping up everywhere as the result of the sentences we utter . . . As soon as a young man gets wind of it, he is delighted as if he had discovered an intellectual gold mine . . .' *Philebus*, 14c. (tr., R. Hackforth).

— **We give names to things.** Wednesday is recalling another perennial focus of philosophical discussion—the significance of the human practice of giving names to the things.

(1) A unique name—'Fido' for an actual particular dog or 'Plato' for an actual particular philosopher—is designed as a label for something which is already seen as unique and particular and actual.

(2) A particular name that is given to many things—'dog', 'philosopher', 'oyster-catcher'—is more obscure. It is evidently intended to express some common feature possessed by the particular things to which it applied, but it implies that those things are *both* actual particular things *and* things capable of sharing a common name.

(3) A particular name which is given to something which is *made by the name* to seem like an actual and particular thing is still more obscure—'mind', 'soul', 'Scotland', 'society', 'music'. It is evidently a label for some complex of ideas, with a more or less direct and necessary connection with actual and particular things.

(4) A particular name which is given to something to which no actual and particular thing corresponds—'truth', 'beauty', 'goodness', 'justice', 'eternity', 'philosophy'—is very obscure indeed, not least because it seems to be entirely a product of the mind, but also seems to be a product of experience of, and reflection on, actual and particular things.

(5) Also problematic is a particular name which is intended to be merely a product of the imagination—seen as the unlimited capacity to invent things having no necessary connection with any actual and particular thing—'Utopia', 'Paradise', 'Faust', 'Hydra'—but corresponding obscurely, within the mind, to actual and particular things to which names in categories (1) and (2) are given. *Paradise* seems to be an instance of a 'place'. *Faust* seems to be an instance of a 'person'. *Hydra* seeming to be an instance of an 'animal'.

Interesting discussions have taken place about the category into which certain particular names should be placed—'God', 'gravity', 'race'—among others.

Socrates and Plato were particularly interested in this problem. They saw that it goes to the root of 'philosophy'—that is, our thinking about the mind, our thinking about thinking.

> 'Well, but do you not see, Cratylus, that he who follows names in the search after things, and analyzes their meaning, is in great danger of being deceived?'
> Plato, *Cratylus*, 438b. (tr., B. Jowett).
> 'How real existence is to be studied or discovered is, I suspect, beyond you and me. But we may admit so much, that the knowledge of things is not to be derived from names. No, they must be studied and investigated in themselves.' 439b.

Socrates is speaking at the end of a long and humorous discussion with Cratylus in which he has made fun of the idea that names have some real relationship with the things that they label. There must be something that corresponds to the word 'justice', but you could not find it by analysing the word itself. (You would be better advised to read Plato, *The Republic*.)

He is also answering in advance the nominalists (see Appendix 1 below), who will say that there is no 'real existence' to be studied and investigated of things which have names, but whose names are not the labels for perceptible things in the 'real' world—names which are not in categories (1) or (2) above.

— **The world ocean inside me**. An echo, perhaps, of S. Freud, *Civilization and its Discontents* (*Das Unbehagen in der Kultur*) (1930). Freud begins that book by discussing something said by the French writer R. Rolland (1866-1944), who had written to Freud commenting on his *The Future of an Illusion* (1927).

In the earlier book, Freud had identified religion as an illusion-filled neurosis directed to the fulfilment of deep instinctive human wishes—wishes that cannot conceivably be fulfilled—hence the word 'illusion'. Rolland regretted that Freud had 'failed to appreciate the real source of religiosity'.

> 'This was a particular feeling of which he himself [Rolland] was never free, which he had found confirmed by many others and which he assumed was shared by millions, a feeling that he was inclined to call a sense of "eternity", a feeling of something limitless, unbounded—as it were "oceanic". This feeling was a purely subjective fact, not an article of faith; . . . but it was the source of the religious energy that was seized upon by the various churches and religious systems . . . On the basis of this oceanic feeling alone one was entitled to call oneself religious, even if one rejected every belief and every illusion . . . It is a feeling, then, of being indissolubly bound up with and belonging to the whole of the world outside oneself.' (tr., D. McLintock).

Freud comments: 'I can discover no trace of this "oceanic feeling" in myself.'

We may compare this with something said by D. Hume (see Appendix 4 below) in 'The Platonist', one of his *Political Essays* (1752):

'The divinity is a boundless ocean of bliss and glory: Human minds are smaller streams, which, arising at first from this ocean, seek still, amid all their wanderings, to return to it, and to lose themselves in that immensity of perfection. When checked in this natural course, by vice or folly, they become furious and enraged; and, swelling to a torrent, do then spread horror and devastation on the neighbouring plains.'

— **The Self and the Other.** Wednesday is recalling yet another perennial challenge which philosophy has struggled with—the problem of explaining the idea of 'I' or 'the self'. How can we explain our sense of our own identity? How can we be both the subject and the object of our thought?

It is fascinating to watch the idea of the *human individual* emerge from within the intense thoughtfulness of the ancient Greek mind. The idea of what it is to be *human* (an *anthropos*, in the universal sense) developed alongside the idea of what it is to be a *unique* human being, a self (*autos*).

The Greeks came to see that all human beings share *humanity*, but each human being has a *soul* (*psyche*), a principle of their own being, of their individual life. We know that we are One, and One among Many, and that each of the Many is also One. We know that we are a Self and that every Other is also a Self.

Descartes identifies the 'I' as the *thinking being*—for a human being who is able to say 'I', to think is to be, to be is to think. I am the subject and the object of my thinking.

As discussed in the Chapter 2 appendices below, this view has caused a succession of philosophers to explore the nature of our identity—*sceptically*, for those (like Hume) who see it as merely a reasonable inference from the form of our thinking; *rationally*, for those (such as Kant) who see it as the necessary condition for the possibility of thinking; *metaphysically*, for those who see it (like Hegel) as the necessary condition of our co-existence with other thinking beings, or who see it (like Schopenhauer) as the necessary condition of our activity in the world that the mind makes by thought and action.

The Greeks also came to identify *human individuals* as *autonomous* (not merely the plaything of the gods or of Fate) and *suffering* (paying the price of their own acts and the acts of others).

And they came to recognise a moral dimension in our shared *humanity*. We have a duty to respect the humanity of other human beings (barbarians, prisoners of war, conquered peoples), just as we expect them reciprocally to respect our humanity. Humanity, in the moral sense, is the right relationship between the self and the other. The Romans took up this idea and speak of *humanitas*, in the moral sense, as a requirement of *natural law* flowing from our common *humanitas*, in the metaphysical sense.

Wednesday may even be aware of Ph. Allott, *Eunomia. New Order for a New World*. The Self and the Other is there identified (§§4.14*ff*) as another of the five Perennial Dilemmas of Society (see above, under 'the One and the Many').

The *Eunomian* dilemma of the Self and the Other is a permanent struggle between a society's constituting of its own identity as a 'self', formed from a partial integrating of the identity of its members, for whom the identity of the society is also part of their own identity, just as their identity is part of the identity of society. Self-consciousness flows in both directions between a society and its members. In this respect also, *a society's self-constituting* reflects the dialectical self-constituting of the personality of the *individual human being*.

S. Freud asserted the connection between the development of the individual and the development of society, but did not himself take the matter much further in his rather limited writings on social questions.

> 'However, if we focus our attention on the relation between the civilization of mankind and the development or upbringing of the individual, we shall conclude, without much hesitation, that the two processes are very similar in kind, if not indeed indeed one and the same process, as it affects different kinds of object . . . Yet in view of the similarity of aims—the one being to create a unified mass consisting of many individuals, the other being to integrate the individual into such a mass—the similarity of the means used in the two processes and the similarity of the resultant phenomena are no surprise . . . Just as the planet still circles round its sun, yet at the same time rotates on its own axis, so the individual partakes in the development of humanity while making his own way through life.' *Civilization and its Discontents* (1930), VIII. (tr., D. McClintock).

— **Self is a crowd**. Edmund is associating himself with many previous affirmations of the experience that one's personality does not always seem to be efficiently integrated. Problems in the self-constituting of one's personality (the 'divided self') are apparently a common experience of ordinary self-consciousness, not merely of states of mind that are conventionally classed as pathological. For an unconventional view of such states of mind, see R.D. Laing, *The Divided Self* (1960).

Nietzsche suggests, in *Human, All Too Human* (2.76) an interesting idea that will play a major part in Freud's anatomy of the mind. '. . . in matters of morality, people treat themselves not as *individuum* [a whole entity] but as *dividuum* [a divided entity].' Freud suggests that we have a virtual father living within us (the super ego).

Goethe's Faust speaks of his own divided personality.

Zwei Seelen wohnen, ach! in meiner Brust, / Die eine will sich von der andern trennen; / Die eine hält, in derber Liebeslust, / Sich an die Welt mit klammernden

Organen; / Die andre hebt gewaltsam sich vom Dust / Zu den Gefilden hoher Ahnen. 'Two souls live, alas! in my breast. Each one wants to separate itself from the other. One holds fast to the world with clinging organs in the crude desire of love. The other strives to raise itself from the dust and return home to its nobler origins.'
J.W. von Goethe, Faust, First Part (Faust speaking). (present author's trans.).

Hamlet's father says: to Hamlet's friends Rosencrantz and Guildenstern:

'Something have you heard / Of Hamlet's transformation; so I call it, / Since nor the exterior nor the inward man / Resembles that it was.'
W. Shakespeare, *Hamlert. Prince of Denmark*, II.ii.

J.-J. Rousseau begins his *Confessions* with the claim: 'the man I shall portray will be myself'. As an epigraph to the whole work he uses a phrase form a Latin poet (Persius): *intus, et in cute* ('inwardly, and on the surface'; 'subcutaneous and cutaneous'). Elsewhere he makes explicit his idea of the divided mind.

'While I meditated upon man's nature, I seemed to discover two distinct principles in it; one of them raised him to the study of the eternal truths, to the love of justice, and of true morality, to the regions of the world of thought, which the wise delight to contemplate; the other led him downwards to himself, made him the slave of his senses, of the passions which are their instruments, and thus opposed everything suggested to him by the former principle. When I felt myself carried away, distracted by these conflicting motives, I said, No; man is not one; I will and I will not; I feel myself at once a slave and a free man; I perceive what is right, I love it, and I do what is wrong; I am active when I listen to the voice of reason; I am passive when I am carried away by my passions; and when I yield, my worst suffering is the knowledge that I might have resisted.'
'Profession of Faith of a Savoyard Vicar', in J.-J. Rousseau, *Émile* (I.19). (tr., B. Foxley).

M Proust, under the influence of H. Bergson (I.19), makes use of a distinction between *le moi extérieur* (the exterior me), shown to other people, and *le moi profond* (the interior and real me). In his *Contre Saint-Beuve*, he discusses the relationship between the biography of a writer or artist and the novel or work of art that the writer or artist creates. Does knowledge of the former help to understand and appreciate the latter? For Proust, the answer is 'no'.
Contre Saint-Beuve was published in 1954, collecting various pieces on literature and aesthetics that Proust had intended to make into a book. Many of his ideas on those subjects were included in his novel *À la recherche du temps perdu*.

Edmund will certainly also recall the words of the American poet Walt Whitman (1819-92) (see ch. 8 above, under 'Shakespearean leaves of grass') in his *Song of Myself*: 'Do I contradict myself? / Very well then I contradict myself, (I am large, I contain multitudes.)' (brackets in the original).

Whitman's main collection—*Leaves of Grass* (1855-92)—is a contra-*Zarathustra*, affirming, in a manic monologue, a certain idea of Americanness as effectively as Nietzsche's work denies, in a manic monologue, a certain idea of Europeanness.

— **No scientist will ever see (a human thought).**

> 'A modern atheistic pretender to wit hath publicly owned this same conclusion, that "mind is nothing but local motion in the organic parts of man's body" . . . as if there were not as much reality in fancy [imagination] and consciousness as there is in local motion. That which inclined these men so much to this opinion was only because they were sensible and aware of this, that if there were any other action besides local motion admitted, there must needs be some substance acknowledged besides body.'
>
> 'But sensible things themselves [things in the outside world presented to the mind by the senses] are not known or understood . . . but by intelligible ideas exerted from the mind itself, that is, by something native and domestic to it . . .'

R. Cudworth (1617-88), *The True Intellectual Ssytem of the Universe*, III. Ralph Cudworth, Fellow of Emmanuel College, Cambridge, was a leader of the Cambridge Platonists, a group of Puritan philosophers in 17th-century Cambridge who sought to reconcile Platonism and Christian theology. They were much admired by, and influenced, both J. Locke and I. Kant. (See Appendices 4 and 8 below.)

> 'Moreover, it must be confessed that perception and that which depends upon it are inexplicable on mechanical grounds, that is to say, by means of figures and motions. And supposing there were a machine, so constructed as to think, feel, and have perception, it might be conceived as increased in size, while keeping the same proportions, so that one might go into it as into a mill. That being so, we should, on examining its interior, find only parts which work one upon another, and never anything by which to explain a perception.'
>
> G.W Leibniz (see above, under 'we class them'), *Mondaology*, §17.

There are natural scientists, and others, who condemn Descartes for supposing that the mind is 'a ghost in the machine', that is, something intrinsically distinct from the brain, but somehow present within the brain (see above, under 'the Self and the Other). They fail to understand that what Descartes did was to re-set the agenda for philosophy, not physiology—re-energising the tradition of philosophy stemming from the ancient Greeks.

Following Descartes, we must say that the products of the *brain* that we think of as the activity of the *mind* can and must be studied in and for themselves, not least because it is the activity of the mind that overwhelmingly determines the activity of the brain as it interacts, through our actions, with the outside world. *Neuroscience is itself an activity of the mind.*

To study the mind is to study the *human world*, the actual and the possible reality made by the mind. The human world exists only in the human mind. Only the mind can know the world made by the mind.

Philosophy is the physiology of the mind.

— *eo ipso*. In Latin, 'in itself'.
— *ipso facto*. In Latin, 'by that very fact'.
— *per definitionem*. In Latin, 'by definition'.
— **Imaginary character (Edmund as)**. 'Why couldn't the world *that concerns us*—be a fiction? And if somebody asked, "but to a fiction there surely belongs an author?"—couldn't one answer simply: *why?* Doesn't this "belongs" perhaps belong to the fiction, too?' F. Nietzsche, *Beyond Good and Evil*, §34.
— **I dream that I am**. 'Once Chuang Chou dreamt he was a butterfly, fluttering here and there just as if he were a butterfly, conscious of following its inclinations. It did not know that it was Chuang Chou. Suddenly he awoke; and then demonstrably he was Chuang Chou. But he does not know now whether he is Choung Chou who dreamt he was a butterfly or a butterfly dreaming he is Chuan Chou.' From a writing of the Chinese Taoist philosopher Chuang Chou (3rd century BCE). (tr., E.R. Hughes). See also I.16, under 'the dream'.
— **Who is Kim ?** Echo of the novel *Kim*, by R. Kipling (see ch. 7 above, under 'little friend of all the world'). 'I am Kim. I am Kim. And what is Kim? His soul repeated it again and again.' (Ch. XV). Edmund may well see Wednesday as a near relative of Kim's *lama*, his guiding holy man or *guru*.

'I went in search of myself.' (εδιςησάμην εμεωυτόν). Heraclitus (see ch. 5 above, under *'geworfen'*), attributed to him by Plutarch. (Diels 101).

'What am I then, O my God? What nature am I?' Augustine, *Confessions*, Bk. X.

— *Qui ça?* In French, 'who is that?' See ch.7 above, under *'Je. Qui ça?'*.
— **Enigma to myself**. 'But do Thou, O Lord, my God, give ear; look and see, and have mercy upon me; and heal me—thou, in whose sight I am become an enigma to myself; this itself is my weakness.' Augustine, *Confessions*, Bk.X.

Augustine also said that man is a *'grande profundum*, a bottomless depth such that he cannot even know himself.' (Bk. IV).

'You could not find the ends of the soul (*psyche*) though you travelled every way, so deep is its report (*logos*).' Heraclitus. (Diels 45).

'One's own self is well hidden from one's own self; of all mines of treasure one's own is the last to be dug up.' (F. Nietzsche).

— **Only half myself.** Edmund will certainly have in mind some words that Leonardo da Vinci wrote in one of his notebooks. 'So that prosperity of body may not ruin prosperity of mind, the painter must live solitary. If you are alone you belong entirely to yourself . . . If you are accompanied by even one companion you belong only half to yourself, or even less. And so you squander yourself according to the indiscretion of your company.'

— **There's no me here.** See ch. 10 above, under 'no self there'.

— **Impulse of Life.** A seemingly universal cultural phenomenon is the idea of 'life' as an active force present in things which are classified as 'living' things. In many cultures, this 'life-force', as it manifests itself in *human beings*, is seen as a specific and distinct human characteristic, epitomised by the word 'soul', and its equivalent in other languages.

Equivalent words in ancient Greek—*psyche*—and Latin—*anima*—and German—*Seele*—together with the Hindu concept of *atman*—carry associations with ideas of spirit, breath, fleeting movement, inwardness, immateriality. (In Greek, *psyche* also means 'butterfly'.) The Greek word also contains ideas about the more substantial aspects of human specificity—mind, reason, understanding, self.

It has accordingly been a central focus of non-religious philosophies to identify the nature of this essential characteristic of human beings as living things.

Spinoza uses the Latin word *conatus* ('effort', 'impulse') an innate striving of each mode of being (not merely living things) to persevere its being, to resist destruction and disintegration, a striving which is its essence.

Fichte uses the idea of 'active power'. Schopenhauer uses a special sense of the word *will* to express the relentless power of the self to make itself, and to make the world that it inhabits. Nietzsche (much influenced by Schopenhauer) uses the idea of 'will to power'. Freud (much influenced by Schopenhauer and Nietzsche) uses the Latin word *libido* ('violent or excessive desire'). Adler uses a special sense of the word *power*. Jung uses the term 'impulse of life', in addition to his emphatic use of the word *soul*. G.B. Shaw uses the term 'life-force' and Bergson élan vital.

For an application of the idea of the 'impulse of life' to the dynamic self-constituting of human societies, including international society, see Ph. Allott, *Eunomia*, §§3.11 ff.

— **Inner Light.** See above, under 'Parmenides'.

— **What is nothing cannot exist.** A saying attributed to Parmenides.

— **Thou art that.** *Tat tvam asi*, in Sanskrit. A fundamental teaching of the Upanishads is that man can enter into the being of God, that the *atman* of man (see above, under 'impulse of life') can be united with the creative energy of the universe (*brahman*).

Such *mystical union* seems to be, in countless different forms, some sort of perennial and universal idea and experience, even within Western culture.

It seems to be a perennial and universal idea that 'man is more than man', in the words of the Priest, in the first scene of *King Oedipus* by Sophocles (c.495-406 BCE), and that we have the capacity to experience a 'mystical' re-union with the divine, however the divine may be conceived.

'We must now conceive of this whole universe as one commonwealth—of which both gods and men are members.' Cicero (106-43 BCE), *Laws* I, 7.23.

'Since the universe is wholly filled with the Eternal Intelligence and the Divine Mind, it must be that human souls are influenced by their contact with divine souls.' Cicero, *On Divination*, I. 49.110.

'Understand that you are god.' Cicero, 'Dream of Scipio', in On the Good Life.

(Cicero came under the strong influence of the Stoic philosopher Seneca—see below under 'a cup of strength'.)

M. Ficino (1433-99), a leading mind of Italian Renaissance humanism, defines man as 'a rational soul participating in the divine mind, employing a body.' Ficino is among those, especially followers of Plato, who use the idea of 'love' (in a specialised sense) to express our potential 'mystical' relationship to God. He sees *amor Dei* ('the love of God') as a spiritual journey (*circuitus spiritualis*) from God to the world and from the world to God. See further in ch. 18 below.

The idea of the absolute integration of humanity with the natural order of the universe is especially associated with the philosophy of B. Spinoza (see above, under 'we class them').

'Most of those who have written about the affects, and men's way of living, seem to treat, not of natural things, which follow the common laws of Nature, but of things which are outside Nature. Indeed they seem to conceive man in Nature as a dominion within a dominion. For they believe that man disturbs, rather than follows, the order of Nature, that he has absolute power over his actions, and that he is determined only by himself.' (Spinoza III, Preface)

'Are not the mountains, waves, and skies, a part / Of me and of my soul, as I of them?' G. Byron, *Childe Harold*, III.

— **Outscape. Inscape.** The English poet G.M. Hopkins (1844-89) uses the word 'inscape' to express the idea of the ultimate individual essence of each individual thing, placing himself in the tradition of Duns Scotus (see above, under 'we class them'). He saw it as a virtually mystical aspect of poetry to enter and to re-present the inscape of things, especially things in the natural world—as he himself did, in his few and beautiful poems. (On his deathbed, he said three times: 'I am so happy'.)

In Sartre's *La Nausée* (see above, under 'we could kill'), the narrator suddenly discovers the nature of 'existence' by seeing the inscape, as one might say, of a chestnut tree in a public park. He sees the tree's existence-in-itself, freed from all associations and generalisations, not simply as a word that we apply to things.

> 'If anyone had asked me what existence was, I should have replied in good
> faith that it was nothing, just an empty form which added itself to external
> things, without changing anything in their nature. And then, all of a sudden,
> there it was as clear as day: existence had suddenly unveiled itself. It had lost
> its harmless appearance as an abstract category: it was the very stuff of things,
> that root was steeped in existence.' (tr., R. Baldick).

And he realises that his own existence is as 'superfluous' (with no reason to exist) and as 'absurd' (with no meaning) as that of the tree. 'Existentialism' is then a therapeutic philosophy (pacifying somewhat the *Angst* of our existence) of how to use the absolute freedom of such existence to construct one's own nature.

— **I am a window**. Edmund has obviously been reading the works of the German philosopher G.W. Leibniz (see above, under 'we class them').

For Leibniz, the ultimate metaphysical individual substances which make up the universe (*monads*) are 'windowless', in the sense that they cannot interact—as cause or effect—with any other part of the universe. But they are 'mirrors', in the sense that they reflect the universal order of the universe. *Every part of the universe contains within it the whole order of the universe.* Even a human being!

The action of every constituent part of the universe—including the human being—forms part of the universal action of the universe—a universal action which, for Leibniz, is an activity in the mind of 'God'. Leibniz's notorious optimism (I.22, under 'a garden to cultivate') is based on this structure of ideas, since such a God would contain the order not merely of a *possible* world, but of the *best possible* world.

Edmund is evidently meaning to say that, on the contrary, he himself, as unique substance, feels able to look out and see the universe, both its inscape (the unique essence of things) and its 'outscape', if there were such a word (the participation of each thing in Nature as a whole).

— **To become what I am**. 'Nature forms us for ourselves, not for others; to be, not to seem.' M. Montaigne, *Essais*, II, 37.

> 'How one will be what one is' (*Wie man wird, was man ist*) is the subtitle of
> F. Nietzsche's *Ecce Homo*. Nietzsche was obsessed with this theme.
>   'Those who do not wish to belong to the mass need only to cease taking
> themselves easily; let them follow their conscience, which calls to them: "Be
> your self [*sei du selbst*]. All that you are now doing, thinking, desiring, is not
> you yourself".' ('Schopenhauer as Educator', in *Untimely Meditations*).
>   'With my best bait I shall today bait the queerest human fish. My
> happiness shall I cast out far and wide . . . For *that* is what I am through

and through: reeling, reeling in, raising up, raising, a raiser, cultivator, and disciplinarian, who once counselled himself, not for nothing: Become what you are!' *Thus Spoke Zarathustra*, Part IV (tr., W. Kaufmann).

Fichte (see ch. 7 above, under 'Ich') had given the idea of self-creation an Aristotelian spin.

'To be free, in the sense stated, means that I myself will make myself whatever I am to be. I must then,—and this is what is most surprising, and, at first sight, absurd in the idea,—I must already be, in a certain sense, that which I shall become, in order to be able to become so; I must possess a two-fold being, of which the first shall contain the *fundamental* determining principle of the second.' J.G. Fichte, *Vocation*.

There may also be an echo of the anguished cry of Oedipus in *King Oedipus*, by Sophocles: 'I ask to be no other man / Than that I am, and *will know who I am*.' (tr., E. F. Watling).

And all such ideas have their source, perhaps, in an often-quoted line (72) in the Second Pythian Ode of the Greek poet Pindar (518-438 BCE): 'Learn: and become what you are.'

Carl Jung (I.20) uses the word 'individuation' to refer to the mind's struggle to integrate itself.

'Individuation means becoming a single, homogeneous being, and, in so far as "individuality" embraces our innermost, last, and incomparable uniqueness, it also implies becoming oneself. We could therefore translate individuation as "coming to selfhood" of "self-realization".'
Relations between the Ego and the Unconscious (1934). (tr., R. Hull).

For the views of Plato and Aristotle on the integration of the personality, see ch. 18 below.

However, it has also often been asserted, not only by Existentialists (see ch. 4 above, under 'bad faith') and not least by Nietzsche, that the search for a real self is mistaken.

'There is no such substratum; there is no "being" behind doing, effecting, becoming; "the doer" is merely a fiction added to the deed—the deed is everything.' F. Nietzsche, *Genealogy of Morals*, I.13.

It may also be recalled that a foundational idea of À *la recherche du temps perdu*, the novel by M. Proust (I.19), is that, behind the names that people bear, there is no continuing entity to which the names, however illustrious, attach.

'I saw human life as a complex from which the support of an individual, identical, and permanent "self" was so conspicuously absent . . .' 'The natural stability which we assume to exist in others is as unreal as our own.' *Le temps retrouvé*, final volume (1927; published posthumously) of *À la recherche du temps perdu*.

Forms of psychotherapy which claim to help people to find 'their true self' encourage delusion—and might cause despair, if people find a 'true self' that they dislike. There is no 'true' self, but only a continuous process of self-constituting which may include generalised ideas about past and present states of that process. The self-constituting of a human personality is remarkably similar to the self-constituting of a human society. See Ph. Allott, *Eunomia*, §§9.2ff.

— **Love yourself.** '. . . *l'homme ne peut pas aimer sans s'aimer.* ('Man cannot love if he does not love himself.') A. Camus, *La Chute*. See also I.19, under 'love ourselves'.

— **False self.** An echo, perhaps, of a piece of unsolicited and improbable advice given by Polonius to his son Laertes in *Hamlet. Prince of Denmark*, by W. Shakespeare. 'This above all: to thine own self be true, / And it must follow, as the night the day, / Thou canst not then be false to any man.'

— **Journey of the soul.** A common idea in major religious traditions is the image of a journey towards enlightenment. In Hinduism, Buddhism, Christianity, and Sufist Islam, the believer may make an inward journey of self-transforming, sometimes requiring rigorous forms of self-discipline, with a view to coming closer to a transcendental, or even divine, goal.

Within the Western philosophical tradition, there is a virtually mystical tradition—not specifically religious—stemming from Plato, as developed by the neo-Platonists (see ch. 2 above, under 'neo-neo Platonist). Dante's *Divine Comedy* (see ch. 3 above, under '*l'amor che muove*') is also an account of a mystical journey.

In language remarkably similar to texts in the other traditions, religious and philosophical, the Italian Franciscan Bonaventure (1221-74) explained the nature of a journey towards God within the Christian tradition.

'The mind in contemplating God has three distinct aspects, stages or grades—the sense, giving empirical knowledge of what is without and discerning the traces (*vestigia*) of the divine in the world; the reason, which examines the soul itself, the image of the divine Being; and lastly, pure intellect (*intelligentia*), which, in a transcendent act, grasps the Being of the divine cause.' Bonaventure, *Itinerarium mentis in Deum* (Journey of the Soul to God). (tr., M. d'Ambrosio).

Others who followed in the Christian journey-of-the-soul tradition are Meister Eckhart (c.1260-c.1327), Ignatius of Loyala (1491-1556), in his *Spiritual Exercises*, Teresa of Avila (1515-82), in her *Way of Perfection* and *Interior Castle*, (see ch. 7

above, under 'becoming a diamond'), and Juan de la Cruz (John of the Cross) (1542-91), especially in his poem *The Dark Night of the Soul*.

— **The grasshopper is a burden**. 'To the weak the grasshopper is a burden.' From 'Imperfect Instruments', in *Parables from Nature* (1855-71) by the English writer Mrs Alfred Gatty.

The remarkable Mrs Gatty (1809-73) was born Margaret Scott, the daughter of Revd. A.J. Scott, who was a friend of Admiral Nelson (I.4) and who served as chaplain on the Royal Naval vessel *Victory*, tending to the Admiral when he was fatally wounded on that vessel at the Battle of Trafalgar (1805).

She married the Revd. A.J. Gatty, who was rector of Ecclesfield (Yorkshire), where she lived until her death, and where she and her father are buried. From early in the 12th century until late in the 14th century, the church and a priory at Ecclesfield had been a dependency of the Benedictine Abbey of St. Wandrille in Normandy (France) (see I.14, under 'Bury St Edmunds').

She was a prolific writer on both scientific and moral matters. Her *History of British Seaweeds* (1863) is still an authoritative work in the field, based on her own studies and observations. There is a Gatty Marine Laboratory at the University of St Andrews. Two species bear her name—an Australian alga and a marine worm.

She was also tirelessly philanthropic, especially in relation to her husband's parishioners, one of whom she and her family helped greatly, to his benefit and to the benefit of his descendants, one of whom is the author of works referred to in I.5 (under 'misanthropology') and I.19 (under 'Eunomia'). His ancestors are most probably products of the Norman connection.

— **Wanderer**. An old man speaking of Zarathustra: 'This wanderer is no stranger to me: he passed by here many years ago. He was called Zarathustra.' Old man speaking to Zarathustra: 'You lived in solitude as in the sea, and the sea bore you.' Zarathustra's shadow speaking: 'I am a wanderer, who has already walked far at your heels: always going without a goal and without a home.' (It is said that the historical Zarathustra lived in solitude for ten years. See below, under 'Zarathustraed'.). F. Nietzsche, *Thus Spake Zarathustra*, Prologue & Part Four.

— **The way of the ideal**. For the idea of the 'ideal', see I.19, ch. 8 above, under 'energising ideal', and ch. 18 below.

— **The way of resignation**. In various mythological and religious traditions, there is a counsel of *resignation*, in the face of the power of the gods or of Nature, the Will of God, Fate or Destiny.

Buddhism and Stoicism propose forms of *acceptance*, intended to have a therapeutic effect on the mind as it meets the challenge of the human condition.

In some religious traditions, there is a counsel of self-denial or self-abnegation or asceticism, designed to lead to a closer association with the transcendental or the divine.

From what we know of Edmund, we are not surprised if he is not attracted by any of the possible ways of resignation.

— **Illusion of time**. Wednesday is invoking another of the perennial problems of religion and philosophy. Is *time* an intrinsic aspect of the order of the material universe? Or is it a product of the human mind enabling us to impose order on the material universe?

Among countless other views—Newton speaks of 'absolute, true, and mathematical time'; Leibniz takes the view that time is inferred from the relation between events; Hume takes the view that time is merely an inference that we draw from observation of events; Kant takes the view that time (with space) is a 'form of perception', that is, a feature of the mind that enables it to find order in its re-presentation of the putative real world.

From the point of view of certain religious traditions, time is nothing more than an illusion, a product of our unenlightened imagination.

— **Every end is a beginning**. 'What we call the beginning is often the end / And to make an end is to make a beginning. / The end is where we start from.' From *Little Gidding*, the fourth of the *Four Quartets*, a poem by T.S. Eliot (I.18).

See ch. 8 above, under 'end and beginning'.

— *Durchlaucht*. See I.13.

— **Apollo is Dionysus**. Nietzsche uses the mythological figures of Apollo and Dionysus to identify two kinds of creative force within nature, which act within the human mind to produce, among other things, corresponding art-forms.

> 'In relation to these immediate creative conditions of nature every artist must appear as "imitator", either as the Apollonian dream artist or the Dionysiac ecstatic artist, or, finally (as in Greek tragedy, for example) as dream and ecstatic artist in one.'
>
> 'Tragedy is an Apollonian embodiment of Dionysiac insights and powers . . .'
>
> F. Nietzsche, *Birth of Tragedy* (1870-71), II, VIII.

The great interest of this idea is that it suggests an alternative (or a complement) to traditional metaphysics in analysing the way in which the human mind reconstructs reality for its own purposes.

The Apollonian is the *ordering* force, using some of the traditional metaphysical categories (including the *principium individuationis;* see above, under 'we class them'), to create a mind-made world which is a sort of dream-world existing only in and for the mind.

The Dionysian force expresses nature *directly and immediately*, as lived and felt experience, closer to poetry than to metaphysics, closer to emotion than to intellect.

Schopenhauer's *idea* and *will* might be seen as Apollonian and Dyonysian in spirit, respectively. (See ch. 4 above, under 'will to know, will to power'.)

Although Jung was certainly no admirer of Nietzsche, there is an echo of these Nietzschean ideas in Jung's 'two kinds of thinking' (explained in final form in his *Symbols of Transformation* of 1956).

Wednesday is, perhaps, suggesting to Edmund that mental healthiness requires the peaceful and fruitful co-existence of both kinds of thinking, both kinds of metaphysics, both kinds of life.

— **Love separates**. Wednesday may have in mind the idea that an anguish intrinsic to the experience of love is the knowledge that the subjective self of the loved one is, and must remain, ultimately unknowable.

— **Ten strings of my soul.** If, as a matter of theoretical physics, the universe can be re-presented mathematically in terms of many more dimensions than the four dimensions familiar to everyday thinking, and if the nature of physical reality can be expressed mathematically using the image of vibrating strings ('string theory'), it seems not unreasonable to suppose that the soul of a human being is at least as complicated and interesting, given that a human being is merely a particular manifestation of the physical reality of the universe.

Edmund, being naturally of a cheerful and optimistic disposition, is entitled to feel that the strings of his soul are vibrating mathematically and merrily.

— **To love yourself**. *L'homme ne peut pas aimer sans s'aimer.* ('One cannot love without loving oneself.') A. Camus, *La chute* (1956).

— **I accept the universe**. Echo of a story told by W. James (see ch. 2 above, under 'pragmatist') in *The Varieties of Religious Experience. A Study in Human Nature* (The Gifford Lectures) (1902), Lecture 2.

> '"I accept the universe" is reported to have been a favourite utterance of our New England transcendentalist, Margaret Fuller; and when some one repeated this phrase to Thomas Carlyle, his sardonic comment is said to have been: "Gad! She'd better!"'

New England Transcendentalism was an American (characteristically Bostonian) movement of a deist character (see ch. 12 below, under 'theism/deism'), integrating idealism, high moral values, and a form of pantheism into something approaching a secular mysticism. Its intellectual leader was R.W. Emerson (1803-82). Th. Carlyle (1795-1881) was a Scottish historian and culture critic noted for his trenchant views on most subjects.

His clinical survey of a vast range of religious attitudes and forms of behaviour leads James, by way of conclusion, to form what he regards as a 'pragmatist' view of religion.

> '. . . the world of our present consciousness is only one out of many worlds of consciousness that exist, and . . . those other worlds must contain

experiences which have meaning for our life also . . . I *can*, of course, put myself into the sectarian scientist's attitude, and imagine that the world of sensations and scientific laws and objects may be all. But whenever I do this, I hear that inward monitor of which W.K. Clifford once wrote, whispering the word "bosh!" . . . the total expression of human experience, as I view it objectively, invincibly urges me beyond the narrow "scientific" bounds.' (Lecture 20).

(W. Clifford (1845-79) was an English mathematician and philosopher. He was a student at, and (briefly) a Fellow of, Trinity College, Cambridge.)

— **Zarathustraed.** Zarathustra, usually known in the West as Zoroaster (died 583 BCE), was the founder of what has come to be called Zoroastrianism, a reformed version of the older Persian religion of Mazdaism. It is yet another instance of the strange coincidence of *enlightenments of the human mind* that occurred in the middle of the first millennium BCE. It is a monotheist religion, with a central emphasis on a moral order founded on ideals, especially the ideal of justice.

Nietzsche explained (in his *Ecce Homo*) why he had used Zarathustra as the vehicle of enlightenment in his *Also sprach Zarathustra* (Thus Spoke Zarathustra).

'Zarathustra was the first to see in the struggle between good and evil the essential wheel in the working of things. The translation of morality into the realm of metaphysics, as force, cause, end-in-itself, is his work . . . Zarathustra created this most portentous of all errors—morality; therefore he must be the first to expose it. Not only because he has had longer and greater experience of the subject than any other thinker—*all history is indeed the experimental refutation of the so-called moral order of things*—but because of the more important fact that Zarathustra was the most truthful of thinkers.' (tr., R. Hollingdale; emphasis added).

The undermining of conventional ideas of morality was a central obsessive aim of Nietzsche's life-work—with a view to finding something beyond the conventional and, in his view, sinister and life-destroying, ideas of so-called 'good' and 'evil'. The sentence italicised above has become a notorious Nietzschean dictum. For another formulation by Nietzsche of the same idea, see ch.6 above, under 'problem of evil'.

The sacred writings of Zoroastrianism include much prophetic speaking of the kind attributed to Zarathustra in Nietzsche's *Also sprach* (and here attributed to the Old Man of the Sea), prefaced by the words (in Sanskrit): *ti vuttakam* ('thus spoke the Holy One').

— **Sea, mother and lover of mankind.** From *The Triumph of Time*, a poem by the English writer A.C. Swinburne (1837-1909).

'I will go back to the great sweet mother, / Mother and lover of men, the sea. / I will go down to her, I and none other, / Close with her, kiss her and mix her with me; / Cling to her, strive with her, hold her fast: . . . / O fair green-girdled mother of mine, / Sea, that art clothed with the sun and the rain, / Thy sweet hard kisses are strong like wine, / Thy large embraces are keen like pain./ Save me and hide me with all thy waves . . . I shall sleep, and move with the moving ships, / Change as the winds change, veer in the tide . . .'

— **I will not die before I have lived**. An echo, perhaps, of something said by J.-J. Rousseau (I.19). *J'étais fait pour vivre, et je meurs sans avoir vécu.* ('I was made in order to live, and I am dying without having lived.') The occasion was a mildly life-transforming event when he was attacked by a dog during one of his walks. *Rêveries du promeneur solitaire* (The Dreaming of the Solitary Walker), 2nd Walk.

In his *Confessions* (bk. 9), he says: 'Devoured by a need to love that I had never been able to satisfy, I saw myself coming to the gates of old age, and dying without having lived.' (tr., J. Cohen).

— ***Genug des Werdens. Laß mich sein!*** In German, 'Enough of *becoming*. Let me *be!*' A line from *Stehe still!* ('Stand still'), one of the *Wesendonk Lieder* (1857-58), five poems by M. Wesendonk set to music by R. Wagner.

— **Like a bird**. 'Like a bird he flew away, just as like a bird he came: that was all.' From a writing of Chuang Chou (see above, under 'I dream that I am'), describing the correct attitude to life and death.

There is an echo of an image in a poem (*Napoléon II*) by the French poet V. Hugo (1802-85).

Toutes les choses de la terre,/Gloire, fortune militaire,/Couronne éclatante des rois,/Victoire aux ailes embrasées,/Ambitions réalisées,/Ne sont jamais sur nous posées/Que comme l'oiseau sur nos toits. ('All the things of the earth, /Glory, military success, / Shining crown of kings, / Victory with blazing wings, / Realised ambitions, / Never rest upon us / Except like a bird upon our roofs.') (present author's trans.).

There is also an echo of a familiar episode in English history (or, at least, English historiography).

'The present life of man upon earth, O king, seems to me, in comparison with that time which is unknown to us, like to the swift flight of a sparrow through the house wherein you sit at supper in winter, with your ealdormen and thegns, while the fire blazes in the midst, and the hall is warmed, but the wintry storms of rain or snow are raging abroad. The sparrow, flying in at one door and immediately out at another, whilst he is within, is safe from the wintry tempest; but after a short space of fair weather, he immediately vanishes out of your sight, passing from winter into winter again. So this life of man appears for a little while, but of what is to follow or what went before we know nothing at all. If, therefore, this new doctrine tells us something more certain, it seems justly to deserve to be followed.'

The words of a speaker at the Council held in York (627 CE) by Edwin, King of Northumbria, to decide whether to accept the Christian faith in his kingdom, as recounted in Bede (c.673-735), *Ecclesiastical History of England* (tr., from Latin, by A. Sellar).

Edwin (584-633) was a son of King Aelle of Deira (Yorkshire, more or less). On his father's death, the kingdom was annexed by the neighbouring king of Bernicia. Edwin recovered the kingdom in 616 and enlarged it, possibly to include most of England (other than Kent) and part of Scotland.

Two forms of Christianity—Celtic and Roman—had coexisted in England. The conversion of England to Roman Christianity had been initiated by Augustine (who became first Archbishop of Canterbury) sent by Pope Gregory the Great (616). (The present Arhcbishop is the 104th holder of the office.)

Edwin had been baptised into Celtic Christianity, but had relapsed into paganism. After his death, both forms of Christianity co-existed in Northumbria. At a synod in Whitby (664) Northumbria accepted the Roman (rather than the Celtic) date of Easter, and attached the Church in England to the Church of Rome—an attachment which would last until the 16th century. See I.16 and Appendix 2 below.

High art and learning flourished in the kingdom of Northumbria, especially in its monasteries. When Alfred the Great, king of Wessex (reigned 878-899), with his administrative capital at Winchester, drove out the occupying Danes and extended his kingdom to cover most of England, he led a cultural renaissance, which formed part of the Carolingian renaissance which extended over much of Europe, originating during the reign of the Emperor Charlemagne (Charles the Great; 747-814). ('Carolingian' from *Carolus,* the Latinised form of Charles).

See ch. 8 above, under 'Allott's Law of Enlightenments'.

— **His wooden staff**. See ch. 16 below, under 'sacred grove'. Edmund may possibly recall a passage in *The Agony*, one of the sacred poems of the English poet G. Herbert (1593-1633) (see ch. 8 above, under 'metaphysical'):

'Philosophers have measured mountains, / Fathom'd the depths of seas, of states, and kings, / Walk'd with a staff to heaven, and traced fountains / But there are two vast, spacious things, / The which to measure it doth more behove: / Yet few there are that sound them; Sin and Love.'

— **A cup of strength.** Echo, no doubt, of 'O may I join the choir invisible', a remarkable poem by George Eliot (see ch. 3 above, under 'God that is dead') in which she celebrates those who leave to humanity a legacy of ideas appropriate to human self-healing and self-perfecting.

> 'May I reach / That purest heaven, be to other souls / The cup of strength in some great agony, / Enkindle generous ardour, feed pure love, / Beget the smiles that have no cruelty—/ Be the sweet presence of a good diffused, / And in diffusion ever more intense. / So shall I join the choir invisible / Whose music is the gladness of the world.'

In causing Edmund to think, perhaps for the first time, about matters of the highest degree of abstraction, the Old Man of the Sea has introduced him to the ultimate questions of metaphysics, which the self-examining human mind has thought about since the beginning of self-directed human thought—how we construct reality with words and ideas; how we bring order to reality by abstract ideas; how we construct identity, individual and collective; how we give a meaning to our own existence; how we relate our existence to the existence of the universe as a whole.

It is no use saying that such matters are merely the arid speculations of dry-as-dust philosophers, having nothing to do with the everyday world, the 'real world'.

Philosophers are explorers of *the world made by the human mind*, the world made from language and ideas, the other world in which all human beings live, whether they are conscious of it or not, the world in which everything human takes place—war, crime, government, religion, education, science, art, love, friendship.

Francis Bacon called it the *radius reflexus* ('the reflexive beam of light')—that 'beam of man's knowledge . . . whereby man beholds and contemplates himself'—a third beam beyond those directed to God and to Nature.

Philosophy is the physiology of the mind. Metaphysics is the physics of the mind-made world.

Philosophers are 'teachers of the human race' (*praeceptores generis humani*). Seneca (c.2BCE-65CE), *Moral Epistles*, LXIV.

In exploring the human mind-made world *as it is*, philosophers reveal the possibilities of the human world *as it might be*—the Eutopianising of Istopia.

Why shouldn't Edmund aspire to become a teacher of the human race, perhaps even a member of the choir invisible who cause succeeding generations to think more perfectly and more creatively?

CHAPTER 12. *San Lazzaro degli Armeni.*

— **San Lazzaro degli Armeni.** In Italian, 'Saint Lazarus of the Armenians'. An island in the Venetian lagoon (see ch. 1 above) which was originally the site of a leper hospital. A monastery was established on the island by Armenian refugees from the Ottoman Empire in the early 18th century.

The monastery was, and remains, a centre of Armenian culture. Armenian Christianity dates from the first century CE.

In a story told in the Christian New Testament, Lazarus is the name of a beggar displaying the symptoms of leprosy.

— **Vaporetto.** In Italian, 'small steamboat'. The name applied to the water buses in Venice has survived from their introduction in the 19th century.

— **Lord Byron.** George Gordon, the sixth Baron Byron (I.15), left England in 1816 under several clouds, including a failed marriage. On 11 November 1816 he arrived in Venice—'the greenest island of my imagination'. He was not dismayed by the city's desolate condition—'I have been familiar with ruins too long to dislike desolation'.

The monastery of San Lazzaro became a haven for him—'studious in the day . . . dissolute in the evening'. He imposed on himself the mental discipline of studying the Armenian language and helping one of the monks to compile an Armenian-English dictionary.

Following visits to other parts of Italy and the sale of his inherited estate in England (Newstead Abbey, Nottinghamshire—a family property since 1540), Byron returned to Venice in 1817, occupying for two years part of the Palazzo Mocenigo on the Grand Canal, where he completed *Childe Harold's Pilgrimage*, wrote the dramas *Beppo* and *Manfred,* and started work on *Don Juan*, another poetical *magnum opus*, which was left unfinished at his death.

He went to Greece to assist insurgents fighting for Greek independence from Turkish rule. He died of marsh-fever in 1824. Greece achieved independence in 1829-30, following the intervention of the major European powers.

— **Terra firma.** See ch. 1 above.

— **Universal Church.** A description applied to the (Christian) Roman Catholic Church, on account of its worldwide presence and multinational membership.

— **Christ's suffering.** In the Christian religious tradition, the life of Jesus Christ ends in physical suffering and death by public execution, followed by resurrection to life.

The paradoxical idea of a 'suffering god' has been an aspect of various religions—a phenomenon much studied by cultural anthropologists, not least in the work of J.G. Frazer (1854-1941). (He was a Fellow of Trinity College, Cambridge, for most of his life.) In his book *The Golden Bough* (1890-1915) and especially in *Adonis Attis Osiris. Studies in the History of Oriental Religion* (1906), an expanded version of one section of his main book, Frazer discusses three of the most striking examples of death-and-resurrection gods in non-Christian religion. To the dismay of some of his first readers, he does not fail to make a connection between aspects of Christianity and various 'pagan' religions.

> 'When we reflect how often the [Christian] Church has skilfully contrived to plant the seeds of the new faith on the old stock of paganism, we may surmise that the Easter celebration of the dead and risen Christ was grafted upon a similar celebration of the dead and risen Adonis . . .'
>
> 'Taken altogether, the coincidences of the Christian with the heathen festivals are too close and too numerous to be accidental. They mark the compromise which the Church in the hour of its triumph was compelled to make with its vanquished but still dangerous rivals.'

For Frazer, annual celebrations of the death and resurrection of a god are natural forms of religious belief and ritual in essentially agricultural societies dominated by the cycle of the seasons.

The dying-and-resurrecting god can readily serve as a powerful archetypal model of the possible self-redeeming of each human being (see below, under 'metanoia').

— **Garden of Eden**. In the Jewish and Christian religious traditions, the *Book of Genesis* (ch. 2) describes the first home of the human race after its creation by God.

> 'And the Lord God formed man of the dust of the ground, and breathed into his nostrils the breath of life, and man became a living soul. And the Lord planted a garden eastward in Eden, and there he put the man whom he had formed.' (King James version, 1611).

— **Ancient Israel**. A Near Eastern people or group of peoples—the Hebrews—with an eventful history characteristic of peoples of that region—full of geographic, ethnic, cultural and institutional complexities and uncertainties. A history reaching back to at least 2000BCE came to be presented in writings which, like the ancient texts of Hinduism, acquired a sacred status within a religion—Judaism.

The words 'Jew' and 'Judaism' are related etymologically to the word 'Judah'. According to the Book of Genesis (see above), Judah, one of the 'twelve tribes' of Israel, was founded by Judah, one of the twelve sons of Jacob. Jacob had taken the name of 'Israel' ('one who has wrestled with God') after experiencing a prophetic dream.

According to the same source, at the beginning of the first millennium BCE, the united kingdom of Israel was ruled by two powerful kings—David and his son Solomon. After the death of Solomon (?10th century BCE) the kingdom separated into two kingdoms—Israel and Judah. These kingdoms co-existed, in intense rivalry, but always subject to the overwhelming power of the neighbouring great powers—especially Egypt, Persia, Babylon, Assyria, and Rome.

The Jewish people were exiled from the land of Israel on several occasions, including their forced exile in Babylon (6th century BCE). A final *diaspora* (in Greek, 'dispersion') began with the military campaigns of the Romans, culminating in the destruction of the Jewish Temple in Jerusalem in 70CE. Following a Jewish revolt of 132-134 CE, the Roman emperor Hadrian forbade any Jew to enter the city of Jerusalem (renamed Aelia Capitolina). The Roman province was renamed Palestina.

(The ancient use of the name 'Palestine' (in ancient Greek, *Palaistine*) to refer to some or all of the area between the Mediterranean coast and the River Jordan reflects the presence in the area of the people known as the Philistines.)

Christianity, which emerged from Judaism through the life and teachings of Jesus Christ, includes among its religious texts parts of the sacred texts of ancient Judaism (referred to as 'the Old Testament'). The 'New Testament' gives an account of the life and teachings of Jesus Christ.

Parts of the Old and New Testaments are also treated as significant religious texts within the religion of Islam.

— **Genesis**. In Greek, 'origin, source, birth'. The Jewish and Christian *Book of Genesis* describes God's creation of the world and of the human race.

— **Original gloom**. Gabi is referring obliquely to the term 'original sin', used to describe the violation of the will of God by the first human being—Adam—in the Garden of Eden, as described in the Book of Genesis (see above).

The concept has given rise to intense controversy throughout the history of Christianity—(a) because it has sometimes been taken to imply that all of Adam's successors—all human beings—have inherited responsibility for Adam's sin; and/or (b) because it has sometimes been taken to mean that all human beings have inherited an innate tendency to sin, that is, to do evil; and/or (c) because it may seem to amount to a form of 'Manichaeism'—a religion founded in the 3rd century CE by (?the Persian) Mani, the central idea of which is that the universe is dominated by ultimate principles of Good and Evil; and/or (d) because it gives rise to fundamental problems about how human beings may overcome their tendency to do evil, including problems about the nature and role of the 'grace of God' as a redeeming force, and hence problems about the nature and role of organised religion.

Gabi draws attention to the depressing fact that the murder of one of the sons of Adam and Eve by the other is the first significant event of their family life recorded in the Book of Genesis (ch. 4).

— **Greek gods**. Gabi is no doubt thinking of the Olympian gods as represented in the (pre-8th century BCE) Homeric epics known as the *Iliad* and the *Odyssey* and in the poetry of Hesiod (8th century BCE; I.19).

The all-too-human nature of the Homeric gods suggests that they were, even more than gods always are, a projection of something peculiar to the ancient Greek mind ('man's own soul turned inside out': J.W. von Goethe, conversation with Riemer), something in the Greek mind which would be transmuted into the extraordinary artistic and intellectual creativity which laid the foundations of European civilisation.

The Olympian gods have none of the gloom and terror of so many of the gods of other civilisations. John (Cardinal) Newman (ch. 19 below, under 'holy places') said that they were 'gay and graceful, as was natural in a civilised age'. They co-exist in a situation of mutual respect with human beings, especially with exceptional human beings, who accept that they may either suffer or benefit from the more or less arbitrary intervention of the gods—a form of understanding which will lead the Greeks to seek better (non-religious) explanations for the human condition and better ways of controlling and improving their own situation by their own efforts.

Ancient Greek philosophy seems to be an exciting exploration of the possibility of a post-mythological understanding of the world—an understanding that post-Homeric Greece would provide in abundance.

— **Bach's Passions**. There are two surviving settings by J.S. Bach (I.20) of the (Christian) New Testament versions of the trial, humiliation and execution of Jesus Christ (called Christ's 'Passion'—in Latin *passio*, from the verb *patior*, 'I suffer')—those of *Matthew* (BWV244) and *John* (BWV 245), based on the accounts in those books of the New Testament. They are much praised for their music and their devotional intensity, not least by non-Christians.

— **Easter Oratorio**. By J.S. Bach (BWV 249). Musical setting of the account of Christ's resurrection from death, commemorated on Easter Sunday, contained in the *Gospel of John*, in the New Testament.

— **Lazarus is us**. The Cardinal is referring to a second biblical figure with the name of Lazarus. According to the *Gospel of John* (ch. 11), he was dead and buried, but was brought back to life by Jesus Christ. (It seems unlikely that the Cardinal is also referring obliquely or ironically to the fact that the name of a major chain of stores selling children's toys—Toys R Us—was evidently chosen by their founder—Charles Lazarus—as a play on his own name. However, we do know that the Cardinal has at least two young great-nephews, and that there is a branch of the store in Rome.)

— **Middle Ages**. A conventional name for the period of European history between the end of the Roman Empire in the West (late 5th century CE) and the Italian Renaissance (from 1453 approx.)—that is, a period between the ancient world of Greece and Rome and the 'modern' world. The triumphalist spirit of the 18th century Enlightenment also referred to the earlier part of the period as 'the Dark Ages', not least because it was seen as a period dominated culturally by institutional Christianity (Christendom). We would now rather recognise that it was also a period of intense artistic and intellectual activity of a high order.

— **1789**. The French Revolution began with the storming of the Bastille prison in Paris on 14 July 1789. There are those who date the beginning of what they call the 'modern' world, or even of what they call 'modernity', from that event.

— **Theism/deism**. Terms which have come to be used to describe two broad categories of religious belief. *Theism* (from the Greek *theos*, 'god') is a belief in a personal God, especially a god made known to believers by self-revelation. *Deism* (from the Latin *deus*, 'god') is a belief, based on the use of human reason, in an impersonal God or god-like universal principle, or a God who or which created the universe but plays no further part in its existence.

In European cultural history, deism arose in the late-17th century as a critical purification of Christianity, designed to remove from religion all elements offensive to reason. It formed part of a revolution of thought flowing from the Renaissance of the 15th century, the Reformation of the 16th century, and the scientific and social revolutions of the 17th century. In the 18th century it appealed to those who saw themselves as enlightened, in the sense of being liberated from what they saw as the tyranny of misguided religious, moral and intellectual traditions.

Deists find it possible to construct codes of morality derived from reason and inner conviction, rather than revelation or authority or tradition. The idea of Shaftesbury, a leading deist (ch. 6 above, under 'pursuit of happiness'), of doing good for good's sake, not because we are 'frighted or bribed into it', influenced I. Kant (Appendix 8 below) in the development of his system of rational morality (*Critique of Practical Reason*).

There have been very many attempts to reconstruct religion on a rational basis—for example, among the most distinguished: J. Locke, *The Reasonableness of Christianity as Delivered in the Scriptures* (1695); I. Kant, *Religon within the Limits of Reason Alone* (1793).

There have also been many efforts to construct a purely rational religion—for example, among the most interesting: M. Robespierre, *Cult of the Supreme Being* (1795) (speech); A. Comte, *Système de Politique Positive* (1851) ('religion of humanity').

The relationship between reason and faith has always been, and remains, a focus of intense investigation—and concern!

For a spirited defence of *theism*, see A. Balfour (1848-1930), *Theism and Humanism* (The Gifford Lectures) (1916). Balfour takes the view that what he calls 'naturalism'—the belief that the universe can be fully explained in scientific terms—is mistaken in denying the capacity of the human mind to think in other terms, especially in terms that transcend the empirical, finding meaning and purpose—in religion, morality, aesthetic experience—of a kind that may be integrated through a belief in God.

Balfour was a student at Trinity College, Cambridge (1866-69) and was connected by marriage (not his own) and friendship with many leading academics and intellectuals of the time. He was an unusual person who combined a lifelong interest in philosophy, especially metaphysics, with an active life in politics. He served as British Prime Minister (1902-1905) and Foreign Secretary (1916-19).

He endeavoured to collect around him in London people (who came to be known as 'the Souls') who were from the most privileged class in society but who were willing to think and talk about things other than hunting and shooting and fishing and themselves. They were forerunners of the group who came to be known as 'Bloomsbury'—but who surely had an over-developed interest in themselves.

For an argument against 'naturalism' in its application to the study of *human* phenomena, in the so-called human and social sciences, see Ph. Allott, *The Health of Nations*, ch. 1.

— **Meism.** The word may already have existed or else Gabi may have invented it. It evidently refers to an extreme emphasis on subjective individuality in the understanding of human life. In European cultural history, it may be said to have taken great strength from the Reformation movement within Christianity (see Appendix 2 below) which stressed individual religious responsibility, as opposed to what it saw as the institutionalised and collectivist (and hence corrupt) religion of the Church of Rome.

The new emphasis on self-consciousness and self-determination fitted well with, and probably contributed much to, the rise of the economic individualism which was a necessary feature of the rapid social and political development of certain European societies from the 14th century onwards. (See, in particular, M. Weber, *The Protestant Ethic and the Spirit of Capitalism* (1904-5) and R. Tawney, *Religion and the Rise of Capitalism* (1934).) See further in ch. 19 below.

The subjectivity of Romantic art and literature in the late-18th and early-19th century, together with 19th-century ego-centred mental philosophy from Fichte to Freud (see above and below *passim*), also contributed much to the idea that the primary focus for the understanding of human life must be the subjectivity of the human individual.

The Cardinal sees as a tragic illusion the perpetuation of the idea that we live in intrinsically individualistic societies, and its cynical propagation as the ideal of economic and social endeavour within the extreme human socialising of the 20th and 21st centuries.

— **Grand illusion.** The Cardinal may have in mind the film *La Grande Illusion* (The Great Illusion) (1937) by the French director J. Renoir (1894-1979), son of the painter A. Renoir (1841-1919). The film presents the horror of the First World War in a form reminiscent of the narrative method of M. Proust, that is, as a panorama of the interaction of actual human beings of different nationalities and different social classes—revealing the tragic relationship between the behaviour and aspirations of individual human beings and the disastrous collective illusions perpetuated by the governments of nations.

Renoir took the title of the film from the title of a book by N. Angell (1872-1967), *The Great Illusion* (1910), in which the author argues that wars between European nations could no longer serve any rational purpose, and the idea that war is biologically natural and necessary is false.

'. . . there exist enormous organised heaps of individuals that are called nations; their life simply amplifies the life of their component cells [the citizens];

and if you are not able to understand the mystery, the reactions, the laws of [the citizens], you will say nothing but empty words when you speak of the struggles between nations.'

M. Proust, *Le temps retrouvé* (ch. 11 above, under 'to become what I am'). (present author's trans.).

— **Leviathans**. The Cardinal will no doubt have in mind the remarkable paradox at the heart of the development of European societies over recent centuries. The rise of individualism has been matched by the rise of collectivism. The 'great illusion' of 'freedom' has been matched by the great reality of socialisation.

The paradox was present in the embryonic genetic programme of what would come to be called 'liberal democracy', that is, in the *Leviathan* of T. Hobbes (Appendix 3 below) and in the embryonic genetic programme of so-called *laissez-faire* capitalism (Appendix 5 below).

The history of the development of modern democracy-capitalism is the history of the ever more intense socialising of human beings, leading even to the socialising of the human *mind* through popular culture, the mass media of communication, and electronic networks (see ch. 6 above, under 'mother-father sign/signal'). See further in ch. 19 below, under 'mind-slaves'.

The paradox is reflected also in the development of some post-Freudian mental philosophy, especially in the United States, which took a strongly social turn, suggesting that mental healthiness of the human individual is primarily a function of good social adaptation.

The professionalisation of 'sociology', again especially in the United States, also propagated the idea that the essential nature of the human being and human consciousnesss is social—an idea whose roots are in American Pragmatism, with still deeper roots in states of mind originating in the earliest colonial period.

For further discussion of the American mind, see ch. 15 below.

Under all these pressures, the individuality of the individual human being has become a fragile idea and a tenuous reality.

— **Liberal Jews**. Judaism, like Christianity and Islam, is practised with different degrees of rigorous adherence to the letter of sacred texts, different degrees of traditional ritual observance, different degrees of openness to aspects of the contemporary world, including non-religious aspects.

— **Metanoia**. Formed from ancient Greek words, meaning 'change of mind, repentance'. It suggests a radical spiritual transformation which brings a person to a 'new life', with a closer experience of the presence of the divine or the transcendental.

— **Bronze Age**. A conventional term which relates cultural history to the history of the development of technology. In the present context, Gabi is probably referring to the second millenium BCE.

— **Sacrificial victimism**. Gabi is presumably referring to a feature of many religions, in which the ritual killing of humans or animals is believed to appease the gods for human failings, or to encourage the gods to act benevolently in relation to human activities. According to one form of presentation of Christian belief, the suffering and death of Jesus Christ constituted a sacrifice which might undo the evil that entered the human condition through the sin of Adam ('atonement'). See above, under 'original gloom'. J.G. Frazer discussed various kinds of such sacrifices in chs. 24-26 of *The Golden Bough* (see above, under 'Christ's suffering').

Gabi may have in mind another view of the redeeming effect of the presence of God in human form (in the person of Jesus Christ)—that it was intended to re-create humanity, as it were. 'He was made man that we might be made gods.' Athanasius (c.295-373), *De incarnatione verbi* (On the Incarnation of the Word).

— **Roman imperialism**. T. Hobbes referred to the Church of Rome as 'the Ghost of the deceased Roman Empire, sitting crowned upon the grave thereof.' (*Leviathan*, ch. 47).

— *inter alia*. In Latin, 'among other things'.

— **Holy Spirit**. 'The Maker and Father of this universe is hard to discover.' Plato, *Timaeus*, 28c (tr., B. Jowett).

In Roman Catholic Christian theology, the unknowable and inexpressible nature of the *One God* is represented as both a unity and a trinity, expressed in the ideas of 'Father', 'Son' and 'Holy Spirit' (in ancient Greek, *hagion pneuma;* in Latin, *spiritus sanctus*). Like the Greek word *pysche* (see ch. 11 above, under 'impulse of life'), the words *pneuma* and *spiritus* have many meanings—spirit, ghost, soul, breath of life, breath of wind. It is believed that, through the Holy Spirit, God is—among other things—constantly made available to the human being, especially in the thinking, willing and acting human mind—giving the human being the capacities necessary to know and to give effect to the will of God.

'God, being generous, desired that all things should become as like as might be to himself.' Plato, *Timaeus*, 29c-30a.

— **The way of all religions**. The Cardinal presumably has in mind the biblical saying—'the way of all earth'—referring to death: for example, among the last words of David to his son Solomon (see above, under 'ancient Israel') (1 *Kings*, ch.2).

The phrase appears in English literature as 'the way of all flesh', a phrase adopted as the title of *The Way of all Flesh* (1903), a novel by the English writer S. Butler (1835-1902). It tells a bitter story of the damage that parents can do to their children, and their children's children.

— **Corruption of the best**. See ch. 5 above.

— **The conversion of the Christians.** Ironical reference to the idea of 'conversion' applied by Christians to non-Christians who are seen as potential Christians.

— **Master of those who know**. Dante's description of Aristotle. See ch. 4 above.

— **After-life**. Life after death. A religion or a metaphysical philosophy which takes the view that the human being is something more than the physical human body may readily also take the view that human life continues, in some sense, after the physical human body has ceased to function as such. The question of the nature of that life after death then becomes a central challenge, and a distingsuihing feature, of many religions and philosphies.

— **Do ut des**. In Latin, 'I give in order that you may give [to me].' In Roman law, and legal systems based on Roman law, the phrase expresses the essential reciprocitiy of a contract.

— **Covenant-based religion**. 'Covenant', from the Latin word *conventum*, 'agreement'. In various religions, there is a foundational idea of an agreement with God. In Judaism (see above), God's various covenants with Israel subtend the belief in the status of the Jews as 'the chosen people' of God.

The Cardinal is, perhaps, referring to the fact that some forms of exposition of Christianity represent it as a 'new covenant', setting terms and conditions of a believer's relationship to God, including provision for rewards and punishments such as 'salvation' and 'damnation'.

A possible reaction to this version of Christianity is expressed by Ivan Karamazov, in *The Brothers Karamazov* by F. Dostoyevsky (see ch. 3 above, under 'from the gorilla'):

'If all are not saved, what good is the salvation of just one?'

— **Already in eternity**. A religion or a metaphysical philosophy which takes the view that *time* is an illusion or merely an aspect of the functioning of the human brain (see ch. 11 above, udner 'illusion of time') may readily also take the view that human beings are already present in timelessness, like every other thing which appears to be time-bound.

— **Do good and avoid evil**. Such an ultimate distillation of the idea of *virtue* occurs in many formulations in many religious and philsophical contexts, where, however, it becomes the focus of intense debate and contention—about the meaning of 'good' and 'evil', and about the problem of the recalcitrance of the human mind which may know what is good, but may incorrigibly choose to do what is evil.

The inescapable and insoluble nature of the problem may be the reason why religions and moral philosphies have typically set such an injunction within powerful metaphysical and transcendental structures of ideas. (See above *passim*, and ch. 6 above, under 'the problem of evil'.)

— **You don't have to believe in the devil**. *Le diable, lui, n'a pas besoin qu'on croie en lui pour le servir.* 'As for the devil, he doesn't need you to believe in him for you to serve him.' A. Gide (ch. 6 above, under 'problem of evil'), *Conversations avec le diable*.

— **Senile dementia**. A progressive deterioration in the functioning of the brain, especially in the form of Alzheimer's Disease, leading to serious disturbances in cognitive functions and memory.

— **Doubt may end as despair**. Doubt is the shadow-form of belief. Despair is the shadow-form of hope. The Cardinal knows that, within the sensitive mind, they co-exist and compete.

— **Dark night**. The beautiful poem *La noche oscura* (The Dark Night) by the Spanish poet and mystic Juan de la Cruz (John of the Cross) (see ch. 11 above, under 'thou art that') is introduced by the words—*Canciones del alma que se goza de haber llegado al alto estado de la perfección, que es la unión con Dios, por el camino de la negación espiritual.* ('Songs of the soul that takes pleasure in having reached the high state of perfection that is union with God, by the way of spiritual negation.')

The poet uses the image of the dark night to express an emptying of his mind and his senses. He surrenders himself to the love of God: *dejéme, / dejando mi cuidado / entre las azucenas olvidado.* ('I left myself, leaving my cares, forgotten among the lilies.')—poetry that sounds very much more beautiful in Spanish than in English translation.

CHAPTER 13. *Beginning to Mean Something.*

— **Beginning to mean something**. Echo of a passage in *Endgame* (1957), a play by S. Beckett (see ch. 7 above, under '*Je. Qui ça?*').

> *Hamm*: 'Clov!' *Clov*: 'What is it?' *Hamm*: 'We're not beginning to . . . to . . . mean something?' *Clov*: 'Mean something! You and I, mean something! (Brief laugh.) Ah that's a good one!' *Hamm*: 'I wonder. Imagine if a rational being came back to earth, wouldn't he be liable to get ideas into his head if he observed us long enough.'

Hamm is paralyzed and blind, dependent on Clov. Hamm's parents are on stage, alive but mostly out of sight inside dustbins. It is a desolate play, apparently about the ever-approaching end of their futile lives, but also (possibly) about the futility of human life in general.

Rupert Brand, on the other hand, is nearer to the beginning of a human life, eager to learn how to build a life intelligently.

> 'Grain upon grain, one by one, and one day, suddenly, there's a heap, a little heap, the impossible heap.' Clov's description of (possibly) the making of a person's life. (Beckett wrote the English version of the play which he had first written in French.)

— **Lycée Michelet**. A secondary school located at Vanves near Paris, with a long and eventful history. It is named after the French historian J. Michelet (1798-1874). On Michelet's general view of French history as an aspect of French constitutional psychology, see Ph. Allott, *The Health of Nations*, §§7.3-4.

— *Jeune homme.* In French, 'young man'.
— *Adolescent.* In French 'adolescent'.
— *Savoir-vivre.* In French, 'knowing how to live [well]'. It implies an exceptional degree of intelligence and refinement in manners and behaviour.

> *Hanc amplissimam omnium artium bene vivendi disciplinam vita magis quam literis persequiti sunt.* ('This greatest art of all, the art of living well, they [the young] learn it best by living rather than by studying.') Cicero, *Tusculan Disputations*, IV.

Cicero's *bene vivendum* (living well) is echoed in the related French phrases—*bon vivant* (someone who enjoys the good things of life) and *bon viveur* (someone who enjoys the good things of life too much).

— **Certain idea.** In French, the equivalent phrase—*une certaine idée*—has a special and familiar resonance. At the beginning of his memoirs, General (later President) C. de Gaulle (1890-1970) writes: *Je me suis fait une certaine idée de la France* ('I formed for myself a certain idea of France.').

There is reason to believe that de Gaulle identified himself rather closely with the idea of France, not least because his surname seems to connect him to the name *Gaule* (Gaul), the French name of the Roman province (*Gallia*, in Latin) which was the forerunner of France.

In French, it is also possible to say *une idée certaine* ('a definite idea').

— *Nuits d'ivresse et d'extase.* Echo of a (nocturnal) love duet in Act IV of the opera *Les Troyens* by the French composer H. Berlioz (1803-69). It is sung by Didon and Énée (Dido and Aeneas) (I.13).

> *Nuit d'ivresse et d'extase infinie! / Blonde Phœbé, grands astres de sa cour, / Versez sur nous votre lueur bénie; / Fleurs des cieux, souriez à l'immortel amour!* ('Night of intoxication and infinite ecstasy! Pale Phoebe [the moon], and the great stars of her court, pour down on us your blessed light; flowers of the heavens, smile on immortal love!') (present author's trans.).

Didon's abandonment by Énée and her choice of self-immolation (in Act V) give rise to rather less restrained music than in the corresponding scene in the opera by Purcell (I.16).

— **Bohemian life.** A life relatively free of social and moral constraints and, unless alleviated by inherited wealth, a life of poverty. Its archetype was created in the novel *Scènes de la vie de bohème* (Scenes from Bohemian Life) (1848) by the French writer H. Murger (1822-61). In a preface, he extols the virtues of such a life, as a purifying and (spiritually) enriching experience for potential writers, artists and musicians.

The novel—like the opera *La Bohème* (1896) by the Italian composer G. Puccini (1858-1924)—sets the scene of such a life in Paris, causing many aspiring writers, artists and musicians to go there to find themselves or, at least, to look for themselves—and to remind themselves of the marginal benefits of a life subject to social and moral constraints—of which Rupert Brand, at least so far, apparently does not need reminding.

— **Stereometaphysics**. Bringing into focus two metaphysical worldviews. From Pythagoras and Heraclitus onwards, to Kant and Hegel, it seems to be a particular feature of metaphysical thinking that a dichotomy of conflicting ideas can become a trichotomy, by producing a third thing which transforms and surpasses the first two ideas. On metaphysiology, see ch. 16 below.

A possible effect of travel to foreign countries is a dialectical enrichment of one's personal metaphysics, especially if one makes the effort to abstract and generalise a foreign 'way of life' and 'state of mind'.

Potentially still more enriching of one's personal metaphysics is close acquaintance with the literature of another country, both imaginative and non-imaginative. Literature reveals the mind of the foreign country in a form more readily conducive to abstraction and generalisation and comparison.

One gets to understand the mind of the Self better by getting to understand better the mind of the Other.

— *Manière de voir*. In French, 'way of seeing'.

— **All France is divided into two parts**. Echo of the opening words of J. Caesar, *De bello gallico* (On the War in Gaul), the Roman general's account of his campaign (58-51 BCE) in Gaul (which, until the 5th century CE, was the Roman province of *Gallia*—more or less, the territory of the future France).

> *Gallia est omnis divisa in partes tres, quarum unam incolunt Belgae, aliam Aquitani, tertiam qui ipsorum lingua Celtae, nostra Galli appellantur. Hi omnes lingua, institutis, legibus inter se differunt.* ('All Gaul is divided into three parts, one of which the Belgae inhabit, the Aquitani another, those who in their own language are called Celts, in our [language] Gauls, the third. All these differ from each other in language, customs and laws.' (trs., W. McDevitte & W. Bohn).

— *La province*. The parts of France which are NotParis, whose inhabitants, unless and until they go to Paris, are likely to be seen by Parisians as 'provincial'.

— *Énarques*. Graduates of the *École nationale d'administration* (ENA). See ch. 19 below, under '*grandes surfaces*'.

— **Cartesian gospel**. Reference to the philosophy of R. Descartes (1596-1650). See ch. 11 above, under 'the self and the other' and Appendix 8.

— **Enlightened pessimism**. The leading minds of the 18th century Enlightenment, especially in France and Britain, found it difficult to reconcile their optimism and their pessimism. They were aware, at one and the same time, of the remarkable creative and progressive capacities of the human being, especially of the human

PHILIP ALLOTT

mind, but also of the inexhaustible awfulness of which human beings have, always and everywhere, proved themselves capable. See I.21.
— *Die Unlust.* In German, 'undesire', 'unpleasure'.
— *Le déplaisir.* In French, 'displeasure', 'unpleasure'.
— **Not serious enough people (the English).**

> 'I fear you will laugh when I tell you what I conceive to be about the most essential mental quality for a free people whose liberty is to be progressive, permanent, and on a large scale; it is much stupidity.'
> 'I need not say that, in real sound stupidity, the English are unrivalled . . . In fact, what we opprobiously call stupidity, though not an enlivening quality in common society, is nature's favourite resource for preserving steadiness of conduct and consistency of opinion.' W. Bagehot (1826-77), *Letters on the French* coup d'état *of 1851* (1852) (letter 3: 'On the new constitution of France, and the aptitude of the French character for national freedom').

Bagehot was later to become the editor of *The Economist* newspaper and the author of a leading work on the British Constitution: *The English* [*sic*] *Constitution* (1865).

> 'It is not at all easy (humanly speaking) to wind up an Englishman to a dogmatic level.' J.H. Newman, *Apologia pro vita sua.* (1864) (see ch. 19 below, under 'holy places').
> *Les anglais me paraissent en général avoir une grande difficulté à saisir les idées générales et indéfinies. Ils jugent parfaitement bien le fait d'aujourd'hui, mais la tendance des faits et leurs conséquences éloignées leur échappent.* ('The English in general seem to me to have great difficulty in grasping general and indefinite ideas. They judge perfectly well today's facts, but the underlying trend of facts and their distant consequences escape them.')

A de Tocqueville, *Voyages en Angleterre et en Irlande* (Journeys into England and Ireland) (1833). (present author's trans.).
De Tocqueville quotes a conversation with J.S. Mill who confirms his view—'The habits or the nature of our mind do not incline us to general ideas.'
— **Pale cast of thought.** Echo of lines in Hamlet's soliloquy—'To be, or not to be'—considering the possibility of suicide. He says that the 'dread of something after death . . . puzzles the will . . .'

> 'Thus conscience does make cowards of us all; / And thus the native hue of resolution / Is sicklied o'er with the pale cast of thought . . .'
> W. Shakespeare, *Hamlet. Prince of Denmark*, III. i.

It has been suggested (A. Bradley) that 'conscience' here means 'consciousness'. But the word is surely intended to have both resonances—too much thinking; *and* conscience in the moral sense of the word.

It has also been suggested (G. Williams) that the word 'cast' refers to cosmetic makeup which, in Elizabethan times, was much used to obtain a pallid complexion, and to conceal imperfections of the skin.

— **The Irish are more lively**. Rupert's characterising of his compatriots has a long pedigree. Compare the meeting of an Englishman, a Scotsman, an Irishman, and a Welshman in W. Shakespeare, *King Henry V*, III. ii (probably written in 1599). Shortly after their conversation, they will engage in the Battle of Agincourt (1415) inspired (according to Shakespeare) by a rousing cry: 'God for Harry, England in the broadest sense, and Saint George!'

The same play characterises the French ruling class as effete. The Dauphin, son of the French king, shortly before the battle, says to the Duke of Orleans: 'I once writ a sonnet in his praise [in praise of his horse] and began thus: "Wonder of nature!".' The Duke says: 'I have heard a sonnet begin so to one's mistress.' (See also ch. 19 below, under '*jeu de paume*'.)

— **Mutual Unlust Society**. An echo of the term 'mutual protection society'—a form of insurance in which the members who face common risks contribute to a fund which is available to be distributed to meet claims arising from accidents.

Rupert presumably has in mind the Freudish idea that a human society may be seen as a system of collective security through shared repression and sublimation of pleasure—with English society as an exceptionally good illustration of the thesis.

> '. . . . it is impossible to overlook the extent to which civilization is built up on renunciation, how much it presupposes the non-satisfaction of powerful drives—by suppression, repression or some other means Such "cultural frustration" dominates the large sphere of interpersonal relations . . .' S. Freud, *Civilization and its Discontents*, III. (tr., D. McLintock). (See ch. 6 above, under 'greatest happiness'.)

— **Survival of the unfittest**. *Survival of the fittest* is a phrase which is not used by C. Darwin himself, but which is used by the English writer H. Spencer (1820-1903). Spencer sees in Darwin's theory of biological evolution by natural selection an explanatory model which could readily and fruitfully be translated into the sphere of human social life.

Darwin's theory does not contain the idea that evolution is necessarily a *progressive* process, necessarily producing *better* living organisms. Species that survive are simply *better adapted* to whatever conditions of habitat they may encounter at a given time. Spencer, on the other hand, believes that society does contain, through the natural phenomenon of social struggle, a natural tendency to self-improvement.

He instances war, capitalism and competitive games as useful tests of fitness to survive.

However, it must be said that it is difficult to conclude that, in actual human societies, those who are seen to 'succeed' to an exceptional degree are necessarily *better* in any way other than in their capacity to seem to succeed.

— **Noble lie**. In *Republic*, Bk. III, 414b-c, Plato uses the phrases (as translated by P. Shorey) 'noble lie' and 'opportune falsehood' (or, one might say, 'socially useful fiction').

With wonderful prophetic insight, Plato saw that, to achieve a stable and successful society, the ruling class must tell itself and the people an effective story about that society—its origins, its nature, its values—not least to explain and justify the society's distribution of wealth and poverty, power and subjection. Such story-telling has been a primary social function of social philosophy and 'ideology' (see below) ever since—always with the possibility that a new and better story might make a new and better society.

— **Charades**. A game in which players mime scenes or phrases which other players endeavour to guess. The singular form of the word has also come to refer to some kind of social performance that conceals its true nature.

— **Narcissism of interesting differences (French/English)**. The Irish writer G. Moore (1852-1933) expressed an opinion on the matter.

> '. . . I will take this opportunity to note my observation, for I am not aware that any one else has observed that the difference between the two races is found in the men, not in the women. French and English women are psychologically very similar; the standpoint from which they see life is the same, the same thoughts interest and amuse them; but the attitude of a Frenchman's mind is opposed to that of an Englishman's; they stand on either side of a vast abyss, two animals different in colour, form, and temperament;—two ideas destined to remain separate and distinct.' *Confessions of a Young Man* (1886), X.
>
> 'It is always possible to bind quite large numbers of people together in love, provided that others are left out as targets of aggression. I once discussed this phenomenon, the fact that it is precisely those communities that occupy contiguous territories and are otherwise closely related to each other—like the Spaniards and Portuguese, the North Germans and the South Germans, the English and the Scots, etc.—that indulge in feuding and mutual mockery. I called this phenomenon "the narcissism of small differences"—not that the name does much to explain it.' S. Freud, *Civilisation and its Discontents* (1930), V (see above).

In fact, Freud did *not* call the phenomenon by that name in discussing it—using the same illustrative examples (and others, less attractive)—in *Group Psychology and the Analysis of the Ego* (1921),VI—if that is the earlier discussion he has in mind.

— **England as a republic**. Voltaire: 'a unique system of government in which they have conserved all that is useful in monarchy, and all that is essential in a republic.' (*Lettres philosophiques*). W. Bagehot (see above): 'A Republic has insinuated itself beneath the folds of a Monarchy.' (*English Constitution*).

— *Pensée unique*. In French, 'single thinking'. The term has come to be used in France in recent years to refer to monolithic sets of ideas with a flavour of ideology (see below, under 'one-dimensional thinking' and 'ideology')—for example, the set of ideas that the French call *libéralisme économique* (dogmatic support of free-market capitalism).

— *Le conformisme*. In French, '[excessive] conformity [of thought or behaviour]'.

— **One-dimensional thinking**. In *One Dimensional Man. Studies in the Ideology of Advanced Industrial Society* (1964), the German philosopher H. Marcuse (1898-1979) identifies a characteristic of advanced capitalist industrial society. The transcendental creative and critical function of thought is suppressed in favour of the thought that the social system itself generates and appropriates for its own purposes.

> 'The productive apparatus and the goods and services which it produces "sell" or impose the social system as a whole . . . . The products indoctrinate and manipulate; they promote a false consciousness which is immune against falsehood . . . Thus emerges a pattern of *one-dimensional thought and behaviour* in which ideas, aspirations, and objectives that, by their content, transcend the established universe of discourse and action are either repelled or reduced to terms of this universe. They are redefined by the rationality of the given system and of its quantitative extension.'

Marcuse was a member of a remarkable group of German thinkers (the Frankfurt School) who extended to 20th-century capitalist society the critical approach opened up by Marx and Engels in relation to early industrial capitalism.

Like Marx and Engels themselves, Marcuse and his colleagues, by their own writings, paradoxically show that it *is* possible, even from within capitalist society, to generate transcendental *anti-social* ideas, ideas which inform and energise their own fierce criticism of its ideological tyranny.

— *N'est-ce pas?* **In French**, 'isn't that so?' ('know what I mean?')

— **Philanthropology**. See I.5. Not to be confused with 'philanthropy'. It seems that Philanthropology is a new philosophy or secular religion dedicated to the purposive improvement of humanity. See generally, Ph. Allott, *Eunomia. New Order for a New World* (I.19). For a philanthropological view of modern European history, see J. Bury, *The Idea of Progress. An Inquiry into its Origins and Growth* (1920).

Philanthropology will always be opposed by a misanthropology which is a default philosophy of human hopelessness.

In Greek, *mis-* is a prefix forming words referring to hatred—including *misanthropos*, 'hating mankind, misanthropic'; *misologos*, 'hating reasoned argument'; *misotheos,* 'hating god, godless'; *misodemos*, 'hating the people, hating democracy'; *misophilippos*, 'hating Philip' (of Macedon, presumably).

And it will always be opposed by those who see any policy of human improvement as merely yet another excuse for arrogant political power.

'The philanthropist [*sic*] is the Nero of modern times.' G. Moore, *Confessions of a Young Man* (see above), VIII.

— **Ontology**. See ch. 8 above.

— *Strapontin*. Fold-down seat in a theatre or in a car.

— **Education**. In concerning themselves with the problem of education, Mr Gray and the Countess join a tradition which reaches back to the beginning of Western social philosophy. Plato's *Republic* contains an extended discussion of the ideal education for those whose social function is to raise *human society* to a higher level of existence, that is to say, to raise *humanity* to a higher level of existence.

There was a similar understanding of the social significance of education in ancient China, Rome, medieval Europe, 17th-century Europe, and in 19th-century Europe, when the privileged classes were able to see that a better society requires not only a better educated ruling class but also better educated citizens in general, as all classes were required to perform ever more complex tasks in industrial capitalism and globalising commerce, and to participate more fully in the political process.

'We must educate our masters.' This was said by W. Forster, industrialist and Liberal politician, introducing into the House of Commons the Bill that became the Education Act 1870, following the second major reform of Parliament in 1867, providing for universal elementary education in Britain.

The problem of the best form of education has never been posed in more difficult circumstances than in the social world of the 21st century. And the problem now, in a globalising world, presents itself as the ultimate challenge, foreseen in hypothetical terms by philosophers in other centuries—'the education of the human race' (*die Erziehung des Menschengeschlechts*) (G. Lessing).

See ch. 19 below, under 'holy places of the new ignorance'.

— **Educate in the holidays**. The *Who's Who* entry of the English writer O. Sitwell (1882-1969) contained the following—'educated during the holidays from Eton'. (Eton College is a British public (that is, private) school, founded in 1440.)

— **Taillevent**. A leading Parisian restaurant in the 8th arrondissement. It is within walking-distance of the Firm's house in the avenue Foch. The motor-car carrying Mr Gray, the Countess and Rupert Brand would no doubt have been delayed by traffic at L'Étoile.

— *Cher fils d'une chère amie à nous*. In French, 'dear son of a dear (female) friend of ours'.

— *Savoir-faire*. In French, 'knowing how to behave'.

— *Je suis là pour perfectionner mon français.* In French, 'I am here to perfect my French.'

— *D'ici deux semaines je le parle couramment.* In French, 'In two weeks time, I will speak it fluently.'

— *Mais vous le parlez déjà à la perfection, mon cher Rupert.* In French, 'But you already speak it to perfection, my dear Rupert.'

— *Chic.* In French, 'chic'.

— *Tenue.* In French, 'clothing, uniform, outfit'. When used to refer to the way in which an elegant woman is dressed, the word already implies approval.

— *Amour.* In French, 'love'.

— *On ne badine pas avec l'amour—avec l'intelligence non plus.* In French, 'one shouldn't play with love—and not with intelligence either.'

   On ne badine pas avec l'amour is the title of a play (1834) by the French writer A. de Musset (1810-57) in which Perdican's unsuccessful campaign to win the love of Camille generates much discussion of the nature of love, with Camille tending to prefer the love of God. Their discussion includes the following charming exchange.

> Camille. Je veux aimer, mais je ne veux pas souffrir; je veux aimer d'un amour éternel, et faire des serments qui ne se violent pas. Voilà mon amant. (Elle montre son crucifix.) Perdican. Cet amant-là n'exclut pas les autres.
>
> (Camille. 'I want to love, but I do not want to suffer. I want to love with an eternal love, and make oaths that are not to be broken. There is my lover.' (She shows her crucifix.) Perdican. 'That lover does not exclude others.') (present author's trans.)

For stereometaphysicians (see above), the place of *amour* at the centre of gravity of French literature is revealing—from the fantasy of medieval courtly love (wellspring of centuries of fatally romanticised 'love', up to and including the 'love' in the music of contemporary popular culture), through the analysis of the destructive power of love in the tragedians of the 17th century, to the analysis of socialised love in the plays and novels of the 18th and 19th centuries and the bleak anomie of personal relations in 20th-century literature.

   One might (controversially, but not arbitrarily) find social relations at the centre of gravity in English literature; the suffering soul in Russian literature; the human spirit in German literature; the soul-before-God in Spanish literature. (Note: a centre of gravity balances extremes however distant, and everything in-between.)

— *Amour amitié. Amitié intime.* In French, 'love-friendship'; 'intimate friendship'.

— *Amour-commerce.* In French, 'love as commerce'.

— *Amour folle.* In French, 'love to the point of madness'.

— **Meaning of love.** Greg Seare might, perhaps, draw Rupert's attention to a poem *The Definition of Love* by the English poet A. Marvell (1621-78) (ch. 8 above, under 'metaphysical') .

'My Love is of a birth as rare / As 'tis for object strange and high / It was begotten by Despair / Upon Impossibility / . . . Therefore the Love which us doth bind / But Fate so enviously debars, / Is the Conjunction of the Mind, / And Opposition of the Stars.'

— **The meaning of meaning**. In writing his prize essay, Rupert will certainly have exposed his mind to *The Meaning of Meaning. A Study of the Influence of Language upon Thought and of the Science of Symbolism* (1923) by C. Ogden and I. Richards.

The authors, members of the first generation of what we may call *post-philosophers*, join a broad trend of 20th-century philosophy which is primarily concerned with the functioning of the phenomenon of *language*, rather than with the substance of the ideas that language is used to express.

Ogden and Richards find that there is no such thing as *meaning* in a general abstract sense—and hence, indeed, no such thing as *truth* in a general abstract sense. There is only a very various repertoire of uses to which language is put, including especially its *symbolic* use (to represent things) and its *emotive* use (to get the listener to have some particular mental experience). The words *true* and *good* are seen as prime examples of language's emotive use. They do not *represent* anything.

The book enjoyed success beyond the circle of professional philosophers because it seemed to destroy, at last and definitively, the charade of philosophy as a 'higher' or 'transcendental' activity of the human mind. It seemed to fit well with the spirit of the times, in so far as that spirit may be seen as an egalitarianising and populist anti-intellectualism in a world full of pathological social phenomena, including war and economic collapse.

We may expect that Rupert, in his essay, will have set out the obvious and necessary response. The power of transcendental words depends on the accumulation of meaning that has come to be associated with them, over the course of centuries or even millennia—incorporating the fruits of humanity's unceasing thinking about its own nature and purposes. Philosophy, of the traditional kind, is concerned with the past, the present, and the future of that meaning.

— **Theory of everything**. Echo of a shorthand term for an enterprise within theoretical physics seeking to find a theory that integrates the theories of 'relativity' and 'quantum mechanics'—a theory which would then, it is said, provide an ultimate explanation of all physical processes in our local universe—perhaps allowing us, at last, to know the 'mind of God'!

— **Ideology**. The word began life in the work of a group of French philosophers ('ideologists') who, following in the line of the thought of Bacon and Locke (Appendices 1 and 4 below), took the view that 'ideas' derive ultimately from the work of the senses ('sensations') and hence that it would be possible to study ideas scientifically, as an extension of biology or zoology.

In his *Éléments d'idéologie* (Elements of Ideology) (1801-15), A. Destutt de Tracy (1754-1836) proposes a 'science of thought' or 'science of ideas' which could become the foundational science of all the human sciences. It would enable human societies to improve themselves rationally and purposefully.

For Hegel (I.19), there is a *history* of ideas, a history which is inherently progressive, with ideas enriching themselves over the course of time.

These approaches influenced the development of the thought of K. Marx and F. Engels (I.19) for whom all ideas, even the most abstract, are socially produced through ascertainable historical processes. And, therefore, a social revolution must be an ideological revolution within the necessity of history.

The idea of *ideology* took on a third life in the 20th century when totalitarian societies took control of the production and distribution of ideas of every kind as an integral part of state power. This led to a more sophisticated assessment of the positive and negative aspects of the study of ideas. See K. Mannheim, *Ideology and Utopia. An Introduction to the Sociology of Knowledge* (1936).

Finally, after 1945, the word came to be used as a general pejorative term, referring to structures of apparently philosophical ideas which are manufactured or appropriated to serve a political purpose, and/or ideas which have, in practice, been used to justify evil social systems. At the extreme, this could be used to condemn some otherwise rather respectable sets of ideas (Plato, Rousseau, Hegel, Marx). See K. Popper, *The Open Society and its Enemies* (1945). Popper was under the happy illusion that an 'open', that is, 'democratic' society freely chooses its own foundational ideas.

— **Q.E.D. CQFD.** In Latin, *quod erat demonstrandum* ('that which was to be shown'). In French, *ce qu'il fallait démontrer* ('that which had to be shown'). Normally used at the end of a mathematical proof.

— **Rite of passage.** An aspect of the social order of certain pre-industrial societies much studied by cultural anthropologists. Young persons are said to perform a 'rite of passage' when they undergo certain ritual ceremonies to mark their passing from the status of child to the status of adult.

Rites of passage in industrial and post-industrial democratic-capitalist societies take many exotic forms.

— **Enter man's estate.** Echo of the charming song sung by the clown Feste at the end of W. Shakespeare, *Twelfth Night, or What You Will* (c. 1601).

'When that I was and a little tiny boy, / With hey, ho, the wind and the rain, / A foolish thing was but a toy, / For the rain it raineth every day./ But when I came to man's estate, / With hey, ho, the wind and the rain, / 'Gainst knave and thief men shut their gate, / For the rain it raineth every day.'

— *Je suis un adulte.* In French, 'I am an adult.'

— **Philosopher's apprentice. Sorcerer of himself.** Echo of 'the sorcerer's apprentice'. See ch. 6 above, under 'help me!' Also, an echo of *le bourreau de soi-même*. See ch. 7 above, under '*plaie et couteau*'.

— *Savoir-être.* In French, 'knowing a good way to be'.

CHAPTER 14. *Meeting of the Ways.*

— **MI6**. See I.3.

— *blackboulage.* In French, 'blackballing' (vetoing a candidate's application to join some body). In a procedure—of ancient origin—used for electing members of an assembly or club, an elector may indicate approval or disapproval of a candidate by surreptitiously placing a ball of a specified colour in a bag or box.

— **Would Abe want to head such an organisation?** An echo here, perhaps, of an immortal paradoxism attributed to the American comic film-actor Groucho (Julius) Marx (1890-1977), in a letter of resignation from a Hollywood club. 'I don't care to belong to any club that will have me as a member.'

— **NSC**. See I.16. Established in 1947, the National Security Council advises the President of the United States of America on national security and foreign policy matters.

— **Secretary of State**. The head of the US Department of State, the foreign ministry of the USA. Thomas Jefferson (I.6) was the first Secretary of State of the new Republic and the first head of the renamed 'Department of State' (1789-93).

In Britain the holder of the ancient office of Secretary of State was originally a dominant royal court official with general responsibilities in national government. In the course of the 18th century, the nature of British government was changing, as a 'cabinet government' of ministers was detaching itself from the royal court under the authority of a figure who held the office of First Lord of the Treasury, and who, in the person of Robert Walpole (1676-1745), emerged, to much consternation, as a 'first or prime minister'. (To this day, the British so-called 'Prime Minister' actually holds the office of First Lord of the Treasury—the title shown on a brass plaque on the front door of 10 Downing Street in London.)

In 1782, two Secretaries of State were appointed—one for Foreign Affairs (the remarkable Whig politician C.J. Fox) and one for Home Affairs (Lord Shelburne). Thereafter, principal functions of government were distributed among an ever-increasing number of ministers, some of whom carried, and carry, the title of Secretary of State.

Originally, the responsibilities of the US Secretary of State were wider than foreign affairs. He was virtually an administrative secretary of the US Government—reflecting the older British conception of the secretary of state. Some of those wider responsibilities remain with the office to this day.

— **IGO. NGO.** Intergovernmental international organisation. Nongovernmental international organisation.

— **Academia**. The Latin form of the Greek word *akademeia*. The rather precious term—and the still more precious *academe*, and the extremely precious *groves of academe*—are used to refer to universities in a general sense. They are derived from the name of the place where Plato taught—a gym (fitness center) in an olive grove near Athens named after Akademos, a hero in Greek mythology.

— **International mafia**. If the term 'mafia' is tactfully limited to referring to masters of traditional forms of international organised crime, it is possible to identify an *international aristocracy* which is exercising disproportionate power in a globalising world—especially including those who control IGO's and NGO's, those who control internationalised industry, commerce, and finance, and those who control international media of communication.

See 'The emerging international aristocracy', in Ph. Allott, *Towards the International Rule of Law*, ch. 5; and 'International law and the international *Hofmafia*. Towards a sociology of diplomacy', in Ph. Allott, *The Health of Nations*, ch. 13. See further in ch. 19 below.

— **Universal Language**. Jim Meehan is speaking of English as a universal language. History suggests that the tendency of a language to be used extra-nationally (beyond its ethnic base) or internationally (for international transactions) is determined circumstantially, and cannot be stage-managed. And the same is true of languages which have expanded to contribute to the formation of other ethnically based languages (for example, Sanskrit, Greek, Latin, German).

Aramaic, Greek, Latin, French and English have, at different times, had substantial extra-national and international use.

The English language originated in England after the immigration of people from northern Europe speaking north-Germanic dialects in the 5th and 6th centuries CE. Those dialects were modified into a succession of distinct forms including so-called Anglo-Saxon and Middle English. Especially among the less-privileged social classes, English survived the introduction of the French language as the official language of the Norman immigration of the late-11th century.

Latin and French (one of the 'Romance' languages deriving from Latin) were the international languages of the Middle Ages (see ch. 12 above). Large numbers of words derived from Latin and French entered the English language. French was the primary language of diplomacy until the 19th century.

English rapidly reasserted itself in England, in preference to Norman French, so that, by the middle of the 14th century, something approaching modern English was the native language of all classes. A statute of 1362 required all pleadings and judgments in the courts of England to be in 'the English tongue', because 'the French tongue is much unknown in the said realm'.

The British Empire (from the 16th century) spread the use of English to many other places, not least to the British colonies in America and to India.

The very many attempts to invent an artificial language to serve as a universal language—not least in response to the notorious difficulties of the English language—have not succeeded, and seem unlikely to succeed in the foreseeable future. The social process known as globalisation makes the need for a universal language—if only as a second language—urgent.

Perhaps there could be a global philological effort to improve the weaker aspects of a universalised English language, without losing its remarkable richness of vocabulary—an amalgamation of Greek, Latin, German, French, and Scandinavian languages, together with words taken from the languages of countries with which Britain was closely associated—and its intensely dynamic quality, producing new words and phrases prolifically and promiscuously as new circumstances require.

— **Unilateral Declaration of Independence**. Jackson's reference to a UDI by Quebec is no doubt intended to be hypothetical. The secession of a member state from a federal state (or, say, from the EU) is a political question as much as, or more than, a legal question.

UDI was the name given to the act by which the government of the British colony of Rhodesia purported to declare its independence from Britain in 1965. The British government—and most other governments—did not recognise the validity of the act. By an act of the British government in 1980 the colony became independent under the name of Zimbabwe.

Quebec (in French, *Québec*) is a province of federal Canada. Britain took possession of the former French territory in Canada (*Nouvelle-France*) after the Seven Years War (1763) (ch. 19 below, under 'Boston lunch-party').

'Loyalists' who had taken the British side in the American War of Independence settled in Canada after recognition of the United States by Britain (1782/1783). A separate province (Quebec) was created in 1791 for the French-speaking inhabitants. The constitutional structure of Canada was formalised in the British North America Act 1867 (an Act of the British Parliament).

The problem of the relationship of Quebec to federal Canada has continued to be a serious political problem.

Among many other historical examples of 'declarations of independence', the Declaration of Independence by British colonies in America in 1776 was not recognised by the British government until 1782.

'His Britannic Majesty acknowledges the said United States, Viz. New Hampshire, Massachusetts Bay, Rhode Island and Providence Plantations, Connecticut, New York, New Jersey, Pennsylvania, Delaware, Maryland, Virginia, North Carolina, South Carolina and Georgia, to be free Sovereign and independent States; That he treats with them as such; And for himself, his Heirs and Successors, relinquishes all Claims to the Government, Propriety, and territorial Rights of the same, and every part thereof . . .' (From Article 1 of the Provisional Articles of Peace of 1782 and Article 1 of the Definitive Treaty of 1783).

It is interesting that the British government here formally acknowledges the independence of the *separate* former colonies, and that the preambles to the two treaties refer to the United States in the plural. However, the preambles to the two documents refer also to 'the two countries'. The legal situation must have been puzzling even for the legal advisers of the parties.

At the time when the peace treaty was concluded, 'the United States of America' was the formal title of a 'confederacy' formed by 'Articles of Confederation and Perpetual Union' agreed by the former colonies in 1777 (entering into force in 1781).

> 'Each state retains its sovereignty, freedom, and independence, and every
> power, jurisdiction, and right, which is not by this Confederation expressly
> delegated to the United States, in Congress assembled.'
> (Article II of the Articles of Confederation).

The federal constitution of the United States was adopted in 1787 and came into force in 1789. Presumably the federal United States succeeded to the rights and obligations, in international law and constitutional law, of the Confederacy and its constituent states under the Treaty of 1783, subject to the interesting question of whether the Constitution (not least its especially obscure Tenth Amendment) leaves with the federalised states any rights and obligations of their own under international law.

The thirteen Southern states that seceded in 1860-61 believed that they at least retained the right of secession from the federation. Eleven of them re-constituted themselves as the Confederate States of America. Following the American Civil War (1861-65) they rejoined the institutions of the federation. The Supreme Court held (in 1869) that their secession had been unconstitutional and a nullity—and hence, presumably, they had never *not* been members of the federal United States.

The problem of secession from composite state-entities continues to be an acute and actual problem to this day.

— **Governor-General**. In certain countries which were formerly British territories and where the British monarch remains as head of state, the monarch's representative is entitled 'Governor-General'.

— **Frankish**. Even if there is no *necessity* to do so, some might think that there could be a marketing advantage in assigning a new brand name to English, in order to identify its USP. Globalese. Worldword. New Latin. Universal Language.

Jackson's suggestion of 'Frankish' reflects the fact that the Franks (in Latin, *Francii*—in German, *die Franken*—in French, *les Francs*) were a tribe which, after the end of the Western Roman Empire, moved into what had been the Roman province of Gaul—and into northern Italy and northern Spain.

On the death of the Frankish emperor Charlemagne (747-814) (see ch. 11 above, under 'like a bird'), his dominions were divided between his two sons—allowing for the emergence of two countries, Germany and France (East Franks, West Franks), with radically different languages—and thereby determining much of subsequent European history and, indeed, much of world history.

The new name 'Frankish' would then indicate a reuniting of the Frankish languages in their descendant, English.

— *Erstes Gremium*. In German, 'first (supreme) committee'. In Latin, *gremium* is '(a person's) lap' and, hence, 'centre' or 'middle'.

— **Global balance of power**. The idea of a 'balance of power' has acted as a self-regulating mechanism of diplomacy, designed to ensure, by means of alliances or competitive territorial acquisition or armaments, that no one state is strong enough to override the interests, or threaten the existence, of other states.

For six centuries, up to and including the *folie à deux* of the Cold War, the idea has had good and bad consequences—sometimes, as in the so-called Alliance System at the turn of the 20th century which led directly to the First World War (1914-18), it has itself had a destabilising effect.

The opportunities for foreign policies based on more or less illusory conceptions of a Balance of Power on a global scale remain in the 21st century, with consequences that are as uncertain as ever—including, as Alison Brand recognises, balances involving not only governments but also non-governmental holders of ultimate global social, cultural, and economic power.

— **Inning**. In baseball, the batting side has an 'inning'. In cricket, the batting side has an 'innings'. They are periods of play in which the batting side seeks to score as many 'runs' as possible.

— **Approach Direct**. Echo, perhaps, of W. Shakespeare, *As You Like It*, V. iv. The clown Touchstone—talking what seems, but only seems, to be nonsense—explains to Jaques the seven 'degrees of the lie', of which the sixth is the 'lie with circumstances' and the seventh is 'the lie direct'.

— **Left-fieldism**. 'Left-field' is a distant part of the playing field in baseball—and so metaphorically, and vaguely pejoratively, an activity or attitude only distantly related to the 'mainstream'.

— **Gulag**. Term applied to penal colonies and concentration camps in Soviet Russia. The word is derived from the Russian *Glavnoe Upravlenie Lagerei* (General Administration of Camps). The word entered general consciousness in the West through the publication (1973) of *The Gulag Archepelago*, a translation of a work by by A. Solzhenitsyn (born 1918) (Nobel Prize for Literature, 1970).

— **My peers are my law**. Abe Green is referring to a distotrtion of the idea reflected in (but not originating in) Article 39 of *Magna Carta*.—an *ad hoc* social contract first concluded (in Latin) in 1215 (and re-affirmed on several later occasions) between the English king and members of the then ruling class.

> *Nullus liber homo capiatur, vel imprisonetur, aut disseisiatur, aut utlagetur,*
> *aut exuletur, aut aliquo modo destruatur, nec super cum ibimus, nec super cum*
> *mittemus, nisi per legale judicium parium suorum vel per legem terre.*
>
> 'No freemen shall be taken or imprisoned or disseised or exiled or in any
> way destroyed, nor will we go upon him nor send upon him, except by the

lawful judgment of his peers [*per legale judicium parium suorum*] or by the law of the land.' (This is one among many differing traditional translations of the text.)

The distortion lies in supposing that the judgment of one's peers ('peer-group pressure') is the same thing as the law of the land.

— **League of Nations**. An ambiguous international system that failed in its main aim. (See I.18).

A league of states formed after the First World War under a Covenant contained in the treaty of peace with Germany (Treaty of Versailles, 1919). Its essential purpose was to communalise certain aspects of inter-state relations, including the most intractable aspect—the tendency of governments to involve their peoples in murderous wars, brought about by incompetence, infantilism, greed, and other forms of emotional immaturity.

The system was dominated by the so-called Great Powers. The United States chose not to become a member of the League. Soviet Russia was not an original member, but became a member in 1934. Germany and Japan were original members, but withdrew from membership in 1933.

— **General and Complete Disarmament**. An ideal that declined into an illusion.

'The maintenance of general peace and a possible reduction of the excessive armaments which weigh down upon all nations present themselves, in the actual present situation of the world, as the ideal toward which should tend the efforts of all governments . . .

'The ever-increasing financial expense touches public prosperity at its very source; the intellectual and physical powers of the people, labour and capital, are, in a great measure, turned aside from their natural functions and consumed unproductively. Hundreds of millions are used in acquiring fearful engines of destruction, which, today considered as the highest triumph of science, are destined tomorrow to lose all their value because of some new discovery in this sphere . . . Economic crises, due in great part to the existence of excessive armaments, and the constant dangers which result from this accumulation of war material, makes of the armed peace of today an overwhelming burden which it is more and more difficult for the people to bear. It therefore seems evident that, if this state of affairs continues, it will inevitably lead to that very cataclysm which we are trying to avoid, and the horrors of which are fearful to human thought.'

Proposal of the Russian Government for a general conference on peace and disarmament (12 August 1898).

Russia (including Soviet Russia) continued to propose what came to be called 'general and complete disarmament'—a proposal that was overwhelmed by events in the 1930's, but was taken up again after World War Two, under the auspices of the United Nations. It remains unrealised and, perhaps, is not now even a generally accepted ideal.

— **Partition of Palestine.** An unsuccessful judgment of Solomon.

Palestine is a territory which has been the subject of contention for a long time (see ch. 12 above, under 'ancient Israel'). In 1922 a League of Nations Mandate (a form of supervisory trusteeship) was assigned to the United Kingdom, the British Government having committed itself to a policy of favouring the establishment in Palestine of a 'national home for the Jewish people'.

> 'His Majesty's Government view with favour the establishment in Palestine of a national home for the Jewish people, and will use their best endeavours to facilitate the achievement of this object, it being clearly understood that nothing shall be done which may prejudice the civil and religious rights of existing non-Jewish communities in Palestine, or the rights and political status enjoyed by Jews in any other country.'
> (Letter from the British Foreign Secretary, A. Balfour, to Lord Rothschild, President of the Zionist Federation (2 November 1917)—commonly referred to as 'the Balfour Declaration'.)
> (On Balfour, see ch.12 above, under 'theism/desim'.)

On 29 November 1947 the UN General Assembly approved, by UNGA Res. 181(II), a Plan of Partition with Economic Union for Palestine—to create an Arab state and a Jewish state, with a Special International Regime for the City of Jerusalem.

This was not accepted as a satisfactory settlement by representatives of the Arab population and neighbouring Arab countries. The state of Israel was proclaimed on 14 May 1948.

An agenda item with the title 'the situation in the Middle East, including the Palestinian question' remains on the agenda of the Security Council to this day.

— **Havana Charter.** An economic revolution that fell at the first fence.

As part of a burst of world-remaking energy at the end of the Second World War, a document was agreed that was designed to reorganise the global economy. A UN Conference on Trade and Employment adopted a Charter (Havana, 24 March 1948) establishing an International Trade Organization, and including provisions (Ch.IV) on the global system of 'free trade' and provisions (Ch.VI) which would have created a system of intergovernmental 'commodity control agreements' to regulate trade in primary products.

The United States decided not to ratify the Charter which, accordingly, did not enter into force. Instead, the Chapter IV provisions were extracted to form (on a provisional basis that lasted for almost forty years) the GATT (General Agreement on Tariffs and Trade). The Chapter VI provisions were distantly reflected in product-by-product 'commodity councils' which were established piecemeal in subsequent years.

A World Trade Organisation was finally established in 1995.

— **Atoms for Peace.** A bright idea that met a dim reality.

In 1953 US President D. Eisenhower proposed an initiative designed to reduce the impact of nuclear weapons. He proposed the establishment of an International Atomic Energy Agency to redirect the use of nuclear power away from military uses towards peaceful uses.

'The more important responsibility of this atomic energy agency would be to devise methods whereby this fissionable material would be allocated to serve the peaceful pursuits of mankind. Experts would be mobilized to apply atomic energy to the needs of agriculture, medicine, and other peaceful activities. A special purpose would be to provide abundant electrical energy in the power-starved areas of the world. Thus the contributing Powers would be dedicating some of their strength to serve the needs rather than the fears of mankind.'

An IAEA was established in 1957 as a UN Specialised Agency. The so-called Cold War had supervened in the meantime.

— **Nuclear Non-proliferation.** A Treaty on the Non-Proliferation of Nuclear Weapons was concluded in 1968.

'Each nuclear-weapon State Party to the Treaty undertakes not to transfer to any recipient whatsoever nuclear weapons or other nuclear explosive devices or control over such weapons or explosive devices directly, or indirectly; and not in any way to assist, encourage, or induce any non-nuclear-weapon State to manufacture or otherwise acquire nuclear weapons or other nuclear explosive devices, or control over such weapons or explosive devices.' (Article I)

'Each of the Parties to the Treaty undertakes to pursue negotiations in good faith on effective measures relating to cessation of the nuclear arms race at an early date and to nuclear disarmament, and on a treaty on general and complete disarmament under strict and effective international control.' (Article VI: see above, under 'general and complete disarmament').

— **Oslo Accords.** Hope springs from time to time, and (hopefully) eternally.

'The Government of the State of Israel and the Palestinian team representing the Palestinian people agree that it is time to put an end to decades of confrontation and conflict, recognize their mutual legitimate and political rights, and strive to live in peaceful coexistence and mutual dignity and security to achieve a just, lasting and comprehensive peace settlement and historic reconciliation through the agreed political process. Accordingly, the two sides agree to the following principles.'

Declaration by Israel and the Palestine Liberation Organization of Agreed Principles for an Agreed Framework for the Interim Period, concluded in Oslo, 13 September 1993. See further above, under 'partition of Palestine'.

'Hope springs eternal in the human breast: / Man never Is [blest], but always To be blest:' A. Pope (I.22), *An Essay on Man*, ep. I.

— **United Nations Organization**. A necessary idea, undone by an unnecessary reality, waiting to be re-imagined.

The founders of the UN had learned lessons from the fate of the League of Nations (see above). Re-founders of the UN might learn lessons from the fate of the UN.

The Security Council was given a more powerful capability than the Council of the League, but still retaining a lesson from the history of the 19th century, in which the exceptional responsibility of a pentarchy (five Great Powers) was recognised as offering the best chance of ensuring the orderly development of a dynamic and dangerous international society—hence the five Permanent Members of the Security Council.

However, the Cold War, and other perennial forms of addictive or deranged behaviour on the part of governments, supervened.

— **European Union**. See I.17. Alison is no doubt fully aware that her suggestion of adding the EU to the litany of international missed opportunities is controversial, especially if it is the suggestion of a British Government official.

She has in mind, no doubt, the counter-factual (might-have-been) picture of a daring innovation in the history of relations between states—a system which might have integrated the best of Europe, past and present, into a new kind of world power, a power whose purpose would be not merely self-aggrandizement or self-protection, but a co-operative enterprise with other leading world powers seeking to make a better world.

Instead, the EU probably seems to Alison to be primarily a system for the haphazard aggregating of the national interests, still fiercely competing, of the member states, acting through institutional systems which mimic national institutional systems—often reproducing the worst aspects of national institutional systems.

Alison—and probably even the British Government—would be bound to see that the EU has not be able to actualise its potentiality as a new kind of Great Power—and seems unlikely to be able to do so in the foreseeable future.

— **Firm-like names**. For example, it seems that MI6 (see I.13) is sometimes referred to as 'the Firm' and the US Central Intelligence Agency is sometimes referred to as 'the Company'. In German, *die Firma*.

— **Langley, Virginia**. Location of the US Central Intelligence Agency, close to Washington DC.

— **Eureka!** In ancient Greek, 'I have found it'. Said to have been uttered by Archimedes of Syracuse when he discovered the principle of what came to be called the 'mass' of matter (*in casu*, the relative masses of gold and silver).

— **USG**. United States Government.

— **Magic Flute.** See I.2.
— **The Met.** The Metropolitan Opera House in New York City.

CHAPTER 15. *North Norfolk.*

— **Norfolk.** A county in East Anglia (I.14), eastern England. In the kingdom of the East Angles, Norfolk was the land of the 'north folk', as Suffolk (I.14) was the land of the 'south folk'. Among those who were born in Norfolk are Horatio Nelson (I.4), Tom Paine (I.20), Robert Walpole (see ch. 14 above, under 'secretary of state'), and William Godwin (see Appendix 6 below).
— **Two last wars.** Greg no doubt has in mind the First World War (1914-1918) and the Second World War (1939-45).
— *Coup de grâce.* In French (and English), 'a blow of grace or kindness [intended to kill someone immediately, to spare them from a lingering death]'.
— **Ghost of post-European civilisation stalking the world.** Greg will have in mind the opening words of K. Marx and F. Engels, *The Communist Manifesto* (1848): 'A spectre is haunting Europe—the spectre of communism. [*Ein Gespenst geht um in Europa—das Gespenst des Kommunismus.*] All the powers of old Europe have entered into a holy alliance to exorcise this spectre: Pope and Tsar, Metternich and Guizot, French Radicals and German police-spies.'

He is, perhaps, referring aphoristically to the fact that the United States of America, starting out in life as a Europe-in-exile, took on its own nature—specific, complex, evolving—always reminiscent of Europe in some ways, but notably alien in other ways (see further below). In the 20th century, particular aspects of post-European Americanism proved to be exceptionally exportable to other countries and now, seemingly, readily globalisable.
— **All the world will be America.** Ironical echo of J. Locke (Appendix 3 below), *Two Treatises of Government* (1689), Second Treatise, §49.

'Thus in the beginning all the World was *America*, and more so than that is now; for no such thing as *Money* was any where known.'

Locke is referring to 'the in-land Parts of America' (§48) and making the point that, without money, trade is not possible. 'Find out something that hath the *Use and Value of Money* amongst his Neighbours, you shall see the same Man will begin presently to *enlarge* his *Possessions.*' (§49). (P. Laslett edition).
— **Perpetual feast of nectar'd fruits.** 'How charming is divine Philosophy! / Not harsh, and crabbed as dull fools suppose, / But musical as is Apollo's lute, / And a perpetual feast of nectar'd sweets, / Where no crude surfet raigns [surfeit reigns].' J. Milton (I.20), *Comus* (1634), first scene.

The idea of philosophy as a dialectical activity—monologue as dialogue—is as old as Heraclitus (see ch. 7 above, under 'all is struggle') and Plato (see above and below, *passim*). Philosophers argue with themselves interiorly, and with each other, contemporaneously and over time, often over long distances of time. (In ancient Greek, *dialektos*, 'conversation, argument'.)

Philosophy is also dialectical in a more substantial sense—since every assertion of an idea necessarily implies the possibility of its contradiction, and the possibility of an unlimited number of intermediate ideas. (On the dialectical method, see ch. 7 above, under '*Ich*'.)

Philosophy is a 'collison of minds' (W. Godwin), including a collision within each separate philosophising mind.

— **Wells-next-the-Sea**. A seaside town, and formerly a substantial port, in Norfolk—now, through no fault of its own, no longer situated next to the North Sea, or any other sea.

— **French cricket**. An informal game played, like cricket, with a bat and ball, but with a single batsman surrounded by fielders.

— **Oceanic feeling**. See ch. 11 above, under 'world ocean inside me'.

— **World Spirit**. For the German idealist philosopher G.W.F. Hegel (I.19 and Appendix 8 below), taking up a leading idea of Herder (Appendix 8 below), the universe has not only a material existence, but also a non-material or 'spiritual' existence—and human beings participate in this dual existential nature. The spiritual universe (the World Spirit—*Weltgeist*) has a history of its own development, reflected in the progressive development of the spiritual, especially mental, aspect of human beings, through the course of history—not least in what Hegel saw as the progressive development of philosophy, religion, and art.

— **March of God in the world**. Hegel's interpretation of human history, in the conventional sense of the word 'history', includes an idea of the progressive development of social forms—both the forms of socialised morality and the forms of social organisation.

If the word 'God' is used to describe the spiritual totality (the World Spirit—see above), then the history of the development of social forms can be seen as a reflection of the history of God's presence in the human world—'the march of God in the world' (*der Gang Gottes in der Welt*). (It is not easy to say how this special Hegelian use of the word 'God' is related to religious uses of the word—or, indeed, to its use by the ancient Greek philosophers.)

In his *Philosophy of Right* (1821), Hegel uses the phrase to describe the development of the advanced (and, perhaps, ultimate) form of social organisation which he calls 'the state' (*der Staat*). (The word *Right*, in the title of Hegel's work, reflects awkwardly the fact that the word *Recht* in the German title refers to both *law* and *morality*.)

> 'The state in and by itself is the ethical whole, the actualization of freedom; and it is an absolute end of reason that freedom should be actual. The state is mind on earth and consciously realizing itself there . . . The march of God

in the world, that is what the state is. The basis of the state is the power of reason actualizing itself as will.'
Addition to §258. (tr., T.Knox).

This is one of the notorious Hegelian passages which—appearing to offer a philosophical basis for the monopoly of the absolute power of the 'state'—came to be seen as prophetic (if not worse) of the totalitarianism of the German Third Reich (1933-45).

In other words, such writing suffered an after-life analogous both to the music-dramas of R. Wagner (see ch. 7 above, under '*Wahn!*'), with their Nordic-Germanic mythologizing, and to the seemingly idolised conception of 'power', and the apparently (but only apparently) pervasive nihilism, in the writings of F. Nietzsche (see ch. 4 above, under 'will to know, will to power', and *passim*).

For an analysis of the German constitutional paradigm of 'state' (and the French and British paradigms of 'nation' and 'society'), see Ph. Allott, 'The crisis of European constitutionalism. Reflections on a half-revolution,' in Ph. Allott, *The Health of Nations*, ch. 7. This conflict of paradigms is at the root of some of the constitutional problems of the European Union.

— **Call no man happy**. 'Call no man happy until he is dead.'

Saying attributed to Solon (I.19). As discussed, in particular, by Aristotle, *Nicomachean Ethics*, I.10, and by Montaigne (I.11, I.21), *Essays*, Bk.I, Essay XIX, the saying has (at least) three possible meanings—(1) it is not possible to be happy in this life-time; (2) given the vagaries of life, one cannot say that one has had a happy life until it is finished; (3) one is only really happy after death (assuming that the next life is (optimistically) imagined as a wholly good experience).

> 'Give ear, then, as they say, to a very fine story, which you, I suppose, will consider fiction, but I consider fact . . . Now in the days of Cronus there was this law about mankind, which from then till now has prevailed among the gods, that the man who has led a godly and righteous life departs after death to the Isles of the Blessed and there lives in all happiness exempt from ill, but the godless and unrighteous man departs to the prison of vengeance and punishment which they call Tartarus . . . Death, in my opinion, is nothing else but the separation from each other of two things, soul and body, and when they are separated from one another, each of them retains pretty much the same condition as when the man was alive, the body retaining its own nature, with all the marks of treatment or experience plainly visible.'
> Plato, *Gorgias*, 523a, 524b (Socrates speaking) (tr., W. Woodhead).

(When Socrates says that things of this kind are 'fact', we are inclined to understand him to mean that they should be taken seriously as inspirations to deeper thinking about matters which are beyond ordinary forms of knowledge.)

— **Angry ape that made the angels weep**. '. . . man, proud man, / Drest in a little brief authority, / Most ignorant of what he's most assur'd, / His glassy essence, like an angry ape, / Plays such fantastic tricks before high heaven / As make the angels weep . . .' W. Shakespeare, *Measure for Measure*, II, ii. (Isabella speaking).

— **Public mind**. See I.19. The phrase came into general use in the 18ᵗʰ century, referring to something close to that which would also be reflected, somewhat later, in the term 'public opinion'—a key term in the explanation of 'liberal democracy'.

   In the writings of the social idealist philosopher Ph. Allott (I.5, I.19), it is used in a different sense—to postulate a real equivalent at the social level to the private mind of the individual human being—with consciousness flowing freely in both directions between the two minds. The self-constituting of a society takes place in the interaction between the public mind of society and the private minds of its citizens. See further in ch. 11 above, under 'the self and the other'.

— **Evolution by natural selection**. Refers especially to the theory proposed in C. Darwin (Appendix 7 below), *On the Origin of Species by Means of Natural Selection, or The Preservation of Favoured Races in the Struggle for Life* (1859). The inter-generational survival of a given species of animal or plant in a given habitat is determined by competition between species, in such a way that it seems as if that species had been 'selected' (? by Nature) as the best adapted to survive in that habitat.

   Given that the *human* species has, to a considerable extent, taken control over its habitat (the natural world), it is uncertain to what extent it remains subject to the principle of evolution by natural selection. There is reason to suppose that the future of the human species is being determined by *very unnatural* selection, and the species may be transforming itself into an *unfavoured race*.

— **We think, therefore** . . . A socialising of the saying of Descartes (Appendix 8 below): 'I think, therefore I am.'

— **Individual self-consciousness**. It is difficult now to appreciate adequately the *originality* of the way in which Plato, especially in the *Republic* but also more generally, proceeds from the individual human being—and the consciousness of the private mind—to construct his ideal structures of human and social well-being.

   This human *atomism*—Democritus (c.460-c.370), with his atomic-materialist explanation of nature, was of the generation before Plato's—is at the root of those religious traditions that rest upon the fundamental responsibility of the human individual, and on those forms of social philosophy (not least 'liberal democracy') that construct society in an *ascending* direction—from the nature and interest of the human individual to the nature and interests of human society—rather than in a *descending* direction, from the power of the ruler to the subjection of the ruled.

— **To disprove the claim of philosophy to find the truth.** David Hume's 'scepticism' spread the perverse (but, to some, reassuring) idea that the perennial philosophical tradition had been a misguided effort to find 'the truth' And it prepared the way for those, especially in the 20th century, who would make the (to some, seductive) claim that philosophy in the perennial form had no further use. See further in Appendix 4 below.

— **America the unphilosophical nation**. What can Greg Seare possibly mean by this? He is, perhaps, recalling the notable prominence of *religion* and *pragmatism* within the American mind.

Although philosophy can play, and often has played, a part in the self-understanding and the presentation of particular religions, *philosophy* in the tradition inherited from ancient Greece is designed to be distinct from other dominant forms of thought, especially *religion* and *natural science*. Philosophy in that tradition—seen as the mind thinking about its own activity—must concern itself with such other forms of thought, such as religion and natural science, without seeing itself as merely an aspect of them.

Greg may be taking the view that pragmatism (see ch. 2 above, under 'pragmatist'), at least in its American form, is, on the contrary, an intrinsically *social* mental activity, designed to develop socially useful ideas, at a more or less abstract level, rather than to think *universally* about the activity of the mind. Generalised thinking is then merely an adjunct, secondary, complementary activity, in relation to religion and social thought generally.

W. James, cool observer of religion and philosophy (see ch. 5 above, under 'Henry's brother William'; and ch. 11 above, under 'I accept the universe'), said:

'When all is said and done, it was English and Scotch writers, and not Kant, who introduced "the critical method" into philosophy, the one method fitted to make philosophy a study worthy of serious men. For what seriousness can possibly remain in debating philosophic propositions that will never make an appreciable difference to us in action?' W. James, *Varieties of Religious Experience* (The Gifford Lectures) (1902), lecture 18.

He goes on to say that C.S. Peirce 'has rendered thought a service by disentangling from the particulars of its application the principle by which these men [the British philosophers] were instinctively guided, and by giving it out as a fundamental and giving to it a Greek name. He calls it the principle of *pragmatism* . . .'

James quotes Peirce on the meaning of this principle.

'Beliefs, in short, are rules for action; and the whole function of thinking is but one step in the production of active habits. If there were any part of a thought that made no difference in the thought's practical consequences, then that part would be no proper element of thought's significance. To develop a thought's meaning we need therefore only determine what conduct it is fitted to produce, that conduct is for us its sole significance.' (From an article by Peirce, 'How to make our ideas clear', in *Popular Science Monthly*, Jan. 1878.)

This profound misunderstanding of British philosophy (and, indeed, British-influenced Continental European philosophy) reflects and embodies a great parting-of-the-ways between the American and the European minds, with consequences that are now of global significance, possibly affecting the whole future of the human species.

Pragmatism, as a socialised after-life of philosophy, shares its place with socialised religion in the American mind. The Puritan 17th-century colonisers established small-scale theocracies, controlling the behaviour of the citizens forcibly in the name of religious beliefs.

A. de Tocqueville (1805-59), clairvoyant observer of the new Republic, its past and its future, identified two circumstances, in particular, that distinguished contemporary America from post-revolutionary France.

> 'It must never be forgotten that religion gave birth to Anglo-American
> society. In the United States, religion is therefore mingled with all the habits
> of the nation and all the feelings of patriotism, whence it derives a peculiar
> force . . . The second circumstance . . . is that the social condition and the
> Constitution of the Americans are democratic, but they have not had a
> democratic revolution. They arrived on the soil they occupy in nearly the
> condition in which we see them at the present day . . .' A. de Tocqueville,
> *Democracy in America* (1835-40), Pt. 2, ch. 1.

(We might recall a deeply English saying attributed to Lord Melbourne (1779-1848), sometime British Prime Minister and sometime tutor in things political to the young Queen Victoria, after he had listened to a sermon on the vices of the age: 'Things are coming to a pretty pass when religion is allowed to invade a gentleman's private life.')

By a fatal chain-reaction, socialised pragmatism leads to human naturalism, and then to laissez-faire scientism.

Human naturalism is a form of human materialism. It treats human phenomena—psychic and social—as essentially natural, and hence capable of being understood and manipulated by methods akin to those of the natural sciences and technology. It reflects an unappeasable longing for certainty and clarity about the painful chaos of human phenomena.

Laissez-faire scientism treats the intensely socialised pursuit of the natural sciences, and their attendant technology, as intrinsically progressive and self-justifying, and self-regulating. It reflects a tragic loss of faith in the creative and regulatory potentiality of any other way of thinking or being.

Both human naturalism and laissez-faire scientism are also powerful presences in the American mind.

— **Americans, a chosen people. Promised land.** The public mind of the United States of America, and the private minds of its citizens, seem to contain a conflicting complex of ideas about their own identity whose roots also seem to lie in the states of mind of some of the original settlers of the land.

'Thus the Puritan was made up of two different men, the one all self-abasement, penitence, gratitude, passion; the other proud, calm, inflexible, sagacious.'

Th. Macaulay (1800-59), in his essay on John Milton (*Edinburgh Review*, 1825). He refers to the Puritans as 'the most remarkable group of men, perhaps, which the world has ever produced'. The word 'perhaps' invites discussion.

Macaulay, historian and public servant, was an undergraduate at Trinity College, Cambridge, and was elected to a Fellowship in 1824, which he left to practise as a barrister.

In assessing the general quality of his intellectual judgment, we may be well advised to note: (a) that he liked reading Plato's dialogues, not for their ideas but for their literary style, rhetoric, and humour; (b) that he faintly praised Cicero ('at the head of the minds of the second order'); (c) that he said of Miss Austen's novels: 'there are in the world no compositions which approach nearer to perfection'; and (d) that he was a liberal *avant la lettre*.

See *The Life and Letters of Lord Macaulay* (1876) by G.O. Trevelyan, Macaulay's nephew (his uncle did not marry) and father of the historian G.M.Trevelyan (Master of Trinity College, 1940-51).

There is in the American public mind the idea of the Americans as a chosen people, the 'chosen vessel' of human redemption. (The phrase is taken from the (Christian) New Testament, *Acts of the Apostles*, 9.15.) And there is the idea of the new society as a 'city on a hill', a promised land. (The phrase is taken from the (Christian) New Testament, *Matthew*, 5.14.)

An 18th-century observer from France asked: What is an American?

'The American is a new man, who acts upon new principles; he must therefore entertain new ideas and form new opinions.'

'Urged by a variety of motives here they [Europeans] came. Every thing has tended to regenerate them. New laws, a new mode of living, a new social system. Here they are become men.'

T. de Crèvecoeur, *Letters from an American Farmer* (1782), Letter III.

(He had settled in America, and had become a British subject and a farmer in New York Colony shortly before Independence.)

The American idea of 'American' as a permanently self-reforming identity—itself a distinctly unEuropean idea—seems to be endemic. O. W. Holmes (1841-1935), Justice of the US Supreme Court, said that the US Constitution 'is an experiment, as all life is an experiment' (in his dissenting opinion in the *Abrams* case, 1919).

Woodrow Wilson said that the Supreme Court is 'a kind of Constitutional Assembly in continuous session'.

There is an irony in these opinions. It is also possible to see the United States as remarkably unchanged over the centuries, by comparison with the permanent revolutionary condition of European countries—a country still ruled by an 18th-century constitution (itself a product of the English 17th century) and by an 18th-century Enlightenment optimism about social progess, against a background of 17th-century moral earnestness.

— **Social control.** A term particularly associated with the name of the American sociologist E. Ross (1866-1951), who uses the term in an article in the first volume of the *Journal of American Sociology* (1896) and in his influential book *Social Control* (1901).

He says that social order is not a natural phenomenon, but is the product of the control of the individual by society—'that ascendancy over the aims and acts of the individual which is exercised on behalf of the group'. It is the job of sociology to study how that control is exercised, and how it might be exercised to improve society. 'Our first duty, therefore, is to explore the field of employment of rewards and punishment as a means of social control.'

American sociologists were impressed by the work of the English social philosopher H. Spencer (see ch. 13 above, under 'survival of the unfittest'). But, for the Americans, what Spencer had called 'social dynamics' is not a natural process, but the product of what Ross calls 'social process', specific social activities which can be investigated and manipulated.

American sociology (national and international!) seems to contain both a *fatalistic realism*—social forces are ultimately beyond control—and a *behaviourist functionalism*—society is always improvable by appropriate social action.

In the words of a first leader in the field—

> 'The great stream of time and earthly things will sweep on just the same in spite of us. It bears with it now all the errors and follies of the past, the wreckage of all the philosophies, the fragments of all the civilizations, the wisdom of all the abandoned ethical systems, the debris of all institutions, and the penalties of all the mistakes. It is only in imagination that we stand by and look at and criticize it and plan to change it . . . That is why it is the greatest folly of which a man can be capable, to sit down with a slate and pencil to plan out a new social world.' W.G. Sumner, 'The absurd attempt to make the world over [to change the world fundamentally]' (1894), reprinted in *War and Other Essays* (1913).

In the first decades of the 20th century, ideas connected with the idea of 'social control' inspired (in the future President W. Wilson, among others) a kind of virulent *conservative socialism*, aiming to improve American society in fundamental ways by aggressive social action, pragmatic and behaviourist in character.

Later, *behaviourism*, a largely American development, became another possible route for social control of the private mind.

'. . . the goal of psychological study is the ascertaining of such data and laws that, given the stimulus, psychology can predict what the response will be; or, on the other hand, given the response, it can specify the nature of the effective stimulus.' J. Watson, *Psychology from the Standpoint of the Behaviorist* (1919).

For the same writer, leader in the field of behaviourism, the function of psychology is '(1) to predict human activity with reasonable certainty, and (2) . . . formulation of laws and principles whereby man's actions can be controlled by organized society.'

For advanced forms of social control, through mass consciousness and 'the market', see ch. 6 above, under 'mother-father sign/signal', and ch.19 below, under 'democracy-capitalism'.

— **Alone in a crowd**. The echo is of an influential book *The Lonely Crowd. A Study of the Changing American Character* (1950) by D. Riesman, with N. Glazer and R. Denney. Together with W. Whyte, *The Organization Man* (1956) and V. Packard, *The Hidden Persuaders* (1957), it drew to general public attention what seemed to be a profound change in American consciousness—a radical *alienation of personal consciousness*, as it comes to be a mere residual effect of mind-forming social phenomena—leading to a population of 'other-directed' citizens (with their thinking and behaviour determined by forces external to their private minds).

The concept of 'alienation' as the loss of personal identity and integrity—from the Latin *alienus* ('the property of another')—had been a central idea of both J.-J. Rousseau and K. Marx. For them, respectively, it was the product of the corrupting effect of corrupt society or of the slavery of industrial capitalism.

But, as noted in several places above and below, the socialising of consciousness had been a constituent element in the making of the American mind from its earliest days. A remarkable feature of that process is the socialising of the Freudian mind-philosophy in America.

In his *Freud: The Mind of the Moralist* (1959; 3rd ed. 1979), ch. 2, P. Rieff discusses *Human Nature and Conduct* (1921) by J. Dewey (see ch. 2 above, under 'pragmatist') and, in particular, his treatment of Freud's *instinct* theory.

'Dewey rejects any such metabiological entity as that which Freud calls "instinct". There is no "separate psychic realm" or force, no "original individual consciousness", Dewey argues, but only a neural potentiality, without effect until it becomes an element in social habits . . . Thus Dewey located in society the critical principle that Freud assigns to human nature, and this divergence accounts for a difference of ethical vision.'

'The idea of the unconscious which forms the cornerstone for Freud's historical conception of sickness, must be got out of the way before the situational or contextual control of sickness, given its most subtle formulation by Dewey and now dominant, in adulterated form, in American social and individual psychology, can prevail.'

Rieff says that Dewey's book is 'the seminal work of American social psychology and still the most widely read book in the field'.

A challenging idea (suggested by a leading American theorist of psychology) is that the socialised view of the practical functioning of the mind might have relevance to the interaction of societies (including so-called 'states'), at least the interaction of what we are here calling the public minds of societies. See the last chapter ('Towards a Psychiatry of Peoples') in H. S. Sullivan, The Interpersonal Theory of Psychiatry (1953).

The divided American mind may explain the strange failure of post-Marxian socialism to take root in America, and also the puzzling mixture of *diffuse idealism* and *crude realism* in American attitudes to international society.

In the light of all the above, it may be that we can express in a few words Greg Seare's troubling diagnosis of the current state of the human condition, which he expresses here, and on other occasions.

Repressed idealism and default materialism are the hallmarks of the mind of American post-European civilisation. The troubling dichotomy of the American mind is liable to become the troubling dichotomy of the human mind.

— **Existing in-oneself.** In the idealist philosophy of Herder and Fichte and Hegel (see ch. 7 above, under '*Ich*'; ch. 11 above, under 'the self and the other'; and Appendix 8 below), the 'I' (personal identity) has various aspects—including the I-in-itself, the I-for-itself, and the I-for-others, reflecting the way in which personal identity is constructed both within individual consciousness and in relation to the consciousness of other people and things.

Greg sees here the danger that, as personal identity comes to be ever more socially determined, a human being's primary source of identity will wither away.

— **Omega point.** *Omega* ('big-o'—as opposed to *omicron* or 'small-o') is the last letter of the Greek alphabet. The French philosopher and palaeontologist P. Teilhard de Chardin (1881-1955) proposed the term *Omega-point* to refer to what he postulated as the ultimate integration of the universe seen as *a system of consciousness.*

'The consciousness of each of us is evolution looking at itself and reflecting upon itself . . . Step by step, from the early earth onwards, we have followed *going upwards* the successive advances of consciousness in matter undergoing organisation. Having reached the peak, we can now turn round and, *looking downwards*, take in the pattern of the whole . . .

'Our habit is to divide up our human world into compartments of different sorts of "realities": natural and artificial, physical and moral, organic and juridical, for instance. In a space-time, legitimately and perforce extended to include the movements of the mind within us, the frontiers between these pairs of opposites tend to vanish . . . .

'Man is not the centre of the universe as once we thought in our simplicity, but something much more wonderful—the arrow pointing the way to the final unification of the world in terms of life . . .

'Man discovers that *he is nothing else than evolution become conscious of itself,* to borrow Julian Huxley's striking expression . . .

'The social phenomenon is the culmination and not the attenuation of the biological phenomenon.'

Extracts from *The Phenomenon of Man* (1955), ch.3. (tr., B. Wall).

(The biologist Julian Huxley (1887-1975) was one of the three remarkable grandsons—with the writer Aldous Huxley (1894-1963) and the Nobel Prize-winning physiologist Andrew Huxley (born 1917; Master of Trinity College, Cambridge, 1984-90)—of the remarkable T.H. Huxley (see ch. 6 above, under 'humanism', and Appendix 7 below).

— **Heinrich Biber**. German composer (1644-1704), especially for the violin. Biber uses *scordatura* (in Italian, 'untuning': tuning the strings of the violin out of their normal tuning) to produce unusual sound effects.

— **Sea-borne Arion**. In ancient Greek mythology, Arion, a poet and musician, was captured by pirates. After singing a song to Apollo, he escaped from the pirate ship on the back of a dolphin.

'Hung on our driving boat, I saw your brother, / Most provident in peril, bind himself,—/ Courage and hope both teaching him the practice,—/ To a strong mast that liv'd upon the sea; / Where, like Arion on the dolphin's back, / I saw him hold acquaintance with the waves / So long as I could see.'

W. Shakespeare, *Twelfth-Night; or What You Will*, I. ii (a sea-captain speaking—to Viola, who hopes that her brother Sebastian has not been drowned; he has not).

Greg will certainly also have called to mind another image from Shakespeare.

'Thou rememberest / Since once I sat upon a promontory, / And heard a mermaid on a dolphin's back / Uttering such dulcet and harmonious breath / That the rude sea grew civil at her song / And certain stars shot madly from their spheres, / To hear the sea-maid's music.' *A Midsummer-Night's Dream,* II. i. (Oberon, speaking to Puck).

And Greg will certainly hear an echo in his mind of the delightful words of
Proteus (one of the eponymous gentlemen) in Shakespeare's *Two Gentlemen of Verona*
(III. ii), on the connection between poetry and music and love.

'Say that upon the altar of her beauty / You sacrifice your tears, your sighs,
your heart. / Write till your ink be dry, and with your tears / Moist it again,
and frame some feeling line / That may discover such integrity: / For Orpheus'
lute was strung with poets' sinews, / Whose golden touch could soften steel
and stones, / Make tigers tame and hugh leviathans / Forsake unsounded
deeps to dance on sands.'

— **Baroque sonata**. The term 'baroque' has been borrowed from architecture to refer
to music which is exceptionally complex and free in form and highly decorated. It
is sometimes used inappropriately to refer to the music of J.S. Bach (1685-1750),
whose music is normally complex and formal and abstract.

In the 18th century, the Italian term *sonata* ('sounded') came to be applied to
relatively short pieces, usually in several movements, for one or two instruments.
Perhaps the violinist here is playing a sonata by D. Scarlatti (1685-1757) or by
C.P.E. Bach (1714-1788), one of J.S. Bach's sons.

— *Freudenmeister* **for** *Trauergeister*. (In German, 'joy-master for sadness-spirits').
Echo of lines in a chorale by J.S.Bach (text by J. Franck), *Jesu, meime Freude* (BWV
227).

*Weicht, ihr Trauergeister, / Denn mein Freudenmeister, / Jesus, tritt herein. / ...
Dennoch bleibst du auch im Leide, / Jesu, meine Freude.* ('Away, you sadness-
spirits, for my joy-master, Jesus, enters . . . you are always, Jesus, even in my
suffering, my joy.')

— **Amechanic trance**. From the Greek *amechanos*, 'physically helpless'. Compare the
word that Homer applies to the crafty, but accident-prone, Odysseus—*polymechanos*,
'resourceful'.

In the *Odyssey*, bk. XII, Odysseus' ship comes within range of the island of
the Sirens, half-woman and half-bird, whose singing puts passing sailors into an
amechanic trance. 'No seaman ever sailed his black ship past this spot without
listening to the sweet tones that flow from our lips, and none that listened has not
been delighted and gone on a wiser man.' (tr., E.V. Rieu).

Warned of the hazard by Circe, Odysseus has himself tied securely to the mast,
and the ears of the sailors filled with wax, and they are able to row safely past.

— **Unheard melody (children dancing to)**.

'For most of us, there is only the unattended / Moment, the moment in and
out of time, / The distraction fit, lost in a shaft of sunlight, / The wild thyme

unseen, or the winter lightning / Or the waterfall, or music heard so deeply / That it is not heard at all, but you are the music / While the music lasts.' T.S. Eliot, *Dry Salvages* (see ch. 7 above, under 'unprayable prayer').

'And the bird called, in response to / The unheard music hidden in the shrubbery, / And the unseen eyebeam crossed, for the roses / Had the look of flowers that are looked at.' T.S. Eliot, *Burnt Norton* (see ch. 9 above, under 'still point').

'Heard melodies are sweet, but those unheard / Are sweeter, therefore, ye soft pipes, play on; / Not to the sensual ear, but, more endear'd, / Pipe to the spirit ditties of no tone . . .' J. Keats (I.17), *Ode on a Grecian Urn* (the poet is describing the scene depicted on an ancient Greek urn).

— **Prison of the children's bodies.** Plato speaks of 'that prison house which now we are encompassed withal, and call a body, fast bound therein as an oyster in its shell.' *Phaedrus*, 250c (tr., R. Hackforth). The words come at the beginning of a highly charged analysis of the effect of physical beauty on the emotions, the mind, and the soul. The experience of beauty is able to free us temporarily by reminding us of the beautiful world we knew before our soul entered the prison of the body. From physical beauty we can ascend through higher forms to its ultimate and real source.

The philosopher-emperor Marcus Aurelius describes the human being as 'a little soul carrying a corpse'. The painter-sculptor-poet Michelangelo speaks of the human body as the *carcer terreno* ('earthly prison').

— **Hidden God.** See I.19.

— ***Holde Geige!*** In German, 'enchanting violin'. Echo of *holde Flöte* ('enchanting flute') said by Tamino in Act I of Mozart's *Die Zauberflöte* (The Magic Flute) (I.2).

> *Wie stark ist nicht dein Zauberton/ Weil, holder Flöte, durch dein Spielen / selbst wilde Tiere Freude fühlen* . . . ('How strong is your magic sound, enchanting flute, for your playing makes even wild animals feel joy'.)

Tamino, the hero, is given a flute to protect him on his journey to initiation in the Temple of Wisdom. The flute charms some otherwise threatening animals into dancing harmlessly. The bird-catcher Papageno, who accompanies him on the first part of his journey, is given a set of tubular bells which charm the evil Monastatos and his minions into dancing harmlessly, when he had seemed to be threatening the virtue of Tamino's potential bride, Pamina.

Despite the title of the opera (more strictly, *Singspiel*—'a play with singing'), these are incidental events, and (as in Weber's *Oberon*) the opera does not take effect as a celebration of the importance of music (compare: R. Wagner's *Meistersinger* or *Capriccio* by R. Strauss), at least 'music' in the conventional sense.

The second level of the Mozart opera (beneath the dream-like events and atmosphere) seems to be exploring different forms of external power over the human mind (religion, science, rationalism, spiritualism, love). The final priests' chorus celebrates the triumph of 'truth and beauty'. Could Mozart's *Zauberflöte* really be a *zauberisch* Idealist Manifesto?

At the third (unconscious) level, the opera seems to be a welter of unconscious archetypes, including elements, not only of the sophisticated religion of ancient Egypt, but of early mystical religion—such as the Orphic mysteries of ancient Greece—Orpheus charmed the Furies with his lyre (compare: Gluck's *Orfeo ed Euridice*). Such mystical religions were ritual explorations of the individual's power and impotence in relation to the natural forces of the universe.

Needless to say, Mozart need not have had such things explicitly present in his mind, or have discussed them explicitly with Schikaneder, the librettist of the opera. Creative artists of the highest order take from the deepest recesses of their mind something which flows, almost autonomously, through their hand on to the page or the canvas or the marble.

— ***Holde Kunst.*** In German, 'lovely art'. Echo of a beautiful *lied* (D547) by F. Schubert (I.7), *An die Musik* (To Music), words by F. von Schober.

Du holde Kunst, in wieviel grauen Stunden, / Wo mich des Lebens wilder Kreis umstrickt, /Hast du mein Herz zu warmer Lieb entzunden, /Hast mich in eine beßre Welt entrückt! 'You lovely art, in how many grey hours, caught up in life's wild embrace, have you ignited in my heart a warmer love, carried me away into a better world!'

From the earliest religions and from the very beginning of philosophy, the mysterious power of music has been recognised.

Transmitted through one of the senses into the mind, music does not directly produce images or ideas, and so bypasses the processes by which the mind otherwise works on the products of the senses, processes we have called 'thinking' and 'knowing', and which have been such central topics of philosophy—as reflected in so much of the Chapter 2 Appendices below.

Music does not present to the mind an idea of 'reality', other than the fact of the sound and its physical source—not even the idea of an imagined or illusory reality. And yet the mind may respond it to it in ways which are the same as, or analogous to, the ways in which it responds to the presentation to it of reality—that is to say, not only rationally and emotionally, but also in terms of moral and aesthetic values. Music is thinking without the anxiety of thinking.

Where does music go to, when it enters in the mind, and what does it do when it gets there? Could it be that music speaks the language of metaphysics?

'. . . education in music is most sovereign, because more than anything else rhythm and harmony find their way to the inmost soul and take strongest hold upon it, bringing with them and imparting grace.' Plato, *Republic*, III, 401d-e. (tr., P. Shorey).

'And harmony, which has motions akin to the revolutions of our souls, is not regarded by the intelligent votary of the Muses as given by them with a view to irrational pleasure, which is deemed to be the purpose of it in our day, but as meant to correct any discord which may have arisen in the courses of the soul, and to be our ally in bringing her into harmony and agreement with herself . . .' Plato, *Timaeus*, 47c. (tr., B. Jowett).

(There is a problem in reading Plato's various discussions of 'music'. The ancient Greek word *mousikos* means 'relating to the (nine) Muses' and can cover the other arts, especially poetry. The passages quoted here seem clearly to refer to 'music' in the modern sense.)

'Music, therefore, if regarded as an expression of the world, is in the highest degree a universal language, which is related indeed to the universality of concepts, much as these are related to particular things. Yet its universality is by no means that empty universality of abstraction, but quite of a different kind, and goes hand in hand with utter precision. In this respect it resembles geometrical figures and numbers, which are the universal forms of all possible objects of experience, and applicable to them all *a priori*, and yet are not abstract, but perceptible and utterly precise.

'. . . . For, as we have said, music is distinguished from all the other arts by the fact that it is not a copy of the phenomenon, or, more accurately, the adequate objectivity of the will [phenomena re-made by the mind], but is the direct copy of the will itself, and therefore represents the metaphysical of everything physical in the world, and the thing-in-itself of every phenomenon . . . .

'This relation may be very well expressed in the language of the schoolmen [medieval followers of Aristotle] by saying: concepts are the *universalia post rem* [universals derived by the mind from perception of the real world], but music gives the *universalia ante rem* [universals present in the mind before our perception of the real world] and the real world the *universalia in re* [universals present in the real world independently of the mind].'

A. Schopenhauer, *The World as Will and Idea*, III, §52. (tr., J. Berman).

Augustine (I.19), Platonist-become-Christian, recognised what he called the *occulta familiaritas* (hidden family relationship) between music and the soul, even if, when he became scrupulously religious later in life, he worried that he was tempted to take too much pleasure in music. Confessions, X.49.

Could it be that Greg has experienced—and has witnessed even in the cricket-playing children—a *conversion of the soul* through music?

'the influence that emanates from works of beauty may waft itself to eye or ear like a breeze that brings from wholesome places health, and so from earliest childhood guide them to likeness, to friendship, to harmony with beautiful reason.' Plato, *Republic* III, 401c.

'. . . there might be an art, an art of the speediest and most effective shifting or conversion of the soul, not an art of producing vision in it [the soul], but on the assumption that it possesses vision but does not rightly direct it and does not look where it should, an art of bringing this about.' Plato, *Republic*, VII, 518d.

Socrates is here discussing the great question of whether the mind-transforming experience of the 'parable of the cave' (*Republic*, VII, 514)—when we gradually discover for ourselves the true nature of 'reality'—could be brought about by a suitably designed system of education—a possibility which is of central interest to the world-changing ambitions of the Firm.

— **Universal harmony.** See ch. 7 above, under '*harmonia mundi*'. Plato learned the power and significance of music from Pythagoras, something which Pythagoras had evidently learned from hearing the music of ancient Egypt. He made the connection between music and mathematics: music produces *harmonia*, because sounds obey universal physical laws capable of being expressed mathematically.

It was then a short step to seeing that the whole earth, and the whole system of heavenly bodies, must obey laws capable of being expressed mathematically. And so to the next steps: that human beings must also, individually and socially, be participants in the order of nature—and hence that our highest purpose must be to produce *harmonia* in society and *harmonia* in the soul of the human individual—ideas which are the stem cells of the whole system of Plato and Platonism.

A more idiosyncratic corollary of such ideas is that the orderly system of the heavenly bodies, moving in their respective 'spheres', being a manifestation of the physics of musical order, must naturally produce its own kind of music—the 'music of the spheres'.

Plato presents this idea directly in the last book of the *Republic*. in the story of the warrior Er who was permitted to visit the places of the after-life and to see the structure of the heavens. He found that each of the eight spheres of the heavens produces a note 'and from all eight there was the concord of a single harmony'. *Republic*, X.617b.

'. . . music is the true idea of the cosmos.' F. Nietzsche, *Birth of Tragedy*, XXI.

It is remarkable that *mathematics* and *music* should be at the root of the deep structure of the world-transforming ideas of the ancient Greek mind, especially its philosophy, of which we are the direct heirs and beneficiaries. It is interesting to think how the human world would now be, if Pythagoras and Plato had not existed, or if nothing had survived of what they had thought.

— **Subunconscious mind.** The Freudian skeletal anatomy of the mind—conscious, subconscious, unconscious—all of them forming themselves in the course of a given person's life, seems to leave unidentified and unexplored an area of the mind which lies behind and beyond and under those areas.

This ultimate mental region is an aspect of the *physiology* of the mind—the built-in wiring of the mind, analogous to the built-in wiring of the brain—a sub-unconscious and pre-unconscious area of the mind, a primary area, deeper even than the unconscious mind—the unconscious mind being formed, for an individual person, by the interacting of the individual mind with the reality that it experiences. The unconscious mind is, therefore, a secondary phenomenon in relation to the *subunconscious,* the deepest-structural functioning of the mind.

It is this fundamental area of the mind which is a natural focus of *philosophy*, especially in the work of the philosophers considered in the Ch. 2 Appendices below. It is an area of the mind that must contain much that is biologically pre-programmed, common to all human minds. And so it is the area of the mind in which C. Jung might better have located the mysterious shared contents of human minds which he places in a puzzling 'collective unconscious' (I.20, under 'valley of the shadow').

The subunconscious mind—where the voice of the soul can be heard—also plays a major part in our appreciation of beauty, and, therefore, of art. See ch. 19 below, under 'soul embracing soul'.

— **Possible personal paradise**. 'Then wilt thou not be loath / To leave this Paradise, but shalt possess / A Paradise within thee, happier far.' J. Milton, *Paradise Lost*, XII.

Milton puts these reassuring words into the mouth of the Archangel Michael, as part of his (Milton's) intellectual struggle with the awful problem of making sense of the story of Adam's sin, and mankind's exclusion by God from the Paradise prepared by God (*Book of Genesis*, see ch. 10 above, and *passim*).

Milton's ingenious argument is that mankind's discovery of good and evil gives human beings the opportunity of creating a good life *for themselves* by the use of faith, morality, and reason.

'Why may not we have our heaven here (that is, a comfortable livelihood in the earth) and heaven hereafter too?' G. Winstanley (1609-76), a leader of the Levellers or Diggers, extreme radicals preaching something close to communist revolution, during the period of the republican interlude in English history, known as the Protectorate (1653-59), between the reigns of the Kings Charles I and Charles II. He was a eutopianist, much influenced by the ideas of Francis Bacon (see Appendix 3 below), suggesting that human beings have an unlimited power to improve the human condition by their own efforts.

— **The empiricists were wrong**. Greg is recalling a slogan of those philosophers for whom the human mind is merely a passive receptor of data received through the senses. *Nihil in intellectus quod prius non fuerit in sensu.* (In Latin, 'there is nothing in the mind that was not formerly in the senses'.) In Appendix 3 below, it is suggested that those philosophers who are reputed to have been 'empiricists' in this sense must rather be seen as, to varying degrees, idealists.

— **Painted veil**. Echo of a sonnet (1818) by P. B. Shelley (I.16).

'Lift not the painted veil which those who live / Call Life: though unreal shapes
be pictured there, / And it but mimic all we would believe / With colours
idly spread,—behind, lurk Fear /And Hope, twin Destinies; who ever weave /
Their shadows, o'er the chasm, sightless and drear.'

Shelley may have borrowed the image of the veil (but not the pessimism) from
F. Bacon (I.11, and Appendix 1 below), for whom natural science is a means of
penetrating the veil of ignorance and delusion. The beautiful image of a 'painted
veil'—the world of mere appearances that conceals a higher reality—also has a
distant echo of Platonism with its postulation of levels of reality and, in the parable
of the cave (*Republic*, bk. 7), the human mind's inherent capacity to see through
and beyond the mere appearances of the world.

— **Haptic/glyptic** In Italian, sculpture *per via di porre* is by way of modelling in clay
or wax; *per forza di levare* is by way of cutting or chiselling into the stone. For
Michelangelo, glyptic sculpture is the only true sculpture, causing the sculpture
to emerge from inside the stone, as if it were already ideally present in the stone, a
spiritual presence within the material. He was a devoted neo-Platonist, seeing the
beauty of the human body as the appearance of an ideal form, radiating from its
earthly prison (see above, under 'prison of their bodies').

Greg is suggesting that an analogous process may occur as we get old, with our
'true or ideal' self emerging from the laying-aside of some of the accreted substance
of everyday life.

— **Ascetic erotic.** A phrase which has been applied, appropriately, to the paradigmatic
personalities of Socrates and Leonardo da Vinci. R.A. Taylor, *Leonardo the Florentine.
A Study in Personality* (1927), V.i.

— **Fifth dimension.** See below, under 'People of the Fifth Dimension'.

— **Purposeless purpose.** A beautiful idea may be found in *The Critique of Judgment*,
by I. Kant (see below, Appendix 8), the third and last part of his great work,
concerned with philosophical problems of purpose and value. The idea is that
there can be a form of *purpose* that is inherent in some process of development, but
which is not merely a chain of causes and effects, and is not present subjectively
as a goal or aim.

An organic system—a living thing—demonstrates such a purpose in the
self-ordering of its growth. Growth is a constant re-ordering of the organism's order.
The idea has a strong Aristotelian echo (I.13)—growth seems to be the unfolding
of a potentiality already present in the organism. It is an idea that resonates strongly
with modern biology, especially genetics.

The 'purpose' element is seen in the fact that the developmental events have
significance in relation to the overall systematic order, not merely as a causal event
(the ingestion of food; leaf fall; the production of seed etc.). It is as if the organism
were choosing the best among alternative possibilities, but choosing in a way that
serves its large-scale self-interest of survival and prospering.

It would not be a mere metaphorical analogy if we were to see such a thing in individual human beings and human societies, given that they are living organisms. For Plato and Aristotle, and for all those who have followed in their footsteps, human beings and human societies are, indeed, the unfolding of inherent potentialities—but an unfolding which, by a quirk of evolution, has become self-conscious.

Human development is both *natural* and *purposelessly purposive* and highly *unnatural* and *purposively purposive*. And that has complicated somewhat the organic self-development of the human species.

These ideas are central ideas in Ph. Allott, *Eunomia*.

— **The sadness of things**. Echo of the Latin phrase *lacrimae rerum*. See ch. 3 above.

— **Imagining of tragedies**. Like all *high art* (expressing something especially complex or new in an especially beautiful way), tragic drama is *metaphysics by other means*, as it constructs an imaginary reality which re-presents crucial aspects of the lived reality of human life.

Greg's views on the nature of the *conflict* contained in tragic drama suggest various influences.

For Goethe (I.12), a conflict of 'the individuality of the self' and 'the necessity of the whole' determines the 'natural' form of Shakespeare's tragic dramas (*Zum Schakespears Tag*, 1771). 'Goethe once remarked that he could think of only thirty-six tragic situations.' F. Nietzsche, *Genealogy of Morals*, Third Essay, XX.

For Nietzsche, there is a 'tragedy at the heart of things . . . an interpenetration of several worlds, as for instance a divine and a human, each individually in the right but each, as it encroaches upon the other, having to suffer for its individuality . . .' Tragic drama is 'an Apollonian embodiment of Dionysian insights and powers' (see ch. 7 above, under 'one must be beautiful').

Of Sophocles' *Oedipus at Colonus* (see ch. 3 above, under 'when godliness is flouted', and ch. 8 above, under 'right not to be born'), Neitzsche says: 'we experience the most profound human joy as we witness this divine counterpart of dialectics'. *Birth of Tragedy*, VIII, IX. (tr., F. Golffing).

Hegel (I.19 and Appendix 8 below) identifies the nature of tragedy by analysing the situation of Socrates, condemned to death by a popular court for disrespect towards the gods and corrupting of the young. 'My trial will be like that of a doctor prosecuted by a cook before a jury of children.' Plato, *Gorgias*, 521e (Socrates speaking) (tr., W. Woodhead).

'The fate of Socrates is tragic in the essential sense, and not merely in that superficial sense of the word according to which every misfortune is called "tragic" . . . In genuine tragedy, then, they [the subject of the tragedy and the powers that destroy him or her] must be powers both alike moral and justifiable, which, from this side and from that, come into collision . . . Two opposed Rights come forth: the one breaks itself to pieces against the other: in this way, both alike suffer loss . . . On the one side is the religious claim,

the unconscious moral habit: the other principle, over against it, is the equally religious claim—the claim of the consciousness, of the reason, creating a world out of itself, the claim to eat of the tree of knowledge of good and evil.'
G.W.F. Hegel, *History of Philosophy*, II.

— **Unhappy consciousness a product of disharmony.** 'Unhappy consciousness' is a term to which Hegel (Appendix 8 below) gave a specialised meaning (mostly linking it to Christianity). Greg is clearly using it here in a quite different sense.

It is remarkable that the ancient Greek philosophers already treated the problem of *happiness* as a philosophical problem, and not merely as what would nowadays be called a 'psychological' problem. They saw it as a problem of the relationship between human consciousness and all that lies beyond human consciousness, up to and including the order of the universe. Happiness is an aspect of our subjective participation in the universe!

On such a view, happiness and goodness and truth and beauty are related—'. . . for the happy are happy inasmuch as they possess the good.' Plato, *Symposium*, 205. (tr., M. Joyce).

Greg's 'five dimensions' of our self-ordering may imply that, on his view, *happiness* is a music of the five spheres of our personal mental universe, which is a solar system of concentric metaphysical spheres, of which our mind is the sun.

Happiness is produced by the harmonious integration of our own minds with the harmonious integration of the universe. See above under 'universal harmony'. It may even be that we recognise this psychologically, when we *feel*, occasionally and for a moment, that everything is in order for-us, sensually and intellectually.

There are many possible triggers of the *sublime*, that is, a sudden sense of the All in One—a Universal Moment, when, for a moment, we feel that all is well with us and the world. A sunset, a scene, a scent, a work of art, a moment in music, a line of poetry, a face, a smile, a word, an idea—the moment when all our mental planets seem to be in perfect alignment.

— **All that is One.** Greg's experience on the beach in North Norfolk is close to a mystical experience of a classical kind—a sudden awareness of the presence of the universe within one's self—the All in the One; the One in the All.

A dark saying of Heraclitus—*haromiē aphanes phanerēs kreitōn*—'hidden harmony is best' (Diels 54)—might be taken as a reflection of one of the central insights of ancient Greek philosophy, from Pythagoras onwards—that the order of the universe is present within every part of the universe, including the human being.

'In this Intelligible World, every thing is transparent. No shadow limits vision. All the essences see each other and interpenetrate each other in the most intimate depth of their nature. Light everywhere meets light. Every being contains within itself the entire Intelligible World, and also beholds it entire in every particular being . . .'

From the neo-Platonist Greek-Egyptian philosopher Plotinus (c.205-270), *Enneads*, V.8.

'The whole is reflected in all the parts; all things keep their own relation and proportion to the universe.' A saying of the German philosopher Nicholas of Cusa (1401-64).

See ch. 11 above, under 'the one and the many' and 'we class them'.

Characteristically, Voltaire (I.15) managed to submerge the ancient idea in a polemic on free will.

> *En effet, il serait bien singulier que toute la nature, tous les astres obéissent à des lois éternelles, et qu'il y eût un petit animal haut de cinq pieds qui, au mépris de ces lois, pût agir toujours comme il lui plairait au seul gré de son caprice.* ('Indeed, it would be very odd if the whole of Nature, all the heavenly bodies should obey eternal laws, and yet there were a little animal, five feet high, which, in defiance of such laws, could act always as it pleased according to its every whim.') *Le philosophe ignorant* (1766). (present author's trans.).

Last words attributed to the dying Plotinus are: 'I am striving to give back the Divine in myself to the Divine in the All.' (Porphyry, *Life of Plotinus*).

— **Impulse of life.** Greg seems here to be connecting the impulse of life (a principle of all organic development: see ch.11 above) with the idea of spirit—a *spiritus intus* (in Latin, 'an inner spirit'), acting as a universal mind that has power over everything—*mens agitat molem.*

> *Principio caelum ac terras camposque liquentis lucentemque globum lunae Titaniaque astra spiritus intus alit, totamque infusa per artus mens agitat molem et magno se corpore miscet.* ('First, the heaven and earth, and the watery plains [the sea], the shining orb of the moon and Titan's star [the sun], a spirit within sustains, and mind, pervading its members, sways the whole mass and mingles with its mighty frame.') Virgil, *Aeneid*, bk. vi (tr., H. Fairclough).

— **The teacher's task—to educate the earth.** *Wir sind auf einer* Mission. *Zur Bildung der Erde sind wir berufen.* 'We are on a mission. We are called upon to educate the earth.' G.F. von Hardenberg (1772-1801), who wrote under the pen-name of Novalis.

The idea of a new kind of education (*Bildung*, in German; 'education' in the widest sense of the word) designed to transform human nature—which had been the subject of Plato's Republic and of much discussion since—was a favourite theme of post-Enlightenment writers, especially in the German post-Enlightenment. J. Herder, *Die Erziehung des Menschengeschlechts* (The Education of the Human Race). F. Schiller, *Über die ästhetische Erziehung des Menschen* (The Aesthetic Education of Human Beings).

— **The teacher's task—how to become immortal.** Echo of a passage in Dante, *Divine Comedy, Inferno*, Canto XV, where Dante meets his revered old teacher Brunetto Latini, to whom Dante owed so much but whom an unnamed vice had consigned to Hell.

> ... *la cara e buona imagine paterna / di voi quando nel mondo ad ora ad ora / m'insgnavate come l'uom s'etterna* ('the dear and kind paternal image of you when many a time in the world you taught me how man makes himself immortal') (tr., J. Sinclair).

— **People of the Fifth Dimension.** Greg evidently sees this spiritual and transcendental dimension of the human being as something quite different from the 'dimensions' in terms of which the human mind reconstructs the physical world—even if he would no doubt want physicists also to recognise that the dimensions they postulate—four, or however many more (see ch. 11 above, under 'ten strings of my soul')—cannot be an adequate model of the universe, if they do not include a transcendental dimension, the dimension that presents itself to the human mind as something that is conveniently called 'mind' or 'spirit'.

(Greg—not least because he does not seem to identify himself as a Christian—would certainly not want to claim any affinity with the *Fifth-Monarchy Men*. In the religious struggles in 17th-century England, they proclaimed the coming of a theocracy ruled by Christ and His Saints—the fifth empire (after Assyria, Persia, Macedonia, and Rome)—as prophesied in the Biblical Book of Daniel.)

— **To re-create the human race is a big task.** Greg may have in mind a line in Virgil, *Aeneid*, I. line 33. *Tantae molis erat Romanam condere gentem.* ('So massive a task it was to found the Roman race.')

— **The other genesis.** Medieval (Christian) philosophers, after the resurrection of the works of the ancient Greek philosophers, struggled with the problem of whether to view the universe in the light of the *Book of Genesis* or in the light of Platonic and Aristotelian ideas about the *logos* of the *cosmos* (see ch. 11 above).

Other cultures and other religions provide us with many other accounts of the origin of the universe. Modern cosmology offers us yet another Book of Genesis, a holy book in the process of being written. It will no doubt resolve all such matters once and for all.

— **World Ocean.** See ch. 11 above.

— **Human world undiscovered.** 'There are a thousand paths that have never yet been trodden—a thousand healths and hidden isles of life. Even now, man and man's earth are unexhausted and undiscovered.' F. Nietzsche, *Thus Spoke Zarathustra*, First Part ('On the gift-giving virtue'). (tr., W. Kaufmann).

CHAPTER 16. *Into the Rose-Garden.*

— **Into the rose-garden.**

'Footfalls echo in the memory / Down the passage which we did not take / Towards the door we never opened / Into the rose-garden . . .'
 T.S. Eliot, *The Four Quartets, Burnt Norton* (see ch. 9 above, under 'still point').

— **Roses are difficult.** The (British) National Rose Society, founded in 1876, disputes the commonly expressed view that roses are difficult to grow, now only expressed by gardeners who still struggle to achieve the level of success that they hope for in the growing of such beautiful plants. It is true that the development of better plant-foods for roses and disease-resistant varieties has improved the lot of the amateur rose-grower.

— **In Aristotelian terms.** Rupert is evidently referring to Aristotelian propositional logic. See ch. 11 above, under 'we class them'

— **A rose by any other name.** In W. Shakespeare's *Romeo and Juliet*, Juliet is considering the significance of the fact that Romeo's family name is Montague, the name of a family who are enemies of her family, whose family name is Capulet. She discusses with herself the relationship of a name to the person who bears it, on similar lines to Gabi and Rupert's discussion (see below).

"Tis but thy name that is my enemy; / Thou art thyself though, not a Montague. / What's Montague? it is nor hand, nor foot, / Nor arm, nor face, nor any other part / Belonging to a man. O! be some other name: / What's in a name? That which we call a rose / By any other name would smell as sweet; / So Romeo would, were he not Romeo call'd, / Retain that dear perfection which he owes / Without that title. Romeo, doff [give up] thy name; / And for that name, which is no part of thee; / Take all myself.' (Act II.2).

(Might we detect the mind, or even the hand, of F. Bacon in this discussion?)
 On a discussion by Socrates/Plato of the problem of names, see ch. 6 above, under 'mother-father' and ch. 11, under 'we give names', and see below.
 When the American writer G. Stein (1874-1946) (see ch. 10 above, under 'no there there') wrote, on several different occasions, that 'a rose is a rose' (or, on one occasion, 'a rose is a rose is a rose is a rose'), it seems that she was seeking to re-establish what she thought of as the original purity of *naming*, in which, she believed, the name and the thing were fused within a human mind less distracted and confused by centuries of allusions, associations, and conflicting conventional ideas attaching to the name.

If the *Book of Genesis* (above, *passim*) suggests that God was the first gardener (see below), it identifies Adam as the first name-giver (on behalf of God).

'And out of the ground the Lord God formed every beast of the field, and every fowl of the air; and brought them unto Adam to see what he would call them: and whatsoever Adam called every living creature, that was the name thereof.' Ch. 2.19. (King James version, 1611).

In the *Cratylus* (see below) Socrates often refers to name-givers as 'legislators'.

— **Rupert addressed as Griselda.** *Socrates*: 'For example, if a person, saluting you [Cratylus] in a foreign country, were to take your hand and say, Hail, Athenian stranger, Hermogenes, son of Smicrion—these words . . . would have no application to you but only to our friend Hermogenes, or perhaps to nobody at all? *Cratylus*: 'In my opinion, Socrates, the speaker would only be talking nonsense.' Plato, *Cratylus*, 429e. (tr., B. Jowett).

Socrates then tries to convince Cratylus that, if he agrees that names can be rightly or wrongly used, then it follows that names are separable from the thing or person named. Hovering behind this light-hearted discussion, there is, as ever, the Platonic thesis that there is a more real reality than that which we see and speak about.

At the end of the dialogue, Socrates suggests that those who take the view of Heraclitus (that everything in the universe is permanently changing) are denying the *possibility of knowledge*. But Cratylus says that, after giving the matter much thought, 'I incline to Heraclitus'.

Socrates: 'Reflect well and like a man, and do not easily accept such a doctrine, for you are young and of an age to learn. And when you have found the truth, come and tell me.'

— **Person known as Rupert.** The problem of the sense in which a name is related to the thing or person to which it is applied has always been a central question in the study of *logic*. Rupert and Gabi seem to have discovered the problem for themselves (like the slave-boy in Plato's *Meno*) (see ch. 11 above, under 'something that he already knew').

Philosophers of logic have asked whether, when we refer to 'Aristotle', we merely mean 'the person known as Aristotle' (as if his name were merely a label)—or are we saying that 'Aristotle' has a potentially definable set of characteristics which entitle us to use the name in relation to a particular person (the person born at Stagira, the pupil of Plato, the writer of certain writings, etc.)? If the latter view is taken, then it would seem to follow that, when we use a name, we are saying something substantive about the thing or person named—that we are uttering implied propositions which have substantive content.

But what is then the position, if we say—in an example much discussed by philosophers of logic—something of the kind: 'the King of France is wise'? Does that imply that there is a King of France? Or are we speaking imaginatively, or lying, or making a mistake? But then the sentence has substantive implications, but of a different kind.

A crucial puzzle has been thought by philosophers of logic to relate to cases where two different names apparently apply to the same thing—the classic instance being the planet *Venus* which is traditionally referred to (for poetically empirical, if misleading, reasons) as both 'the evening star' and 'the morning star'. This particular instance was discussed at length by the English mathematician and philosopher Bertrand Russell (I.16), responding to ideas of the German mathematician and philosopher G. Frege (1848-1925). Can we be saying something substantive about a thing or person, in using a name, if two names can apply to the same thing?

It is difficult to say, in general terms (e.g., in mathematical terms) what it means to say that A=B. It seems to imply, at one and the same time, that A and B are *the same thing* (despite being referred to as 'A' and 'B') and also that they are *not the same thing* (given that they are referred to as 'A' and 'B'), and are merely *capable of being equated* (whatever 'equated' may mean).

If they are *the same thing*, they are *not capable of being equated*. This principle has even been given a name by the philosopher G. Leibniz (see ch.11 above, under 'we class them')—*the principle of the identity of indiscernibles* (if it is not possible to detect a difference between two things, they must be the same thing!).

Underlying the debate among philosophers of logic—and the debate between Gabi and Rupert—is another kind of question, also much discussed by philosophers—how *do* we identify the unique identity of a *thing* and, still more difficult, of a *human individual*? (See ch. 11 above, under 'we class them' and ch. 2 Appendices below, *passim.*)

We are most interestingly told (by B. Schweitzer, as noted by B. Snell in *The Discovery of Mind*, 1953) that, at some point in time in ancient Greece, inscriptions incised on memorial stone figures changed their form—from 'I am X' to 'I am the image of X'. Was this the beginning of the discovery of the idea of the intrinsic individual essential identity of human beings, distinct from their name?

— **Existence—essence.** Rupert is referrring to the classical theme of philosophical metaphysics—the nature of the essential being-in-itself of an existing thing. See above and below, *passim.*

— **DNA.** See I.13.

— **Morphology.** From the Greek, *morph* ('form', 'shape', 'figure'). A central feature of biology and zoology is the classification (taxonomy) of plants and animals by reference to their shared physical characteristics.

Aristotle was a great classifier of plants and animals. The modern science of morphology owes much to the work of John Ray (1627-1705). Ray was a student and (from 1649) a Fellow of, Trinity College, Cambridge (resigning in 1662, being unwilling to take an oath of adherence to the rites and ceremonies of the Church of England, as required by an Act of Parliament of 1661).

The study was much advanced by the Swedish and French naturalists Linnaeus (C. von Linnée; 1707-78) and G. Buffon (1707-88). It was Linnaeus (*System of Nature*, 1735), who put 'man' into the class of 'primates' (with apes, lemurs, and bats) and who began to identify the characteristics of different human 'races'. His work had a great effect on the (non-scientific) public mind of Enlightenment Europe, which wanted to believe in the possibility of, at last, *rationalising* both Nature and Humanity.

Gabi is right in saying that, since the discovery of the chemical and molecular basis of genetic development (especially in the form of DNA), there are now more sophisticated and precise ways of classifying organic forms.

— **Prize roses**. In Spring and Summer, England is awash with flower shows, at which flowers and plants are displayed, and prizes are awarded—culminating in the Chelsea Flower Show, in London in May, organised by the Royal Horticultural Society. We are not told where Edmund's roses were prized, or at what level (gold, silver, or other).

— **Summer-house**. The (revealingly) English name for a small wooden structure in a garden, designed for sitting and contemplating, weather permitting. Knowing Edmund as we do, we may assume that his summer-house evokes associations.

For the same thing, the Germans use the word *die Laube*—the title of a *lied* by F. Schubert (D214), setting a poem by L. Hölty (1748-76), in which the summer-house is associated by the poet with lost love and 'tears' (*Tränen*), a word which occurs *very frequently* in German Romantic poetry.

> *Nimmer werd' ich, nimmer dein vergessen,/ Kühle, grüne Dunkelheit,/ Wo mein liebes Mädchen oft gesessen, /Und des Frühlings sich gefreut . . .* ('Never, never will I forget you, cool green shade, where my beloved often sat, taking delight in the Springtime.')

The French say *le pavillon*—and that word is sometimes borrowed in German, as (delightfully) in Act 3 of the operetta *Die lustige Witwe* (The Merry Widow) by the Hungarian composer F. Lehàr (1870-1948), where a *pavillon* is the scene of confused assignations:

> *Sieh dort den kleinen Pavillon /Er kann höchst diskret verschwiegen sein! / O, dieser kleiner Pavillon /Plaudert nicht ein Wörtchen aus, o nein!*
> ('See there that little *pavillon*, it can keep secrets with utmost discretion! Oh, little *pavillon*, do not give away a single little word in chatter, oh no!')

— **Simianism**. See I.13. Cicero was not the first, nor the last, to notice the remarkable similarity between human beings and monkeys. *Simes quam similes, turpissima bestia, nobis* ('Monkeys, the most shameful of animals, how similar to us.') Cicero, *De natura dei* (On the nature of God), I.35.

— **Metaphysiology**. See I.5. Of course, in forming complex judgments about other people, we cannot forget the view of B.Spinoza (see ch.11 above, under 'we class them') to the effect that the idea that human beings form of God tells us more about human beings than about God. Paul's idea of Peter tells us more about Paul than about Peter.

— **Plato Quotient—Aristotle Quotient**. From the Latin *quot*, 'how many?'

— *Plato und Aristoteles! Das sind nicht bloß die zwei Systeme, sondern auch die Typen zweier verschiedenen Menschennaturen, die sich, seit undenklicher Zeit, unter allen Kostümen, mehr oder minder feindselig entgegenstehen. Vorzüglich das ganze Mittelalter hindurch, bis auf heutigen Tag, wurde solchermaßen gekämpft, und dieser Kampf ist der wesentlichste Inhalt der christlichen Kirchengeschichte.*

> 'Plato and Aristotle! They are not merely two systems, but also the types of two different human natures, which, since time immemorial, have been opposed to each other. Throughout the Middle Ages, up until today, there has been this struggle between them, and this struggle has been the most important substantive content of Christian church history.'
>
> H. Heine (1797-1856)(see ch. 2 above, under '*Dahin*', and Appendix 8), in an essay entitled *Deutschland* ('Germany'), originally published in French, in the *Revue des deux mondes* (1834). (present author's trans.).

In ancient Greek thought before Plato, there had already arisen deep differences of view as to the relationship between *mind* and *matter* ('mind makes reality'; 'mind is the product of matter')—differences argued out by Heraclitans and Pythagoreans, by the followers of Anaxagoras and Protagoras.

The two kinds of explanation of the world—transcendental and rational—and the two kinds of human nature represented by Platonism and Aristotelianism were already in existence—the one liable to be more congenial to the religious spirit, the other liable to be more congenial to the scientific spirit.

> 'Plato comports himself in the world like a blessed spirit . . . He moves longingly to the heights, to participate once again in his source. Everything that he utters is related to an eternal One, Good, True, Beautiful, whose demands he strives to enliven in his bosom . . . Aristotle, on the contrary, stands in the world like a man, an architect. He traces round a monstrous circle for his foundation, gathers materials from all sides, sorts them, piles them up, and thus ascends to the heights like a pyramid, in a geometric form, while Plato reaches for the heavens like an obelisk, indeed like a pointed flame.
>
> 'When two such men, who apportion human nature between them to a certain extent, appeared as distinct representatives of glorious qualities

which are not easy to combine, when they had the fortune . . . to utter their education fully, not in short laconic sentences like oracular sayings but in exceptional, extensive numerous works; when these works for the best part remain to mankind and are more or less continuously studied and reflected on: it naturally follows that the world, insofar as it is regarded as feeling and thinking, was obliged to devote itself to one or the other, to acknowledge one or the other as master, teacher, leader.'

J.W. Goethe, *Materielen zur Gechischte der Farbenlehre*. (Elements relating to the History of Colour Theory). English version of the quoted passage taken from J. Haden's trans. of E. Cassirer, *Kant's Life and Thought* (1918/1981).

Goethe, poet and novelist and public official and public intellectual, spent twenty years in the elaboration of his ideas about the nature and effects of colour, a central and obsessive theme of which is a rejection of Isaac Newton's explanation of colour as the product of a composite phenomenon within white light.

'But the most surprising, and wonderful composition was that of *Whiteness* . . . 'Tis ever compounded, and to its composition are requisite all the aforesaid primary Colours, mixed in due proportion.'

I. Newton, *Opticks*, published in 1704, reporting experiments done in Cambridge in 1666.

Greg and Edmund are suggesting that it is possible, even today, to find the dominating and competing metaphysical presences of Plato and Aristotle in our minds, even if we know nothing of classical philosophy.

— **Gilbertian law**. See ch. 5 above, under 'every child'. According to the lyric by W.S. Gilbert, every child is born 'either a little Liberal, / Or else a little Conservative.'
— **Born again**. A term used, especially by Christians, to describe a personal spiritual transformation, a metanoia (see. ch. 12 above). 'Verily, verily, I say unto thee, Except a man be born again, he cannot see the kingdom of God . . . Except a man be born of water and of the Spirit, he cannot enter into the kingdom of God.' *Gospel of John*, ch.3. (King James version, 1611).
— **Rorschachery**. The Swiss psychiatrist H. Rorschach (1884-1922) devised a form of clinical investigation in which the patient responds to the sight of ready-made ink-blots, spontaneously, and (he and his followers believe) self-revealingly.
— **Neo-behaviourist**. See ch. 15 above, under 'social control'.
— **Traumocrancy**. Combination of German (*Traum*, a dream) and Greek (*manteia*, 'divination'). See ch. 1 above, under 'Freudian interpretation'.
— **Diarchic Indicators**. *Diarchy*, from Greek roots, 'rule by two'.
— **PQ↔AQ**. The list of diarchies given here is illustrative only. It will no doubt be added to, or subtracted from, as the study of *metaphysiology* sophisticates itself.

— **Flotsam and jetsam**. Abandoned objects floating in the sea (French, *flotter*) or thrown overboard from a vessel (French, *jeter*), and liable to be washed up on the seashore.

— **Trojan exiles. Boat-people**. Neither the *Odyssey* nor the *Aeneid* suggest that Trojan exiles settled in South-west Spain. Greek legend did suggest that the port city of Cádiz was founded by Hercules following his slaying of the monstrous Geryon. Cádiz, the most ancient inhabited city in Europe, was founded by the Phoenicians (see ch. 9 above, under 'Carthage'), under the name of *Gadir* in the 12th century BCE. Thereafter it was a desired target for very many of the subsequent civilisations.

The Andalusian coast to the south of the city, as far as Tarifa, has been a desired target for refugees trying to reach Europe from Africa in small boats, often at the cost of their lives. At their closest in that area, where the Atlantic Ocean and the Mediterranean Sea meet, Africa and Europe are separated by some nine miles (fourteen kilometres).

— ***Animi exercendo levantur***. In Latin, 'the mind is improved by exercise'. From a saying by Cicero in his book on old age, suggesting that the elderly should keep their minds active. *Et corpora quidem exercitationum defatigatione ingravescunt, animi autem exercendo levantur.* Cicero, *De senectute*, 1.36. ('And exercise may weigh down the body with exhaustion, but exercise lifts up the mind.')

Compare Rousseau's horticultural analogy. 'We shape plants by cultivation, and men by education.' *Émile*, bk. 1.

Edmund is apparently taking the sensible view that discussion of philosophical puzzles—whatever other value it may have in helping us to face the perennial problems of human existence—has an important incidental effect, in increasing the agility and creative power of our minds. (*Disputations* in medieval universities, about matters more substantial than the number of angels on a pinhead, were also extreme exercises in mental agility.)

And the same can be said of the study of foreign languages, which empowers us in the use of language in general, and hence in our capacity to think (using language inwardly), leading also to the sophisticating of our stereometaphysics (see ch. 12 above).

See ch. 19 below, under 'the holy places of the new ignorance'.

— **Newmarket Heath**. Large areas of grass-covered heath land surrounding Newmarket, used for the daily exercise of racehorses. They have been maintained as such, and for that use, since the 17th century. See ch. 17 below, under 'Newmarket'.

— **Dementia. Deficia**. From the Latin, *dementia* ('foolishness, insanity') and *deficere* ('to grow weak').

— **Mental laterals**. Supposing that the mind has muscles equivalent to lateral muscles in the human body, which may be strengthened by exercise.

— **Purposeless**. See ch. 15 above, under 'purposeless purpose'.

— **To become what I am**. See ch. 11 above.

— **Shape of something true**. 'I take no sides. I am interested in the shape of ideas. There is a wonderful sentence in Augustine: "Do not despair; one of the thieves was saved. Do not presume; one of the thieves was damned." That sentence has a wonderful shape. It is the shape that matters.' S. Beckett, quoted by A. Schneider, *Samuel Beckett: the Critical Heritage* (1979).

This fine insight of Beckett's—that we are liable to assent most easily to ideas expressed in a *form* that seems to have a quality of 'rightness' about it—is surely confirmed by experience.

'Man is born free, but everywhere he is in chains'. (Rousseau). *Man ist was er isst* ('We are what we eat.') (Feuerbach). *Credo quia absurdum* ('I believe it *because* it is not reasonable.') (Tertullian). 'Rose-red city—half as old as time.' (Burgon, about Petra).

Ideas such as these would not be so effective if they had been expressed in a different form. They are more than the sum of their parts. The shape of the words is part of their meaning—a definition of poetry, perhaps?

— **Process of becoming**. Despite his recent initiation into French metaphysiology, Rupert may not be familiar with the thoughts and works of Simone de Beauvoir (1908-86). *On ne naît pas femme. On le devient.* ('One is not born a woman. One becomes it.') *Le deuxième sexe* (The Second Sex) (1949). It is a truth that applies much more widely than merely to gender.

— *Ipse dixit*. In Latin, 'he himself has said it'. Usually referring to a sententious saying by someone of significance. Cicero uses the phrase ironically (*ipse dixit Pythagoras*) in referring to the very-much quoted (and creatively quoted) ancient Greek philosopher. Cicero, *De natura dei*, I.5.

— **Death the purpose of life**. See ch. 19 below, under 'death wish'.

— **Roses think we are immortal?** It may be that Gabi's very English education nevertheless introduced her to the French writer B. de Fontenelle (1657-1757), nephew of the great French dramatist P. Corneille (1606-84).

> *Si les roses, qui ne durent qu'un jour, faisaient des histoires, et se laissent des mémoires les unes aux autres, les premières auraient fait le portrait de leur jardinier d'une certaine façon et, de plus de quinze mille âges de roses, les autres qui l'auraient encore laissé à celles qui les devaient suivre, n'y auraient rien changé. Sur cela, elles diraient: Nous avons toujours vu le même jardinier, de mémoire de rose on n'a vu que lui, il a toujours été fait comme il est, assurément il ne meurt point comme nous, il ne change seulement pas.'*

> ('If roses, which last only a day, wrote histories, and handed on memorials from one to another, the first ones would have described their gardener in a certain way and, in the fifteen thousand ages of all roses, the others which had handed on that picture to those which followed, would have said nothing different. And so, they would say: We have always seen the same gardener, so far as the rose-memory goes we have seen no other, he was always the same

as he is, certainly he never dies like us, he does not even change.') (present author's trans.).

> *Entretiens sur la pluralité des mondes* (Discussions on the Plurality of Worlds) (1686).

— **Actualise the ideal of beauty**. F. Schiller, in his *Äesthetische Erziehung*, letter 15 (see ch. 15 above, under 'teacher's task') uses a fine phrase—*lebender Gestalt* ('living form'). Edmund may be suggesting that we should apply that idea to explain the beauty of a garden. Schiller defines the phrase as 'the union of the ideal and the actual'. On the ideal of beauty, see further in ch.18 below.

— **Gardening to defeat time**.

> 'To be conscious is not to be in time / But only in time can the moment in the rose-garden, / The moment in the arbour where the rain beat, / The moment in the draughty church at smokefall / Be remembered; involved with past and future./Only through time time is conquered.'
>
> T.S. Eliot, *Burnt Norton* (see above).

— **For a while**. Edmund would not be able to use this phrase in isolation without thinking of the opening lines of a poem by J. Dryden (I.16): 'Music for a while / Shall all your cares beguile.' The poem was set to beautiful music by H. Purcell (I.16).

— **Agony in the garden**. Inappropriate echo of the traditional name given to an episode in the life of Jesus Christ. Shortly before his trial and execution, he suffered extreme anguish when he went, with his friends, to a place called the Mount of Olives. 'And being in an agony he prayed more earnestly: and his sweat was as it were great drops of blood falling down to the ground.' *Gospel of St Luke*, 22.44. (King James version, 1611.)

— **Nature to be commanded must be obeyed**. Saying of F. Bacon (I.16; Appendix 1 below), *New Organon*, I.III. It epitomises one aspect of the mentality of the natural scientist, who must display *humility* in relation to the data which observation of Nature reveals, or refuses to reveal. (Another aspect is *pride*, in relation to the seeming omnipotence and omniscience of the scientific method.)

— **World without roses**. *Il resterait peu de choses / A l'homme, qui vit un jour, / Si Dieu nous ôtait les roses, / Si Dieu nous ôtait l'amour!* ('Not much would remain to man, who lives for a day, if God took away roses, if God took away love.') V. Hugo (ch. 11 above, under 'like a bird'), *Je sais bien*, a poem in his collection *Les Contemplations*, XVIII.

— ***Voilà les roses! Conjuguant le verbe aimer***. In French, 'Look, there are the roses—conjugating the verb "to love".' Echo of lines in Hugo's *L'âme en fleur*, a poem in *Les Contemplations*, II. *Tout conjugue le verbe aimer. Voici les roses.* ('Everything conjugates the verb "to love". Look at the roses.')

Could it be that Hugo knew the story of the response of a prince at the court of Frederick the Great in Potsdam (I.6), when asked how they occupied their time? *Nous conjuguons le verbe s'ennuyer* ('we conjugate the verb "to be bored"')—meaning: 'I am bored, you are bored, he is bored etc.'
— **God the first gardener**.

> 'God Almighty first planted a garden. And indeed it is the purest of human pleasures. It is the greatest refreshment to the spirits of man; without which, buildings and palaces are but gross handiworks; and a man shall ever see, that when ages grow to civility and elegancy, men come to build stately sooner than to garden finely; as if gardening were the greater perfection.'
>
> F. Bacon, essay on *Gardens* (1625).

Bacon gives detailed advice on garden-design, albeit for a garden whose ideal area should apparently be some thirty acres. In the great debate about *lawns* as part of the design of the ideal garden, he takes the better view (in their favour): 'because nothing is more pleasant to the eye than green grass kept finely shorn.'
— **Garden of the soul**.

> 'A beginner must look upon himself as making a garden, wherein our Lord may take His delight, but in a soil unfruitful, and abounding in weeds. His Majesty roots up the weeds, and has to plant good herbs. Let us, then, take for granted that this is already done when a soul is determined to give itself to prayer, and has begun the practice of it. We have, then, as good gardeners, by the help of God, to see that the plants grow, to water them carefully, that they may not die, but produce blossoms, which shall send forth much fragrance, refreshing to our Lord, so that He may come often for His pleasure into this garden, and delight Himself in the midst of these virtues.'
>
> From *The Life* of Teresa of Avila (1515-82), her spiritual autobiography. (tr.(from the Spanish), D. Lewis).

Teresa, here and elsewhere, uses an extremely extended metaphor of a 'garden' to suggest the nature of the soul, a place where human beings act as assistant gardeners, as it were, to God as the principal gardener of their souls. See ch. 11 above, under 'becoming a diamond'.

L'esprit du jardinier parfume le parfum! ('The spirit of the gardener perfumes the perfume!'). A. Lamartine (see ch. 6 above, under 'mother-father sign'), in his poem *Lettre à Alphonse Karr, jardinier.* (Letter to Alphonse Karr, [Lamartine's] gardener) (1857).

> *L'orateur du forum, le poète badin, / Horace et Cicéron, qu'aimaient-ils ? un jardin :/ L'un à Tibur trempé des grottes de Neptune, / L'autre en son Tusculum plein d'échos de tribune. / Un jardin qu'en cent pas l'homme peut parcourir, / Va! c'est assez pour*

vivre et même pour mourir ! ("The orator of the forum, the playful poet, Horace and Cicero, what did they love? a garden: one [Horace] at Tibur [Tivoli] refreshed by Neptune's grottoes, the other [Cicero] in his Tusculum echoing with the sounds of the tribune, a garden of no more than a hundred paces. Fine! That's enough for living and even for dying!') (present author's trans.).

The Romans' love of gardens is one of their more attractive features—Statius, Pliny, Horace, Cicero (especially as revealed in his letters). They saw the garden not merely as an escape from the dreadful urbanism of Rome. They recognised its artistic and metaphysical significance. And they recognised the garden as the scene of humble, and sometimes rewarded, effort.

'. . . I might be singing what artful tillage decks rich gardens, singing of the rose-beds of twice-blooming Paestum . . . [But] I call to mind how under the towers of Oebalia's citadel, where dark Galaesus waters his yellow fields, I saw an old Corycian, who had a few acres of unclaimed land, and this a soil not rich enough for bullocks' ploughing, unfitted for the flock, and unkindly to the vine. Yet, as he planted herbs here and there about among the bushes, with white lilies about, and vervain, and slender poppy, he matched in contentment the wealth of kings and, returning home in late evening, would load his board with unbought dainties. He was first to pluck roses in spring and apples in autumn; and when sullen winter was still bursting rocks with the cold, and curbing running waters with ice, he was already culling the soft hyacinth's bloom, chiding laggard summer and the loitering zephyrs.' Virgil, *Georgics*, IV (tr., H. Fairclough).

— **Where God walks**. 'And they heard the voice of the Lord God walking in the garden in the cool of the day: And Adam and his wife hid themselves from the presence of the Lord God amongst the trees of the garden.' From the (biblical) *Book of Genesis*, 3.8.
— **Metaphysical Garden**. Echo of the Chelsea Physick Garden, established by the Society of Apothecaries in 1673, close to the river Thames in Chelsea (London), as a botanical garden, bringing together plants used for medical purposes from around the world, with a view to the training of apprentice apothecaries.
— *Illuminati / cognoscenti / dilettanti*. In Italian, 'enlightened ones'. 'knowing ones', 'delighting ones'. All terms that have been used in English to describe privileged intellectual and artistic enthusiasts.
— *Lyceum / Academy*. Edmund has obviously borrowed these names from Cicero's garden at Tusculum (near present-day Frascati, in Italy). The gardens of Cicero's villa were laid out in terraces, and in groves which he called Lyceum and Academy. For 'academy, see ch. 14 above, under 'academia'. Lyceum was the name of a gymnasium with covered walks in an eastern suburb of Athens, close to a temple

of Apollo, to whom the epithet *lykeios* (of uncertain meaning) was applied (among many others).

— **Scents merging**. 'Nor had nature only painted there, but of the sweetness of a thousand odours there it made one, blended and unknown to men.' Dante, *Divine Comedy: Purgatory*, Canto VII. (tr., J. Sinclair). Virgil is leading Dante through the place where are assembled those of the dead who, for one not very grave reason or another, have not reached Paradise.

In the *Divine Comedy: Paradiso*, XXXII, 'the mystical rose' is one of the final forms that appears in Dante's visionary Heaven. It is Beatrice who 'imparadises' Dante's mind (*quella che 'mparadisa la mia mente*), XXVIII. He watches as the Virgin Mary, 'mother and daughter of God' (see below), takes her place as one of the petals of the mystic rose—before Dante himself approaches (but does not reach) the final stage, closest to God—the Beatific Vision.

— ***Rosa centifolia.*** An old multi-petaled rose, highly scented. Its oil is used to produce rose oil, the basis for many commercially produced scents. Grasse (southern France), leading centre of the global scent-making industry, grows and uses vast quantities of *rosa centifolia* every year.

Grasse has two other particular claims to fame. It is the place where Napoleon, having set foot in France again at nearby Golfe-Juan, after his escape from exile in Elba, proclaimed his return to power, at the beginning of the Hundred Days which would end in defeat at Waterloo (1815) and new exile (on the rather more remote island of St Helena). It is also the birthplace of the splendidly elegant painter J.H. Fragonard (1732-1806).

— **Blood-red water**. We may be inclined to avoid the question of how and where, at what cost, at what price, Edmund obtained a block of polished purple porphyry. Presumably it was polished by the hands of craftsman in the ancient world—but who knows where it may have been in the meantime, and how it found itself in England.

Edmund will certainly have designed the scene with care, and with multiple metaphysical, not to say mythological, meanings.

> 'At that season the red earth washed down from the mountains by the rain tinges the water of the river, and even the sea, for a great way with blood-red hue, and the crimson stain was believed to be the blood of Adonis, annually wounded to death by the boar on Mount Lebanon. Again, the scarlet anemone is said to have sprung from the blood of Adonis, or to have been stained by it; . . . The red rose also was said to owe its hue to the same sad occasion; for Aphrodite, hastening to her wounded lover, trod on a bush of white roses; the cruel thorns tore her tender flesh, and her sacred blood dyed the white roses for ever red.'
>
> J. Frazer (see ch. 12 above, under 'Christ's suffering'), *The Golden Bough. A Study in Magic and Religion* (1922), ch. XXXII.

We may suppose that Edmund, like countless other visitors to Venice, will have looked closely, and wondered, at the two porphyry sculptures, apparently representing four (Roman Imperial) tetrarchs, set at an outside angle of the Treasury of the Doge's Palace. It is now thought that they were made in Egypt in the 4th century, and were brought to Venice as loot in the 13th century.

Or else it may be that he is trying to recapture something of the troubling presence (nearby) of the rough block of porphyry, brought to Venice from Acre in the 13th century—the *Pietra del Bando*, on which a public official stood to proclaim the decrees and verdicts of the Signoria, the governing oligarchy of Venice.

— *Sehnsucht nach Süden*. See ch. 7 above, under '*Italienische Reise*', and below.

— **Hampstead**. See below.

— **Green and flowering hamrony**. Edmund has formed this phrase from a much longer inscription on an arcade in the Garden of the Generalife. The Generalife (its Spanish name) is a small palace constructed (12th-14th centuries) by the Arab rulers of Spain in their city of Granada (Andalucía, Spain). It was situated beside the main palace complex of the Alhambra. With its beautiful gardens, it was designed to be peaceful and spiritually inspiring. (Large parts of Spain were under Arab rule from the late 8th century until 1492.)

— **Misanthropologising**. See I.5.

— **Anatomy of optimism**. *The Anatomy of Melancholy. What it is, with all kinds [of] causes, symptomes, prognostiches and several cures of it* was published (originally in 1621, but revised and expanded thereafter) by Robert Burton (1577-1640), under the pseudonym Democritus Junior. Having been an undergraduate at Brasenose College, Oxford, he spent his life ('a silent, sedentary, solitary, private life') as a Student (=Fellow) of Christ Church, Oxford, which he describes as 'the most flourishing College in Europe'.

The book is a massive compendium (1200 pages) of idiosyncratic discussion and quotations and literary and philosophical allusions (from ancient Greece onwards) relating in any way to melancholy (nowadays known as 'depression') of which Burton claimed to be a chronic sufferer—although the book itself has throughout a gently playful tone of voice. He is particularly sound on the effects of 'overmuch study'.

'. . . hard students are commonly troubled with gouts, catarrhs, rheums, cachexia, bradypepsia, bad eyes, stone, and colic, crudities, oppilations, vertigo, winds, consumptions, and all such diseases as come by overmuch sitting; they are most lean, dry, ill-coloured, spend their fortunes, lose their wits, and many times their lives, and all through immoderate pains and extraordinary studies . . . How many poor scholars have lost their wits, or become dizzards, neglecting all worldly affairs and their own health, *esse* and *bene esse* [being and well-being], to gain knowledge for which, after all their pains, in this world's esteem they are accounted ridiculous and silly fools, idiots, asses, and (as oft they are) rejected, contemned, derided, doting, and mad!' (I.2.3.15—it is a very organised book).

He is also sound on the contemporary disdain for true education. He quotes Lipsius (Flemish humanist: 1547-1606), on how students are made to study law and divinity in order to get on in life:

'The hope of gain overrides all scholarly studies, and a pile of money gives more pleasure that anything written by crazy Greeks and Romans. And from these people come those who are called on to govern the state, and to act as the counsellors of kings. Gosh, what a world! [*O pater, o patria!*].' (Lipsius original in Latin; present author's trans.).

Explaining the title of his book, he says: 'it is a kind of policy in these days to prefix a phantastical title to a book which is to be sold—for as larks come down to a day-net, many vain readers will tarry and stand gazing, like silly passengers, at an antic picture in a painter's shop, that will not look at a judicious piece.'

Dr Johnson said that the *Anatomy* was 'the only book that ever took him out of bed two hours sooner than he wished to rise'. (From Boswell's *Life*, here reproducing Dr Maxwell's recollections of Dr Johnson, 1770). We may imagine Greg and Edmund reading passages form the book to each other in Greg's rooms in Cambridge.

As optimists, they would also be familiar with the following.

'For I am building in the human understanding a true model of the world, such as it is in fact, not such as a man's own reason would have it to be; a thing which cannot be done without a very diligent dissection and anatomy of the world. But I say that those foolish and apish images of worlds which the fancies of men have created in philosophical systems must be utterly scattered to the winds.' F. Bacon, *New Organon*, I.CXXIV.

However, Greg and Edmund would, of course, *see* this thought and *raise* it—to borrow language from the card-game known as Poker. Well-founded *optimism* overcomes corrosive doubt and mere common sense in building *the true model of a better world*.

— *Fría y pura,—cálida y dura*. In Spanish, 'cold and pure', 'warm and hard'.

Echo of a poem by the fine Spanish poet A. Machado (1875-1939), member of a remarkably creative group of Spanish writers and artists and composers known as *la Generación de 1898* (The Generation of 1898). The year 1898 was a traumatic year for Spain, the year of a war with the United States in which Spain lost control, among other things, of Cuba, the Philippines, and Puerto Rico. It heralded a century in which the United States intervened repeatedly, with force of arms, in the Caribbean and Central and South America.

> *¡Soria fría. Soria pura. / Cabeza de Extremadura. / . . . con sus murallas roídas / y sus casas denegridas ! / . . . Soria, ciudad castellano / ¡tan bella! bajo la luna.* (Cold Soria, pure Soria, at the head of Extremadura . . . with its broken walls and its derelict houses! . . . Soria, city of Castille, so beautiful in the moonlight!') (present author's trans.). *Campos de Soria*, VI.

Soria, where Machado lived for a while, is an isolated town in central Spain, in the harsh La Mancha region of the ancient kingdom of Castille. Andalucía, on the other hand, the most southerly province (now 'autonomous region') of Spain, is normally hot and dry.

— **Virgin Birth**. Parthenogenesis. With capital initial letters, the reference is probably to the birth of Jesus Christ, son of Mary, who said to the angel Gabriel : 'I know not a man.' From the (Christian) *Gospel of Luke*, 1.34.

— **Evolution by natural Selection**. See ch. 13 above, under 'survival of the unfittest', and Appendix 7 below.

— **True serpent in the Paradise Garden**. In the (biblical) *Book of Genesis*, chs. 2 and 3, God told Adam not to eat the fruit of the Tree of the Knowledge of Good and Evil at the centre of the Garden of Eden (Paradise). Among the creatures made by God was a serpent. When Eve, the first woman, had been made, the serpent tempted her, and through her Adam, to eat the fruit of the Tree—the 'original sin'. The (English) King James version says that the serpent was 'more subtle' than any of the other creatures. The (Latin) Vulgate version says the serpent was *callidior* ('cleverer, more cunning'). On 'original sin', see I.19 and above, *passim*.

The idea that the propensity of human beings to do evil is *biologically* determined is much discussed and widely accepted, especially among people who do not subscribe to religious views on the subject.

Such a view turns our biological inheritance into a form of Fate. It cites *selfishness* and *aggression* as *necessary* features of the biological struggle to survive, as evidenced by our observation of the way of life (and death) of countless animal species—and, indeed, by the tragic side of the history of the human species itself. On this view, it would not be possible for the human species, as an evolved animal species, to have avoided the inheritance of such features.

It has been noted above (in various contexts) that S. Freud propagates a sort of metaphysical version of this thesis—suggesting that each human being begins life with characteristics of a potentially self-destructive and interpersonally conflictual kind which strongly affect, or even determine, the subsequent development of personality.

Greg Seare and Edmund Jenning are representatives of another school of thought, taking the view that the human species has also inherited a self-determining and self-transcending capacity, as a result of the generous act of evolution in conferring on us a brain which allows us to think and communicate, with no as-yet-known limit. They are not *endaimonists* (possessed by bad demons) but *eudaimonists* (possessed by the good demon of happiness) and *enthusiasts* (possessed by a sort of godliness). (See ch. 19 below, under 'enthusiasts').

— **Particular paradise**. See ch. 9, above, under 'the clicking and the tapping'.

— **Sacred grove**. 'And it came to pass, that on the morrow Moses went into the tabernacle of witness; and, behold, the rod of Aaron for the house of Levi was budded, and brought forth buds, and bloomed blossoms, and yielded almonds.' The (biblical) *Book of Numbers*, ch. 17.8. (The 'rod' was one of twelve formed by God by splitting the branch of a tree.)

Rods appear rather frequently in the Old Testament, and branches of sacred trees occur rather frequently in various more or less mystical religions—no doubt reflecting something in the Jungian *collective unconscious*, if not also something less metaphysical in the Freudian *personal unconscious*, or something universal in what has been referred to here as the *subunconscious mind* (ch. 15 above).

The nine hundred pages of J. Frazer's *Golden Bough* are required to explain a strange ritual described in its first chapter, and which, Frazer says, 'the divine mind' of the English painter J. Turner (1775-1851) had represented in his painting known as *The Golden Bough* (1834). (It now seems that Frazer may have misunderstood the iconography of the painting.)

> 'In antiquity this sylvan landscape was the scene of a strange and recurring tragedy. On the northern shore of the lake . . . stood the sacred grove and sanctuary of Diana Nemorensis, or Diana of the Wood . . . In this sacred grove there grew a certain tree round which at any time of the day, and probably far into the night, a grim figure might be seen to prowl . . . He was a priest and a murderer; and the man for whom he looked was sooner or later to murder him and hold the priesthood in his place. Such was the rule of the sanctuary.'

The story, which sounds like a dream fit for the scalpel of a Freud or Jung, contains within it the potentiality of countless religious and philosophical and social ideas—hence the scale of Frazer's book.

In Virgil's *Aeneid*, Aeneas cannot enter Hell to search for Proserpine, unless he carries a golden bough.

> 'There lurks in a shady tree a bough, golden in leaf and pliant stem, held consecrate to nether Juno . . . But 'tis not given to pass beneath earth's hidden places, save to him who hath plucked from the tree the gold-tressed fruitage . . . When the first is torn away, a second fails not, golden too, and

the spray bears leaf of the selfsame ore [golden colour] . . . Only so shalt thou survey the Stygian groves and realms the living may not tread.' Virgil, *Aeneid*, VI. (tr., H. Fairclough).

It is generally thought that the bough in question was of mistletoe, growing on an oak tree.

— **Olive-tree**. With these unappetising precedents, Edmund must be relieved that the wooden staff of the Old Man of the Sea has produced a *Silver-Green* Bough—an *olive-tree* with *silver-green* leaves. The olive-tree was cherished and venerated throughout the ancient world. In the (biblical) *Book of Judges*, the olive is invited to become the king of trees, and it was sometimes so regarded in Greece and Rome, because of its longevity, its self-sufficiency, its utility, and its fruitfulness (as if these were ever characteristics of kings). As global climate change begins to change the British climate, it becomes possible (*in principle*) to grow olive-trees in southern England.

— **Hampstead**. A London suburb, formerly a village outside London, high on a hill, with a large area of open grassland (Hampstead Heath). Home for two centuries to many thoughtful and creative people.

Hampstead is an exceptionally unlikely place in which to find a *sacred grove*. But it is quite common for its more thoughtful and creative inhabitants to have a longing for (and a second home in) the *warm south* (also known as *der Süden*) where olive-trees are profusely at home.

'O for a beaker full of the warm South! / Full of the true, the blushful Hippocrene, / With beaded bubbles winking at the brim, / And purple-stainèd mouth; / That I might drink, and leave the world unseen, / And with thee fade away into the forest dim.' J. Keats (see ch.1 above, under 'Venice observed'), *Ode to a Nightingale* (1819). In ancient Greek mythology, Hippocrene was the fountain of the Muses on Mount Helicon in Greece.

Keats was briefly a resident of Hampstead, in a house that may be visited. Suffering from tuberculosis, he moved to Rome and died there in 1821, at the age of twenty-five.

CHAPTER 17. *Gnostalgia for the Future*

— **Gnostalgia**. ?New word. Pronounce as 'nostalgia' (silent 'g'). 'Anguished longing for the old wisdom.' From ancient Greek, *gnosis*, 'knowledge, wisdom' (from *gignosco*, 'to know', 'to get to know') and the modern English word *nostalgia* (from ancient Greek *nostos*, 'return home', and *algos*, 'pain, sorrow').

Gnostics were heterodox sects in the early centuries of Christianity who believed in a dualism of good and evil, in the superiority of mind over the evil contained in matter, and in the capacity of the mind to have access to a special knowledge (*gnosis*) of the divine.

— **Newmarket**. Town in Suffolk (I.14) which has been the principal location of horse-racing in England since the royal patronage of horse-racing there began under King James I in 1604. It is 12 miles from Cambridge and 12 miles form Bury St Edmunds (I.14).

The town and, in particular, its High Street are situated on the route of the Icknield Way, regarded as one of the oldest long-distance roads in Britain, linking Buckinghamshire (Ivinghoe Beacon) and Norfolk (Knettishall Heath)—part of it taking the form of the modern A11. The remarkable Roman road-builders turned it into one of their major cross-country roads. There are relics of human occupation of the area in the Stone Age and the Bronze Age (see below, under 'Neolithic times').

The area to the north of Newmarket (Norfolk; ch.15 above) is thought to be the main location of the (ancient British) Iceni tribe. (The Roman settlement at Norwich was known as *Venta Icenorum*.). Boudica (or Boadecia), queen of the Iceni, almost succeeded in driving the occupying Romans out of England (60-61 CE). After burning to the ground three of their towns (at London, St Albans, and Colchester), her army was defeated, and she and some 60,000 other Britons were killed, at the Battle of Watling Street (another pre-Roman road paved by the Romans—part of it linking London and Dover—the modern A2). The occupying Romans remained in *Britannia* until the year 410, when their (Western) Empire had declined, and would soon finally fall.

The town of Newmarket began to be developed (as a 'new market' under a royal charter) in the year 1200, when the land was given by the (Anglo-Norman) lord of the manor of Exning (three miles from Newmarket) as a dowry on the marriage of his daughter.

The Romans constructed a bridge over the river at Cambridge (now the site of Magdalene Bridge) and established a settlement nearby. In 1068, the invading Normans built a castle on the hill overlooking the river-crossing. Its exiguous remains are now adjacent to the Cambridgeshire County Council offices. The county of Cambridge was an Anglo-Saxon shire, listed in the Norman taxation-register known as Domesday Book (1086) under the name G*rentebrigescire* = 'shire of Granta bridge'. (The river Cam was then known as the Granta.)

The Anglo-Saxons, who had succeeded the Romans as occupying invaders in Britain, established thmeselves on the site of the old Roman settlement, calling it *Grantaceastr* in the 7th century, *Grantabrycge* in the 9th century. Invading Danes occupied Cambridge for part of the 9th century.

The Roman Empire in the East (Byzantium) survived until 1453, the dawn of an Enlightenment that came to be called the Italian Renaissance. By that date, over a period of three centuries, a university—a product of another European Renaissance, in the 12[th]century—had been establishing itself at Cambridge.

— **Crackling excitement (horse racing).** Greg Seare evidently has in mind a brilliant and troubling account of a race meeting in the Prater in Vienna in *Phantastische Nacht* (1922) (Fantastic Night), a short story by the Austrian writer S. Zweig (1881-1942). 'All I wanted was to experience the spectacle, the crackling sensuous excitement that pervaded the heightened emotion of the hour . . .'

The horse on which the narrator had placed a bet won the race. 'Ecstasy such as I had never known before flooded through me, a mindless joy at seeing chance bow to my challenge with such slavish obedience . . .' (tr., A. Bell).

— **Quantum mechanics.** Mystical hypothesis about the behaviour—and hence the nature—of matter at the sub-atomic level. *At that level* energy changes states in ways which are, in principle, unpredictable, but which are capable of producing *larger-scale effects* which are predictable within the scientific hypotheses which are designed to make them predictable, but those effects are then able to produce *even larger-scale effects*, such as those at the level of whole bodies, including the human being or the horse, that are less predictable or not predictable at all.

Freedom of the will is the quantum mechanics of the human mind. For some religions, the Will of God is quantum mechanics at the level of the universe.

— **Racing Post.** A daily newspaper in the United Kingdom dedicated to horse-racing (and greyhound racing).

— **Marsh Harrier** (UK). *Circus aeruginosus.* **Northern Harrier** (US). *Circus cyaneus.* Large hawk-like birds, feeding on birds and small mammals. Found especially in areas of marshland.

— **Audubon friends.** The Audubon Society is a society in the United States originally devoted to the protection of birds and, now, to the protection of wild-life in general. It takes its name from J. J. Audubon (1785-1851), an ornithologist whose *Birds of America* contains beautiful and accurate paintings of almost five hundred species of birds.

— **Who can frame (discontents).** Three words inevitably echoing words in the poem *The Tiger* by W. Blake (I.16). 'Tiger, tiger, burning bright / In the forests of the night, / What immortal hand or eye / Could frame thy fearful symmetry?'

— **Microcosms.** From late-Latin *microcosmus*—from the ancient Greek, *micros* ('small') and *kosmos* ('world, universe').

— **Nostalgia.** See above, under 'gnostalgia'.

— **Silly sheep.**

> 'Priests were the first deluders of mankind, / Who with vain faith made all their reason blind; / Not Lucifer himself more proud than they, / And yet persuade the world they must obey; / Of avarice and luxury complain, / And practise all the vices they arraign. / Riches and honour they from laymen reap, / And with dull crambo feed the silly sheep. / As Killigrew buffoons his master, they / Droll on their god, but a much duller way. / With hocus-pocus, and their heavenly light, / They gain on tender consciences at night. / Whoever has an over-zealous wife / Becomes the priest's Amphitryo during life.'

A. Marvell (see ch. 13 above, under 'meaning of love'), *Poems on Affairs of State* (1689, posthumous).

In ancient Greek mythology, Zeus impersonated Amphitryon to have his way with the latter's wife. Thomas Killigrew was a contemporary dramatist.

The word 'crambo' means 'cabbage' (from the Latin *crambe*, from the Greek *crambe*)—and hence, in this context, 'worthless religious teaching'. In English, Crambo was also the name of a rhyming game—because the Roman poet Juvenal (c.60-c. 130 CE) had applied the word to boring poetry, calling it *crambe repetita* ('repetitious cabbage').

Marvell was a serious Protestant (except for a brief flirtation with Catholicism when he was an undergraduate). It was presumably by Catholic priests that 'silly sheep' were misled. 'Silly' in the 17th century meant 'easily led', rather than 'silly' in the modern sense. Shakespeare had used 'silly sheep' in the word-play scene in *Love's Labour's Lost* (1595/96), V. i.

— **Asymptotically**. In geometry, an asymptote is a line which approaches ever closer to a curve without meeting it.

— **Hope and experience**. Inappropriate echo of Samuel Johnson's saying (worthy of Oscar Wilde). A second marriage is 'the triumph of hope over experience.' Boswell's *Life* (Dr Maxwell's recollections; see ch. 16 above, under 'anatomy of optimism').

— **The eye sees itself**. On Bacon's *radius reflexus*, see ch.11 above, under 'cup of strength'.

— **Pride in being irrational**. Echo of the saying: *credo quia absurdum* (in Latin, 'I believe it because it is not supported by reason'; in Latin, *absurdus* means 'unreasonable, foolish').

This saying has traditionally been attributed to the Christian writer Tertullian (c.155-c.222); son of a Roman centurion in Africa, he was born and died in Carthage (see ch. 9 above). The saying is not to be found *ipsissimis verbis* in his extensive surviving writings.

However, the phrase does reflect one of his essential ideas. *Faith*, as a mode of knowing, is distinct from *Reason*. (See ch.12 above, under 'theism/deism').

For instance, he applied this idea to what he refers to as the 'impossible' fact of the 'resurrection from the dead' of Jesus Christ. The belief of those who believe in that fact, he said, is founded on the testimony of those who actually witnessed the event, and were believers in it as a manifestation of the divinity of Christ.

Compare S. Freud's discussion of the saying attributed to Tertullian.

'It maintains that religious doctrines are outside the jurisdiction of reason—are above reason. Their truth must be felt inwardly, and they need not be comprehended. But this *Credo* is only of interest as a self-confession. As an authoritative statement it has no binding force. Am I to be obliged to believe *every* absurdity? And if not, why this one in particular? There is no appeal to a court above that of reason. If the truth of religious doctrines is dependent on an inner experience which bears witness to the truth, what is one to do about the many people who do not have that rare experience? One may require every man to use the gift of reason which he possesses, but one cannot erect, on the basis of a motive that exists only for a very few, an obligation that shall apply to everyone.'

The Future of an Illusion (1927), V. (tr., W. Robson-Scott) (see ch.11 above, under 'world ocean').

Another commonly held view is that of W. James (see ch. 5 above, under 'Henry's brother William'). 'In its inner nature, belief, or the sense of reality, is a sort of feeling more allied to the emotions than to anything else.' It is 'intimately connected with subsequent practical activity'. Principles of Psychology (1890), II.

— **Royal Ballet.** The principal ballet company in the United Kingdom, based at the Royal Opera House, Covent Garden, in London.
— **Holy water.** Water that has been blessed by an appropriate religious ritual. Hilda Greene is no doubt referring to 'holy water' in the Christian use of the expression.
— **Odour of sanctity.** Originally referring to a Christian belief that the corpse of a saintly person emits a sweet smell, the phrase came to be used, usually sarcastically (as here by David Greene), to refer to people who make a show of their piety, possibly masking hypocrisy (compare: 'Pharisee').
— **One True Faith, definitive and infallible.** No doubt Alison, a 'Catholic sometimes' (IP, ch. 2) has in mind the awful problems posed by the general idea of a 'One True Faith'.

A religion would not be much of a religion if it were not believed by its believers to be the one true faith. But there then arises a separate question of whether believers should decide simply to co-exist with non-believers or should to seek to *convert* non-believers into believers. Again, it is not unreasonable, but not necessary, that believers should want to share their faith with non-believers.

But there then arises a further question of whether to seek to *compel* non-believers to become believers by the use of physical force, or other forms of extreme pressure, or even to seek to destroy other faiths or to exterminate believers in other faiths. History shows numerous examples of all these forms of behaviour. It would not be unreasonable for non-believers—and even believers—to regard such behaviour as simply a criminal abuse of public power, if it is the work of some public authority, or common crime, if it is the work of anyone else.

It is a matter for each religion, within its own limits, to decide these questions. A justification for any such decision, from *inside* a given religion, may have no meaning or value *outside* that religion—for non-believers, for international law, for criminal law, or for law in general.

In the case of the Roman Catholic Church, its organisational structure includes authorities and systems designed for the purpose of taking such decisions (see ch. 1 above). That structure also includes an office-holder—the Pope, Bishop of Rome—whose status is as of a first among equals (bishops), but whose authority is very much more than that status would imply. In particular, the Pope's decision on certain matters is believed to be final and binding—so-called 'Papal Infallibility' (from Italian *Papa*, 'Pope', and a negative form of the Latin *fallere*, 'to be mistaken').

A decree of the First Vatican Council (1869-70) defined the nature of Papal Infallibility. When the Pope decides that a particular 'doctrine of faith or morals' is to be held by the entire Church, then that doctrine becomes an infallible (unchallengeable, invariable) doctrine of the Church. The decision to define the doctrine formally at the Council was intensely controversial, as is the meaning of the words used. It was warmly supported by Cardinal Manning (1808-92), Archbishop of Westminster, head of the Roman Catholic Church in England.

The civil rights of Catholics in England having only been restored in 1829, the Roman Church in England set about reasserting itself with remarkable vigour. A tendency within Anglicanism (see Appendix 2)—the Oxford Movement (from 1851)—sought to move closer to Roman forms, and there were conversions from Anglicanism to Roman Catholicism, not least of the future Cardinals Manning and Newman.

As a student at Oxford, Henry Manning had been a close friend of W.E. Gladstone, the future Prime Minister, who, as a schoolboy at Eton College, had been the closest friend of A. Hallam who, as a student at Trinity College, Cambridge, had been the closest friend of the future Poet Laureate, A. Tennyson ('as near perfection as mortal man could be', Tennyson said) (see I.18).

Manning was also a friend of another Oxford student S. Wilberforce (son of W. Wilberforce, the campaigner against slavery), who, as Bishop of Oxford, would take part in a famous public debate in Oxford (1860) with T.H. Huxley (see below) on the subject of Darwinism—the former challenging the latter to say whether it was through his grandfather or his grandmother that he claimed descent from a monkey.

The ethos of Oxford University seems to be especially apt to produce both ambitious politicians *and* High Church aesthetes (see I.19, under 'religion of beauty'). The English writer Lytton Strachey (1880-1932) (an undergraduate at Trinity College, Cambridge, 1899-1903), in writing about Cardinal Manning, contrasts the ethos of Cambridge University 'whose cloisters have ever been consecrated to poetry and common sense'.

Certainly, the bracing air of Cambridge seems to have produced a remarkable number of successful poets and of scientists and mathematicians—the activities of the latter being, perhaps, manifestations of both 'common sense' and 'poetry'.

But it also produced various members of the so-called Bloomsbury Group (including Strachey), whose cultural and moral ethos was self-consciously ambiguous. Maynard Keynes (King's College, Cambridge) was an economist, an aesthete, and rich.

In post-[King-]Edwardian England (after 1910), the Bloomsbury Group were a mutual-admiration society of more or less admirable people, exceptionally devoted to high culture, with a centre of gravity in the Bloomsbury district of London, but with socio-cultural outposts in other places, including Cambridge and East Sussex.

They were epigones of the denizens of the Parisian *salons* of the 18th and 19th centuries, the (Cambridge) Apostles, The Metaphysical Society (a sounding-board, in particular, for T.H. Huxley), and The Souls (a refuge from the mindlessness of London society for the benefit, in particular, of A.J. Balfour—see in ch. 12 above).

— **Iconoclasts**. From ancient Greek, *eikōn*, 'image, likeness'; *klasō*, 'to break'. Destroyers of religious images, especially images of persons. In the 8th century, in the Eastern (Byzantine) part of the Christian Church there was a movement led by the Eastern Emperors to destroy all such images. As an aspect of the Protestant Reformation in Europe (16th and 17th centuries), there was much destroying of images, especially sculpture and paintings, on the ground that they were sacrilegious.

— **They will manufacture people**. Greg Seare is referring to the fact that it is now certain that, sooner or later, the relevant natural sciences will come together to enable human beings to be manufactured, in accordance with pre-determined specifications, in much the same way as machines are manufactured. An interesting consequence is that the aspects of human personality and behaviour related to sexual reproduction will then have to be directed elsewhere!

The idea that machines will eventually take over from human beings is not a new idea. 'In the course of ages we will find ourselves the inferior race.' S. Butler (see ch.12 above, under 'the way of all religions'). In a letter to a New Zealand newspaper, Butler compared the evolution of machines to the (Darwinian) evolution of human beings.

T.H. Huxley (see next entry) said: 'we shall, sooner or later, arrive at a mechanical equivalent of consciousness'. 'I protest that if some great Power would agree to make me always think what is true and do what is right, on condition of being turned into a sort of clock and wound up every morning before I got out of bed, I should instantly close with the offer.' (speaking to the Cambridge YMCA in 1870).

— **World without religion**. Passionate and/or scornful and/or rational rejection of religion is an ancient phenomenon—and yet religion survives. Even 19th-century nihilism was unable to deliver the *coup de grâce* (see ch. 3 above, *passim*). This has led to another ancient idea: that religion must satisfy some psychological need. From this it has seemed to follow that it will be difficult to get rid of religion so long as the psychological need persists, or until some other way of satisfying that need is found.

The failure of attempts to suppress established religions suggests that the *suppression* of religion is not likely to offer a general solution to the problem, at least in the foreseeable future. In ancient Egypt, the Pharaoh Amenophis IV (Akhenaton) (1372-54) failed. In the Eastern Roman Empire, Julian 'the Apostate' (331-363) failed—*vicisti Galilaee* ('You won, Galilean [Jesus Christ]', dying words attributed to Julian. In Revolutionary France, Robespierre and the Jacobins failed. Even in the ruthless Stalinist Russian and Maoist Chinese Empires, religion persisted within the minds of many of the people.

In a letter (2 January 1910) to Jung, Freud had said:

'It has occurred to me that the ultimate basis of man's need for religion is *infantile helplessness*, which is so much greater in man than in animals. After infancy he cannot conceive of a world without parents and makes for himself a just God and a kindly nature, the two worst anthropomorphic falsifications he could have imagined.'

In reply (2 February 1910) Jung said:

'Religion can be replaced only by religion.'
The Freud/Jung Letters (1974). (trs., R.Manheim and R. Hull).

K. Marx recognised the scale of the problem.

'Religion is the general theory of this world, its encyclopaedic compendium, its logic in popular form, its spiritual point d'honneur, its enthusiasm, its moral sanction, its solemn complement, and its universal basis of consolation and justification. It is the fantastic realization of the human essence since the human essence has not acquired any true reality. The struggle against religion is, therefore, indirectly the struggle against that world whose spiritual aroma is religion. Religious suffering is, at one and the same time, the expression of real suffering and a protest against real suffering. Religion is the sigh of the oppressed creature, the heart of a heartless world, and the soul of soulless conditions. It is the opium of the people [*das Opium des Volkes*].'
K. Marx, *Zur Kritik der Hegelschen Rechtsphilosophie* (*Critique of Hegel's Philosophy of Right*). One of the so-called 1844 Manuscripts, not published in his lifetime, reflecting the early stages of Marx's thinking (still under the influence, among others, of Rosuseau).

As did F. Nietzsche.

'Christianity, in particular, might be called a great treasure house of ingenious means of consolation: it offers such a collection of refreshments, palliatives, and narcotics; it risks so much that is most dangerous and audacious; it has displayed such refinement and subtlety, such southern subtlety, in guessing what stimulant affects will overcome, at least for a time, the deep depression, the leaden exhaustion, the black melancholy of the physiologically inhibited. For we may generalize: the main concern of all great religions has been to fight a certain weariness and heaviness grown to epidemic proportions.'

F. Nietzsche, *Genealogy of Morals*, Third Essay, §17. (tr., W. Kaufmann).

Scientism, Marxism, Freudianism and Capitalism have seemed, at different times and in different ways, to offer a possible replacement for religion, a possible methadone for the opium religious addiction.

But there seems now to be no reason to believe that any of these—*isms* is likely to replace religion, at least in the foreseeable future.

Scientism.

Baconism (see Appendix 1) gave a philosophical basis to the orderly uncovering of the order of the natural world (the 'laws of nature'), including the human animal as an aspect of the natural world. But Bacon himself recognised that other aspects of human experience, especially the area that human consciousness sees as the *supernatural* realm, are a separate province, beyond the reach of 'natural philosophy' (the natural sciences).

Especially in France, in the 18th century, it came to seem that this reticence to extend rigorous study to things human and divine was unnecessary. It must be possible to find the laws governing not only economic phenomena (see Appendix 5), but human phenomena in general—an approach we may call *human scientism.*

C. Condorcet 1743-94), C. Saint-Simon (1760-1825), and A. Comte (1798-1857) argue that the emancipation of the human mind from the fantasies of metaphysics and religion makes it possible, at last, to consider human phenomena abstractly and objectively—to chart and extrapolate the trajectory of human progress—from religion to metaphysics to science (Condorcet), to affirm a 'religion of science' (Saint-Simon), to practise a quasi-scientific discipline of 'sociology' (Comte), creating the possibility of a new kind of scientifically coherent and godless religion, a 'religion of humanity' (Comte).

Subsequent experience has shown that none of the human sciences—not even historiography, anthropology or psychology—can do more than analyse and synthesise, and make hypotheses about, religious phenomena. There is no reason to suppose that they will ever be able to eliminate the religious phenomenon.

Darwinism (from 1859) then encouraged the idea that the natural sciences themselves could simply take possession of human phenomena in general, with no pre-determined limit to their capacity to determine the nature and causes of human phenomena of all kinds—an approach we may call *natural scientism.*

T.H. Huxley (see ch. 15 above, under 'omega point' and Appendix 7) came to be seen as (and to behave as) the prophet of this new scientific triumphalism.

'Science takes the place of dogmatic religion. Mr Huxley is the favourite and popular apostle of this new creed.'
The Tablet (a Roman Catholic magazine founded in 1840), writing in1871. Quoted in A. Desmond, *Huxley: From Devil's Disciple to Evolution's High Priest* (1994).

Huxley insisted vehemently that *agnosticism* (the word he himself had coined) was not the same thing as *atheism*. Atheism, he said, is as unprovable as polytheism. An agnostic simply suspends judgment on matters that are not, in principle or not yet, provable or disprovable.

Huxley was the high priest of what was already described as a 'priesthood of science' and, later, when Whewell's new word (see Appendix 7) came to be a commonplace, a 'priesthood of *scientists*'.

What struck his contemporaries powerfully was that Huxley's devotion to science was itself of a virtually religious character, the product of what one is tempted to call a Protestant Science Ethic.

'. . . his nature is essentially Puritanic, if not Calvinistic. He has the moral earnestness, the volitional energy, the absolute confidence in his own convictions, the desire and determination to impress them upon all mankind, which are the essential marks of Puritan character.'
T.Baynes, writing in 1873, quoted in Desmond (above).

Late in life, Huxley's contrasted the purity of Science, uncovering the hidden eternal order of things, with the rapidly accumulating, amazing, and often unpleasant achievements of *technology*, seen as applied science—the 'froth and scum' of science, as he put it, in one of his less perceptive and less prescient judgments.

As Greg Seare witnessed at Goldberg Pynch, in the 20th century natural scientism has acquired a self-justifying and irreversible hegemony over the human future, of a kind which even Bacon and Huxley, in their most propagandising mood, could not have imagined. And its technical by-products now regularly surpass the most urgent human needs and desires. But these products are not always judged to be a good thing, and are sometimes judged to be a very bad thing indeed. See ch.4 above, under 'academy of projectors', and ch.19 below.

It is possible that these developments in natural scientism, far from curing or even displacing the human hunger for religion, are themselves now contributing to an intensifying of the neurotic and desperate aspects of religion's attraction for the human mind.

Marxism.

'Examined closely, Marxism is not just *one* among many hypotheses replaceable tomorrow by another; it is a simple statement of the conditions without which there will be no humanity in the sense of a reciprocal relationship between men and no rationality in history. In a sense it is not *a* philosophy of history, it is *the* philosophy of history, and to refuse to accept it is to blot out historical reason. After which there will be nothing left but dreams or aimless adventure.'

M. Merleau-Ponty, *Humanism and Terror. An Essay on the Communist Problem* (1947). (tr., J. O'Neill).

In *The Opium of the Intellectuals* (1955), the French writer R. Aron (1905-83) cites this passage as an example of the effort to turn Marxism (or, at least, a supposedly 'humanised' version of Marxism) into a virtual religion. He links his own opinion to the thesis of J. Benda in his *La trahison des clercs* (The Treason of the Intellectuals) (1927).

Benda argues that intellectuals 'had ceased to care for higher things and had come to regard the organisation of the temporal city as the ultimate goal. They taught people to prize earthly goods, national independence, the political rights of the citizen, the raising of living standards.' It was 'the secularisation of thought' by 'a humanity which is giving itself up to realism with a unanimity, a lack of reserve, a sanctification of its passion utterly unprecedented in history.' On the contrary, the mission of intellectuals is to serve higher permanent values, such as truth and justice.

Any radical emancipatory potentiality of Marxism has been much damaged, perhaps fatally, by its association with tyrannical and corrupt social orders in the 20th century.

Freudianism.

In his intellectual autobiography *Memories, Dreams, Reflections* (1961), C. Jung recalls the moment when he felt that he had truly analysed Freud's obsession with sexuality.

'One thing was clear: Freud, who had always made much of his irreligiosity, had now constructed a dogma; or rather, in place of a jealous God whom he had lost, he had substituted another compelling image, that of sexuality. It was no less insistent, exacting, domineering, threatening, and morally ambivalent than the original one. Just as the psychically stronger agency is given "divine" or "daemonic" attributes, so the "sexual libido" took over the role of a *deus absconditus*, a hidden or concealed god. The advantage of this transformation

for Freud was, apparently, that he was able to regard the new numinous
principle as scientifically irreproachable and free from all religious taint.'
(ch. V; trs., R. and C. Winston).

Any radical emancipatory potentiality of Freudianism has been damaged,
perhaps fatally, by its association with pathological mental phenomena flowing from
a socialising, a universalising, and now a globalising, of an obsession with human
sexuality to which Freudianism contributed much psychic energy.

Capitalism.

Twentieth-century philosophers of capitalism are as far from Adam Smith
(see Appendix 5 below) as is Thomas Aquinas from Paul of Tarsus among the
philosophers of Christianity. The Austrian school of conservative economists—in
particular, L. von Mises (1881-1973) and F. Hayek (1899-1972)—have taken
the ideological struggle between Capitalism and Socialism to a philosophical level
ironically reminiscent of the work of K. Marx and F. Engels, involving views of the
most universal kind about the nature and purpose of social life and the potentiality
of human happiness.

However, the lived reality of advanced capitalism—with its high values of
materialism, Darwinian struggle, and insatiable desire—suggests that it is not, and
never will be, capable of meeting the psychic need to which religion, for better and
for worse, has traditionally responded.

On the contrary, by propagating an illusory idea of happiness, often at great
personal psychic cost to workers and consumers, it is contributing to an intensifying
of the neurotic and desperate aspects of religion's attraction for the human mind.
See further in ch.19 below.

Indifferentism.

As noted above, 19th-century agnosticism was anything but indifferentist. It
knew that the concern of the human mind with the matters traditionally dealt with
by religion could not be simply ignored. It was an intensely serious concern, to
which natural and human science must apply itself, so far as possible, with a view
to finding some form of psychotherapy.

In the late-20th century, it began to seem that the problem of religion would
become bound up with an apparently unrelated social phenomenon—the gradual
emptying of the human mind—a phenomenon that Alison and Greg refer to in
this conversation.

As the mind is gradually emptied of memory, including historical memory,
knowledge, thinking, and education—which had been the main processes of human
psychic development—the phenomenon of religion might also wither away. Religion
may wither away as the capacity to think about difficult things withers away—the
capacity to think about anything other than actual situations and immediate desires.

In the future, people may be left knowing nothing at all, and hence believing nothing at all.

— **Philosopher-kings**. Echo of Plato's most concise statement of one of the central theses of his *Republic*.

> 'Unless, I [Socrates] said, either philosophers become kings in our states or those whom we now call our kings and rulers take to the pursuit of philosophy seriously and adequately, and there is a conjunction of these two things, political power and philosophical intelligence . . . there can be no cessation of troubles, dear Glaucon, for our states, nor, I fancy, for the human race either.' 473d. (tr., P. Shorey).

Strange as it may seem, the idea is still regarded as controversial—the idea that the higher powers of the mind might be applied to the exercise of political power—an idea reflected in the ancient Chinese, and modern European, institution of a professional civil service of public officials, educated in such a way as to have the capacity to bring rational intelligence to the business of government.

Plato's own ideas on the practical application of the ideas of transcendental social philosophy have also been severely criticised. See ch.13 above, under 'ideology'.

> 'Plato's philosophy is the most savage and the most profound attack upon liberal ideas which history can show. It denies every axiom of "progressive" thought and challenges all its fondest ideals. Equality, freedom, self-government—all are condemned as illusions which can be held by idealists whose sympathies are stronger than their sense. The true idealist, on Plato's view, will see men as they are, observe their radical inequalities, and give to the many not self-government but security, not freedom but prosperity, not knowledge but the "noble lie". The perfect State is not a democracy of rational equals, but an aristocracy in which a hereditary caste of cultured gentlemen care with paternal solicitude for the toiling masses.'
>
> 'I still find the *Republic* the greatest book on political philosophy which I have read. The more I read it, the more I hate it: and yet I cannot help returning to it time after time.'
>
> R. Crossman, *Plato Today* (1937), chs. IV, X.

In an Introduction to a second edition (1959), Crossman said:

> 'I see now more clearly than I did twenty years ago that my irreverent hostility to Plato was just as prejudiced as the adulation of my elderly colleagues [at Oxford University, where Crossman was an academic, before he became a Labour Party politician]. If I was right to portray him as a failed politician,

they were equally justified in calling him the founder of what we now call theology, theory of knowledge, ethics and semantics.'

— **Sociobiologically advantageous**. Greg Seare is here drawing attention to the fact that a *sociobiologist* might take the view that *religion* serves the biological purpose of assisting human beings or human societies, or the human species in general, to survive and prosper.

A leader in the field of *sociobiology* has defined the field of study.

'Sociobiology is defined as the systematic study of the biological basis of all social behaviour.' E.O. Wilson, *Sociobiology. The New Synthesis* (1975).

The definition obviously includes the possibility that such a study may be applied not only to the social behaviour of non-human animal species but also to the social behaviour of the human species.

As the human species is closely related, through evolution, to other animal species and hence, ultimately, to all animal species, what we can know of the social behaviour of other animal species must obviously be relevant to our understanding of the social behaviour of human beings.

Such a conclusion is also obviously supported by the fact that other animal species appear to behave in ways that are remarkably similar to ways in which human beings behave, including ways that evidently involve instinct and thought and memory and purpose, and meaningful communication.

The conclusion is also supported by the fact that human behaviour itself is obviously determined to a considerable extent by the biological constitution of each human being (ontogeny) and of human beings in general (phylogeny).

However, the application of such considerations to human beings, especially to human social behaviour, gives rise to several serious problems.

(1) Hypotheses about such matters have a problematic *epistemological* status. Biology, as a field of study, extends over a vast range of levels of organisation of living things, from the molecular level to the level of social behaviour. Hypotheses about matters at the more general level are incapable of either verification or falsification, as those terms are applied to the hypotheses of 'hard' science, including those relating the more fundamental levels of biological organisation.

(2) The exceptional level of development of the *thinking capacity* of the human being, and the vast volume of accumulated human thought, obviously distinguish human behaviour from animal behaviour, but to what extent, and with what consequences?

(3) Hypotheses which are produced, notwithstanding (1) and (2) above, are liable to be treated as having a *deterministic* effect—'since this is how things biologically are, this must be how things humanly are, and will be, and shall be'.

For example—

(a) the struggle involved in *economic* processes—is it, or is not, a reflection of the struggle of biological species-survival? Ironically, both Darwin and Wallace were strongly influenced by the determinist capitalist economics of T. Malthus (see Appendix 5) in assigning a central place to struggle in their accounts of the origin of species;

(b) the *social dominance* of the male human gender or of certain racial or ethnic groups—are they, or are they not, a reflection of inequalities of power in non-human animal species?

(c) the human propensity to *aggressive behaviour*, up to and including inter-societal war—is it, or is it not, a reflection of biologically programmed aggressive instincts in non-human animal species?

Hypotheses on such matters are liable to have very substantial effects on the self-constituting of human personality and human societies, especially if those hypotheses are treated deterministically.

— **Puritans in American colonies**. See ch. 15 above, under 'Americans, a chosen people'.

— **Darker age**. Reference to the 'Dark Ages', a term applied at one time, by those who did not know better, to most of the 'Middle Ages' (see ch. 12 above) of European history (5th to 12th centuries) or else to a more limited period around the time of the invasion of the territories of the Roman Empire by so-called 'barbarian' tribes (c. 5th century), a period from which there survive relatively few remains of art and literature.

— **Ideology**. See ch. 13 above, under 'ideology'.

— *Passim*. In Latin (and English), 'here and there'.

— *A la carte*. In French (and English), 'choosing from a list of choices'.

— **Beyond politics**. An idea, which is gaining wider acceptance, is to the effect that the form of 'politics' which has been a central feature of liberal democracy is being superseded by new forms of collective will-formation. See further in ch. 19 below.

— **The Ark**. Reference to a story in the (biblical) *Book of Genesis*, chs. 6-8. 'God saw that the wickedness of man was great in the earth, and that every imagination of the thoughts of his [man's] heart was only evil continually.' God decided to flood the face of the earth to destroy every living thing, including all human beings, 'for it repenteth me that I have made them' (King James version, 1611). But he singled out Noah as a good man, ordering him to build an ark (a ship-like vessel) to save his family and two examples of various species of animals.

It would not be surprising if God had repented himself of his creation of human beings on many other subsequent occasions. But this we may never know.

— **End of History**. See I.19.

— **Neolithic times**. In Greek, *neos*, 'new'; *lithos*, 'stone'. The later part of the Stone Age in the history of human social and technical development. It includes the beginning of agriculture, and hence of fixed human settlements. In the Middle East, the cradle of urban civilisation, it occurred at about 12,000-10,000 BCE. In Europe, especially Northern Europe, it occurred much later. It was followed by the Bronze and Iron Ages, again referring to stages of technical development.

— **Without wrong there can be no right**. 'It is important to remember that evil is essential to the order of the world and to the birth of the good.' Voltaire, *Zadig* (1747) (the angel Jesred speaking). *Zadig* is, like *Candide* (I.21), one of Voltaire's *contes philosophiques* (philosophical stories), in which a story is used to explore a philosophical theme (though without the benefit of an *explanation of allusions*), in this case the problem of evil.

— **To be loved you must love**. See ch. 8 above, under '*si vis amari*'.

— **C'est son métier**. *Dieu me pardonnera, c'est son métier*. In French, 'God will forgive me. It's his job.' Dying words attributed by A. Meißner to H. Heine (see ch. 2 above, under '*dahin*'; ch. 15 above, under 'Plato Quotient'; and Appendix 8).

— **What would the universe say?** The Cardinal is probably not thinking, on this occasion, of the beautiful idea in Hindu philosophy that, at the creation of the universe, the universe emitted the sound *Aum* or *Om,* the original sound that contains all other sounds, all words, all languages.

He may possibly have in mind the words of Psalm19, in the (biblical) *Book of Psalms*. 'The heavens declare the glory of God; and the firmament sheweth his handywork. Day unto day uttereth speech, and night unto night sheweth knowledge.' (King James version, 1611).

— **Process of becoming**. A central idea of Aristotle's metaphysics is the idea that existence is the unfolding of a potentiality of becoming, that potentiality being, as it were, an *essential* order or self-ordering, leading to self-fulfilment. (See I.13.)

This idea seems to reconcile a number of ideas that he found in earlier philosophers—the ultimate nature of reality as *change* (Heraclitus); the nature of reality as *self-creating* (Parmenides); the universality of *order* (Pythagoras); existence as a reflection of something that *transcends* existence and contains *universal value* (Plato).

Such a process applies to all existence, even if it is most apparent in organic growth and, in particular, in the life of human beings, who have the special characteristic that they are able to be conscious of their becoming, and to take responsibility for their becoming (see next entry). To the modern mind, such ideas resonate powerfully with the idea of *genetic programmes* at the root of organic forms.

Only 'God' (in the ancient Greek abstract sense of the term, rather than the Judeo-Christian highly personalised God) is exempt from the process of becoming—God's *essence* and *existence* being one and the same thing.

These ideas constitute, perhaps, a 'moment' (see ch. 11 above) in which Western philosophy parted company with some forms of Eastern philosophy in which the *self* is seen as an illusion, and the ideal of *becoming* is an extinguishing of the selfishness which is the source of suffering. Those aspects of Western culture which enshrine ideas of *fierce individualism* and *relentless progressivism* are surely born out of this 'moment'.

The self-understanding of the human being might have been—and might be—otherwise in a world not dominated by fierce individualism and relentless progressivism.

Western culture experienced another significant 'moment', when the Hellenic stream of consciousness met the Hebraic stream of consciousness to form Christianity. See ch. 3 above, under 'Hellenic and Hebraic'.

— **Ethics, a philosophy of what to do next.** The remarkable nature of Aristotle's mind, not to speak of his evidently inexhaustible intellectual energy, led him to seek to bring order to every known aspect of human knowledge—knowledge of the natural world, of the social and political worlds, of the world of the mind. His universalising achievement is another 'moment' (see previous entry) in the development of the human species-mind—the moment when the human mind decides that it has the capacity to take stock of the whole of its content, and to put the whole contents of the mind in order.

Aristotle was even responsible for organising our knowledge into the heuristic compartments which have ever since proved to be more or less convenient. One of those compartments is *politics* (how to organise human social life in the *polis*). Another is *ethics*—how to organise our capacity to *will* our *actions*.

The ancient Greek word *ēthos* (in the plural, *ēthea*) was used in two different senses which are delightfully reflected in the long history of the study of ethics.

The word was used to mean both 'custom, usage, and habit' and 'disposition, temper and character'. Is morality conventional—accumulated social rules or standards—or is it something to do with the inner life of the particular human being? Or is it, perhaps, a reflection of a form of *order* which transcends the individual human being and human society? All three have been advocated as the basis of morality.

Aristotle himself, in the *Nichomacean Ethics* (at least in the rather confused form in which it has come down to us), wanders among the three, the third being, we may suppose, the product of the influence of his teacher Plato (see ch. 18 below).

A similar problem arose in Latin, where the word *mos* (plural *mores*) was used to mean both 'a person's will' and a society's 'custom or usage'.

Cicero (see ch. 11 above, under 'thou art that', and *passim.*) resolved the matter, in characteristic fashion, by inventing a new word to reflect the inheritance from the Greek philosophers—a plural word *moralia* (which, like Aristotle, he identified as a *pars philosophiae*—a department within philosophy). Cicero's word gave us in English a second word, *morality*, in addition to the Greek-derived word *ethics*.

Cicero struggled nobly with the problem of rendering into Latin the rich inheritance of abstract concepts in Greek philosophy. He was obliged to invent a whole series of new words to reproduce the Greek concepts. Many of his inventions have been used, like *moralia*, to form words in the English language.

> *Quality. Individual, Vacuum. Property. Induction. Element. Definition.*
> *Difference. Notion. Comprehension. Infinity. Appetite. Instance. Science. Image.*
> *Species.* English-speakers have to thank Cicero for all of these words.
> (See M. Grant, intro. to Cicero's *On the Good Life*, 1971).

The triploid conception of morality (custom—character—universal order) makes a notable appearance in the philosophy of Hegel (see Appendix 8). He distinguishes *Sittlichkeit* (socially or traditionally based morality) and *Moralität* (the intuitive morality of the individual human being), both of them being subject to the transcendental ordering of the World Spirit.

— *Synousia. Synoikia. Sympathia. Symmetria. Symphonia.* In ancient Greek—'being together'—'living together'—'feeling together'—'symmetry'—'harmony, sounding together'.

— *Harmonia. Eunomia.* In ancient Greek, 'harmony, agreement'; 'the good order of society' (see I.19).

The number of words in ancient Greek expressing these related ideas is remarkable. The ancient Greeks seem to have had a powerful attachment to the idea of *order*, in everything from the self-constituting of the human individual through the order of society to the order of the universe. This mind-set generated the possibility of explaining everything in the universe in a single coherent system of ideas.

This Greek form of universalism offers a possible explanation of everything in the universe, a universalism which is apart from all religious forms of universalism.

It has been a fundamental structural component in the self-constituting of all societies whose structure can be traced, directly or indirectly, to ancient Greek ideas.

It is thus a mind-set of world-historical significance, a leading element in the making of the human-made world as we know it—and hence in the possible re-making of that world!

— **Binding force**. In the current state of *theoretical physics*, four fundamental binding forces of matter are recognised—the *strong nuclear*, the *electromagnetic*, the *weak nuclear*, and *gravitation*. It is an aim of theoretical physics to reduce these four into one single and ultimate binding force. See ch. 13 above, under 'theory of everything'.

F. Bacon (Appendix 1 below) proposed a special conception of 'metaphysics'—the system of *abstractions* that the mind constructs in re-constructing the *order* of the natural world.

He says that people have criticised Plato wrongly for looking for the ultimate 'forms' or 'ideas' of things. Like Aristotle, he says that Plato's mistake was to suppose that they existed 'absolutely abtracted from matter', that is, existing in some higher sphere separately from the things of which they are ultimate forms or ideas. In this way, Bacon says, Plato strayed into the field of theology, 'wherewith all his natural philosophy is infected'.

> 'So of [the pyramid of] natural philosophy [science], the basis is natural history [observation]; the stage next the basis is physics; the stage next the vertical point is metaphysics. As for the vertical point . . . , the summary law of nature, we know not whether man's inquiry can attain unto it . . . And therefore the speculation was excellent in Parmenides and Plato, although but a speculation in them, that all things by scale did ascend to unity.'
> F. Bacon, *The Advancement of Learning* (1605), Second Book (spelling slightly modernised).

It would be delightful to be able to accept the Cardinal's suggestion that, in the current state of *metaphysics*, we have already unified the binding forces of the human universe in a force that we call *love*.

— **The soul is ageless**. No doubt the Cardinal has in mind the idea of the *soul* as intrinsically distinct from the body, and hence not subject to the body's process of aging, whereas Miss Spurgeon is probably thinking of the *soul* as an expression of the totality of our inward lives, which may seem to be very much subject to a process of aging, bearing the scars of all that we have endured.

CHAPTER 18. *Ideal Affinities.*

— **Ideal affinities**. *Dialectic*—new ideas formed from the interaction of old ideas—is central to the mental activity known as philosophy (see ch. 15 above, under 'perpetual feast', and *passim*). But a striking feature of the long life-story of philosophy is a series of particularly close creative intimacies, outside place and beyond time, between specific philosophers.

There are very many examples of such *intellectual affinities* (*Geistesverwandschaften*— I.21) among those philosophers whose ideas have been especially influential in forming the *ideal reality* of the *human world* that we inhabit.

Socrates and Plato. Pythagoras and Plato. Parmenides and Plato. Plato and Aristotle. Aristotle and Carneades. Seneca and Cicero. Jesus Christ and Paul of Tarsus. Plato and Plotinus. Aristotle and Boethius. Aristotle and Albertus Magnus. Albertus Magnus and Aquinas. Bernard of Clairvaux and Dante. Plato and Marsilio Ficino. Erasmus and Luther. Luther and Calvin. Suárez and Grotius. Descartes and Pascal. Aristotle and Bacon. Hobbes and Locke. Bacon and Voltaire. Locke and Voltaire. Voltaire and Rousseau. Rousseau and Voltaire. Locke and Jefferson. Wolff and Vattel. Locke and Hume. Hume and Kant. Rousseau and Kant. Rousseau and Marx. Proudhon and Marx. Marx and Engels. Bentham and J.S.Mill. Shakespeare and Schiller. Kant and Hegel. Hegel and Schopenhauer. Schopenhauer and

Nietzsche. Schopnehauer and Freud. Nietzsche and Freud. Freud and Jung. Darwin and Spencer. Ruskin and Proust. Marx and Lenin.

As discussed in the Chapter 2 Appendices below, even those philosophers who refuse to be *Platonic* or *Aristotelian* idealists accept, openly or tacitly, the idea that it is *ideas* that create human reality, given that the production of ideas is the central *creative* function of the *brain*, whether or not *the idea of the mind* is regarded as being separable from *the idea of the brain*.

It is our own personal *metaphysiology* (ch. 16 above) that will tend to condition our own intellectual affinities, our own *Gesitesverwandschaften*.

— **Category of quantity**. For the philosophical concept of *category*, see Appendices 4 and 8 below.

— **Forms of love**. Edmund, having discovered his *metaphysical self* with the help of the Old Man of the Sea, is now able to experience, for himself, a Platonic-Aristotelian 'moment'—the great *integrating* of metaphysics, ethics, and aesthetics.

He can, at last, become the *philosopher of love* that he has always aspired to be—of *love* in all its forms, from the love of myself, to the love of the mother and the child, through the love of one human being for another, to the love of self-ordering society and the self-ordering universe, and the love of the ideal, and even, possibly, the love of a universe-ordering God.

— **Syncope**. Heart-stopping. Breath-taking. Mind-blowing.

— **Happiness**. We have seen that Edmund has, metaphysiologically, a particular affinity to the great intellectual affinity that is Plato-Aristotle. Their understanding of *happiness*—the ultimate self-integrating of the human soul—is that it is not an emotional state of mind but a state of *being*, that is to say, a state of *becoming*.

CHAPTER 19. *World Mind Revolution.*

— **Holland Park**. A residential area in the Western part of inner London. Its demography has recently become similar to that of Hampstead (see ch.16 above).

— *Jeu de paume*. In French, 'tennis (court)'—for an ancient form of tennis, played indoors—in French, *jeu de paume*; in English, 'real tennis'—as opposed to *le tennis* ('tennis'), the modern form, played outside on grass or clay.

In W. Shakespeare, *Henry V*, a French Ambassador, addressing King Henry, says—

> 'Your highness, lately sending into France, / Did claim some certain dukedoms,
> in the right /of your great predecessor, King Edward the Third / In answer of
> which claim, the prince our master [the Dauphin] . . . / sends you, meeter
> for your spirit, / This tun of treasure . . .'

The King asks his uncle, the Duke of Exeter, 'What treasure, uncle?' The Duke replies—'Tennis-balls, my liege.' (Act I, sc. ii).

The King is not amused, and the Battle of Agincourt (1415) takes place shortly after—in Act IV, sc. iv.

On 20 June 1789 the representatives of the *Tiers état* swore an oath not to disperse until they had obtained a constitution for France. The Revolution itself began with the storming of the Bastille prison in Paris on 14 July 1789. The *Tiers état* (the Third Estate, the respresentative body of the commoners) was one of three bodies (the clergy, the nobility, the commons) in the traditional hierarchy of the French *ancien régime* ('old order', before the Revolution).

Over the centuries, the three 'estates' had met together very occasionally as the *États généraux* ('general estates'). (Before the fateful meeting in 1789, they had last met in 1614.) On this occasion, the Commons, meeting without the other estates, were obliged to swear their revolutionary oath in the *tennis-court* at the Palace of Versailles, the usual meeting place of the Estates being unavailable.

The significance of the French Revolution, generally and in its details, remains a matter of intense controversy to this day, not least in France. 'The French have long memories; for them politics are the continuation of history. Royalist, Bonapartist, Republican—most French writers belong to one of these categories.' D. Cooper, *Talleyrand* (1932), ch.14.

But it is clear that the new self-consciousness of the *Tiers état* was a necessary moment in the eventual transformation of the political system into that of a liberal democracy. A leading propagandist of a new order told them that they represented the 'nation' (E. Sieyès, *Qu'est-ce que le Tiers état?* (What is the Third Estate?) (1789). The Declaration of the Rights of Man and of the Citizen (1789) told them that 'sovereignty lies with the nation'. The Constitution of 1791 said that 'national sovereignty lies with the people'. On French constitutional psychology, see Ph. Allott, *The Health of Nations*, §§7.29-31.

However, as with the 'other view' of the so-called Glorious Revoution of 1688 in England, there are those who argue that, after the French Revolution, the privileged and the powerful under the *ancien régime* re-emerged, in the course of the 19th century, in various new disguises. The Firm, and LOSC and MOTH, will have to hope that this is not an Iron Law of Revolutions.

— **Nailing of theses to the door.** Reference to pre-revolutionary gestures by J. Wyclif and M. Luther. See Appendix 2 below.

— **Boston lunch-party.** Echo of another pre-revolutionary event. By the Tea Act 1773, the (British) East India Company was authorised to export tea 'to any of the British colonies or plantations in America, or to foreign parts, discharged from the payment of any customs or duties whatsoever'.

This legislation was not well received in the colony of Massachusetts. Tea-ships of the Company were boarded in Boston harbour, and their cargo of tea was thrown overboard. This has ever since been called 'the Boston tea-party'. In a British context, a 'tea-party' is (or, probably, was) a minor social event, usually in the late afternoon, involving the drinking of tea and, perhaps, a modest amount of eating. For further information, see 'The Hatter's Mad Tea-Party', in L. Carroll, *Alice in Wonderland* (I.19), ch. VII.

The 1773 Act was one of a number of ill-advised acts of the British Government in relation to the American colonies, which declared their independence from Britain in 1776. See ch. 14 above, under 'unilateral declaration of independence'.

In mitigation of the failings of the Britsh Government in its dealings with the American colonies, it must be said that Britain had paid a very great short-term economic price for its apparent success in the Seven Years War (1756-63)—a pan-European war, with worldwide theatres of conflict. The imposition of burdensome taxation in Brtain and in the colonies was part of a general effort of national economic recovery.

This situation was a foretaste of the devastating economic cost of Britian's apparent successes in the Napoleonic Wars (1793-1815), the First World War (1914-18), and the Second World War (1939-45). (A tax on income was introduced by the British government for the first time in 1798 to help to meet the cost of the Napoleonic Wars.)

None of the four conflicts was initiated or desired by Britain. Whether British diplomacy might have dealt with King Frederick II of Prussia (as instigator of the Seven Years War), Napoleon Bonaparte, Kaiser Wilhelm II of Germany, or Adolf Hitler in some other and better way is a matter for discussion.

— **Tout passe**. Part of a French proverbial saying—*tout passe, tout casse, tout lasse* ('everything goes away, everything breaks down, everything becomes boring').

— **Haute cuisine**. In French, 'high-level cookery'. Cooking of the most sophisticated kind.

— **The party's over**. Echo of a charming song (in the musical *Bells are Ringing*, 1956), music by Jule Styne (1905-94). The lyric, by B. Comden and A. Green, includes the following—'The party's over / It's time to call it a day / They've burst your pretty balloon / And taken the moon away / It's time to wind up the masquerade.'

— **Death wish**. See ch . 6 above, under 'Wyczwycz'. Freud had idenitifed what he believed to be a frequent component of *dreams*—a repressed desire for the death of other people, especially close relatives. After (perhaps, because of) the horrors of the First World War, he later took the view that human personality is ruled not only by what he had called a 'pleasure principle' (*Lustprinzip*) but also by a *Todestriebe* (a 'death drive'). *Jenseits des Lustprinzips* (Beyond the Pleasure Principle) (1919).

He distinguishes this from what many others before him had identified as an apparently biological (evolutionary) component of *aggression* in human personality, which he himself accepted—in the widest form (including war, violence of all kinds, but also jokes, slips of the tongue and mistakes in general (parapraxis), academic disputes, family quarrels, etc.). But Freud's *death drive* is a fundamental tendency of living things to seek their own death, to rejoin inorganic matter.

— **Unwritten constitution** Neither Athens nor Rome had a written constitution. The *ius internum* (internal public law) in the Canon Law of the Roman Church might be said to be a form of written constitution—in the Middle Ages, a written *European* constitution. The Instrument of Government (1653) was a written constitution during the brief period of republicanism in Britain (1649-60).

The British colonies in America had written constitutions. The confederal (1781) and federal (1787) constitutions of the new United States of America were written constitutions. Together with the written constitutions of revolutionary France, they established the idea that a well-ordered nation should have a written constitution.

Experience shows that written constitutions are no guarantee of social stability or governmental propriety. The obvious advantages of an *unwritten* constitution have always been recognised.

The Roman constitution was not reached 'by any process of reasoning, but by the discipline of many struggles and troubles, always choosing the best in the light of the experience gained in disaster.' Polybius (c.200-c.120 BCE).

> 'In history a great volume is unrolled for our instruction, drawing the materials of future wisdom from past errors and infirmities of mankind.'
>
> 'We have an inheritable crown; an inheritable peerage; and a House of Commons and a people inheriting privileges, franchises, and liberties, from a long line of ancestors. This policy appears to me to be the result of profound reflection; or rather the happy effect of following nature, which is wisdom without reflection, and above it.'
>
> E. Burke, *Reflections on the Revolution in France* (1790) (see Appendix 6 below).

— **Constitutional Convention**. Probably a reference to the conference held in Philadelphia in 1787 to draft a new constitution for the United States of America. It may also refer to National Constitutent Assembly in revolutionary France (from 1789) or the National Convention (from 1792) which drafted a constitution (1793).

— **Pilgrims and pioneers**. See ch. 5 above, under 'Connecticut'.

— **Atlantis**. In two of his dialogues (*Timaeus* and *Critias*), Plato recounts the legend of the conquest of Atlantis by Athens, in the very distant past. Atlantis (named after the god Atlas) was an island in the Atlantic Ocean.

> 'Now in this island of Atlantis there was a great and wonderful empire . . .
> This vast power, gathered into one, endeavoured to subdue at a blow our country and yours [Athens].'
> *Timaeus*, 25a-b (Critias speaking). (tr., B. Jowett).

Athens led the resistance and defeated the armies of Atlantis. And then earthquakes caused the island of Atlantis to sink into the depths of the sea—and disappear form history. In the *Critias*, Socrates uses the social and political organisation of Atlantis as a possible example of a well-ordered state—until it became corrupted.

The New Atlantis (1626) by F. Bacon (I.19, and Appendix 1 below) explores the possible arrangements of a modern well-ordered society. It is dominated by a (Baconian) think-tank or university—Salomon's House.

> 'The end of our foundation is the knowledge of causes, and secret motions
> of things; and the enlarging of the bounds of human empire, to the effecting
> of all things possible.'

— **Mind-slaves in iron-cages**. Echo of a phrase used in a work by the German sociologist M. Weber (1864-1920), *The Protestant Ethic and the Spirit of Capitalism.* (1904-5/1920-21). (See ch. 6 above, under 'Weberian sociology'.)

He discusses 'the tremendous cosmos of the modern economic order'.

> 'This order is now bound to the technical and economic conditions of machine
> production which today determine the lives of all individuals who are born
> into this mechanism, not only those directly concerned with economic
> acquisition, with irresistible force.'

Weber quotes another writer saying that care for external goods should lie on the shoulders 'like a light cloak'.

> 'But fate decreed that the cloak should become an iron cage.'

Earlier capitalism had been a form of 'rational conduct on the basis of the idea of calling'—'calling' in the religious sense of a *vocation* in life, reflecting an ascetic ethical spirit within Protestant Christianity. The calling manifested itself as a pious *duty* to create prosperity by rational effort. But that tendency had since been subverted and perverted.

> 'Since asceticism [as part of the Protestant ethic] undertook to remodel the
> world and to work out its ideals in the world, material goods have gained
> an increasing and finally an inexorable power over the lives of men as at no
> previous period in history. Today the spirit of religious asceticism—whether
> finally, who knows?—has escaped from the cage. But victorious capitalism,
> since it rests on mechanical foundations, needs its support no longer. The rosy
> blush of its laughing heir, the Enlightenment, seems also to be irretrievably
> fading, and the idea of duty in one's calling prowls about in our lives like the
> ghost of dead religious beliefs . . .
> 'No one knows who will live in this cage in the future, or whether at
> the end of this tremendous development entirely new prophets will arise, or

there will be a great rebirth of old ideas and ideals, or, if neither, mechanized petrification, embellished with a sort of convulsive self-importance. For of the last stage of this cultural development, it might well be truly said: "Specialists without spirit, sensualists without heart; this nullity imagines that it has attained a level of civilization never before achieved".' (ch. V)' (tr., T. Parsons).

It is certainly a part of the great strength of *capitalism* that it contains *its own high values*—economic freedom, competition, wealth, rationality, efficiency, nationalism, internationalism—which make *traditional high values* unnecessary, or even undesirable, except to the extent that they are useful, and internalised, in the *totalitarian* capitalist social system.

Even *liberal democracy* becomes a necessary adjutant and co-conspirator, efficiently producing the vast volumes of law, government, and administration that totalitarian advanced capitalism requires.

See Ph. Allott, *Eunomia*, §§18.27*ff*, on the possible (or impossible) humanising of capitalism.

— **Middle class (revolution).**

'Thus it is manifest that the best political community is formed by citizens of the middle class, and that those states are likely to be well-administered, in which the middle class is large, and larger if possible than both the other classes . . .'

Aristotle, *Politics*, IV. ii. 10. (tr., B. Jowett).

In the 17th century, when British society was undergoing a permanent and self-conscious social revolution, there was much interest in the social organisation of Holland—a very successful society, apparently based on commerce, with a dominant middle class. (Observers were also sent to Venice, another commercial society, but which was found to be too authoritarian in its political structure.)

F. Bacon was one of the admirers of Holland, and wanted an England where wealth 'resteth in the hands of the merchants, burghers, tradesmen, freeholders, farmers in the country, and the like.'—the middle class being inclined to use their wealth 'sparingly and fruitfully to the general public benefit.'

Indeed, political change in *England*, from the 14th century onwards, may be seen as an accumulating effect of the aspirations of the middle class. The *American* rebellion and the founding of the United States may be seen as the work of the middle class, urban and rural.

T. Jefferson saw that the middle class has a special interest in a well-ordered society. 'Every one, by his property, or by his satisfactory situation, is interested in the support of law and order.' (letter to J. Adams; 28 October 1813). But he also hoped that America might be a society which also includes a 'natural aristocracy'—'the most precious gift of nature, for the instruction, the trusts and government of society'.

In the *French* Revolution, a middle class, broadly defined, dominated the Third Estate (see above), sagaciously supporting the deep popular urge to get rid of the abusive privileges of the nobility and the clergy, but determined to create a new kind of society, based on rational and effective law and order.

K. Marx (*18th Brumaire of Louis Bonaparte*, 1852) characterised as 'bourgeois' the English Revolution of 1688, the American Revolution of 1776, and the French Revolution of 1789.

— **Communist Manifesto**. See ch.15 above, under 'ghost of post-European civilisation'.

— **Fundamentalist pragmatism**. See ch.2, under 'pragmatist'. The word 'fundamentalist' is applied generally to religious believers who take a strictly dogmatic or literalist view of their religious beliefs.

— **Man is unhappy**. See ch.6 above, under 'greatest happiness', and ch.15 above, under 'call no man happy', and *passim*.

— **Holy Land**. For Christians, Palestine, where Jesus Christ lived. (See ch.12 above, under 'ancient Israel'.) Other religions have had, and have, holy places.

— **Everyone is interested in Shakespeare**. May Gaunt could possibly have in mind—but it is more likely that Greg Seare would hear in her words an unintended allusion to—an anecdote relating to the publication of C. Darwin, *The Origin of Species*, in 1859.

John Murray, his prospective publisher, did not think much of the work when he saw it in manuscript, having consulted a publisher's reader, who said that Darwin would be better advised to concentrate on his work on pigeons. 'Everybody is interested in pigeons.'

Murray was the son of John Murray, who was the long-suffering publisher of the works of George, Lord Byron, and who supervised the burning, in his offices, of the manuscript of Byron's scurrilous memoirs, an event which has ever since been regretted by right-thinking people.

— **Nihilism**. From the Latin, *nihil* ('nothing'). A state of mind—especially of the European public mind in the latter part of the 19th century—which denies traditional ideas produced by religion, philosophy, or social custom, and despairs of the possibility of replacing them.

F. Nietzsche, see above *passim*, has seemed to be a representative figure of this state of mind—but he passionately believed in the *necessity* and, perhaps (but always on the borderline of despairingly), the *possibility* of replacing the old ideas. Like Dostoevsky and Weber, and so many others of their contemporaries, familiarity with spiritual despair caused episodes of mental breakdown.

— **Social animals**. Echo of Aristotle, *Politics*, I.2. 'Hence it is evident that the state is a creation of nature, and that man is by nature a political animal [*zoon politikon*: naturally inclined to live in a *polis*, an orderly society].

— *Homme moyen sensuel*. In French, 'an average person, with average intellectual and emotional characteristics'. A classic, somewhat elusive, category in French discourse. Another example is *honnête homme*, a 'decent person', somewhat equivalent to the English 'gentleman', in its looser sense.

— **Gloom of Schopenhauer. Scream of Nietzsche.** Echo of W. Shakespeare, *Macbeth* (1603-06). The action of the tragedy is punctuated—in a stroke of dramatic genius—by the episodic appearance of three Witches. In Act IV, sc. I, they are presiding over a boiling cauldron.

'Fillet of a fenny snake, / In the cauldron boil and bake; / Eye of newt, and toe of frog, / Wool of bat, and tongue of dog, / Adder's fork, and blind-worm's sting, / Lizard's leg, and howlet's wing, / For a charm of powerful trouble, / Like a hell-broth boil and bubble.'

A fine example of Shakespeare's delight in the possibiltiies of the English language (see below under 'Edmund Euphues').

— **Sweep back a sea.** Echo of a legend concerning King Canute (Cnut or Knut), a Danish (Viking) king who invaded England in 1015, became king of most of England, and died in 1035. The Vikings had been invading England since the last years of the 8th century.

The legend is that the king symbolically demonstrated to his courtiers the limits of his royal power by (ineffectively, but predictably) ordering the sea to stop in its tracks. The story was first told by Henry of Huntington in his *Historia Anglorum* (History of the English) (1139).

— **Leading to good fortune.** Echo of an image in W. Shakespeare, *Julius Caesar*. (IV. iv).

'There is a tide in the affairs of men, / Which, taken at the flood, leads on to fortune; / Omitted, all the voyage of their life / Is bound in shallows and in miseries./ On such a full sea are we now afloat; / And we must take the current when it serves, / Or lose our ventures.'

(Brutus, leader of Caesar's assassins, speaking after the event.)

— **Great Game of Government**. 'Great game' is a 19th-century term for diplomacy among the Great Powers, especially between the British and Russian Empires. The term figures prominently in *Kim* (1901), a novel by the English writer R. Kipling (1865-1936) set in India, in which the Great Game is diffusely manifested in the very secondary activity of espionage. See ch. 7 above, under 'little friend'.

— **Rousseau's General Will. Adam Smith's Invisible Hand.** See Appendix 5 below. The interesting link between the two ideas, in political and economic theory respectively, is that they both postulate the *systematic* integration of intensely disintegrated human activity, nevertheless producing what seems to be a coherent, even a rational, outcome.

— *Manière de voir. Manière de vivre.* In French, 'way of seeing' ; 'way of living'. See ch. 13 above.

— *Curriculum vitae meae.* 'The course of my life'. In Latin, *curriculum* is a running-race, from *currere*, 'to run'.

— **Other-determined.** See ch. 15 above, under 'alone in a crowd'.

— **Class of all classes.** B. Russell (I.16) and the American mathematician-philosopher A.N.Whitehead (1861-1947), in their *Principia Mathematica* (1910-13), considered a paradox stemming from the idea of a class (of objects). A class of objects may or may not be a *member* of that class The class of all human beings *is* a member of the class of all human beings. A number (2,3,4 . . .) is a class of things having that number of members, but *is not* itself a member of that class.

There must be a class of all classes that are *not members* of themselves. But that class cannot be a member *of itself* (by definition), but then the class of all classes is not a class of *all* such classes. So there cannot be a class of all classes that are not members of themselves. Or can there?

Russell's suggested solution is to redefine a class (*theory of types*). A *class* is a class of things of the same *type* (*e.g.*, at the same level of abstraction). The class is not of the same *type* as the things that are its members. A *number* is a class which is not of the same *type* as the class of things that are its members. But does this solve the paradox, given that the class of all classes that are *not* members of themselves *could* be said to be of the same *type* as its members?

— **John Rawls.** An American social theorist (1921-2002) who, in *A Theory of Justice* (1971), proposed a rationalised pragmatic non-transcendental liberal theory of justice, according to which social inequalities may only be considered to be justified if they are the product of a bona fide search for social equality. Equality sometimes justifies inequality.

— **Jacques Derrida.** A French post-philosopher (1930-2004) who took the view that the meaning of a product of the human mind (a text, an art work . . .) is constructed in the course of the search for its meaning ('deconstruction'), as is the meaning of that deconstruction—including the meaning of Derrida's own work.

— **Ludwig Wittgenstein.** I.20. Austrian-British post-philosopher who (eventually) took the view that philosophy is an investigation of the puzzles which langugage creates, as we think and talk about abstract matters. Language is not a potential representation of reality (as he had at one time supposed) but a multi-purpose tool that we use pragmatically in communicating thought and feeling.

It is better (he says) to remain silent than to treat the puzzles of human existence as if they contained something more interesting (a 'truth', perhaps) than their effect as linguistic phenomena. See ch. 6 above, under 'mother-father sign/signal', and ch.13 above, under 'the meaning of meaning'.

— *Iter vitae suae.* In Latin, 'the course of his life'.

— **Botanical garden of the mind**. William James (ch. 5 above, under 'Henry's brother William', and *passim*) referred to the university as a 'botanical garden of the mind' where thoughts are 'precious seeds'. (*Essays in Radical Empiricism*).

— **Holy places of the New Ignorance**. The new ignorance at university level may not be entirely new.

J. Milton (1608-74) (Christ's College, Cambridge) condemned the 'intellective abstractions of logic and metaphysics' taught at Cambridge—'an asinine feast of sowthistles and brambles'.

'In the present age, whatever flatters the mind in its ignorance of its ignorance, tends to aggravate that ignorance.' S.T. Coleridge (1772-1834) (Jesus College, Cambridge); in a letter to T. Poole, 1810).

A.Tennyson (1809-92) (Trinity College, Cambridge) wrote a sonnet about his time as an undergraduate at Cambridge, including the lines: 'Because you do profess to teach, / And teach us nothing, feeding not the heart.'

In Britain there was a great mid-19th-century debate about the nature and purpose of a university. Should the university be a place of high scholarship taken to its limits (following what the British saw as the German ideal)? Or should it be a place for training the governing class? Royal Commissions on the Universities of Oxford and Cambridge (1852-3), having considered the options, recommended (characteristically) that British universities should aim to be both things. It is a puzzle that is still puzzling.

J.H. Newman (1801-90) (Trinity and Oriel Colleges, Oxford; see also ch. 20 below) made a substantial contribution to the debate, in a series of lectures published as *The Idea of a University* (1852). He describes the condition of the university students of his day.

'. . . ill-used persons, who are forced to load their minds with a score of subjects against an examination, who have too much on their hands to indulge themselves in thinking or investigation, who devour premises and conclusion together with indiscriminate greediness, who hold whole sciences on faith, and commit demonstrations to memory, and who too often, as might be expected, when their period of education is passed, throw up all they have learned in disgust, having gained nothing really by their anxious labours, except perhaps the habit of application.

'Yet such is the *better* specimen of the fruit of that ambitious system which has of late years been making way among us: for its result on *ordinary* minds, and on the common run of students, is less satisfactory still; they leave their place of education simply dissipated and relaxed by the multiplicity of subjects, which they have never really mastered, and *so shallow as not even to know their shallowness*. How much better, I say, is it for the active and thoughtful intellect, where such is to be found, to eschew [avoid] the College and the University altogether, than to submit to a drudgery so ignoble, a mockery so contumelious.'

(Discourse VI, emphasis added).

In a characteristic Victorian aphorism, J. Ruskin (I.16) said: 'You do not educate a man by telling him what he knew not, but by making him what he was not.'

— **Private vice—public benefit**. On Mandeville's ingenious justification of economic individualism, see Appendix 5 below.

— **Prince of Darkness**. 'The prince of darkness is a gentleman; Modo he's called, and Mahu.' W. Shakespeare, *King Lear*, III. iv. (Edgar speaking, pretending to be mad.) The play was probably written between 1603 and 1606.

L. Theobald (1688-1744) uncovered the remarkable connection between exotic words and phrases used in *King Lear* (including those used here) and S. Harsnett's *Declaration of Egregious Popish Imposters* (1605), a pamphlet inveighing against what he took to be the Roman Catholic practice of exorcisim. Harsnett (1561-1631) was a Fellow and then Master of Pembroke Hall (founded 1347), Cambridge (now Pembroke College), and was made Archbishop of York in 1629.

There are those who believe, on rather slight evidence, that Shakespeare was a closet Roman Catholic, in times when it was dangerous to come out as such. If so, he may have taken particular pleasure in reading Harsnett's wild invective.

— **Dismal alchemy of money breeding money**.

> 'The most hated sort [of money-making], and with the greatest reason, is usury, which makes a gain out of money itself, and not from the natural use of it. For money was intended to be used in exchange, but not to increase at interest. And this term usury [*tokos*] which means the birth of money from money, is applied to the breeding of money because the offspring resembles the parent. Wherefore of all modes of making money this is the most unnatural.' Aristotle, *Politics*, I.10. (tr., B. Jowett).

This opinion—and Aristotle's discussion of money in his *Ethics*—gave rise to much difficulty for his Christian followers, especially Thomas Aquinas (ch. 8 above). Given economic realities of property-based societies, let alone the realities of developing captalism, they had to find ingenious ways to mitigate the natural sinfulness of the economic exploitation of one human being by another.

The word 'dismal' in this kind of context inevitably echoes the characterisation by T. Carlyle (in an article on slavery, 1849) of 'political economy' as 'the dismal science'. Later in the 19th century, 'political economy' became more exclsuively technical, and changed its name to 'economics'. Carlyle was one of many 19th-century culture critics who were appalled by the materialism and cruelty of the new industrial capitalist society. See Appendices 5 and 6 below.

Having quoted, on many occasions, from the elegant translations by Benjamin Jowett of works of Greek philosophy, we may take this last opportunity to recall a tribute paid to his work by Alfred Housman (see ch. 4 above, under 'darkness made visible')—'the best translation of a Greek philosopher which has ever been executed by a person who understood neither philosophy nor Greek.'

Jowett (1817-93), Master of Balliol College, Oxford, was celebrated for his (awareness of his own) omniscience—and for a directness of speech at least as acerbic as Housman's.

— **State-sponsored slavery.**

> 'The great capitalist, the owner of a manufactory, if he operated with slaves instead of free labourers, like the West India planter, would be regarded as owner both of the capital, and of the labour. He would be owner, in short, of both instruments of production: and the whole of the produce, without participation, would be his own.
>
> 'What is the difference, in the case of the man, who operates by means of labourers receiving wages? The labourer, who receives wages, sells his labour for a day, a week, a month, or a year, as the case may be. The manufacturer, who pays these wages, buys the labour, for the day, the year, or whatever period it may be. He is equally therefore the owner of the labour, with the manufacturer who operates with slaves.
>
> 'The only difference is, in the mode of purchasing. The owner of the slave purchases, at once, the whole of the labour, which the man can ever perform: he, who pays wages, purchases only so much of a man's labour as he can perform in a day, or any other stipulated time. Being equally, however, the owner of the labour, so purchased, as the owner of the slave is of that of the slave, the produce, which is the result of this labour, combined with his capital, is all equally his own.
>
> 'In the state of society, in which we at present exist, it is in these circumstances that almost all production is effected: the capitalist is the owner of both instruments of production: and the whole of the produce is his.'

James Mill (1773-1836), Scottish historian and philosopher, father of J.S. Mill, in his *Elements of Political Economy* (1821), ch 1. In economic theory, J. Mill was a follower of D. Ricardo (Appendix 5 below).

In *Zur Kritik der politischen Ökonomie* (Contribution to a Critique of Political Economy) (1859), Karl Marx expressed, in a wonderfully simple formula, what we now recognise as the great and devastating *secret of capitalism*. (The word 'devastating' is derived from the Latin verb *devastare*, 'to lay waste'.)

> *'the exchange-value of labour is less than the exchange-value of its product.'*

In other words, by turning labour into a *commodity*, like any other commodity, the capitalist can give it any value that the labour-market will allow, but making sure that the amount he pays for the labour is less than the amount he can get for the commodity produced by the labour. The *surplus value* goes to the capitalist, not to the labourer. The payment to the labourer is not determined by his needs, or by considerations of social justice.

(It is an unfortunate feature of the German language that the word for 'employer' is *Arbeitgeber* ('work-giver'), and the word for 'employee' is *Arbeitnehmer* ('work-taker'). The contrary is surely their true relationship.)

But, even if considerations of social justice *were* to be taken into account, who would determine what social justice is? Marx and Engels deal with that question in another brilliant formula (like the first, distilling much pre-Marxian thought).

> 'The ideas of the ruling class are in every epoch the ruling ideas, i.e. the class which is the ruling *material* force of society, is at the same time its ruling *intellectual* force. *The class which has the means of mental production at its disposal, has control at the same time over the means of mental production . . .*'
>
> K. Marx & F. Engels, *The German Ideology*, Pt. I (written in 1845-6, but not published until the 20th century). (tr., W. Lough; emphasis added).

Thomas More had noticed the same phenomenon.

> 'Consequently, when I consider and turn over in my mind the state of all commonwealths flourishing anywhere today, so help me God, I can see nothing else than a kind of conspiracy of the rich, who are aiming at their own interests under the name and title of the commonwealth. They invent and devise all ways and means by which , first, they may keep without fear of loss all that they have amassed by evil practices and, secondly, they may then purchase as cheaply as possible, and abuse, the toil and labour of all the poor. These devices become law as soon as the rich have once decreed their observance in the name of the public—that is, of the poor also! . . . What is worse, the rich every day extort (*abradunt*) a part of their daily allowance from the poor not only by private fraud but by public law . . . and finally *by making laws, [the rich] have palmed it off as justice.*
>
> T. More, *Utopia* (1516). (emphasis added).

And so had Adam Smith.

> 'Laws and government may be considered . . . as a combination of the rich to oppress the poor, and preserve to themselves the inequality of goods which would otherwise be destroyed by the attacks of the poor. The government and

laws . . . tell them [the poor] that they must either continue poor or acquire wealth in the same manner as they [the rich] have done.'

A. Smith (Appendix 5 below), *Lectures on Jurisprudence* (lecture of 22 February 1763).

More and Smith and Marx and Weber could not have foreseen the *extreme finance capitalism* (national and global), of the late-20th and early-21st centuries—not directly connected to the *production* of anything, and not involving much *labour*, in which *money* itself becomes a *commodity*, and in which considerations of *social justice*, or even the *common good* of society (national or international), play no part.

On the *perennial dilemma* (see ch. 11 above, under 'the One and the Many') of Justice and Social Justice, see Ph. Allott, *Eunomia*, §§5.32*ff.*

— **The wealth/health of nations**. For *The Wealth of Nations*, see Appendix 5 below. For *The Health of Nations*, see ch. 6 above, under 'focus group', and *passim*.

— *Homo economicus*. In Latin, 'economic human being'. A term used to suggest that human beings have specific natural characteristics manifested in their participation in economic transactions.

— **The end times**. The Countess is referring to religious beliefs about the 'end of the world' (at least, of the human world), especially the beliefs of those Christians who see in the present state of the world the accumulating presence of phenomena matching those which, in the Bible, are seen as presaging the end of the (human) world.

— **Wishful thinking**. 'Thy wish was father, Harry, to that thought.' W. Shakespeare, *King Henry VI, Part Two*, IV. v. (the King speaking). The Prince of Wales, the future Henry V, finds the king, his father, sleeping, and thinks that he is dead. Awake, the King reads his son's mind.

For S. Freud, always looking on the bright side, everything that we say and do conceals thoughts that constitute our real desires, mostly desires of the more unpleasant kinds.

— **Clash of Civilisations**. A phrase associated with the name of S. Huntington (born 1927), an American political theorist. In *The Clash of Civilizations and the Remaking of World Order* (1996; based on an article originally published in 1993), he suggests that the post-Cold War world faces conflict, not of the traditional kind among sovereign states, but a life-and-death struggle among competing cultures. In particular, he warns that 'Western' culture is at risk from other cultures, including Chinese and Islamic cultures.

— **Prometheus**. I.22.

— **Pareto twenty per-cent**. The Italian economist V. Pareto (1848-1923) calculated that, normally, 20% of the population hold 80% of the wealth of a country. This observation has been extrapolated into a generalisation found to be applicable in many social fields—20% of the population commit 80% of crimes; 20% of the population create 80% of new ideas, wealth, inventions, or whatever.

— **Revaluation of values**. It is important to note that Nietzsche (I.19, and above *passim*) was not proposing a mere 're-thinking' of the corrupt values of Western society. His obsessive theme was *die Umwertung aller Werte*—normally but not satisfactorily, translated as 'the transvaluation of all values'.

He preached a 'revaluing'; of the very idea of 'value', that is to say, of the system of ideas which underlie our judging of things and people—for example, good and bad, right and wrong, true and false. He suggests that the present condition of human beings is a direct product of the history of human values—a history which is, of course, contingent, in the sense that it has been produced by the cultures that happen to have dominated the human mind through the course of history.

For Nietzsche, human history shows that our inherited idea of value, and our inherited values, are the cause of the debased state of humanity. What, he asks, might be the nature of *value*, as the source of *values*, if we started again, and tried to choose the idea of value, and the values, that would make a *better* kind of human being—an *Übermensch*, a human being (*Mensch*) the idea and the fact of whose nature is beyond (*über*) the impoverished idea and the wretched fact of the nature of human beings as they have become hitherto.

— **The only power over power is the power of ideas**. A slogan that reflects a central theme of the social idealism of Philip Allott. See *The Health of Nations*, §7.127.
— **A revolution in the mind, not in the streets**. A slogan that reflects a central theme of the social idealism of Philip Allott. See *The Health of Nations*, §14.58.
— **Oscar Wilde. Beautiful untrue things**. '. . . Lying, the telling of beautiful untrue things, is the proper aim of Art.' In O. Wilde (I.19), *The Decay of Lying* (1889 / 1905).
— **André Malraux. Creating the world**. *L'artiste surmonte l'angoisse en refaisant le monde à sa mesure et tel que l'homme l'eut fait s'il avait été dieu.* ('The artist overcomes anxiety by re-making the world to suit him/herself, and as a human being would have made it if he/she had been God.') A. Malraux (1901-76), *Les voix du silence* (The Voices of Silence) (1951).
— **Camus. Live a second time**. *Créer, c'est vivre deux fois.* ('To create is to live twice.') A. Camus (ch.11 above, under 'gratuitous existence'). From the chapter entitled 'Absurd creation', in *Le Mythe de Sisyphus* (The Myth of Sisyphus) (1942).

> 'The philosopher, even if he is Kant, is a creator. He has his characters, his symbols and his secret action. He has his plot-endings. On the contrary, the lead taken by the novel over poetry and the essay merely represents, despite appearances, a greater intellectualization of the art . . . . The number of bad novels must not make us forget the value of the best. These, indeed, carry with them their universe. The novel has its logic, its reasonings, its intuition, its postulates. It also has its requirements of clarity.' (tr., J. O'Brien).

— **Beckett. It is something**.

'You complain that this stuff is not written in English. It is not written at all. It is not to be read—or rather it is not only to be read. It is to be looked at and listened to. His writing is not about something, it is that something itself.'

S. Beckett (ch.7 above, under '*Je. Qui ça?*'), writing about *Finnegan's Wake* by J. Joyce (ch. 9 above, under 'artist as young man'). In 'Dante . . . Bruno . . . Vico . . . Joyce', (1929) in *Disjecta: Miscellaneous Writings and a Dramatic Fragment* (1983).

Joyce's novel was finally published in its entirety in 1939. It had appeared in parts from 1922. It is at, or way beyond, the limit of comprehensibility, in language and structure. It is certainly 'something', but *what* exactly is a matter of keen debate.

— **Plato. State of the imagination in society.** Especially in bk. X of the *Republic*, Plato/Socrates discusses the place of 'poetry' in society, including 'poetry' in the widest, ancient Greek, meaning of the word—works of the imagination in general (see above, 'Epigraphs', under 'Aristotle'). It is a discussion of a phenomenon of which we have immeasurably more experience—the power of consciousness to make society, and the power of society to make consciousness.

In considering the actual state and the possible state of society, we know that we must take account of the forces that mould—

— the consciousness of the *ruling* class (who have general power over the state of the *public mind* of society),
— the consciousness of the *governing* class (who exercise public, especially legal, powers in the public interest, under the influence of general states of the public mind),
— and the consciousness of the *people* in general, whose consciousness helps to form, and is powerfully formed by, the state of the public mind. (See ch. 15 above, under 'public mind', and *passim*.)

A main theme of the *Republic* is the question of how the consciousness of the *ruling* class, in particular, should be formed, especially through *education*. (Compare above, under 'holy places of the new ignorance'.)

Plato/Socrates says that he is as much affected by poetry and the other arts as anyone else, but the problem is that they may have two negative effects—the risk of causing us to become unable to distinguish between reality and fantasy; and the risk that people will come to be dominated by the pursuit of sensuous pleasure.

Our experience of two things—the relentless efforts of totalitarian regimes to control consciousness, and the effects (personal, social, and global) of 'popular culture'—may make us think that the discussion of the problem of the formation of social consciousness is far from finished and more urgently necessary than ever.

— **Jamesianism.** See ch. 5 above, under 'Henry James mode'.

— **Soul embracing soul**. Greg evidently has in mind a tradition of aesthetic philosophy beginning, in the modern world, with Anthony Cooper, 3rd Earl of Shaftesbury (1671-1713) (see ch. 6 above, under 'greatest happiness'). He allowed himself to be much influenced by both Plato and John Locke (Appendix 4 below).

> 'Nor will you deny beauty to the wild field, or to these flowers which grow around us, on this verdant couch. And Yet, as lovely as are these forms of nature, the shining grass or silvered moss, the flowry thyme, wild rose, or honey-suckle; 'tis not their beauty allures the neighbouring herds, delights the brouzing fawn, or kid and spreads the joy we see amidst the feeding flocks: 'Tis not the *Form* rejoices; but that which is beneath the form: 'tis savouriness attracts, hunger impels; . . . for never can the *Form* be of real force where it is uncontemplated, or unjudged of, unexamined, and stands only as the accidental note or token of what appeases provoked sense . . . If brutes therefore . . . be incapable of knowing and enjoying beauty, as being brutes, and having sense only . . . ; it follows, that neither can man by the same *sense* . . . conceive or enjoy *beauty*; but all the *beauty* he enjoys, is in a nobler way, and by the help of what is noblest, his mind and reason.'
> Earl of Shaftesbury, 'The Moralists', II.3, in *Characteristicks* (1714), II.

Kant (Appendix 8 below, and above *passim*) adapted this idea of *beauty*, as the product of both *sense* and *reason*, to fit into his most general philosophy of mind. Our recognition of beauty is both a personal experience and a universal experience—universal, because it is generated by a universal, and universalising, capacity of the human mind.

For this aesthetic tradition, beauty is not a matter of mere subjective feeling, or cultural convention, or shared opinion, or a generalisation from experience of things that have been called beautiful.

It is the activity of an *a priori* (built-in) potentiality of the mind, shared by all human minds. And, hence, an aesthetic judgment, like judgments of *reason* in general, is made by each individual mind, but is made in a way that is the same for all minds. My aesthetic judgment is a claim that a particular beautiful thing is capable of being seen as beautiful by everyone.

Kant calls this 'subjective universality'. An aesthetic judgment is also akin to a *moral* judgment which, according to Kant, is also a claim to the *possible universality* of the principle underlying the moral judgment that I make.

When we make an *aesthetic* judgment, we are, as it were, speaking into an identical area deep inside the mind of the person to whom we communicate that judgment—located in what we have referred to above as the *subunconscious* mind, where we listen to the *voice of the soul* (see ch. 15 above, under 'subunconscious mind').

'Hence he will talk about the beautiful as if beauty were a characteristic of the object [the "beautiful" thing] and the judgment were logical (namely, a cognition of the object through concepts of it), even though in fact the judgment is only aesthetic and refers to the object's presentation merely to the subject [the person judging that it is "beautiful"]. He will talk in this way because the judgment does resemble a logical judgment inasmuch as we may presuppose it to be valid for everyone . . . In other words, a judgment of taste must involve a claim to subjective universality.'

    I. Kant, *Critique of Judgment* (1790/93), Pt. I, Bk. I, §6. (tr., W. Pluhar).

Greg evidently also has in mind the third party involved—namely, the artist (painter, writer, composer . . .). In seeking to make a beautiful thing, the artist must be participating in the same subjective-universalising process—the soul of the artist speaking, as it were, to the souls of those who will share in the judgment of the beauty of the thing—soul speaking to soul, subunconscious mind communicating with subunconscious mind

From the above, it follows that there may be disagreement about matters of aesthetic judgment—as there are about matters of moral and rational judgment. But it also follows, of course, that not everyone's judgment of taste—no more than everyone's judgment of morality or rationality—is of equal value.

— **Blake. Tree of Life**. 'Art is the Tree of Life. Science is the Tree of Death.' Text accompanying an engraving by W. Blake (I.16, and above *passim*) entitled *Laocöon* (see ch.9 above, under 'knot of vipers'). The 'Tree of Life' is one of Blake's powerful symbols, epitomising the coming of a 'new kingdom' of 'mercy, pity, peace, and love'.

— **City of Good**. Echo of the title (and central theme) of Augustine's *City of God* (see ch.3 above, under '*città terrene*').

— **Cleopatra's Nose**. 'Cleopatra's nose: if it had been shorter the whole face of the earth would have been different.' B. Pascal (I.19), *Pensées*, II.162 (tr., A. Krailsheimer).

    J.B.Bury (1861-1927; Fellow of Trinity College, Cambridge, from1893; Regius Professor of Modern History in the University, from1902) wrote an essay entitled 'Cleopatra's Nose' (1916), on the world-historical consequences of contingent circumstances, such as the love of the Roman general Antony (Marcus Antonius) (83-30 BCE) for the Egyptian queen Cleopatra (69-30 BCE).

    Antony killed himself after losing the battle of Actium in 31BCE, which enabled Octavian (Caius Julius Caesar Octavianus Augustus) (63 BCE-14 CE), great nephew and adopted heir of Julius Caesar (who had also been a close friend of Cleopatra; he made her Queen of Egypt), to become sole ruler of Rome. (He had previously been a member of a triumvirate with Antony and Lepidus.)

    Octavian was at first called *Princeps* ('leader', 'prince', 'first citizen'), and then *Imperator* ('Emperor'), under the name Augustus. He was the first Roman Emperor,

Imperator being a title previously given to military commanders (*imperare*, 'to command', 'to lead') after victory in a major battle.

— **Martin Luther's Constipation.** The idea that Luther's poor digestion was the cause of the Protestant Reformation of the 16th century is associated particularly with the name of the German-Danish-American pyschiatrist E. Erikson (1902-94). However, his *Young Martin Luther. A Study in Psychoanalysis and History* (1958) gives more prominence to Luther's problematic relationship with his father. The book follows in the wake of S. Freud's *Leonardo. A Study in Psychosexuality* (1910), which led the field in what has come to be called pyschobiography (see I.20, under 'the vulture and the child').

— **People know perfectly well what is right.**

> 'While I meditated upon man's nature, I seemed to discover two distinct principles in it; one of them raised him to the study of the eternal truths, to the love of justice, and of true morality, to the regions of the world of thought, which the wise delight to contemplate; the other led him downwards to himself, made him the slave of his senses, of the passions which are their instruments, and thus opposed everything suggested to him by the former principle. When I felt myself carried away, distracted by these conflicting motives, I said, No; man is not one; I will and I will not; I feel myself at once a slave and a free man; I perceive what is right, I love it, and I do what is wrong; I am active when I listen to the voice of reason; I am passive when I am carried away by my passions; and when I yield, my worst suffering is the knowledge that I might have resisted.'
>
> J.-J. Rousseau, 'Profession of faith of a Savoyard priest', in *Émile* (1762), bk. IV. (tr., B. Foxley).

— *Reform.* In German, 'reformation', especially the 16th-century Protestant Reformation within Christianity.
— **Fallen existence.** See ch. 5 above, under 'fall of man', and *passim.*
— **Crimes and follies of mankind.** See I.13.
— **Sad pageants of men's miseries.** Echo of a phrase in *The Faerie Queene* (bk. II, canto I) by the English poet E. Spenser (1552-99) which honours the life and times of Queen Elizabeth (daughter of Henry VIII and Anne Boleyn; reigned 1558-1603)—who is also represented as Gloriana.

Gloriana is an opera by the English composer B. Britten (1913-76) composed to celebrate the coronation of Queen Elizabeth II (1953). The story of the opera is based on *Elizabeth and Essex. A Tragic History* (1928) by L. Strachey (see ch. 17 above, under 'one true faith'). The second Elizabeth may not have been amused to find that the opera, like the book, is about the first Elizabeth's 'love life'.

Spenser, yet another Cambridge poet, had been an undergraduate at Pembroke Hall (College), Cambridge (see above, under 'prince of darkness'). The echoed words are spoken by a fatally wounded woman, longing for death, but wondering whether the heavens take delight in making us endure suffering and torment.

In his poem, *The Vision of Don Roderick* (1811), the Scottish writer W. Scott (1771-1832), intentionally echoes the Spenserian image. The poem describes a tempting of fate by Rodrigo, the last Visigoth king of Spain, who is shown a vision of the dreadful consequences that will follow, including the loss of Spain to the Arabs, which would, indeed, occur in the year 714.

Scott links the story to the struggle to remove Napoleon from Spain—known in Britain as the Peninsular War, in Spain as the *Guerra de la Independencia*—that aim being finally achieved, oddly enough, in the year 1814.

> 'For that sad pageant of events to be / Showed every form of fight by field and flood; / Slaughter and Ruin, shouting forth their glee, / Beheld, while riding on the tempest scud, / The waters choked with slain, the earth bedrenched with blood!'

— **Journey of the mind.** See ch. 11 above, under 'journey of the soul'.
— **People-devouring kings and foolish peoples.** Echo of Homer, *Iliad*, Bk. I.

> '"Wine-bibber," he cried, "with the face of a dog and the heart of a hind, you never dare to go out with the host in fight, nor yet with our chosen men in ambuscade. You shun this as you do death itself. You had rather go round and rob his prizes from any man who contradicts you. You devour your people, for you are king over a feeble folk . . .".'
> (Achilles speaking). (tr., S. Butler).

Achilles is excoriating Agamemnon, leader of the Greek forces who are attacking Troy, in order to rescue Helen, wife of Agamemnon's brother Menelaus, who has been abducted by Paris. Achilles is renowned for his fierce anger, but shows another side of his character in his grief over the death of Patroclus, his comrade and friend.

> 'A dark cloud of grief fell upon Achilles as he listened. He filled both hands with dust from off the ground, and poured it over his head, disfiguring his comely face, and letting the refuse settle over his shirt so fair and new. He flung himself down all huge and hugely at full length, and tore his hair with his hands.' (Bk. XVIII).

Echo also of Horace (I.5), *Epistles*, I. ii (to Lollius). He refers to an unidentified writer's history of the Trojan War, which speaks of Greece being devastated by a pointless war—*fabula . . . stultorum regum et populorum continet aestum* ('a story of the turbulence of stupid kings and peoples').

In *The Tragical Historie of Dr Faustus* by C. Marlowe (I.20), the Doctor, on seeing Helen appear (accompanied by two cupids, which may or may not be significant) asks:

'Was this the face that launcht a thousand shippes / And burnt the topless
Towres of Ilium [Troy]?'
Like Paris, he cannot resist her—
'Sweet Helen, make me immortal with a kiss.' [He kisses her.] 'Her lips
suck forth my soul: see, where it flies!'

— *Grandes surfaces.* In French, 'supermarkets', 'hypermarkets'.
— *Grandes écoles.* In French 'great schools', a term referring to a group of university-level specialised colleges with highly competitive admission and high professional standards.
    They include the École Nationale d'Administration (ENA), founded in 1945 to prepare the most senior French public officials, many of its graduates becoming leaders in politics and public administration of all kinds. The elitism of the ENA system and the remarkable social and political prominence of its graduates (referred to as *énarques*) have made it controversial. Edmund has apparently formed the view that the ENA system leads to an ingrained narrowness of mind and vision.
— *Noblesse oblige.* In French (and English), 'nobility imposes an obligation' ; 'from those to whom much is given much is expected'.
— **A better world.**

'Even in the mere consideration of the world as it is . . . there arises within me
the wish, the desire—no, not the mere desire, but the absolute demand—for a
better world . . . A voice within me proclaims with irresistible conviction: "It
is impossible that it can remain thus; it must become other and better".'
    J.G. Fichte (see ch.7 above, under '*Ich*'), *Vocation of Man*, III. (tr., W.
Smith).

— **The pity of it all.** Greg will have in mind Othello's self-torturing as he realises that he must kill Desdemona, the wife whom he loves, but who, he wrongly believes, has been unfaithful to him. 'O! Iago, the pity of it, Iago!' *Othello* IV. i. (Othello speaking, not knowing that it is Iago who has misled him.)
— **Edmund Euphues.** In Greek, *euphuēs*; 'graceful, shapely, goodly, clever, witty'.
    Gregory Seare, Shakespearean scholar, will certainly be invoking the Greek meaning of the word, rather than its use as the name of the hero of the two novels by the English author J.Lyly (1554-1606)—*Euphues. The Anatomy of Wit* (1578) and *Euphues and his England* (1580), about a young man who has every advantage of person and wealth, but who spends his time in the pursuit of love, but mostly in *talking* about love.

The over-elaborate and pedantic prose-style of the novels caused the word *Euphuism* to be applied to overwrought prose or verse, the writing of which became fashionable in Elizabethan England. It is surely reflected in those aspects of the style of W. Shakespeare which seem to display his sheer delight in the possibilities of the English language.

Compare *Gongorismo* in Spanish literature, named after the poet Luis de Góngora y Argote (1561-1627), one of the great writers of Spain's *siglo d'oro* (Golden Age), whose poetry shows a similar delight in the possibilities of the Spanish language.

It is a delight which is also manifested in *Don Quijote* (1605, and 1615), where Cervantes seems to enjoy the pleasure of telling the story as much as he wants us to enjoy reading it (see ch. 2 above, under 'true author').

— **Beautiful in body and mind.**

> 'Then, said I [Socrates], when there is a coincidence of a beautiful disposition in the soul and corresponding and harmonious beauties of the same type in the bodily form—is not this the fairest spectacle for one who is capable of contemplation?' Plato, *Republic*, III, 402d.

— **Moral elegance.** Proust dedicated his first published work—*Les plaisirs et les jours* (1896) (The Pleasures and the Days—a title ironically recalling Hesiod's *The Works and the Days*—see ch. 3 above, under *'o tempora, o mores'*)—to Willie Heath, a young Englishman who had been a close friend, but who had recently died at the age of twenty-two. In the dedication, he compares Heath to 'young lords painted by Van Dyck, whose pensive elegance you shared'.

> *Leur élégance, en effet, comme la vôtre, réside moins dans les vêtements que dans le corps, et leur corps lui-même semble l'avoir reçue et continuer sans cesse à la recevoir de leur âme : c'est une élégance morale.* ('Indeed, their elegance, like yours, resides less in their clothes than in their body, and their body itself seems to have received it, and to keep receiving it, from their soul: it is a moral elegance.') (present author's trans.).

— **Self-transforming Edmund.**

> 'Something have you heard / Of Hamlet's transformation; so I call it, / Since nor the exterior man nor the inward man / Resembles that it was.' W. Shakespeare, *Hamlet*, II. ii. (King Claudius speaking).

— **All-too-human.** Echo of F. Nietzsche, *Menschliches, Allzumenschliches. Ein Buch für freie Geister* (Human, All-Too-Human. A Book for Free Spirits) (1878).
— **String theory of the soul.** See ch. 11 above, under 'ten strings of my soul'.

— **Binding force of love**. See ch. 17 above, under 'binding force'.
— **Eutopia**. See I.22.
— **We are becoming**. See ch. 7 above, under 'I think I'm becoming'.
— **Enthusiasts**. Formed from the ancient Greek word *entheos*—'full of the god, inspired, possessed'.

In the *Phaedrus*, Plato discusses what he calls the best form of 'divine madness' (*enthousiasmos*), in which the awareness of *beauty* causes us to become aware of the eternal and transcendental world, beyond the senses and beyond ordinary consciousness.

> 'Now, as we have said, every human being has, by reason of her nature, had contemplation of True Being: else would she never have entered into this human creature; but to be put in mind thereof by things here [on earth] is not easy for every soul; some, when they had the vision, had it but for a moment; some when they had fallen to earth consorted unhappily with such as led them to deeds of unrighteousness, wherefore they forgot the objects of their vision. Few indeed are left that can still remember much: but when these discern some likenss of the things yonder, they are amazed, and no longer masters of themselves, and know not what is come upon them by reason of their perception being dim.'
>
> Plato, *Phaedrus*, 249d. (tr., R. Hackforth).

It seems that Greg and Edmund *will* retain a permanent memory of their self-transforming experiences in the presence of different parts of the World Ocean—and Ingo would no doubt also have remembered his oceanic experience in some self-transforming way, had he survived the experience.

— **Idealists of the world unite!** Echo of the closing words of K. Marx & F. Engels, *The Communist Manifesto*, usually translated into English as 'Workers of the world, unite!'. *Proletarier aller Länder, vereinigt euch!* ('Proletarians of all countries, unite!').

Greg evidently has in mind that, in the 21st century, before it is too late, humanity must find a state of mind beyond terminal despair.

We—and the Firm and LOSC and MOTH—will need a new breed of human beings, highly educated in several of the world's leading civilisations, able to think through and beyond all existing thinking, filled with a rare zeal of human self-transcending and self-perfecting—philosophers beyond philosophy, kings beyond kings, believers beyond belief, human beings of the future beyond human beings of the past.

— **Wakened by a kiss.** Echo of the story of the Sleeping Beauty who, after sleeping for one hundred years, is wakened by the kiss of an intrepid prince—in the version by the brothers Jacob (1785-1863) and Wilhelm Grimm (1786-1859). They published a collection of folk-tales. The elder brother was also the founder of German philology!

C. Perrault (1728-1803) also published a collection of stories for children, including a version of the Sleeping Beauty story. The intrepid prince is not present in the Perrault version.
— **Did May Gaunt blush?**

> 'Thrasymachus made all these admissions not as I now lightly narrate them, but with much balking and reluctance and prodigious sweating, it being summer, and it was then I beheld what I had never seen before—Thrasymachus blushing.'
>   Plato, *Republic*, 350c, Socrates speaking. (tr., P. Shorey).

In the discussion in Book I of the *Republic*, between Socrates and several interlocutors, about the nature of justice, it is Thrasymachus who has vigorously argued for the tough realistic (proto-Machiavellian-Hobbesian-Marxian-May Gauntian) approach—'the just is nothing else than the advantage of the stronger.' (338c).

(In fairness, it should be said that the underlying intention of N. Machiavelli (1469-1527) in *Il principe* (The Prince) (1513/1532) is not beyond dispute. One view is that he is subliminally propagating an idea of democracy by explaining so convincingly the intrinsic and necessary selfish immorality of a monarch. His writings were notably deconstructed and (generally) defended in a review essay (1827) by the Liberalish historian T.B. Macaulay—see ch. 15 above, under 'Americans, a chosen people'.)

By his characteristic form of cross-questioning, Socrates makes Thrasymachus come close to admitting that, after all, justice must have something to do with fairness and goodness, and not merely power.

The discussion is an important step in the exposition of Plato's general philosophy, in inviting us to realise that we already recognise, and use and value, values that transcend everyday reality—that is, values that are not merely by-products of everyday reality.

CHAPTER 20. *Tying the Knot.*

— **Brompton Oratory**. I.14. Unofficial name of a Roman Catholic church in the Kensington district of London. It was established (1884) by the congregation known as 'the Oratory', originally founded in Italy in the 16th century. In 1845 an English Oratorian congregation was founded in Birmingham by the future Cardinal Newman (see ch. 19 above, under 'holy places').

He also founded (1859) the Oratory School, a public (that is, private) school, intended as a Catholic alternative to Eton College (ch. 13 above, under 'educate in the holidays'). The school moved to Caversham Park, Berkshire, in 1922, and then to Woodcote, Oxfordshire, in 1942. During the Second World War, the school briefly took refuge at Downside School (I.3).

— **Tying the knot**. In French, *nouer*, 'to tie, to knot'. In French (and English), *dénouement*, 'untying'; 'resolution of the plot of a drama or story'.

Nouement ('tying of a knot') might, on the other hand, mean the beginning, or first tying up, of the plot of a new drama or story.

> 'Then think not long in taking little pain, / To knit the knot, that ever shall remain.' E. Spenser (see ch. 19 above, under 'sad pageants'), from one of his *Amoretti* sonnets (1595), addressed to his potential bride—'the knot' refers here to marriage.

To celebrate their actual wedding-day, he wrote *Epithalamion* (1597). (In ancient Greek, *epi*, 'near, before'; *thalamos*, 'bridal-chamber'.)

> 'Open the temple gates unto my love, / Open them wide that she may enter in, / And all the postes adorne as doth behove, / And all the pillours deck with girlands trim, / For to receyve this saynt with honour dew, / That commeth in to you.'

— **Victoria and Albert Museum**. I.14.
— **[Edmund] takes hold of her [Gabi's] hand.**

> 'But then suppose he takes her hand. This act of her companion risks changing the situation by calling for an immediate decision. To leave the hand there is to consent in herself to flirt, to engage herself. To withdraw it is to break the troubled and unstable harmony which gives the hour its charm. The aim is to postpone the moment of decision as long as possible. We know what happens next; the young woman leaves her hand there, but does not notice that she is leaving it. She does not notice because it happens by chance that she is at this moment all intellect . . . And during this time the divorce of the body from the soul is accomplished; the hand rests inert between the warm hands of her companion—neither consenting nor resisting—a thing.'
> J.-P. Sartre, *L'Être et le Néant* (Being and Nothingness) (1943), ch.2. (tr., H. Barnes).

The book contains the discussion by Sartre (see ch. 11 above, under 'outscape, inscape') of the great Parmenidean problem (ch. 11 above, generally)—how does the human mind conjure the *being* of something (including our 'self') from out of *nothing*?

The quoted passage (obviously based on much personal experience) is part of his discussion of what he calls 'bad faith' (*mauvaise foi*)—our capacity to make ourselves *exist fully* as two quite different persons *at the same moment*. His better-known example is of the waiter in a characteristic French café, who performs the role of 'waiter' with total, seemingly exclusive, commitment and efficiency, while half-revealing the rather desolate figure of his other, non-waiter self.

— **Look with the mind**. Echo of W. Shalespeare, *A Midsummer-Night's Dream*, I. i.

> 'Love looks not with the eyes, but with the mind, / And therefore [for that reason] is wing'd Cupid painted blind.' (Helena speaking).

— **Mysterious smile of interior voluptuousnesses**. Echo, perhaps, of a poem *Aimons toujours* (Let us always love) by V. Hugo, in his collection *Les Contemplations* (see ch.16 above, under '*voilà les roses*').

> *Aime, afin de charmer tes heures! /Afin qu'on voie en tes beaux yeux / Des voluptés intérieures / Le sourire mystérieux!* ('Love, to bring charm to your hours! So that one may see in your beautiful eyes the mysterious smile of interior voluptuous pleasures!').

— **Anglican**. See Appendix 2 below.
— *Qui ça?* See ch. 7 above.
— **DNA**. I.13.
— **Alchemy of the soul**. Echo, perhaps, if only metaphorical, of the intense attention that C. J. Jung (I.20 and above, *passim*) devoted to *alchemy* and *Gnosticism*, including the idea that mystical *psychic* transformations may occur, analogous to the mystical *physical* transformations which alchemists sought to cause (such as, turning some other metal into gold).
— **The story of a life**. Edmund's wealth now includes a wealth of wisdom.

> 'Beloved Pan, and all ye other gods who haunt this place, give me beauty in the inward soul; and may the outward and inward man be at one. May I reckon the wise to be the wealthy, and may I have such a quantity of gold as a temperate man and he only can bear and carry.'
> Plato, *Phaedrus*, 279b. (tr., B. Jowett). Socrates speaking (praying).

EPIGRAPHS

— **Sophocles**. From *Oedipus at Colonus*. Oedipus is speaking to Theseus, king of Athens, shortly before Oedipus is mysteriously taken away by the gods. (tr., E.F. Watling).
— **George Eliot**. From 'A College Breakfast-Party', a poem (1874) which contains a re-imagined version of a discussion about metaphysics among a group of (19th-century!) Cambridge undergraduates.
— **William Godwin**. From *Things as They Are, or, The Adventures of Caleb Williams* (1794). See Appendix 6 below.)

— **Aristotle**. From the *Politics*, I.5. J.-J. Rousseau places it as an epigraph at the beginning of his *Discourse on the Origin of Inequality* (1754) (here, in the trans. of G.D.H. Cole).

— **Gerrard Winstanley** (1609-1676). English anarchist, communist, revolutionary. In the social unrest following the execution of King Charles I (1649), he challenged every aspect of the institutional order of England, especially the institution of property. He and his associates (so-called Levellers and Diggers) sought to impose by direct action the people's right to use the land for their own benefit. They were suppressed by the use of public force.

   The quotation (from *The New Law of Righteousness*, 1649) reflects a populist version of a view held by those influenced by Francis Bacon, to the effect that humanity has within itself an unlimited power to improve human life, and to undo the supposed 'Fall of Man'. The delightful, and characteristically English, phrase 'comfortable livelihood' was much used by Winstanley to express a sensibly radical spiritual and social and human ideal.

— **John Smith** (1618-52), one of the Cambridge Platonists, Fellow of Queens' College, Cambridge. The quotation is from his 'Discourse on the Knowledge of God', in his (posthumous) *Select Discourses* (1659).

— **Epicurus** (341-270 BCE). The quoted text is Fragment 54, in C. Bailey, *Epicurus. The Extant Remains* (1926).

— **Rudyard Kipling** (1865-1936). The quotation is from his poem *The Fairies' Siege*.

> 'I'd not give way for an Emperor, / I'd hold my road for a King—/ To the Triple
> Crown [the Pope] I would not bow down—/ But this is a different thing. / I'll
> not fight with the Powers of Air, / Sentry, pass him through! / Drawbridge let
> fall, 'tis the Lord of us all, / The Dreamer whose dreams come true!'

— **Cicero**. In Latin, 'there is a lot I haven't said.' From Cicero's Fourth Oration against Catiline in the Roman Senate.

CHAPTER 2 APPENDICES

APPENDIX 1. William of Occam and Francis Bacon.

William of Occam (1285-1349) continues to be an active participant in philosophy's permanent conversation, in which the particular contribution of a given philosopher may or may not survive as an audible voice.

He challenged the intellectual basis of a new metaphysics of Christianity stemming from the acceptance by the Roman Church of a new school of philosophers, among whom the Italian philosopher Thomas Aquinas (1225-1274) was the most influential, who sought to reconcile Aristotelian rationalism with the traditional theology of Christianity.

The perennial debate to which Aquinas and William contributed goes far wider than the theology of Christianity. It is about the nature of what we suppose to be reality. What is the connection between the ideas in our minds concerning 'reality' and the reality that we suppose to exist independently of the mind? William rejected the Aristotelian notion (itself a dilution of Plato's views) that the ideas we use to make sense of reality correspond to something contained within reality itself—such ideas as essence, substance, cause, species, man, soul, space, time, good, evil, truth, justice.

So-called nominalists dispute this notion, saying that the fact that we give a name (*nomen*—'name' or 'noun', in Latin) to something does not mean that there is necessarily anything in reality corresponding to the name (cf. 'unicorn'). So-called 'universals' (abstract generalisations) are nothing more than words (*voces*), conventional generalised names that we give to collections of particulars—and only particular things are real.

William himself seems to have arrived eventually at what we may call a modified nominalist view, to the effect that universals do have some sort of reality in that they are evidently a way in which the mind connects itself to some actual aspect of non-mind reality—'for them [generalisable particulars] to be is to be known': *eorum esse est eorum cognosci*—an idea with a prolific philosophical future (see Appendices 4 and 8 below).

William, who was a pugnacious polemicist, attacked the Church on grounds going far beyond philosophy. He was investigated at length for heresy, not least for attacking the central tenet of Aquinas (and now of the Church) that the attributes of God (existence, infinity, perfection, uncaused cause, and so on) were a matter of faith and yet capable of being supported by reason. For William, faith and reason are intrinsically separate and different.

The debate between idealism and materialism about the nature of reality has been staged with sectarian vigour from the very beginning of Western philosophy in Greece.

> 'One party define reality as the same thing as body, and as soon as one of the opposite party asserts that anything without body is real, they are utterly contemptuous. On this issue an interminable battle is always going on between the two camps.' Plato, *Sophist*, 246b. (tr., F.M. Cornford).

(Confusingly, 'idealists', believing in the reality of ideas, were, especially in the Middle Ages, also known as 'realists', whereas Plato is referring here to Greek philosophers known to us as 'materialists', believing only in the reality of the physical world.)

In William we may detect early signs of characteristic features of that English (later, British and American) philosophical mind that so disgusted Nietzsche—scepticism (authority or logic are the sources of nothing but illusory forms of 'truth'), empiricism (real reality is not made by the mind; truth can be nothing more than the mind's orderly representation of that reality), pragmatism (truths arise from the everyday process of truth-seeking, especially the social aspect of that process, and have no greater claim to respect than the process that produces them).

However, in those same countries and on such modest philosophical foundations, three great idea-worlds have prospered, under the names of Natural Science, Democracy, and Capitalism—*nomina* or *voces* that represent and/or produce overwhelmingly real phenomena of the human-made world!

Francis Bacon (1561-1626) was born into the highest ranks of the English ruling class (he himself became Lord Chancellor and was made Viscount St Albans) at a time (the reign of Queen Elizabeth I, 1558-1603) when a storm of creative energy had manifested itself in English society, leading to substantial economic development and the first phase of an overseas empire, but leading also to a remarkable artistic and intellectual effervescence. The Italian Renaissance (from about 1453) and the German Reformation (from about 1520) were experienced as a form of intellectual liberation, freeing the mind to begin again in its thinking about every possible subject of thought. A vogue word was 'new'.

The novelty of Bacon's intellectual revolution was not merely something that we identify retrospectively. It was his explicit philosophical purpose.

> 'There was but one course left, therefore—to try the whole thing anew upon a better plan, and to commence a total reconstruction of sciences, arts, and all human knowledge, raised upon proper foundations' (F. Bacon, Proem to *The Great Instauration*).

Bacon's 'proper foundations' are a new epistemology, that is to say, a new theory of knowledge, a new theory of truth. We must at last reject the idea that the source of truth is to be found in submission to authority, tradition, common opinion, logical sophistry, metaphysical speculation, or wishful thinking—which are merely 'sciences as one would', based on 'an infusion from the will and affections'. (*New Organon*, XLIX).

A main rhetorical target is Aristotle, whose tyrannising presence he had encountered as a student at Cambridge. (In the Middle Ages, Aristotle's system of logic had come to be known by the Greek name *organon*—'instrument'—*sc.*, of good thinking.)

> '. . . in the physics of Aristotle you hear hardly anything but the words of logic, which in his metaphysics also, under a more imposing name, and more forsooth as a realist than a nominalist, he has handled over again. Nor let any weight be given to the fact that in his books on animals and his problems, and other of his treatises, there is frequent dealing with experiments. For he had come to his conclusion before [*a priori*]; he did not consult experience as he should have done, for the purpose of framing his decisions and axioms, but having first determined the question, according to his will, he then resorts to experience, and bending her into conformity with his placets [orders], leads her about like a captive in a procession. So that even on this count he is more guilty than his modern followers, the schoolmen [medieval academic followers of Aristotle], who have abandoned experience altogether.' (*New Organon*, LXIII).
>
> '. . . the reasoners resemble spiders, who make cobwebs out of their own substance.' (XCV).

Bacon called for a radical reform of the universities and their 'professory learning' and deplored the conversion of philosophy into 'an occupation or profession', isolated from the real problems of the real world (*The Advancement of Learning*, Second Book).

Why had human knowledge made so little progress over the last two thousand years? Bacon asks. His answer is that the purpose of the search for knowledge had not been understood.

> 'Now the true and lawful goal of the sciences is none other than this: that human life be endowed with new discoveries and powers.' (LXXXI) 'For I am building in the human understanding a true model of the world, such as it is in fact, not such as a man's own reason would have it to be . . . Truth, therefore, and utility are here the very same things.' (CXXIV).

He put his most general prophecy in what now seems to be a delightfully laconic form, given the subsequent overwhelming triumphs of the natural sciences (referred to in his day as 'natural philosophy'):

> 'From a natural philosophy, pure and ummixed, better things are to be expected.' (XCVI).

Bacon redefines the word 'metaphysics'. Natural philosophy must necessarily concern itself with more generalised ideas about what it discovers by experiment and through experience.

> 'Thus, let the investigation of forms, which are (in the eye of reason at least, and in their essential law) eternal and immutable, constitute *Metaphysics;* and let the investigation of the efficient cause [Aristotle's term for the most material form of causation], and of matter, and of the latent process, and the latent configuration . . . constitute *Physics.*' (IX).

He was inclined to regard mathematics as a sort of ultimate metaphysics.

He accepts that metaphysics must lead to ever more general theories of the natural universe. Knowledge of the natural world forms a pyramid.

> 'So of natural philosophy, the basis is natural history [observation]; the stage next is physique; the stage next the vertical point is metaphysique. As for the vertical point, . . . the summary law of nature, we know not whether man's inquiry can attain unto it . . . And therefore the speculation was excellent in Parmenides and Plato, although but a speculation in them, that all things by scale did ascend to unity. So then always that knowledge is worthiest which is charged with least multiplicity; which appeareth to be metaphysique.' (*The Advancement of Learning,* Second Book).

Bacon says that to do physics without metaphysics (as he has defined it) is like 'discoverers that think there is no land, when they can see nothing but sea'—a trope echoed delightfully by Lewis Carroll in his poem *The Hunting of the Snark* (1876) where the ship's crew of snark-hunters were grateful to the Bellman for bringing on board a large map representing the sea without the least vestige of land: 'And the crew were much pleased when they found it to be, / A map they could all understand.'

Needless to say, this Baconian *ascending* form of metaphysics—closely controlled generalising from closely controlled observing of particulars—is intended to be the very negation of the *descending* form—whether the Platonic/Arisotelian postulation of a real metaphysical reality behind apparent physical reality or the still more extreme form of metaphysical deduction from general religious beliefs.

Bacon himself was a religious believer after his own fashion (as all religious believers are, at least in England), and accepted the social and moral significance of religion, but his central intellectual purpose was to establish the independence and specificity of what would come to be recognised as the *scientific method* of reasoning—a method, or methods, whose nature would itself become the focus of much philosophical controversy.

The English essayist and cultural commentator William Hazlitt (1778-1830) said of Bacon (in his *Lectures on English Philosophy*):

'He was one of the most remarkable instances of those men, who, by the rare privilege of their nature, are at once poets and philosophers, and see equally in both worlds—the individual and the sensible, and the abstracted and intelligible forms of things. And thus, by incorporating the abstract with the concrete, and general reasoning with individual observation, [was able] to give to our conclusions that solidity and firmness which they otherwise always want.'

It is interesting to compare the project of the very English Francis Bacon with those of the French mathematician and philosopher René Descartes (1596-1650) and the German mathematician and philosopher Gottfried Leibniz (1646-1716), both of whom also argued for a radical purification of the thinking process, but who believed that such purified thinking could re-establish, on a new secure footing, a form of *a priori* rational metaphysics which owes much to the metaphysical tradition inherited from ancient Greece.

They were leading exponents of what Nietzsche, in the passage quoted as an initial Epigraph to this volume, regarded as a distinct and superior Continental philosophical tradition (see Appendix 8 below).

APPENDIX 2. **Wyclif and Cranmer**.

John Wyclif (1330-1384) was an academic theologian who taught intermittently at Oxford University (briefly Master of Balliol College, 1360-61).

Like William of Occam and Francis Bacon, he was an intellectual revolutionary. His was a powerful voice in a double crisis—in the Church of Rome and in English society.

The Church was in a state of schismatic disorder with two rival Popes—at Rome and at Avignon in France (1378-1417)—and, briefly, a third (Parisian) Pope (1410). The English state was at war with the French state, in what came to be called the Hundred Years War, and opposed the claims of the French Pope. Serious social unrest in England expressed itself in public violence (the Peasants Revolt, 1381), but also in a storm of condemnation of the wealth, privileges and abuses of the Roman Church in England.

Wyclif gained popular support (the Lollards) in his campaign for fundamental 'reformation' of the Church. In 1395 a paper containing twelve 'conclusions' reflecting some of Wyclif's radical proposals was attached by his followers to the doors of St Paul's Cathedral and Westminster Abbey in London, and presented to Parliament. But, as a theologian, Wyclif went further—supervising a translation of the Bible into English (to undermine the authority of the Latin-speaking priesthood) and challenging fundamental doctrinal positions of the Church, including the Church's teaching on 'transubstantiation' in the Church's central ritual act (the Eucharist).

Wyclif was thus a progenitor of the Reformation of the early sixteenth century. Martin Luther, whose ninety-five disputatious theses were nailed to the door of the Schlosskirche (castle church) in Wittenberg in 1517, and whose anti-clerical German translation of the Bible greatly influenced the development of the German language, acknowledged his debt to Wyclif and to the man he called 'Holy Johannes Hus' (c.1371-1415), the Czech radical reformer who had been condemned by the Church as a heretic and burned to death.

Wyclif managed to avoid such a fate, at least during his lifetime. The Council of Constance (1414-18) condemned some of his writings as heretical and ordered that his body be exhumed and thrown onto non-consecrated ground, a sentence carried out by the Bishop of Lincoln in 1428. John Hus had learned of Wyclif's work through what might be called the Bohemian connection, following the marriage of the sister of King Wenceslaus of Bohemia to England's King Richard II in 1382.

Thomas Cranmer (1489-1556). The separation of England from the institutional structure of the Church of Rome was effected by Acts of Parliament (from 1534) in the reign of King Henry VIII (reigned 1509-47).

Cranmer had been a student and Fellow of Jesus College, Cambridge. In 1533 he was appointed by the King as Archbishop of Canterbury, the head of the Roman Church in England—an office then already almost one thousand years old. In 1521 the Pope has conferred on Henry the title *Defensor fidei* (Defender of the Faith) to reward him for a work of orthodox Catholic theology (probably written by Thomas More). In 1531 Henry caused the English bishops to recognise him as 'Supreme Head of the Church in England'. This title was changed by Parliament to 'Supreme Governor of the Church of England' in the reign of his daughter Elizabeth. Improbably, both titles are still held by the British monarch.

Cranmer played a major part in establishing a form of religion (Anglicanism) retaining better features of medieval Roman Christianity while extirpating what were seen as its vices. He was executed (by burning) in Oxford in the reign of Henry's daughter Mary (1553-58) who married the very (Roman) Catholic King Philip II of Spain and sought to restore Roman Catholicism in England.

The new Anglican form of religion was epitomised in Cranmer's Book of Common Prayer (1559) which is still used (with revisions) throughout the world-wide Anglican community of churches. That Book, and a new English-language version of the Bible (the King James Bible, 1611), played a significant part in the development of the modern written and spoken English language, helping it to become something close to a world-wide *lingua franca*.

APPENDIX 3. Hobbes and Locke and Jefferson.

Thomas Hobbes (1588-1679) proposes a *metaphysics* of society and government and law that would serve as the groundwork, and a vigorous stimulus, for most subsequent thinking about the philosophical basis of human society. Not least, it would form the groundwork of an untidy profusion of ideas that are referred to under the convenient label of 'liberal democracy'.

The debate, which began in ancient Greece, has continued without interruption until the present day, enriched now by experience of countless actual societies and their remarkable achievements, both admirable and terrible.

Just as Plato, in particular, had written his dialogues against the background of Athenian social unrest and a class struggle liable to unsettle even the most philosophical of conservative minds, so the minds of each generation participating in the subsequent debate have been conditioned by contemporary social conditions.

Hobbes lived at a time of intense social unrest in England—a Civil War that would lead to the public execution of a King (1649) by extra-legal order of the House of Commons, and the establishment of a temporary republic (until the monarchy was restored in 1660). He proposed an integrated metaphysics of society focused on a question which was a central feature of the perennial great debate—and, indeed, the contemporary public debate in England. What is the ultimate source of the authority of law in a society?

Plato has Socrates lead a discussion on this very question in Book I of the *Republic*, where he discusses three already familiar answers—inherited custom, implied contract, the will of the strongest in society. Plato/Socrates then argues that the best answer is much more complicated—the source of all authority in society rests on something in the nature of a society, in the purpose of social organisation, in the nature and purpose of human existence.

For Plato, that something is to be found in the world of transcendental values, including the transcendental value known as 'justice' seen as a general moral order of the universe, but which is available as an ideal for the making of social and moral order in the human world.

His pupil Aristotle, in his surviving writings known as *Politics* and *Ethics*, follows a less elevated route, but also taking the view that the nature of human society reflects the nature of human beings as social animals, for whom society is the way of achieving the 'good life', that is, the full flourishing of human potentiality judged by transcendental ideals of social and moral order—ideals which the human mind's capacities, including its capacity of 'reason', allow us to present to ourselves as motivating forces of our actions.

In the subsequent phases of the perennial debate, other answers to the question of the ultimate source of authority in society had been suggested—God, Nature, Reason, the god-ordained monarch, the people. Hobbes returns almost to Aristotle in arguing that the nature of human society is explained by the nature of human beings.

In *Leviathan* (1651), he sets out a devastating series of axioms about human nature intending that, as in Euclid's textbook of geometry, everything else will logically follow if you assent to those axioms. He is saying that one can abstract and generalise the working of the minds of individual human beings to find the essentials of human nature. In so doing you will find the essential nature of society, since society is nothing other than 'artificial man', human nature magnified and collectivised.

Without society, human beings would be bound to act only in pursuit of their own self-interest, seeking to use whatever natural advantage of power they may have to dominate everyone else. They would be in a state of war. We may have a natural inclination to avoid war, but also a natural right of self-defence, in order to protect what is ours. We are naturally free, but we may voluntarily limit our freedom or agree to share it with someone else, but always as the result of a prudential calculation about how we might live more safely.

For Hobbes society can only be a prudential arrangement in which our freedom is shared, and in which we are all subject to a government that acts on our behalf to enforce the shared limitations on our freedom. We limit our freedom in order to secure our freedom against the abuse of their freedom by others. As citizens we authorise the authority of the government (the 'sovereign') that acts on our behalf, in particular the acts that take the form of law.

It follows that each society is self-contained. The authority of the law arises from the constitution of the society and is not due to, or subject to, any external or transcendental source of authority. Ideas of 'justice' or 'natural law' have only the meaning and effect that society itself gives to them.

It follows also that our personal identity becomes a social identity and that society must be concerned with all socially significant ideas, including the ideas that the people have about the nature and purpose of society. Religion and education are necessarily matters subject to social determination and control. A given society is self-explaining and self-justifying.

A society is not simply the sum total of its present members—a Many acting as One. It is virtually a living thing, a person, an organism with its own form of life and growth to be found in its constitution, its form of self-constituting. It follows finally that society has a more or less Aristotelian inherent (logically necessary) *purpose*—to bring about the best possible life for human beings.

John Locke (1632-1704). Locke lived in more peaceful times—albeit that Parliament was extra-legally disposing of another king: James II was caused to abdicate in 1688.

By ingenious, but not very convincing, means, Locke puts a warmer gloss on the cold Hobbesian worldview, allowing believers in liberal democracy—not least the rural gentry of British America who would become the revolting British colonists of 1776—to believe that society can be seen as reflecting a much more optimistic picture of human nature.

In the Lockeian worldview, we human beings naturally respect the rights of others—including their right to life and liberty and the enjoyment of what they regard as theirs and they regard as ours ('estate' or 'property', in Locke's vocabulary). As citizens we retain our individual identity and our private life but we participate in public life, in the exercise of the authority of public authorities. Government and laws are instruments that we use to create the conditions of our survival and prosperity—our happiness, as it were.

In his characteristically off-hand manner, Locke suggests a series of benign, vaguely Aristotelian guiding principles which have proved to be profoundly influential in social practice. (Off-handedness is to British philosophy what rigorous obscurity is to German philosophy, and obscure clarity is to French philosophy.)

> 'The end of government is the good of mankind.' *Two Treatises on Government* (1689) (P. Laslett edition), II, §229.
>> Government 'is for the good of the governed'. (I, §92).
>> Laws can only be made 'for the Public Good' (II, §3).
>> Government is intrinsically limited by its purpose and we have a right to enforce those limits even against the power of government. Those who make the laws 'are themselves subject to the laws' (II, §143).

J.-J. Rousseau reconciles the organic unity of the Hobbesian state (with its totalitarian potentiality) with the consensual unity of the Lockeian society in a General Will which is 'always right' and its determinations become *law*, but in the formation of which the citizens may participate in a diffuse sort of way. (On the General Will, see further in Appendix 5 below.)

It is important to understand that the nature of the writing of Hobbes and Locke and Rousseau is not 'scientific', in the spirit of Bacon, nor rigorously 'rational', in a Cartesian or Leibnizian sense. Social theory of this kind is not a hypothesis based on the facts of social experience.

In introducing his own version of a theory of the consensual basis of society (I.1), Rousseau clearly recognises that social theory is not about *explaining* the phenomenon of society but about providing a good *ideal basis* for a society's survival and prospering. At the beginning of his *Social Contract*, he asks—how does it happen that we give up our natural freedom in belonging to society?

> 'I do not know. What can *justify* it? I believe I can answer that question.'

I. Kant (Appendix 8 below), much influenced by Rousseau in this respect, suggests a useful way of understanding a theory such as that of the contractual (consensual) basis of society and government.

> '[It is] an idea of reason, which nevertheless has undoubted practical reality; for it can oblige every legislator to frame his laws in such a way that they could have been produced by the united will of a whole nation, and to regard each subject, in so far as he can claim citizenship, as if he had consented within the general will.' I. Kant (see Appendix 8 below), 'On the common saying: "This may be true in theory, but it does not apply in practice".' (1793).

Like the writing of Plato and Aristotle, such writing offers what should strictly be called *metaphysical social theory* as a set of ideas to live by—'science as one would' or 'truth as utility', to use Baconian formulas. We live by such ideas today, even if we have never heard of Hobbes or Locke (or Kant or Rousseau). It is for each of us to judge whether the best way to justify the contemporary lived reality of the massive systems of law and government and social control that we persist in calling 'liberal democracy' is the theoretical model of Hobbes, of Locke, or of Rousseau—or none of the above.

Thomas Jefferson (1743-1826). An instigator of the rebellion of British colonists in America (1776-1783). Thanks to the failure of the British government to suppress the rebellion by force, the rebellious colonists avoided trial for treason and sedition. Jefferson survived to become the third President (1801-1809) of a federation of the former colonies, called 'the United States of America'—the name that the colonies asserted in first declaring their 'independence' in 1776.

There are three kinds of revolution, if a 'revolution' is defined as an abrupt, non-linear, unconstitutional change in the power-structure of a *polis*, other than change caused by conquest or colonisation by a foreign power.

There are revolutions in which *ideas are a secondary cause*, at most, and whose main means is the use of force under the authority of a charismatic leader—Alexander, Julius Caesar, Charlemagne, Cromwell, Robespierre, Napoleon, Bolívar, Bismarck, Hitler.

There are revolutions involving *the imposition of non-indigenous ideas* under the inspiration of a charismatic indigenous leader—Meiji Tenno, Lenin, Kemal Atatürk, Mao Tse Tung.

And there are revolutions which arise from an assertion, usually by charismatic figures, of *ideas already present* within the social structure which is the target of the revolution—Solon, Ashoka, the Gracchi, Caesar Augustus, Jesus Christ, Luther, Sieyès and Mirabeau and Robespierre (in the first phase of the French Revolution), Gandhi and Nehru.

The American Revolution has generally been seen as a revolution of the third kind. It is possible also to see it as a revolution of the first kind—the use of force to bring about a restructuring of power within the British-plus-American political-economic ruling class, with George Washington as the charismatic leader. Jefferson and Washington were certainly not natural tribunes of the people. They were from the privileged colonial land-owning gentry. It is not difficult to discern—and there are those who have discerned—a self-interested economic programme underlying the Revolution and, indeed, the federal Constitution which emerged from it.

Much the same ambiguity surrounded the previous and analogous 'revolutions' in England, involving the removal of three kings—Richard II (1399), Charles I (1649), and James II (1688). In each case, the peculiarly similar self-justifying rhetoric claimed that the unconstitutional events were the assertion of the true principles of the ancient constitution (revolution as restoration). Jefferson was even one of those who have taken the view that the true Anglo-Saxon nature of the English polity was subverted by the alien intrusion of the Normans in and after the year 1066.

> 'Charles Stuart, the now king of England . . . hath had a wicked design totally
> to subvert the ancient and fundamental laws of this nation and in their place
> to introduce an arbitrary and tyrannical form of government'.

(Act of the House of Commons—not a valid Act of Parliament—establishing a 'court' to try the king, 1649).

'The history of the present King of Great Britain is a history of repeated injuries and usurpations, all having in direct object the establishment of an absolute Tyranny over these States.'

US Declaration of Independence, 1776, of which Jefferson was the principal author. The then following list of alleged offences of George III is remarkably similar to the tone and substance of the offences alleged against Richard II in 1399.

The colonies had a long memory of British misrule in America, including a botched attempt to federate them as a Dominion in 1688, and the suppression of their rebellious response, a response that had been encouraged by the example of the so-called Glorious Revolution in Britain centred on the removal of James II (1688).

But the Americans were also perfectly familiar with English constitutional history and, not least, with the amazing ferment of political ideas in books and pamphlets which flooded the English public mind in the seventeenth century, and among which it is only posterity that has raised the writing of Hobbes and Locke to such a predominant place.

Those ideas ranged from extreme conservatism to extreme radicalism, from the advocacy of theocracy to the advocacy of communism. They included discussion of the possible re-constituting of Great Britain as a republic, with a President and a Senate.

The people of Massachusetts even considered re-naming it Oceana, a name taken from the title of a remarkable book by James Harrington (1656) which anticipated some of the most significant structural features of the eventual federal US constitution (1787). See Ph. Allott, 'The fate of democratic republicanism in a globalising world', in *Towards the International Rule of Law*, ch. 4.

Jefferson and the other founders of the American republic were models of the late-eighteenth century British ruling class at its best, with a sort of intellectual clairvoyance about social and political organisation distilled from the best of English and Dutch and French thought of the seventeenth and eighteenth centuries, and hence from the best of all such thought since the days of Plato and Aristotle—but with the immense advantage that they had given themselves a clean sheet on which to write a Constitution.

It was a clairvoyance that produced the federal Constitution of 1787, with its first ten amendments: (the Bill of Rights, 1791). It was a clairvoyance that produced the Federalist Papers (1788-9), a wonderfully articulate exposition, for the benefit of the newspaper-readers of New York, of what their authors claimed to be the principles underlying the new constitution. They are a perfect epitome of what the American state-makers supposed Baconian *truth* and *utility* to be in the re-making of a particular human society.

APPENDIX 4. **Locke and Berkeley and Hume**.

John Locke (1632-1704). Locke wrote not only on the philosophy of society (Appendix 3 above) but also on general philosophy in the tradition originating in ancient Greece, including epistemology, metaphysics, and ethics. His *Essay concerning Human Understanding* was published in the same year (1689) as the *Two Treatises on Government*. The following quotations from the *Essay* are taken from the edition by R. Woolhouse (Penguin Books, 1997) which is based on the fifth edition (1706)—the last on which Locke himself worked.

Western philosophy is a prolonged and continuing discussion, explicit or implicit, of *the ideas of Plato and Aristotle*. It is not possible to think about those ideas as if they were newly minted and pristine.

Even Christian theology, the Christian religion's philosophising about itself, which dominated the European mind for some fourteen centuries, would not have become what it has been without the ideas of Plato and Aristotle. For example, the *consubstantiality* of the three persons of the three-in-one God and the *transubstantiation* at the heart of the central ritual act (the Eucharist) of Roman Catholic Christianity invoke the idea of *substantia*, the Latin word which came to be used by theologians to represent the Aristotelian category *ousia*.

The Romans had previously translated *ousia* by the invented Latin word *essentia*. They saw the Latin word *substantia* as the etymological equivalent of the Greek *hypostasis*, both words suggesting something that underlies something else. These problems of philology were at the heart of a great theological dispute of the fourth century. The Council of Nicea (I.16) used the word *homoousios* (*consubstantialis*, of the same divine substance) to represent the unity underlying the three 'persons' of the Christian God. The Council thereby rejected the dissenting view—that the three 'persons' of God were 'of *like* substance' (*homoiousios*)—one small letter, an *iota* (Greek letter "i"), big with historical consequences.

The dispute about the nature of God continued and continues. It led to a doctrinal separation and, later, an institutional separation of the Roman Church in the West and the Eastern Orthodox Church which continues to the present day. (The 'Arian heresy' had taken the view that the persons of God were of different nature (*heteroousios*) and hence that the person of the living Christ was not a manifestation of God. A denial of the Nicene concept of the Trinity and of the divinity of Christ continues in a number of dissenting Christian faiths.)

Modern Western philosophy (since 1689) is a prolonged and continuing discussion, explicit or implicit, of *the ideas of John Locke*. It is not possible to think about those ideas as if they were newly minted and pristine. Even the philosophy of science has been obliged to treat as a central question the central Lockeian problem of the nature and the functioning of the ideas that we use to re-present to the mind the presumptive reality of the physical world.

Unlike Francis Bacon, Locke claimed for himself, with a modesty corrected by posterity, a humble purpose in offering his general philosophy of knowledge. He said that, in the commonwealth of learning, not everyone can be among the 'master-builders, whose mighty designs, in advancing the sciences, will leave lasting monuments to the admiration of posterity . . . ; 'tis ambition enough to be employed as an under-labourer in clearing the ground a little, and removing some of the rubbish that lies in the way of knowledge.' (*Epistle to the Reader*).

However, like Bacon, Locke did claim that he was saying something *new*.

> 'The imputation of novelty, is a terrible charge amongst those, who judge of men's heads, as they do of their perukes [wigs], by the fashion; and can allow none to be right, but the received doctrines. Truth scarce ever yet carried it by vote anywhere at its first appearance: new opinions are always suspected, and usually opposed, without any other reason, but because they are not already common.' (*Dedication*, to his patron, the Earl of Pembroke).

Locke devotes more than six hundred pages to the task of 'clearing the ground a little and removing some of the rubbish'. It leads him to investigate every aspect of the functioning of the mind. But it also turns out to be a prescriptive or regulatory task. He will explain how it is that we *may* claim to 'know' anything, and how it is that we *may* determine that what we claim to know is 'true'. In so doing, he will uncover inherent *limits* to the capacity of the human mind. Locke will, he assures us, tell us what it is that we *can and cannot* know for certain.

In an epigraph on the title-page, he quotes from Cicero who says that we would do better to confess 'not to know what we may not know' (*nescire quod nescias*). Our minds prepared by William of Occam and Bacon, we may guess that 'what we may not know' includes, above all, the kind of 'metaphysics' that Plato and Aristotle, and their followers, have propagated.

> 'Let us look into the books of controversy of any kind, there we shall see that the effect of obscure, unsteady, or equivocal terms is nothing but noise and wrangling about sounds, without convincing or bettering a man's understanding. For if the idea be not agreed on, betwixt the speaker and hearer, for which the words stand, the argument is not about things, but names.' (III.XI.§6).

It is interesting, and hazardous, to summarise the thought of the most influential philosophers in a few words. *Plato* (echoing the Pythagoreans and Parmenides)—real reality is something much more than reality seems to be. *Aristotle*—being is becoming, but the becoming of something that itself *is*. *Aquinas*—(Christian) faith and reason can be reconciled. *Bacon*—true knowledge comes from the rational generalisation of orderly observation of the physical world. *Rousseau*—human society need not necessarily be a system for corrupting human beings. *Marx*—society need not necessarily be the exploitation of the many by the few. *Freud*—the unconscious mind has reasons that the conscious mind does not know. *Locke*—the mind is a machine for processing ideas.

In its descriptive aspect, the *Essay* is an amiable amble through the strange workings of the human mind. As such, it might best be considered as a treatise in cognitive psychology, a discipline invented by Aristotle and culminating in the less daring side of the work of Freud. Like Aristotle and Freud, Locke discusses such things as dreams, errors, illusions, delusions, errors, verbal confusions, trite maxims, conventional thinking, wishful thinking, myth and religion. In a description that has usefully been applied to Freud, Locke might be said to be a *biologist of the mind*, investigating the functioning of an organic system. (F. Sulloway, *Freud, Biologist of the Mind*, 1979.)

However, it is the other aspect of the *Essay*—its prescriptive theory of knowledge—that places Locke in a still more unexpected and seemingly improbable category—*metaphysician of the mind*.

Locke's foundational, not to say obsessive, idea is that there are no *innate ideas*—that is to say, ideas that are built into our brains with a seal of absolute truth. He says that all our 'ideas' are produced in the everyday operation of the mind.

> 'There is nothing more commonly taken for granted than that there are certain principles, both speculative and practical (for they are both) ['practical' here means 'moral'] universally agreed upon by all mankind; which therefore they argue, must needs be constant impressions, which the souls of men receive in their first beings, and which they bring into the world with them, as necessarily and really as they do any of their inherent faculties.' (I.II.§2)

On the contrary, says Locke, the mind we are born with is 'white paper, void of all characters, without any ideas.' (II.I.§2). 'Children, idiots, savages and the grossly illiterate' do not innately know metaphysical propositions such as 'whatsoever is, is' or 'it is impossible for the same thing to be, and not to be.' 'Such kind of general propositions . . . are the language and business of the [philosophical] schools, and academies of learned nations, where disputes are frequent.' (I. II.§27).

Even the proposition that 'one and two make three' cannot be innate since it requires a complex structure of rational thought to make sense of it. Even the idea of 'God' cannot be innate, since it varies so much from time to time and from place to place, and is apparently not present at all in some minds. (I.IV.§7ff.).

(Plato, in his dialogue called *Meno*, had suggested that certain fundamental aspects of mathematics are innately present within us. With appropriate guidance, anyone can be led to 'unforgetting' (*anamnesis*) of such things and—more importantly—of ultimate *ideas* of a transcendental nature (beauty, truth, the good, justice . . .). For the German philosopher Edmund Husserl (1859-1938) also, finding the 'truth' involves an uncovering or unforgetting (*aletheia*) of something which is, in some form, already within us.)

So where does the content of our minds come from—

> 'that vast store, which the busy and boundless fancy of man has painted on it, with an almost endless variety? Whence has it all the materials and reason and knowledge? To this, I answer, in one word, from *experience*: in that, all our knowledge is founded; and from that it ultimately derives itself.' (II. I.§2). (The italicised emphasis in this and subsequent quotations is in the original text.)

This is Locke's most notorious idea—the idea that supposedly identifies him and his followers as post-Baconian 'empiricists'—from the Greek: *en* (by) and *peira* ('experiment', 'experience').

But Locke goes on to make a distinction between two sources of knowledge, a distinction which means that he is certainly not merely an empiricist, if that word is to retain any worthwhile meaning. It is a distinction that will provide the groundwork for the work of later philosophers, including Berkeley, Hume, Kant, Hegel and Schopenhauer (discussed hereafter).

The problem is latent in the word 'ultimately' in the passage quoted above. If our ideas are 'ultimately' derived from external physical reality, how ultimate is ultimate? How far can 'true knowledge' be allowed to stray from physical reality?

> 'Our observation employed either about *external sensible objects; or about the internal operations of our minds perceived and reflected on by ourselves, is that, which supplies our understandings with all the materials of thinking.* These two are the fountains of knowledge, from whence all the ideas we have, or can naturally have, do spring.' (II.I.§2)
>
> 'In time, the mind comes to reflect on its own *operations* about the ideas got by *sensation*, and thereby stores itself with a new set of ideas, which I call ideas of *reflection*.'

So 'the original of all knowledge' is *sensations* (our *perceptions* of 'the *impressions* that are made on our *senses* by outward objects that are extrinsical to the mind') and *ideas of reflection* (our 'perception of the operations of our own minds', that is to say, ideas 'proceeding from powers intrinsical and proper to itself [to the mind] which, when reflected on by itself, become also objects of its contemplation'). (II.I.§2 andI. I.I.§24).

For Locke 'perception' is the first stage of mental production, producing ideas about the 'sensations' which are the immediate 'impressions' that we receive about external reality by way of our senses. But the mind then goes on to produce 'ideas of reflection'—our ideas about our ideas, the second 'fountain of knowledge'. And these can presumably be produced *ad infinitum*, getting ever more remote from our immediate impressions of external reality. And they can include feelings about our ideas—'some sort of passions arising from them, such as is the satisfaction or uneasiness arising from any thought' (II.I.§4).

Locke explicitly sets himself an apparently impossible task by seeking to explain every possible kind of mental content at every possible level of particularity or generality, all subsumed under the single word 'ideas'.

> 'But, before I proceed on to what I have thought on this subject, I must here in the entrance beg pardon of my reader for the frequent use of the word *idea*, which he will find in the following treatise. It being that term, which, I think, serves best to stand for whatsoever is the object of the understanding [the operation of the mind] when a man thinks, I have used it to express whatever is meant by *phantasm, notion, species*, or whatever it is, which the mind can be employed about in thinking; and I could not avoid frequently using it.' (I.I.§8).

This new perfectly general use of the word 'idea' incurred the displeasure of Samuel Johnson (1709-84), English writer and lexicographer and a man of the better sort of common sense. He was 'particularly indignant against the almost universal use of the word *idea* in the sense of *notion* or *opinion*, when it is clear that *idea* can only signify something of which an image can be formed in the mind. We may have an *idea* or *image* of a mountain, a tree, a building; but we cannot surely have an *idea* or *image* of an *argument* or *proposition*.' (J. Boswell, *Life of Johnson* (1791), entry for 23 September 1777).

But subsequent practice would prove to be on the side of Locke. We have come to use the word 'idea' in its most general possible sense.

Johnson might also have mentioned that the word 'idea' already had a notorious past. Plato had used the Greek word *idea*, which English translators rendered as 'idea' or 'form', to stand for his ultimate metaphysical concept—the eternal and immutable patterns that lie behind reality, including such ideas as 'justice', 'the good', 'the beautiful'. From Plato to Locke, beginning with his pupil Aristotle, Plato's idea of Ideas had been an intensely fruitful presence in the great dialectical debate of philosophy.

Having described the working of the mind as thinking about ideas of every possible kind, and at every possible level of generality, Locke might seem to face a difficult task in seeking to find a general prescription for identifying 'true' ideas, or what he calls 'certain knowledge'.

It is not only a difficult task but, one might think, an intrinsically impossible task. He is offering a set of ideas—presumably themselves intended to be 'true' ideas—for determining the truth of ideas. Such a claim must surely be a breach of a general principle that we may extrapolate from a principle of mathematical logic proposed by the Austrian mathematician Kurt Gödel (1906-78) and known as the principle of *incompleteness* or *undecidability*. A system of ideas cannot contain the proof of its own validity. Even Aristotelian logic cannot prove the truth of Aristotelian logic.

Locke's prescription for determining true knowledge cannot simply be a requirement of some kind of direct 'correspondence' between our ideas and external physical reality, since, by his definition, ideas of reflection are only ideas about ideas. So his criteria for controlling the truth of ideas must be twofold—not only *correspondence* to external reality but also *agreement* among ideas.

> '*Knowledge* then seems to me to be nothing but *the perception of the connexion or agreement, or disagreement or repugnancy of any of ideas*. Where this perception is, there is knowledge, and where it is not, there, though we may fancy, guess, or believe, yet we always come short of knowledge.' (IV.I.§2).

We acquire knowledge either by *intuition* or by *reason*. Intuition means that we spontaneously see the agreement or disagreement between ideas. Reason means that we test the question by reference to some third, higher idea. And we can, of course, have knowledge also by *sensation*, which tells us about 'the existence of things actually present to our senses', but such knowledge is much more limited than knowledge by intuition or reason.

Locke realises that some people may see a problem with such a line of argument.

> 'I doubt not but my reader, by this time, may be apt to think that I have been all this while only building a castle in the air; and be ready to say to me: "To what purpose all this stir? Knowledge, say you, is only the perception of the agreement or disagreement of our own ideas: but who knows what those ideas may be? Is there anything so extravagant as the imaginations of men's brains? Where is the head that has no chimeras in it? Or if there be a sober and a wise man, what difference will there be, by your rules, between his knowledge and that of the most extravagant fancy in the world? They both have their ideas, and perceive their agreement and disagreement one with another. If there be any difference between them, the advantage will be on the warm-headed man's side, as having the more ideas, and the more lively. And so, by your rules, he will be the more knowing. If it be true, that all knowledge lies only in the perception of the agreement or disagreement of our own ideas, the visions of an enthusiast and the reasonings of a sober man will be equally certain".' (IV.IV.1)

Locke's answer takes up the fourth and final book of the *Essay*—one hundred and sixty pages of dense prose which has provided much grist to the mills of professional philosophers.

He rejects as a general test of truth the comparison of our ideas with observations of the external physical world. They can only generate 'particulars' in our minds. Even to make them into 'substances' (the Aristotelian word again) we have to form the idea of a substance and then compare it with the particulars.

He rejects the idea that truth can be found, other than exceptionally, by reconstructing all the mental steps that led to a particular proposition.

He says that we rarely, if ever, decide the truth of anything on the grounds of Aristotelian formal logic, even if Aristotle was 'one of the greatest men amongst the ancients; whose large views, acuteness, and penetration of thought and strength of judgment, few have equalled.'

And, in his main assault on the old philosophy of the Aristotelians, he rejects (Chapters VI and VII of Book Four) the idea that there are any universal concepts or principles or axioms or maxims shared by all minds that make thinking possible or determine some part of its content.

> 'Mr Newton, in his never enough to be admired book [published two years before Locke's], has demonstrated several propositions, which are so many new truths, before unknown to the world, and are further advances in mathematical knowledge: but for the discovery of these, it was not the general *maxims*, "what is, is"; or "the whole is bigger than a part", or the like, that helped him.' (IV.VII.§11).

Locke's solution to the problem of the relationship between knowledge and truth is to suggest that the mind's complex ideas are themselves patterns in relation to which we can judge other ideas. He calls these patterns 'archetypes'. They are distinct from 'abstractions'—'whereby ideas taken from particular beings, become general representatives of all of the same kind' so that we can use these abstracted patterns of reality 'to rank real existences into sorts, as they agree with these patterns, and to denominate them accordingly'. (II.XI.§9).

The archetypal patterns in our ideas are the mind's own invention and their function is to be, as it were, *normative*. They put other ideas into order. So, on this view, the idea of 'truth' is an archetypal idea designed to identify true ideas or, if the degree of conformity is not complete, probable truths.

Locke suggests that the mind also has a capacity to form various characteristic *relations* between ideas (II.XXV, XXVI). These prove to be a strange mixture of linguistic relationships (*brother, near, soon* etc.), and very complex ideas which had been central to classical metaphysics—*existence, substance, cause and effect, time, space* etc. These relations are a strong echo of the *categories* of Aristotle (whom Locke does not mention in this context) and a strong prefiguring of Kant's *categories*. See further in Appendix 8 below.

Using modern terminology, we might say that Locke's sees the brain as a self-ordering integrating machine using self-generated algorithms or programmes designed to establish relations between self-generated events within the brain, and to remove inconsistencies and incompatibilities among them. He gives his own definition of *reason*, as the mind's purposive effort to find truths in an orderly way, a process that is otherwise *intuitive*.

What the mind tells us to be true cannot be untrue if it conforms to a relevant archetype of truth. The truth-making capacity of ideas is a natural urge in the mind, but sometimes (more often than not!) the system does not produce clarity or certainty or even probability but leaves us in a state of 'confusion of ideas'.

We may be reminded of Freud's 'economic' or 'hydraulic' picture of the mind as a system for finding stable states in response to instinctual drives. The mind's search for truth would then be seen as a tension-reducing mechanism.

In a charming discussion, rejecting Descartes' idea that 'the soul is always thinking', Locke says that his is one of those dull souls that is not always thinking. He cannot see why it is 'any more necessary for the *soul always to think*, than for the body always to move; the perception of ideas being (as I conceive) to the soul, what motion is to the body, not its essence, but one of its operations.' (II.I.§10).

(Voltaire strongly preferred Locke's opinion. However, it is difficult to imagine Voltaire not-thinking for a single instant in the whole of his life. He was not a great admirer of Descartes as a philosopher: *Le premier des mathématiciens ne fit guère que des romans de philosophie.* ('The first of mathematicians hardly produced anything but romantic stories of philosophy.' Voltaire, *Siècle de Louis XIV*, ch. XXXI.)

Locke suggests that all operations of the mind are of the same interactive character, including even moral ideas. Morality is a system of self-regulating regulatory ideas whose conflicts and obscurities are the result of imperfections in our ways of thinking about moral problems. Religious ideas are the product of reason or of faith, the latter being submission to an external source of truth, especially 'revelation'.

The idea of God is a product of reason.

> 'Thus from the consideration of ourselves, and what we infallibly find in our own constitutions, our reason leads us to the knowledge of this certain and evident truth, that "there is an eternal, most powerful, and most knowing being"; which whether any one will please to call *God*, it matters not.' (IV.X.§6).

Locke says that it follows that the extent of our knowledge is intrinsically limited: by our capacity to form ideas, by our capacity to process ideas (by agreement and disagreement among them), and by the fact that we cannot ever know all our ideas, either intuitively or rationally. But we have the inherent capacity always to improve our thinking.

> 'Nevertheless, I do not question, but that human knowledge, under the present circumstances of our beings and constitutions may be carried much further, than it has hitherto been, if men would sincerely, and with freedom of mind, employ all that industry and labour of thought, in improving the means of discovering truth, which they do for the colouring or support of falsehood, to maintain a system, interest, or party they are once engaged in.' (IV.III.§6).

Since, as he himself makes clear, nothing that Locke himself says is merely a perception of sensations about physical reality (say, about the brain), his system must be classed as a system of *mental metaphysics*, like those of Aristotle and Freud, an imaginary picture of quasi-material ideas functioning through quasi-physical interactions to serve quasi-organic functions. Locke the so-called 'empiricist' is truly, if surprisingly, Locke the *idealist*.

To Voltaire, and others, Locke seemed like the miraculous messenger of a new truth.

> 'It is especially in philosophy that the English are the masters of other nations . . . . Chancellor Bacon had begun by saying that we must investigate nature in a new way, that we must make experiments.'
>
> 'Locke alone could serve as a great example of the advantage that our century has had over the finest ages of Greece. From Plato to him, there is nothing: no one, in the meantime, had made any progress on the working of the mind.' (*Siècle de Louis XIV*, ch. XXIV).

Thomas Jefferson (Appendix 3 above) said that Bacon, Newton and Locke were 'the three greatest men the world had ever produced' (letter to B. Rush, 16 January 1811).

George Berkeley (1685-1753) published his most influential works at a remarkably young age—*An Essay Towards a New Theory of Vision* (1709) and *Treatise concerning the Principles of Human Knowledge* (1710).

Berkeley, who studied and taught at Trinity College, Dublin (founded 1592), is often referred to as Bishop Berkeley, although he only became Bishop of Cloyne in the (Anglican) Church of Ireland in 1743.

His early work has another remarkable characteristic. It has been misunderstood, wilfully or negligently, by countless philosophers and commentators.

Aristotle discusses the nature of sense perception (in the treatise known by its Latin title as *De Anima*—'On the Soul'). The relationship between the mind and the reality that seems to present itself to us through the senses has always been one of the most fascinating puzzles addressed by philosophy. Berkeley focused on an obvious weakness in Locke's model of the relationship.

Locke has suggested that bodies in the 'external' world 'produce ideas' in our minds because of the presence of *qualities* in those bodies. Our senses 'convey into the mind' such qualities (yellow, heat, cold, soft, hard, bitter etc.). (Locke, *Essay*, II.I) The qualities may be 'primary' (such as bulk, figure, extension, number, motion) because 'they are in the things themselves' and they produce ideas in our minds that are 'resemblances' of those qualities.

For Locke, other qualities are productions of the mind processing information from the senses, such as heat or colour. (*Essay*, II.VIII). This is similar to Aristotle's view that a *quality* of the object—an aspect of its 'substance'—enters the sensing organ and is then transmitted to the mind that interprets it as the quality in question. (In Latin, *qualitas*, from *qualis*, meaning 'of what kind?' = *poiotes*, from *poios*, in ancient Greek.)

Berkeley rejects this model completely. How can we possibly know what is 'in the things themselves', given that our only knowledge of those things is what we know of them through the senses, and what we know of them through the senses is only what the mind presents to us as the product of the senses?

The eye receives some sort of image on the retina which it communicates to a part of the brain designed to interpret that image. But the image is not a reproduction of the thing of which it is an image, or of some aspect of that thing's substance.

The only thing our mind knows is 'ideas'.

> '[And such ideas are] either ideas actually imprinted on the senses; or else such as are perceived by attending to the passions and operations of the mind; or lastly, ideas formed by help of memory and imagination.' (*Principles*, §1).

What we call an object is merely a collection of ideas in our minds.

> 'For as to what is said of the absolute existence of unthinking things, without any relation to their being perceived, that is to me perfectly unintelligible. Their *esse* is *percipi* [the being of a thing is its being perceived by a human mind]' (§3).

Berkeley argues strongly against 'materialists' who believe in the existence of the material world independent of the human mind—'*the absolute existence of sensible objects in themselves, or without the mind*' (§24). Materialism, he says, leads to Scepticism, Fatalism, Idolatry, Atheism, and Irreligion (§94).

The idea of 'things in themselves' would have a busy subsequent philosophical life-story (see below and Appendix 8 below).

Berkeley's views attracted fierce opposition. He was accused of preaching a ludicrous form of idealism, suggesting that the material world does not exist, and that I can know nothing but my own mind—a sort of bleak *solipsistic idealism* (from *solus* ('alone') and *ipse* ('self'), in Latin).

Denis Diderot (1713-84), leader of the *philosophes* of the French Enlightenment and main editor of the *Encyclopédie* that was its essential embodiment, said:

> 'Those philosophers are called idealists who, conscious only of their own existence and of the sensations which succeed each other within themselves, do not admit of anything else: a peculiar system which, it seems to me, could only have been invented by the blind; a system which, to the shame of the human mind and of philosophy, is the most difficult to combat, although the most absurd of all.'

D.Diderot, *Lettre sur les aveugles à l'usage de ceux qui voient* (1749) ('Letter on the blind for the use of those who can see'). (present author's trans.).

Diderot himself preached a splendidly thorough materialism, arguing that not only the mind but also what we call 'life' (including sexual reproduction) are merely particular manifestations of inert matter. See especially his *Conversation with d'Alembert and d'Alembert's Dream* (1830).

Deemed too scandalous to be published in his lifetime, it was copied for the eyes of a limited number of his friends. The manuscript was sent, with the rest of his papers, to Catherine the Great in St. Petersburg after his death. Jean le Rond d'Alembert (1717-83), Diderot's close collaborator, is remembered as a mathematician and sceptical philosopher. He wrote the *Discours préliminairee*, a manifesto of the new intellectual climate, in vol. I of the *Encyclopédie*. He is also remembered for the unusual fact that his Christian name is that of the church in Paris on whose steps he was abandoned as a baby, the illegitimate child of the extraordinary Madame de Tencin.

James Boswell recalls a discussion with Dr Johnson.

> '[We discussed] Bishop Berkeley's ingenious sophistry to prove the non-existence of matter, and that every thing in the universe is merely ideal. I observed, that though we are satisfied his doctrine is not true, it is impossible to refute it. I never shall forget the alacrity with which Johnson answered, striking his foot with mighty force against a large stone, till he rebounded from it, "I refute it *thus*".' (*Life of Johnson*, entry for 6 August 1763).

Needless to say, dear Samuel Johnson, the very model of 18th-century good sense, probably understood that his foot had not refuted Berkeley's idealist epistemology, but only a commonplace parody of Berkeley's ideas.

Berkeley's philosophy is more subtle and more sensible than his detractors suppose.

Strangely, it is V.I.Lenin, of all people, who argues this convincingly in his *Materialism and Empirio-Criticism. Critical Comments on a Reactionary Philosophy* (1908). He speaks more respectfully of Berkeley, the idealist, than of contemporary positivists. He is attacking neo-Kantian and post-Kantian philosophers, especially philosophers of science (Avenarius and Mach), who purport to dismiss as meaningless and/or unnecessary the question of the reality of the material world. Lenin says that they do not seem to know that Berkeley (and Locke and Hume) had dealt with these matters long ago.

> 'That the things I see with my eyes and touch with my hands do exist, really exist, I make not the least question. The only thing whose existence we deny is that which *philosophers* call Matter or corporeal substance.' (Berkeley, *Principles*, §34)

Berkeley is not denying our knowledge that there are things in the external world. What he is rejecting is the idea that some intrinsic form of those things *causes* the particular form that our knowledge has of them—as if matter were primary and the operation of our mind only a secondary and tributary effect. He is rejecting a philosophical *materialism* inherited from certain of the ancient Greek philosophers. And he is rejecting the Aristotelian idea of 'substance' if that is meant to refer to an ultimate underlying reality, existing independently of the 'substance' that we create by fitting our ideas of a thing together. (§37).

He is suggesting an idea of great interest—and philosophically prophetic. He says that there is a *symbolic parallelism* between the external things and their re-presentation in our minds. It is a relation of 'a mark or *sign* with the thing *signified*'. (§65). We may detect here an echo of what we referred to above as William of Occam's *modified nominalism* (see Appendix 1).

The thing signified is not merely matter. And the signifying mind is not merely matter in another form. They are both closer to what has traditionally been called *spirit*, a universal substance in relation to which matter is a secondary form of existence. Berkeley suggests, as did Descartes, that it is the goodness of God that has made the human mind capable of such a relationship to the external world.

Natural science is possible because our mind fits such ideas together into a 'train and succession of ideas' which allow us to make 'well-grounded predictions' (§59). And, in any case, we are not alone in our thinking. We check on our own ideas of reality by comparing them with other people's ideas. (§84).

In his *Lettre sur les aveugles* (see above), Diderot, starting from a radically different philosophical position, discusses Berkeley's own theory of vision and proposes an explanation which is remarkably similar to the Berkeleyan model as presented above.

David Hume (1711-76). A leading figure of the Scottish Enlightenment, Hume made his main contribution to the philosophy of mind at a remarkably early age. His *Treatise of Human Nature* was published in 1739-40, a young man's breezy and bold reaction to the new ferment of philosophy, to what we are here calling the new British *metaphysics of the mind*.

> 'This book seems to be wrote upon the same plan with several other works that have had a great vogue of late years in England. The philosophical spirit, which has been so much improved all over Europe within these last fourscore years, has been carried to as great a length in this kingdom as in any other. Our writers seem even to have started a new kind of philosophy, which promises more both to the entertainment and advantage of mankind, than any other with which the world has been yet acquainted.' (D. Hume (probably), *An Abstract of the Treatise* (1740). (Hume had been disappointed with what he saw as a lack of interest in his more-than-six-hundred-page book when it was published. The Abstract explains some of his main ideas in simple terms.)

Hume mentions the fierce and interminable disputes among philosophers.

> 'From hence in my opinion arises that common prejudice against metaphysical reasonings of all kind, even amongst those, who profess themselves scholars. By metaphysical reasonings, they do not understand those on any particular branch of science, but every kind of argument, which is in any way abstruse, and requires some attention to be comprehended.' (*Treatise*, Introduction).
>
> 'There is no question of importance, whose decision is not comprised in the science of man; and there is none, which can be decided with any certainty, before we become acquainted with that science. In pretending therefore to explain the principles of human nature, we in effect propose a compleat system of the sciences, built on a foundation almost entirely new, and the only one upon which they stand with any security.' (Introduction).

Hume says that 'the only solid foundation' for the new science of human nature is the same as that for the natural sciences—'experience and observation'. He refers to the new philosophy of the natural sciences of 'my Lord Bacon' and to

> 'some late philosophers in England, who have begun to put the science of man on a new footing . . . Nor ought we to think, that this latter improvement in the science of man will do less honour to our native country than the former in natural philosophy [the natural sciences], but ought rather to esteem it a greater glory, upon account of the greater the importance of that science, as well as the necessity it lay under of such a reformation.'

The *Treatise* has a subtitle: *Being an Attempt to introduce the experimental Method of Reasoning into Moral Subjects*. But Hume acknowledges that it is not possible to set up experiments on human matters like those applied to the natural world.

> 'We must therefore glean up our experiments in this science from a cautious observation of human life, and take them as they appear in the common course of the world, by men's behaviour in company, in affairs, and in their pleasures.' (Introduction).

However, it must be said that the rest of the book is almost identical in style and method to countless other previous and subsequent works in the field, including those of Hobbes and Locke and Berkeley—namely, intelligent introspection and common-sense generalisation. It is writing designed to win the comfortable assent of a particular audience—people as sensible and worldly-wise as Hume and his friends—rather than to convince dogmatists of all kinds or the high-priests of what Bacon had called 'professory learning', who were, and are, beyond intellectual redemption.

The *Treatise* is divided into three Books—on the Understanding, on the Passions, and on Morals. Book I accordingly traverses much the same ground as Locke's *Essay* and Berkeley's *Principles*.

Hume uses the word *perceptions* as the most general name for the contents of the mind, but he draws an axiomatic distinction between two kinds of 'perception' which he calls *impressions* and *ideas*, distinguished by 'the degree of force and liveliness, with which they strike upon the mind.' (*Treatise*, Bk.I, I.1).

An *impression* is a direct unreflective event in the mind, including sensations and emotions. An *idea* is a thought that may or may not be a thought about an impression. Ideas may be *simple* or *complex*, the latter being divisible into simpler ideas.

In a footnote he explains:

> 'I here make use of these terms . . . in a sense different from what is usual, and I hope this liberty will be allowed me. Perhaps I rather restore the word *idea*, to its original sense, from which Mr Locke had perverted it in making it stand for all our perceptions.'

Ideas can exist separately from each other or can be joined together by *association*. The associating of ideas occurs spontaneously or through mental effort. The famous Aristotelian idea of 'substance' and all other such ideas are, for Hume as they were for Locke, merely names given to a collection of ideas, a sort of composite *fiction*.

It follows also that, for Hume as it was for Berkeley, *abstraction* is a way of thinking and speaking about collections of ideas. An abstraction—*triangle, government, space, time*—does not itself become a thing because we customarily talk about it as if it were such.

Hume's discussion of these preliminary matters is unimpressive. It soon becomes clear that the distinctions between 'impressions' and 'ideas' and between 'simple' and 'complex' ideas have no rigorous basis of distinction. And Hume's explanations of 'abstraction' and the 'association' of ideas seem arbitrary and no more convincing than anyone else's ideas on the subject. It is almost as if he knew that he was now, after Locke and Berkeley and the other new metaphysicians of the mind, pushing at an open door, as entitled as anyone else to postulate his own structural ideas about the working of the mind, without much call for rigorous intellectual effort.

It is difficult to say that Hume adds much of fundamental value to the ideas of his predecessors on what we may call the *physics* of the mind (how does the mind function?).

Notwithstanding several thousand years of philosophical debate on the subject, he restates, as if it were now beyond dispute, the *idealist* position on the nature of reality that we have found in the other British philosophers who are traditionally, and bizarrely, classed as *empiricist* philosophers.

> 'The idea of existence, then, is the very same with the idea of what we conceive to be existent. To reflect on any thing simply, and to reflect on it as existent, are nothing different from each other.'

'A like reasoning will account for the idea of *external existence* [external to the mind]. We may observe, that 'tis universally allowed by philosophers, and is besides pretty obvious of itself, that nothing is ever really present with the mind but its perceptions or impressions and ideas, and that external objects become known to us only by those perceptions they occasion. To hate, to love, to think, to feel, to see; all this is nothing but to perceive.' (Bk. I, I. vi).

However, Hume's *Treatise* contains *three notorious ideas* on the *metaphysics* of the mind (what is the nature of the reality that the mind constructs?) that have played a major role in the next phase of the perennial debate of philosophy, especially in the subsequent development of German philosophy. (See Appendix 8 below.)

(1) *Causation*. Hume treats the phenomenon of *causation* as the crucial example of the mistaken, but normal, way of thinking that treats our ideas as ideas about actual structural features of external reality (i.e., external to the human mind) rather than as inventions of the human mind.

What we think of as a relation of cause and effect

'can never operate on the mind, but by means of custom, which determines the imagination to make a transition from the idea of one object to that of its usual attendant . . .' (I.III.xiv).

The inference from cause to effect

'is nothing but the effects of custom on the imagination' (II.III.i).

Hume explicitly rejects Aristotle's ingenious (and controversial) distinction between kinds of causes (Aristotle's *Physics*, 195a). He implicitly differs from Locke's more 'realist' view—

'a *cause* is that which makes any other thing, either simple idea, substance, or mode, begin to be; and an *effect* is that, which had its beginning from some other thing' (Locke, *Essay*, II.XXVI, §2).

For Hume, it is *habit*—that is, our habitually associating ideas derived from our experience of ourselves and the external world—which leads us to believe that the future will *probably* resemble the past. And so all we think we *know* about ourselves and about the world is properly seen as a register of *probabilities*. Even our *personal identity* (when we say 'I') is, like causation, a product of our mind as it associates ideas that have been present in our minds and have been retained in our memory.

'Had we no memory, we should never have any notion of causation, nor consequently of that chain of causes and effects, which constitute our self or person.' (IV.I.vi).

In his (?) *Abstract* of the *Treatise* (see above), Hume uses the example of billiards.

'Here is a billiard-ball lying on the table, and another ball moving towards it with rapidity. They strike; and the ball, which was formerly at rest, now acquires a motion. This is as perfect an instance of the relation of cause and effect as any which we know, either by sensation or reflection.'

What happens when we see one billiard-ball approaching another? We infer that the latter will be set in motion.

'This is the inference from cause to effect; and of this nature are all our reasonings in the conduct of life: on this is founded all our belief in history: and from hence is derived all philosophy, excepting only geometry and arithmetic.' 'We are determined by CUSTOM alone to suppose the future conformable to the past.'
'It is not, therefore, reason, which is the guide of life, but custom.'

The proper default attitude of the true philosopher is *scepticism*, a sort of humility in the face of the strict limits that the nature of the human mind imposes on our capacity to know anything, let alone to know anything for certain, given that all our supposed knowledge is ultimately the product of our *imagination*.

Hume even reproves himself (IV.I.vii) for a fault that he may have fallen into 'after the example of others' by using such expressions as: 'it is evident, it is certain, it is undeniable'. (Locke, like Hume, was a serial offender in this regard. It is remarkable that, to this day, philosophers who reject the idea of 'truth' as meaningless pepper their own argumentative writing to that effect with the words 'true' and 'false' and 'proved' and 'disproved'.)

(2) *Truth and reason and feeling.* A vast philosophical tradition, going back to Aristotle and beyond, explores the nature of 'truth', as if it were something that transcends the individual human mind, and 'reason', as a sort of self-transcending capacity of the mind, enabling us to discover 'truth'. But, for Hume, the human mind cannot possibly transcend its rather limited capacities.

He offers his own version of Locke's idea of 'relations' (see above), itself a re-working of Aristotle's 'categories' and a prefiguring of Kant's 'categories' (Appendix 8 below).

For Hume, 'relations' (*resemblance, identity, space and time, cause and effect, quantity, difference,* etc.) are complex ideas produced by the association of ideas and which we use like templates to compare and integrate other ideas.

'Reason' is a purposive effort to make use of such relations, a process whose goal is 'truth', where 'truth' is what we feel to be a satisfactory conformity between these preformed relations and our ideas, including our ideas formed from sensations received from the external world.

This seeking for 'truth' is classified by Hume among our 'passions' (II.III). Our aim may be 'utility', but we may be led by other passions—including our desire to experience 'pleasure' and to avoid 'pain'. Indeed, philosophising, which requires effort and does not always succeed, is like 'hunting or gaming or curiosity about our neighbours'. 'To illustrate all this by a similar instance, I shall observe, that there cannot be two passions more nearly resembling each other, than those of hunting and philosophy.'

Hume says that mere 'reason' can never cause us to choose to do anything. That is always the work of the passions (our feelings, emotions, desires).

> 'Human life is so tiresome a scene, and men generally are of such indolent dispositions, that whatever amuses them, though by a passion mixed with pain, does in the main give them a sensible pleasure.' (III.X).
>
> 'We speak not strictly and philosophically when we talk of the combat of passion and reason. Reason is, and *ought* only to be the slave of the passions, and can never pretend to any other office than to obey them' (II.III). (Emphasis added; Hume's peculiar use of the word 'ought' here deserves our particular attention—what can it possibly mean in this context?.)

Hume immediately acknowledges that this may seem a 'somewhat extraordinary' opinion. It became one of his most notorious and most quoted sayings.

(3) *Morality*. 'Morality' is traditionally seen as a set of ideas operating as a motivating force causing us to behave in particular ways. Plato and Aristotle and their countless followers devote much attention to its nature and purpose and substance.

In Book II of his *Treatise*, Hume catalogues and analyses, at great length, human dispositions and motives ('passions'), as an amusing, but not particularly useful, part of his 'experimental' approach to 'human nature'. His discussion is remarkably similar in style and content to Aristotle's *Ethics*. But, in Book III, he offers a philosophy of morality that associates him with an ancient sceptical tradition which denies the *rationality of morality*.

Moral rationality is yet another of Aristotle's ingenious inventions—*practical reason*—the idea that the well-developed human mind can find moral principles within itself by the use of the mind's reasoning capacity. Hume devotes only twenty-two pages to what would prove to be an intensely provocative, if intensely unconvincing, line of counter-argument.

Moral judgments are not the product of reason, since they are designed to control our actions and, as he claims already to have proved, our actions are determined by our feelings, not by reason. Reason can help to determine our actions only by helping us to analyse the implications of a morally challenging situation or the possibilities of action in that situation. The choice we make in that situation cannot itself be *determined* by reason.

> 'The rules of morality, therefore, are not conclusions of our reason. No one, I believe, will deny the justness of this inference; nor is there any other means of evading it, than by denying that principle, on which it is founded. As long as it is allowed, that reason has no influence on our passions and actions, it is in vain to pretend, that morality is discovered *only* by a deduction of reason.' (III.I.1).

Emphasis added. The word 'only' reveals a deep, and much discussed, confusion in Hume's argument. Reason *is* so much involved in our making of moral judgments, as he later admits, that it is not of much interest to say that our moral judgments are not 'only' determined by reason.

> 'Reason *is* the *discovery* of truth or falsehood. Truth or falsehood *consists* in an agreement or disagreement either to the real relations of ideas, or to real existence and matter of fact. Whatever, therefore, is not susceptible of this agreement or disagreement, is *incapable* of being true or false, and can *never* be an object of our reason. Now it is evident our passions, volitions, and actions, are not susceptible of any such agreement or disagreement. It is *impossible*, therefore, they can be pronounced either true or false, and be either contrary or conformable to reason.' (III.I.1). (emphasis added).
>
> Hume here reveals that he has forgotten the lessons of scepticism and nominalism in his own Book I, and is treating *his own ideas* prescriptively, so that his ideas of reason and truth have become virtual *real things*—things-in-themselves—in the systematic structure of the mind.

Hume then offers a supplementary, and off-hand, 'observation, which may, perhaps, be found of some importance'. (III.I.1). It is a passage which has become mysteriously famous, and has given rise to countless interpretations and re-interpretations.

He says that authors often draw what they suppose to be *moral conclusions* from what they suppose to be *statements of fact*.

> 'I have always remarked, that the author proceeds for some time in the ordinary way of reasoning, and establishes the being of a God, or makes observations concerning human affairs; when of a sudden I am surprised to find, that instead of the usual copulations of propositions, *is*, and *is not*, I meet with no proposition that is not connected with an *ought*, or an *ought not*.'
>
> '. . . a reason should be given, for what seems altogether *inconceivable*, how this new relation *can* be a deduction from others, which are entirely

different from it. But as authors do not commonly use this precaution, I shall presume to recommend it to the readers; and am persuaded, that this small attention would subvert all the vulgar systems of morality, and let us see, that the distinction of vice and virtue is not founded on the relation of objects, nor is perceived by reason.' (III.I.1). (Emphasis added.)

If Hume were really what he claims to be—a quasi-scientific observer of human nature—he would want to explain why vast systems of morality, including some that were much acclaimed in his own time, so frequently take the form he derides.

It seems rather that he was actually pursuing a personal campaign against traditional forms of religion, repudiating all those deductive systems of morality derived from the intellectual structures of revealed religion, their revelations being constantly framed in the form of statements about metaphysical realities and conventionally expressed in sentences, containing forms of the verb *to be*.

But surely *systems of morality*, however formed and however questionable, are as much a part of observable *human nature* as is scepticism or atheism. Indeed, the *feelings* that, according to Hume, cause us to make judgments in terms of *virtue* and *vice* are themselves robust and ancient and interesting phenomena of human nature, surely worthy of investigation by *the experimental method*. You do not effectively 'subvert' systems of morality by saying that they have foundations which are convincing for those who believe in such systems, even if you (Hume) do not agree with those foundations.

Hume, echoing Hobbes but less trenchantly, finds the source of the distinction between *virtue* and *vice*, not in any natural phenomenon or in any matter of fact, other than in a feeling we have about different actions.

'An action, or sentiment, or character is virtuous or vicious; why? because its view causes a pleasure or uneasiness of a particular kind.'

'To have the sense of virtue, is nothing but to *feel* a satisfaction of a particular kind from contemplation of a character.'

'Morality, therefore, is more properly felt than judged of.' (III.I.II).

'Take any action allowed to be vicious: Wilful murder, for instance. Examine it in all lights, and see if you can find that matter of fact, or real existence, which you call *vice*. In whichever way you take it, you find only certain passions, motives, volitions and thoughts. There is no other matter of fact in the case. The vice entirely escapes you, as long as you consider the object. You can never find it, till you turn your reflexion into your own breast, and find a sentiment of disapprobation, which arises in you, towards the action. Here is a matter of fact; but it is the object of feeling, not of reason. It lies in yourself, not in the object.' (III.I.1).

Hume was a notoriously nice person.

'Upon the whole, I have always considered him, both in his lifetime and since his death, as approaching as nearly to the idea of a perfectly wise and virtuous man, as perhaps human frailty will permit.' (Adam Smith (Appendix 5 below), letter to W. Strahan, 1776).

And yet David Hume's youthful philosophising has had an effect on Western philosophy which we may now see as intensely stimulating, but also laying the groundwork for the abandoning of the very idea of philosophy in the great tradition.

Philosophical scepticism has always been an essential part of the powerfully dialectical and dynamic character of the Western philosophical tradition. Unlike mythology and religion, but not unlike the natural sciences, Western philosophy enriches itself through negation. Every philosophical idea contains the possibility of its negation by another philosophical idea. The pre-Socratic philosophers in Greece were already engaged in complex and lively debate and dispute about every kind of philosophical problem.

The Pythagoreans, and then Socrates and Plato, articulate their philosophical positions in conscious opposition to other (especially materialist and relativist) positions.

Aristotle is a sceptic in relation to what he sees as the mysticism and dogmatism of the Pythagoreans and Plato. A later leader of the Platonic Academy, Carneades (c.213-c.129 BCE), was a sceptical Platonist and a Hume *avant la lettre*. He had an extreme form of dialectical teaching method—echoing the method (but not the aim) of Socrates, and prefiguring the method (but not the aim) of medieval scholasticism (*disputatio in utramque partem*), in which opposing arguments on each issue are set against each other.

A leading figure of the Aristotelian renaissance of the 12th century, Pierre Abélard (1079-1142), in *Sic et Non* ('Yes and No'), treats the problem of apparently conflicting opinions within Christian theology, consideration of which can (sometimes!) lead to an enrichment of thought. *Dubitando enim ad inquisitionem venimus; inquirendo veritatem percipimus* ('For in doubting we are led to investigate; in investigating we discover the truth.') (Prologue).

Carneades' lectures in Rome, as a member of a delegation of Greek philosophers (156-155 BCE), had a great intellectual effect (not least on Cicero). We might even speculate that they played some part in causing a defeatist 'end of philosophy' feeling in Rome (there could not much more to be said beyond Greek philosophy), and hence the relative poverty of Roman philosophy.

Carneades taught that the best we can know of reality is as a form of probability which we may act on as a reasonable working hypothesis (*pithane phantasia*, 'a plausible idea'). He rejects what he sees as the theological dogmatism of the Stoics and, in particular, the idea that sense-impressions can sometimes produce something that we regard as certainty (*kataleptike phantasia*, 'a sound idea'), rather as Hume rejects the suggestion that we have a capacity for forming intuitive certainties by means of what some of his contemporaries were calling a 'common sense'.

Hume's ideas—or, perhaps, his philosophical style and his attitude—invaded the minds of a remarkable group of German philosophers (see Appendix 8 below), but their powerful new thinking faded away in the late-nineteenth century, leaving the field open to a sad effusion of unphilosphies and anti-philosophies—

positivism (human phenomena are to be studied quasi-scientifically);

utilitarianism (the human mind is a pre-programmed calculating machine programmed to serve self-interest);

pragmatism (the human mind is an inseparable part of a social idea-processing system);

reductionism (the human mind is determined by human physiology);

nihilism (we cannot know or value anything, except as an expression of arbitrary and incomprehensible choice);

logical positivism (so-called philosophical problems are mental illusions).

In the 20th century, it was possible for some to proclaim 'the end of philosophy'.

Hume's debonair and infuriatingly common-sense philosophising recalls the style and attitude of another inexhaustibly interesting public intellectual of the eighteenth-century Enlightenment.

Voltaire's perverse refusal to philosophise seriously was the hallmark of his sardonic and sceptical personality. Voltaire was definitely not a nice person of the Humean kind, even if there was a powerful streak of benevolence somewhere inside him, but writing and talking flowed from him like magma from a volcano.

To Hume and Voltaire we might be inclined to apply Samuel Johnson's judgment of Voltaire and Rousseau: 'Why, Sir, it is difficult to settle the proportion of iniquity between them.' (*Life of Johnson*, entry for 15 February 1766).

APPENDIX 5. **Adam Smith and Ricardo**.

Adam Smith (1723-90), a leading figure of the Scottish Enlightenment, studied at the University of Glasgow (first founded in 1451) and Balliol College, Oxford. He was Professor of Logic and then Professor of Moral Philosophy at Glasgow from 1751 to 1764. He is the prophet of a new socio-economic order, a socio-economic order from which the present 'Western' social order derives. Adam Smith's vision is of a particular form of *totalitarian socialism*.

David Ricardo (1772-1823) worked as a stockbroker (until 1812), his first publication on economic theory dating from 1809. He is a progenitor of what may be called *economic positivism*, the idea that economic phenomena are explicable independently of other social phenomena, albeit that such explanations may have—and, in Ricardo's case, did have—very substantial implications for public policy.

Adam Smith is a perfect example of eighteenth-century humanistic rationalism. The full title of the work which has come to be known as *The Wealth of Nations* (1776)— *An Inquiry into the Nature and Causes of the Wealth of Nations*—could not be more characteristic of the British eighteenth-century intellectual climate which was perfectly described by John Stuart Mill as 'innovative, infidel, abstract, metaphysical, and prosaic'. (*Westminster Review*, March 1840).

It is not possible to overstate the impact on general consciousness of the worldview expressed and implied in Smith's *The Wealth of Nations*. In style and method it is indistinguishable from the work of his friend David Hume, and of countless other writers over the course of the two preceding centuries—that is to say, intelligent common-sense speculation about human phenomena, written in the form of discursive and non-technical, almost conversational, not to say rambling, prose. Such writing is 'amateur' writing, in the sense that it is not addressed to a restricted professionalized audience. It is designed to enter fruitfully into the minds of a small, relatively cohesive elite of well-educated and well-intentioned readers with broad interests.

Smith's book is yet another six-hundred-page blockbuster. The literate leisured class of his time must have had little else to do, other than to write and read such books. It also has what may now seem to us a peculiar characteristic, given nineteenth-century conventions of 'scholarship' that we have inherited. It is characteristic also of Hume's writing, and of the writing of so many others of their kind.

It draws on much that has already been written—especially, in Smith's case, by a number of French and English writers—for example, R. Cantillon, *Essai sur la nature du commerce en général* (Essay on the Nature of Commerce in General) (1755); A-R-J. Turgot, *Réflexions sur la formation et la distribution des richesses* (Reflections on the Formation and Distribution of Wealth) (1766); or P. de la Rivière, *L'ordre naturel et essentiel des sociétés politiques* (The Natural and Essential Order of Political Societies) (1767)—or, indeed, a remarkable (and notably Humean) work by Smith himself—*The Theory of Moral Sentiments* (1759).

But it seems to take the previous writings for granted, rarely citing them explicitly or identifying points of agreement and disagreement—with no sign yet of the symptoms of Teutonic Foot-and-Note Disease (borrowing this useful nosological term from James 'Behaviourism' Watson).

The appeal and the impact of such a book as Hume's *Treatise* or Smith's *Wealth of Nations* come from their integration of carefully selected familiar, or readily comprehensible, ideas into a striking new intellectual totality.

The new intellectual totality of *The Wealth of Nations* is a new vision of society, a new way of looking at society. From Plato and Aristotle onwards, general theories of society had been explanations of the possible and preferable forms of government and law in a society which is seen essentially as a *political system*, a *polis*, a general arena for the organised living-together of human beings. Smith contributed to that perennial debate in his other writings, but, in *The Wealth of Nations*, discussion of government and law is only incidental, at most, to the construction of an idea of society as an *economic system*, an *oikos*, a household. (The English word 'economics' is derived from the Greek words *oikos* and *nomos*, the latter meaning, in this context, 'law' or 'regulation'.)

In Hobbesian and Humean fashion, Smith starts with what he considers to be two essential elements of *human nature*—self-interest and the commercial instinct. He treats these as axiomatic, the rest of the system following as a more or less necessary deduction.

In postulating self-interest as a primary aspect of human nature, Smith takes issue with his own teacher and professorial predecessor at Glasgow—Francis Hutcheson—and their friend David Hume, both of whom treat *sympathy*, human fellow-feeling, as a primary aspect of human nature.

For Smith, we are naturally self-interested but we are also utterly dependent on other people. This means that we have to engage their self-interest to serve our self-interest. This gives rise to the commercial nature of our relationship with other people—'a certain propensity in human nature . . . to truck, barter and exchange one thing for another.'

> 'But man has almost constant occasion for the help of his brethren, and it is in vain for him to expect it from benevolence only. He will be more likely to prevail if he can interest their self-love in his favour, and show them that it is for their own advantage to do for him what he requires of them. Whoever offers to another a bargain of any kind, proposes to do this. Give me what I want, and you shall have this which you want, is the meaning of every such offer; and it is in this manner that we obtain from one another the far greater part of those good offices which we stand in need of. It is not from the benevolence of the butcher, the brewer, or the baker that we expect our dinner, but from their regard to their own interest. We address ourselves, not to their humanity but to their self-love, and never talk to them of our own necessities but of their advantages.'
> *Wealth of Nations*, Bk.I, ch. II.

We may recognise this depth psychology of enlightened selfishness as the foundational characteristic of the self-understanding, and self-justifying, of what we have come to call 'capitalism'. It is a foundational idea in the metaphysics of capitalism. Capitalism is a theory of the systematic exploitation of self-interest in the service of the common interest of society.

Smith's *Wealth of Nations* is a metaphysical vision. Like Hobbes and Locke and Berkeley and Hume, Smith is a prophet of a form of *prescriptive metaphysics,* as we may call it—a work of the imagination designed to change our understanding of the human world and, hence, to change our behaviour as actors in the human world.

That *private vice* may serve the *public interest* was a familiar idea in the 18th century. In Bernard de Mandeville's satirical poem *The Grumbling Hive: Or, Knaves Turned Honest* (1705), he had described the social life of a hive of bees which had been richly productive so long as every bee, performing its own socially appointed task, acted out of the crudest self-interest.

'Thus every part was full of vice, / Yet the whole mass a paradise.'

One day, the bees decided that they should reform themselves and live honestly. The result was disaster. Nobody did their appointed work and the gross domestic product of the hive was reduced to zero (in modern terms).

'[To] live in ease / Without great vices, is a vain / Eutopia seated in the brain.'

In Smith's ideal society, as in de Mandeville's, the secret of society's capacity to create the ever-increasing wealth of the nation is *the division of labour*.

> 'This great increase of the quantity of work which, in consequence of the division of labour, the same number of people are capable of performing, is owing to three different circumstances; first, to the increase of dexterity in every particular workman; secondly, to the saving of the time which is commonly lost in passing from one species of work to another; and lastly, to the invention of a great number of machines which facilitate and abridge labour, and enable one man to do the work of many.' (Bk. 1, ch. I).

But the division of labour means that we become dependent on the labour of others for what we cannot produce ourselves.

> 'Observe the accommodation of the most common artificer or day-labourer in a civilized and thriving country, and you will perceive that the number of people of whose industry a part, though but a small part, has been employed in procuring him this accommodation, exceeds all computation.' To accommodate the life of 'the very meanest person in a civilized country' requires 'the assistance and co-operation of many thousands.' (Bk. I, ch. 1).

So it seems that the so-called 'division of labour' is really an *integration of labour*. Our natural dependence on each other becomes a systematic dependence, if we are to live beyond the bare minimum of subsistence. Society is a systematic integration of labour.

We recognise this *subjection* of the work of the individual to the working of the collective economic system as a second fundamental characteristic of the metaphysics of what we have come to call capitalism. Capitalism is a ruthless transformation of human individuals into integral parts of a collective social system. Capitalism is *absolute collectivism*. Capitalism is the ultimate form of *slavery—human beings made into machine-parts.*

Efficiency of production means that the worker produces a *surplus* of goods beyond his own personal and immediate needs. But he needs other goods for his own personal use. He is in a position to exchange his own surplus for the surplus produced by other workers.

'He supplies the far greater part of them [his needs] by exchanging that surplus part of the produce of his own labour, which is over and above his own consumption, for such parts of the produce of other men's labour as he has occasion for. Every man thus lives by exchanging, or becomes in some measure a merchant, and the society itself grows to be what is properly a commercial society.' (Bk. I, ch. iv).

Humanity invented *money* to store the surplus produce of labour. A *market* is necessary to determine its *value*.

'The word VALUE, it is to be observed, has two different meanings, and sometimes expresses the utility of some particular object, and sometimes the power of purchasing other goods which the possession of that object conveys. The one may be called "value in use"; the other, "value in exchange". The things which have the greatest value in use have frequently little or no value in exchange; and, on the contrary, those which have the greatest value in exchange have frequently little or no value in use. Nothing is more useful than water: but it will purchase scarce anything; scarce anything can be had in exchange for it. A diamond, on the contrary, has scarce any value in use; but a very great quantity of other goods may frequently be had in exchange for it.' (Bk. I, ch. iv).

From these few words whole libraries of writing would accumulate. From these few words social revolutions would take fire, and the course of the history of the human world would be changed for ever.

How should the surplus produce of labour be valued and who should benefit from its value?

A third feature of the metaphysics of capitalism is that it is a particular system for determining and distributing the *surplus value* produced through the collectivisation of labour.

The *market* is a mythical monster at the heart of the metaphysics of capitalism. The market digests the products of *labour*, processes them into *money-value*, and regurgitates them as *wealth*. Society, which determined the organisation of *labour*, then determines how *wealth* is to be *distributed* as *property*. The organisation of labour and the distribution of wealth are determined by social struggle.

Capitalism as an -ism is not only a system of metaphysics—a reality made by, for and in the human mind. It is also an ethics. The market-monster has its own inherent enzyme-values—economic self-determination, competition, efficiency, innovation, wealth-maximising—which enable it to digest the infinite variety of the products of labour. It is omnivorous. Its insatiable diet can include religions, art, sex, interpersonal relations, ideas of every kind, everything in the natural world—all of which it can value and re-value and transform into species of wealth and property.

In a laconic passing reference, Adam Smith uses a powerful metaphor—the Invisible Hand—which has come to epitomise the essence of the Smithian vision of society. (Did Smith get the idea from Rousseau's behaviourist educational principle of the *main cachée* (hidden hand)?)

Smithian society has a *systematic* existence, a method of functioning that is virtually *organic*, a totalising mechanism which is virtually that of a living thing. The market is more intelligent than those who participate in it. The wonder-working *market* is *natural* and *rational* and *benign*. In an economically totalitarian Smithian society, the increasing wealth of the nation as a whole is a fortunate, but inevitable, by-product of the increasing wealth of the economically-determined citizens. The benignest of eighteenth-century rationalists has revealed the true 'nature and causes' of the wealth of nations.

> 'As every individual, therefore, endeavours as much as he can both to employ his capital in the support of domestic industry, and so to direct that industry that its produce may be of the greatest value; every individual necessarily labours to render the annual revenue of the society as great as he can. He generally, indeed, neither intends to promote the public interest, nor knows how much he is promoting it. By preferring the support of domestic to that of foreign industry, he intends only his own security; and by directing that industry in such a manner as its produce may be of the greatest value, he intends only his own gain, and he is in this, as in many other cases, led by an invisible hand to promote an end which was no part of his intention.' (Bk. IV, ch xx).

David Ricardo, in *On the Principles of Political Economy and Taxation* (1817), sets out a number of important disagreements with the views of Adam Smith,

> 'but he hopes it will not, on that account, be suspected that he does not, in common with all those who acknowledge the importance of the science of Political Economy, participate in the admiration which the profound work of this celebrated author so justly excites.' (Preface).

Smith's separation of economic philosophy from the rest of social philosophy means that 'the science of Political Economy' would, in the course of the nineteenth century, come to be called simply 'Economics', most influentially in A. Marshall's *Principles of Economics* (1894), purporting to discover neutral and natural rules, 'laws' even, governing the operation of the economic machine, that is to say, the principles of functioning of what it supposes to be quasi-natural economic phenomena. The age-old vision of society-as-metaphysics becomes a new vision of society-as-physics.

'To determine *the laws which regulate* this distribution [of rent, profit and wages] is the principal problem in Political Economy: much as the science has been improved by the writings of Turgot, Stuart, Smith, Say, Sismondi, and others, they afford very

little satisfactory information respecting the *natural course* of rent, profit, and wages.'
Ricardo, *Principles*, Preface. (emphasis added).

In a letter to Thomas Malthus (9 October 1820), Ricardo had said that 'political economy' is not 'an enquiry into the nature and causes of wealth' but 'into the laws which determine the division of the produce of industry among the classes who concur in [share in] its formation'. Malthus treated his own favoured economic hypotheses ('laws') deterministically, as bases for predicting the future of capitalist societies, especially in relation to their levels of population growth, with important consequences for general public policy.

In the *Principles*, Ricardo develops a naturalistic theory of *value*, a value-free theory of value, as one might say—borrowing an epithet (*wertfrei*, in German) from what would be the exposition by the German writer Max Weber (1864-1920) of the intellectual aspiration of a 'sociology' which would seek to treat the *subjective values active* in human social activity as part of that activity, as distinct from the values of *objectivity and neutrality* animating the work of the *observing* 'sociologist'.

(Two French writers, Claude de Saint-Simon (1760-1825) and Auguste Comte (1798-1857) had laid the foundations of a science of society ('sociology') whose claim to the status of a science was, as in the case of economics, a claim of theoretical independence from the values systems of religion or politics. The German historian Leopold von Ranke (1795-1886) was the prophet of an analogous re-imagining of a scientific form of historiography. On the controversial nature of historiography, see Ph. Allott, 'International law and the idea of history,' in *The Health of Nations*, ch. 11.)

The 19th-century obsession with explaining and justifying society in terms of a quasi-scientific economic metaphysics inspired many dissenting voices.

> '. . . mumbling to ourselves some vague janglement of Laissez-faire, Supply-and-demand, Cash-payment the one nexus of man to man: Free-Trade, Competition, and the Devil take the hindmost, our latest Gospel yet preached.'
> T. Carlyle, *Past and Present* (1843).

> 'Among the delusions which at different periods have possessed the minds of large masses of the human race, perhaps the most curious—certainly the least creditable—is the modern *soi-disant* [so-called] science of political economy, based on the idea that an advantageous code of social action may be determined irrespectively of the influence of social affection.' J. Ruskin, *Unto This Last* (1860).

John Maynard Keynes had been Marshall's student at Cambridge but distinguished himself from what he called 'the classical school' of economists, 'those, that is to say, who adopted and perfected the theory of Ricardian economics' (J.M. Keynes, *The General Theory of Employment Interest and Money* (1936), ch.1). He urged a younger economist to repel attempts 'to turn [economics] into a pseudo-natural-science' (letter to Roy Harrod, 4 July 1938).

Ricardo's theory of 'value' gave overwhelming prominence to the factor of *labour*, a prominence which would become a central issue in socio-economic philosophy (not least in the work of Karl Marx) and which Ricardo himself, and many other writers, would subsequently modify, giving prominence to other factors, including the contribution of so-called 'capital'. In the division of labour, what is the function of those who, according to Mandeville's fable of the bees (see above), 'cunningly convert to their own use the labour of their good-natured heedless neighbour'?

Ricardo's other seminal contribution to the new science of economics was the extrapolation of the Smithian enterprise to *international trade*. There could surely be naturalistic explanations of patterns of international trade.

Ricardo suggested that, when particular goods are produced in a place where production has a *comparative cost advantage* over the production of the same goods elsewhere, goods from that place would be liable to be traded internationally. This suggested the Smithian inference that it would benefit the wealth of the world, as it were, if there were an international division of labour, a freedom to trade internationally, so that particular goods would tend to be produced where they were most efficiently produced, by reason of climate, natural resources, relevant skills or other factors. The liberated self-interest of *laissez faire* (in French and English, 'let people get on with making it') within the nation could form a fruitful alliance with the liberating *laissez aller* (in French and English, 'let it go where it may') of international free trade.

Ricardo was expressing these ideas at a time when 'free trade' was at the centre of social struggle in and beyond Britain. In the economic crisis following the end of the Napoleonic Wars (1815), Britain experienced a struggle of classes and interests which hovered on the edge of revolutionary violence.

The 'Corn Laws' were Acts of Parliament protecting the agricultural interest from competition from imported grain, and so supporting a higher price for bread, a key factor in the standard-of-living of wage-earners. (An interesting feature of the Laws is that they contained market-control mechanisms remarkably similar to those of the (original) Common Agricultural Policy of the European Union.)

They were the focus of what would become a worldwide struggle between free trade and protectionism that continues to the present day. The Corn Laws were finally repealed in 1846. (A substantial part of the urban middle class had come to be more directly represented in the House of Commons following the passing of the Reform Act of 1832.)

Ricardo, still discussed, often deplored, set the agenda of a fundamental debate about the proper place of economic factors in explaining and justifying human society—a debate that is as vigorous today as it has ever been.

APPENDIX 6. **Burke and Owen and Bentham**.

Whether or not 'economics' or 'sociology' could gain acceptance for their claim to some sort of quasi-scientific apolitical status, 'politics'—public value-based debate about social issues designed to affect the exercise of public power—flourished in the nineteenth century as never before or since.

Edmund Burke was the apostle of what would come to be called 'conservatism'. Robert Owen was the apostle of what would come to be called 'socialism'. Jeremy Bentham was the apostle of what would come to be called 'liberalism'.

Together they shaped the structure of political debate within the public mind of a society living through revolutionary self-transforming, permanent revolution, a nervous condition that has turned out to be the normal condition of 'Western' societies, and is now infecting the whole human world.

Edmund Burke (1729-1797), sympathetic to the claims of the rebellious American colonists, and fiercely hostile to the impending tragedy of the French Revolution, asks us to venerate the wisdom that a society accumulates over the course of time, learning from its experience, its trials and errors. For Burke, a society is an evolutionary self-creating, whose best future potentiality is contained in the best of its past. The American rebellion reflected the better principles of the British constitution. The French Revolution flew in the face of the constitutional experience of France.

> 'A man full of warm, speculative benevolence may wish his society otherwise constituted than he finds it; but a good patriot, and a true politician, always considers how he shall make the most of the existing materials of his country. *A disposition to preserve, and an ability to improve, taken together,* would be my standard of a statesman. Everything else is vulgar in the conception, perilous in the execution.'
>
> 'Old establishments are tried by their effects. If the people are happy, united, wealthy, and powerful, we presume the rest. We conclude that to be good from whence good is derived. In old establishments various correctives have been found for their aberrations from theory. Indeed they are the results of various necessities and expediences. They are not often constructed after any theory; theories are rather drawn from them.'
>
> 'We are afraid to put men to live and trade each on his own private stock of reason; because we suspect that this stock in each man is small, and that the individuals would do better to avail themselves of *the general bank and capital of nations and of ages.*' (emphasis added).

These quotations are from Edmund Burke, *Reflections on the Revolution in France* (1790), a sustained polemic about current events which also presents a timeless theory of society and government. In his *Thoughts on French Affairs* of 1791, Burke offered two further, prophetic analyses of the events in France.

> 'The present revolution in France seems to me to be quite of another character and description [as compared with previous revolutions]; and to bear little

resemblance or analogy to any of those which have been brought about in Europe, upon principles merely political. *It is a revolution of doctrine and theoretic dogma.* It has a much greater resemblance to those changes which have been made upon religious grounds in which a spirit of proselytism makes an essential part.'

Burke had detected the emergence of what would come to be called *ideology*.

'The monied men, merchants, principal tradesmen, and men of letters (hitherto generally thought the peaceable and even timid part of society), are the chief actors in the French revolution. But the fact is, that as money increases and circulates, and as the circulation of news, in politics and letters, becomes more and more diffused, *the persons who diffuse this money, and this intelligence, become more and more important . . .* Their eyes were dazzled with this new prospect. They were, as it were, electrified and made to lose the natural spirit of their situation. A bribe, great without example in the history of the world, was held out to them—the whole government of a very large kingdom.' (emphasis added).

Burke had also detected the rise and rise of the *middle class*. What could be the future of a society (French or British or American) whose constitutional centre of gravity had hitherto been the aristocratic or, else, the land-owning or, at least, the most privileged class?

William Hazlitt said of Burke (essay on Burke, 1817):

'In the American war, he constantly spoke of the rights of the people as inherent, and inalienable: after the French Revolution, he began by treating them with the chicanery of a sophist, and ended by raving at them with the fury of a maniac.'

Dr Johnson admired Burke as a person.
'His stream of mind is perpetual.' J. Boswell, *Life of Johnson* (entry for 20 March 1776).

Robert Owen
Before Owen launched the word 'socialism' on its remarkable journey, there were already powerful voices in England pleading the case of purposive social *progress* through rational social *reform*, the case that would be taken up in the 19th century under the name of *socialism*.

Thomas Paine (1737-1809), British (later also American and French) polemicist, invigorated both the American and French revolutions with a torrent of bright and simple ideas amounting to a moderate theory of popular revolution. He was the author of two best-sellers—*Common Sense* (1776) and *The Rights of Man* (1791)—rivalling Burke in the fertility of his ideas and in polemical eloquence, but in favour of a root-and-branch populism as opposed to Burke's paternalist conservatism.

William Godwin (1756-1836) built a bridge between philosophy and politics, setting the tone and laying the foundation of all subsequent idea-centred and value-based political debate in mature liberal democracies. Politics as a dialectic of practical theory—that is, of applied philosophy—would become the ideal public discourse of liberal democracy.

Of Godwin's *An Enquiry concerning Political Justice, and its Influence on General Virtue and Happiness* (1793), William Hazlitt said:

> 'No work in our time gave such a blow to the philosophical mind of the country.'

Godwin's central, not to say obsessive, idea is simple to state. Human beings are the product of social circumstances. Improve the social circumstances and you will improve the human being.

> 'The vices and moral weakness of man are not invincible: Man is perfectible, or in other words susceptible of perpetual improvement.'
>
> 'We are born unequal in our personal characteristics and we are born unequal in our social circumstances. But we share a natural sociability and a natural rational capacity. It follows that we can act together to improve society and to improve humanity. Social and individual behaviour is conditioned by our ideas. It follows that we can improve behaviour, social and individual, by improving our ideas.'

Godwin, although a proto-socialist, admired Burke as a person.

> 'In all that is most exalted in talents, I regard him as the inferior of no man that ever adorned the face of earth; and, in the long record of human genius, I can find for him very few equals. In subtlety of discrimination, in magnitude of conception, in sagacity and profoundness of judgement.'

But he utterly rejected Burke's attachment to the virtues of the aristocracy and his veneration for the inherited wisdom of the constitution.

> 'Law we sometimes call the wisdom of our ancestors. But this is a strange imposition. It was as frequently the dictate of their passion, of timidity, jealousy, a monopolizing spirit, and a lust of power that knew no bounds. Are we not obliged perpetually to revise and remodel this misnamed wisdom of our ancestors? to correct it by a detection of their ignorance, and a censure of their intolerance?'

Godwin rejected de-humanising (Smithian) philosophies that suggested that human beings are merely self-seeking and mindless automata caught up in impersonal social machines.

'Again, it has been said that self-love is innate. But there cannot be an error more easy of detection.'

He also rejected de-humanising trends in general philosophy.

'Some persons have of late suggested doubts concerning the propriety of the use of the word mind. An accurate philosophy has led modern enquirers to question the existence of two classes of substances in the universe, to reject the metaphysical denominations of spirit and soul, and even to doubt whether human beings have any satisfactory acquaintance with the properties of matter. The same accuracy, it has been said, ought to teach us to discard the term mind. But this objection seems to be premature. We are indeed wholly uncertain whether the causes of our sensations, heat, colour, hardness and extension (the two former of these properties have been questioned in a very forcible manner by Locke, Human Understanding, the two latter by Berkeley and Hume) be in any respect similar to the ideas they produce. We know nothing of the substance or substratum of matter, or of that which is the recipient of thought and perception. We do not even know that the idea annexed to the word substance is correct, or has any counterpart in the reality of existence. But, if there be any one thing that we know more certainly than another, it is the existence of our own thoughts, ideas, perceptions or sensations (by whatever term we may choose to express them), and that they are ordinarily linked together so as to produce the complex notion of unity or personal identity. Now it is this series of thoughts thus linked together, without considering whether they reside in any or what substratum, that is most aptly expressed by the term mind; and in this sense the term is intended to be used throughout the following work.'

'It has appeared that an enquiry concerning the principles and conduct of social intercourse is the most important topic upon which the mind of man can be exercised; that, upon these principles, well or ill conceived, and the manner in which they are administered, the vices and virtues of individuals depend; that political institutions, to be good, must have constant relation to the rules of immutable justice; and that those rules, uniform in their nature, are equally applicable to the whole human race.'

'The object proposed in the following work is an investigation concerning that form of public or political society, that system of intercourse and reciprocal action, extending beyond the bounds of a single family, which shall be found most to conduce to the general benefit. How may the peculiar and independent operation of each individual in the social state most effectually be preserved? How may the security each man ought to possess, as to his life, and the employment of his faculties according to the dictates of his own understanding, be most certainly defended from invasion? How may the individuals of the human species be made to contribute most substantially to the general improvement and happiness? The enquiry here undertaken has for its object to facilitate the solution of these interesting questions.'

Godwin's prescription for the new kind of society was based on a fine idea which he borrowed explicitly from a famous passage in the writing of his friend Tom Paine—a crucial distinction between *society* and *government*.

'Some writers have so confounded society with government, as to leave little or no distinction between them; whereas they are not only different, but have different origins. Society is produced by our wants and government by our wickedness; the former promotes our happiness positively by uniting our affections, the latter negatively by restraining our vices . . . Society in every state is a blessing, but government even in its best state is but a necessary evil . . . Government, like dress, is the badge of lost innocence; the palaces of kings are built on the ruins of the bowers of paradise.' (Thomas Paine, *Common Sense*).

Godwin built this characteristically British (and American) idea into a prophecy of an ideal anarchism, the withering-away of government as human beings were led to become rational and well-intentioned self-governing beings.

'Government is nothing but regulated force.'
    'It is earnestly to be desired that each man should be wise enough to govern himself, without the intervention of any compulsory restraint; and, since government, even in its best state, is an evil, the object principally to be aimed at is that we should have as little of it as the general peace of human society will permit.'
    (Compare, improbably: J.W. Goethe: 'Which is the best government? That which teaches us to govern ourselves.')
    'With what delight must every well informed friend of mankind look forward to the auspicious period, the dissolution of political government, of that brute engine which has been the only perennial cause of the vices of mankind, and which, as has abundantly appeared in the progress of the present work, has mischiefs of various sorts incorporated with its substance, and no otherwise removable than by its utter annihilation!'

(For further discussion of British and American visceral distrust of public authority (*misarchy*), see 'The crisis of European constitutionalism. Reflections on a half-revolution', in Ph. Allott, *The Health of Nations*, ch. 7.)

The above quotations form Godwin's chaotically revised and published writings are mostly from the 1793 edition of *Political Justice*. Godwin substantially revised his text in a 1796 edition and thereafter. The 1793 edition and Godwin's revisions are presented in Vols. 3 and 4 respectively of *Political and Philosophical Writings of William Godwin* (ed., 1993).

But it was **Robert Owen** (1771-1858) who led the way in ensuring that the rigorous naturalistic economism of Smith and Ricardo and the 'social science' of St Simon and Comte, and their ilk, would be matched, throughout the 19th century, by a permanent dialectical negation in favour of *progressive political thought* and *progressive political action*.

Owen was one of the new breed of wealthy industrialists produced by what came to be known as the Industrial Revolution. But he was enough of a product of the 18th century to know that in a good society social organisation and public policy must be purposively determined on the basis of both reason and value.

His axiomatic principle is set out with relentless emphasis in *A New View of Society, Or, Essays on the Principle of the Formation of the Human Character, and the Application of the Principle to Practice* (1813).

> 'This principle is, that "Any general character, from the best to the worst, from the most ignorant to the most enlightened, may be given to any community, even to the world at large, by the application of proper means," which means are to a great extent at the command and under the control of those who have influence in the affairs of men.'
>
> 'No: the time is now arrived when the public mind of this country, and the general state of the world, call imperatively for the introduction of this all-pervading principle, not only in theory, but into practice.'
>
> 'The present Essays, therefore, are not brought forward as mere matter of speculation, to amuse the idle visionary who thinks in his closet, and never acts in the world; but to create universal activity, pervade society with a knowledge of its true interests, and direct the public mind to the most important object to which it can be directed to a national proceeding for rationally forming the character of that immense mass of population which is now allowed to be so formed as to fill the world with crimes.'

Owen said that *crime is caused* by the poor social conditions of the mass of the people and could be more or less eradicated by the introduction of universal education and the raising of standards of working and living.

'In those characters which now exhibit crime, the fault is obviously not in the individual, but the defects proceed from the system in which the individual was trained. Withdraw those circumstances which tend to create crime in the human character, and crime will not be created. Replace them with such as are calculated to form habits of order, regularity, temperance, industry; and these qualities will be formed. Adopt measures of fair equity and justice, and you will readily acquire the full and complete confidence of the lower orders. Proceed systematically on principles of undeviating persevering kindness, yet retaining and using, with the least possible severity, the means of restraining crime from immediately injuring society . . . and by degrees even the crimes now existing in the adults will also gradually disappear: for the worst formed disposition, short of incurable insanity, will not long resist a firm, determined, well-directed, persevering kindness. Such a proceeding, whenever practised, will be found the most powerful and effective corrector of crime, and of all injurious and improper habits.'

'How much longer shall we continue to allow generation after generation to be taught crime from their infancy, and, when so taught, hunt them like beasts of the forest, until they are entangled beyond escape in the toils and nets of the law? when, if the circumstances of those poor unpitied sufferers had been reversed with those who are even surrounded with the pomp and dignity of justice, these latter would have been at the bar of the culprit, and the former would have been in the judgement seat.'

'Those who have duly reflected on the nature and extent of the mental movements of the world for the last half-century, must be conscious that great changes are in progress; that man is about to advance another important step towards that degree of intelligence which his natural powers seem capable of attaining. Observe the transactions of the passing hours; see the whole mass of mind in full motion; behold it momentarily increasing in vigour, and preparing ere long to burst its confinement. But what is to be the nature of this change? A due attention to the facts around us, and to those transmitted by the invention of printing from former ages, will afford a satisfactory reply.'

'The end of government is to make the governed and the governors happy.'

'That government, then, is the best, which in practice produces the greatest happiness to the greatest number; including those who govern, and those who obey.'

William Hazlitt was not impressed.

'The doctrine of Universal Benevolence, the belief in the Omnipotence of Truth, and in the Perfectibility of Human Nature, are not new, but "Old, old," Master Robert Owen;—why then do you say that they are new? They are not only old, they are superannuated, they are dead and buried, they are reduced to mummy, they are put into the catacombs of Paris, they are sealed up in patent coffins, they have been dug up again and anatomised, they have been drawn, quartered, and gibbeted, they have become black, dry, parched in the sun, loose, and rotten, and are dispersed to all the winds of Heaven!'

Owen practised what he preached in organising his cotton-mills at New Lanark in Scotland and in later, unsuccessful projects in America (which were rather the fruit of what Bernard de Mandeville (see Appendix 5 above) would have called 'vain Eutopias seated in the brain'.) He was a relentless polemicist and activist, inspiring social reforms that would take most of the rest of the century to achieve.

Owen used the word 'socialism' for the first time in an essay published in 1827. In 1841 he took part in a public debate in Bristol on the topic—'What is socialism; and what would be its practical effects upon society?'

Jeremy Bentham (1748-1832) was an Owen sympathiser, but his was a different form of benevolent rationalism, a rationalism without the visionary and milleniarist spirit. The apostle of what came to be called *Utilitarianism* believed that the organisation of society had an identifiable goal—'the greatest happiness of the greatest number'—a goal the route towards which could be determined rationally, almost as a matter of intelligent calculation.

This idea came to be called *the principle of utility*, a name of which Bentham himself did not entirely approve (see, an added 'note' in the 1822 edition of the *Fragment* and footnote to ch. 1 in the New Edition (1823) of his *An Introduction to the Principles of Morals and Legislation,* 1780).

To measure some social arrangement or act or some legal provision in terms of 'happiness' implies, he said, a measuring of the amounts of 'pleasure and pain' that it produces, not merely a determination of its 'utility' in some other practical sense.

'The age we live in is a busy age; in which knowledge is rapidly advancing towards perfection. In the natural world, in particular, every thing teems with discovery and with improvement. The most distant and recondite regions of the earth traversed and explored the all-vivifying and subtle element of the air so recently analyzed and made known to striking evidences, were all others wanting, of this pleasing truth. Correspondent to discovery and improvement in the natural world, is reformation in the moral; if that which seems a common notion be, indeed, a true one, that in the moral world there no longer remains any matter for discovery. Perhaps, however, this may not be the case: perhaps among such observations as would be best calculated to serve as grounds for reformation, are some which, being observations of matters of fact hitherto either incompletely noticed, or not at all would, when produced, appear capable of bearing the name of discoveries: with so little method and precision have the consequences of this fundamental axiom, *it is the greatest happiness of the greatest number that is the measure of right and wrong*, been as yet developed.'

'Be this as it may, if there be room for making, and if there be use in publishing, discoveries in the natural world, surely there is not much less room for making, nor much less use in proposing, reformation in the moral. If it be a matter of importance and of use to us to be made acquainted with distant countries, surely it is not a matter of much less importance, nor of much less use to us, to be made better and better acquainted with the chief means of living happily in our own: If it be of importance and of use to us to know the principles of the element we breathe, surely it is not of much less importance nor of much less use to comprehend the principles, and endeavour at the improvement of those laws, by which alone we breathe it in security.'

The *Fragment on Government* is an attack on what Bentham considers to be the self-satisfied and sinister conservatism of William Blackstone (1723-80), whose lectures Bentham had been obliged to attend at Oxford, and whose *Commentaries on the Laws of England* were all the more troubling for being regarded as a work of great learning and even greater authority.

'While with this freedom I expose our Author's [Blackstone's] ill deserts, let me not be backward in acknowledging and paying homage to his various merits: a justice due, not to him alone, but to that Public, which now for so many years has been dealing out to him (it cannot be supposed altogether without title) so large a measure of its applause. Correct, elegant, unembarrassed, ornamented, the style is such, as could scarce fail to recommend a work still more vicious in point of matter to the multitude of readers. He it is, in short, who first of all institutional writers, has taught Jurisprudence to speak the language of the Scholar and the Gentle man: put a polish upon that rugged science: cleansed her from the dust and cobwebs of the office: and if he has not enriched her with that precision that is drawn only from the sterling treasury of the sciences, has decked her out, however, to advantage, from the toilette of classic erudition: enlivened her with metaphors and allusions: and sent her abroad in some measure to instruct, and in still greater measure to entertain, the most miscellaneous and even the most fastidious societies.'

Bentham explains the principle of utility with blithe but deceptive clarity. The obvious and overwhelming problems of its practical application reveal its fatal obscurity. What is 'pleasure'? What is 'happiness'? How can they be measured?

'III. By utility is meant that property in any object, whereby it tends to produce benefit, advantage, pleasure, good, or happiness, (all this in the present case comes to the same thing) or (what comes again to the same thing) to prevent the happening of mischief, pain, evil, or unhappiness to the party whose interest is considered: if that party be the community in general, then the happiness of the community: if a particular individual, then the happiness of that individual.

'IV. The interest of the community is one of the most general expressions that can occur in the phraseology of morals: no wonder that the meaning of it is often lost. When it has a meaning, it is this. The community is a fictitious *body*, composed of the individual persons who are considered as constituting as it were its *members*. The interest of the community then is, what is it?—the sum of the interests of the several members who compose it.

'V. It is in vain to talk of the interest of the community, without understanding what is the interest of the individual. A thing is said to promote the interest, or to be *for* the interest, of an individual, when it tends to add to the sum total of his pleasures: or, what comes to the same thing, to diminish the sum total of his pains.

'VI. An action then may be said to be conformable to the principle of utility, or, for shortness sake, to utility, (meaning with respect to the community at large) when the tendency it has to augment the happiness of the community is greater than any it has to diminish it.

'VII. A measure of government (which is but a particular kind of action, performed by a particular person or persons) may be said to be conformable to or dictated by the principle of utility, when in like manner the tendency which it has to augment the happiness of the community is greater than any which it has to diminish it.'

Bentham says that the principle of utility obviously cannot be proved: 'for that which is is used to prove everything else, cannot itself be proved'—a charmingly Gödelesque argument (Appendix 4 above), meaning that it is not possible to say whether the principle of utility itself satisfies the principle of utility.

> 'Not that there ever is or ever has been that human creature breathing, however stupid or perverse, who has not on many, perhaps on most occasions of his life, deferred to it.'

In a (presumably) half-humorous example of the application of the principle, Bentham relates that Alexander Wedderburn, then Attorney General and later Lord Chancellor, had said that Bentham's principle was 'dangerous'. Wedderburn was commenting on the *Fragment on Government* at the time of its first publication in 1776. Bentham replied *ad hominem*.

'In a Government which had for its end in view the greatest happiness of the
greatest number, Alexander Wedderburn might have been Attorney General
and then Chancellor: but he would not have been Attorney General with
£15,000 a year, nor Chancellor, with a peerage with a veto upon all justice,
with £25,000 a year, and with 500 sinecures at his disposal, under the name
of Ecclesiastical Benefices, besides *et coeteras*.'

Bentham laboriously proposes formulas for calculating pleasure and pain, for the
individual and for societies. But, more remarkably and much more influentially, he
proceeds to re-imagine the criminal law and its system of punishments on a utilitarian
basis—more or less on the basis of what we would now call a cost-benefit analysis. (In
this new enlightened view of the criminal law, Bentham acknowledged that he was
following in the revolutionary footsteps of Bonesana Beccaria (1738-94), the Italian
philosopher of the criminal law.)

Bentham's 'Rule 1' for the calculation of punishments in the criminal law is—

'The first object, it has been seen, is to prevent, in as far as it is worth while,
all sorts of offences; therefore, *The value of the punishment must not be less in
any case than what is sufficient to outweigh that of the profit of the offence*.'

Bentham objected to the idea of 'natural rights' conceived as being an ultimate test,
other than utility, for the validity of all laws. Elsewhere he called them 'nonsense on
stilts'. In the *Principles* (added note of 1823) he regrets that the United States—'that
newly created nation, one of the most enlightened, if not the most enlightened, at
this day on the globe'—should have chosen this path. (A Bill of Rights had been
added to the US federal constitution of 1787, drawing on the precedents of such
documents in several of the constituent American states, which had themselves drawn
inspiration from English precedents, such as Magna Carta of 1215 and the Bill of
Rights of 1688).

As to the dreadful mess and accumulated injustices of the English Common Law,
Bentham's prescription was a written constitution and codification. But Bentham also
revived a Hobbesian (Appendix 3 above) command theory of law—law as the command
of the sovereign and *legislation* as the natural expression of the sovereign's will. This was,
yet again, prophetic. Although the United Kingdom did not adopt a written constitution
(and, God and the calculation of utility permitting, never will), the wholesale reform
of the law and social institutions was a great achievement of the 19th century—with
Britain following the example of France and Prussia in espousing its own brand of legal
rationality.

The chief agent of reform was a mass of legislation produced by a parliament which,
after 1832, contained a significant presence of the middle class and which Engels would
call 'the most revolutionary body in Europe'. What the Duke of Wellington, clear-eyed
pillar of the British *ancien régime*, foresaw in the 1830's as a 'revolution by due process

of law' became a revolution by way of Benthamite legislation, within the context of an intensely lively and intensely political British public mind.

Burke and **Owen** and **Bentham** had laid the groundwork of an efficient form of permanent political confrontation—'politics'—in which 'utility' or the 'common good' would be the dialectical resultant of the interaction between a moderate *stabilising conservatism*, a moderate *idealising socialism,* and a moderate *progressive liberalism.* Such a triploid form of right-left-centre politics came to seem like an appropriate way of actualising the new theory of democratic capitalism, an organisation of the public mind which proved capable of being adapted to the different circumstances of other societies, across Europe and across the world.

Politics is the incorporation of a metaphysics of value into the physics of a dynamic society. *Politics* is society's public mind arguing with itself about the potentialities of social power.

APPENDIX 7. **Newton and Lyell and Darwin.**

Newton, Lyell and Darwin. Isaac Newton, Charles Lyell, and Charles Darwin caused the human mind to re-imagine its relationship to the natural world and thereby changed humanity's idea of its self.

The universe has an explanation. The planet Earth has a history. The human species has an origin.

The human mind is able to expound that explanation, to recount that history, to identify that origin. The human being that found itself able to do these things seemed to have become a new kind of human being

Even if, as Voltaire said, very few people had read Newton's *Philosophiae Naturalis Principia Mathematica* (1687), even in translation, all educated people in 18th-century Europe were talking about it—not least because of Voltaire's own public relations effort in his *Lettres philosophiques, ou Lettres anglaises* (Philosophical Letters, or English Letters) (1734), especially Letters XII-XIV. (Voltaire attended Newton's state funeral in Westminster Abbey in 1727.)

As with all other powerful innovators, **Isaac Newton** (1642-1727) owed much to his great predecessors and freely acknowledged that debt. In a scintillating review of challenges to be addressed by the newly conceived natural science, Francis Bacon (Appendix 1 above) had included two, among very many others:

— finally determining whether 'we may take the attraction of the mass of the earth as the cause of weight' (*New Organon*, XXXVI);

— finally determining 'if there be any magnetic power which operates by consent between the globe of the earth and heavy bodies, or between the globe of the moon and the waters of the sea (as seems highly probable in the semimenstrual ebbs and floods), or between the starry sphere and the planets whereby the latter are attracted to their apogees, all these must operate at very great distances.' (XLV).

When he was President of the Royal Society (from 1703), Newton also drew up a list of the immediate problems to be addressed by natural science, and prefaced his list with his own slightly revised version of the Baconian scientific method.

> 'Natural Philosophy [natural science] consists in discovering the frame & operations of Nature, reducing them (as far as may be) to general Rules or Laws, establishing those Rules by observations & experiments, & thence deducing the causes & effect of things.'

But what is the epistemological status of the 'rules and laws' of science? Bacon had said—

> 'There is no soundness in our notions, whether logical or physical. Substance, Quality, Action, Passion, Essence itself, are not sound notions; much less are Heavy, Light, Dense, Rare, Moist, Dry, Generation, Corruption, Attraction, Repulsion, Element, Matter, Form, and the like; but all are fantastical and ill defined.' (*New Organon*, XV).

And yet Newton saw that by giving names such as 'attraction' or 'gravity' or 'force' to the phenomena of nature, scientists were still *not* purporting to know what the real reality of those things might be. He said that he had used

> 'the words *attraction, impulse,* or *propensity* of any sort towards a centre indifferently and interchangeably one for the other, considering these forces not in the *physical* but only in the mathematical sense. Hence let the reader beware lest he think that by words of this kind I define a type or mode of action or cause or physical reason of any kind.'
>
> I. Newton, *De Motu Corporum*; trans. and quoted in J. Herivel, *The Background to Newton's* Principia.

David Hume (Appendix 4 above) said that, 'if the Newtonian philosophy be rightly understood', it consists of 'rational constructions', since we know only the appearances and not their 'real nature' (*Treatise of Human Nature*, I.II.v).

Adam Smith (Appendix 5 above) said:

> 'A system [of ideas] is an imaginary machine invented to connect together in the fancy [imagination] those different movements and effects which are already in reality performed.'
>
> Essay on the 'History of Astronomy', in *Essays on Philosophical Subjects*.

Scientists create ideal hypotheses. Scientists are also metaphysicians. This philosophically idealist theory of science, which Einstein apparently also accepted, was propagated in the late 19th century by Avenarius and Mach, and was a main target of V.I. Lenin in his *Materialism and Empirio-Criticism* (Appendix 4 above).

The Scottish geologist **Charles Lyell** (1797-1875) was a powerful consolidator, at a moment in the history of the relatively new science of geology, when a dramatic conspectus had become possible. The full title of his main work affirms his scientific method—*The Principles of Geology. An Attempt to Explain the Former Changes of the Earth's Surface by Reference to Causes now in Operation* (1830-33).

The new conspectus revealed a planet *Earth* which had evolved over hundreds of millions of years, and was still evolving. Over a shorter period, *organic life* had left the (fossil) traces of its own evolution. And the evolution of the organic life that we call *human life* had evidently occupied only a remarkably brief period. And the evolution of *civilised* human life had occupied a very brief period indeed.

Such ideas are now so familiar to us that it is difficult to imagine the shock that they produced in public consciousness. Some advances in science produce a corresponding change in the general paradigms of public consciousness, and thereby of private consciousness, a new consciousness which may not contain any very substantial comprehension of the complexity of the corresponding scientific ideas—the Copernican revolution, the circulation of the blood, gravitational attraction at a distance, electro-magnetism, genetic inheritance, the 'uncertainty' aspect of quantum mechanics, the electro-chemistry of the brain, explosive nuclear fission, the structure of DNA, climate change . . . .

One of Lyell's keenest readers was **Charles Darwin** (1809-1882), who read the first two volumes of the *Principles* during his time on the *Beagle* (1831-36) and who himself, at that time, still had a major interest in geology.

Darwin's *On the Origin of Species by Natural Selection, or The Preservation of Favoured Races in the Struggle for Life* (1859) suggests that the human species also has a determinable history, and that the 'natural selection' that produced all other animal species had also produced the human species. Darwin was another great consolidator. There had already been much discussion, in many European countries, of the idea of the 'evolution' of species. But his consolidation was so far-reaching and profound that he was immediately recognised, like Isaac Newton, as a great innovator. The intense shock produced in public and private consciousness by this new view of human prehistory is not difficult to understand.

The intellectual and moral challenge of the ideas of Newton, Lyell and Darwin stems from the fact that they were proposing authoritative explanations of the reality of the universe and of humanity's place in the universe which were not those that had been proposed by religion and philosophy. Whatever their personal attitude to the ideas of religion and philosophy, they produced ideas that were liable to be seen as not merely distinct in their intellectual groundwork from religious and philosophical ideas but also, to a greater or a lesser extent, as incompatible with many such ideas. In all three centuries—17th, 18th and 19th—such a challenge collided with profound developments in both religion and philosophy themselves.

Developments in *metaphysical philosophy*—especially concerning the mind's relationship to the putative reality of the universe—are considered in Allusions Explained above, and in Appendices 1 and 4 above, and Appendix 8 below.

During the same period, *religion* was in a state of permanent crisis, not merely through antagonistic sectarianism within Christianity but also through a swelling tide of more or less openly admitted *disbelief.* In the 19th century the mental crisis surrounding religion reached an acute state, with profound effects in social life and in the tormented psychology of thoughtful people. The crude intrusion of the new metaphysical 'truths' of natural science into public consciousness raised doubt and confusion to pathological levels.

It came to seem that there is a choice among three possible intellectual responses

— the two truth-realms view (the more or less peaceful co-existence of scientific truth and religious/philosophical truth);
— the final abandoning of the supposed truths of religion and philosophy in favour of the truer truths of science;
— or else, as a third possible response, benevolent neutrality. As suggested by Darwin's friend and champion and fellow scientist Thomas Huxley, this third response came to be known as *agnosticism*—from the words *agnoeō* (not to know, in ancient Greek) or *agnoia* (not-knowledge), words related to the word *gnōsis* (knowledge).

However, it soon became clear that to claim not to be able to choose finally between the truths of science and the truths of religion is liable to be seen, by the more determined kind of religious believer, as nothing but an affirmation of disbelief, as anything but benevolent or neutral, as a mask for atheism.

In the meantime (1833), the remarkable William Whewell (1794-1866; Master of Trinity College, Cambridge from 1841-66) had, among his other newly invented words, conferred the title of 'scientist'—and hence a new basis for their collective self-consciousness and self-confidence—on the practitioners of the extremely diverse forms of 'natural sciences', but who could now see themselves as the fellow-clergy of a new non-religious religion.

Whewell had imperiously appropriated the Latin word *scientia*, meaning 'knowledge' in the most general sense (from the verb *scire*, 'to know'). Philosophers were left as 'lovers of *sophia*'—in Greek,'wisdom, knowledge, cleverness'—a more obscure social status.

Whewell proposed an explanation of the scientific method which is a modification of those of Bacon and Newton, noted above, and which must be close to the average scientist's own understanding of the matter: He himself, in honour of Bacon, referred to his own theory as the *Novum Organon Renovatum* (The New Organon Renewed), in *The Philosophy of the Inductive Sciences* (3rd ed., 1858).

APPENDIX 8. **Continental European mind.**

Nietzsche was right in supposing that Continental European philosophy had followed a different course from that of British philosophy in the 17th, 18th and 19th centuries. While British philosophy pursued an intense and prolonged dialectical struggle with the problem of *the physiology of the mind*, seeking to create a *metaphysics* (in the Baconian sense) of the *physics* of the mind, the Continental European mind had continued to pursue substantive metaphysics in the unbroken philosophical tradition stemming from the pre-Socratic philosophers and Plato and Aristotle, through Epicureanism and Stoicism, to the scholastic Aristotelian philosophy of the High Middle Ages.

René Descartes (1596-1650), Baruch Spinoza (1632-77), Gottfried Leibniz (1646-1716), and Christian Wolff (1679-1754)—to name only the most influential of the new metaphysicians—constructed their particular mind-made worlds, each a well-furnished other-world which is neither the world of things nor merely a world in the mind. These metaphysical mind-made other-worlds are imagined as, in some sense, *existing*, as such and in themselves. They are, in some sense, *real*.

The furniture of these metaphysical mind-worlds varies, but it is of a kind which Platonists and Aristotelians and neo-Platonists and neo-Aristotelians would recognise.

> *Mind. Matter. God. Nature. Idea. Spirit. Substance. Essence. Being. Soul. The Absolute. Mode. Necessity. Reason. Freedom. Will. Truth. Immortality. Good. Evil. Time. Space.*

The fact that so many of these concepts are present also in Christian theology—and, indeed, in the theology of other religions, especially Eastern religions—suggests that they form part of some intellectual phenomenon parallel to religion, some sort of sublimated religion, some sort of deracinated theology.

This, in turn, suggests that they are designed to satisfy some psychological need analogous to the psychological need that religions are able to satisfy—the need to have an explanation of everything, an explanation that is coherent, comprehensible and convincing, and which does not offend our intelligence or our feelings at their best, and may affect the way we live our lives—and, above all, an explanation that is not merely the rationalising of the phenomena presented to the human mind by the senses, which is the task so remarkably performed by the natural sciences.

The Continental European Megametaphysicians, as we might call them, were really the New Realists, believing in the 'reality' of ideas. They were also Orientalising Mystics. They believed in the real reality of a third world behind the human mind and the physical world, a 'supersensible' world beyond the reach of the human senses, an 'intelligible' world more or less available to the human mind through the intuitive and rational capacities of the mind.

> *Der Gedanke ist die unsichtbare Natur, die Natur der sichtbare Gedanke*—to quote the German Romantic poet Heinrich Heine (1797-1856). ('Thought is invisible Nature, Nature visible Thought.')

However, it has been suggested, in the Allusions Explained above and in the preceding Chapter 2 Appendices, that the supposedly Anti-Metaphysical British Empiricists were really New Idealists, reaching a not-wholly-dissimilar destination as the Contientnal European philosophers, but by a very different route.

The British philosophers believed that we have to face, coldly and directly, the fact that the world as we know it is the world *made by our ideas*, and our knowledge of the world is limited by the *limited capacities* of a human mind whose limits that mind cannot, however, know. Above all, the British philosophers believed that we are *responsible*—socially and morally—for the world that our ideas create.

And then came **Immanuel Kant** (1724-1804). He would seek to unite the British and the Continental European mind-worlds and would thereby make possible two apparently incompatible futures for philosophy in the 19th and 20th centuries—on the one hand, a new kind of human mind-world; on other hand, a post-philosophy which denies the possibility of philosophy in the traditional sense of the word.

Having lectured in Königsberg (East Prussia) from an early age, Kant was appointed Professor of Logic and Metaphysics in the University in 1770. He published *The Critique of Pure Reason*, the first of his three major works, in 1781, at the age of fifty-seven. His philosophy was his life.

> 'He molded his whole life with the strength and purity of an indomitable will and infused it with a single ruling idea; but this will, which in the formation of his philosophy proved itself to be a maximally positive and creative element, affects his personal life with a restrictive and negative cast. All the stirrings of subjective feeling and subjective emotion comprise for him only the material which he strives with ever-growing determination to subject to he authority of "reason" and of the objective dictates of duty.'
>
> E. Cassirer, *Kant's Life and Thought* (1918); tr. J. Haden (1981).
>
> '. . . nothing worth knowing was indifferent to him; no cabal, no sect, no prejudice, no ambition for fame had the least seductiveness for him in comparison with furthering and elucidating truth. He encouraged and engagingly fostered thinking for oneself; despotism was foreign to his mind.'
>
> J.G. Herder (1744-1803), himself a profoundly influential German writer of the period, in Letter 79 of his *Letters on the Advancement of Humanity* (quoted approvingly by Ernst Cassirer).

Heinrich Heine coldly said that it would be impossible to write a life history of
Kant, since he had neither a life nor a history. Did Heine know the description of a
philosopher by Erasmus, in his relentlessly ironical *Praise of Folly* (1515)?

'[He first describes the happy life of a fool.] Let's now compare the lot of a
wise man with that of this clown. Imagine some paragon of wisdom to set
up against him, a man who has frittered away all his boyhood and youth in
acquiring learning, has lost the happiest part of his life in endless wakeful
nights, toil and care, and never tastes a drop of pleasure even in what's left of
him. He's always thrifty, impoverished, miserable, grumpy, harsh and unjust
to himself, disagreeable and unpopular with his fellows, pale and thin, sickly
and blear-eyed, prematurely white-haired and senile, worn-out and dying
before his time. Though what difference does it make when a man like that
does die? He's never been alive. There you have a splendid picture of a wise
man.' (Commentators suggest that Erasmus has here set out his own idea
of himself.)

Kant noted that 'the illustrious Locke' had failed to disentangle the problem,
discussed above, of how the mind can produce ideas *about* the outside (non-mind) world
which mysteriously seem not have been derived from experience *of* the outside world.
He had failed to explain how the mind can 'obtain knowledge which far transcends
all limits of experience.' *Critique of Pure Reason.* (tr., N. Kemp Smith). (This was in a
passage—conventionally numbered B127-8—that Kant himself added in the second
edition of his work.)

'David Hume recognised that, in order to be able to do this, it was necessary
that these concepts should have an *a priori* origin [not based on experience].
But since he could not explain how it can be possible to think concepts . . .
and since it never occurred to him that the understanding might itself,
perhaps, through these concepts, be the author of the experience in which
its objects are found, he was constrained to derive them from experience,
namely, from a subjective necessity (that is, from *custom*), which arises from
repeated association in experience, and which comes mistakenly to be regarded
as objective . . . '.
'While the former of these two illustrious men [Locke] opened a
wide door to *enthusiasm* [*Schwärmerei*, in the German text; *imaginative*
thinking]—for if reason once be allowed such rights, it will no longer allow
itself to be kept within bounds by vaguely defined recommendations of
moderation—the other [Hume] gave himself over entirely to *scepticism*,
having, as he believed, discovered that what had hitherto been regarded as
reason was but an all-prevalent illusion infecting our faculty of knowledge.
We [Kant] now propose to make trial whether it be not possible to find

for human reason safe conduct between these two rocks, assigning to her [reason] determinate limits, and yet keeping open for her the whole field of appropriate activities.' (Kant said elsewhere that Hume had awakened him from his [Kant's] 'dogmatic slumbers'.)

Kant then claimed to undertake 'an enterprise never before attempted', namely, to establish the *conditions* that make *knowledge* possible or, to put it in other words, that make *rational thought* possible. This word 'possible' is the clue to the whole Kantian enterprise. Unlike his British predecessors, Kant is not purporting to investigate the working of the mind, as an empirical task. (We have suggested above that the idea that the British philosophers were doing any such thing is false. They were metaphysicians of the mind, not cognitive psychologists.).

Instead, Kant is trying to find the *logically necessary* steps allowing us to claim to 'know' for certain something about the outside world (i.e., a reality that we suppose to exist outside the human mind). He is offering a 'transcendental critique' of 'pure reason'—that is to say, reason's only possible explanation of itself to itself, and hence a delimitation of the intrinsic boundaries of rational thinking.

For us to 'know' an object in the outside world several things are required.

(1) There must be a thinking subject, with a 'unity of consciousness'—a self-contained 'I' that is location of the total thinking process.

(2) There must be a capacity ('perception') to receive 'appearances' of the outside world through the senses.

(3) There must be a capacity ('intuition') that recognises appearances as being produced by the outside world.

(4) There must be a capacity ('understanding') that synthesises these appearances into unities ('manifolds'—one from many).

(5) There must be 'concepts' which are applied to the products of the understanding, and these concepts must be *a priori*—that is, not themselves derived from thinking about the outside world. (For Kant space and time are '*a priori* forms of intuition'—see (3) above.)

(6) These concepts or 'categories' (such as 'quantity', 'quality', 'existence', 'possibility', and so on) are patterns or templates which are themselves 'pure'—that is, they are themselves empty of substantive content and capable of being applied to an infinite number of products of the understanding. (Kant borrowed the word 'category' from Aristotle, but he says that he is using it in a quite different way. Aristotle had been finding something intrinsic in the nature of the propositions that we regard as 'true', rather than in the processes of the mind.)

(7) The *a priori* concepts must turn the products of the understanding into objects of thought to which the mind can apply 'reflection': that is, a higher capacity of the mind which can compare and contrast them with other objects of thought.

(8) This process then implies that the mind has a universalising and unifying capacity—fitting together all its contents in an orderly way—which is a 'regulative' function, allowing the mind to police its own activity.

Several important consequences flow from this hypothesis.

(9) We cannot know anything about 'things-in-themselves' in the outside world other than the appearances ('phenomena') that they present to our mind, and in the form that the mind re-presents those appearances to itself. All we can do is *rationally to suppose* that there are objects in the outside world which we may call 'noumena'—rationally postulated by our *nous* (Greek for 'mind')—of which we, at least, know that they have the characteristic that they are able to produce the phenomena which we transform into 'objects'.

(10) The mind is capable of producing object-like things which are simply outside the control of rational thinking—not merely what we traditionally classify as works of the imagination, but also metaphysical entities, in what we have above called the mega-metaphysical tradition from Plato to Wolff and Leibniz.

> 'Leibniz erected an *intellectual system of the world*, or rather believed that he could obtain knowledge of the inner nature of things by comparing all objects with the understanding and with the separated, formal concepts of its thought . . . In a word, Leibniz *intellectualised* appearances, just as Locke . . . *sensualised* all concepts of the understanding, *i.e.* interpreted them as nothing more than empirical or abstracted concepts of reflection.' (282-3).

Kant joins in the criticism of the Lockeian use of the word 'idea' to cover all kinds of mental content.

> 'I beseech those who have the interests of philosophy at heart that . . . they be careful to preserve the expression 'idea' in its original meaning, that it may not become one of those expressions which are commonly used to indicate any and every species of representation, in a happy-go-lucky confusion, to the consequent detriment of science.' The word should be sued to express only a higher form of mental product—an 'idea of reason', a concept 'transcending the possibility of experience'. (314).

In the *Critique of Pure Reason*, Kant might thus be said to have provided, incidentally, a metaphysics of natural science, in pursuance of the project proposed by Francis Bacon (Appendix 1 above)—that is to say, an explanation of how the mind *processes rationally* information received from external reality.

But has he provided anything else? Has he solved the great puzzle set by his British predecessors—a puzzle that (we have suggested above) they failed to solve, because they found it to be insoluble? How can the mind set *limits* for itself? How can the mind find the limits of its own capacity? How can the mind find the *true* meaning of 'truth'?

In two other works, Kant offers a metaphysics of morality (*Critique of Practical Reason*) and a metaphysics of value, especially aesthetic value (*Critique of Judgment*). These again are hypotheses as to the *logical conditions that make possible* moral and aesthetic judgments. They are not concerned with the psychology of such judgments (the 'passions' in Hume's terminology) or with the analysis or advocacy of any particular substantive moral or aesthetic systems, principles or propositions.

In all three works, Kant thus steered a course between the Scylla of extreme idealism (*we can only know for certain the contents of our minds*) and the Charybdis of extreme empiricism (*the only sound basis of knowledge is our experience of the outside world*) by what he regarded as a revolutionary strategy (a 'Copernican Revolution', as he himself claimed in the Introduction to the second edition of *Pure Reason*)—*sound knowledge is a co-operative project between the outside world and the human mind, each making possible the other.* The mind is not merely a passive receiver of impressions nor merely an active inventor of ideas. It is both. The 'understanding' is 'the lawgiver of nature' (148).

We may distinguish Kant's metaphysical model of *rationality*—which is splendidly illuminating and helpful—from his attempt to establish *reason* as a law-giver unto itself, that is, his attempt to establish a *morality of rationality,* capable of ruling out improper (i.e. non-rational) thinking—a very much more difficult project.

In the latter part of *Pure Reason*, he suggests a number of ways in which the mind controls the validity of its own activity, other than by merely checking it against actual experience of the external world.

(11) Kant admits the possibility of 'ideals'.

> '. . . human reason contains not only ideas but ideals also, which although they do not have, like the Platonic ideas, creative power, yet have *practical* power (as regulative principles), and form the basis of the possible perfection of certain *actions* . . . Although we cannot concede to these ideals objective reality (existence), they are not therefore to be regarded as figments of the brain; they supply reason with a standard which is indispensable to it, providing it, as they do, with a concept of that which is entirely complete in its kind, and thereby enabling it to estimate and to measure the degree and the defects of the incomplete.' (486).

In other words, Kant goes a considerable way down the Platonic road.

> 'The ideal is, therefore, the archetype (*prototypon*) of all things, which one and all, as imperfect copies (*ectypa*), derive from it the material of their possibility, and while approximating to it in varying degrees, yet always fall very far short of actually attaining it.' (492).

He tells us what Plato *meant* to say or *should* have said (310*ff*):

'I need only remark that it is by no means unusual, upon comparing the thought which an author has expressed in regard to his subject . . . to find that we understand him better than he has understood himself.'

(We may be inclined to say the same thing of Kant himself!)

'Plato very well realised that our faculty of knowledge feels a much higher need than merely to spell out appearances according to a synthetic unity, in order to be able to read them as experience. He knew that our reason naturally exalts itself to modes of knowledge that so far transcend the bounds of experience that no given object can ever coincide with them, but which must none the less be recognised as having their own reality, and which are by no means mere fictions of the brain.'

(A remarkable statement by one who is supposed by some commentators to have finally disposed of the delusional claims of 'metaphysics'!)

(12) Kant is even willing to accept that *reason* may produce an *idea of God*.

Obviously, the three leading alleged 'proofs' of God's existence cannot possibly 'prove' God's *existence*. (500ff.). But a *possible idea* of 'God' can be seen as the last term of a logical progression of the *unifying thinking* which is inherent in rational thought.

There is no way of proving the 'existence' of God in the way that we must suppose the existence of 'objects' in the outside world whose phenomena we perceive through the senses and process in our thinking. But 'God' seems to be a logical and natural conclusion to the way that the mind acts essentially as an integrating mechanism, from its simplest operations in synthesising sense-experiences into particular unities ('objects') through its more and more abstract joining-up of ideas and ideas-about-ideas.

So, in this respect, *I* am somewhat like God. My *self—I*—my *soul*—is also something that we cannot know as if it were an internal version of an 'object' in the outside world, or as if it were some sort of 'inner sense' by which we can look at our selves as we look at the (supposed) external world.

'I think' is merely my acknowledgement of the logical and necessary unity of the thinking process, the *necessarily supposed* integrator of the integrating process.

'Self-consciousness in general is therefore the representation of that which is the condition of all unity, and itself is unconditioned' (365).

(13) Kant's central regulative idea is that we cannot assert the *existence* of something that cannot be the subject of *possible experiencee*. To the extent that theology

and metaphysics talk about the *existence* of things that cannot be the subject of possible experience that are a form of fantasy.

'. . . all those conclusions of ours which profess to lead us beyond the field of possible experience are deceptive and without foundation.' (532).

'. . . human reason has a natural tendency to transgress these limits, and . . . transcendental ideas are just as natural to it as the categories are to understanding—though with this difference, that while the categories lead to truth, that is, to the conformity of our concepts with the object, the ideas produce what, though a mere illusion, is none the less irresistible, and the harmful influence of which we can barely succeed in neutralising even by means of the severest criticism.' (532).

'Thus pure reason, which at first seemed to promise nothing less than the extension of knowledge beyond all limits of experience, contains, if properly understood, nothing but regulative principles, which, while indeed prescribing greater unity than the empirical employment of understanding can achieve, yet still . . . carry its agreement with itself, by means of systematic unity, to the highest possible degree. But if, on the other hand, they [the regulative principles of reason] be misunderstood, and be treated as constitutive principles of transcendent knowledge [proving the existence of things not capable of being found in experience], they give rise, by a dazzling and deceptive illusion, to persuasion and a merely fictitious knowledge, and therewith to contradictions and eternal disputes.' (569).

However, we are bound to ask (as we were also bound to ask—Appendix 4 above—in relation to the supposedly regulative principles of Locke and Hume)

— (a) how does the mind determine what is *possible* experience?
— (b) how does the mind determine what is the *highest possible* degree of the unifying activity of the mind?
— (c) how does the mind determine the *proper* meaning of its own self-regulating principles?

To know its own limits the mind must apparently be able to go beyond those limits.

(14) Kant thus seems to think that he has disposed of perennial traditions of both theology and metaphysics—and he is often admired for having done so successfully. But, once again, the ghost of the Platonic baby seems mysteriously to remain when the water has been thrown out of the metaphysical bath.

'I accordingly maintain that transcendental ideas [not capable of being the subject of possible experience] never allow of any constitutive employment . . . On the other hand, they have an excellent, and indeed indispensably necessary, regulative employment, namely, that of directing the understanding towards a certain goal upon which the routes marked out by all its rules converge, as upon their point of intersection.' (533).

Kant calls this 'the hypothetical employment of reason'.

'The hypothetical employment of reason has, therefore, as its aim the systematic unity of the knowledge of understanding, and this unity is the *criterion of the truth* of its rules . . . Its function is to assist the understanding by means of ideas, in those cases in which the understanding cannot by itself establish rules, and at the same time to give to the numerous and diverse rules of the understanding unity or system under a single principle, and thus to secure coherence in every possible way.' (535-6).

Kant thus here sees the mind as desperately seeking to put all of its contents into good order, to make sense, as one might say, of its very various contents. And he seems to be saying that transcendental ideas may be used as dreadful illusions and fictions (as in much of traditional theology and metaphysics), but they may also be used in a good way, if they help us to fit together into meaningful patterns and structures the intense complexity and diversity of our ideas.

(In his analysis of the working of the human mind, Augustine (I.19) referred to a supposed etymology of the Latin verb *cogitare* (to think)—formed from *cogere* (to collect) and *agitare* (to cause to move), itself a livelier form of *agere* (to move, to act, to do). Augustine, *Confessions*, bk. 10.)

It might thus be possible, if hazardous, to state in the following form Kant's hypothesis of the human mind in its most general form—his answer to the most general questions which philosophy asks itself—the *medulla* (in Latin, 'bone-marrow' or 'kernel') of his thinking.

Reductio ad medullam Kantiensem

Our *knowledge* is based, not only on the *orderly re-presenting* by the mind to itself of the phenomena that it receives from external reality, *but also and necessarily* on the total process of the mind, including its capacity to *re-order its own contents systematically*, a capacity whose limits the mind itself cannot know. It follows that 'truth' is not something that the mind discovers or uncovers but is rather an *ideal* of the mind's orderly thinking, that is to say, the ideal of *thinking rationally*. It also follows that *existence* is not an attribute or characteristic that something 'has' or 'does not have'. It is a way of expressing a particular product of the mind's thinking-about-its-thinking about particular phenomena which it has formed into the idea of a particular thing. It follows also that the mind is able to use the mind to improve its thinking, and hence its action in relation to the 'external' world.

It is humbling to recall that the Latin philosopher and poet Boethius (c.480-524) had already arrived at similar conclusions.

> 'As when light strikes upon the eye / Or voices clatter in the ear: / The active power of mind then roused / Calls forth the species from within / And fitting them to marks impressed / From outside, mingles images / Received with forms it hides within.' *The Consolation of Philosophy*, bk. V. (tr., V. Watts).

(Boethius is also to be remembered with reverence for having said that 'the court orators of today . . . try to excite the sympathy of the court for those who have suffered grievous and painful injury, although a juster sympathy is more due to those who are guilty. They ought to be brought to justice not by a prosecution counsel with an air of outrage, but by a prosecution kind and sympathetic, like sick men brought to the doctor . . . [for] wickedness is a disease of the mind' (bk. IV)—a proposal that recalls that of S. Butler (1835-1902), in his utopian-satirical novel *Erewhon*, to the effect that sick people should be treated as criminals, and criminals should be treated as sick people.)

The nature of the Kantian solution to philosophy's central problem—and repeated misunderstanding of the nature of that solution—might help to explain the course of development of post-Kantian Continental European philosophy, which would travel in three main directions—

(a) to German mega-metaphysical idealism—especially in the work of G.W. F. Hegel (1770-1831)—denying the Kantian idea of the intrinsic unknowability of external reality, replacing it with Hegel's view that the mind is itself an integral part of the reality that it experiences—and hence reality/mind (*Geist*, 'spirit', 'mind') has a single form of life, a single history, a single future;

(b) to positivism (emanating especially from France)—especially in the form of the 'human sciences'—treating human phenomena (including human mental phenomena) as if they were themselves phenomena of a reality external to the mind—the quasi-scientific or pseudo-scientific study of things human as if it were the study of things;

(c) to the denial of the possibility of philosophy—(i) *given* that all of philosophy's attempts to find an unchallengeable ground of 'truth' have failed and must fail; and (ii) *given* that the natural sciences have a reasonable claim to be uncovering 'truth', if only to a form of provisional truth (a Whewellian hypothetical truth derived from direct and collective observation of the phenomena of the external world, which may be corrected if and when other, inconsistent phenomena are observed, and a different hypothesis is required); and (iii) *given* that it seems that the only form of certainty that the mind can produce is to be found (paradoxically) in the pure abstractions of mathematics—and in the illusionary certainties of religion;

(d) to extreme nihilism and extreme pessimism.

Fortunately, however, philosophy in the great tradition remains available to us, not only in the surviving works of the most creative and influential philosophers, but also in our minds, in countless inherited ideas, of whose origins we may be wholly ignorant, but whose potentiality for making a better human world we have also inherited. New mind-worlds always have been, and always will be, possible human worlds.

*   *   *

INDEX

of Names and Subjects

Crystallography of a human reality
containing genomes of countless other possible human realities

NAMES

Abélard, 423

Académie des Sciences, 180

Academy of Projectors, 180

Accademia dei Lincei, 180

ACKWO, 64

Adam, 71, 191, 228, 250, 251, 282, 287, 325, 332, 341, 345

Aeneas, 65, 156, 157, 241, 290, 346

Aeschylus, 136

Aesop, 7, 136

Akhenaton, 354

Albert (Albertus Magnus), 151, 365

Alfred the Great, 278

Allott, Ph., 35, 142, 194, 201, 208, 218, 232, 233, 251, 260, 264, 268, 272, 285, 289, 295, 301, 311, 312, 327, 367, 371, 379, 403, 430, 437

Allott, R, 199

Andalucía (Andalusia), 24, 105, 150, 241, 337, 343, 345

Angell, N, 285

Antibes, 20

Apollo, 76, 104, 206, 211, 274, 309, 319, 327, 342

Aquinas, Th., 35, 169, 224, 358, 365, 376, 393, 406

Arendt, H, 173, 179

Arion, 97, 319

Aristotle, Aristotelian, 7, 35, 100, 101, 102, 103, 105, 133, 136, 148, 151, 166, 169, 174, 182, 185, 193, 194, 200, 203, 214, 224, 232, 235, 242, 243, 257, 258, 259, 271, 287, 311, 323, 326, 330, 331, 332, 333, 335, 336, 362, 363, 364, 365, 366, 371, 372, 376, 381, 392, 393, 395, 396, 399, 400, 401, 403, 404, 405, 406, 408, 409, 410, 412, 415, 417, 419, 420, 423, 425, 447, 450

Armenia, 280

Arnold, M, 160, 161, 179, 247

Aron, R, 357

Athanasius, 287

Athens (Athenian), 26, 99, 157, 164, 182, 201, 203, 301, 332, 341, 368, 369, 391, 399

Atoms for Peace, 92, 307

Augustine of Hippo, 35, 143, 151, 169, 191, 195, 224, 267, 278, 323, 383, 455

Augustus, 155, 156, 383, 402

Bach, J S, 78, 151, 226, 283, 320

Bacon, F (Baconian), 21, 104, 145, 163, 180, 209, 240, 279, 298, 325, 326, 331, 339, 340, 344, 350, 355, 356, 364, 365, 370, 371, 392, 393, 394, 395, 396, 397, 401, 403, 405, 406, 407, 412, 416, 443, 444, 446, 447, 451

Bagehot, W, 146, 292, 295

Balfour, A, 284, 306, 353

Balliol College, Oxford, 377, 397, 424

Barbarossa, 145

Baudelaire, C, 219, 230, 247

Bauer, F, 216

Bayreuth, 56, 226

Beckett, S, 126, 156, 186, 211, 256, 338, 380, 381

Beckford, W, 219

Bede, 278

Beerbohm, M, 228

Benda, J, 357

Benedict (Benedictine), 140, 233, 273

Bentham, J, 21, 102, 145, 205, 365, 431, 432, 439, 440, 441, 442, 443

Bentley, R, 172, 202

Bergson, H, 265

Berkeley, G, 21, 145, 174, 175, 407, 412-417, 426, 435

Berlioz, H, 290

Bernard of Clairvaux, 169, 365

Bessette, H, 232

Biber, H, 97, 319

Bismarck, O von, 144, 153, 169, 402

Blackstone, W, 440

Blake, W, 127, 156, 159, 248, 253, 349, 383

Bloomsbury, 285, 352, 353

Blunt, A, 193

Boethius, 365, 456

Bonaparte, N, 144, 159, 169, 170, 342, 368, 385, 402

Bonaparte, L, 372

Bonaventure, 272

Borges, J, 152

Boswell, J, 414 (see also Johnson, S)

Brasenose College, Oxford, 343

Brompton Oratory, 131, 389

Bronowski, J, 158

Browning, E B, 167, 210

Browning, R, 170, 230

Buddha, 163

Buffon, L, 334

Burke, E, 21, 102, 369, 431-434, 443

Burton, R, 343

Bury, J, 295, 383

Bury St Edmunds, 240, 273, 348

Butler, R A, 154

Butler, S, 209, 287, 353, 385, 456

Buxtehude, D, 55, 226

Byron, G, 77, 144, 158, 159, 170, 209, 210, 212, 257, 269, 280, 372

Byzantium, 139, 159, 169, 241, 348, 353

Caesar Augustus (Octavian), 383, 402

Calderón, P, 102, 227

Calvin, J, 46, 102, 108, 201, 356, 365

Cambridge University, 95, 151, 154, 163, 172, 182, 183, 199, 209, 210, 230, 231, 232, 241, 245, 266, 276, 280, 284, 315, 319, 333, 344, 348, 352, 353, 375, 376, 383, 391, 392, 395, 398, 430, 446

Camus, A, 126, 153, 252, 257, 272, 275, 380

Canterbury, Archbishop of, 193, 398

Cantillon, R, 425

Canute, 373

Carlyle, Th., 206, 237, 275, 376, 430

Carneades, 365, 423

Carroll, L, 199, 208, 259, 368, 396

Carthage, 65, 157, 240, 241, 255, 256, 337, 350

Cassirer, E, 336, 448

Castor and Pollux, 142

Catholic (Roman), 28, 58, 62, 102, 139, 140, 161, 163, 166, 167, 169, 191, 196, 202, 249, 287, 350, 351, 356, 376, 389, 398, 404

Catiline, 155, 392

Cato, 248, 255, 270

Catullus, 151, 230

Central Intelligence Agency, 308

Cervantes, M de, 153, 387

Chamfort, N, 181

Charlemagne, 143, 169, 278, 303, 402

Chekhov, A, 39, 187

Christ Church, Oxford, 343

Chuang Chou, 267, 277

Churchill, W, 146, 224

Church of England (Anglican), 84, 131, 161, 231, 291, 333, 398, 412

Cicero, 35, 133, 155, 166, 185, 228, 248, 256, 269, 290, 315, 334, 337, 338, 340, 341, 363, 364, 365, 392, 405, 423

Claudel, P, 195, 196

Cleopatra, 127, 248, 383

Clarke, H, 210

Clifford, W, 276

Coleridge, S, 255, 375

Commynes, Ph. de, 144

Comte, A, 204, 237, 284, 355, 430, 437

Condorcet, C, 355

Confederate States, 303

Connecticut, 36, 37, 90, 182, 302, 369

Constantine, 139, 169

Copernicus, 445, 452

Corneille, P, 171, 338

Cranmer, Th., 21, 397, 398

Crèvecoeur, T, 315

Crossman, R, 244, 359

Cudworth, R, 266

d'Alembert, J, 414

Dante (Alighieri), 27, 30, 31, 35, 144, 159, 161, 162, 168, 169, 174, 178, 182, 228, 254, 272, 287, 330, 342, 365, 381

Darwin, C, 21, 144, 145, 158, 166, 293, 312, 352, 353, 355, 358, 361, 366, 372, 443, 445, 446

Davies, L, 242

de la Rivière, P, 425

de Tocqueville, A de, 292, 314

Defoe, D, 255

Democritus, 253, 312

Derrida, J, 123, 374

Descartes, R, 83, 266, 267, 291, 312, 365, 397, 401, 411, 415, 447

Destutt de Tracy, A, 299

Dewey, J, 147, 317, 318

Dickens, C, 237

Diderot, D, 205, 414, 415

Dido, 65, 157, 240, 241, 290

Diogenes Laertius, 147, 148, 235

Dionysus, 76, 211, 274, 327

Dostoyevsky (Dostoevsky), F, 162, 165, 166, 257, 288, 372

Downside School, 389

Drummond, H, 158, 188

Dryden, J, 159, 232, 339

Dublin, 241

Egypt, 182, 199, 209, 248, 281, 322, 324, 329, 343, 353, 354

Einstein, A, 192, 445

Eisenhower, D, 307

Eliot, G, 57, 133, 163, 229, 279, 301

Eliot, T S, 169, 219, 220, 221, 222, 223, 224, 230, 238, 274, 321, 331, 339

Elizabeth I, 183, 240, 394, 398

Emerson, R W, 185, 275

Emmanuel College, Cambridge, 182, 184, 209, 266

Engels, F, 242, 295, 299, 309, 358, 365, 372, 388, 442

Epicurus, 133, 148, 168, 207, 234, 392

Erasmus, D, 141, 142, 182, 209, 365, 449

Erikson, E, 384

Eton College, 296, 352, 389

Euripides, 136, 195, 235

European Union, 90, 92, 141, 189, 302, 308, 311, 431, 463,

Eve, 71, 191, 228, 250, 282, 345

Existence, 58, 59, 70, 71, 73, 83, 97, 98, 99, 101, 113, 127, 136, 157, 162, 167, 171, 175, 176, 177, 190, 209, 211, 212, 218, 231, 236, 250, 252, 257, 259, 260, 262, 263, 270, 275, 279, 284, 296, 304,

305, 310, 333, 335, 337, 362, 374, 380,
384, 393, 399, 409, 410, 413, 415, 417,
418, 429, 435, 446, 453, 454, 456
Èze, 20, 145
Feuerbach, L, 163, 338
Fichte, G, 213, 214, 233, 257, 259, 260, 271,
    285, 318, 386
Ficino, M, 203, 269, 365
Fielding, H, 137
Fitzgerald, S, 186
Fifth-Monarchy Men, 330
Flaubert, G, 181, 247
Fontenelle, B, 338
Forster, W, 296
Frazer, J, 280, 281, 287, 342, 346
Freedom, 22, 23, 34, 53, 124, 125, 149, 162,
    169, 171, 191, 215, 218, 270, 286, 292,
    303, 310, 349, 359, 371, 400, 401, 411,
    431, 440, 447
Frege, G, 333
Freud, S, 15, 24, 69, 83, 102, 121, 138, 152,
    153, 167, 168, 170, 174, 178, 179, 188,
    190, 196, 205, 213, 216, 227, 229, 238,
    242, 246, 247, 262, 264, 268, 285, 286,
    293, 294, 317, 318, 324, 336, 345, 346,
    350, 354, 355, 357, 358, 366, 368, 379,
    384, 406, 412
Fry, C, 142
Fuller, M, 275
Gatsby, J, 38, 186
Gatty, M, 273
General and Complete Disarmament, 92,
    305, 307
Gesuati, 28, 162
Gibbon, E, 26, 156
Gide, A, 144, 195, 196, 257, 288
Gilbert, W S, 102, 187, 209, 336
Girton College, Cambridge, 245
Glasgow University, 204, 424, 426
God, 18, 26, 28, 29, 30, 31, 41, 53, 54, 71,
    78, 79, 80, 81, 95, 104, 105, 108, 109,
    112, 122, 124, 126, 128. 129, 132, 142,

143, 151, 158, 160, 163, 164, 165, 166,
167, 168, 169, 170, 183, 188. 191, 192,
195, 197, 207, 210, 211, 213, 215, 216,
217, 221, 212, 215, 216, 217, 221, 222,
225, 229, 234, 235, 236, 237, 239, 244,
249, 250, 251, 258, 259, 261, 267, 268,
269, 270, 272, 273, 279, 280, 281, 282,
283, 284, 287, 288, 289, 293, 296, 297,
298, 310, 321, 325, 332, 334, 335, 336,
339, 340, 341, 342, 345, 346, 349, 354,
357, 361, 362, 366, 369, 378, 380, 383,
388, 392, 393, 399, 404, 406, 411, 415,
421, 442, 447, 453
Gödel, K, 408, 441
Godwin, W, 133, 161, 309, 310, 391, 434-437
Goethe, W von, 144, 145, 150, 205, 206, 215,
    216, 224, 248, 249, 264, 265, 282, 327,
    336, 436
Goldsmith, O, 387
Góngora y Argote, L, 387
Gounod, C, 149
Greece (Greek, Hellenic), 24, 78, 102, 139,
    148, 150, 155, 157, 160, 162, 172, 179,
    194, 196, 203, 209, 211, 215, 220, 224,
    234, 235, 238, 250, 251, 252, 263, 274,
    280, 282, 283, 301, 318, 319, 330, 322,
    333, 335, 337, 343, 347, 363, 364, 377,
    385, 394, 397, 399, 404, 412, 423
Green, J, 195
Grimm, J & W, 388
Hahn, R, 170
Hall, J, 209
Hampstead, 66, 104, 105, 343, 347, 366
Hardenberg, G von, 329
Harvard University, 146, 184, 186, 239
Havana Charter, 92, 306
Hayek, F, 358
Hazlitt, W, 152, 396, 433, 434, 438
Hebraic, 27, 160, 173, 196, 363
Hegel, G W F, 29, 102, 145, 151, 174, 213,
    220, 263, 291, 299, 310, 318, 327, 328,
    364, 365, 407, 456

Heidegger, M, 190

Heine, H, 151, 216, 335, 362, 448, 449

Helvétius, A, 205

Hemingway, E, 255

Henry of Huntington, 373

Henry VIII, 240, 384, 398

Heraclitus, 190, 218, 221, 224, 234, 235, 236, 267, 268, 291, 309, 328, 332, 362

Herbert, G, 230, 278

Herodotus, 209

Herrick, R, 222

Hesiod, 155, 250, 282

Hesse, H, 226

Hindemith, P, 228

Hobbes, Th., 21, 102, 145, 184, 192, 205, 286, 287, 365, 389, 398, 399, 400, 401, 402, 403, 416, 422, 426, 442

Hölderlin, F, 157

Holmes, O W, 315

Hölty, L, 334

Homer (Homeric), 136, 150, 162, 172, 191, 282, 283, 320, 395

Hooker, T, 182

Hopkins, G M, 269

Horace, 7, 137, 155, 222, 237, 340, 341, 385

Housman, A, 172, 173, 377

Hugo, V, 277, 339, 340, 391

Hume, D, 21, 145, 164, 174, 200, 201, 203, 204, 207, 263, 274, 365, 404, 407, 414-426, 435, 444, 454

Huntington, S, 379

Hus, J, 398

Husserl, E, 407

Hutcheson. F, 200, 204, 205, 426

Huxley, Aldous, 152, 202, 319

Huxley, Andrew, 319

Huxley, J, 319

Huxley, T H, 204, 352, 353, 356, 446

Huysmans, J-K, 149

Ibsen, H, 244

Ignatius of Loyola, 272

James, H, 36, 37, 57, 152, 184, 185, 186, 228, 229, 247, 381

James, W, 147, 179, 184, 185, 192, 275, 313, 351, 375

Jean Paul (P F Richter), 164

Jefferson, Th., 21, 145, 205, 300, 365, 371, 398, 402, 403, 412

Jerusalem, 26, 154, 155, 282, 306

Jesus Christ, 99, 102, 151, 154, 157, 161, 164, 169, 186, 216, 226, 234, 236, 243, 280, 282, 283, 287, 329, 339, 345, 350, 354, 365, 372, 402

Jesus College, Cambridge, 375, 398

John of Salisbury, 193

John of the Cross (Juan de la Cruz), 273, 289

Johnson, S, 179, 230, 344, 408, 414, 424, 433

Jowett, B, 377

Joyce, J, 188, 241, 246, 381

Julian (the Apostate), 354

Julius Caesar, 156, 169, 247, 248, 255, 291, 383, 402

Jung, C J, 138, 154, 166, 170, 188, 226, 229, 238, 255, 268, 271, 275, 325, 346, 354, 357, 366, 391

Justinian, 30, 159, 169

Juvenal, 243, 350

Kahn, G, 152

Kant, I, 35, 96, 102, 145, 174, 200, 213, 263, 266, 274, 284, 291, 313, 326, 365, 380, 382, 383, 401, 407, 448, 449, 450, 451, 452, 453, 454, 455

Keats, J, 143, 152, 213, 230, 321, 347

Kern, J, 210

Key, S, 189

Keynes, J M, 353, 430

Kipling, R, 133, 223, 267, 373, 392

Kreuzberg, 55, 69, 226, 244

Laing, R D, 264

Lamartine, A, 199, 253, 340

Lazarus, 78, 280, 283

League of Nations, 92, 217, 305, 306, 308

League of Sensible Countries (LOSC), 63, 89, 90, 91, 92, 93, 117, 118, 119, 125, 127, 131, 367, 388

Lehàr, , 334

Leibniz, G W, 177, 259, 266, 270, 274, 333, 397, 447, 451

Lenin, V.I., 169, 366, 402, 414, 445

Leonardo da Vinci, 101, 268, 326, 384

Lessing, G, 216, 242, 296

Levellers, 325, 392

Linnaeus, 334

Lipsius, 344

Locke, J, 21, 102, 145, 164, 166, 174, 184, 191, 200, 204, 205, 266, 284, 298, 309, 365, 382, 398, 400-412, 414, 416, 417, 418, 419, 426, 435, 449, 451, 454

Lollards, 397

Lorca, F G, 66, 241

Louis XIV, 193, 411, 412

Lourdes, 56, 226

Ludwig I, 187

Ludwig II, 187

Luther, M, 18, 27, 140, 143, 167, 365, 367, 384, 397, 402

Lycée Michelet, 82, 289

Lyly, J, 306

Macaulay, T B, 315, 389

Machado, A, 344, 345

Machiavelli, N, 389

Magritte, R, 137

Mallarmé, S, 216, 222

Malraux, A, 126, 380

Malthus, Th., 361, 430

Mammon, 239

Mandeville, B de, 439

Mann, Th., 178, 211, 216, 219

Mannheim, K, 299

Manning, Cardinal, 352

Marcus Aurelius, 321

Marina di Ravenna, 27, 159

Marshall, G, 239

Marcuse, H, 295

Márquez, G G, 152

Marsh Harrier, 107, 349

Marx, G, 300

Marx, K, 102, 174, 203, 242, 295, 299, 309, 317, 354, 358, 365, 366, 372, 377, 378, 379, 388, 406, 431

Massachusetts, 182, 183, 184, 219, 302, 367, 403

Massari, G, 162

Mauriac, F, 195, 196, 242

Mayrhofer, J, 150

McMarthy, M, 143

McLuhan, M, 199

Meister Eckhart, 272

Méridoux, J, 196

Merleau-Ponty, M, 357

MI6, 62, 64, 89, 237, 300, 308

Michelangelo (Buonarroti), 102, 206, 223, 321, 326

Mill, J, 377

Mill, J S, 292, 365, 377, 425

Miller, M, 238

Milton, J, 150, 158, 171, 195, 228, 309, 315, 325, 375

Minerva, 220

Mises, L von, 358

Monk, R, 198

Montaigne, M de, 270, 311

Moore, G, 152, 294, 296

More, Th., 209, 378, 398

Movement of Thinking Humans (MOTH), 119, 120, 127, 128, 367, 388

Mozart, W A,150, 162, 213, 321, 322

Mumtaz Mahal, 192

Murger, H, 290

Murray, J, 372

Musset, A de, 297

Nelson, H, 272, 309

Nero, 229, 296

New Lanark, 439

Newman, J.H., 283, 292, 352, 375, 389

Newmarket, 103, 106, 337, 348

Newnham College, Cambridge, 245
Newton, I, 21, 145, 253, 274, 336, 410, 412, 443-446
New Issuea (NI), 64, 67, 68, 91
Nicholas of Cusa, 329
Nicolson, H, 239
Nietzsche, F, 7, 21, 28, 29, 45, 55, 121, 136, 144, 145, 153, 158, 160, 161, 163, 164, 165, 166, 168, 174, 177, 178, 179, 195, 201, 203, 211, 213, 214, 216, 224, 247, 258, 259, 264, 267, 268, 270, 271, 273, 274, 275, 276, 311, 324, 327, 330, 354, 355, 366, 372, 380, 387, 394, 397, 447
Norton, C E, 186
Nuclear Non-proliferation, 307
Odysseus, 65, 150, 241, 254, 256, 320
Ogden, C K, 198, 298
Olympus, 68, 244, 282, 283
Oratory School, 389
Orczy, Baroness, 237
Oriel College, Oxford, 375
Orthodox Church, 139, 140, 398, 404
Orwell (Blair, E), G, 209
Oslo Accords, 92, 307, 308
Owen, R, 21, 145, 431, 432, 433, 437, 438, 439, 443
Oxford University, 85, 144, 162, 180, 343, 352, 359, 375, 397, 398, 424, 440
Packard, V, 317
Paestum, 26, 154, 341
Palestine, 63, 92, 282, 306, 308, 372
Palladio, A, 162
Pandora, 250
Pareto, V, 126, 379
Parmenides, 72, 190, 250, 251, 252, 268, 362, 396, 390
Peirce, C, 147, 185, 197, 313
Pembroke College (Hall), Cambridge, 376, 384, 405
Petrarch, F, 144, 203, 231
Philo, 234
Pico della Mirandola, G, 150

Pilgrim Fathers, 183
Pindar, 271
Pineta di Classe, 27, 159, 254
Plato, 7, 26, 51, 101, 102, 105, 126, 127, 136, 143, 148, 151, 152, 154, 169, 174, 176, 179, 194, 196, 197, 201, 203, 204, 208, 209, 211, 222, 236, 249, 261, 262, 269, 271, 272, 287, 294, 299, 301, 309, 311, 312, 322, 323, 324, 327, 328, 330, 331, 332, 335, 336, 359, 362, 363, 364, 365, 366, 369, 381, 382, 387, 388, 389, 391, 394, 396, 399, 401, 403, 404, 405, 406, 408, 412, 420, 423, 425, 447, 451, 452, 453
Plotinus, 151, 211, 329, 365
Polybius, 369
Pope, A, 308
Popper, K, 182, 299
Pound, E, 222
Poussin, N, 193
Powell, A, 193
Protagoras, 203, 335
Proust, M, 57, 184, 193, 228, 248, 265, 271, 285, 286, 366, 387
Purcell, H, 290, 339
Pythagoras, 203, 335
Pythia, 47, 206
Quebec (Québec), 90, 302
Rank, O, 187
Ranke, L von, 430
Ravenna, 27, 30, 159, 161, 169
Rawls, J, 123, 374
Reid, Th., 200
Renoir, A, 285
Renoir, J, 285
Ricardo, D, 21, 145, 377, 424, 429, 430, 431, 437
Richards, I A, 198, 298
Richardson, S, 137
Rieff, Ph., 317, 318
Riesman, D, 317
Rimbaud, A, 212, 213, 221, 222
Robbe-Grillet, A, 151

Robespierre, M, 284, 354, 402

Rome (Church of), 18, 77, 138, 139, 140, 162, 167, 169, 202, 278, 280, 285, 287, 352, 368, 389, 393, 397, 398, 404

Ross, E, 316

Rousseau, J-J, 7, 136, 137, 167, 174, 192, 193, 195, 242, 243, 251, 253, 265, 277, 299, 317, 338, 365, 384, 392, 401, 402, 406, 424

Royal Society, 180

Ruskin, J, 144, 238, 366, 376, 430

Russell, B, 123, 333, 374

Saint-Simon, C, 355, 430

Sartre, J-P, 171, 190, 204, 257, 390

Saussure, F de, 197

Schelling, F von, 145

Schiller, F, 329, 339, 365

Schober, F von, 322

Schopenhauer, A, 121, 145, 159, 168, 174, 175, 177, 178, 179, 213, 227, 259, 260, 263, 268, 270, 323, 365, 373, 407

Schubert, F, 150, 256, 322, 334

Scott, W, 385

Secretary of State, 239, 300, 309

Segesta, 26, 154

Seidl, G, 256

Selinunte, 26, 154

Seneca, 35, 234, 269, 279, 365

Seven Years War, 189, 302, 368

Shaftesbury (A. Cooper), 204, 284, 367, 382

Shakespeare, W, 22, 38, 58, 99, 102, 121, 146, 150, 152, 162, 166, 168, 173, 186, 193, 199, 202, 227, 231, 240, 249, 265, 266, 272, 292, 293, 299, 304, 312, 319, 350, 365, 366, 372, 373, 376, 379, 386, 387

Shaw, G B, 268

Shelley, M, 161

Shelley, P B, 144, 161, 253, 325, 326

Shirley, J, 158

Sicily, 24, 154

Sidi Bou Said, 65, 240

Sieyès, E, 367, 402

Sitwell, O, 296

Smith, A, 21, 122, 145, 244, 358, 378, 379, 423-426, 429, 437, 444

Smith, J, 133, 392

Snell, B, 333

Socrates, 136, 147, 174, 196, 197, 199, 201, 203, 235, 250, 255, 261, 262, 311, 324, 326, 327, 331, 332, 359, 365, 370, 381, 387, 389, 391, 399, 423

Solomon, 154, 281, 287, 306

Sophocles, 133, 136, 164, 182, 227

Spencer, H, 293, 316, 366

Spengler, O, 227

Spenser, E, 384, 385, 390

Spinoza, B, 177, 259, 268, 269, 335, 447

St Thomas d'Aquin (church), 55, 224

Stein, G, 190, 248, 331

Stevenson, R L, 152

Strachey, L, 352, 384

Strauss, D, 163

Strauss, R, 321

Styne, J, 368

Suárez, F, 35, 174, 365

Suetonius, 215, 248

Sullivan, A, 187, 209

Sullivan, H S, 318

Sulloway, F, 178, 406

Sumner, W, 316

Surtees, R, 239

Swift, J, 178, 180, 181

Swinburne, A C, 276

Syracuse, 26, 154, 308

Tacitus, 229

Taillevent, 86, 296

Taine, H, 162

Tawney, R, 285

Teilhard de Chardin, P, 318

Tennyson, A, 352, 375

Teresa of Avila, 139, 215, 272, 340

Tertullian, 338, 350

Thirty Years War, 17, 138, 141

Thrasymachus, 389

Tolstoy, L, 142

Treitschke, H von, 216

Trevelyan, G M, 315

Trevelyan, O, 315

Trevisan (family), 139, 140

Tricoteuse, 47, 206

Trinity College, Cambridge, 154, 172, 173, 183, 210, 230, 232, 276, 280, 284, 315, 319, 333, 352, 375, 383, 412, 446

Trinity College, Oxford, 375

Troy (Trojan), 103, 150, 155, 156, 157, 240, 241, 337, 385, 386

Turgot, A, 425, 429

Turner, J M W, 162, 346

United Nations, 63, 92, 189, 217, 238, 239, 306, 308

Universal Declaration of Independence, 90, 302, 368

University College, London, 172

University College, Oxford, 144

University of Paris, 224, 233

UNPAST, 63, 239

Valéry, P, 210, 254

Vatican, 18, 144, 257, 352

Venice, 15, 16, 17, 18, 26, 27, 28, 30, 31, 77, 138, 140, 142, 143, 144, 154, 159, 161, 162, 170, 171, 211, 230, 280, 340, 343, 347, 371

Verlaine, P, 222

Vermont, 40, 189

Vico, G, 174, 381

Virgil, 155, 156, 191, 232, 254, 329, 330, 341, 342, 347

Vishnu, 53, 217

Voltaire, 29, 102, 137, 166, 167, 195, 209, 251, 295, 329, 362, 365, 411, 412, 424, 443

Wadham College, Oxford, 180

Wagner, R, 154, 170, 185, 187, 216, 226, 277, 311

Walpole, R, 300, 309

Wars of Religion, 17, 140

Washington, G, 402

Watson, J, 317, 425

Weber, M, 201, 285, 370, 372, 379, 430

Wesendonk, M, 277

Westport, 37, 59, 185

Wharton, E, 229

Whewell, W, 446, 457

Whistler, J, 238

Whitby, 278

Whitehead, A N, 374

Whitman, W, 230, 266

Whyte, L, 178

Wilcox, E W, 58, 230

Wilde, O, 126, 181, 350, 380

William of Occam, 21, 145, 175, 393, 397, 405

Wilson, E O, 360

Wilson, W, 316

Winstanley, G, 133, 325, 392

Winthrop, J, 183

Wittgenstein, L, 123, 173, 198, 199, 374

Wolf, H, 223

Wolff, C, 174, 447, 451

Woolf, V, 57, 229, 245

Wordsworth, W, 217, 231

Wyatt, Th., 231

Wyclif, J, 21, 145, 397, 398

Wyczwycz, W, 45, 196, 368

Yeats, W B, 149

Zattere, Le, 27, 161, 162

Zeno, 149

Zeus, 142, 250, 350

Zoroaster, 276

Zweig, S, 349

SUBJECTS

Abstraction, 18, 291, 323, 374, 417

Academia, 90, 301, 341

Academy, 35, 104, 151, 180, 181, 203, 341, 356, 423

Aesthetic, 22, 59, 123, 149, 176, 184, 204, 242, 265, 284, 322, 329, 366, 382, 383, 452

Agnostic, 29, 167, 356, 358, 446

All, The, 29, 52, 54, 76, 99, 105, 109, 110, 328, 329, 439

Altermondialisme, 209

American Mind, 96, 121, 126, 148, 286, 313, 314, 315, 317, 318

A Midsummer-Night's Dream, 150, 319, 391

Amor Dei, 269

Amour, 86, 87, 290, 297

Anatomy of Melancholy, The, 343

Anatomy of optimism, 105, 343, 350

Anatomy of the mind, 264

Angst, 42, 146, 191, 193, 270

Anthropotheism, 168

arche, 174, 235, 236

Archetype (archetypal), 19, 124, 145, 186, 255, 281, 290, 322, 410, 411, 452

Arianism, 157, 169, 404

Art (artist), 7, 29, 37, 41, 42, 90, 118, 126, 127, 136, 137, 142, 144, 152, 154, 162, 168, 177, 179, 180, 181, 184, 193, 198, 222, 231, 238, 241, 242, 244, 265, 274, 278, 279, 285, 290, 310, 322, 323, 324, 325, 327, 328, 361, 374, 380, 381, 383, 394, 428

As You Like It, 220, 304

Ascetic, 98, 163, 326, 370

Ascetic erotic, 98, 236

Atheism, 29, 144, 173, 266, 356, 413, 422, 446

Atman, 225, 268

Atomism, 253, 312

Atonement, 287

Bad faith (see also *mauvaise foi*), 32, 171, 271, 390

Balance of power, 91, 304

Baroque, 28, 55, 97, 162, 320

Beautiful, 28, 30, 37, 39, 40, 41, 43, 51, 52, 76, 79, 80, 84, 93, 104, 106, 107, 114, 115, 126, 127, 128, 129, 143, 144, 151, 152, 162, 170, 177, 204, 210, 211, 213, 214, 218, 247, 269, 289, 321, 322, 323, 326, 327, 331, 335, 339, 343, 345, 349, 362, 380, 382, 383, 387, 391, 408

Beauty, 52, 53, 97, 104, 114, 127, 144, 154, 157, 160, 163, 173, 179, 184, 186, 203, 205, 210, 211, 230, 261, 320, 321, 322, 323, 325, 326, 328, 339, 352, 383, 388, 389, 391, 406

Becoming, 75, 102, 103, 104, 112, 113, 128, 129, 130, 152, 177, 190, 218, 271, 277, 362, 363, 366, 388

Behaviourism, 102, 190, 316, 317, 336, 425, 429

Bible, The, 155, 216, 234, 379, 397, 398

Bildung, 329

Binding force, 113, 115, 129, 168, 350, 364, 365, 388

Biology, 32, 34, 96, 121, 138, 178, 195, 218, 293, 298, 319, 326, 333, 345, 360, 361, 368

Birth of Tragedy, The, 136, 211, 259, 274, 324, 387

Body, 46, 52, 55, 71, 72, 73, 102, 103, 113, 114, 115, 120, 129, 130, 138, 165, 166, 185, 207, 211, 214, 215, 218, 224, 239, 249, 266, 268, 269, 287, 288, 311, 321, 326, 337, 365, 387, 390, 394, 398, 411

Body politic, 42, 183, 192, 193, 441

Brain, 26, 34, 48, 74, 146, 156, 193, 220, 221, 251, 257, 266, 267, 288, 325, 346, 366, 410, 412, 413, 427, 439, 445, 452, 453

Brand Nominalism, 64

Bronze Age, 79, 80, 286, 348

Buddhism, 53, 163, 196, 215, 225, 239, 250, 272, 273

Calvinism, 46, 102, 201, 356

Cambridge Platonists, 151, 266, 392

Candide, 24, 137, 153, 188, 362

Capitalism (capitalist), 21, 22, 23, 48, 49, 53, 68, 96, 122, 123, 124, 147, 171, 208, 215, 216, 244, 285, 286, 294, 295, 296, 317, 355, 358, 370, 371, 377, 379, 394, 426, 427, 428, 443

Categories (Aristotelian/Kantian), 175, 236, 257, 366, 404, 406, 410, 419, 450, 454

Cause (causation), 171, 175, 208, 216, 244, 295, 299, 378, 379, 394, 396, 410, 418, 419, 420, 422, 426, 427, 430, 443, 455

Cherry Orchard, The, 39, 187, 188

Chosen people, 96, 288, 314, 315, 361, 389

Christianity, 29, 79, 80, 84, 108, 124, 139, 140, 142, 157, 163, 164, 167, 168, 169, 173, 178, 191, 196, 202, 203, 204, 216, 221, 224, 251, 272, 278, 280, 281, 282, 283, 284, 286, 288, 328, 347, 354, 358, 363, 370, 384, 393, 398, 404, 446

City of God, 31, 142, 169, 170, 383

City on a hill, 315

Civilisation, 142, 169, 205, 262, 264, 293

Civilization and its Discontents, 205, 264, 293, 295

Clash of Civilisations, 125, 379

Cognitive, 197, 259, 288, 450

Cognitive biology, 33, 34

Cognitive engineering, 33, 34

Collective unconscious, 145, 255, 325, 346

Common good, 218, 379, 443

Communism (communist), 96, 194, 244, 309, 325, 357, 392, 403

Communist Manifesto, The, 120, 305, 372, 388

Conatus, 268

Confession, 27, 161, 242, 350

Confessions (Augustine), 151, 224, 267, 323, 455

Confessions (Rousseau), 195, 251, 265, 277

Consciousness (108 references—not listed)

Conservativism (conservative), 38, 102, 107, 129, 316, 336, 358, 399, 403, 432, 434, 440, 443

Continental European mind, 6, 22, 146, 447, 448

Contradiction (principle of), 258

Conversion, 80, 244, 278, 323, 324, 395

Corn Laws, 431

Cosmology, 330

Counter-Reformation, 140, 162

Covenant, 80, 183, 238, 239, 298, 305

Cratylus, 197, 262, 332

Crime (criminal), 141, 154, 218, 227, 279, 301, 351, 437, 438

Criminal law, 218, 351, 442

Critias, 369, 370

Custom, 102, 111, 201, 363, 364, 372, 399, 418, 419, 449

Cynics, 148, 151, 168, 207, 234, 255

Dark Ages, 283, 361

Darwinism, 84, 158, 352, 355

Death, 55, 57, 58, 59, 69, 72, 85, 103, 104, 127, 143, 145, 157, 158, 161, 165, 170, 172, 180, 187, 194, 195, 196, 199, 211, 217, 218, 223, 224, 225, 227, 231, 240, 249, 257, 258, 273, 277, 278, 280, 281, 287, 292, 298, 303, 309, 311, 327, 342, 345, 368, 379, 383, 385, 398, 414, 423

Death of Christ, 78, 191, 281, 283, 287

Death of God, 29, 165, 258

Death of the mind, 85

Death wish (instinct), 119, 196, 388

debita nostra, 28, 161

Dehumanising, 46, 61, 124, 171, 195, 435

Deism, 78, 165, 167, 185, 192, 275, 283, 284, 350

Democracy (democratic), 21, 42, 49, 61, 84, 96, 122, 123, 124, 125, 183, 184, 192, 194, 208, 215, 233, 260, 286, 296, 299, 312, 314, 317, 359, 361, 367, 371, 389, 394, 398, 400, 402, 403, 434, 443

Democracy-capitalism, 215, 296, 434

Despair, 26, 81, 119, 129, 142, 148, 157, 229, 272, 289, 298, 338, 372, 388

Devil (Satan), 38, 80, 124, 158, 169, 171, 187, 202, 237, 251, 288, 430

Dialectic, 21, 123, 124, 148, 162, 204, 209, 213, 218, 258, 260, 264, 291, 309, 310, 365, 408, 423, 434, 437, 443, 447

Diarchic Indicators, 102, 336

Diaspora, 282

Divine, 18, 29, 143, 157, 159, 167, 168, 182, 185, 210, 218, 253, 269, 272, 273, 286, 327, 329, 330, 342, 346, 348, 355, 357, 358, 404

Divine Comedy, The, 159, 182, 272, 330, 342

Division of labour, 427, 431

Dream (dreaming), 15, 25, 40, 58, 60, 74, 85, 102, 133, 138, 149, 151, 154, 158, 166, 170, 177, 189, 267, 269, 274, 277, 281, 306, 321, 336, 346, 392, 414, 430

Dystopia, 209

Ecce Homo, 195, 270, 276

Economics (see also Political Economy), 21, 23, 208, 361, 376, 426, 429, 430, 431

Education, 85, 111, 119, 122, 137, 205, 211, 233, 251, 296, 322, 324, 329, 336, 337, 338, 344, 358, 375, 381, 400, 437

élan vital, 268

Empiricism, 175, 203, 272, 284, 333, 375, 394, 407, 412, 417, 451, 452

End of History, 111, 361

End times, 125, 379

English elite, 84

English mind, 145, 294

Enlightenment (see also Law of Enlightenments), 46, 60, 61, 95, 127, 163, 164, 204, 205, 216, 225, 226, 233, 252, 272, 276, 278, 283, 291, 316, 329, 334, 348, 370, 413, 424

Enthusiasm.38, 120, 146, 346, 354, 409, 449

Enthusiasts, 129, 341, 346, 388

Epicurean, 23, 47, 61, 148, 151, 168, 297, 234, 255

Epistemology, 218, 250, 360, 394, 404, 414, 444

Equality, 86, 87, 359, 374

Essay Concerning Human Understanding, 404, 435

Essence, 101, 160, 162, 179, 190, 200, 218, 260, 268, 269, 270, 333, 354, 362, 396, 404, 411, 444, 447

essentia, 404

Eternity (eternal), 41, 68, 80, 166, 176, 192, 219, 224, 233, 253, 261, 262, 265, 269, 288, 297, 308, 328, 335, 356, 384, 388, 396, 408, 411

Ethics (ethical) (see also Morality), 32, 33, 34, 44, 45, 46, 48, 65, 112, 136, 194, 195, 196, 197, 200, 218, 310, 316, 317, 360, 363, 366, 370, 404, 428

Ethics (Nicomachean), 232, 311, 363, 376, 399, 420

Eunomia, 9, 11, 113, 218, 232, 260, 264, 268, 272, 273, 295, 327, 364, 371, 379

Eunomian, 22, 24, 146, 260, 264

Eunomianism, 20

Euphues, 129, 373, 386

Eutopia, 46, 129, 202, 209, 388, 427

Evil (see also Problem of Evil), 23, 29, 30, 45, 47, 67, 69, 78, 79, 80, 123, 125, 126, 127, 128, 141, 145, 153, 158, 170, 178, 191, 195, 196, 200, 207, 218, 221, 222, 239, 242, 247, 250, 267, 276, 282, 287, 288, 299, 321, 362, 378, 393, 436, 441, 447

Evolution, 95, 96, 105, 182, 188, 218, 249, 293, 312, 318, 319, 327, 345, 346, 353, 360, 368, 432, 445

Existence, 58, 59, 70, 71, 73, 83, 97, 98, 99, 101, 112, 136, 157, 162, 167, 171, 231, 236, 250, 252, 257, 259, 260, 262, 263, 270, 275, 279, 284, 296, 304, 305, 310, 333, 335, 337, 362, 374, 380, 384, 393, 399, 409, 410, 413, 415, 417, 418, 429, 435, 446, 453, 454, 456

Existentialism, 64, 193, 204, 252, 270

Fall of Man (see also Original Sin), 26, 191, 250, 384, 392

Fantasy, 17, 22, 68, 82, 96, 125, 135, 162, 187, 219, 297, 381, 454

Father, 36, 39, 46, 47, 56, 95, 102, 105, 138, 150, 161, 163, 164, 168, 182, 188, 197, 215, 218, 240, 242, 254, 264, 265, 273, 286, 287, 317, 331, 340, 374, 377, 379, 384

Father-figure, 39, 188

Federalist Papers, The, 403

Fifth Dimension, 99, 129, 326, 330

Focus group, 48, 208, 379

Foot-and-Note Disease, 425

Frankish, 91, 303, 304

Free trade, 306, 430, 431

Free will, 34, 41, 177, 191, 192, 195, 329, 349

French mind, 86, 294

French Revolution, 161, 206, 224, 237, 283, 367, 372, 402, 432, 433

Freudianism (Freudian), 15, 24, 102, 138, 152, 167, 170, 188, 190, 227, 238, 246, 286, 317, 324, 355, 357, 358

Friendship, 59, 87, 208, 234, 284, 297, 323

Fundamentalist, 84, 96, 120, 204, 372

Future, the, 17, 18, 27, 46, 49, 53, 54, 64, 65, 71, 76, 82, 91, 106, 119, 125, 126, 128, 132, 146, 156, 161, 202, 206, 210, 217, 222, 238, 241, 262, 291, 298, 302, 308, 312, 314, 316, 339, 347, 351, 354, 355, 356, 359, 369, 370, 388, 419, 430, 432, 433, 456

Future of an Illusion, The, 262, 351

Garden (gardener), 24, 39, 42, 51, 58, 59, 78, 80, 100, 104, 105, 117, 123, 153, 163, 167, 178, 188, 193, 210, 231, 270, 281, 282, 331, 332, 334, 338, 340, 341, 343, 345, 351, 375

Garden of Eden, 78, 80, 281, 282, 345

Geistesverwandschaften, 365

Genealogy of Morals, On The, 160, 166, 178, 258, 271, 327, 355

General Will, 41, 96, 122, 191, 192, 373, 401

Generalife, 343

Genesis, Book of, 71, 78, 81, 99, 158, 191, 228, 231, 249, 250, 281, 282, 325, 330, 332, 341, 345, 361

Generic, 107

Genetic, 34, 38, 107, 210, 240, 241, 286, 334, 362, 445

Genetics, 33, 34, 46, 326

Geology, 445

Giorno della Repubblica, 17

Globalisation, 209, 217, 302

Gnosis, 347, 348, 446

Gnostalgia, 106, 347, 349

Good, the (goodness), 22, 30, 34, 44, 45, 67, 114, 115, 121, 125, 126, 128, 147, 148, 149, 166, 174, 194, 195, 203, 204, 211, 222, 247, 261, 269, 290, 328, 362, 401, 406, 408, 415

Gorgias, 311, 327

Governing class, 96, 375, 381

Government, Two Treatises on, 205, 309, 401, 404

Grace (of God), 30, 168, 191, 282, 322

Great Game, 122, 373

Greatest happiness, 46, 204, 205, 293, 372, 382, 438, 439, 440, 442

Haiku, 230

Hamlet, 99, 231, 238, 272, 292, 387

Happiness (happy), 42, 46, 56, 57, 65, 76, 95, 99, 115, 120, 121, 124, 128, 131, 149, 165, 177, 178, 179, 180, 201, 202, 204, 205, 206, 225, 239, 249, 254, 256, 269, 270, 284, 293, 299, 311, 328, 346, 358, 366, 369, 372, 382, 400, 432, 434, 436, 438, 439, 440, 441, 442, 449, 451

Harmonia, 324, 364

Harmonia animi, 52, 214

Harmonia mundi, 52, 214, 324

Harmony, 98, 104, 179, 214, 215, 322, 323, 324, 328, 364, 390

Health of Nations, The, 10, 124, 201, 208, 233, 251, 285, 289, 301, 311, 367, 378, 380, 430, 437

Hinduism (Hindu), 53, 163, 177, 185, 217, 225, 226, 239, 260, 268, 272, 281, 362

Holy Spirit, 79, 287

Homo economicus, 124, 379

homoiousios, 404

homoousios, 404

Hope, 54, 87, 99, 109, 111, 117, 123, 129, 171, 226, 289, 307, 308, 319, 326, 350

Human being, 24, 29, 38, 45, 59, 67, 69, 70, 71, 72, 77, 78, 95, 103, 106, 115, 121, 122, 124, 125, 127, 129, 130, 149, 157, 173, 177, 188, 195, 211, 213, 227, 246, 250, 252, 259, 260, 263, 264, 270, 275, 281, 283, 286, 287, 291, 312, 328, 330, 345, 349, 360, 363, 364, 366, 376, 379, 380, 388, 434, 443

Human nature, 29, 67, 78, 153, 205, 275, 282, 317, 329, 335, 399, 400, 416, 420, 422, 426

Human Nature, Treatise on, 176, 415, 416, 417, 418, 419, 420, 425, 444

Human race, 67, 99, 124, 152, 168, 174, 218, 232, 279, 281, 282, 296, 329, 330, 359, 430, 435

Human reality, 24, 127, 135, 252, 366

Human sciences, 46, 121, 299, 355, 456

Human species, 29, 42, 95, 115, 119, 158, 312, 327, 345, 360, 363, 436, 443, 445

Human world, 21, 24, 46, 64, 82, 99, 118, 119, 124, 126, 127, 128, 129, 146, 153, 158, 168, 174, 179, 202, 236, 237, 267, 279, 310, 319, 324, 330, 365, 379, 399, 426, 428, 432, 457

Humanism (humanist), 46, 47, 118, 129, 144, 201, 203, 204, 269, 284, 319, 344, 357

Humanity, 21, 29, 46, 59, 78, 96, 97, 99, 104, 119, 120, 124, 128, 143, 163, 173, 174, 179, 191, 194, 195, 204, 217, 252, 263, 264, 269, 279, 296, 334, 355, 357, 380, 388, 392, 426, 428, 434, 448

Hypostasis, 404

Iconoclasts, 110, 353

Idea(s) (728 references—not listed)

Ideal, 18, 20, 24, 25, 34, 48, 57, 60, 64, 75, 76, 79, 85, 102, 104, 114, 124, 125, 127, 129, 152, 153, 161, 162, 163, 185, 297, 209, 220, 226, 233, 234, 249, 273, 276, 285, 296, 305, 306, 312, 326, 329, 366, 375, 392, 399, 401, 414, 434, 436, 445, 452, 455

Ideal Form, 48, 129, 207, 326

Ideal Realism, 24, 152

Idealism (idealist), 24, 35, 99, 129, 130, 146, 175, 176, 200, 203, 213, 218, 225, 232, 248, 249, 251, 259, 275, 310, 312, 318, 322, 325, 359, 366, 380, 388, 394, 412, 413, 414, 417, 445, 448, 452, 456

Idealist Manifesto, 322

Ideology, 87, 111, 294, 295, 298, 299, 359, 361, 378, 433

Illusion, 18, 75, 76, 78, 79, 123, 125, 135, 167, 199, 202, 212, 262, 274, 285, 286, 288, 299, 305, 351, 363, 449, 454

Imagination (imagine), 22, 23, 24, 25, 31, 52, 60, 68, 69, 70, 73, 75, 78, 80, 88, 96, 101, 104, 108, 112, 114, 119, 123, 127, 128, 154, 162, 170, 192, 194, 230, 242, 243, 252, 258, 259, 261, 266, 274, 276, 280, 289, 316, 361, 381, 413, 418, 419, 426, 442, 443, 444, 449, 451

Immortality (immortal), 28, 39, 99, 104, 143, 163, 166, 173, 218, 230, 231, 255, 290, 300, 330, 338, 349, 386, 447

Impulse of Life, 30, 59, 75, 99, 122, 268, 287, 329

Incarnation, 157, 235, 236, 287

Indifferentism, 24, 358

Individualism, 75, 108, 285, 286, 363, 376

Individuation (principle of), 259, 271

Industrial Revolution, 218, 437

Innate, 196, 200, 246, 250, 268, 282, 406, 435

Inner Light, 75, 251, 268

Inscape, 75, 269, 270, 390

Instinct, 101, 165, 196, 227, 317, 360, 426

Intellectual, 20, 27, 29, 34, 49, 59, 62, 87, 96, 120, 127, 169, 171, 177, 178, 182, 184,

185, 194, 197, 198, 199, 203, 204, 216, 218, 220, 223, 224, 276, 230, 232, 244, 252, 261, 266, 275, 283, 284, 305, 315, 325, 336, 341, 357, 365, 366, 373, 378, 393, 394, 396, 397, 403, 414, 416, 417, 422, 423, 417, 422, 423, 424, 425, 430, 445, 447, 451

Intelligent Design, 249

Intelligible system (of the world), 266, 451

Intuition, 380, 409, 450

Invisible Hand, 122, 192, 373, 429

Inward eye, 115

Inward perfection, 115

Islam (Moslem), 53, 216, 272, 282, 286

Italienische Reise, 52, 215, 343

Joy, 54, 55, 97, 99, 155, 166, 177, 222, 223, 228, 230, 320, 321, 327, 349, 382

Judaism (Jewish, Hebraic), 27, 158, 160, 168, 173, 196, 234, 249, 281, 282, 306, 363

Judgment, Critique of, 326, 383, 452

Julius Caesar, 247, 373

Justice, 34, 64, 214, 261, 262, 265, 276, 357, 374, 378, 379, 384, 389, 393, 399, 400, 408, 434, 435, 437, 438, 440, 442, 456

Katha Upanishad, 55, 225, 260

King Henry V, 293, 366, 379

King Henry VI, Part Two, 240, 379

King Lear, 99, 193, 194, 227, 249, 376

Law (laws), 30, 92, 96, 100, 102, 110, 142, 146, 148, 163, 169, 179, 181, 183, 187, 191, 192, 193, 201, 203, 204, 205, 208, 218, 243, 244, 249, 256, 263, 269, 288, 291, 301, 303, 304, 305, 310, 311, 315, 317, 324, 329, 344, 351, 355, 365, 367, 368, 371, 372, 378, 379, 392, 396, 398, 399, 400, 401, 402, 403, 425, 426, 429, 430, 431, 434, 438, 440, 442, 443, 444, 452

Law of Enlightenments, 60, 233, 276, 278

Laws, 208

Leviathan, 192, 286, 320

Leviathans, 78, 286, 320

Liberal democracy, 192, 208, 233, 286, 312

Liberalism (liberal, *libéralisme*), 38, 79, 102, 123, 187, 192, 208, 233, 286, 295, 296, 312, 315, 336, 359, 361, 367, 371, 374, 398, 400, 402, 432, 434, 443

Libido, 148, 243, 268, 357

Life (394 references—not listed)

Life-force, 268

Limbo, 202

Lingua franca, 398

Logic, 148, 218, 257, 258, 331, 332, 333

Logical positivism, 190, 424

logos, 197, 234, 235, 236, 237, 268, 330

Lohengrin, 186, 187

Love (214 references—not listed)

Love of God, 30, 71, 80, 112, 128, 129, 160, 188, 269, 289, 297

Love's Labour's Lost, 350

Macbeth, 99, 373

Madame Bovary, 69, 247

Magic Flute, The, 94, 309, 321

Magic Idealism, 24

Manichaeism, 282

Market (free-market), 21, 41, 68, 109, 192, 208, 244, 235, 317, 378, 428, 429, 431

Marxism (marxist), 111, 147, 190, 247, 318, 355, 357, 378, 389

Materialism, 173, 176, 218, 227, 249, 251, 312, 314, 318, 358, 376, 394, 413, 414, 423, 415, 445

Mathematics, 158, 179, 214, 258, 324, 396, 406, 457

Mauvaise foi, 171, 390

Mazdaism, 276

McCalvinism, 108

Meaning of meaning, 87, 198, 298, 374

Measure for Measure, 166, 312

Megametaphysicians, 447

Meism, 78, 285

Meno, 255, 256, 332, 406

Mental hormonal balance, 102

Metanoia, 281, 286, 332, 406

Metaphysical, 22, 52, 53, 58, 59, 61, 72, 75, 76, 77, 95, 97, 98, 102, 103, 104, 113, 114, 115, 126, 142, 146, 148, 169, 174, 177, 200, 230, 232, 234, 249, 253, 255, 260, 263, 270, 274, 278, 287, 288, 291, 297, 323, 328, 336, 341, 342, 345, 346, 353, 366, 395, 396, 397, 401, 406, 408, 416, 422, 425, 426, 435, 446, 447, 448, 451, 452, 454

Metaphysical Revolution, 59, 61

Metaphysics, 22, 53, 87, 88, 96, 101, 102, 112, 125, 136, 147, 166, 178, 203, 206, 208, 218, 250, 251, 252, 274, 275, 276, 279, 284, 291, 322, 327, 333, 355, 362, 364, 366, 375, 391, 393, 396, 397, 398, 399, 404, 405, 410, 412, 415, 418, 426, 427, 428, 451, 452, 453, 454, 455

Metaphysics, 203, 214

Metaphysiology, 101, 102, 105, 252, 291

Microcosm, 30, 218

Mid-Atlantic Ridge Syndrome, 126

Middle Ages (medieval), 31, 53, 78, 145, 162, 170, 173, 174, 197, 203, 215, 244, 283, 296, 297, 301, 323, 335, 337, 361, 369, 394, 395, 398, 423, 447

Middle class, 46, 90, 117, 119, 120, 230, 371, 372, 431, 438

Mind (mental) (848 references—not listed)

Misanthropology, 123, 273, 295

Misarchy, 437

Moment, 72, 250, 251, 252, 257, 328, 362, 363, 366

Morality (moral) (see also Ethics), 23, 24, 34, 45, 47, 75, 84, 86, 88, 96, 98, 101, 121, 123, 129, 136, 137, 146, 148, 149, 156, 167, 193, 195, 200, 201, 204, 205, 207, 214, 215, 227, 233, 234, 247, 255, 257, 263, 264, 265, 273, 275, 276, 279, 284, 288, 290, 291, 293, 310, 316, 319, 322, 325, 327, 328, 352, 354, 356, 363, 364, 382, 383, 384, 387, 396, 399, 406, 411, 416, 420, 421, 422, 424, 425, 434, 439, 440, 445, 452

Moral order, 276, 399

Moral rationality (see also Practical Reason), 420

Moral responsibility, 98, 121

Moral sense, 200, 204, 263, 293

Morphology, 101, 249, 333

Mother, 39, 46, 47, 52, 55, 56, 62, 65, 76, 102, 105, 157, 158, 161, 182, 188, 197, 221, 226, 228, 231, 246, 257, 276, 277, 286, 317, 331, 340, 342, 366, 374

Mother-father, 46, 47, 197, 286, 311, 331, 340, 374

Mother-figure, 158, 188, 226

Music, 22, 41, 42, 97, 98, 129, 131, 150, 154, 162, 170, 179, 185, 192, 193, 198, 209, 214, 217, 218, 222, 223, 226, 238, 242, 261, 277, 279, 283, 290, 297, 309, 319, 320, 321, 322, 323, 324, 328, 339, 368

Name (217 references—not listed)

Nandinatha Sutra, 217

Narcissism, 84, 85, 294

Natural law (laws of nature), 122, 263, 269, 355, 365, 396, 400

Natural philosophy, 206, 355, 365, 395, 396, 416, 444

Natural sciences, 46, 99, 173, 174, 179, 190, 198, 206, 234, 248, 313, 314, 353, 355, 376, 394, 395, 415, 416, 423, 430, 443, 444, 446, 447, 451, 457

Natural selection, 95, 105, 312, 345, 445

Naturalism, 222, 284, 285, 314

Nature (426 references—not listed)

Neo-neo-Platonism, 24, 151, 203, 211, 234, 272,

Neo-Platonism, 151, 203, 234, 272, 326, 329, 447

Neuroscience, 267

New Atlantis, The, 370

New Egolatry, 29

New Enlightenment, 61, 233

New Ignorance, 123, 296, 337, 375, 381

New Issues, 64, 67, 68, 91

New Organon, The, 339, 344, 395, 443, 444, 447

New Testament, 78, 154, 163, 234, 235, 280, 282, 283, 315

New Theism, 80

Nihilism (nihilist), 29, 121, 129, 252, 311, 353, 372, 424, 457

Noble lie, 84, 294, 359

nomen, 393

Nominalism, 64, 197, 393, 395, 415, 421

Noumenon(a), 190, 451

Oceana, 403

Oceanic feeling, 95, 262, 310, 388

Old Testament, 234, 249, 282, 346

Olympian gods, 282, 283

Omega point, 96, 318, 356

One, The, 264, 287, 313, 328, 329, 379

One and the Many, The, 260, 261, 264, 329, 379

One True Faith, 110, 351, 384

Ontology, 60, 61, 85, 232, 296

Optimism (optimist), 35, 42, 85, 99, 102, 105, 153, 156, 177, 204, 270, 275, 291, 316, 343, 344, 350, 400

Order, 30, 46, 97, 98, 105, 112, 113, 117, 124, 129, 149, 160, 162, 187, 188, 194, 195, 204, 214, 233, 234, 235, 236, 237, 269, 316, 324, 326, 328, 355, 356, 362, 363, 364, 370, 371, 372, 379, 392, 399, 410, 424, 425, 438, 455

Original sin, 250, 282, 345

Othello, 99, 386

ousia, 404

Outscape, 75, 269, 270, 390

Pagan, 79, 202, 281

Papal Infallibility, 352

Paradise, 27, 46, 98, 105, 158, 202, 261, 325, 342, 345, 346, 436

Paradise Lost, 150, 158, 169, 171, 195, 202, 228, 325

Passions, 128, 129, 219, 243, 265, 384, 408, 413, 417, 420, 421, 422, 452

Past, the, 17, 18, 27, 28, 49, 53, 58, 64, 66, 71, 76, 109, 132, 173, 206, 217, 238, 272, 298, 308, 314, 316, 339, 369, 388, 408, 418, 419, 430, 432

Pensée unique, 85, 295

Perception, 266, 274, 323, 388, 407, 409, 411, 412, 417, 418, 435, 450

Perennial Dilemmas of Society, 218, 260, 264

Pessimism, 80, 83, 87, 164, 178, 291, 326, 457

Phaedo, 222

Phaedrus, 196, 199, 321, 388, 391

Phenomenology, 190, 198, 200, 203

Philanthropology, 61, 85, 102, 233, 295,

Philebus, 262

Philosopher-kings, 110, 359

Philosophical nation, 57, 59, 98, 116, 130

Philosophical Revolution, 59

Philosophy (428 references—not listed)

Philosophy of mind, 153, 167, 382, 415

Physics, 22, 112, 206, 218, 275, 279, 298, 324, 365, 395, 396, 411, 417, 429, 443, 447

Physiology, 24, 191, 248, 267, 279, 325, 424, 447

Platonism, Platonist (see also 'Plato' under Names), 24, 102, 105, 151, 203, 211, 233, 234, 256, 263, 266, 272, 323, 324, 326, 329, 335, 423

Platonising, 233

Pleasure principle, 156, 368

Poetry, 57, 136, 151, 152, 154, 167, 168, 169, 173, 181, 210, 221, 222, 230, 231, 242, 245, 269, 274, 280, 282, 289, 320, 373, 328, 334, 338, 350, 352, 380, 381, 387

Political animal, 372

Political Economy, 192, 193, 376, 377, 429, 430

Politics, 21, 22, 24, 42, 49, 83, 111, 118, 119, 128, 147, 153, 154, 201, 284, 361, 367, 399, 430, 431, 433, 434, 443

Politics, 166, 185, 214, 243, 371, 372, 376

Popular culture, 125, 128, 296, 297, 381

Positivism, 164, 190, 424, 456

Possible (possibility) (247 references—not listed)

Power (440 references—not listed)

PQ/AQ, 101, 102, 103, 105, 336

Practical fascism, 315

Practical realism, 35

Practical Reason, Critique of, 207, 284, 452

Practical Reason (see also Moral rationality), 39, 102, 207, 214, 420, 452

Pragmatism (pragmatist), 23, 35, 86, 96, 120, 147, 148, 185, 190, 197, 203, 204, 275, 286, 313, 314, 317, 372, 394, 424

Prayer, 16, 41, 54, 76, 119, 132, 140, 151, 161, 189, 219, 221, 223, 224, 231, 321, 340, 391, 398

Prescriptive metaphysics, 426

Private mind, 24, 95, 96, 121, 128, 312, 317

Problem of Evil, 45, 195, 207, 242, 250, 276, 288, 362

Promised Land, 96, 314, 315

Protagoras, 203, 335

Protestantism (Protestant), 140, 160, 162, 167, 185, 191, 202, 285, 350, 353, 356, 370, 384

Proustian, 57, 184, 193, 228

psyche, 263, 268

Psychology (psychological), 24, 33, 34, 79, 111, 120, 121, 164, 178, 201, 207, 220, 245, 246, 247, 289, 294, 317, 318, 328, 351, 353, 355, 367, 406, 426, 441, 446, 452

Public mind, 60, 95, 96, 121, 128, 194, 204, 312, 314, 334, 372, 381, 403, 432, 437, 443

Pure Reason, Critique of, 147, 448, 449, 451, 452

Pure reason, 122, 225, 450, 454

Puritan, 110, 182, 209, 266, 314, 315, 356, 361

Purpose, 46, 48, 49, 59, 64, 72, 90, 98, 101, 102, 103, 104, 111, 119, 123, 142, 167, 184, 193, 197, 204, 245, 252, 284, 285, 299, 305, 307, 308, 323, 324, 326, 337, 338, 352, 358, 360, 374, 375, 394, 395, 396, 399, 400, 401, 405, 409, 420

Purposeless purpose, 98, 326, 337

Quantum mechanics, 106, 298, 349, 445

Quotient, 335

Rational, 45, 83, 109, 112, 128, 152, 157, 164, 167, 173, 180, 190, 197, 205, 207, 213, 236, 248, 258, 269, 284, 285, 289, 335, 353, 359, 370, 372, 373, 383, 397, 401, 406, 429, 433, 434, 436, 444, 448, 450, 451, 452, 453

Rationalism, 321, 393, 425, 439

Rationality, 22, 34, 96, 109, 180, 201, 207, 295, 357, 371, 383, 420, 442, 452

Realism, 24, 35, 129, 152, 218, 247, 316, 318, 357

Reality (real) (231 references—not listed)

Reality principle, 196

Reason (reasonable) (167 references—not listed)

Reductionism, 424

Religion (religious) (341 references—not listed)

Religion beyond religions, 27, 99, 108, 112

Renaissance, 61, 78, 102, 139, 151, 161, 162, 164, 203, 215, 233, 240, 252, 269, 278, 283, 284, 348, 398, 423

Republic, 209, 214, 262, 294, 296, 312, 322, 323, 324, 326, 329, 359, 381, 387, 389, 388

Revaluation, 126, 213, 380

Revolution (communist, constitutional, democratic, ideological, industrial, intellectual, mental, metaphysical, middle class, permanent, philosophical, religious, scientific, social), 59, 61, 102, 117, 118, 119, 125, 126, 141, 165, 204, 206, 218, 224, 242, 284, 299, 306, 311, 314, 316, 325, 366, 367, 371, 380, 392, 394, 397, 402, 403, 431, 432, 437, 442, 445, 452

Revolution (American), 402, 433

Revolution (English), 372, 403

Revolution (French), 161, 206, 224, 237, 283, 314, 354, 367, 369, 372, 402, 432, 433

Revolutions, Iron Law of, 367
Romeo and Juliet, 189, 231, 331
Rorschachery, 102, 336
Rosa centifolia, 102, 336
Rose, 58, 79, 86, 100, 101, 210, 230, 331, 339, 341, 342, 382
Ruling class, 84, 90, 96, 127, 226, 293, 294, 296, 304, 381, 394, 402, 403
Sacred grove, 105, 278, 346, 347
Scepticism, 29, 83, 120, 146, 207, 312, 394, 413, 419, 421, 422, 423, 449
Scientism, 204, 314, 355, 356
Scientist, 74, 121, 151, 206, 266, 339, 446
Self, the, 51, 52, 55, 70, 71, 74, 75, 78, 83, 85, 86, 98, 99, 113, 120, 124, 128, 129, 143, 171, 194, 205, 213, 218, 233, 248, 249, 263, 264, 266, 268, 272, 279, 291, 312, 318, 326, 361, 363, 364, 366, 426
Self and the Other, The, 74, 218, 263, 264, 266, 291, 312, 318
Self-consciousness, 72, 96, 101, 198, 212, 229, 264, 285, 312, 367, 446, 453
Self-constituting, 233, 252, 260, 264, 272, 312, 361, 364, 400
Self-creating, 24, 46, 59, 75, 85, 98, 113, 119, 128, 171, 211, 362, 432
Self-forming, 249
Self-ordering, 30, 96, 98, 99, 113, 124, 194, 258, 326, 328, 362, 366, 410
Self-perfecting, 70, 120, 125, 143, 203, 211, 279, 388
Self-revealing, 132, 143
Self-transcending, 120, 346, 368, 419
Semantic Existentialism, 64
Semiology (semiotics), 197, 198, 199
Sensation, 53, 98, 166, 218, 242, 276, 298, 407, 409, 412, 413, 417, 419, 420, 435
Sexuality, 46, 101, 138, 178, 246, 276, 298, 338, 353, 357, 407, 412, 413, 414, 417, 420, 428, 435
Siddha, 215
Sign/symbol, 46, 47, 197, 286, 340, 374

Simianism, 101, 334
Slavery, 66, 90, 96, 124, 242, 243, 317, 352, 376, 377, 427
Social animal, 121, 166, 372, 399
Social consciousness, 121, 122, 184, 381
Social control, 84, 96, 316, 317, 336, 402
Social process, 173, 187, 217, 302, 316
Socialism, 102, 129, 205, 316, 318, 358, 424, 432, 433, 434, 439, 443
Society (social) (543 references—not listed)
Sociobiology, 360
Sociology, 46, 120, 121, 201, 286, 299, 301, 316, 355, 370, 430, 431
Son-figure, 39, 188
Sophism (sophist), 46, 201, 203, 433
Sophist, 394
Soul (153 references—not listed)
Stereometaphysics, 83, 252, 291, 297, 337
Stoicism (stoic), 23, 61, 148, 149, 151, 168, 174, 204, 207, 234, 255, 269, 273, 423, 447
String theory, 129, 275, 387
Subjective universality, 382, 383
Sublimation, 122, 213, 246, 293, 447
Substance, 49, 70, 132, 138, 177, 194, 198, 200, 220, 229, 234, 239, 243, 257, 259, 266, 270, 298, 326, 393, 395, 403, 406, 410, 412, 413, 414, 415, 417, 418, 420, 435, 436, 441, 447
substantia, 406
Subunconscious, 98, 127, 129, 324, 325, 346, 382, 383
Suffering god, 280
Super-ego, 39, 188, 213
Syllogism, 258
Symbolism (symbolist, symbolic), 11, 20, 21, 22, 24, 138, 152, 161, 163, 188, 222, 298, 415
Symposium, 136, 211, 328
Taoism, 225, 250
Technology, 47, 53, 64, 122, 157, 158, 286, 314, 356
The Tempest, 189, 207

Theism, 78, 80, 165, 192, 275

Theology, 46, 96, 139, 151, 169, 181, 191, 203, 216, 217, 224, 227, 234, 250, 266, 287, 360, 365, 393, 398, 404, 423, 447, 453, 454, 455

Theory of types, 374

Things-in-themselves, 9, 174, 176, 190, 323, 451

Thought (think, thinking) (367 references—not listed)

Thus Spoke Zarathustra, 153, 158, 163, 166, 227, 254, 271, 273, 276, 330

Timaeus, 143, 207, 287, 323, 369

Time (237 references—not listed)

Todestriebe, 368

Totalitarianism (totalitarian), 42, 60, 85, 96, 110, 299, 311, 371, 381, 401, 424, 429

Towards the International Rule of Law, 142, 301, 403

Tragedy, 98, 99, 128, 182, 229, 249, 274, 327, 346, 373, 432

Transcendental, 98, 103, 104, 148, 175, 187, 194, 203, 232, 233, 256, 272, 273, 286, 288, 295, 298, 330, 335, 359, 364, 374, 388, 399, 400, 406, 450, 454, 455

Transcendental value, 103, 399

Transcendentalism, 185, 275

Transubstantiation, 236, 397, 404

Transvaluation, 380

Traumocrancy, 102, 336

Tristan und Isolde, 170

Truth (true) (230 references—not listed)

Twelfth Night, 168, 299, 319

Two Gentlemen of Verona, 320

Übermensch, 213, 380

Umwertung, 380

Undecidability, 409

Unhappy consciousness, 96, 99, 328

Universal Language, 90, 91, 301, 302, 303, 323

Universal Legislator, 47, 207

Universals, 100, 323, 393

Universe (185 references—not listed)

University, 32, 44, 105, 118, 184, 244, 301, 337, 348, 352, 359, 370, 375, 376, 383, 395

Universities of Misanthropology, 123

Unphilosophical nation, 96, 313

Unwritten constitution, 119, 368, 369

Upanishads, 177, 225, 268

Usury, 124, 376

Utilitarianism (utilitarian), 46, 186, 201, 424, 439, 442

Utility (principle of), 439, 440, 441

Utopia, 209, 261, 299, 378

Vajrayâna, 215

Virtue, 90, 137, 149, 156, 157, 183, 204, 205, 255, 288, 321, 330, 422, 434

War, 17, 41, 61, 80, 110, 141, 142, 150, 159, 166, 172, 180, 189, 201, 218, 224, 225, 239, 240, 241, 263 279, 285, 291, 294, 298, 302, 303, 304, 305, 306, 307, 308, 309, 316, 344, 361, 368, 379, 385, 389, 391, 399, 400, 433

Western Civilisation, 26, 199, 215, 227, 253

Will to power, 34, 159, 174, 177, 214, 268, 274, 311

World Ocean, 74, 76, 99, 262, 310, 330, 351, 388

World Spirit, 95, 310, 364

Zoroastrianism, 276